Dracula
Curse of the Vampire

Dracula – Curse of the Vampire is unlike other books. In fact, it is the gateway to a world of gothic horror, and an interactive adventure inspired by the works of Bram Stoker.

As well as the book itself, you will need two dice (or a standard pack of playing cards), a pencil and an eraser. Using these tools, and a simple set of game rules contained within the book, you will undertake a perilous quest to thwart the eponymous Count's evil plans, or perhaps become the blood-sucker himself and battle the Vampire-Hunters instead.

YOU decide which route to take, which perils to risk, and which of the terrifying creatures ranged against you to engage in battle. But be warned – whether you succeed in your quest, or succumb to the curse of the vampire, will be down to the choices YOU make.

Do not tarry, for the dead travel fast. And remember, the blood is the life!

Proudly Published by Snowbooks in 2021

Copyright © 2021 Jonathan Green
Illustrations © 2021 Hauke Kock
Jonathan Green asserts the moral right to be identified as the author of this work.
All rights reserved.

Snowbooks Ltd.
email: info@snowbooks.com
www.snowbooks.com

British Library Cataloguing in Publication Data
A catalogue record for this book is available from the British Library.

HARDBACK 978-1-913525-00-2
PAPERBACK 978-1-913525-01-9
EBOOK 978-1-913525-02-6

With thanks to the Play-Testers of Transylvania:
林立人　Lin Liren ✚ KJ Shadmand ✚
Tim Shannon ✚ Laurent JALICOUS aka Warlock-man ✚
Simon Scott ✚ René Batsford ✚
JASON VINCE A.K.A. 'DREAM WALKER SPIRIT' ✚
Candela/Victoria ✚ Shane "Asharon" Sylvia ✚ Ron White ✚
Stuart Warren ✚ Fabrice Gatille ✚ Nasser Khalid Al Alawi ✚
Reba Phillips ✚ Kim Newman ✚ Suguru Oikawa ✚
Nicholas Chin ✚ Emma Owen

With special thanks to Mike Bingham, Victor Cheng, Emma Owen, Paul Simpson, and Ron White.

Printed in the UK by CPI Antony Rowe

Dracula
Curse of the Vampire

Written by **JONATHAN GREEN**
Illustrated by **HAUKE KOCK**

ALSO BY JONATHAN GREEN

ACE Gamebooks
Alice's Nightmare in Wonderland
The Wicked Wizard of Oz
NEVERLAND – Here Be Monsters!
Beowulf Beastslayer
'TWAS – The Krampus Night Before Christmas

Snowbooks Fantasy Histories
You Are The Hero – A History of Fighting Fantasy Gamebooks
You Are The Hero Part 2

Snowbooks Anthologies
Sharkpunk (edited by Jonathan Green)
Game Over (edited by Jonathan Green)
Shakespeare Vs Cthulhu (edited by Jonathan Green)

Fighting Fantasy Gamebooks
Spellbreaker
Knights of Doom
Curse of the Mummy
Bloodbones
Howl of the Werewolf
Stormslayer
Night of the Necromancer

Sonic the Hedgehog Adventure Gamebooks
Theme Park Panic (with Marc Gascoigne)

Stormin' Sonic (with Marc Gascoigne)

Doctor Who Adventure Gamebooks
Decide Your Destiny: The Horror of Howling Hill
Choose The Future: Night of the Kraken

Star Wars: The Clone Wars – Decide Your Destiny
Crisis on Coruscant

Gamebook Adventures
Temple of the Spider God

Warlock's Bounty
Revenge of the Sorcerer

Path to Victory
Herald of Oblivion
Shadows Over Sylvania

Dedicated to
Master David Peterson 丁超塵 師傅,
Peerless Mentor of Heroes and Warriors

Dracula
Curse of the Vampire

Beyond the Forest
11

Dracula – Curse of the Vampire Adventure Sheets
30

Dracula – Curse of the Vampire
37

Acknowledgements
643

He is Legend: Breathing New Life into an Undead Classic
648

About the Author
690

Beyond the Forest

Introduction

The book you hold in your hands is a gateway to a world of gothic horror, and an adventure inspired by Bram Stoker's ***Dracula***. Within its pages you will undertake a perilous quest to thwart the eponymous Count's evil plans, or perhaps become the bloodsucker himself and battle the Vampire-Hunters ranged against you.

For this is no ordinary book. Rather than reading it from cover to cover, you will discover that at the end of each narrative section you will be presented with a series of choices that allow you to control the course of the story.

In ***Dracula – Curse of the Vampire*** you will take on the role of one of three Vampire-Hunters – either young solicitor Jonathan Harker, his fiancée Mina Murray, or Doctor John Seward – or the undead Count Dracula himself! You decide which route to take, which perils to risk, and which of the terrifying creatures you will meet along the way to fight.

Success is by no means certain and you may well fail to complete the adventure at your first attempt. However, with experience, skill, and maybe even a little luck, each new attempt should bring you closer to your ultimate goal.

In addition to the book itself, you will need two six-sided dice, or a conventional pack of 52 playing cards, a pencil, an eraser, and a copy of the ***Dracula – Curse of the Vampire*** Adventure Sheet (spare copies of which can be downloaded from **www.acegamebooks.com**).

Playing the Game

There are three ways to play through *Dracula – Curse of the Vampire*. The first is to use two six-sided dice. The second is to use a conventional pack of 52 playing cards. The third is to ignore the rules altogether and just read the book, making choices as appropriate, but ignoring any combat or attribute tests, always assuming you win every battle and pass every skill test. (Even if you play the adventure this way, there is still no guarantee that you will complete it at your first attempt.)

Where *Dracula – Curse of the Vampire* differs from other titles in the **ACE Gamebooks** series is that if you play as one of the three Vampire-Hunters, you will be able to change which of the three characters you are playing as at regular points throughout the adventure. However, if you choose to play as Count Dracula, you will experience a unique adventure from the vampire's point of view.

If you are opting to play through *Dracula – Curse of the Vampire* using the game rules, you first need to determine the strengths and weaknesses of the various characters in the game.

Playing as the Vampire-Hunters

Each of the three Vampire-Hunters has five attributes that you will need to keep track of during the course of the adventure, using their Adventure Sheets. Some of these will change frequently, others less so, but it is important that you keep an accurate record of the current level for all of them.

Agility – This is a measure of how athletic and agile a character is. If they need to leap across a chasm or dodge a deadly projectile, this is the attribute that will be employed.

Combat – This is a measure of how skilful a character is at fighting, whether it be wielding a keen-edged blade in hand-to-hand combat or firing a gun.

Endurance – This is a measure of how physically tough a character is and how much strength they have left. This attribute will vary more than any other during your adventure.

ESP – Also known as Extra-Sensory Perception, this is a measure of the strength of a character's psychic sixth sense; in other words, how capable they are of receiving information directly with their mind, rather than via any of the recognised physical senses.

Terror – This is a measure of how scared a character is. The more terrified a character becomes, the less likely they are to be able to cope in frightening or traumatic situations.

Unlike some adventure gamebooks, in **Dracula – Curse of the Vampire** characters' strengths and weaknesses are not determined randomly. However, everyone's *Terror* score starts at zero.

In addition to the five basic attributes, each of the Vampire-Hunters may employ **The Pen is Mightier** special ability at critical moments during the adventure, which allows them to avoid coming to blows with an enemy, by altering the narrative of the encounter and enabling them to escape unscathed. However, this special ability can only be used three times by each character during an adventure; each time you call upon it, you must cross off one use on the relevant character's Adventure Sheet.

On the following pages you will find each of the three playable Vampire-Hunter characters in **Dracula – Curse of the Vampire** described in turn, along with their strengths and weaknesses. Each one will affect the course of the narrative in quite different ways as you read the book and play through the adventure.

If you decide to read through the adventure as one of the Vampire-Hunters, before you begin you will need to decide which character you want to play as. You will soon discover that there are places where you are given the opportunity to swap characters.

You are free to either play as the same character throughout, or to chop and change, whenever you are given that option. However, it is very important that you keep track of which character you are playing as at any one time, and that you update the correct character's Adventure Sheet. For example, if Mina Murray gains 2 *Terror* points, make sure you don't add them to Jonathan Harker's total. Likewise, if Jonathan Harker loses 1 *ESP* point, do not deduct it from Dr Seward's *ESP* score.

Mr Jonathan Harker

Jonathan Harker has not long qualified as a solicitor and has recently taken a junior position at the firm of Hawkins, Oldman & Lee in the English city of Exeter, in Devon. He is hardworking and has a meticulous eye for detail. He is engaged to Miss Mina Murray.

Whenever you see a cross icon beneath a section number, rather than read that section, add 10 to the number, turn to this new section immediately, and read that one instead.

AGILITY	9
COMBAT	10
ENDURANCE	24
ESP	7

Miss Mina Murray

Mina Murray is engaged to be married to the dashing young solicitor Jonathan Harker. To aid him in his work, she is practising her secretarial skills. She is devoted and dedicated, and possesses a keen intellect and logical mind.

Her best friend since childhood is Miss Lucy Westenra, who is everything that Mina isn't – flighty, illogical, and lacking in erudition – having been born into a wealthy family and being blessed with a beauty that makes any man – other than Mina's fiancé Jonathan, it seems – instantly fall in love with her at first sight.

Whenever you see a bat icon beneath a section number, rather than read that section, add 20 to the number, turn to this new section immediately, and read that one instead.

AGILITY	8
COMBAT	8
ENDURANCE	20
ESP	8

Doctor John Seward

Despite his young age, Doctor John Seward – known as 'Jack' to his close friends – runs the Carfax Asylum, in Purfleet, Essex, having focused on diseases of the mind since qualifying as a medical practitioner.

A man of science, he holds no truck with the supernatural. When he was at medical school, one of his tutors was Professor Van Helsing of Amsterdam, the renowned physician and psychiatrist.

Whenever you see a skull icon beneath a section number, rather than read that section, add 30 to the number, turn to this new section immediately, and read that one instead.

AGILITY	10
COMBAT	9
ENDURANCE	22
ESP	6

Blood Points and the Vampire-Hunters

There is one more statistic you will need to keep track of during your adventure, and that is the number of *Blood* points you have. You begin the adventure with zero *Blood* points.

While each Vampire-Hunter has their own unique set of stats to keep track of, they share the same *Blood* score. The *Blood* score keeps track of how powerful Dracula is becoming, as the Vampire-Hunters battle to stop his plans coming to fruition. If you do something that alerts Dracula to the fact that you are hunting him, the *Blood* score will increase, whereas destroy one of the vampire's agents and the *Blood* score will decrease.

Be warned – while playing as more than one of the Vampire-Hunters during the adventure can have certain benefits, it can also result in Dracula becoming more powerful more quickly. For example, if Doctor John Seward does something that causes the *Blood* score to increase, Jonathan Harker may suffer later, as a direct consequence of the former's actions.

Playing as Count Dracula

Dracula has four basic attributes – *Agility, Combat, Endurance* and *ESP* – and these work in the same way as they do for the Vampire-Hunters. You will also notice a *Suspicion* score on his Adventure Sheet; the purpose for this will be explained during the course of the adventure.

Count Dracula

Born in the fifteenth century, Vlad Tepes III was the ruthless ruler of the principality of Wallachia, whose fondness for skewering his enemies on blunted stakes earned him the moniker 'The Impaler'. By sorcerous means he was transformed into one of the undead and has survived to the present day by drinking the blood of the living.

AGILITY	8
COMBAT	9
ENDURANCE	24
ESP	7

Blood Points and Count Dracula

If you are playing as Count Dracula, the *Blood* score is a measure of how powerful you are becoming, so in this case, a high *Blood* score can be of benefit. When Dracula accumulates enough *Blood* points, his rank increases, which in turn enables him to bring other dark powers to bear against his enemies. Dracula begins the adventure with zero *Blood* points.

Please note, if having achieved a certain rank Dracula's *Blood* score drops below the number of points required to reach that rank, he does not go down a rank and he does not lose any special abilities he may have already acquired. However, to progress to a new higher rank, Dracula's *Blood* score would still have to reach the required number of points for that to happen.

The following table shows you the number of *Blood* points required to achieve each rank.

Blood Score	Rank
0	Son of the Dragon
10	Lord Impaler
20	Voivode of Wallachia
30	Nosferatu
40	Count Dracula
50	Prince of Darkness
60	King of Vampires
70	Emperor of the Dead

Testing Your Attributes

At various times during your adventure, you will be asked to test one or other of the attributes of the character you are playing as at the time.

If it is your *Agility*, *Combat* or *ESP* that is being tested, simply roll two dice. If the total rolled is equal to or less than the attribute being tested, you have passed the test; if the total rolled is greater than the attribute in question, then you have failed the test. (If you are using playing cards, draw one card; picture cards are worth 11 and an Ace is worth 12.)

If it is your *Endurance* score that is being tested, roll four dice in total. If the combined score of all four dice is equal to or less than your *Endurance* score, then you have passed the test, but if it is greater, then what is being asked of you is beyond your current capabilities and you have failed the test. (If you are using playing cards, draw two cards and add their values together; picture cards are worth 11 and an Ace is worth 12.)

Terror Tests

Testing your *Terror* score works differently from other attribute tests. If it is your *Terror* score that is being tested, roll four dice in total. If the total rolled is equal to or greater than your *Terror* score, you have passed the test; if the total rolled is less than your *Terror* score, then you have failed the test. (If you are using playing cards, draw two cards and add their values together; picture cards are worth 11 and an Ace is worth 12.)

Please note, your *Terror* score may not drop below zero and may not exceed 24 points.

Restoring Your Attributes

In general, a character's *Agility*, *Combat* and *Endurance* scores may not exceed their starting values, unless specifically stated by the text. However, a character's *ESP* score may exceed its initial level.

There are various ways that you can restore lost attribute points, or even be granted bonuses that take a character's attributes beyond their starting scores, and these will be described during the course of the adventure.

An easy way to restore lost *Endurance* points is to find sustenance. However, in **Dracula – *Curse of the Vampire***, there is another way to restore *Endurance* points, and that is via journal entries.

If you are playing as one of the Vampire-Hunters, whenever you read a section that starts with an extract from someone's journal, a letter, a telegram or a newspaper extract – **and is printed in this typeface** – you may restore up to 4 *Endurance* points. This only applies when a section starts with an extract of text and does not apply to any telegram or other piece of text that appears in this way in the middle of a section. (Count Dracula cannot restore *Endurance* points in this way.)

Remember, a character cannot exceed their starting *Endurance* score unless specifically stated by the text, so this *Endurance* boost does not apply to the very first extract you read as you begin an adventure.

Hand-to-hand Combat

You will repeatedly be called upon to defend yourself against all manner of horrors in **Dracula – *Curse of the Vampire***. Sometimes you may even choose to attack these monsters yourself. After all, as they say, the best form of defence is attack.

When this happens, start by filling in your opponent's *Combat* and *Endurance* scores in the first available Encounter Box on pages 35-36.

Whenever you engage in combat, you will be told in the text whether you or your enemy has the initiative; in other words, who has the advantage and gets to attack first.

1. Roll two dice and add your *Combat* score. The resulting total is your *Combat Rating*.

2. Roll two dice and add your opponent's *Combat* Score. The resulting total is your opponent's *Combat Rating*.

3. For each Combat Round, add a temporary 1 point bonus to the *Combat Rating* of whichever of the combatants has the initiative for the duration of that round.

4. If your *Combat Rating* is higher than your opponent's, you have wounded your enemy; deduct 2 points from your opponent's *Endurance* score and move on to step 7.

5. If your opponent's *Combat Rating* is higher, then you have been wounded; deduct 2 points from your *Endurance* score and move on to step 8.

6. If your *Combat Rating* and your opponent's *Combat Rating* are the same, roll one die. If the number rolled is odd, you and your opponent deflect each other's attacks; go to step 10. If the number rolled is even, go to step 9.

7. If your opponent's *Endurance* score has been reduced to zero or below, you have won; the battle is over, and you can continue the adventure. If your opponent is not yet dead, go to step 10.

8. If your *Endurance* score has been reduced to zero or below, your opponent has won the battle. If you want to continue your adventure you will have to start again from the beginning, maybe changing the character you are playing as. However, if you are still alive, go to step 10.

9. You and your opponent have both managed to injure each other; deduct 1 point from both your *Endurance* score and your opponent's *Endurance* score. If your *Endurance* score has been reduced to zero or below, your adventure is over; if you want to play again you will have to start again from the beginning. If you are still alive but your enemy's *Endurance* has been reduced to zero or below, you have won; the battle is over, and you can continue the adventure. If neither you nor your opponent are dead, go to step 10.

10. If you won the Combat Round, you will have the initiative in the next Combat Round. If your opponent won the Combat Round, they will have the initiative. If neither of you won the Combat Round, neither of you will gain the initiative bonus for the next Combat Round. Go back to step 1 and work through the sequence again until either your opponent is dead, or you are defeated.

Fighting More Than One Opponent

Sometimes you may find yourself having to fight more than one opponent at the same time. Such battles are conducted in the same way as above, using the ten step process, except that you will have to work out the *Combat Ratings* of all those involved. As long as you have a higher rating than an opponent you will injure them, no matter how many opponents you are taking on at the same time. Equally, any opponent with a *Combat Rating* higher than yours will be able to injure you too.

However, for every two opponents you have to fight simultaneously, you must deduct 1 point from your *Combat Rating* for the duration of the battle.

For example, Dr Seward finds himself having to fight two lunatics at Carfax Asylum; for the duration of the fight, he must deduct 1 point from his *Combat Rating*. If Mina Murray found herself fighting three wolves, she would still only have to deduct 1 point from her *Combat Rating*. But if Count Dracula found himself having to fight four Vampire-Hunters at the same time, he would have to deduct 2 points from his *Combat Rating*, for the duration of the battle.

Ranged Combat

If you acquire a revolver, a rifle, or another gun of some kind during the course of your adventure, you may use it when instructed by the text, but also during some combats. They all behave in the same way.

If you find yourself in battle, and you have the initiative in the opening Combat Round, you may choose to fire your gun before engaging in hand-to-hand combat. *Take a Combat test* and if you pass the test, you cause your opponent 3 *Endurance* points of damage; if you fail the test you have simply wasted your shot.

If you hit your opponent you may take a second shot, but no more after this.

An Alternative to Dice

Rather than rolling dice, you may prefer to determine random numbers during the game using a pack of playing cards.

To do this, when you are called upon to roll dice, simply shuffle a standard 52-card deck (having removed the Jokers) and draw a single card. (If you are asked to roll four dice, draw two cards.) Number cards are worth the number shown on the card. Jacks, Queens and Kings are all worth 11, and if you draw an Ace, it counts as being worth 12 (for example, if you are engaged in Combat), and is an automatic pass if you are testing an attribute – any attribute.

After drawing from the deck, you can either return any cards you have drawn or, using the Pontoon method, leave those drawn cards out of the deck. Both styles of play will influence how lucky, or unlucky, you may be during the game, when it comes to determining random numbers.

Equipment

During the course of your quest, you will no doubt come across all manner of curious items that you will want to pick up and take with you, just in case they prove to be of use later on.

Anything that you do collect should be recorded on your Adventure Sheet, including any weapons and other miscellaneous unusual objects.

Code Words

You will also come across various clues and useful pieces of information, or be forced to endure unusual or unpleasant experiences, during the course of your adventure. The knowledge you have acquired and the experiences you have endured are tracked in the form of code words, a list of which appears on page 33.

Whenever you acquire a particular code word, you will be instructed to tick off on this list.

Code words are cumulative and not necessarily restricted to specific characters. For example, if Jonathan Harker, Mina Murray and Doctor John Seward all discover useful information about Count Dracula, they can share that information, which could then be of benefit to any of them later on.

Hints on Play

There is more than one path that you can follow through the adventure to reach your ultimate goal, but it may take you several attempts to actually complete the adventure, so it is advisable to make notes as you progress.

Keep a careful eye on your attributes throughout the game. Beware of traps and setting off on wild goose chases. However, it would be wise to collect useful items along the way that may aid you further on in your quest.

Lastly – and although this has been mentioned already, it bears mentioning again – it is very important that you keep a careful track of which character you are playing as during the course of your adventure. You do not want to accidently increase Doctor Seward's *ESP* score if you are playing as Mina Murray at the time.

Ending the Game

There are several ways that your adventure can end. If the *Endurance* score of the character you are playing as ever drops to zero or below, they have been killed and your adventure is over. If this happens, stop reading at once.

There may also be occasions where you are prevented from progressing any further through the adventure thanks to the choices you have made, or if you meet a sudden and untimely end. In all these cases, if you want to have another crack at completing the adventure you will have to begin the story afresh from the start, perhaps choosing a different character this time.

There is of course one other reason for your adventure coming to an end, and that is if you successfully complete your quest, the very same quest that awaits you now…

Adventure Sheet
Mr Jonathan Harker

Add 10 to the section number and read that one instead.

| Agility = 9 | Combat = 10 | Endurance = 24 |

| ESP = 7 | Terror = |

The Pen is Mightier

Equipment and Notes

Adventure Sheet
Miss Mina Murray

Add 20 to the section number and read that one instead.

| Agility = 8 | Combat = 8 | Endurance = 20 |

| ESP = 8 | Terror = |

The Pen is Mightier [ ] [ ] [ ]

Equipment and Notes

Adventure Sheet
Dr John Seward

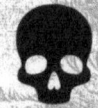

Add 30 to the section number and read that one instead.

| Agility = 10 | Combat = 9 | Endurance = 22 |

| ESP = 6 | Terror = |

The Pen is Mightier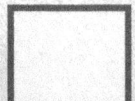

Equipment and Notes

Blood

Code Words

Anthropophagy	Desmodontinae	Orvos	Strigoi
Apáca	Elesett	Pestis	Succubus
Arachnophilia	Eptesicus	Psychopathia	Suicide
Árulás	Exsanguination	Quinquaginta	Superstition
Auxilia	Gonosz	Rabszolga	Szerencse
Azrael	Haemorrhage	Rejtett	Térkép
Babona	Inventa	Sárkány	Țigani
Barbastella	Kereszt	Scientia	Transfusion
Barghest	Lángok	Sedative	Tükör
Bogey	Lunatic	Slave	Vânători
Borzalom	Lycanthropy	Somnambulism	Varázslat
Cadaver	Lyssavirus	Spectre	Vârcolac
Demeter	Monomania	Stratégia	Zoophagous

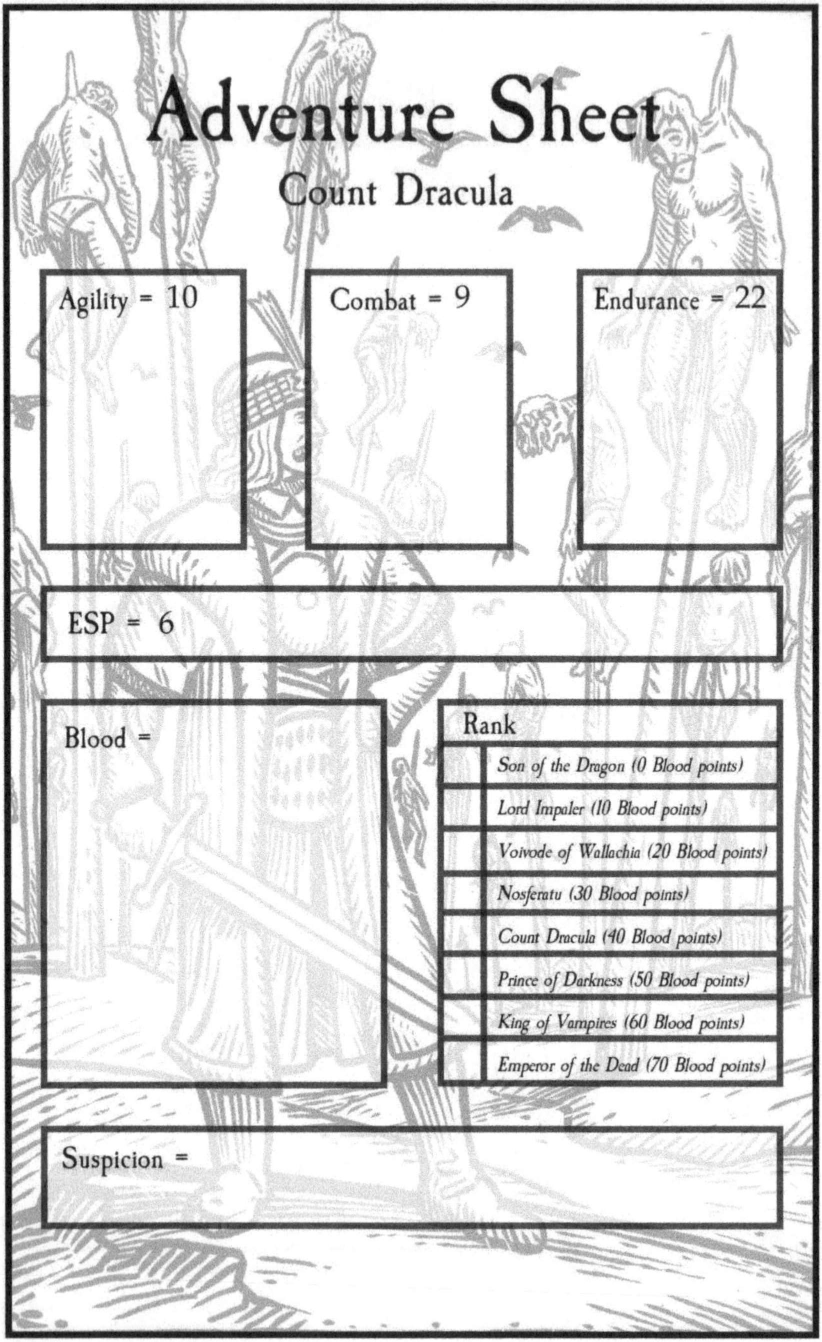

Adventure Sheet
Count Dracula

Agility = 10

Combat = 9

Endurance = 22

ESP = 6

Blood =

Rank

- Son of the Dragon (0 Blood points)
- Lord Impaler (10 Blood points)
- Voivode of Wallachia (20 Blood points)
- Nosferatu (30 Blood points)
- Count Dracula (40 Blood points)
- Prince of Darkness (50 Blood points)
- King of Vampires (60 Blood points)
- Emperor of the Dead (70 Blood points)

Suspicion =

Encounter Boxes

Combat =
Endurance =

Combat =
Endurance =

Combat =
Endurance =

Combat =
Endurance =

Combat =
Endurance =

Combat =
Endurance =

Combat =
Endurance =

Combat =
Endurance =

Combat =
Endurance =

Combat =
Endurance =

Combat =
Endurance =

Combat =
Endurance =

Combat =
Endurance =

Combat =
Endurance =

Encounter Boxes

Combat = Endurance =	Combat = Endurance =
Combat = Endurance =	Combat = Endurance =
Combat = Endurance =	Combat = Endurance =
Combat = Endurance =	Combat = Endurance =
Combat = Endurance =	Combat = Endurance =
Combat = Endurance =	Combat = Endurance =
Combat = Endurance =	Combat = Endurance =

Dracula
Curse of the Vampire

Do not tarry, for the dead travel fast…

If you are playing as Jonathan Harker, turn to **1**.
If you are playing as Mina Murray, turn to **250**.
If you are playing as Doctor John Seward, turn to **500**.
If you are playing as Count Dracula, turn to **750**.

1

JONATHAN HARKER'S JOURNAL

30 April 1897

When we started for our drive the sun was shining brightly on Munich, and the air was full of the joyousness of early summer...

Having arrived in the Bavarian capital of Munich, with a day to spare before your train departs for Bistritz, in the region of Transylvania in Romania, you decide to make the most of your enforced sojourn and instruct Herr Delbruck – the maitre d'hotel of the Quatre Saisons, where you are staying – to hire a carriage, so that you might go for a drive in the surrounding countryside, it being such a glorious day.

Herr Delbruck does as you ask and, just as you are about to depart, comes down to the carriage and wishes you a pleasant drive.

His hand still on the handle of the carriage door, he says to the coachman, "Johann, remember you are back by nightfall. The sky looks bright but there is a shiver in the north wind that says there may be a sudden storm. But I am sure you will not be late" – he smiles, before adding – "for you know what night it is."

Johann answers with an emphatic, "*Ja, mein Herr,*" and, touching his hat, drives off quickly.

If you want to ask the coachman what is so special about tonight, turn to **31**. If not, turn to **92**.

2

There is no one in the kitchen or the servants' rooms, which are close at hand. You then try all the other rooms, one by one, until finally you reach the dining room.

It is there you find the four servant women, lying on the floor, their throats torn out as if by a rabid dog.

(Add 2 points to your *Terror* score and tick off the code word *Anthropophagy*.)

"We can attend to them later," Van Helsing says, in a wavering whisper, "but now, we must see to Miss Lucy!"

Turn to **72**.

3

Although they bear the patina of age upon their blades, the swords are surprisingly well-preserved. They are *kilij*, a type of one-handed, single-edged and moderately-curved sabre used by the soldiers of the Ottoman Empire.

Hoping that you might feel a little more confident and a little less fearful with such a weapon in your hand as you explore the Count's haunted home, you take one from its place within the arrangement on the wall, and make a few practice sweeps with it, slicing it through the air. It is light and finely-balanced, so you can still carry your lamp as well as the sword.

If you want to take it with you, record the Sabre on your Adventure Sheet, deduct 1 point from your *Terror* score, and as long as you are wielding the blade in battle you may add 1 point when calculating your *Combat Rating*. Make a note that you may only carry one weapon at a time and then return to **672** to make another choice.

4

"And now for you, Madam Mina," Van Helsing says, turning to your wife, "this marks the end of your part in the proceedings, until all is well. You are too precious to risk taking with us. We are men and are able to bear what must happen this night. But you must remain our star and our hope, and we shall act all the more freely knowing that you are not in the danger."

You feel greatly relieved, upon hearing the Professor's pronouncement, even though Mina appears less than happy with the situation. But she does not want her mere presence among the party to put the rest of you in harm's way, and though it is a bitter pill for her to swallow, she agrees to remain behind in your rooms at the asylum.

Turn to **159**.

5
The True History of Vlad the Impaler

The Sultan's army entered the Forest of the Impaled. There were large stakes there on which twenty thousand men, women, and children had been spitted. Shocked by the sight, the Sultan said that it was not possible to deprive a country of a man who had done such great deeds, and who had such a diabolical understanding of how to govern his realm and its people. The rest of the Turks were dumbfounded when they saw the multitude of men on the stakes. There were infants too affixed to their mothers on the stakes, and birds had made their nests in their entrails.

Horrified by the theatrical display of cruelty that greets them on the approach to Târgoviște, the Turks turn tail, Mehmed ordering a rapid, strategic withdrawal from Wallachian territory.

(Gain 10 *Blood* points.)

"This is a great day!" Captain Petru declares, as you stand together on the parapet outside your throne room, watching the Conqueror's forces as they head south for Ottoman lands once more. "News of what you have done here will spread like the plague, and not only throughout the Ottoman Empire; it will reach the ears of any neighbouring ruler who might think they can challenge the might of the Voivode of Wallachia."

"I know Mehmed," you say, sullenly. "He'll be back. He is not done with Wallachia yet."

"Then we shall prepare for war," Petru replies, "and it shall be glorious!"

"A war of attrition could be the end of us," you point out. "We defeat an army of 150,000 men and he will send another 300,000. If there are two things Mehmed has an endless supply of, it is men and an inbred sense of superiority."

"What you need is an advantage, husband," says Erzebet, a cruel smile curling her ruddy lips. "Something the Sultan cannot anticipate. Something that will take him by surprise."

"You have something in mind, my queen?"

"You are a great and powerful ruler. You wield great temporal power, and your people obey your every command. But what if you could be something more?"

Erzebet spends her days in esoteric study. While there is nothing you do not know about war-craft, she is a scholar of the arcane and supernatural, like the women in her family before her.

"Go on."

"There is a place in the mountains to the north, over Lake Hermanstadt – a place where it is rumoured a man might become something more than a man."

"What is this place?" you ask.

"Its ancient name is the Scholomance, and it is said that if a supplicant sheds their earthly trappings and makes their way there, alone, and if they can overcome the trials that will be set before them, then they might gain power over the lesser things of the earth and even gain mastery over the elements."

Radu gasps in horror. "Prince Vlad, I too have heard of that accursed school of witchcraft and you cannot even consider trying to find it. You must not! For the price you would have to pay for such unnatural power would be your very soul."

Which adviser will you listen to? Your good angel or your bad angel?

Will you seek out the Scholomance, so that you might acquire the means to halt the invasion of your lands by the Ottomans once and for all? If so, turn to **271**; if not turn to **696**.

6

"Join us, sister! Join us!" the sirens shriek. "Become his bride!"

And then the Sisters' faces melt and merge into one and you are staring into the hideous, wizened, bat-like visage of the bloodthirsty Count.

A dreadful, high-pitched screaming tears the night apart but several long moments pass before you realise that it is you who is doing the screaming.

Gain 3 *Blood* points and turn to **900**.

7

"I am younger and stronger, Professor," you tell your mentor. "It must be me."

"Then get ready at once."

Van Helsing is well-prepared, having brought with him his bag, in which are many instruments and drugs – or, as he puts it, "The ghastly paraphernalia of our beneficial trade."

He takes some things from his bag and lays them out on a little table. Then he mixes a sleeping draught, and helps Lucy drink it: "Now, miss, here is your medicine. Swallow it all down."

She passes into unconsciousness and he works swiftly, with absolute method, to perform the operation.

The pain and discomfort you must put up with are nothing compared to the joy you feel at seeing the colour start to return to Lucy's cheeks, even as you start to feel dizzy from blood loss yourself.

The Professor stands, with watch in hand, and with his eyes fixed now on Lucy, then on you, shifting back and forth between the two of you.

Your eyes half-closed, you are dimly aware of someone else entering the room. It takes you a moment to realise it is Arthur, come down from Ring to see how Lucy is for himself, having received your letter, and read between the lines, fearing the worst.

Presently you hear Van Helsing say in a soft voice, "It is enough. You attend to your friend, Mr Holmwood. I will look to her."

Once the Professor has dressed the wound the procedure made in your arm, Arthur takes you downstairs, holding on to you the whole way, for he can see how much the operation has weakened you, and gives you port wine, as you lie down on a sofa for a while.

The light-headedness you are feeling soon passes, and you start to feel a little more like yourself, but the transfusion has taken its toll. (Deduct half your remaining *Endurance* points, rounding fractions down, and tick off the code word *Transfusion*.)

Arthur tells you that he must return to his ailing father, but asks you to keep him informed as ever of any developments regarding his beloved. And you promise you shall, for she is your beloved too.

Turn to **56**.

8

It is late in the afternoon on the sixth day of November when you finally catch up with your quarry.

You have been climbing steadily ever since following the spur road from the Borgo Pass that leads to Castle Dracula. From this height, as you approach the top of the peak of the crag, it is possible to see a great distance; and far off, beyond the white waste of snow, you can see the river lying like a black ribbon in kinks and curls as it winds its way through the mountains.

The snow starts to fall more heavily, and swirls about fiercely, for a high wind has started to blow. And then, straight ahead of you, through pauses in the snow flurries, you see your quarry – a band of Szgany gypsies accompanying a leiter-wagon – and your heart leaps when you see the great square chest, bound to it. This must be the last remaining box of earth!

Beyond the swirling wall of snow, you make out the looming sinister, shadowy presence of the Count's decaying home, silhouetted against the sinking red orb of the sun.

"They are racing for the sunset!" Arthur shouts over the panting of the horses, the pounding of their iron-shod hooves on the road, the clatter of the wagon, the moaning wind, and the howling of wolves. "We may be too late!"

If the *Blood* score is 12 or higher, turn to **23**. If it is lower than 12, turn to **76**.

9

It would seem that Renfield is in the middle of a psychotic episode. He is immensely strong, more like a wild beast than a man. He comes for you, teeth bared like a wolf and foaming at the mouth. (Your patient has the initiative in this battle.)

RENFIELD   COMBAT 8   ENDURANCE 10

After 5 Combat Rounds, or if you manage to reduce Renfield's *Endurance* score to 6 points or fewer, whichever is sooner, turn to **292**.

10

Presently you come to a wide stretch of open country, shut in by hills all around. Their sides are covered with trees, which spread down to the plain, dotting in clumps the gentler slopes and hollows that are visible here and there. The winding road curves close to the densest of these thickets before vanishing behind it.

And then the snow begins to fall. Thinking of the miles and miles of bleak country you have passed, you hurry on, seeking shelter in the wood. Darker and darker grows the sky, while the snow falls faster and heavier until the ground all around you is a glistening white carpet, the furthest edge of which is lost in misty vagueness.

In only a little while, you realise that you must have strayed from the road, for you miss the hard surface underfoot and your feet sink deeper into the snow. The wind grows stronger, the air becomes icy cold, and in spite of your exertions, you begin to suffer its ill-effects. (Deduct 2 points from your *Endurance* score.)

The snow is falling thickly and whirling around you in rapid eddies, so that you can barely see your hand in front of your face, while every now and again the heavens are torn asunder by vivid lightning. In the flashes you can see ahead of you a great mass of trees, chiefly yew and cypress, all heavily coated with snow.

As soon as you are in the shelter of the trees, the rush of the wind is muffled by their snow-bent boughs. You realise that the darkness of the storm has merged with the darkness of the night. As the storm dies down, you hear the weird wolf-sound again, which is now echoed by many similar sounds that come from all around you. (Add 1 point to your *Terror* score.)

Now and again, a straggling ray of moonlight pierces the black mass of drifting cloud, lighting up your surroundings with its otherworldly monochrome luminescence. Skirting the edge of the copse, you find that a low wall encircles it, and following this you soon come upon an opening. Here the cypresses form an alley that leads up to the square mass of a building.

Just then, the drifting clouds obscure the moon again and you pass along this path in darkness. Shivering from the cold – and nothing more, you are sure – knowing that there is at least the hope of shelter up ahead, you grope your way blindly on.

And then, suddenly the moonlight breaks through the clouds once more, revealing to you that you are not in a village, but a graveyard! The edifice ahead of you isn't a house, but a massive tomb of marble, as white as the snow that lies on and around it.

With the moonlight, there comes a succession of long, low howls, as you might expect a whole pack of wolves to make.

Impelled by some form of fascination, you approach the sepulchre. Etched in German into the lintel above the Doric door are the words:

COUNTESS DOLINGEN OF GRATZ
IN STYRIA
SOUGHT AND FOUND DEATH
1801

On top of the tomb, seemingly driven through the solid marble, is a great iron spike, while on the back wall, graven in great Russian letters you see:

THE DEAD TRAVEL FAST

There is something so unsettling about this whole place that you start to wish you had taken the coachman's advice and stayed away. You feel the cold perceptibly grow upon you, until it seems to grip you by the heart, and your whole body starts to shake from fear as much as the freezing effects of exposure.

You start to back away from the tomb, moving towards the trees that mark the boundary of the graveyard, when the storm decides to unleash all its fury upon you. The ground shakes, as though thousands of horses are thundering across it, and the storm bears upon its icy wings great hailstones that beat down both leaf and branch.

If you want to run for cover within the trees, turn to **48**. If you would prefer to seek shelter within the sepulchre itself, turn to **77**.

11

As the captain is showing you and Arthur to the cramped cabin you are to share for this leg of your journey, as you travel up the Sereth, you spy a near-bald, short, misshapen figure emerge from another cabin, further along the corridor, and head towards the cargo hold. You bring him to Arthur's attention.

When the two of you are alone you say under your breath, "Arthur, that hunchback was on the train from Varna to Galatz. And now here he is again, on the same boat as us, travelling towards Castle Dracula."

"Do you think he could be an ally of our enemy?" Lord Godalming asks.

"All I know is that we cannot trust anyone in this land of mysteries and monsters," you reply.

"And you think he might be up to no good?"

If you want to follow the hunchback with the intention of finding out precisely what he is up to, turn to **41**. If you would rather ignore your suspicions and not risk drawing attention to yourselves while you are aboard the steam-launch, turn to **788**.

12

The road soon climbs away from the river, as the Sereth enters a steep-sided gorge, and you find yourselves within a range of steep-sided wooded hills.

It does not feel like you have gone many miles from Galatz when you become aware of a slavering panting sound chasing after you along the road.

"They're back," Quincey mutters and you both know to whom he is referring.

Twisting in the saddle and looking behind you, you see lean dark-furred shapes loping along the road on all fours after you, red eyes blazing from the darkness.

If you are in possession of some Silver Bullets, turn to **32**. If not, turn to **52**.

13

LETTER, MINA HARKER TO LUCY WESTENRA, BUDA-PESTH

24 August

My dearest Lucy,

I know you will be anxious to hear all that has happened since we parted at the railway station at Whitby. Well, my dear, I got to Hull all right, and caught the boat to Hamburg, and then the train on here. I can hardly recall anything of the journey, except that I knew I was coming to Jonathan.

I found my dear one, oh, so thin and pale and weak-looking. All the resolution has gone out of his dear eyes, and that quiet dignity which I told you was in his face has vanished. He is only a wreck of himself, and he does not remember anything that has happened to him for a long time past. At least, he wants me to believe so, and I shall never ask.

He has had some terrible shock, and I fear it might tax his poor brain if he were to try to recall it. Sister Agatha, who is a good creature and a born nurse, tells me that he raved of dreadful things whilst he was off his head. I wanted her to tell me what they were; but she would only cross herself, and say that the ravings of the sick were the secrets of God.

She is a sweet, good soul, and the next day, when she saw I was troubled still, after saying that she could never mention what my poor dear raved about, added: "I can tell you this much, my dear: that it was not about anything which he has done wrong himself; and you, as his wife to be, have no cause to be concerned. His fear was of great and terrible things, which no mortal mind can bear."

I waited by his bedside, until he awoke. After we had remade our promises of love to each other, he asked me for his coat, as he wanted to get something from the pocket; I asked Sister Agatha, and she brought all his things. I saw that amongst them was his notebook, and was going to ask him to let me look at it, in the hope that I might find some clue to his trouble contained within, when he said to me very solemnly:

"Wilhelmina," – I knew then that he was in deadly earnest – "you know, dear, my ideas of the trust between husband and wife: there should be no secret, no concealment. I have had a great shock, and when I try to recall what it was, I do not know if it was all real or the dreaming of a madman. You know I have had a brain fever, and that is to be mad. The secret is here, and I do not want to know it. I want to take up my life again here, with our marriage.

"Here is the book. Take it and keep it, read it if you will, but never let me know; unless, indeed, some solemn duty should come upon me to go back to the bitter hours, asleep or awake, sane or mad, recorded here."

He fell back exhausted, and I put the book under his pillow, and kissed him. I asked Sister Agatha to beg the Mother Superior to let our wedding be that afternoon, and so the chaplain of the English mission church was sent for.

Jonathan woke a little after the hour, and all was ready, and he sat up in bed, propped up with pillows. He answered his "I will" firmly and strongly. I could hardly speak; my heart was so full that even those words seemed to choke me.

When the chaplain and the sisters had left me alone with my husband, I took the book from under his pillow, and wrapped it up in white paper, and tied it with a little bit of pale blue ribbon which was round my neck, and sealed it over the knot with sealing-wax, and for my seal I used my wedding ring. Then I kissed it and showed it to my husband, and told him that I would keep it so, and that it would be an outward and visible sign for us all our lives that we trusted each other; that I would never open it unless it were for his own dear sake or for the sake of some stern duty.

Then he took my hand in his and said that it was the dearest thing in all the wide world, and I told him that he had made me the happiest woman in all the wide world. And, my dear, when he kissed me, and drew me to him with his poor weak hands, it was like a very solemn pledge between us.

Lucy dear, I tell you all this because you have been, and are, very dear to me. Please Almighty God, may your life be all it promises: a long day of sunshine, with no harsh wind, no forgetting duty, no distrust. I must not wish you no pain, for that can never be; but I do hope you will be always as happy as I am now. Goodbye, my dear.

I must stop, for Jonathan is waking and I must attend to my husband!

Your ever-loving

Mina Harker.

Turn to **44**.

14

The leiter-wagon slews to a halt in the snow and at another command from their hetman, the gypsies instantly surround the cart, jostling one another in their eagerness to carry out his orders.

Do you want to try to leap onto the cart, to get to the box of earth secured there (turn to **366**), or will you prepare to fight the gypsies (turn to **733**)?

15

Despite having once been Van Helsing's student, you can't help agreeing with Arthur; that it seems foolish to quit the tomb again in search of Lucy, when she will return here herself, in time.

The four of you secrete yourselves behind other sarcophagi and within as yet unfilled coffin-niches, in the wall of the tomb, while Van Helsing shutters his lantern.

You do not have to wait very long before you hear the creak of hinges and the rustle of chiffon on the marble floor of the tomb.

Peering out from your hiding place, you see a red-haired woman in a white gown, descending the steps into the crypt, with something dark held to her breast. Your heart grows cold as ice; you would know those tumbling red locks anywhere.

But Lucy is not alone; she is accompanied by half a dozen children, ranging in age from three to seven, or so it would appear. By the moonlight that enters the tomb through the open door, you see that their clothes are dishevelled, and their faces appear unnaturally pale.

Reaching the bottom of the steps she stops. You recognise the features of Lucy Westenra, but they are somehow changed; the sweetness has turned to adamantine cruelty, and her purity to voluptuous wantonness. You also see that her lips are crimson with fresh blood, and that the stream has trickled over her chin and stained the white of her death-robe.

(Add 1 to your *Terror* score.)

At a shout of "Now!" from Van Helsing, you emerge from your hiding places, ready to confront the evil that has taken root in this resting place of the dead.

When the thing that now bears Lucy's shape becomes aware of you all, it draws back with an angry snarl, eyes blazing with unholy light. The unnatural monster callously drops the child in her arms, the infant giving a sharp cry as it hits the stone floor. It does not move but lies there wailing, the cold-blooded act wringing a groan from Arthur.

Turning her attention to Lord Godalming then, the Lucy-creature advances towards him with outstretched arms, and a wanton smile on her lips. "Come to me, Arthur," she says languorously.

"My arms are hungry for you. Come and we can lie together. Come, my husband, come!"

There is something diabolically sweet in the tone of her voice, something of the tinkling of glass when struck, which rings through your brain even though the words are addressed to another.

As for Arthur, he appears to be under a spell, his arms open wide as if to accept her embrace and draw her to him.

"Arthur, these others mean me harm," she says. "Protect me, my husband." And too late, you realise what the Lucy-creature has done.

"Yes, my beloved," Arthur says, turning towards you, the club he is carrying gripped tight in his hand.

The changed children surround Quincey and Van Helsing, while Arthur focuses his attention on you.

If you want to use *The Pen is Mightier* special ability, and you still can, turn to **38**. If not, turn to **68**.

16

DR SEWARD'S DIARY

(Kept in phonograph)

4 October

Come the afternoon, Van Helsing, Lord Godalming, Quincey Morris and I set off to find out what ship the Count had boarded and whither it was bound...

"I am sure the Count wishes to return to his Transylvania," says Professor Van Helsing when the four of you arrive at the Port of London, "and I feel sure that he must go by the mouth of the Danube, or somewhere else in the Black Sea, since that is the way by which he first came to your England."

And so, you begin your search by trying to ascertain which ships left for the Black Sea last night, following Arthur's advice and paying a visit to Lloyd's of London, where a record is kept of all ships that sail, no matter how small they might be.

Sure enough, there you discover that only one Black-Sea-bound ship went out with the tide, the *Czarina Catherine*, and she set sail from Doolittle's Wharf for the Bulgarian port of Varna, and thence to other places along the Danube.

"So!" the Professor exclaims. "This is the ship the Count is travelling on."

At Doolittle's Wharf you find a large man sitting in a small wooden office and ask him about the *Czarina Catherine*. Red of face and loud of voice, accompanied by much swearing – having been given a little something by Quincey to loosen his tongue – he asks about among the stevedores until you are able to piece together what the Count has been up to.

* * * *

Yesterday afternoon, at about five o'clock, a man arrived at the wharf, who was clearly in a desperate hurry, with a great box upon a cart. He was tall, thin and pale, with a high nose, gleaming white teeth, and eyes that seemed to burn, so intense was his stare, and dressed all in black. He too was free with his money, making quick inquiries as to which ships were sailing for the Black Sea, which led him to an introduction with Captain Donelson of the *Czarina Catherine*.

He astounded everyone by lifting the great box down from the cart by himself. Having stowed it on board, the man told the captain he would return to check upon his cargo when he had seen to the business of filling in the necessary shipping forms. But having been paid, Donelson was keen to set sail, and had no intention of waiting for the man to return.

But a thin mist began to creep up from the river, and it grew, and grew, until a dense fog enveloped the ship and all around her. Indeed, the fog did not depart until the tall, thin man returned. He boarded to check on his cargo and went down with the mate and saw where it was placed, and then came up and stood awhile on deck in the fog. It was assumed he had left again by himself, for none saw him leave.

The fog began to melt away, and all was clear once more. The ship left on the ebb tide and by morning would doubtless have been far out in the mouth of the Thames.

"The *Czarina Catherine* will be well out to sea by now," the Professor says, his bushy eyebrows bunching.

And so, having gleaned as much information as you can, the four of you return to Purfleet and Carfax Asylum.

* * * *

The following evening, Van Helsing calls another meeting of the Vampire-Hunters in your private study.

Turn to **96**.

17

Clearly Quincey is suffering some maddening side-effect from the snake bite; that can be the only possible explanation for his sudden change in character. Foaming at the lips, the blade of his knife flashing in the firelight, while the gypsies watch from the edge of the circle and do nothing to intervene, he launches himself at you. (In this battle, Quincey has the initiative.)

QUINCEY MORRIS   COMBAT 8   ENDURANCE 9

You do not really want to hurt your companion, so you must reduce your *Combat Rating* by 1 point for the duration of this battle. If you win two consecutive Combat Rounds, or if you manage to reduce the Texan's *Endurance* score to 4 points or fewer, turn to **37** at once.

18

With five of you working together, you manage to force the door and thereby gain entry to Carfax House – the splintering of the wood around the lock, and the clatter of the mechanism falling to the floor, echoing through the passageways of the old mansion.

Gain 2 *Blood* points and turn to **301**.

19

And then your blade is in your hand and you slice its keen edge through the vampire's throat.

A look of horror on his face, Dracula stumbles away from you, clutching at the wound, as blood pumps between his clawing fingers. Suddenly Quincey Morris is there beside you, and with a shout of rage and effort, he plunges his great Bowie knife into the monster's heart.

Before your very eyes, and almost in the drawing of a breath, the vampire's entire body crumbles into grave dust – first the flesh and then the skeleton beneath – which disperses on the wind, and in a moment is gone.

Turn to **75**.

20

The asylum is silent when your party returns, save for some poor creature who is screaming away in one of the distant wards, and a low, moaning sound coming from another wretch's room. The poor soul is doubtless torturing himself, after the manner of the insane, with needless thoughts of pain.

You tiptoe into your own room and find Mina asleep. She is breathing so softly that you have to put your ear down to hear it. She also looks paler than usual, and you hope the meeting tonight did not upset her too much.

You settle down to sleep on the sofa, so as not to disturb her. You are truly thankful that she is to be left out of your future work, and even any deliberations. It is too great a strain for a woman to bear.

* * * *

It is only to be expected that you would oversleep, for the previous day was a busy one, and the night had no rest at all. Even Mina must have felt its exhaustion, for though you sleep until the sun is high, you are still awake before her, and have to call several times before she stirs.

Having breakfasted, you leave your wife in Dr Seward's safekeeping and set off for London once more, determined to find out what happened to the twenty-one boxes that were missing from the chapel of Carfax House.

You know that fifty boxes of earth were received by Mr Billington in Whitby and that these were passed on to Carter Paterson, who was responsible for having them delivered to Purfleet. The question is, who then took twenty-one of those boxes away again, and where did they take them?

The vital clue required to solve the mystery is amidst Mina's transcriptions of Dr Seward's phonograph cylinders, specifically in a report made by his colleague, Dr Hennessey. The carriers who came to take the boxes away were involved in an altercation with one of Dr Seward's patients, who had managed to break out of the asylum. Thankfully, Dr Hennessey took their names and addresses, in case they might be needed.

The men you need to interview are Jack Smollet and Thomas Snelling, who are both in the employ of Harris & Sons, Moving and Shipment Company, Orange Master's Yard, Soho.

Upon arriving in London, you make your way first to Mr Snelling's house and then Mr Smollet's, interviewing each in turn, but what they tell you only confirms what you had started to suspect yourself. Dracula has had the 'missing' boxes of earth transported to the very properties you aided him in purchasing around London.

* * * *

You return to Purfleet later that evening, much to your wife's delight. After dinner, while you meet with the others again in Dr Seward's study to discuss developments, Mina retires to bed, complaining that she feels terribly tired, the poor dear.

Your meeting is soon interrupted, however, when a wild yell from the ward below, brings Simmons, one of the hospital attendants, to Dr Seward's study.

"Come quickly, Doctor," he says, breathlessly, having run here as fast as he could. "It's Renfield. He's been involved in some kind of accident."

Turn to **676**.

21

You hand over your Silver Crucifix (strike it from the Equipment Box on your Adventure Sheet) but you return the following day to be given three dozen silver-plated bullets, in return for a few folded notes from Arthur's seemingly inexhaustible fortune.

Record the Silver Bullets on your Adventure Sheet and then turn to **703**.

22

The boom of Arthur's rifle discharging almost makes you jump out of your saddle.

The wolf's legs give way beneath it and it bowls along the road into a snowdrift.

Cross off one use of *The Pen is Mightier* special ability and turn to **64**.

23

All around you, you can see wolves gathering – singly, as well as in twos and threes, and even greater numbers – and moving in for the kill. If you are going to stop the wagon, you are going to have to fight your way through the wolves first.

If you want to use *The Pen is Mightier* special ability, cross off one use and turn to **76**. If not, turn to **51**.

24

There is no time to lose, and your situation has become even more desperate, as the longer you take to find the remaining boxes of earth, the greater the risk that your dear wife could become like poor Lucy Westenra, or one of the Weird Sisters you fell prey to whilst imprisoned within Castle Dracula.

Fortunately, you are sure you know where the remaining twenty-one boxes have been taken – to the very properties you helped the Count acquire, and that are located in the London districts of Piccadilly, Walworth, and Mile End.

Turn to **84**.

25

You reconvene later that evening in your suite after supper, at Mina's request. (Restore up to 4 *Endurance* points.)

She comes to the meeting armed with all manner of notes, maps and other papers.

"I have been carrying out my own investigation into the matter of how the Count intends to return to Castle Dracula, and I believe I have made a discovery," she says. "My surmise is this – that in London the Count decided to get back to his castle by water, as the most safe and secret way. He was brought from the castle by Szgany gypsies, and they probably delivered their cargo to Slovaks who took the boxes of earth to Varna, to be shipped to London. Thus, the Count knew who could arrange this service again for the return journey.

"When the box was on land, before sunrise or after sunset, the vampire came out from his makeshift coffin and met with Skinsky, instructing him to arrange carriage for the box upriver. When this was done, he covered his tracks..."

She spreads the map out on a table so that all of you can see it quite clearly.

"I have examined this chart and find that the river most suitable for the Slovaks to have ascended is either the Pruth or the Sereth. Of these two, the Pruth is the more easily navigated, but the Sereth is, at Fundu, joined by the Bistritza which runs up round the Borgo Pass. It makes a loop around Castle Dracula and so is the closest that can be got to his home by water."

"Now we are on his trail once again!" Van Helsing exclaims in delight. "We may yet succeed in our mission. Our enemy has the start on us, so here and now we must plan what we are all going to do and do it tonight!"

"I shall book passage on a boat travelling upstream and follow him," says Arthur.

"And I shall hire horses, to follow on the bank in case he puts ashore," says Quincey.

"Good!" says the Professor. "But neither of you must go alone. There may be the Count's allies to overcome; the Szgany is strong and rough, and he carries rude arms."

You speak up quickly, volunteering yourself to accompany one of your fellows, but who do you want to travel with? Will it be Arthur (turn to **219**), or Quincey (turn to **249**)?

26

You push your horses hard, barely resting, so desperate are you to reach Castle Dracula before your quarry does.

At dawn on the sixth day of November, from your position atop the Carpathian crags, you see a party of Szgany ahead of you, dashing away from the river with their leiter-wagon. They are surrounding it in a cluster, and hurry along as though beset.

The snow is falling lightly and there is a strange excitement in the air. Far off you hear the howling of wolves; the snow brings them down from the mountains, and they present another danger you may have to face in time.

Your horses ready, you are soon off, in pursuit of the wagon and the gypsies.

If you have the code word *Lángok* ticked off, turn to **991**. If not, turn to **207**.

27

"I am younger and stronger, Professor," you tell your mentor. "It must be me."

"Then get ready at once. I will bring up my bag."

But as Van Helsing goes downstairs, there is a knock at the hall door. The maid opens it and in rushes Arthur Holmwood.

"Jack!" he calls, upon seeing you on the landing. "I was so anxious. I read between the lines of your letter and have been in agony. My father is better, so I ran down here to see for myself. Is this gentleman Professor Van Helsing? I am so thankful to you, sir, for coming."

"And you, sir, have come just in time," Van Helsing says, holding out his hand, "for our dear Miss Lucy is in a very bad way. But you can help her."

"What can I do?" Arthur asks hoarsely. "Tell me and I shall do it. My life is hers, and I would give the last drop of blood in my body for her."

"My young sir," the Professor says with a gruff laugh. "I do not ask so much as that, not the last drop! But Miss Lucy is in need of blood, and blood she must have, or she will die. We must perform what we call a transfusion of blood, from the full veins of one to the empty veins of the other. John was going to give his blood, but now you are here. Our nerves are not so calm and our blood not so bright as yours."

You all go up to Lucy's room together. Van Helsing takes some things from his bag and lays them out on a little table. Then he mixes a sleeping draught, and helps Lucy drink it: "Now, miss, here is your medicine. Swallow it all down."

Her eyelids start to flicker, as the narcotic begins to manifest its potency, and she falls into a deep sleep. Then with swiftness, but with absolute method, Van Helsing performs the operation.

As the transfusion goes on, some colour returns to Lucy's cheeks, and through Arthur's growing pallor, the joy shines from his face.

The Professor stands, with watch in hand, and with his eyes fixed now on Lucy, then Arthur, and back again, constantly.

You start to grow anxious as you can tell the blood loss is taking its toll on Arthur, strong though he is, and it gives you some idea of the terrible strain Lucy's body must have been under that what weakens her lover does not restore her fully.

Presently Van Helsing says in a soft voice, "It is enough. You attend him. I will look to her."

Having dressed the wound the procedure made in Arthur's arm, you take him downstairs, holding on to him the whole way, for you can see how much the experience has weakened him. You give him port wine and let him lie down a while. When the light-headedness has passed, you send him home to rest, sleep much and eat much.

Turn to **56**.

28

Having sat up all night, as the sun rises above the snow-clad trees, a great weariness overcomes you and you lie down beside the embers of the fire, wrapped up in your thick fur coat, and soon fall asleep…

* * * *

You open your eyes to total darkness.

"Professor?" you call. "Professor Van Helsing?" But there is no reply.

Getting up from your place by the fire, you cross the holy circle without suffering any ill-effects and set off towards the castle in search of your missing guardian. You glide over the snow, leaving no trace upon the white blanket covering the ground.

Ahead of you stands the castle, black and forbidding, but an open archway beckons to you. As you draw closer, faces coalesce from the shadows, white as bone, their eyes sunken, mouths open, so that they look almost like skulls.

"Come to us, sister!" the vampyre women whisper. "Come to us. Join us. Be as one with us."

And then the sisters' skull-like faces are all you can see, as they swell to fill your vision, elongating and distorting, long snake-like fangs pushing through bleeding gums, and you feel that they will swallow you whole.

Take a Terror test. If you pass the test, turn to **900**. If you fail the test, turn to **6**.

29

You have strayed too close. Hearing your footsteps on the gravel path, Renfield suddenly spins around, white fire burning in his eyes, and, shrieking like a banshee, he throws himself at you.

If you want to use *The Pen is Mightier* special ability, cross off one use and turn to **292**. If not, turn to **9**.

30

"Come to me!" the vampire commands, and you feel something primal and feral snarl and writhe within you as it strains to obey Dracula's summons.

Take a Combat test. If you pass the test, turn to **100**. If you fail the test, turn to **65**.

31

When you are clear of the town, you signal the driver to stop.

"Tell me, Johann," you say, when you have the coachman's full attention, "what is tonight?"

He crosses himself before answering: *"Walpurgisnacht."*

Taking out his watch – a great, old-fashioned German silver thing as big as a turnip – he looks at it, with his eyebrows gathered together and an impatient shrug of his shoulders, clearly unhappy about this unnecessary delay.

If you want to press him to tell you more about this Walpurgisnacht, turn to **63**. If you merely want to motion him to proceed, turn to **92**.

32

Fortunately, you have already loaded your revolver with the silver ammunition. Unholstering the gun, you fire at the creatures pursuing you, holding them at bay. You know you have hit one of them when you hear a sharp yelp of pain.

Turn to **102**.

33

Whimpering in fear, the Sultan's pet sorcerer scuttles back into the shadows.

"You would stoop so low as to use black magic to defeat me, Mehmed?" you challenge your nemesis. "You must fear me a very great deal."

"I fear no man," the Conqueror rails, "no matter what the mystics might have told me about you – about what you will become. I will cut you down like the dog you are and take your throne like I have taken so many others before it!"

And with that, Mehmed the Conqueror runs at you, his scimitar flashing in his hand. (In this battle, the Sultan has the initiative.)

MEHMED THE CONQUEROR   COMBAT 10   ENDURANCE 10

If you are still alive after 6 Combat Rounds, or as soon as you reduce the Sultan's *Endurance* score to 4 points, whichever is sooner, turn to **113** at once.

34

You and Professor Van Helsing close on the cart, your weapons trained on the gypsies. In response, the gypsies draw their own weapons – all manner of knives and pistols – and hold themselves ready to attack.

Suddenly all is confusion, and the Szgany engage your brave companions in battle.

In the midst of it all you see Jonathan on one side of the ring of men, and Quincey on the other, forcing their way to the cart, clearly bent on finishing their task before the sun sets. Nothing hinders them, not the levelled guns or flashing knives of the gypsies, nor the wolves.

If the *Blood* score is 15 points or higher, turn to **959**. If it is lower than 15, turn to **956**.

35

Loading the Silver Bullets into your pistol, you will be able to dispatch another two of the shape-changers.

If all the Werewolves have been dealt with now, turn to **568**. If not, turn to **492**.

36

Exiting the room, do you want to try the door opposite you – the one bearing the dragon crest – if you haven't already done so (turn to **529**), or do you want to descend the steps to the next chamber (turn to **59**)?

37

You land a savage blow against the side of Quincey's head that knocks him out cold, but not for long.

As the American comes round muttering, "Where am I? What's going on?", you help him to his feet. Keeping your pistol trained on the Szgany witch, you make your way back to where you tethered your horses and help Quincey into the saddle.

An eerie stillness hangs over the camp and none of the gypsies makes a move to stop the two of you as you remount your horses and set off into the Borgo Pass.

Tick off the code word *Ţigani* and turn to **26**.

38

It is as if Arthur no longer knows you, no matter how much you cry his name, desperately hoping to make him see sense somehow. You realise you have no choice but to defend yourself against the bewitched Arthur.

But just as you raise your cudgel, Quincey leaps over the heads of the hissing urchins, and brings the hilt of his big Bowie knife down on the back of Arthur's head. His knees immediately give away and he crumples to the floor, in an unconscious heap.

Before he can do any more, the children leap onto Quincey's back, sending him sprawling on the cold marble floor of the tomb as well.

Cross off one use of *The Pen is Mightier* special ability and turn to **98**.

39

Faced by the horror that is the King of Vampires, the Prince of Darkness, Dracula the Un-Dead, your resolve shatters, and you cannot resist as he exerts his will against you.

You walk willingly to meet your end, a cruel smile spreading across the vampire's lips as you do so. But rather than sink his fangs into your throat and drink your blood, with one vicious thrust of his claw-fingered hand, he plunges it straight into your chest. When he pulls it free again, he has your still beating heart clutched in his gory grasp.

Having done all you can to stop the Count, thwarting his plans at every turn, there can be no place for you in Dracula's Empire of the Dead...

Your adventure ends here, in blood and snow and darkness.

THE END

40

Tearing out Skinsky's throat with your teeth, and slitting his belly open from sternum to groin, you leave his eviscerated corpse atop a tomb in the cemetery as a warning to any who might come after you, and then return to your box to await the arrival of the Slovaks.

Turn to **140**.

41

The corridor outside your cabin is empty. Unobserved by anyone else, the two of you make your way down the steps at the far end into the hold of the steamboat, where you find several more doors. The chugging of the engine reverberates through the structure of the vessel and the air is thick with the acrid smell of coke.

Indeed, the door closest to you opens onto a fuel store, with coke piled in partitioned stalls. The next door leads to the boat's stinking bilges, while the third takes you into the cargo hold itself.

By the light of a swaying oil lantern, you can make out several large packing crates and cases of scientific equipment. They are the same large cases and packing crates you discovered in the luggage van of the train from Varna. Lying on top of one of the cases is a crowbar, which has clearly been used to jemmy open the largest of the crates. Clouds of icy mist are escaping from the crack in the crate, where it has been partially-opened.

If you want to finish what someone else has clearly already started and use the crowbar to prise open the crate, turn to **816**. If you would rather leave well-enough alone, turn to **97**.

42

Hearing the rapid *pit-pat* of a swiftly driven horse's feet, you become aware of a carriage pulling up at the gate, and a few seconds later see Van Helsing running up the avenue.

"Have you only just arrived? Are we too late? Did you not get my telegram?"

You answer as quickly and as coherently as you can, explaining that you have been unable to make anyone in the house hear you.

Raising his hat solemnly, the Professor says, "Then I fear we are too late. Come, if there be no way open to get in, then we must make one."

At the back of the house, you find a kitchen window. The Professor produces a surgical saw from his bag and handing it to you, directs you to attack the iron bars that guard it. Having cut through three of them, Van Helsing uses a long thin knife to push back the fastening of the sashes. In this way, you open the window and make your way inside, followed by the Professor.

Do you want to search the ground floor of the house first (turn to **2**), or do you want to head straight upstairs to Lucy's room (urn to **72**)?

43

You fight off the dire wolf as best you can, whilst clinging onto your mount's reins with one hand. (You must reduce your *Combat Rating* by 1 point for the duration of this battle, but you have the initiative.)

DIRE WOLF   COMBAT 7   ENDURANCE 7

If you manage to kill the wolf within 6 Combat Rounds, turn to **64**. If the wolf is still alive after 6 Combat Rounds, turn to **64** anyway.

44

It is September before you return to England, but when you set foot on English soil again, it is as a married couple. You have never felt happier, despite all you have been through.

As a wedding gift, the Sisters of St Joseph and Ste Mary gave you each a phial of holy water. (Add the Holy Water to your Adventure Sheet.)

When you arrive in Exeter, you find a carriage waiting for you, and in it, although he has not been well himself, Mr Hawkins. He takes you to his house, where comfortable rooms have been readied for you, and that evening you dine together.

After dinner, Mr Hawkins raises his glass, saying, "My dears, I want to drink to your health and prosperity, and may every blessing attend you both. I have known you both since you were children, and now I want you to make your home here with me. I have neither wife nor child, and in my will I have left you everything."

It is a very happy evening indeed.

*   *   *   *

But the following morning makes you as sad as the previous evening made you happy, when poor Mr Hawkins is found to have died unexpectedly during the night.

In accordance with his will, together you inherit everything – the house, the business, and a fortune which to people of your modest upbringing is wealth beyond the dream of avarice.

Mr Hawkins also stipulated in his will that he wanted to be buried next to where his father lies interred, in London.

* * * *

The service is very simple and very solemn. There are only yourselves and the servants in attendance, along with one or two of Mr Hawkins' old friends from Exeter, his London agent, and a gentleman representing the Incorporated Law Society.

The two of you stand together, hand in hand, and feel that your best and dearest friend is gone.

Turn to **60**.

45

When you are safely ensconced inside your hotel, you go back over the notes you have taken and, with the aid of a map of the region, try to work out where the vile Count could be. And slowly you come to what seems like the only possible conclusion.

Sending your husband to reconvene the Vampire-Hunters after supper, in a private dining room at the hotel, you join the meeting armed with your notes, as well as the map. (Restore up to 4 *Endurance* points.)

"I have been carrying out my own investigation into the matter of how the Count intends to return to Castle Dracula," you explain, "and I believe I have made a discovery. My surmise is this – that in London the Count decided to get back to his castle by water, as the most safe and secret way. He was brought from the castle by Szgany gypsies, and they probably delivered their cargo to Slovaks who took the boxes of earth to Varna, to be shipped to London. Thus, the Count knew who could arrange this service again for the return journey.

"When the box was on land, before sunrise or after sunset, the vampire came out from his makeshift coffin and met with Skinsky, instructing him to arrange carriage for the box upriver. When this was done, he covered his tracks..."

You pause to spread out the map on a table so that everyone can see it clearly.

"I have examined this chart and find that the river most suitable for the Slovaks to have ascended is either the Pruth or the Sereth. Of these two, the Pruth is the more easily navigated, but the Sereth is, at Fundu, joined by the Bistritza which runs up round the Borgo

Pass. It makes a loop around Castle Dracula and so is the closest that can be got to his home by water."

Professor Van Helsing clasps your hands in his, saying, "Our dear Madam Mina is once more our teacher. Her eyes have seen what the rest of us were blind to. But now we are on his trail once again! We may yet succeed in our mission. Our enemy has the start on us, so here and now we must plan what we are all going to do, and do it tonight!"

"I shall book passage on a boat travelling upstream and follow him," says Arthur.

"And I shall hire horses, to follow on the bank in case he puts ashore," says Quincey.

"Good!" says the Professor. "But neither of you must go alone. There must be force to overwhelm force, if needs be, for there may be the Count's allies to overcome; the Szgany is strong and rough, and he carries rude arms."

"I think I had better go with Quincey," says Dr Seward. "We have been accustomed to hunt together, and we two, well-armed, will be a match for whatever may come along."

The Professor addresses your husband then: "Friend Jonathan, you should go with Lord Godalming up the river, and whilst John and Quincey guard the bank where perchance our enemy might be landed, I will take Madam Mina right into the heart of the enemy's country."

But hearing this, your dear husband breaks his silence and cries out in distress: "Do you mean to say, Professor Van Helsing, that you would bring Mina, tainted as she is with that devil's illness, right into the jaws of his death-trap? Not for the world! Not for Heaven or Hell!"

He becomes almost speechless for a minute, before finding the wherewithal to continue.

"Do you know what the place is? Have you seen that awful den of hellish infamy with the very moonlight alive with grisly shapes, and every speck of dust that whirls in the wind a devouring monster in embryo? Have you felt the vampire's lips upon your throat?"

Here he turns to you and, as his eyes alight on your forehead, he throws up his arms with a cry of, "Oh, my God, what have we done to have this terror upon us?"

"Oh, my friend, it is because I would save Madam Mina from that awful place that I would go," explains the Professor, the tone of his voice calming you all. "God forbid that I should take her into that place, but there is much to be done, and many places to be sanctified, so that his nest of vipers be obliterated. I will take Madam Mina by carriage, following the route you yourself took, Jonathan, when you travelled from Bistritz over the Borgo Pass, and that way we will find our way to Castle Dracula. There, Madam Mina's hypnotic power will surely help, for we shall find our way all dark and unknown otherwise after the first sunrise when we are near that fateful place."

* * * *

Less than two hours after your macabre visit to the graveyard of St Peter's, you and Professor Van Helsing board the last train to Veresti, where you will acquire a carriage to drive to the Borgo Pass. It takes all your courage to say goodbye to your darling husband, for there is a very real possibility you may never meet again. (Add 1 point to your *Terror* score.)

You have plenty of money with you, as you intend to buy a carriage and horses and drive yourselves. The Professor knows a smattering of words in a great many languages, so you should get on all right. And you are armed; Quincey Morris has furnished you with a large-bore revolver, while Arthur has leant you a lady's untipped fencing sabre.

(Add the Revolver and the Sabre to your Adventure Sheet.)

You do not delay in settling into your compartment in the last carriage on the train, hoping to get at least some rest before arriving in Veresti, while the Professor goes to the lounge car to enjoy a drink and a smoke before retiring.

However, you have not been travelling for even an hour when you hear a cry and come to with a start, fearing the worst.

Do you want to leave your compartment to investigate (turn to **704**), or do you think it would be wiser to remain where you are (turn to **67**)?

46

JONATHAN HARKER'S JOURNAL

4 October

Professor Van Helsing instructed me to stay with my dear Mina, while the rest of them set off for the Port of London...

Your wife has brightened up considerably and the certainty that the Count is out of the country has given her great comfort. And such comfort is strength to her.

For your own part, now that you are no longer face to face with the horror the Count embodies, it seems almost impossible to believe that the threat he once posed was real. Even your own terrible experiences in Castle Dracula seem like a long-forgotten dream.

(Deduct 1 point from your *Terror* score.)

But then your eye falls upon the red scar that now blemishes your poor darling's white skin. Alas! How can you disbelieve when confronted with such evidence? While the imprint of the holy wafer remains upon her forehead there can be no disbelief.

But nonetheless, the pain and the fear are reduced. There is some guiding purpose manifest throughout, which is in itself comforting.

* * * *

The following evening, when the others have returned to the asylum, a meeting of the Vampire-Hunters is convened once again in Dr Seward's private study.

Turn to **96**.

47

When you get to the porch, the Professor opens his bag and takes out all manner of items, which he lays on the step, sorting them into four groups, evidently one for each of you.

"My friends," he says, in a barely audible whisper, "we are heading into terrible danger, and we need to arm ourselves accordingly. Remember, our enemy has the strength of twenty men, and we must guard ourselves from his touch. Keep this near your heart," he says, giving each member of your party a small silver crucifix, "and put these flowers round your neck" – he hands each of you a wreath of withered garlic blossoms – "and of all *this*, which we must not desecrate needlessly."

'This' is a portion of Sacred Wafer, blessed during the Holy Eucharist, which he has put into envelopes, and which he shares out among your brave band now.

(Record the Silver Crucifix, the Garlic Garland and the Sacred Wafer in the Equipment Box on your Adventure Sheet.)

"And now we must gain ingress to the house."

If you have a set of Skeleton Keys, turn to the number stamped on the tag they are attached to. If you do not have a set of Skeleton Keys, turn to **18**.

48

You rush to the nearest cypress, but find it affords you barely any shelter at all from the hammering hailstones, leaving you no choice but to run for the refuge offered by the tomb.

Take an Endurance test. If you pass the test, turn to **77**, but if you fail the test, turn to **106**.

49

You catch sight of Renfield again as he disappears behind the angle of the old house and set off after him.

On the far side of the manse, you are surprised to find him pressed close against the old iron-bound oak door of a chapel. He seems to be talking to someone, although you can see no one else there.

"I am here to do your bidding, Master," you hear him say. "I am your slave, and you will reward me, for I shall be faithful. I have worshipped you long and afar off. Now that you are near, I await your commands, and you will not pass me by, will you, dear Master, in your distribution of good things?"

His obsequious pleadings send a shiver down your spine. (Add 1 point to your *Terror* score but deduct 2 *Blood* points.)

If you have the code word *Auxilia* ticked off, turn to **292**. If not, turn to **29**.

50

The asylum is silent when your party returns, save for some poor creature who is screaming away in one of the distant wards, and a low, moaning sound coming from another wretch's room. The poor soul is doubtless torturing himself, after the manner of the insane, with needless thoughts of pain.

With the dawn close at hand, you retire to your private quarters to sleep.

* * * *

It is almost noon when you are awakened by the Professor walking into your room. He is more jolly and cheerful than usual, and it is evident that the night's work has helped take some of the brooding weight off his mind.

After going over the details of your nocturnal adventure again, he suddenly announces, "Your patient interests me greatly. May I visit him with you this morning? I want to talk to him about his delusion of consuming living things to prolong his own life."

"But the answer is here," you say, laying your hand on Mrs Harker's typewritten transcription of your phonograph diary. "When our learned lunatic made that very statement of how he used to consume life, his mouth was actually nauseous with the flies and spiders he had just eaten."

Van Helsing smiles then. "Good! Perhaps I may gain more knowledge out of the folly of this madman than I shall from the teaching of the most wise. Who knows?"

While the Professor takes the typewritten manuscript away with him to study, you get up and set about your day's work – the business of running the asylum.

* * * *

That evening, after dinner, and with Mrs Harker having gone to bed, the rest of you gather round the fire in your study to discuss the day's developments. But a wild yell, and the arrival of Simmons, one of the hospital attendants, at your door interrupts your meeting.

"Come quickly, Doctor," he says, breathlessly, having run here from the ward. "It's Renfield. He's been involved in some kind of accident."

Turn to **676**.

51

As you spur your horse forward, one of the largest of the animals leaps up at you. (You have the initiative in this battle.)

WOLF   COMBAT 7   ENDURANCE 6

If you defeat your opponent, turn to **76**.

52

Spurring your steed onwards, you race along the road through the night as the twig-fingers of branches reach for you from the side of the road.

Take an Agility test. If you pass the test, turn to **102**, but if you fail the test, turn to **82**.

53

"Look! Madam Mina, look!" the Professor suddenly shouts.

From your vantage point it is possible to see a great distance; and far off, beyond the white waste of snow, you can see the river lying like a black ribbon in kinks and curls as it winds its way through the mountains.

However, straight in front of you, and not too far off, you can make out a group of mounted men hurrying along through the snowstorm. In their midst is a cart, a long leiter-wagon that sweeps from side to side as it races along the rough road towards the castle. From the men's clothes you can tell that they are gypsies – no doubt the Szgany Jonathan encountered during his first visit to Transylvania.

On the cart is a great square chest, and your heart leaps when you set eyes upon it, for you feel that the end is near.

"They are coming quickly," says the Professor, watching the progress of the wagon and its attendants like you. "They are flogging the horses and galloping as hard as they can."

Beyond the swirling wall of snow, you can make out the sinister, shadowy presence of the Count's decaying stronghold, silhouetted against the red orb of the sun.

"They are racing for the sunset. We may be too late," he says hollowly.

Hearing a sudden cry, you catch sight of two horsemen following hard on the gypsies' heels, coming up from the south. It is Quincey Morris and Dr Seward! And then, from the north you see two more riders, galloping at break-neck speed along the pass, and you know at once that it is your beloved Jonathan and the noble Arthur.

"They are all converging!" the Professor shouts in glee, reloading his rifle, while you make sure you have your revolver to hand.

But it is not only the fearless Vampire-Killers who are converging on this spot before Castle Dracula, for you can see, here and there, dots moving singly and in twos and threes, and larger numbers, as the wolves gather for the kill.

The wind comes in fierce bursts, furiously driving the snow before it and sweeping around you in circling eddies. You can clearly distinguish the individuals of each party now, the pursued and the pursuers, the former redoubling their efforts as the sun drops lower and lower over the mountain tops.

Closer and closer they come, and all at once two voices call out: "Halt!" One is Jonathan's, raised in passion, the other Mr Morris's resolute tone of quiet command.

The gypsies rein in their horses, and in that instant Arthur and Jonathan draw alongside the wagon on one side, as Dr Seward and Quincey join it on the other.

The leader of the gypsies waves them back, and in a fierce voice commands the Szgany to keep going. But the four men raise their guns and order them to stop.

* * * *

If you want to continue the story as Mina Harker, turn to **34**. If you would rather continue the story as either Jonathan Harker or Dr Seward, turn to **14**.

54

There is no time to lose, and your situation has become even more desperate, as the longer you take to find the remaining boxes of earth, the greater the risk that Mrs Harker will end up like your own dear Lucy, and you could not bear to see that happen to another man's beloved.

However, your party may actually be one step ahead of the Count in this regard, for Harker helped Dracula acquire not just Carfax House, but three other properties, all located in London: one in Piccadilly, one in Walworth, and one in Mile End.

Turn to **84**.

55

Mehmed earned the epithet 'the Conqueror' for a reason. You are not able to resist the temporal strength he wields and Târgoviște falls to his forces. Despite offering to pay him what the Sultan believes he is due, in terms of both money and boys, it is too little too late.

But not one to beg, you make a defiant last stand against the Sultan's forces, leading your men into battle in a last ditch attempt to salvage your reputation and ensure your legacy. You are ultimately cut down on the steps of your own palace.

Your adventure, like your life, is over.

THE END

56

When Arthur has gone, you return to Lucy's room, and find her sleeping gently, her breathing already stronger. Van Helsing sits at her bedside, looking at her intently.

You notice that the narrow black band Lucy always wears round her throat, fastened with an old diamond buckle given to her by Arthur, has been dragged up a little, revealing an unpleasant red mark on her throat.

"What do you make of it?" Van Helsing asks, encouraging you to take a closer look.

Just over the external jugular vein there are two puncture marks, not large, but not wholesome looking either. There is no sign of disease, but the edges of the holes are white and appear worn, almost reminding you of something that has been gnawed at.

Could this wound be the reason for Lucy's anaemia? But then if that were true, the whole bed should be scarlet with her blood, for her to be as pale and as emaciated as she was before the transfusion.

"I can make nothing of it," you reply.

"I must go back to Amsterdam tonight," the Professor says, rising to his feet. "There are books and things there which I need. You must keep watch all night. See that she is well-fed and that nothing disturbs her. I shall be back as soon as possible, and then we may begin."

"May *begin*? What on earth do you mean?"

"We shall see!" is all he will say as he hurries out of the room. But he comes back a moment later, putting his head inside the door and holding up a warning finger says, "Remember, she is your charge. If you leave her, and harm befalls her, you shall not sleep easy hereafter!"

Turn to **86**.

57

One of the snakes latches onto your face, sinking its long fangs into your cheek and releasing its venom into your bloodstream. You cry out in pain even as you yank the serpent free and hurl it into the hungry flames of the gypsies' campfire.

Lose 2 *Endurance* points and turn to **78**.

58

"Come to us, sister. Come!" the weird women call again, but you resist their siren lure. God be thanked, you are not like them. Not yet.

Van Helsing advances towards them, the piece of burning firewood held out before him in one hand and another piece of holy wafer in the other.

They draw back into the darkness then, laughing their low horrid laugh. You busy yourself feeding the fire, knowing that you are safe as long as you remain inside the circle.

Presently the horses begin to scream, as the unnatural women indulge their savage passions by killing the animals. Their whinnying moans cease at last, and you know that the poor beasts will never feel terror again, but you do.

(Add 1 point to your *Terror* score.)

* * * *

You remain beside the fire until the red glow of the dawn begins to permeate the snowy gloom.

Van Helsing leaves the circle to check on the horses, but when he returns not many minutes later, he merely tells you what you already know: "The horses are dead, all of them slaughtered by those monsters."

His bushy eyebrows beetle in rage and frustration, and anger clouds his expression.

"I will make my way to the castle, while the sun is up, and put an end to them where they lie," he says. "Madam Mina, wait here until I return, and whatever you do, do not step outside the circle."

Do you want to do as the Professor says (turn to **28**), or will you insist that you go with him, into Castle Dracula, in search of the Weird Sisters (turn to **872**)?

59

You move as if in a trance, your footsteps carrying you down the flight of steps, and enter the opulently adorned chamber. Stopping at the bottom, you take in your surroundings by the lamp held in your hand.

This was evidently the portion of the castle occupied by the ladies in bygone days, for the furniture has more an air of comfort than any you have seen so far. Before you, beneath a canopy like that of some battlefield-pitched pavilion, are strewn all manner of rugs, and dust-covered cushions, couches and divans, while silken drapes hang like cobwebs from the ceiling.

The sense of sleep is upon you, and the obstinacy that comes with it, and you determine to sleep here, where, of old, ladies sat and sang, and lived sweet lives whilst their gentle breasts were sad for their menfolk, away in the midst of remorseless wars.

Soft moonlight streams through the diamond panes of a great window, soothing you and only feeding your desire to lay down and turn the tables on your nocturnal existence, and so you lie down upon one of the great couches.

Take an ESP test. If you pass the test, turn to **200**, but if you fail the test, turn to **166**.

60

After the funeral, you take a bus to Hyde Park Corner and from there walk down Piccadilly, with you holding Mina by the arm.

And then you see him.

He appears far younger than the last time you saw him, but there can be no mistaking that aquiline nose and thick moustache, although he now looks more like the portrait of his ancestor that was hung over the fireplace in your quarters at Castle Dracula and has acquired a pointed beard.

"My God!" you gasp, clutching your wife's arm so tightly that she gives a gasp of pain herself.

"Whatever is the matter?" she asks, wincing.

But you cannot tear your eyes away. "Do you see who it is?"

"No, dear," Mina replies, following your terrified, unblinking gaze. "I don't know him. Who is it?"

"It is the man himself! It is the Count, but he has grown young!"

Add 2 points to your *Terror* score and then *Take a Terror test*. If you pass the test, turn to **103**. If you fail the test, turn to **133**.

61

Reaching the deep Doric doorway of the tomb, you crouch against the massive bronze door, gaining at least some protection from the pummelling hailstones, for now they only drive against you as they ricochet from the ground or the marble walls.

But as you lean against the door, with a groaning of ungreased hinges, it opens inwards. The shelter of even a tomb is welcome in the midst of such a pitiless tempest, and you are about to enter when there comes a flash of forked lightning that lights up the whole expanse of the heavens.

In that instant, as the darkness of the tomb is banished, you catch sight of a beautiful woman, with plump cheeks and full red lips, seemingly asleep upon a stone bier.

As the thunder breaks overhead, she stirs and rises from her marble bed, but you are not even sure that her feet are touching the ground.

But how can this be? Surely to have been lying in a stone cold tomb, in the graveyard belonging to a village that was depopulated centuries ago, the woman must have been dead. But then how is it that she can appear as fresh as if she has just woken from a sleep?

(Add 1 point to your *Terror* score and tick off the code word *Succubus*.)

She suddenly fixes you with eyes that seem to burn red, and glides towards you, her hair and gown streaming out behind her in the gale that has found its way into the sepulchre. Her pristine features twist into a demonic snarl and, speaking German, she shrieks, "Who would disturb my sleep this Walpurgis Night?"

And then, hands outstretched before her, reaching for you with fingers twisted into claws, she flies at you screaming: "No matter! You will pay with your life's blood!"

If you want to use *The Pen is Mightier* special ability, cross off one use and turn to **131**. If not, turn to **91**.

62

Realising that the young Englishman is in danger from another of the undead, with her own sinister plans, your anger manifests as a deep-throated growl.

Thunder rumbles overhead, as if in reply, and a bolt of brilliant white light streaks down from out of the clouds, finding the iron spike surmounting the tomb, and pours through it into the earth. The mausoleum explodes with a roar of incandescent flame and shattered masonry.

The Englishman is hurled backwards to land in the snow, while the occupant of the tomb emerges from the wreckage of the broken building, her face on fire, the vellum white skin blackening and turning to ash and embers, like parchment. The undead mistress of this dead place flies at you, on huge, bat-like wings, shrieking with banshee-fury, and with claws and teeth bared.

You meet the furious Countess in brutal battle. (You have the initiative.)

COUNTESS DOLINGEN   COMBAT 9   ENDURANCE 9

If you slay the undead Countess, turn to **884**. Alternatively, you may choose to deduct 3 *Blood* points and turn to **907** straightaway, without having to engage in battle.

63

Johann shakes his head, clearly unwilling to divulge anymore, but you are insistent.

Through a combination of the coachman's broken English and your little knowledge of German, you learn that, according to the belief of millions of people, Walpurgis Night is when the Devil walks abroad, when graves open, and the dead come forth from them and walk. It is a time when all evil things of earth, and air, and water, hold their revels.

Seeing the terrified look on the coachman's face as he shares what he knows of this accursed night with you, leaves you feeling unnerved. (Add 1 point to your *Terror* score and tick off the code word *Superstition*.)

Wishing that you had paid more heed to the old adage "a little knowledge is a dangerous thing", you instruct Johann to drive on.

Turn to **92**.

64

The wolves fall back and vanish back into the forest whence they came.

Turn to **483**.

65

"Come to me!" comes the Count's voice again, and you cannot resist him.

As you slink through the snow towards the vampire, your body starts to morph and change, muscles and bones reshaping themselves, your clothes falling from you, useless to you now that you are a wolf.

You open your mouth, now an elongated muzzle, and raise a howl of praise to your master's glory.

"The children of the night," he laughs cruelly. "What music they make!"

And then, impelled by your new master's sheer force of will, you join your wolf brethren in turning on your former companions.

Your adventure, like their lives, is over.

THE END

66

MINA HARKER'S JOURNAL

5 October

Our meeting for report. Present: Professor Van Helsing, Lord Godalming, Dr Seward, Mr Quincey Morris, Jonathan Harker, Mina Harker...

A meeting of the Crew of Light is convened in Dr Seward's private study, three nights after Count Dracula attacked you in your bedchamber, bestowing upon you the curse of the vampire.

You are pleased to be busy again, as to you has fallen the task of taking the minutes of the meeting.

Turn to **96**.

67

In only a matter of moments Van Helsing appears at your compartment door. He looks relieved to see that you are unharmed.

"Madam Mina, did you hear that cry?" he asks.

You confirm that you did and in return he tells you that there has been a death.

"I'm going to investigate," he says.

"You believe it to be the work of Count Dracula?" you ask, your heart pounding within your chest.

"I do not know. But I intend to find out."

You are confused; surely if the vampire was on board the train you would have sensed his presence, so strong is the connection between you.

If you want to go with the Professor to find out more, turn to **704**.
If you would rather persuade him not to get involved, turn to **87**.

68

It is as if Arthur no longer knows you, no matter how much you cry his name, desperately hoping to make him see sense somehow. You realise you have no choice but to defend yourself against your confused friend. (In this battle you have the initiative.)

ARTHUR   COMBAT 8   ENDURANCE 9

You do not want to hurt the poor man, and you certainly don't want to kill him, so you fight merely to incapacitate him and put him out of the fight.

For the duration of this battle, you must reduce your *Combat Rating* by 1 point, as you are trying to knock Arthur out, rather than kill him. If you win two consecutive Combat Rounds, or if you reduce Arthur's Endurance score to 4 points or fewer, whichever happens first, you succeed in knocking him out – turn to **98** immediately.

69

Watching from the window, you catch sight of Renfield darting between the trees that proliferate within the asylum grounds as he makes for the high wall that separates your property from the abandoned manse that is Carfax House.

Quick as a flash, he scrambles up and over the wall, as if he were a gecko, and vanishes into the grounds of the derelict house.

Fearing that Renfield could be both a danger to himself and others, you tell Barlow to gather the other attendants and follow you into the Carfax estate.

Leaving the asylum, you hurry down the road to the gates of Carfax House, which stand chained and padlocked shut. However, the chains are loose enough that you are able to squeeze between the gates and sprint along the drive towards the great shadow of the empty house.

Tick off the code word *Auxilia* and then turn to **49**.

70

Arriving at the shuttered warehouse, you are horrified to find that vermin have gnawed their way through the crates and devoured the preserved corpses hidden within.

Having subsisted on a diet of strigoi flesh for some weeks, the rodents have mutated and become monstrous examples of their kind, their bloated flesh bursting with suppurating boils, their eyes cloudy with cataracts, and their naked tails covered in ulcers.

You take out your fury on the rats, killing every single last one of them, but it does not change the fact that your plans of conquest have been dealt a significant blow by the hungry rodents. (Deduct 4 *Blood* points.) You can only hope that the same thing hasn't happened at the other properties.

Choosing somewhere you haven't visited yet, which property do you want to check next?

The end-of-terrace house in Walworth? Turn to **274**.

Carfax House in Purfleet, Essex? Turn to **155**.

71

You are so appalled by the body parts that have been put on ice inside the crate that you do not think to wonder where the person is who was clearly halfway through opening the crate before you disturbed them, until you feel the blow that lands on the back of your head, sending you reeling.

Lose 2 *Endurance* points, 1 *Agility* point and 1 *Combat* point, and, if you are still alive, turn to **119**.

72

You race up the stairs to Lucy's room, and, with white faces and trembling hands, open the door and enter.

On the bed lie two women, Lucy and her mother. Mrs Westenra's face is drawn and white, with a look of terror fixed upon it. She is quite clearly dead, her heart having given out at last, no doubt.

Lucy is lying at her mother's side. The garlic flowers that had been about her neck lie discarded on her mother's bosom, and her throat is bare. You can see the two mysterious wounds quite clearly, for they are horribly white and mangled.

Without a word, the Professor bends over the bed, his head almost touching Lucy's breast, and you fear the worst. The thought of Lucy losing her battle for life scares you more than anything else. (Add 1 point to your *Terror* score.)

Van Helsing gives a quick turn of his head, as if listening, and suddenly leaping to his feet, he cries out, "It is not yet too late! Quick! Quick! Bring the brandy!"

You fly back downstairs and return less than a minute later. Van Helsing rubs the brandy on Lucy's lips and gums, and then on her wrists and the palms of her hands.

"I can do no more for the time being," he says. "She is nearly as cold as her mother. We will need to warm her up before we can do anything more."

At the Professor's instruction, you draw a hot bath and place Lucy in it, as she is. As the heat begins to have some effect, you hear her heartbeat more audibly through your stethoscope, and her lungs show perceptible movement.

"She must have another transfusion of blood," Van Helsing snaps, "and soon, but you and I are both exhausted. Who is left to open his veins for her now?"

"Will my blood do?" comes a voice from the threshold of the bathroom.

"Quincey Morris!" you cry in joy and relief, upon seeing Arthur's American friend, who was once a suitor for Miss Lucy's affections, like yourself. "What brings you here?"

"I guess Art is the cause," he replies, handing you a telegram.

Have not heard from Seward for three days and am terribly anxious. Cannot leave. Father still in same condition. Send me word how Lucy is. Do not delay. – Holmwood.

"I think I came just in the nick of time. Just tell me what to do."

Van Helsing strides forward and, taking his hand, looks him straight in the eyes: "A brave man's blood is the best thing on this earth when a woman is in trouble. The devil may work against us for all he's worth, but God sends us men when we need them."

Turn to **112**.

73

Snarling, the wolves attack. While the Professor battles one of the beasts, you take on the other. (In this battle you have the initiative.)

WOLF   COMBAT 6   ENDURANCE 6

If you kill the wolf, turn to **53**.

74

As Van Helsing rummages in his bag, you warily approach the coffin and peer inside.

Lucy's corpse lies there, beautiful again in death. But there is no love left in your heart; it has been replaced by a deep loathing for the foul thing that has taken Lucy's shape and banished her soul.

She is a nightmare of Lucy; the points of elongated teeth resting on the full red lips of her voluptuous mouth, the blood stains that besmirch her cheeks and chin, her carnal appearance a devilish mockery of Lucy's virginal purity.

The ever methodical Van Helsing takes from his bag a cleaver, then a hammer, and finally a round stake, some three inches thick, one end of it having been sharpened to a fine point, which has then been hardened by charring it in a fire.

Placing the hammer and the stake in your unresisting hands he says in an urgent whisper, "A moment's courage and it is done. The stake must be driven through her."

"Go on," you answer him hoarsely, for you are a man of healing and not a purveyor a death. "Tell me what to do."

"Take the stake in your left hand, place the point over her heart, and then strike in God's name. And do not falter when once you have set upon that path."

You do as your tutor instructs – master and student once again – placing the tip of the stake against the soft flesh of her breast, as Van Helsing opens a missal and begins to recite a prayer for the dead.

As you raise the hammer in your right hand, Lucy's eyes suddenly flick open, and a viperous hiss escapes her rosy lips.

Add 1 point to your *Terror* score and then *Take a Terror test*. If you pass the test, turn to **508**. If you fail the test, turn to **94**.

75

Against all the odds, you have put an end to the undead tyranny of Dracula, the King of Vampires.

Turn to **380**.

76

Your heart leaps when you realise that the other members of your party, separated from each other for almost a week, are converging on this spot as well. Mina and Professor Van Helsing are rushing down the snowy slope from the direction of the castle, kicking up great flurries of white powder as they descend, while you can hear the remainder thundering along the road behind you, also on horseback.

The wolves scatter, while the Szgany are momentarily thrown into disarray. Perhaps you are not too late after all!

(Add one use of *The Pen is Mightier* special ability to your Adventure Sheet.)

The wind comes now in fierce bursts, furiously driving the snow before it and sweeping around you in circling eddies. You can distinguish the individual gypsies quite clearly now, as they redouble their efforts to reach the castle as the sun drops lower and lower in the sky.

"Halt!" you shout as you catch up with the cart at last.

The gypsies rein in their horses, and at the same instant the two of you draw up on one side of the wagon, as your companions come alongside it on the other.

The leader of the gypsies waves them back, and in a fierce voice commands the Szgany to keep going. But your party of fearless Vampire-Killers raise their guns and order the Transylvanians to stop.

* * * *

If you want to continue the story as Mina Harker, turn to **34**. If you would rather continue the story as either Jonathan Harker or Dr Seward, turn to **14**.

77

What before you sought to avoid, you now sprint towards, seeking shelter from the hailstorm. However, before you reach the marble mausoleum, you are struck by the full force of the icy bombardment.

(Roll one die and add 1, then divide the total by 2, rounding fractions up; deduct this many *Endurance* points. Alternatively, pick a card and deduct its face value from your *Endurance* score, unless it is 5 or above, or a picture card, in which case deduct 4 points from your *Endurance* score.)

Turn to **61**.

78

The gypsy camp suddenly melts away and you unexpectedly find yourself in a dank crypt, staring into an open stone sarcophagus. You are holding a sharpened stake of whitethorn wood in one hand.

Lying within the sarcophagus is the monster you have travelled all this way to kill, the tips of his elongated fangs resting on his full, ruddy lips.

The monster's eyes snap open and he rises from his tomb, giving a snake-like hiss of triumph. You lash out in fear, plunging the tip of the stake into his left eye. But rather than recoiling in agony or giving a cry of pain, the vampire starts to laugh. You are paralysed with fear, unable to tear your gaze from the Count's remaining, pulsing red eye, and at the periphery your vision starts to dim.

And then the glowing red eye is no longer an eye but the sun, setting behind the familiar silhouetted skyline of London, capital of the British Empire. You can see no signs of life as you gaze out across the deserted city, until the sun disappears beneath the horizon, as the inhabitants of the necropolis awaken and rise from their graves. London has become a city of the dead, populated by walking cadavers. An animated corpse, wearing the rot-ruined face of your beloved, reaches for you, white worms wriggling free of her decayed flesh, a fat maggot writhing within the pit of a hollow eye-socket.

And then it isn't a grave grub emerging from her eye-socket but a monstrous albino serpent emerging from the mouth of a shadowy cave, jaws opening wide, deploying fangs as large as elephant's tusks, ready to sink them into your helpless body.

Add 2 points to your *Terror* score and then *Take a Terror test*. If you pass the test, turn to **111**, but if you fail the test, turn to **222**.

79

Making it to the top of the wall, you discover a tree growing close to it on the other side, which means that your descent is much easier than it might have been, and soon you are safely back on the ground.

Turn to **49**.

80

After the funeral, you take a bus to Hyde Park Corner and from there walk down Piccadilly, Jonathan holding you by the arm.

You are looking at a very beautiful girl, in a big cartwheel hat, sitting in a carriage outside Guiliano's the jewellers, when Jonathan suddenly clutches your arm so tightly that you give a startled gasp of pain, and he hisses under his breath, "My God!"

Always living with the fear that some nervous fit may upset him again at any moment, you quickly turn to your husband and ask him what it is that has disturbed him so.

He is very pale, his eyes bulging from his head, half in terror and half in amazement, and you realise he is staring at a tall, thin man, with a beaky nose, black moustache and pointed beard, who is also observing the pretty girl. He is looking at her so hard that he does not see either of you, and so you have a good view of him. His face is hard, and cruel, and sensual, and his big white teeth – that look all the whiter because his lips are so red – are pointed like an animal's!

"Do you see who it is?" says Jonathan, who is staring so intently at the stranger that you start to worry the man will notice.

"No, dear," you reply, "I don't know him. Who is it?"

His answer both shocks and thrills you. "It is the man himself!" he hisses in abject terror.

Take an ESP test. If you pass the test, turn to **164**. If you fail the test, turn to **187**.

81

The bats fly off towards the shadowy silhouette of Carfax House, and you can't help wondering if they are going to report back on your presence here. (Gain 2 *Blood* points.)

It is then that the others arrive, summoned by your whistle. With no one having found any sign of the boxes having been stored anywhere else within the grounds, you all hasten to the house.

Turn to **47**.

82

Then your head hits a tree branch, and you are almost knocked out of the saddle.

Lose 2 *Endurance* points, 1 *Agility* point, and 1 *Combat* point. If you are still alive, turn to **102**.

83

Having formed a bond with Lucy Westenra, you continue to feed from her when you can, even transporting yourself to the house where she is staying, in the form of a bat, in order to drink her blood.

Her friend Mina becomes increasingly distressed by Lucy's strange behaviour and worsening condition, but whatever she tries to do to thwart your plans is always too little too late.

Gain 4 *Blood* points, restore up to 8 *Endurance* points, and turn to **341**.

84

"I think the house in Piccadilly is key," Professor Van Helsing says, when the six of you meet again later that morning, in the study that has become the Vampire-Hunters' makeshift committee room. "He must have many belongings hidden somewhere, and why not somewhere so central, so quiet, and from where he can come and go by the front or the back at all hours? I think we should search there."

"But what of the properties in Walworth and Mile End?" asks Arthur. "We cannot risk leaving any earths for that old fox to run to. Professor, if you would go to the house in Piccadilly, I volunteer to search the Walworth address."

"Then I will visit Mile End," says Quincey.

"Then it is decided," says the Professor. "We will split up and between us we ensure that the fiend has nowhere left to hide on English shores."

Van Helsing turns to you. "I would appreciate your help at the house in Piccadilly," he says. "Will you accompany me there?"

Where do you want to visit, and with whom?

Piccadilly with Van Helsing?	Turn to **741**.
Walworth with Lord Godalming?	Turn to **116**.
Mile End with Quincey Morris?	Turn to **136**.

85

And so it is that, on a baking hot summer's day, the Sultan, Mehmed the Conqueror, still believing the Ottomans' superior military force will prevail in the end – despite his invading army having sustained heavy losses and worsening morale, due to the guerrilla warfare tactics you have employed in your skirmishes against his forces so far – marches on the capital.

If your rank is that of *Son of the Dragon*, turn to **55**. If your rank is that of *Lord Impaler* or higher, turn to **5**.

86

DR SEWARD'S DIARY

(Kept in phonograph)

8 September

I sat up all night with Lucy. The opiate worked itself off towards dusk, and she waked naturally...

When she wakes, Lucy looks like a different person from the emaciated husk of a human being she had been before she received the blood transfusion. Her spirits have lifted, and she is full of a happy vivacity.

Despite Mrs Westenra pooh-poohing the idea that you need to sit up with her all night, pointing out her daughter's renewed strength and excellent spirits, you insist, and having prepared for your long vigil, you take a seat by her bedside.

But it soon becomes apparent that Lucy does not want to sleep, and so you ask her why she would not want to, when it is a boon everyone craves.

"All this weakness comes to me when I sleep, until I dread the very thought of it," she explains.

"But, my dear girl, you may sleep tonight," you tell her. "I am here watching you, and I can promise that nothing will happen. On top of that, I promise that if I see any evidence of bad dreams, I will wake you at once."

Upon hearing that, she gives a deep sigh of relief, and sinks back onto her pillow. She is soon fast asleep.

* * * *

You watch her all night long. She never stirs but enjoys a deep, tranquil, life-giving sleep. There is a smile on her face that you take as evidence that no bad dreams disturb her peace of mind this night.

In the morning, you leave her in the care of her maid and return home, and your work at Carfax Asylum takes you all day to clear. But that night you return to Hillingham to keep watch at Lucy's bedside again.

* * * *

When the duty falls on you for a third night, you quail at the thought, for you are beginning to feel the numbness that marks cerebral exhaustion.

Upon reaching Hillingham, you find Lucy up and in good spirits. Looking at you sharply, she says, "No sitting up tonight for you. You are worn out and I am quite well again. Indeed, if there is to be any sitting up, it is I who will sit up with you."

Will you insist on maintaining your night-time vigil (turn to **101**), or will you give in to tiredness at Lucy's insistence (turn to **161**)?

87

You explain your reason for not believing the Count to be involved, finishing with, "We have our own urgent mission. We cannot let anything distract us from that, lest it lead to failure."

"My dear Madam Mina," he says, clasping your hands in his, "once more you teach me that caution is more prudent than curiosity in this instance. We will spend the rest of the journey in our own company and not interfere in matters others are more than capable of dealing with. We should arrive in Veresti in only a matter of hours. Now, try to get some rest."

Turn to **107**.

88

You cannot resist the mesmeric voices of the wanton women. Rising from your seat by the fire, you walk towards them, as they beckon you onward.

"No! No! Do not go without," comes Van Helsing's plaintive voice from behind you. "Here you are safe!"

"Do not fear for me," you reply dreamily. "There is none safer in all the world from them than I."

But then you reach the edge of the sanctified circle. As you try to cross it, your body is wracked with the most terrible pain; it feels as if the scar on your forehead is on fire!

You recoil from the holy barrier, your body contorting in agony. But the Weird Sisters' spell is broken.

(Lose 4 *Endurance* points and deduct 1 *Blood* point.)

If you are still alive, turn to **58**.

89

Shaking with cold and shock, you struggle to your feet. But as you do so, you find yourself surrounded by a vague, white, moving mass. It is as if all the graves around you have opened and sent forth the phantom forms of their shrouded dead, and they are closing in on you.

One of the ethereal spectres draws near and you begin to make out details – a skull-like visage beneath the hood of a grave-sheet, and fleshless fingers reaching for you.

(Add 1 point to your *Terror* score.)

If you want to use *The Pen is Mightier* special ability now, cross off one use and turn to **263**. If not, turn to **204**.

90

Despite their unearthly, ethereal beauty, there is something about the women that makes you feel uneasy; you feel a deep longing swelling within you, but at the same time a nerve-shredding fear.

Turn to **228**.

91

As the woman you can only suppose might once have been the Countess Dolingen of Gratz rushes towards you, her elongated eye-teeth bared like fangs within a bestial grimace of a face, you prepare to defend yourself as best you can, using your stout oak stick. (In this battle, your assailant has the initiative.)

THE COUNTESS   COMBAT 9   ENDURANCE 11

If you are still alive after 6 Combat Rounds, or if you reduce the Countess's *Endurance* score to 5 points or fewer, whichever is sooner, turn to **131** at once.

92

Johann urges the horses forwards and the carriage bounces over the rutted road. Every now and then the horses throw up their heads and sniff the air suspiciously, causing you to scan the countryside you are passing through for any sign of what might have startled them. But there is nothing there – at least not anything that you can see.

The road is quite bleak, for you are traversing a high, windswept plateau. As you drive, you catch sight of a road that appears little used and which dips through a winding valley. It looks so inviting that you call to Johann to stop, and when he has pulled up, you tell him that you would like to drive down that road.

The coachman starts to make all sorts of excuses and frequently crosses himself as he speaks, as well as looking at his watch, as if in protest.

Then the horses start to become restless again, their nostrils flaring as if they can smell something unpleasant on the breeze, and Johann grows pale. Jumping down, he takes the frightened animals by the bridles and leads them on some twenty feet.

If you want to ask Johann what has spooked the horses, turn to **122**. If you do not want to know what has upset the animals, turn to **154**.

93

Incredibly the wolf starts to whimper and then suddenly takes off into the blizzard, quickly followed by its fellow.

Deduct 1 *Blood* point and turn to **53**.

94

You recoil in horror. Seizing upon your moment of weakness, the creature strikes, slashing at you with fingernails that have become talons, raking the flesh of your forearm, a spray of blood spurting from the wound. (Lose 2 *Endurance* points.)

You stumble backwards, the dread tools of death Van Helsing had given to you, for the express purpose of putting an end to the monster, falling from your hands and clattering onto the floor of the tomb.

And then suddenly Arthur is there beside you. He picks up the executioner's tools and, as the Professor holds the horror back with his golden crucifix, Lord Godalming places the point of the stake over the heart and brings the hammer down on the blunt end hard.

The thing in the coffin writhes in agony and a hideous, blood-curdling screech comes from its open lips. The body shakes as it twists in wild contortions, the sharp white teeth champing together till the lips are cut, and the mouth is smeared with a crimson foam.

But Arthur never falters. He looks like the figure of Thor as his arm rises a second time to drive the stake deeper and deeper with every blow. Foul, black blood wells up from the pierced heart, some of it spurting into his face, but even then he does not stop.

At last, the writhing and quivering of the body dies down, until finally it lies still, and the terrible task is done.

The hammer falls from Arthur's hand, and he collapses against the side of the coffin, his forehead dripping with sweat, his breath coming in broken gasps.

Turn to **124**.

95

The wolves and the gypsies have flown, other than those whose corpses litter the ground around about you, while Castle Dracula is nothing more than a grim silhouette against the darkening sky.

But then there comes a terrible convulsion of the earth that sends your party falling to their knees. At the same moment, with a roar that seems to shake the very heavens, the whole castle and even the crag upon which it stands seem to rise into the air and scatter into fragments, while a mighty cloud of black and yellow smoke blasts upwards from the sundered ground. When the smoke clears, nothing of Dracula's bat-haunted lair remains.

After the cataclysmic destruction of the castle, an eerie stillness falls like a funeral pall over the mountains, as the thunder-clap of the castle's destruction rolls away over the valleys and chasms of the Carpathians.

While the rest of you get to your feet, Quincey Morris remains on the ground, leaning on one elbow, a hand pressed to his side. You can see the blood still gushing through his fingers and hurry over to him – as do Dr Seward, Arthur, Professor Van Helsing, and your dear Jonathan, who kneels behind him so that the wounded man might lay his head against your husband's shoulder.

With a sigh of effort, the Texan takes your hand in his, and reading the anguish of your heart in your face, he smiles. "I am only too happy to have been of any service! Oh, God!" he cries suddenly, struggling into a sitting posture and pointing at you. "It was worth dying for this. Look!"

It is suddenly as if your face is being bathed by a rosy glow. With one impulse, the other gentlemen sink to their knees and a deep and earnest "Amen" breaks from their lips, as their collective gaze follows Quincey's pointing finger.

Tentatively you put a hand to your forehead and gasp yourself. Where before there was the knotted skin of the wafer burn, now it is smooth, and you feel no pain as you touch the spot.

"Now God be thanked that all has not been in vain!" breathes the American. "See! The snow is not more stainless than her forehead! The curse has passed away!"

And to your bitter grief, but with a smile on his lips, Quincey dies, a gallant gentleman to the last.

Turn to **1000**.

96

Professor Van Helsing begins by recounting what he discovered when he visited the Port of London, that the Count is even now on board the *Czarina Catherine* and sailing for the Black Sea and the Bulgarian port of Varna.

"And so, my dear Madam Mina, it is that we have to rest for a time, for our enemy is on the sea, with the fog at his command, on his way to the mouth of the Danube," he explains. "To sail a ship takes time, and when we set off we will travel by land, thereby making much quicker progress. Indeed, we shall reach his destination before him.

"That last box of earth we seek is to be landed in Varna and given to an agent, one Ristics, who will there present his credentials; and so, our merchant friend will have done his part."

"I ask again, Professor," says Arthur, when Van Helsing is done speaking, weariness etched into his face, "is it really necessary we pursue the Count now that he has departed English shores?"

"Yes, it is necessary!" the Professor answers with growing passion. "For Madam Mina's sake and for the sake of humanity. This monster has done much harm already. He has infected Madam Mina with his vampiric curse. Even if he does no more direct injury, having lived out her allotted lifespan, death, when it comes, will make her a vampire, just like poor Miss Lucy. We cannot allow this to come to pass! Only Dracula's death will free Madam Mina from this fate and redeem her immortal soul."

"But will not the Count take his rebuff wisely?" asks Quincey Morris. "Since he has been driven from England, will he not avoid it, as a tiger does the village from which he has been hunted?"

"Your man-eater, as they call the tiger in India, once it has tasted human blood, it cares for no other prey. We hunt a man-eater too, and he is not one to retire and stay far off. In his life – his living life – he travelled beyond the Turkish frontier and attacked his enemy on his own ground. He was beaten back, but returned again, and again, and again. Look at his persistence and endurance. Who knows how long ago he conceived the idea of coming to London? But having set his mind to it, he deliberately set himself down to prepare for the task. He studied new tongues, taught himself modern social etiquette, along with politics, law, finance, the sciences, the habits and customs of a new land and a new people who have come to be since his blood still pumped hot and red in his veins. What he has seen here, in England, will have only whet his appetite and deepened his desire. He has achieved all that he has achieved to this point from a ruined tomb in a forgotten land. Imagine what more he could do now that he better understands what awaits him here, at the heart of the British Empire; he that can smile at death, who can flourish in the midst of diseases that kill off whole peoples.

"But we have pledged to set the world free. Our toil must be in silence, and our efforts all in secret; for in this enlightened age, when men believe not even what they see, the doubting of wise men would be his greatest strength. It would be at once his sheath and his armour, and his weapons to destroy us, his enemies, who are willing to imperil even our own souls for the safety of one we love, for the good of mankind, and for the honour and glory of God."

Turn to **130**.

97

You spin around, as someone makes to strikes you with a hammer.

Turn to **119**.

98

The thing that now wears Lucy's form suddenly gives an angry snarl, eyes blazing with unholy light. But in the next moment she regains some measure of self-control and turns her attention towards you.

"Come to me, John," she purrs, a wanton smile on her crimson lips, as she crosses the vault towards you. "It is you I want. Only a doctor can give me what I need."

You cannot tear your eyes away from her penetrating gaze, even though you know you must, or else succumb to her hypnotic beauty.

Take an ESP test. If you pass the test, turn to **138**, but if you fail the test, turn to **346**.

99

Your heart pounding inside your chest, you nonetheless stand your ground and listen intently to the head's whispered utterances. While your ears hear the guttural desert tongue of Arabia, inside your head you hear the words spoken in the Queen's English.

"Beware, for the accursed lord of this place is a ghoul, a demon who drinks the blood of the living to sustain his own life after death."

You have heard enough. Your pulse pounding in your ears, you back out of the room, closing the door firmly behind you. You wonder what other impossible secrets the castle hides within its walls.

Add 1 point to your *Terror* score, deduct 1 *Blood* point, and then turn to **59**.

100

"Children of the night!" the vampire's voice carries over the wailing of the wind. "Answer my call! Defend your master from these, his enemies."

The surviving members of the wolf pack close on your party from all sides. You are going to have to act fast.

If you have the code word *Vârcolac* ticked off, turn to **151**. If not, turn to **245**.

101

That night, after supper, which is enlivened by Lucy's charming presence, you take your place at her bedside and watch her as she drifts off into a deep sleep.

But you are feeling exhausted yourself and have to fight against every natural instinct, just to stay awake.

Take an Endurance test. If you pass the test, turn to **121**, but if you fail the test, turn to **141**.

102

"Look!" shouts Quincey and there, two hundred yards away, you make out a wooden bridge wide enough for a cart to cross, spanning the crevasse where a waterfall tumbles down between the hills.

But your attention is drawn back to the pack pursuing you when you hear a savage snarl to your right and realise that one of the Werewolves has caught up with you.

If you want to use *The Pen is Mightier* special ability, and you still can, turn to **134**. If not, turn to **156**.

103

The rejuvenated Count is observing a pretty girl, in a big cartwheel hat, sitting in a carriage outside Guiliano's, the jewellers.

As you watch, a man comes out of the shop, carrying a small parcel, which he gives to the lady, who then drives off. The Count keeps his eyes fixed on her, and when the carriage moves off up Piccadilly he follows in the same direction and hails a hansom.

In that moment you realise that everything you endured whilst a guest at Castle Dracula really did happen, and that the fiend is going through with his vile plans.

There and then you resolve to do all you can to thwart his dark ambitions, and you feel the fire of crusading zeal blaze through your weary body.

Add 1 point to your *Combat* score, deduct 1 point from your *Terror* score, deduct 1 *Blood* point, and then turn to **218**.

104

Flailing about you with your knife, you defend yourself against the shrieking bats. (In this battle, you have the initiative.)

CAULDRON OF BATS   COMBAT 6   ENDRUANCE 8

If you manage to reduce the cauldron's *Endurance* score to zero, the surviving bats break from the fight and flee. Turn to **81**.

105

The wolves and the gypsies have flown, leaving the corpses of those that fell littering the ground all about you, while Castle Dracula is nothing more than a grim silhouette against the darkening sky.

But then there comes a terrible convulsion of the earth that sends your party falling to their knees. At the same moment, with a roar that seems to shake the very heavens, the whole castle and even the crag upon which it stands seem to rise into the air and scatter into fragments, while a mighty cloud of black and yellow smoke blasts upwards from the sundered ground. When the smoke clears, nothing of Dracula's wolf-haunted lair remains.

After the cataclysmic destruction of the castle, an eerie stillness falls like a funeral pall over the mountains, as the thunder-clap of the castle's destruction rolls away over the valleys and chasms of the Carpathians.

While the rest of you get to your feet, Quincey Morris remains on the ground, leaning on one elbow, a hand pressed to his side, and you can see blood gushing through his fingers. You hurry over to him – as does Lord Godalming, Professor Van Helsing, and Jonathan Harker, who kneels behind him, resting Quincey's head against his shoulder.

With a feeble sigh of effort, Quiney takes Mina's hand in his, and seeing the anguish of her heart in her face, he smiles and says, "I am only too happy to have been of any service! Oh, God!" he cries suddenly, struggling up into a sitting position and pointing at the distraught woman. "It was worth dying for this. Look!"

Mrs Harker's face is suddenly bathed in a rosy light. You join Arthur and the Professor in sinking to your knees, a deep and earnest "Amen" breaking from your lips as your eyes follow Quincey's finger to rest upon the unblemished skin of Mina's forehead.

"Now God be thanked that all has not been in vain!" your American friend gasps. "See! The snow is not more stainless than her forehead! The curse has passed away!"

And to your bitter grief, but with a smile on his lips, Quincey dies, a gallant gentleman to the end.

Turn to **1000**.

106

What before you sought to avoid, you now sprint towards, in search of shelter from the hailstorm. However, before you reach the marble mausoleum, you are struck by the full force of the icy bombardment.

(Roll one die and divide the result by 2, rounding halves up; add 3 to this total and deduct that many points from your *Endurance* score. Alternatively, pick a card and deduct that many *Endurance* points, unless it is greater than 6 or a picture card, in which case deduct 6 *Endurance* points.)

Turn to **61**.

107

MINA HARKER'S JOURNAL

31 October

Arrived at Veresti at noon. The Professor tells me that this morning at dawn he could hardly hypnotise me at all, and that all I could say was, "dark and quiet"...

Later that afternoon you prepare for the off, Professor Van Helsing having sequestered a carriage and horses. Your guardian has also purchased meat and drink for the journey ahead, as well as fur coats, and wraps, and all sorts of warm things.

You still have something more than 70 miles before you. The country is lovely, and most interesting – if only you were visiting under different conditions, how delightful it would be to see it all – while snow-flurries come and go as if forecasting worse weather to come.

* * * *

You travel westwards, the country growing ever wilder as you climb higher and higher towards the ragged broken tooth peaks of the Carpathian Mountains.

It is cold now, so cold that the heavy sky is full of snow – which, when it falls, will settle for all winter as the ground is hardening to receive it – and you sleep for much of the time.

You reach the Borgo Pass just after sunrise on the third day since leaving Veresti. Stirring, you point to a particular road.

"This is the way."

"How do you know it?" the Professor challenges you.

"Of course, I know it!" you answer. "Did not my husband travel the same road and write of it in his record of his time in this terrible country?"

The byroad is very different from the coach road from Bukovina to Bistritz – which is wide and firm underfoot – and is clearly little used. Taking this route, you travel for many more hours – moving into a more and more wild and desert land, a place of great frowning precipices and tumbling waterfalls – until finally, as twilight is settling over the mountain peaks, as you are climbing a steeply rising hill, you catch sight of the summit, upon which stands the forbidding ramparts of an ancient castle.

The place appears deserted, as quiet as the grave. You have clearly beaten everyone else here, including the Count.

(Deduct 1 *Blood* point.)

Before night falls, the Professor feeds the horses while you make a fire, one hundred yards from the great gates of the castle. He then proceeds to have something to eat as well, but you have no appetite for food. Van Helsing draws a great circle around you and the fire, in the settling snow, and taking a holy wafer, he crumbles it up into a fine powder and sprinkles it over the ring he has just made.

Then there is nothing for the two of you to do but wait.

* * * *

Darkness descends, the heavy snow-clouds blotting out the light of the moon. Hours pass, during which the horses become unsettled and tear at their tethers, and the fire begins to die.

Peering out into the night, it seems to you that the snow-flurries and wreaths of mist take on the shape of three women, clad in trailing grave garments. The horses whinny and cower in terror, and Van Helsing takes up a burning brand from the fire, coaxing it into life, as if he intends to defend himself with it.

And now the women before you are of solid flesh and you know then that they are the same three women that sought to lay their lips upon Jonathan's throat!

You feel as if you recognise their swaying forms yourself, their bright hard eyes, pronounced white teeth, and their ruddy, voluptuous lips. All three of them are smiling at you, and the musical laughter of their voices comes to you through the snow-muffled silence of the night. They point at you and say in sweet, tinkling tones, that possess the intolerable sweetness of water glasses, "Come, sister. Come to us. Come!"

Take an ESP test. If you pass the test, turn to **58**, but if you fail the test, turn to **88**.

108

Utterly terrified, you turn and run back the way you have just come, towards the entrance to the graveyard.

Hearing a savage snarl behind you spurs you on, as you then become aware of something pursuing you. In the desperate hope of somehow evading the unnatural beast, you dodge and weave between the graves.

Take an Agility test. If you pass the test, turn to **171**, but if you fail the test, turn to **148**.

109

You are a man of books and academic study, not adventure, and do not have the strength to be an adventurer. You are almost at the top of the wall when your tired muscles fail you and you lose your grip.

In desperation, you make a lunge for the top. You manage to grab hold but graze your body against the broken bricks as you save yourself from falling. (Lose 2 *Endurance* points.)

You take a few moments to gather yourself and then finally haul yourself up.

Turn to **79**.

110

You throw your victim onto the bed and spring at the men. Ignoring you, Harker rushes to aid his wife, leaving you to face the other four.

You must fight the Vampire-Hunters all at the same time. While you have the initiative in this battle, you must deduct 1 point when calculating your *Combat Rating*, for some of them are armed with crucifixes and protected by fragments of communion wafer.

	COMBAT	ENDURANCE
DOCTOR SEWARD	9	10
HOLMWOOD	8	9
QUINCEY THE AMERICAN	9	9
THE PROFESSOR	8	8

At any time during the battle, if you wish, you may deduct 4 *Blood* points to eliminate one of the Vampire-Hunters; however, you may only use this ability against one of your opponents.

If you kill all of the Vampire-Hunters, gain 8 *Blood* points and turn to **400**. If you lose the battle, turn to **605**.

111

And then the nightmarish visions fade, and you find yourself back in the gypsy camp.

You are horrified to see that Quincey is putting the golden goblet to his lips, moving as if in a trance.

Without a second thought, you smash the cup from his hands. He looks at you then, blinking repeatedly, as if coming to from a drowsy reverie.

Shrieking in rage, the gypsy-witch throws herself at you, trying to rake your face with her long fingernails.

If you want to use *The Pen is Mightier* special ability, and you still can, turn to **167**. If not, turn to **144**.

112

DR SEWARD'S DIARY

(Kept in phonograph)

18 September

Once again we went through that ghastly operation, and though plenty of blood went into her veins, Lucy did not respond to the treatment as well as on the other occasions. Her struggle back into life was something frightful to see...

While Van Helsing tends to Lucy, you go downstairs with Quincey. When the two of you are alone, and as he has a lie down after a restorative glass of wine, he says to you, "Jack Seward, I don't want to shove myself in anywhere where I've no right to be, but this is no ordinary case. You know I loved that girl and wanted to marry her, and so I can't help feeling anxious about her. What's wrong with her?"

"Lucy has lost a lot of blood," you tell him as calmly as you can, for the poor fellow is clearly terribly anxious.

"And how long has this been going on?"

"About ten days."

"Ten days!" Quincey exclaims. "Then I guess, Jack Seward, that poor pretty creature that we all love has had put into her veins within that time the blood of four strong men. Man alive, her whole body wouldn't hold it." Drawing close to you, in a fierce whisper he says, "What took it out?"

"That," you say, shaking your head, "is the crux. I can't even hazard a guess. There has been a series of little circumstances which have thrown out all our calculations as to Lucy being properly watched. But these shall not occur again. Here we stay until all be well or ill."

Quincey holds out his hand. "Count me in. You and the Dutchman will tell me what to do, and I'll do it."

* * * *

When Lucy wakes later that afternoon, her eyes light upon Van Helsing and then on you, and she is gladdened. But then, as she looks around the room and realises where she is, she shudders and gives a cry of grief, throwing her poor thin hands in front of her pallid face. And between great, wracking sobs, cries out for her mother, while you do your best to comfort her.

Turn to **137**.

113

A sudden stabbing pain, just below your ribs, causes you to take a sharp breath. The Sultan takes a step back from you, laughing cruelly. You feel the pressure in your side increase and then a voice close to your ear says, "You didn't see that coming, did you cousin?"

You pull away – the dagger that had been thrust up and under your ribcage sliding free in a rush of blood – and your horrified gaze falls on a familiar face. It is Basarab, another of the Dracul line with his own claim to the throne of Wallachia.

"What have you done?" you gasp, as an icy sensation starts to spread from the wound in your side throughout your chest, making you gasp for air. (Deduct 4 *Endurance* points.)

"What you should have done long ago. Made a deal with his Excellency Mehmed the Conqueror, rather than condemn my countrymen to years of famine, privation and fear," Basarab declares, a mad gleam in his eyes.

"You... you have killed me," you gasp, struggling to stay on your feet.

"And in doing so I have brought an end to this pointless war and saved Wallachia!"

Your vision blurring, your head starts to spin, and you realise you have to get out of there as fast as you can or face certain death.

Take a Combat test and an Endurance test. If you pass both tests, turn to **165**, but if you fail either test, turn to **135** at once. Alternatively, you can deduct 3 *Blood* points and turn to **165** without having to take either test.

114

You feel a wicked, burning desire swell within your heart, wishing that they would kiss you with those ruby red lips, even though deep down you know it would cause your dear Mina pain if she were party to that knowledge.

The women whisper together, as they glide across the room towards you, and then all three of them laugh. It is a silvery, musical laugh, like the intolerable, tingling sweetness of water-glasses when played by a cunning hand. But nonetheless, your body answers their siren call.

The fair-headed one shakes her head coquettishly, as the other two urge her on.

"Go on!" one of the dark-haired beauties says. "You are first, and we shall follow. Yours is the right to begin."

"He is young and strong," adds the other. "There are kisses for us all."

You remain where you are upon the couch, peering out from under your eyelashes in an agony of delighted anticipation. The fair girl advances and reaching the couch, she bends over you, her décolletage looming large, closer and closer, until you feel the movement of her breath upon your skin.

She smells as sweet as honey and her scent sends the same tingling through your nerves as her tinkling laughter.

If you are wearing a Golden Crucifix, turn to **143**. If not, turn to **182**.

115

At your command, the jails and dungeons are emptied and, no matter the crime, the prisoners are flung onto stakes outside the city gates. Just for good measure, you order that the graves of the recently deceased be dug up and their rotting carcasses mounted on stakes at the side of the road as well.

When the Sultan's army reaches Târgoviște, he will be confronted by not only men impaled on stakes, but women and children as well...

Gain 10 *Blood* points and turn to **85**.

116

It is agreed. You will accompany Lord Godalming to the house in Walworth, Van Helsing will go to the Piccadilly property and meet you there, as soon as you can join him, while Quincey Morris and Jonathan Harker set off for Mile End.

* * * *

When you arrive, you are surprised to find a cart and horses pulled up in the gateway to the side of the property, beyond which lies an enclosed cobbled yard. The wagon is painted with the words

'Harris & Sons, Moving and Shipment Company, Orange Master's Yard, Soho'.

Two cart-men are securing a tarpaulin over the back when you arrive.

"Good afternoon, gentleman," says Arthur, demonstrating a confidence the aristocracy are born with. "You wouldn't happen to be calling on my friend Mr Cushing would you, by any chance?"

Rather than doff their caps respectfully, as they should when addressed by a peer of the realm, the two men eye you both suspiciously, which immediately raises your suspicions, and mutter something about being in a hurry and having to deliver their cargo before nightfall.

"And may I enquire as to what it is you are transporting?" your companion continues.

Without waiting for a reply, he lifts the end of the tarpaulin, using his cane, and you step forward to peer into the back of the cart with him.

An audible gasp escapes your lips when you see six wooden crates, like the ones you found stored in the chapel of Carfax House.

Take an ESP test. If you pass the test, turn to **177**, but if you fail the test, turn to **206**.

As the coach continues to fly along, the driver leans forward in his seat while the passengers on each side crane their heads, peering eagerly into the darkness.

At last, the pass opens out on the eastern side. Dark clouds roll overhead, and the air becomes heavy with the expectation of thunder.

You peer out into the darkness as well, searching for any sign of the conveyance that is to carry you to the Count, expecting to see the glare of lamps through the blackness at any moment. But all remains dark.

And then the driver brings the carriage to an abrupt stop and you can make out a sandy spur road, lying white before you, but there is no sign of any other vehicle.

Your fellow passengers draw back into their seats, sighing as if with relief. It would appear that the conveyance you were expecting to meet you here, in the Borgo Pass, to take you on to Castle Dracula, has not turned up.

The driver looks at his watch muttering – "An hour less than the time" – and then, turning to you, says in German that is worse than yours, "There is no carriage here. The Herr is not expected after all. He will now come on to Bukovina and return tomorrow or the next day."

But while he is speaking, the horses begin to neigh and snort wildly, pawing at the ground with their hooves.

Accompanied by a chorus of screams from the other passengers, a caleche, pulled by a team of four, coal-black horses, appears as if from nowhere out of the night and draws up alongside the coach. It is driven by a tall man, with a long brown beard and wearing a great black hat, which hides his face from you, although his deep-set eyes appear to gleam red in the lamplight.

"You are early tonight, my friend," he says to the coachman.

"The English Herr was in a hurry," the wretch stammers in reply.

"That is why, I suppose, you wished him to go on to Bukovina," says the bearded stranger.

The driver blanches but says nothing.

"You cannot deceive me, my friend. I know too much, and my horses are swift."

He smiles, and the lamplight reveals a hard-looking mouth, with full red lips and sharp-looking teeth, as white as ivory.

You half-hear one of your companions whisper to another peasant, *"Denn die todten reiten schnell"* – 'For the dead travel fast'.

"Give me the Herr's luggage," says the stranger, and with startling alacrity your bags are put into the caleche. As soon as you are on board as well, the bearded man shakes his reins, the splendid coal-black horses turn, and you are swept away into the darkness of the pass.

You cannot help but look back, where you see your late companions crossing themselves, before the coach driver cracks his whips, calling to his horses, and they are swept on their way to Bukovina.

You feel a strange chill and an inexplicable feeling of loneliness come over you. A cloak is suddenly thrown over your shoulders, a rug is laid across your knees, and the driver says in excellent German, "The night is chill, *mein Herr*, and my master the Count bade me take all care of you. There is a flask of slivovitz underneath the seat, if you should require it."

Putting a hand under the seat, you find the flask, and take it out. Opening it, you sniff the vapours that rise from within; the smell reminds you of plum brandy.

If you want to take a swig, turn to **139**. If you would prefer to put the flask back where you found it, turn to **168**.

118

Once you are done drinking your fill of the dead man's blood (gain 2 *Blood* points and restore up to 4 *Endurance* points), you drag his corpse to the bows of the ship, and there cast it into the waves.

As you stand there for a moment, watching for any sign of the English coast – knowing that you must be close to your destination now – sensing movement behind you, you make yourself as smoke just as the First Mate tries to run your corporeal body through with his knife.

You are about to take solid form again, in order to deal with the upstart sailor, when he mutters something in Romanian.

You freeze. The man is praying! He continues to pray, out loud, whilst holding his knife out in front of him. And the force of his belief is palpable! Where many find their faith built on foundations of sand when they actually come face to face with a creature of the night, such as yourself, seeing you like this has only strengthened the First Mate's righteous resolve.

The power of his faith repels you and so you vanish into the air and the darkness, only resuming your physical form when you are back inside the hold, in your box of unconsecrated earth.

Turn to **162**.

119

Standing before you are the hunchback and another man. This second individual appears to be wearing a butcher's apron and in one hand he holds a bone-saw. His henchman is wielding a hammer that he has taken from a belt of tools at his waist.

"Spies!" the taller man cries out in German, his eyes wild. "You would steal Doktor Frankenstein's life's work? Have at them, Igor!"

"At once, Herr Doktor!" the other replies and they go for the pair of you.

If you want to use *The Pen is Mightier* special ability, and you still can, turn to **153**. If not, turn to **183**.

120

The Sisters abandon their plaything, and hurry to prostrate themselves at your feet. But their hubris has awoken the beast within you, and now they will suffer its wrath.

Grasping Lilith's slender neck in your steely grip, you hurl her from you, while Lamia and Melusina retreat from you in fear.

Turn to **175**.

121

For Lucy you would do anything and staying up for a third night in a row is but a trifle to ensure her continued well-being. But it still takes its toll on your weary mind.

(Deduct 1 point from your *Combat* score.)

As the clock chimes twelve in the hall downstairs, you become aware of something banging against Lucy's window. Getting up to see what it is, you are startled to find a huge bat – many times larger than any native species you know of – clawing at the glass.

Upon seeing you, the creature bares its elongated fangs and then takes off, disappearing into the night.

(Tick off the code word *Eptesicus* and add 1 point to your *Terror* score.)

As the first fingers of dawn poke through the blinds of Lucy's room, you lose your battle with sleep at last, only to wake again when you feel a hand on your head.

You start awake to find Van Helsing standing there.

"And how is our patient?" he asks.

Lucy is sleeping soundly, and her cheeks are tinged with a subtle bloom of rose.

Turn to **212**.

122

For an answer, Johann crosses himself again, points to the spot you have just left, and then to a wooden cross, set up at the road junction. "Buried him... him what killed themselves."

You have heard of the old custom of burying suicides at crossroads, but for the life of you, you cannot understand why that would frighten the horses.

Tick off the code word *Suicide* and turn to **154**.

123

Meeting the blazing gaze of the larger of the two wolves approaching the cleft, you will it to turn around and leave this place.

Take an ESP test. If you pass the test, turn to **93**. If you fail the test, turn to **73**.

124

The great cleaver gripped tight in his hand, with one sharp blow the Professor removes the corpse's head and, having filled its mouth with garlic, sets about resealing the coffin.

When all is done, the four of you make your way out of the tomb, Van Helsing locking the door behind you.

Outside the air is sweet, and the first pinkish hues of morning are colouring the eastern sky, as the birds begin their dawn chorus.

As you make your way out of the churchyard, Van Helsing says, "Now, my friends, one step of our work is done – and a most harrowing one – but there remains a greater task; to hunt down the author of all our sorrow and put an end to him.

"Two nights hence let us meet again and dine together at seven of the clock, and John shall be our host. I shall entreat two others to join our number.

"Tonight, I leave for Amsterdam, but shall return tomorrow night. And then begins our great quest, for there is a terrible task before us, and once our feet are on the ploughshare we must not draw back."

Turn to **809**.

125

With the vampire dead, rather than feed on his rot-ravaged flesh, you take your payment in kind for his affrontery from his dazed thrall, Penny. Dreadful though your animalistic ways might be, you cannot help but relish the taste of her blood in your mouth.

(Gain 4 *Blood* points and restore up to 6 *Endurance* points.)

But what Varney said, about knowing what you are up to, has planted a seed of doubt in your mind. If he had even an inkling of what you have planned, who else might know?

Turn to **189**.

126

It is agreed. You will accompany Lord Godalming to the house in Walworth, Van Helsing will go to the Piccadilly property and meet you there, as soon as you can join him, while Quincey Morris and Dr Seward set off for Mile End.

* * * *

When you arrive, you are surprised to find a cart and horses pulled up in the gateway to the side of the property, beyond which lies an enclosed cobbled yard. The wagon is painted with the words 'Harris & Sons, Moving and Shipment Company, Orange Master's Yard, Soho'.

Two cart-men are securing a tarpaulin over the back when you arrive. You recognise them at once; they are the pair you interviewed in Bethnal Green, Mr Smollet and Mr Snelling.

"Good afternoon, gentlemen," you say, approaching them confidently. "How's business?"

The second they realise who it is that's addressing them, the cart-men panic. They leap up into the driver's seat of the cart and, whipping the horses with the leather reins, drive the animals out of the gate and straight towards you.

Take an Agility test. If you pass the test, turn to **264**, but if you fail the test, turn to **295**.

127

Several pistol-shots ring out through the night, sounding loud in the darkness, and shrieking, the bats flee.

Cross off one use of *The Pen is Mightier* special ability and turn to **81**.

128

It is all you can do not to scream in terror, and you run from the room fearing that you will never escape this cursed castle.

Add 2 points to your *Terror* score and turn to **59**.

129

You had never really considered how tall the wall between the two properties was until now, but you can't let yourself be put off – Renfield is getting away!

Taking a deep breath, you begin to climb, finding hand- and footholds in the mouldering brickwork.

Take an Endurance test. If you pass the test, turn to **79**, but if you fail the test, turn to **109**.

130

After a general discussion, the six of you determine that your next course of action will not definitely be settled upon until you have all slept on the matter, and spent some time considering the consequences of whatever actions may be taken.

You agree to meet again tomorrow at breakfast, and after making your conclusions known to one another, only then shall you settle upon the appropriate path.

Turn to **185**.

131

Just then there comes another blinding flash, which strikes the iron spike surmounting the tomb and pours through it into the earth, shattering the marble edifice in an explosion of incandescent flame. You are hurled out into the storm, as if you have been grasped by the hand of a giant and pulled backwards.

For a moment you catch sight of the Countess, contorted in agony as she is lapped by the flames, and then her bitter scream of pain is drowned by another thunder-crash.

The relentless hailstones beat down upon you again while the air reverberates with the howling of wolves.

(Roll one die and deduct this many points from your *Endurance* score. Alternatively, pick a card and deduct that many *Endurance* points, unless it is greater than 6 or a picture card, in which case deduct 6 *Endurance* points.)

If you are still alive, turn to **89**.

132

You realise that you must take action, or other forces will see to it that you never leave Castle Dracula. And so, you determine to search the Count's sepulchral stronghold once more, but this time during the hours of daylight, to find a way out no matter what.

As the sun grows high in the sky the next morning, and strikes the top of the great gateway opposite your window, your fear falls from you as if it is a vaporous garment dissolved by the dawn.

No man can know, till he has suffered during the night, how sweet and dear to his heart and eye the morning can be. (Deduct 1 point from your *Terror* score.)

You decide to take action whilst the courage of the day is upon you.

Considering you have never seen the Count out and about by daylight, you are intrigued to know what secrets lie within the chamber from which he emerges to crawl down the castle wall at night. But there is only one sure way you know of to get there.

If you want to climb out of your window and descend to the Count's chamber this way, turn to **163**. If you would prefer not to attempt something so reckless and want to try to find a way into his chambers from within the castle, turn to **547**.

133

In that moment you realise that the living nightmare you were forced to endure whilst a guest at Castle Dracula was real and not some hallucination brought on by the brain fever.

It is evident that the fiend intends to press home his villainous plans. You are the only one who knows the truth, but how can a mere mortal like you possibly hope to stand against his dark ambitions?

That terrible knowledge saps the strength from your bones. Mina is so worried about you that she takes you to sit a while in the Green Park as waves of exhaustion suddenly overcome you, and you briefly lose consciousness.

Turn to **218**.

134

The boom of Quincey's Winchester going off sets your heart racing even faster.

The Werewolf's legs give way under it and it skids to a lifeless halt in the middle of the road.

Cross off one use of *The Pen is Mightier* special ability and turn to **188**.

135

It is no good, you are too weak. You collapse onto your knees and from there onto the floor. The last thing you are aware of, before you pass out from blood loss, is the insane expression on your traitorous cousin's face, and Mehmed's cruel laughter echoing in your ears.

Your adventure, like your life, is over.

THE END

136

And so, it is agreed; you will join Quincey Morris in visiting the property in Mile End, while the rest of the Vampire-Hunters will head to Walworth, apart from Van Helsing, who will go to the Piccadilly property and meet the rest of you there, as soon as you can join him.

* * * *

The address is that of a former printers, the offices being located on the first floor, above the warehouse that occupies the ground floor; the perfect place to store a number of boxes of earth.

Indeed, upon entering the warehouse, your companion having forced the lock with the swift application of a crowbar, in the shadows created by dirt-smeared windows and half-closed shutters, you find six boxes, identical to those you purified in the chapel of Carfax House.

But it looks like someone has done your work for you. Something has chewed its way through the planks from which the boxes have been constructed and appears to have eaten what was hidden inside. For among the clods of mouldering clay strewn about the floor sit a number of rats, gnawing on the human remains that were hidden within the crates.

You cannot believe that the vermin were as large as they are now when they began feasting on the corrupted Transylvanian corpses and determine that it must have been their diet of Strigoi flesh that has changed them so terribly. Each one is big enough to swallow an infant whole.

(Add 1 to your *Terror* score.)

If the *Blood* score is equal to or greater than 8, turn to **502**. If it is lower than 8, turn to **532**.

137

That night she sleeps fitfully. You and the Professor take turns to watch over her, never leaving her unattended for even a moment, while Quincey Morris patrols the house and its grounds, in case Lucy's attacker should return.

When daylight comes again at last, Lucy barely even reacts to it, and spends much of the day dozing. You watch her as she sleeps, and, her mouth open, you notice that her gums are pale and drawn back from the teeth, which you are sure look longer and sharper than is natural.

When she wakes in the afternoon, she asks for Arthur and you telegraph for him to come at once, while Quincey goes off to meet him at the station.

* * * *

When her betrothed arrives, it is almost six o'clock, and the sun is setting. And when he realises how desperate the situation is, he is choked with emotion, and none of you find yourselves able to say anything.

Arthur's presence causes Lucy to rally a little, and she speaks to him more brightly than she has to anyone else since you arrived after she was attacked.

However, you fear that tomorrow will see an end to your watching.

Turn to **157**.

138

Somehow you manage to break free from her mesmerising stare, and you see her beguiling charms for what they really are. Her soulless beauty is nothing but a porcelain mask behind which hides a monstrous, blood-sucking leech.

In that moment, what remains of your love for Lucy is burned away by unadulterated hatred, and you determine to put an end to her yourself, here and now.

The complexion becomes livid, and the eyes seem to throw out sparks of hellfire. The brows become wrinkled, as though the folds of flesh were the coils of Medusa's snakes, and the blood-stained mouth stretches wide, as in the passion masks of the Ancient Greeks. If ever looks could kill, you see it in that moment.

If you want to employ *The Pen is Mightier* special ability, and you still can, turn to **208**. If not, turn to **178**.

139

The flask does indeed contain plum brandy, which warms you from the inside and helps to ease your anxieties. (Gain 3 *Endurance* points.)

The flask contains four further measures, and each measure will restore 3 *Endurance* points. However, if you drink more than one measure in one go, you must also reduce your *Combat* score by 1 point for every measure over the initial one that you drink, until after your next battle; you may also deduct 1 point from your *Terror* score, but this is not cumulative. (For example, if you drank two measures in one go, you would have to temporarily reduce your *Combat* score by 1 point, whilst permanently reducing your *Terror* score by 1 point, but if you emptied the bottle in one go, you would have to reduce your *Combat* score by 3 points but would still only reduce your *Terror* score by 1 point.)

If you want to keep the Flask of Plum Brandy with you, record it on your Adventure Sheet.

Now turn to **303**.

140

True to their word, the Slovaks have your box sent upriver, aboard a steam-launch, which finally puts into the village of Strasba one afternoon – a week after you arrived in Galatz – and you find your ever-faithful Szgany waiting to meet it. They load the crate onto a leiter-wagon of their own, securing it with hefty ropes, and set off for Castle Dracula.

You know that the Vampire-Hunters are still in pursuit, but if you can just reach your fortress home in time, you will be able to awaken the strigoi that still lie in the catacombs beneath the crag and put an end to the meddling Englishmen, American and Dutchman, once and for all!

As the wagon bumps and bounces over the rocky track that leads from Strasba and the river ultimately to Castle Dracula, it thrills you to hear the wolves calling to their master from their forest home, welcoming you back to the land of your forefathers.

Take an ESP test. If you pass the test, turn to **210**. If you fail the test, turn to **286**.

141

It is no good. The excellent meal you enjoyed, and the glasses of the more than adequate port you enjoyed with it, combine to send you into your own desperately-needed slumber.

* * * *

Conscious of someone's hand on your head, you start awake to find Professor Van Helsing standing there beside the bed.

"And how is our patient?" he asks, turning his attention to Lucy. "*Gott in Himmel!*"

Hearing his exclamation of horror, a deadly fear shoots through your heart. (Add 1 point to your *Terror* score.)

Turn to **181**.

142

Van Helsing agrees that it might be wise not to assume that the boxes have been stored in the house and so the five of you split up to search the grounds, each of you promising to give a whistle if you find anything.

You head north, to where an ancient apple orchard has grown into a copse of tangled, lichen-barked trees. Hearing a sound like the flapping of laundry on a line has you looking upwards and there, silhouetted against the moon, you see dozens of leathery-winged bats descending from out of the night's sky.

You manage to remember to give a shrill whistle and then the bats attack.

If you want to use *The Pen is Mightier* special ability, and you still can, turn to **127**. If not, turn to **104**.

143

Your seducer might be honey-sweet, but there is a bitter offensiveness underlying the sweetness, like the coppery smell of blood.

As she presses her body against yours, she pulls open your shirt, exposing the crucifix upon its beaded rosary.

The instant her eyes fall upon the holy symbol, she recoils from you, hissing and spitting like a hell-cat, and lashing out with her fingernails, which are sharpened to chiselled points, leaving bloody gouges across your chest.

(Lose 2 *Endurance* points.)

Turn to **228**.

144

You only just have time to arm yourself before the witch is upon you. (In this battle the witch has the initiative.)

SZGANY WITCH   COMBAT 7   ENDURANCE 7

If you kill the witch, turn to **191**.

145

You try the skeleton keys one after another, until you find one that fits the lock. After a little play back and forth, the bolt yields, and shoots back with a rusty clang. Ancient hinges creaking, the door slowly opens.

Turn to **301**.

146

The light and warmth of the Count's courteous welcome has dissipated all your doubts and fears, and you realise that you are indeed half-famished with hunger. Having made your toilet, you make your way into the other room.

Supper is already laid out. Your host is standing on one side of the great fireplace, leaning against the stonework. With a graceful wave of his hand he says, "I pray you, be seated and sup how you please. You will, I trust, excuse me that I do not join you, but I have dined already. And I do not drink… wine."

You hand him the sealed letter that Mr Hawkins entrusted to you, before you left England for Transylvania, informing the Count that you have recently qualified as a solicitor.

As he digests the contents of the letter, you fall upon a most excellent roast chicken. This, with some cheese and a salad, and a bottle of old tokay – of which you have two glasses – is your supper. (Restore up to 3 *Endurance* points.)

When you have finished eating, at your host's behest, you draw up a chair and join him by the fire. He proceeds to ask you many questions about your journey, and you tell him by degrees of all you experienced on the way to Castle Dracula, while you study his striking physiognomy more closely. His face is aquiline, with a thin nose and peculiarly arched nostrils. He has a lofty, domed forehead and he wears his hair long, in the fashion of the boyars of the past. The mouth is rather cruel-looking, with peculiarly sharp white teeth, which protrude over the lips, whose remarkable ruddiness shows astonishing vitality for a man of his years. His ears are pale, and extremely pointed. The chin is broad and strong, the cheeks firm though thin. The general effect is one of extraordinary pallor.

You also notice his hands, where they rest upon his knees; the nails are long and fine, cut to a sharp point, and curiously there are hairs growing at the centre of the palms.

A horrible feeling of nausea comes over you, which you are unable to conceal.

The Count offers you a grim smile, which shows off his protuberant teeth even more than before.

(Add 1 point to your *Terror* score.)

You are both silent for a while, and looking towards the window, you see the first dim streak of the coming dawn colour the sky.

From beyond the walls of the castle, you hear the howling of many wolves down in the valley below.

The Count moves towards the window, his eyes gleaming: "Listen to them, the children of the night. What music they make!"

Seeing the look of appalled horror on your face, he adds, "You must be tired. Your bedroom is all ready, and tomorrow you shall sleep as late as you will. I have to be away till the afternoon, so sleep well and dream well!"

With another courteous bow, he leaves the room.

You are lost in a sea of wonders, your mind awhirl with strange things, which you dare not even confess to yourself. You pray that God keeps you safe, if only for the sake of your dear Mina back in England, so many, many miles away.

* * * *

If you wish to continue the story as Mina Murray, turn to **278**. If you would prefer to continue the story as Jonathan Harker, turn to **371**.

147

You seize hold of the unnatural women and drag them off their plaything, hurling them to the corners of their boudoir, but not without them retaliating and lashing out at you.

Deduct 6 *Endurance* points, 2 *Blood* points and 1 *ESP* point, and then turn to **175**.

148

You can hear the panting of the beast right behind you now, and then, performing an almighty leap, it strikes you from behind. You are sent crashing to the ground, winded and wounded, with blood seeping through the torn fabric of your clothes where the thing has torn open your right shoulder with its raking claws.

Lose 3 *Endurance* points and, if you are still alive, turn to **211**.

149

Returning to the main hospital building, you tell the night watchman to gather three or four others at once, and follow you into the grounds of Carfax House, convinced, as you are, that Renfield could be both a danger to himself and others.

Then, not wanting to lose track of your patient's whereabouts entirely, you return to the wall that separates the asylum's grounds from those of the Carfax estate.

Tick off the code word *Auxilia* and then turn to **129**.

150

At your command, either side of the road that leads to the gates of Târgoviște, your men plant great stakes in the ground – each one over ten feet tall. Upon these, all the Turkish soldiers they captured are impaled and left to die in agony, creating a veritable forest of the impaled. Any enemy commander who sees it will surely think twice about attacking so ruthless a ruler.

(Gain 6 *Blood* points.)

But those wretches who have been impaled on the stakes at your behest were all prepared to die in battle for their Sultan. Perhaps there is something more you could do to really drive home the message that your authority is not to be challenged within your own dominions.

If you want to order your men not to stop at the bodies of the dead Turks and captured Janissaries, turn to **115**. If you think the message you are sending is already quite clear enough, turn to **85**.

151

Hearing a strange snarling sound, you immediately look to Arthur and see that he is undergoing the same hideous transformation that threatened to take over his body before.

His face has become a lupine snout, while his fingernails are now bleeding claws, and his eyes are jaundice-yellow spheres.

Snarling, he attacks.

If you want to call on *The Pen is Mightier* special ability, and you still can, cross off one use and turn to **215**. If not, turn to **180**.

152

Your final task is to arrange everything into date order – including the cuttings you kept from *The Dailygraph* and *The Whitby Gazette*, and pieces from *The Westminster Gazette* and *The Pall Mall Gazette* that you found in Dr Seward's study – so that anyone reading it will have a clear understanding of the matter and how all aspects of it are connected.

Turn to **592**.

153

"What is going on down here?" comes a voice from behind you.

Standing at the entrance to the hold are the boat's captain and his two sons, who are both built like wrestlers.

"These men were going to kill us!" Arthur exclaims, speaking up quickly. "And I dread to think what they were planning on doing with the contents of these crates. If I were you, captain, I would throw them off your ship."

Doktor Frankenstein tries to protest his innocence, but when the captain sees dissected human remains in the largest crate, he will not be swayed.

"Lock them in their cabin," he tells his sons, "and we will put them ashore as soon as we reach Fundu."

The insane doctor and his murderous assistant dealt with, you and Arthur gladly leave the hold again.

Cross off one use of *The Pen is Mightier* special ability and turn to **788**.

154

"Well, Johann, I want to go down this road," you tell the coachman, as you exit the carriage. "I shall not ask you to come unless you like; but tell me why you do not like to go, that is all I ask."

At that he stretches out his hands appealingly to you and implores you not to go. There is just enough English mixed with the German for you to follow the drift of his talk. He seems on the verge of telling you something – the very idea of which evidently frightens him – but pulls himself up saying simply, "*Walpurgisnacht!*"

You suddenly hear a sound, somewhere between a yelp and a bark. It comes from far off, but it upsets the horses nonetheless, and it takes all Johann's skill to quieten them again.

"That sounded like a wolf," you say.

"Yes, but there are no wolves here now," Johann replies, his face pale.

"Is it a long time since the wolves were so near the city?" you ask.

"Long, long," the coachman answers, "in the spring and summer; but with the snow the wolves have been here not so long."

As Johann struggles to calm the horses, dark clouds rapidly cross the sky, the sunshine passes away, and a breath of cold wind teases at your hair and clothes.

But it proves to be only a breath – a warning of worse weather to come perhaps – for once the clouds have passed the sun comes out brightly again.

Johann squints as he gazes at the horizon. "The storm of snow, he comes before long time," he grumbles.

Then he checks his watch and, keeping a tight hold on the horses' reins, climbs onto the driver's box.

You do not immediately get back into the carriage.

"Tell me about the place where this road leads," you say.

Johann crosses himself yet again and mumbles a prayer before answering: "It is unholy."

"What is?"

"The village."

"There is a village?"

"No. No one lives there hundreds of years."

"But you said there was a village," you persist.

"Yes. Was."

"So where is it now?"

Whereupon the coachman embarks upon a long story, in both German and English, and so mixed up you struggle to understand exactly what he is saying.

As far as you can tell, hundreds of years ago much of the populace had died there and been buried in their graves; but sounds were heard under the clay, and when the graves were opened, men and women were found rosy with life, their mouths red with blood. And so, in haste to save their lives – and their souls! – those who were left fled to other places, to where the dead were dead, and not… "Something else."

Johann is evidently afraid to speak the last words. In fact, he is in a perfect paroxysm of fear – white-faced, perspiring, trembling, and looking round constantly, as if expecting some dreadful presence to manifest itself there, in the bright sunshine on the open plain.

Finally, in agonised desperation, he cries, "*Walpurgisnacht!*" and points to the carriage for you to get in.

Your English blood rises at this, and standing back you say, "You are afraid, Johann. Go home. I shall return alone. The walk will do me good." Taking your oak walking stick and closing the carriage door, pointing back to the city you say, "Go home, Johann. *Walpurgisnacht* does not concern Englishmen."

There is nothing the poor fellow can do to dissuade you from the course of action you have decided upon, and so, with a despairing gesture, he turns the horses towards Munich.

Do you want to watch him depart, to make sure he does as you have bidden (turn to **179**), or will you set off down the winding road into the valley (turn to **209**)?

155

In the form of a bat – *Desmodontinae gigantica*, to be precise – you follow the winding path of the Thames from central London to Purfleet.

You see the smoke rising from the burning building before you even come within sight of Carfax House. When you do eventually arrive, it is to discover that the chapel adjoining the house – and in which twenty-nine boxes of earth had been stored – has been put to the torch. Everything that was in it has been destroyed.

Deduct 8 *Blood* points and then turn to **425**.

156

You have no choice but to fight off your pursuer as best you can, whilst clinging onto your mount's reins with one hand and taking your sword in hand with the other. (You must reduce your *Combat Rating* by one point for the duration of this battle, but you have the initiative.)

WEREWOLF   COMBAT 7   ENDURANCE 8

If you manage to slay the Werewolf within 6 Combat Rounds, or you reduce the Werewolf's *Endurance* score to 3 points or fewer, whichever is sooner, turn to **188** at once.

157

DR SEWARD'S DIARY

(Kept in phonograph)

20 September

`Only resolution and habit can let me make an entry tonight. I am too miserable, too low-spirited, too sick of the world and all in it...`

At one o'clock in the morning, you take over from Van Helsing, and continue to sit with Lucy while the Professor and Arthur get some much-needed rest.

At six o'clock, Van Helsing comes to relieve you of your solemn duty. When he sees Lucy's face he says to you in a sharp whisper, "Draw up the blind. I want light!"

Then he bends down and, with his face almost touching Lucy's, he examines her carefully. Upon removing the garland of garlic flowers, he gives a cry: "*Mein Gott*! The wounds on her throat have vanished!"

He turns to you, his face set and stern.

"She is dying. It will not be long now. Wake her beloved and let him come and see the last. We have promised him."

When you return only a matter of minutes later with Arthur, Lucy opens her eyes and, seeing him, whispers softly, "Arthur! Oh, my love, I am so glad you have come! Kiss me!"

Take an ESP test. If you pass the test, turn to **184**, but if you fail the test, turn to **214**.

158

"Look! Madam Mina, look!" the Professor suddenly calls. "We have company."

Springing to your feet, you join him at the entrance to the cleft. He hands you the field-glasses and points out into the snow.

It is falling more heavily now, and swirling about fiercely, for a high wind is beginning to blow. However, there are times when there are pauses between the flurries and it is during one of these lulls that you see the dark shapes padding through the snow towards you. There are two of them, and as they draw closer, they start to growl with sinister intent.

How do you want to deal with the wolves? Will you:

Arm yourself and prepare to fight?	Turn to **73**.
Use *The Pen is Mightier* special ability (if you still can)?	Turn to **260**.
Try to impose your will upon the wolves?	Turn to **123**.

159

Under the cover of darkness, the five of you leave Carfax Asylum and help each other clamber over the boundary wall the hospital shares with Carfax House.

Each of you is armed with a revolver and a large knife – "For other enemies more mundane," as Van Helsing put it – and you all carry a small electric lamp, fastened to your breast just in case.

(Record the Revolver, the Large Knife and the Electric Lamp in the Equipment Box on your Adventure Sheet.)

Taking care to keep to the shadows cast by the trees that grow close to the wall, you discuss where to look for the boxes of earth.

What do you want to suggest? To search the grounds first (turn to **142**), or head to the house straightaway (turn to **47**)?

160

After a general discussion, the six of you determine that your next course of action will not definitely be settled upon until you have all slept on the matter, and spent some time considering the consequences of whatever actions may be taken.

You agree to meet again tomorrow at breakfast, and after making your conclusions known to one another, only then shall you settle upon the appropriate path.

* * * *

You rise early, with the feeling that sleep has done you the power of good much. (Restore up to 3 *Endurance* points and deduct 1 point from your *Terror* score.)

When you all meet again at breakfast, there is more general cheerfulness than you ever expected to experience again. It is truly wonderful how much resilience there is in the human character. It is only when you catch sight of the red blotch on Mrs Harker's forehead that you are brought back to reality with a bump.

Van Helsing comes to your study later that morning. You can see that he has something on his mind.

"Friend John," he says at last, "there is something that you and I must talk of alone, although later we may have to take the others into our confidence. I fear that our poor, dear Madam Mina is changing."

A cold shiver runs through you.

"With the sad experience of Miss Lucy, we must this time be warned before things go too far. Our task is now in reality more difficult than ever. I can see the characteristics of the vampire coming into her face. It is now but very slight, but it is still there for those with the eyes to see it. Her teeth are somewhat sharper, and at times her eyes appear harder.

"But my greatest fear is this. If she can, by our hypnotic trance, tell what the Count sees and hears, is it not also true that he who hypnotised her first, and who drank her blood, and made her drink of his, should, if he willed it, compel her mind to disclose to him that which she sees and hears?"

You nod weakly. (Add 2 points to the *Blood* score.)

"In that case, we must keep her ignorant of our intent, for she cannot divulge that which she does not know."

The Professor wipes his forehead, which has broken out in profuse perspiration at the thought of the pain which he might have to inflict upon the poor soul already so tortured, before leaving to prepare for the next meeting of your exclusive and terrible secret society.

Turn to **185**.

161

You will not argue with her, and so go and have your supper. Lucy joins you and, enlivened by her charming presence, you enjoy an excellent meal, finishing it off with a couple of glasses of a more than satisfactory port.

When you are done, Lucy takes you upstairs and shows you to a room next to her own, where a cosy fire is burning. "Now," she says, "you must stay here. I shall leave this door open and my door too. You can sleep on the sofa and if I want anything I shall call out, and you can come to me at once."

You cannot do anything but acquiesce, for you are dog-tired, and could not have stayed up if you had tried. So, on Lucy renewing her promise to call you if she should want anything, you lie down on the sofa, and forget about everything.

* * * *

Conscious of someone's hand on your head, you start awake to find Professor Van Helsing standing there beside the sofa.

"And how is our patient?" he asks.

"Well, when I left her…" – you begin – "or rather, when she left me."

"Come, let us see," he says, and together you enter Lucy's room.

The blind is down, and you go over to raise it gently, while Van Helsing steps with his soft, cat-like tread over to the bed. Hearing his exclamation of horror, "*Gott in Himmel!*" a deadly fear shoots through your heart. (Add 1 point to your *Terror* score.)

Turn to **181**.

162

Your deathless sleep is disturbed when the lid of the box you are lying in is prised open by the First Mate, a crowbar gripped in his strong hands.

If your *Suspicion* score is 9 points or higher, turn to **192**; if not, turn to **226**.

163

While your courage is still fresh, you go to the window and ease through it onto the sill beyond. The stones are big and roughly cut, and time and the weather has washed the mortar from between them, providing you with numerous hand- and foot-holds. And so, you begin your descent.

Take an Agility test. If you pass the test, turn to **223**. However, if you fail the test, turn to **193**.

164

Although you are sure you have never seen the man before, nonetheless there is something strangely familiar about him. It is as if he projects an aura that your subconscious mind senses, and in doing so finds something familiar about the dark stranger.

The sensation is most unsettling, and an ice-water chill trickles down your spine.

(Add 1 point to your *Terror* score but deduct 1 *Blood* point.)

"It is the Count," says Jonathan, his voice barely more than a whisper, "but he has somehow turned back the years and grown young again!"

He is patently very distressed and so you gently draw him away, finding a comfortable seat in a shady place, in the Green Park. It is a hot day for autumn, and Jonathan soon falls asleep, with his head on your shoulder.

Seeing him like this causes you great anxiety, for you fear his condition could cause, or equally be the result of, some injury to the brain.

Perhaps the time has come when you must open the parcel wrapped in white paper, and tied with a pale blue ribbon, and learn what is written within Jonathan's notebook.

Turn to **218**.

165

Drawing on your final reserves of strength, you somehow fight your way free of the Sultan's tent, where you are spotted by Captain Petru. But even as he pulls you up onto his horse behind him, you already know that you are dead, and by the time he makes it back to the palace, you have succumbed to your wounds.

* * * *

Your body is laid out in state, your queen, Erzebet sobbing hysterically over your lifeless corpse, while Radu averts his gaze. Your cousin Basarab steps up to take your place and, your body barely cold, negotiates a truce with the Turks, the people of Wallachia completely unaware of the fact that he is the very traitor who murdered you, even when you were on the verge of defeating Mehmed the Conqueror and freeing your country from the Ottoman Empire forever.

You are interred within a great black granite sarcophagus in a crypt of Dealu Monastery in the hills above Târgoviște. But not long after, stories start to circulate that the vault was broken into and the mortal remains of Prince Vlad Tepes stolen away by persons unknown.

If your rank is that of *Nosferatu* or higher, turn to **230**. If not, turn to **195**.

166

You give in to sleep and are transported by the most wonderful dream – although if Mina were to learn of its nature it would cause her great sadness and pain.

You are no longer alone. The room is the same, unchanged in any way since you first entered it, and in the brilliant moonlight you can see your footsteps where they have disturbed the long accumulation of dust. Illuminated by the moonlight are three young women – ladies, you judge, by their dress and manner – but they cast no shadow on the floor; you can still see only your own footsteps.

Two are dark, and have high aquiline noses, like the Count, and great dark, piercing eyes, that glow red like hot coals. The other is fair, with great masses of golden hair and eyes like pale sapphires.

All three have brilliant white teeth that shine like pearls against the ruby of their voluptuous lips.

They advance towards you with slow, graceful steps, smiling seductively, the tips of their tongues playing over their exposed teeth and plump lips. The moonlight shining through the window behind them makes their diaphanous robes translucent, revealing their shapely forms beneath.

You feel a wicked, burning desire swell within your heart, wishing that they would kiss you with those ruby red lips, even though deep down you know it would cause your dear Mina pain if she were party to that knowledge.

The women whisper together, as they glide across the room towards you, and then all three of them laugh. It is such a silvery, musical laugh, your body answers their siren call.

The fair-headed one shakes her head coquettishly, as the other two urge her on.

"Go on!" one of the dark-haired beauties says. "You are first, and we shall follow. Yours is the right to begin."

"He is young and strong," adds the other. "There are kisses for us all."

You remain where you are upon the couch, peering out from under your eyelashes in an agony of delighted anticipation. The fair girl advances and reaching the couch, she bends over you, her décolletage looming large, closer and closer, until you feel her breasts brushing your face, only a thin shift keeping the firm nipples from touching your quivering lips directly.

The hairs on your arms stand on end then as several hands start to caress your body, and the soft supplication of kisses too. The skin at your wrists begins to tingle as the kisses become more passionate. There is a fleeting sensation of pain, but no more than a pinprick, and it passes in a moment, as the sucking lips and tongues tease at your flesh.

But at the back of your mind, a small voice of doubt registers the pain more completely and begins to question whether you are asleep at all, or in some hypnotic trance.

(Lose 2 *Endurance* points and gain 3 *Blood* points.)

But the voice is silenced again when the fair-haired beauty straddles your waist and pulls her shift over the top of her head, her supple body appearing like marble in the deceitful moonlight.

She smells as sweet as honey and her scent sends the same tingling through your nerves as her tinkling laughter.

If you are wearing a Golden Crucifix, turn to **143**. If not, turn to **182**.

167

The witch-queen of the Szgany tribe throws herself at you, as you struggle to raise your blade in time to defend yourself. But in doing so, she unwittingly skewers herself on your sword.

Cross off one use of *The Pen is Mightier* special ability and turn to **191**.

168

The carriage goes at a hard pace, and in this way, you continue your unknown night journey. Despite the cloak and rug, you start to shiver from the cold. (Lose 1 *Endurance* point.)

Curious to know how time is passing, you strike a match, and by its flame read your watch face. You are shocked when you see that it is only a few minutes to midnight.

Then, far off in the distance, from the mountains on either side, rises the howling of wolves, which affects both you and the horses in the same way, for you are almost minded to jump from the caleche and run, whilst the horses rear and plunge madly, so that the driver is forced to use all his iron strength to keep them from bolting.

How many of the following code words do you have ticked off? *Babona, Kereszt, Gonosz, Varázslat.* (If you have the code word *Szerencse* ticked off, you may deduct 1 from the total.)

None?	Turn to **303**.
One?	Turn to **197**.
Two?	Turn to **216**.
Three of more?	Turn to **246**.

169

Roll one die (or pick a card). If the number rolled is odd (or the card is red), turn to **849**. If the number rolled is even (or the card is black), turn to **806**.

170

Harker cowers before you, in fear not just of his life but also his wife's soul. But the other Vampire-Hunters have rallied themselves and close in like a pride of lions, ready to make the kill.

During the hours of daylight, your powers are seriously limited; you cannot reduce your physical form to mist or transform yourself into a creature of the night.

Do you want to make a break for it, while you still can (turn to **485**), or are you prepared to face the Vampire-Hunters in battle (turn to **235**)?

171

As if warned by some sixth sense, you know the thing is about to leap and, heart pounding, throw yourself sideways, landing on your side among the thick grass between the overgrown tombstones.

Turn to **211**.

172

You feel that your near-nocturnal existence is taking its toll on you. It is destroying your nerve, it has you starting at every shadow, and your mind is full of all sorts of horrible imaginings. God knows that there are grounds for your overwhelming sense of dread in this accursed place!

Suddenly desiring a breath of fresh air, you throw open a window and fill your lungs with cold night air. You look out over the beautiful expanse of this region of the Carpathian Mountains. Everything is bathed in soft yellow moonlight, that seems to cause the distant hills to melt into obscurity, and the shadows in the valleys and gorges are of velvety darkness.

But as you lean from the window, something catches your eye – something that is moving a storey below your position. Drawing back behind the weatherworn stonework, you peer out warily.

What you glimpsed is the Count's head coming out from a window. But revulsion and terror threaten to overwhelm you when you see the man slowly emerge from the window and begin to crawl down the castle wall, headfirst, over the dreadful abyss, with his cloak spreading out around him like great wings.

Take a Terror test. If you pass the test, turn to **225**. If you fail the test, turn to **196**.

173

Take an ESP test. If you pass the test, turn to **240**, but if you fail the test, turn to **203**.

174

Fighting their way through the clouds of buzzing, black, bristly-bodied flies that still fill the room, the attendants rush into Renfield's cell and grab hold of him by the arms, before he can do you any more harm.

And in that instant the fight goes out of him, the swarming flies escape between the bars of the window, and the remaining spiders disappear into cracks in the corners of the room.

You stagger out of the chamber, even more determined to put an end to the evil that has robbed the wretch of his sanity and caused the downfall of your own dear Lucy.

The echo of Renfield's voice pursues you along the passageway beyond his cell: "You will, I trust, bear in mind, later on, that I tried to warn you, Dr Seward. Remember, I did try to warn you!"

Turn to **159**.

175

Climbing like a spider into the shadows that cluster at the dome of the chamber like cobwebs, Lilith turns and challenges you: "You yourself never loved. You never love!" And a mirthless, soulless laughter rings through the room from the Sisters.

"Yes, I too can love," you reply. "You yourselves can tell it from the past. Is it not so?" And then, with a guttural growl, you add: "I promise that when I am done with him you shall kiss him at your will. Now go!"

"Are we to have nothing tonight?" Lamia says, pointing at the bag you dropped on the floor when you arrived, which moves suddenly.

You say nothing, but merely nod. Melusina pounces on the bag at once, tearing it open to discover the 'little something' you found for them whilst out hunting.

The Sisters gather round the bag, muttering almost motherly, soothing sounds, but which could equally be the purrs of hunting felines, and then begin to feed.

Harker himself has fainted, the sound of the infant's wailing too much to bear after all that he has endured this night. But more importantly than that, Harker now knows your secret.

* * * *

From that moment on, you make sure that Harker remains confined to his rooms. You even have the foresight to cajole him into writing three more letters: one saying that his work is almost done, and that he will start for home again, within a few days; another saying that he is setting out the morning after the date the letter is sent; and the third saying that he has left the castle and is back in Bistritz.

Such subterfuge will mean that none can interfere with your plans, no matter what the Sisters' visions might claim.

* * * *

A month later, at your behest, the Szgany bring a consignment of large wooden boxes to the castle and proceed to fill them with mouldering earth taken from the catacombs beneath Castle Dracula. Not only that, but inside each crate you have them place one of the bodies of the dead, preserved by esoteric means by the Cult of Balaur in the catacombs of the Scholomance, that now lie beneath the castle, and bind their undead spirits to serve you in death.

* * * *

A week or so later, long before sunset, your diurnal rest is disturbed when Harker somehow finds his way into your crypt and pushes back the lid of your black granite sarcophagus, waking you.

You can only imagine that he exited his prison via a window and from there found the way into the crypt from your own long-abandoned chambers in the castle. But of more pressing concern is the fact that he is holding a shovel in his hands, as if he intends to use the sharp edge of the tool to strike your head from your shoulders.

If you have the code word *Rabszolga* ticked off, turn to **238**. If not, but you have the code word *Árulás* ticked off, turn to **268**. If you have neither of these code words ticked off, turn to **305**.

176

Carried on leathery wings six feet wide, you swoop down to attack the doctor, slashing at his face with your cruel claws. (You have the initiative in this battle.)

DOCTOR SEWARD   COMBAT 9   ENDURANCE 10

If you wish, you may deduct 3 *Blood* points and automatically win – turn to **221**.

If not, the wolf will assist you in your battle against the young doctor. Each Combat Round you will have two attacks rather than just one; if one or other of the attacks is successful, you will injure your opponent, but if both attacks are successful, you cause double damage that Combat Round. However, Dr Seward is focusing his attacks on you, so if he wins a Combat Round, you will be the one who is injured and not Bersicker.

If you are still alive after five Combat Rounds, or as soon as you reduce Dr Seward's *Endurance* score to 4 points, whichever is sooner, turn to **221** at once.

177

Feeling the hackles on the back of your neck rise, you turn round just as one of the men tries to bring the butt of his horse-whip down on your head. Catching his arm in your left hand, you push him away from you, as Arthur draws his sword-stick and threatens the other fellow with the sharp end, making them think twice about trying anything else.

"Come on, Smollet!" shouts the other, leaping into the driver's seat of the wagon.

"I'm coming, Snelling!" your attacker barks back, as he lumbers after him.

The cart-men geeing the horses forward, the wagon lurches out of the gate and away down the street.

Turn to **236**.

178

The handmaiden of death goes for you then, fast as a striking cobra, claws and teeth bared, determined to rip out your throat. (In this battle, you have the initiative.)

THE BLOOFER LADY   COMBAT 9   ENDURANCE 10

After 5 Combat Rounds, or if you manage to reduce the Lucy-creature's *Endurance* score to 5 points or fewer, whichever is sooner, turn to **208**.

179

Leaning on your stick, you watch Johann leave. He drives slowly along the road for a while, but then you catch sight of a figure coming over the crest of the hill; a man, tall and thin. When he draws near the horses, they begin to jump and kick about, and even to whinny in terror. Johann is clearly unable to hold them, and they bolt down the road, fleeing this place at a mad run.

You watch, concerned for the coachman, until the carriage passes out of sight, and then look for the stranger again; but he too has gone.

There is something unnerving about the man's sudden appearance and subsequent disappearance.

Add 1 point to your *Terror* score and turn to **209**.

180

You prepare to fight your friend, knowing that in doing so you will not only be saving yourself, but him too. (In this battle, you have the initiative.)

ARTHUR   COMBAT 8   ENDURANCE 9

Because you are trying not to hurt Arthur, you must reduce your *Combat Rating* by 1 point for the duration of this battle. If you win two consecutive Combat Rounds, or if you manage to reduce Arthur's *Endurance* score to 4 points or fewer, turn to **215** at once.

181

The Professor raises his hand, his iron face drawn and ashen.

There on the bed, seemingly in a swoon, lies poor Lucy, more white and wan-looking than ever. Even her lips are white, and the gums seem to have shrunk back from the teeth, as can be seen in a corpse after a prolonged illness.

"Quick!" Van Helsing barks. "Bring some brandy."

You fly to the dining room and return with the decanter, but Lucy is in need of a more fortifying pick-me-up than mere alcohol.

"It is not too late. Her heart still beats, though but feebly. All our work is undone, and we must begin again."

He is already dipping into his bag and takes out the instruments of transfusion. You roll up your shirt sleeve and without a moment's delay, there being no need for an opiate to sedate Lucy, the operation commences.

No man knows, till he experiences it himself, what it is to feel his own lifeblood drawn away into the veins of the woman he loves. But it is with a sense of personal pride that you see a faint tinge of colour steal back into Lucy's pallid cheeks and lips.

The Professor watches you critically until he says at last, "That will do." He attends to Lucy, while you press your fingertips to the incision in your arm and lie down, for you feel faint and a little sick.

At his leisure, he binds up your wound and sends you downstairs to get a glass of wine for yourself, but it will take more than Mrs Westenra's finest claret to restore you fully.

(Deduct half your remaining *Endurance* points, rounding fractions down, and tick off the code word *Haemorrhage*.)

If you have the code word *Transfusion* ticked off, turn to **244**. If not, turn to **212**.

182

Her voluptuousness thrills you to the very root of your being, and as she arches her neck she licks her lips. In the moonlight you can see the moisture shining on her scarlet lips and on her pink tongue as it licks the sharp, white teeth.

She lowers herself onto you and you feel the soft, shivering touch of her lips on the super-sensitive skin of your throat, and the hard dents of two sharp teeth, just touching and pausing there.

You close your eyes in languorous ecstasy and wait, with beating heart, for the longed for moment of blissful agony, when the tips of those sharp teeth puncture your skin.

And when it comes it does not disappoint, as the unnatural women start to feed…

Roll one die and add 2; deduct this many *Endurance* points.

(Alternatively, pick a card and deduct its face value from your *Endurance* score, unless it is 9 or above or a picture card, in which case deduct 8 points from your *Endurance* score.)

If you are still alive, turn to **618**.

183

You must fight Doktor Frankenstein and Igor at the same time. (Your opponents have the initiative in this battle.)

	COMBAT	ENDURANCE
DOKTOR FRANKENSTEIN	8	7
IGOR	7	6

Because Arthur is fighting with you, each Combat Round you will have two attacks, which means you have two chances to injure your opponents. If you lose a Combat Round, roll one die (or pick a card); if the number rolled is even (or the card is black), you may reduce the damage done to you by one point.

If you win the fight, turn to **213**.

184

There is something the matter. You have never heard such seductive words pass from her lips.

Turn to 2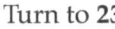

185

When the Vampire-Hunters meet again it is without Mina. She passes on her apologies, saying that she thought it better that the rest of you should be free to discuss your movements without being embarrassed by her presence, considering those discussions will inevitably have to include the matter of what should be done with her, should she succumb to the vampire's curse.

And so, with one member down, you discuss your plan of campaign, with Van Helsing putting the facts before you:

"The *Czarina Catherine* left the Thames yesterday morning. It will take her at least three weeks to reach Varna, but we can travel overland to the same place in just three days. Even allowing for two days less for the ship's voyage, owing to the way in which the Count can influence the weather, and if we allow another whole day and night for any delays that may threaten to impede our journey, then we have a margin of nearly two weeks. And so, in order to be quite safe, we must leave here on the seventeenth at the latest. That way we shall reach Varna a day before the ship arrives, which will give us time to make such preparations as may be necessary. Of course, we shall all go armed against evil things, both physical and spiritual."

"I understand that the Count comes from a wolf country," says Quincey, "and it may be that he shall get there before us. I propose that we add Winchesters to our armament. I have a kind of belief in a Winchester when there is any trouble of that sort around."

"Good!" says Van Helsing. "Winchesters it is. In the meantime, we can do nothing here. And I suspect Varna is unfamiliar to all of us, so let us go there sooner. It is as long to wait here as there. Tonight and tomorrow we can get ready, and then, if all be well, we will be ready to set out on our journey."

Add the Winchester Rifle to your Adventure Sheet and turn to **227**.

186

At five o'clock that evening, when you present the finished bundle of typewritten pages to your host, you recognise it as the perfect opportunity.

"Dr Seward, may I ask you a favour? I want to see your patient, Mr Renfield. What you have said of him in your diary interests me greatly. Do let me see him."

It seems that he cannot refuse you, and so, to your great relief, he accedes to your request.

You enter Renfield's cell to find Dr Seward's patient sitting on the edge of his bed, head down, but with his eyelids raised so that his eyes follow you as you enter the chamber.

Although his dishevelled condition takes you aback, you nonetheless hold out your hand to him, and address him: "Good evening, Mr Renfield."

Take an ESP test. If you pass the test, turn to **217**, but if you fail the test, turn to **241**.

187

Your poor husband is evidently terrified, and if you were not there to support him, you feel he would have sunk down to his knees.

He keeps staring as a man comes out of the jeweller's carrying a small parcel, which he gives to the young lady, who then drives off. The dark man keeps his eyes fixed on her, and when the carriage moves off up Piccadilly he follows, hailing a hansom of his own.

"I believe it is the Count," says Jonathan, who has become frozen to the spot, "but he has grown young!"

He is patently very distressed and so you draw him away quietly, and find a comfortable seat in a shady place sit for a while in the Green Park. It is a hot day for autumn, and after a few minutes spent staring at nothing, Jonathan's eyes close, and he goes to sleep, with his head on your shoulder.

To see him like this – like he was when you were reunited with him in Buda-Pesth – puts you in a state of high anxiety, for you fear his condition could cause or exacerbate some injury to the brain.

(Add 1 point to your *Terror* score.)

Perhaps the time has come when you must open the parcel wrapped in white paper, and tied with a pale blue ribbon, and learn what is written within Jonathan's notebook.

Turn to **218**.

188

Reaching the bridge, you spur your horse across it as Quincey uses his lighter to set fire to the rag you realise he has stuffed into the neck of an open bottle of Bourbon rum. Raising his arm, he hurls the bottle behind him.

The Texan's improvised bomb smashes against the wooden planks, the alcohol splashing across the entire width of the bridge as it bursts into flames.

You hear the Werewolves howl in shock and see the lupine forms of your pursuers come to a sudden stop behind the wall of flames.

Turn to **981**.

189

It is too long since you last checked on the strigoi-boxes you have stored in and around London, and a creeping sense of paranoia that is almost as strong as the desire to drink the blood of mortals tells you that you should check on them.

But which location do you want to visit first?

The end-of-terrace house in Walworth?	Turn to **274**.
The former printers' warehouse in Mile End?	Turn to **70**.
Carfax House in Purfleet, in the county of Essex?	Turn to **593**.

190

In your bloodlust, you take the man's head from his shoulders, and you do not even recoil in horror when his still beating heart sends a ruddy torrent fountaining into the air, spraying you with gore. In fact, you lick some of the dying man's blood from your face, so lost are you in the heat of battle. (Gain 2 *Blood* points.)

* * * *

The massacre continues throughout the night – from three hours after sunset until four bells the following morning. With the cavalry routed, you give the command for your troops to retreat.

"We have won a great victory today, my lord!" Captain Petru declares, as you quit the battlefield.

"We may have won this battle, but we have yet to win the war," you replied sagely. "Mehmed escaped my sword and his forces still massively outnumber our brave sons of Wallachia."

"Then we will return to the palace and the Sultan will not find us wanting when he comes knocking at our gates. We will raise the banners of the ancient Order of the Dragon above the city walls. This simple act of defiance will be a sign to the heathen that we Wallachians are not so easily conquered."

"Yes," you ponder, "a sign."

Warriors and strength of arms are not the only tools at a wise warlord's disposal. Sometimes, a psychological advantage can be the most powerful weapon of all.

Do you want to send Sultan Mehmed a message that says you are a formidable foe, regardless of how many men you have at your command (turn to **150**), or do you want to return to the palace and prepare to be besieged (turn to **85**)?

191

The gypsy hetman and his tribe stare at you in horror as the witch slides free of your blade and falls to the ground, dead. But not one of them makes a sound or moves to stop you as you back out of the camp – Quincey keeping his Winchester trained on them the whole time – and return to your waiting horses.

Mounting up, you spur your steeds into action and gallop away into the Borgo Pass.

Turn to **26**.

192

The First Mate is not alone. Standing at his shoulder, peering into your crate, is the gruff Captain. In one hand he holds aloft a lantern; in the other, a crucifix.

While the Captain's crucifix and the prayers of the babbling First Mate keep you trapped within the box, the Romanian takes a heavy-headed hammer and a large ship's nail from his tool-chest and, demonstrating a righteous zeal that would put many a priest to shame, uses the one to drive the other through your chest and into your heart.

That done, he picks up an axe and takes your head from your shoulders. Then he and the Captain consign your rapidly decaying remains to the waves.

Your adventure, like your unnatural life, is over.

THE END

193

You are within reach of the Count's window when your foot slips and you lose your grip on the wall. You fall past the opening and, trying to grab the windowsill, tear your fingernails on the rough stones.

And then you are plummeting into the gorge, the castle vanishing above you, the rushing wind loud in your ears. It is a fall you cannot hope to survive.

Your adventure is over.

THE END

194

It is late in the afternoon when you sense that others are drawing near the castle, although whether it is your husband or that monster the Count that you can sense you do not know. You and the Professor set off towards the east, intending to intercept the Count before he can reach his decaying stronghold. You do not travel fast, for the way takes you steeply downhill.

It is hard-going, trudging through the snow, and having gone about what you judge to be a mile you sit down to rest on a large rock. Looking back, you see the clear outline of Dracula's castle cut the sky in all its grandeur, perched a thousand feet up on the summit of a sheer precipice, and with seemingly a great gap between it and the adjacent mountains. There is something wild and uncanny about the place.

Far off you can hear the distant howling of wolves. Even though the sound is muffled by the deadening snowfall, it still unnerves you deeply. Professor Van Helsing is busy searching for some strategic point, where you will be less exposed, in case the wolves track you through the snow.

You continue to watch the road, which you can just trace through the drifting snow, until the Professor gives a whistle. Getting up again, you join him at what appears to be a natural hollow in a rock, with an entrance like a doorway between two boulders.

"See," he says, taking you by the hand and drawing you inside, "here we can wait out of the cold and the wind; and if the wolves do come we can meet them one by one."

Taking his field-glasses from their case, from the shelter of the rocks, he begins to search the horizon.

If the *Blood* score is 12 points or higher, turn to **158**. If the *Blood* score is lower than 12, turn to **53**.

195

The mystery of the disappearance of your body is never solved, and while your legend lives on after your death, you do not.

Your adventure is over.

THE END

196

You cannot believe your eyes! Is it some trick of the moonlight, some weird effect created by the moon-cast shadows?

You keep looking and are convinced what you are witnessing is not some night-born delusion. You can see the Count's clawed fingers and toes grasp the corners of the stones, worn clear of mortar by the stress of years, and using every projection he moves downwards with considerable speed, just as a lizard might move along a wall.

The overwhelming dread that hangs about this horrible place overwhelms you, and you fear there can be no escape, encompassed all about, as you are, with terrors you dare not dwell upon.

Lose 1 *Combat* point and 2 *Endurance* points from fear, add 1 to your *Terror* score, and then turn to **225**.

197

Roll one die (or pick a card). If the number rolled is odd (or the card is red), turn to **246**. If the number rolled is even (or the card is black), turn to **216**.

198

An invocation of your will sends Bersicker leaping at the doctor, with jaws slavering and snarling savagely.

Deduct 2 *Blood* points and turn to **221**.

199

You land safely and set off after the fugitive madman.

"Last I saw, Mr Renfield went left and then headed straight towards the old house," Barlow calls down to you.

Setting off at a run, not wanting to give your quarry the chance to escape, as you pass through the belt of trees that rings the asylum grounds, you see a white figure disappear over the top of the high wall that separates your property from Carfax House.

Do you want to run back to the asylum to rally the troops (turn to **149**), or do you want to go it alone and follow Renfield over the wall before he can get any further away (turn to **129**)?

200

Just as you are on the verge of giving in to sleep entirely, the Count's warning comes to mind again: *"Let me warn you, my young friend, that should you leave these rooms you will not fall asleep in any other part of the castle. It is old, and has many memories, and there are bad dreams for those who sleep unwisely."*

As you struggle to rouse yourself from the unnatural lethargy that has beset your body, you realise that you are not alone.

In front of you, illuminated by the moonlight, are three young women – ladies, you judge, by their dress and manner – but they cast no shadow, and on the floor you can see only your own footsteps have disturbed the long accumulation of dust.

Two are dark, and have high aquiline noses, like the Count, and great dark, piercing eyes, that glow red like hot coals. The other is fair, with great masses of golden hair and eyes like pale sapphires. All three have brilliant white teeth that shine like pearls against the ruby of their voluptuous lips.

All three advance towards you with slow, graceful steps, smiling seductively, the tips of their tongues playing over their exposed teeth and plump lips. The moonlight shining through the window behind them makes their diaphanous robes translucent, revealing their shapely bodies beneath.

Take a Combat test. If you pass the test, turn to **90**. If you fail the test, turn to **114**.

201

The following evening, you provide your guest with some sheets of note paper and three envelopes, telling him, "It will please your friends to know that you are well, and that you look forward to getting home to them."

He obediently writes two letters – one to his employer, Mr Hawkins, and one to his fiancée, a certain Mina Murray – while you yourself compose several notes. One is directed to Samuel F. Billington of Whitby; another to Herr Lautner of the Bulgarian port of Varna; a third to Coutts & Co., the London bankers; and the fourth to Herren Klopstock & Billreuth, bankers of Buda-

Pesth. All of them are required in preparation for the next part of your plan.

Adding the missives he has penned to those you have scribed, you rise and make your excuses. At the door you stop and turn, saying, "Let me warn you, my young friend, that should you leave these rooms you will not fall asleep in any other part of the castle. It is old, and has many memories, and there are bad dreams for those who sleep unwisely."

* * * *

With a living, breathing mortal soul in the castle once more, it is all you can do not to devour your guest and drink his blood. The beast within must be fed, and so you are forced to leave the castle and go hunting. And you are aware that it would be wise to return with something for the Sisters to feast on, to keep them docile, lest they seek out Harker themselves.

But when you return some hours later, having fed yourself (restore up to 6 *Endurance* points), and with a little something for the Sisters to dine on, you are perturbed when you sense Harker's heartbeat not in the guest quarters, but in the east wing of the crumbling castle. And he is not alone; you clearly underestimated the Sisters' guile and gluttonous bloodlust.

You burst into the Sisters' chamber, with all the force of a hurricane, extinguishing the lanterns that are burning in the room. The Sisters cannot hide their true forms from you, and you see them for the snake-worshipping horrors they are.

Your fury is as terrible as the tornado that carried you into the room – for you still have need of Harker and you cannot bear for something to happen to the man, as it did to Renfield before him – and you take it out on the disobedient vampyres.

"How dare you touch him, any of you?" you scream at them in your native tongue. "How dare you cast eyes on him when I had forbidden it? He is mine! Beware how you meddle with him, or you will have to deal with me!"

Divide your *Blood* score by 10, rounding fractions up. Then roll 1 die, and if the number rolled is equal to or less than the resulting total, turn to **120**. If it is greater, turn to **147**.

202

Renfield pummels you with his fists, and you have no choice but to defend yourself against the madman's brutal assault. (In this battle Renfield has the initiative.)

RENFIELD   COMBAT 8   ENDURANCE 10

If you are still alive after 6 Combat Rounds, or if you reduce Renfield's *Endurance* score to 3 points or fewer, whichever is sooner, turn to **174** at once.

203

You attempt to insinuate your way into the terrified First Mate's mind, but he has decked himself all about with holy charms – having rifled through the belongings of the dead crewmen in search of anything that might serve him in his battle against you – and so he is able to resist your psychic probing.

As you struggle to escape the confines of the box, the First Mate attacks. (Your opponent has the initiative in this battle.)

FIRST MATE   COMBAT 9   ENDURANCE 9

If you are still alive after 6 Combat Rounds, or if you reduce your opponent's *Endurance* score to 4 points or fewer, whichever is sooner, turn to **240** at once.

Alternatively, if you wish, you may spend 3 *Blood* points and turn to **240** without having to fight the Romanian.

204

Taking your stout stick in hand once more, you lash out at the phantom as it glides towards you over the icy ground. (In this battle the Phantom has the initiative.)

PHANTOM   COMBAT 8   ENDURANCE 9

If you manage to make a successful strike against the ethereal entity, turn to **233** immediately. After 4 Combat Rounds, even if you haven't managed to lay a single blow against the wraith, turn to **263**.

205

You excuse yourself from the next meeting, suspecting that the men will want to discuss the part you will have to play in all this as well as their plan to catch up with the Count and put an end to him.

While the meeting is taking place, you confine yourself to your rooms and your own thoughts on the matter.

When Jonathan returns, the meeting concluded, you waste no time in sharing the conclusions you have come to, and how the two of you should proceed.

"Jonathan, I want you to promise me something on your word of honour. Promise me that you will not tell me anything of the plans formed for the campaign against the Count. Not by word, or inference, or implication; not at any time whilst this remains!" You point to the scar on your forehead.

"I promise!" he declares with great solemnity. From that moment it feels like a door has been shut between the two of you.

You go on: "There is a poison in my blood, in my soul, which may destroy me – which must destroy me, unless some relief comes to us. My soul is at stake, and I shall tell you plainly what I want, my beloved husband. Should the time come, I want you to kill me."

"And what time is that?" Jonathan asks, his voice low and strained.

"When you are convinced that I am so changed that it is better that I die. And when I am dead in the flesh, then you must drive a stake through my heart and cut off my head or do whatever else may be necessary to grant me rest!"

Jonathan looks at you, wan-eyed and with a greenish pallor. "Must I make such a promise, Mina?"

"You must, my dearest," you insist. "When the time comes you must not shrink from the task. You are the nearest and dearest to me and mean all the world to me; our souls are knit into one, for all time. If it is to be that I must meet death at any hand, let it be at the hand of him that loves me best."

"I swear to you by all that I hold sacred and dear," he says, and there is steel in his voice now, "that, should the time ever come, I shall not flinch from that dread duty."

Hearing your husband speak those words fills you with a sense of calm and you know that, no matter what happens, he will do all to guard the fate of your immortal soul.

Deduct 1 point from your *Terror* score and turn to **227**.

206

You hear the swoosh of something cutting through the air behind you the instant before the butt of a horse-whip is brought down hard on the back of your head.

(Lose 2 *Endurance* points, and for the duration of the next battle you have to fight, reduce your *Combat Rating* by 1 point.)

Reeling from the blow you turn and, through blurred eyes, see what appears to be two identical cart-men both raising their right-arms, ready to strike you again.

Somehow you manage to catch your attacker's wrist in your left hand, preventing him from landing the blow. You shove him away from you, as Arthur unsheathes his sword-stick and threatens the other fellow with the sharp end, in case either of them try anything else.

"Come on, Smollet!" shouts the leaner of the two, leaping into the driver's seat of the wagon.

"I'm coming, Snelling!" your attacker barks back, as he lumbers after him.

The two cart-men geeing the horses forward, the wagon lurches out of the gate and away down the street.

Turn to **236**.

207

It is late in the afternoon when you finally catch up with your quarry.

You have been climbing steadily ever since following the spur road from the Borgo Pass that leads to Castle Dracula. From this height, as you approach the top of the peak of the crag, it is possible to see a great distance; and far off, beyond the white waste of snow, you can see the river lying like a black ribbon in kinks and curls as it winds its way through the mountains.

The snow starts to fall more heavily, and swirls about fiercely, for a high wind has started to blow. And then, straight ahead of you, through pauses in the snow flurries, you see your quarry – a band of Szgany gypsies accompanying a leiter-wagon carrying the great square chest, inside which Count Dracula must be hiding.

Beyond the swirling wall of snow, you make out the looming sinister, shadowy presence of the Count's decaying home, silhouetted against the sinking red orb of the sun.

"They are racing for the sunset!" Quincey shouts over the panting of the horses, the pounding of their iron-shod hooves on the road, the clatter of the wagon, the moaning wind, and the howling of wolves. "We may be too late!"

If you have the code word *Tigani* ticked off, turn to **304**. If not, turn to **234**.

208

The Bloofer Lady abruptly breaks from the fight, seeking solace in the coffin that birthed it.

Turn to **74**.

209

Turning down the side road, you head through the deepening valley. You do not see any reason for the coachman's objection to the route and walk for a couple of hours without having any care of the time or distance covered, and without seeing a single person or even a house. The place is desolation itself.

And then, on turning a bend in the road, you come upon a scattered fringe of woodland. You sit down to take a moment's rest and begin to look around. It suddenly strikes you how much colder it is now than at the commencement of your walk, and something like a strange sighing sound that seems to come from all around you is your constant companion.

Thick clouds are massing in the sky overhead, and sensing that a storm is coming, you resume your journey. Having lost all track of time, it is only when the deepening twilight forces itself upon you that you begin to consider how you might find your way back to the Quatre Saisons. The air is cold, and a sound is carried on the wind, not unlike the mysterious cry you thought was made by a wolf, and for a moment you hesitate.

If you want to retrace your steps, back along the road that brought you into the valley, turn to **239**. If you would prefer to press on, determined to at least see the deserted village, having walked all this way, turn to **10**.

210

You suddenly give voice to an agonised howl as the very essence of your being is torn apart by the most abject soul-rending pain, your scream accompanying the death-cries of the Weird Sisters.

The vampyre women are dead, leaving you with a hole in your heart as surely as if one of the Vampire-Hunters had driven a stake through it.

Deduct 6 *Blood* points and then turn to **286**.

211

Warily you pick yourself up off the ground – your breath coming in ragged gasps – and face the monster that has cornered you.

It is some nightmarish amalgam of man and beast, neither one thing nor the other, but something altogether much worse. The creature is crouched, ready to pounce, its strength wound up in its muscular body like the potential energy trapped within a watch spring. Lips curl back from teeth that have become part of a blunt snout, while strings of thick saliva dangle from its glistening teeth.

If you want to call on *The Pen is Mightier* special ability, and you still can, turn to **261**. If not, turn to **231**.

212

Lucy sleeps well into the day, and when she does finally awake she appears fairly well and strong. She chats with you quite freely, and you try to keep her amused.

When Mrs Westenra comes up to see her she says, "We owe you so much Dr Seward, for all you have done, but you really must now take care not to overwork yourself. You are looking pale yourself."

* * * *

"Now you go home, and eat much and drink enough," Van Helsing tells you, when the two of you are alone again. "Make yourself strong. I shall stay here tonight and sit up with Miss Lucy."

You return to Purfleet in time for a late dinner, and then make your rounds, before retiring to the welcome embrace of your own bed. But both waking and sleeping, your thoughts always come back to the puncture marks on Lucy's throat, and the ragged appearance of their edges.

* * * *

The following afternoon you go over to Hillingham and find Lucy much better and Van Helsing in excellent spirits after taking delivery of a large parcel from abroad. Opening it, he takes out a great bundle of white flowers.

"These are for you, Miss Lucy," he says, giving them to her.

"For me? Oh, Professor Van Helsing!"

"Yes, my dear, but they are not for you to play with. These are medicines. I will put them in your window, and I will make them into a wreath and hang it round your neck, so you sleep well."

"Oh Professor, I believe you are playing a joke on me," she says with a laugh, throwing the flowers down as if in disgust, having smelt them. "Why, these flowers are only common garlic!"

To your surprise, Van Helsing rises up and, his iron jaw set, says sternly, "I never jest! There is grim purpose in what I do, and I warn you to take care, for the sake of others, if not your own. I only do this for your own good, for there is much virtue in these so common flowers."

You assist the Professor in decking Lucy's room with the garlic – which, you learn, have come all the way from Haarlem – while he fastens the windows and latches them securely. Next, taking a handful of the flowers, he rubs them over the sashes, as if he intends every whiff of air that might get in would be laden with their potent scent. He then treats the door and even the fireplace in the same way.

It seems grotesque to you and feel you must say something. "Professor, I know you always have a reason for everything you do, but it seems to me that you are working some spell to keep out an evil spirit."

"Perhaps I am!" comes his quick reply.

When Lucy is ready for bed, he fixes a wreath of garlic around her neck, telling her, "Take care not to disturb it, and even if the room feels close, do not open the window tonight, or the door."

As you leave Hillingham by carriage, Van Helsing says, "Tonight I can sleep in peace. And after two nights of travel, with much reading in the day between, and a night to sit up, sleep is what I need. But call for me early tomorrow nonetheless, and we will come together to see whether my 'spell' has worked."

Turn to **357**.

213

The insane surgeon and his hunchbacked servant both dead, you and Arthur hide the bodies as best you can, behind the pile of packing cases, confident that you will put ashore and be gone long before their deaths are discovered by the crew.

Turn to **788**.

214

You draw closer, as Arthur eagerly bends over to do her bidding, and it is then that you see the pale gums again and the pointed teeth as she opens her mouth.

Your heart racing, you know you have to act fast.

Take an Agility test. If you pass the test, turn to **237**, but if you fail the test, turn to **267**.

215

As the transformed wolf-man throws himself at you again, you bring the hilt of your weapon down hard on top of his head, and he drops to the ground, stunned.

Turn to **245**.

216

You are terrified by the howling of the wolves, and you cannot help but think of how everyone you have met of late crossed themselves and made signs against the Evil Eye when they learned where you were going.

Add 1 point to your *Terror* score and turn to **303**.

217

He makes no immediate reply, but studies you intently with a frown on his face. His expression soon gives way to a look of wonder, which then merges with apparent doubt.

"You're not the girl the doctor wanted to marry, are you?" Renfield says at last. "You can't be, you know, for she's dead."

"Oh no! I have a husband of my own," you say, trying to smile through the tears welling in your eyes at mention of poor Lucy's passing. "I am Mrs Harker."

"Then what are you doing here?"

"My husband and I are staying with Dr Seward for a short while."

"Then don't stay."

The lunatic's pronouncement is as unexpected as it is compassionate.

"But why not?" you ask him.

"I used to believe that by consuming a multitude of living things, no matter how low in the scale of creation, I might indefinitely prolong my life," he says, changing the subject, a distant look coming into his bulging eyes. "At times I held the belief so strongly that I actually tried to take human life. The doctor here will bear me out that on one occasion I tried to kill him for the purpose of strengthening my vital powers, by assimilating his life by consuming his blood. For the blood is the life, is that not true, Doctor?"

"It is time we left," Dr Seward says uneasily, looking at his watch.

"Goodbye," you say, as you make to follow the doctor out of the cell, "and I hope I may see you again, under auspices pleasanter to yourself."

To your astonishment, Mr Renfield replies, "Goodbye, my dear. I pray to God I may never see your sweet face again. May He bless and keep you!"

Dr Seward escorts you back to your own room and then leaves to collect Van Helsing while you wait for your husband to arrive.

Tick off the code word *Psychopathia* and then turn to **592**.

218

You head home after the traumatic encounter, but more bad news awaits you when you return to Exeter, in the form of a telegram.

```
TELEGRAM, VAN HELSING, LONDON, TO MR AND MRS HARKER,
                        EXETER

                     22 September

You will be grieved to hear that Mrs Westenra died five
days ago, and that Lucy died the day before yesterday.
They were both buried today.
```

Oh, what a wealth of sorrow in a few words! Poor Mrs Westenra! Poor Lucy! Gone, never to return!

* * * *

If you wish to continue the story as Mina Harker, turn to **242**. If you want to continue as Jonathan Harker, turn to **329**.

219

"Excellent!" says Van Helsing once you are paired up. "I will take Madam Mina to Veresti by train, and then by carriage, following the route Jonathan journeyed, from Bistritz over the Borgo Pass, and thus we will find our way to Castle Dracula. There, Madam Mina's hypnotic power will surely help, for we shall find our way all dark and unknown otherwise after the first sunrise when we are near that fateful place. There is much to be done, and many places to be sanctified, so that his nest of vipers be obliterated."

* * * *

Less than two hours after your macabre visit to the graveyard of St Peter's you are at the river harbour, waiting to board a steamship that is travelling upriver to Strasba.

The wharf is busy with the hustle and bustle of river-workers and travellers even after dark, and an old woman bundled up in an assortment of shawls and blankets catches your eye. In broken German, she makes it clear that she is a pedlar and has all manner of superstitious charms and supposedly medicinal remedies to sell.

Most of it is tat, but one of her home-brewed concoctions does grab your attention. With the aid of some dramatic sign language, she explains that it will take away a fever brought on by the bite of a mad dog, and that it contains wolfsbane.

If you want to buy the phial of the wolfsbane potion, turn to **353**. If you decide that it is probably best to avoid indulging in any local remedies, turn to **413**.

220

The True History of Vlad the Impaler

Calling his men together, Vlad easily persuaded them to enter the enemy camp. He divided the men so that either they should die bravely in battle with glory and honour or else, should destiny prove favourable to them, they should avenge themselves against the enemy in an exceptional matter. So, at nightfall, the Prince entered the Turkish camp.

Your plan works. Accompanied by blaring buglers and blazing torches, under cover of darkness your forces penetrate the enemy encampment before the Turks even know they are under attack. Your Carpathian Guard speed like lightning in every direction, slaughtering the enemy in their hundreds.

With the Ottomans taken entirely by surprise, you realise that you may never get a better opportunity to put an end to Mehmed's invasion of Wallachia: cut off the head of the serpent and it will die. And so, you make your way through the camp until you are standing before the Sultan's pavilion once more.

As your bodyguards dispatch the Janissaries on sentry duty there, you force your way into the marquee, ready to put an end to Mehmed the Conqueror himself.

Only he's not there. The wily snake has fled! Instead, you find yourself facing one of his viziers.

As the Turk unsheathes his scimitar, you tighten the grip on your own sword and prepare to vent your fury upon the Sultan's servant. (You have the initiative in this battle.)

VIZIER   COMBAT 7   ENDURANCE 7

If you kill the vizier, turn to **190**.

221

Dawn is turning the sky to the east of London a muted shade of pink. Twilight, the time around dawn and dusk, is when you are at your weakest. Deciding that the upstart doctor can wait until a more suitable occasion presents itself for you to do away with him, you signal to the wolf that it is time to leave with a piercing cry and take off into the night. The wolf responds with a deep-throated howl and takes off after you, the two of you disappearing along the road.

Turn to **277**.

222

Before your eyes, the monstrous white worm metamorphoses again, taking on the guise of your erstwhile companion, Quincey Morris. The Texan strides towards you, hissing angrily, and he fixes you with a horrid ophidian stare, his pupils no more than black, snake-like slits.

Able to move again, you prepare to defend yourself.

If you want to call upon *The Pen is Mightier* special ability, cross off one use and turn to **282**. If not, turn to **868**.

223

You look down only once, just to make sure that a sudden glimpse of the awful depth will not overcome you, but after that keep your gaze firmly from it.

Having a fairly assured sense of the direction and distance to the Count's window, you make your way towards it as best you can. And then, before you know it, you are slipping through the arched opening into the Count's secret chamber.

Looking around, you are surprised to see by the morning light, coming in through the window, that the room appears to have never been used! The furniture is of the same style as that in the women's wing and covered with dust as well. There are also chains and ornaments, some of them jewelled, but all antiques stained with the patina of age.

In one corner of the room, you stumble upon a great heap of gold, gold of all kinds. You uncover Roman, British, Austrian, Hungarian, Greek, and Turkish money among the hoard, all of it covered with a film of dust, and none of what you find is less than three hundred years old.

But you are not interested in stealing from the Count; you are here to learn the truth of what he is, and what he is about.

What you take to be the door that connects the chamber to the rest of the castle is locked, and there is no sign of a key, but at another corner of the room there is another heavy door. This one is open and leads through a stone passage to a circular stairway, which goes steeply down.

Descending, taking care where you tread – for it is dark here, the stairwell lit only by loopholes in the heavy masonry – at the bottom you find yourself at one end of a tunnel-like passage, from which comes the odour of old earth newly turned.

You feel compelled to follow the passage, wherever it may lead, the mildew smell growing heavier until you enter an old, ruined chapel that has evidently been used as the castle graveyard in the past. The roof is broken, and in two places you can see steps leading to vaults, but the ground has recently been dug over, and the mouldering earth placed into the wooden boxes brought to Castle Dracula by the Slovaks.

There is no sign of the Szgany, who you take it have been the ones tasked with the work that has been undertaken here.

Do you want to make a thorough search of the chapel (turn to **251**) or, if you feel that you have seen enough, do you want to quit this place of death without further ado (turn to **567**)?

224

Brushing the moths away from you, you rush back down the stairs and are relieved when the insects do not follow.

Turn to **273**.

225

What manner of man is this Count Dracula? Or what manner of creature in the semblance of a man?

At that moment you determine to do all you can to escape or die trying. You are convinced the Count has left the castle now and decide to use the opportunity to explore more than you have dared to do as yet.

Taking up a lamp, you descend the stone stairs to the hall. Although you find you can pull back the bolts easily enough, and unhook the great chains, the great door is locked, and the key gone. It must be in the Count's possession!

So instead, you set out upon a thorough examination of the various stairs and passages that interlace the gloomy castle and try all the doors that open from them. One or two small rooms near the hall are open, but there is nothing to see in them except old furniture, dusty with age and moth-eaten. At last, however, you find a door at the top of a stairway which, though it appears locked, gives under a little pressure.

You have entered a wing of the castle further to the right than the rooms you know, and a storey lower down, its tall windows overlooking the great precipice.

The castle is built on the corner of a great rock, so that on three sides it is quite impregnable. Great windows were placed here during its construction, where sling, or bow, or culverin could not reach. To the west is a great valley, and ascending in the distance, great jagged mountain fastnesses, rising peak on peak, the sheer rock studded with mountain ash and thorn, whose roots cling to cracks and crevices in the stone.

Exploring this portion of the castle, you come to a bend in the passage you are following. There is an iron-studded oak door to your left, in the south-facing wall, a chill wind blowing through the cracks between the planks. To your right, the passage continues to a suite of rooms at its end.

Do you want to try the door to your left (turn to **248**), or will you keep following the passageway to the right (turn to **489**)?

226

Meeting your blood-red gaze, the First Mate abruptly freezes.

If your rank is that of *Prince of Darkness* or higher, turn to **266**. If not, turn to **173**.

227

12 October, London

Your party of six Vampire-Hunters leaves Charing Cross on the morning of the 12 October and arrives in Paris the same night. There you take the places that have been secured for you aboard the Orient Express.

If the *Blood* score is 8 or higher, turn to **306**. If it is lower than 8, turn to **257**.

228

Now fully alert, you watch as before your very eyes, the women's features appear to shift and change, like melting wax, their bodies changing also, and you see them as they really are.

One appears to have taken on the aspect of a snake, her jaw dislocating as it hinges unnaturally wide, with thick serpentine coils where her legs were before. A tearing sound accompanies the transformation of another of the creatures, as great bat-like wings unfold from behind her back, while the fair-haired beauty is revealed to be little more than an animated corpse, her skull-like visage ruddy with gore.

The unnatural women stalk, crawl and slither towards you.

Take a Terror test. If you pass the test, turn to **276**. If you fail the test, turn to **299**.

229

"And now for you, Madam Mina," the Professor says, addressing you directly, "this marks the end of your part in the proceedings, until all is well. You are too precious to risk taking with us. We are men and are able to bear what must happen this night. But you remain our star and our hope, and we shall act all the more freely knowing that you are not in the danger."

All the men, but especially your husband, seem relieved, but it does not make sense to you that they should brave any danger without you, and perhaps lessen their strength in numbers by excluding you. Nonetheless, their minds are made up and, although it is a bitter pill for you to swallow, you can do nothing save accept their well-intentioned care of you.

As the five of them prepare for what must be done this very night, you retire to your rooms, although you doubt you will be able to sleep, when the man you love is in peril! In the end you settle for lying down and pretending to sleep.

You do not feel at all sleepy but are possessed of a devouring anxiety. You keep going over in your mind everything that has occurred, and it all seems like some horrible tragedy.

If you had not gone to Whitby, perhaps poor dear Lucy would still be alive, for she didn't take to visiting the churchyard until after

you arrived, and if she hadn't gone there during the day with you, she would not have walked there in her sleep. And if she had not gone there at night, the Count would not have destroyed her as he did.

And so it is that, in the end, you cry yourself to sleep...

* * * *

Your sleep is disturbed by the sound of praying – coming, you believe, from Mr Renfield's cell – but it is the sudden, profound silence that startles you, and causes you to get up.

You look out of the window. All is dark and silent, the black shadows thrown by the moonlight possessed of a soundless mystery of their own. Not a thing seems to be stirring, but all is grim and fixed as death.

But there is one thing moving in the still of the night. A thin white mist is creeping with an almost imperceptible slowness across the lawn towards the asylum, as if it has a sentience and a vitality of its own.

You return to bed and pull the bedclothes over your head, as a leaden lethargy comes over you and you fall back to sleep. And as you sleep, you dream...

* * * *

You are lying in bed, but your limbs are so heavy you feel you could not move even if you wanted to. It begins to dawn on you that the air is heavy, and dank, and cold. All is dim, the gaslight you left lit for Jonathan, appearing as a tiny red spark through the thick fog that fills the room.

As you watch, the fog gets thicker and thicker, until it looks like a concentrated pillar of cloud in the middle of the room, through the top of which you can just make out the light of the gas, which then divides and seems to shine on you like two red eyes. And then the eyes are not shining through the fog but are set within a livid white face, bending over you from out of the mist.

As the horror seizes you, everything fades to darkness...

* * * *

When Jonathan wakes you late the following day, you do not feel rested at all. In fact, you feel more weary than when you retired to bed last night, and the face in the mist, with its blazing red eyes, returns to haunt you every time you close your eyes.

Deduct 2 *Endurance* points, add 1 to your *Terror* score, and then turn to **269**.

230

Your body carried away by the followers of the Great Serpent, you are buried once again in the soil of your homeland, beneath Broken Tooth Mountain. But your death-sleep is not a contented one and your corpse becomes restless...

* * * *

You wake from violently gruesome dreams – in which you are a bloated leech drawing sustenance from the body of a dead plague victim – with a mouth full of soil, and in a panic, dig yourself out of the shallow pit in which you have been buried. As the shock of your reawakening passes, you notice how wizened your hands are, looking like nothing more than skeletal digits covered with the thinnest, most desiccated covering of skin. You flex your fingers, marvelling at how you are still able to move them, whilst recalling your last moments among the living as if it were a lingering dream.

Rising from your grave, you find the dark-eyed priestess watching you.

"What has happened to me?" you ask her, your voice cracking with age. "What have I... become?"

"You have ascended," she says. "You are a man no longer. You are now nosferatu, the chosen of Balaur – immortal. You no longer need food or drink as men do. Not only that, but you are faster and stronger than you were before, able to resist wounds that would prove fatal for ordinary men. The life-blood of others is an elixir to you that can restore your strength and youth, and help you recover from what would otherwise be mortal injuries. You possess the power to have your revenge against your mortal enemies, so go. Now!"

As the sun is setting over the Carpathian mountains you discover that you only need will something and it is so; you wish to return to your royal seat and, your body assuming a more suitable form, you fly over the peaks and valleys of Wallachia, soaring above forests and farms that pass beneath you in the blink of an eye.

In no time at all, or so it seems, as the moon rises over the turrets of Târgoviște, you arrive at the royal palace and enter the bedchamber of Prince Basarab. But as you gaze upon your cousin's sleeping form it quickly becomes clear that many years, rather than weeks or months, have passed since you went into the earth, for the man you are looking at has aged noticeably. In your fury, you rip out his throat and gorge yourself on his blood before he becomes conscious of how his own actions have doomed him.

And yet you realise that, even with Basarab dead, you can never rule Wallachia again, as you once did, although you will always be bound to your homeland.

Leaving the abattoir that Basarab's bedchamber has become, you set out in search of the one who drove you to seek such accursed power as now resides within your undying form.

* * * *

The hunt is long, and your search lasts many years. You are forced to hide in the dark places of the world during the day, going out as darkness falls to feed the insatiable need for blood that has transformed you into something more savage beast than man.

But at last, almost twenty years after the fateful night attack at Târgoviște, you finally catch up with the Conqueror again, hundreds of leagues to the south in Constantinople, as he is planning campaigns to capture Rhodes and southern Italy, and even conquer the Mamluk Sultanate of Egypt and claim the Caliphate as well.

Although somehow, deep down, you know that it is your 'brother' Mehmed, you barely recognise the old man, he has aged so much since your last encounter. But this time you are sure to wake him, so that he is fully aware of who has returned from the dead to have his revenge before taking his life. And this time, when you leave the Sultan's tent unseen, you take a trophy with you – Mehmed's head.

* * * *

Discovering that your queen Erzebet died years ago and realising there is no place for you in the world now, you return to the near-impenetrable depths of the Carpathian mountains. Finding the descendants of the snake-cult susceptible to your will, and easily dominated, you have them raise a new fortress home for you, atop the crag beneath which lie the catacombs of the Scholomance, and there you hide away from the rest of the world.

Over time you discover that you are not the only one of your kind and that there are more horrors than just vampires abroad in the forests and deep, shadowed valleys of this mountainous region. And in time you learn that there are those who have sworn to rid the world of your kind, religious zealots who prosecute witch-hunts, burning and beheading many of those who have enjoyed a second life after their first death.

But, ever the cunning strategist, you remain locked within your mountain fastness and bide your time, determining that one day you shall take your rightful place as ruler once again, learning all you can about those who might oppose you in the interim. For if there is one thing that is not in short supply now, it is time.

* * * *

The years pass, and then the decades, and then whole centuries, and while you do not die, your body does begin to age, although your youthful looks and vigour return after you have gorged yourself on blood.

However, the population of the Carpathians is not great, with settlements being few and far between. You cannot risk taking too many, for fear of arousing the suspicions of what passes for the authorities in these more enlightened times, where communication is possible by wire, with messages taking mere days to travel from the nearest town of Bistritz to Buda-Pesth, over four hundred miles away, and in which whole armies can cover great distances by means of the railway networks that cover the continent, from Paris to Constantinople.

And so, you are forced to limit yourself to only one or two peasants a month, and spend much of the rest of your time sleeping the sleep of the dead in the black granite sarcophagus in which you were originally buried, the gypsy-folk of the Szgany tribe having transported it to Castle Dracula for you long ago. The Szgany are a proud people, who swear allegiance to a noble leader, unto death. They are not without their secrets either, for their bloodline carries its own dark taint.

But eternity is a long time, and it is not only your thirst for blood that drives you to perform appalling acts of barbarism, treating people as nothing more than a source of sustenance. You thirst for power too, just as you did in your mortal life, and so you set about making your plans of conquest...

But the world has changed since you cut yourself off from it. The Ottoman Empire has long since fallen, as has the House of the Draculs. You are the last of that royal bloodline. The greatest empire in the world now is ruled from an island in northern Europe, an empire that covers a quarter of the globe and claims a quarter of its one and a half billion inhabitants as its citizens – the British Empire. And its undisputed ruler is the Widow of Windsor, Queen Victoria of the House of Hanover.

Understanding full well that knowledge will always give you the advantage over your enemy, you set about building a library of reference books – everything from the *London Directory* and *Whitaker's Almanac* to the *Army and Navy Lists* and the *Law List* – and cultivate all manner of potentially useful contacts. If you are to conquer the British Empire, and become the ultimate ruler of the world, you will need a base of operations close to its capital in England, if not a number of bolt-holes you can retreat to, if needs be. You always favoured guerrilla warfare, when dealing with Mehmed the Conqueror's attempts to invade Wallachia, attacking his forces from behind enemy lines, and so you formulate a plan to acquire several properties in and around London that will enable you to do just that. But to help bring your plan to fruition you will require an unwitting ally, someone to work on your behalf from within. An inside man, if you like.

You have an advertisement placed in *The Dailygraph* –

Gentleman of an ancient Eastern European family, seeks assistance with relocation to England...

– which results in an ambitious Mr Peter Hawkins of Exeter writing to you, offering most reasonable terms for his firm to act on your behalf in purchasing property in and around London. At your request, Mr Hawkins sends a solicitor in his employ to liaise with you – to go through the necessary paperwork and acquire your signature and seal where required – a certain Mr R. M. Renfield.

Gain 6 *Blood* points and turn to **265**.

231

Cornered, you have no choice but to draw your weapons and defend yourself as the wolf-man pounces. (In this battle, the Werewolf has the initiative.)

WEREWOLF   COMBAT 9   ENDURANCE 9

If you manage to slay the beast, turn to **291**.

232

Batting aside the flies and crushing the scuttling spiders beneath your feet, you move towards the madman, the only thought in your mind that this nightmare will come to an end if you can just make him shut his mouth.

And then he is there in front of you, consumed by a paroxysm of desperate rage: "Let me out of this house at once! You don't know what you do by keeping me here. You don't know whom you wrong, or how! Can't you hear me, man? Can't you understand? Will you never learn? Let me go! Let me go! *Let me go!*"

If you want to use *The Pen is Mightier* special ability, and you still can, cross off one use and turn to **174**. If not, turn to **202**.

233

You strike the spectre, but your stick passes straight through it, leaving nothing but a trail of clinging mist in its wake. You are incapable of injuring the phantom!

Tick off the code word *Spectre*, add 1 point to your *Terror* score, and turn to **263**.

234

If the *Blood* score is 15 points or higher, turn to **304**. If it is lower than 15, turn to **76**.

235

Harker's companions come to his aid, while he recovers himself, and engage you in battle.

You must fight them all at the same time, and while you have the initiative in this battle, you must deduct 1 point when calculating your *Combat Rating*, for they are protected by silver crucifixes and garlands of garlic, that would repel you completely were it not for the very desperate nature of this battle. (The Vampire-Hunters have the initiative.)

	COMBAT	ENDURANCE
ARTHUR HOLMWOOD	8	9
QUINCEY MORRIS	9	9
DOCTOR SEWARD	9	10
PROFESSOR VAN HELSING	8	8

After 8 Combat Rounds, or as soon as you manage to reduce the *Endurance* score of one of the Vampire-Hunters to 3 points or fewer, whichever is sooner, turn to **330** at once.

236

With one deft flick of his rapier blade, Arthur catches the bolt holding the back of the cart in place as it hurtles past him and pulls it back. The tailboard of the cart drops down and, as the wagon bounces over the cobbles, the boxes of earth come tumbling out onto the ground, where they smash open, spilling their contents across the yard.

You glimpse grey limbs desperately struggling to claw the earth back over pallid flesh that is beginning to crinkle and blacken as it is exposed to the sunlight that suddenly fills the yard. But as the undead things that had been buried in the boxes begin to burn, so they thrash about, mouths open in silent screams of agony, thereby exposing more of their wretched remains to the sun's purifying touch.

(Deduct 1 point from your *Terror* score.)

While you are mesmerised by the destruction of the Strigoi, the two burly men jump down from the cart and advance on you and Arthur.

Choose your opponent! Will you:

Attack Mr Smollet?	Turn to **317**.
Attack Mr Snelling?	Turn to **349**.
Use *The Pen is Mightier* special ability (if you can)?	Turn to **369**.

237

Sensing danger, you swoop upon Arthur, and drag him back with a strength you never knew you possessed.

"Not on your life! Not for your living soul and hers!" Van Helsing roars, as he rushes to help you, standing between Lucy and her fiancé like a lion at bay.

Turn to **297**.

238

Harker seems possessed of a resolve you have never seen in a mortal man before and will not be shaken from his grim purpose. Before you can rouse yourself fully, he brings the shovel down with both hands, slicing through your neck with one clean blow.

That done, he breaks the handle of the digging implement over his knee and plunges the splintered shaft into your heart, your undead body crumbling to dust as he does so.

Now nothing stands between Countess Dolingen of Gratz – for it is she who has turned Harker into her puppet – and her undead claim on your ancestral lands.

Your adventure, like your life-in-death, is over.

THE END

239

And so, you set off back the way you have just come. But as you do, it is as if the twilight deepens with every hurrying step you take.

You hear the sound of the wolf more clearly now, for it seems to be circling you. You can hear its claws scraping the ground, and the low, guttural growl of its breathing, and you fear that you are heading into danger, rather than away from it.

Panting for breath now, you decide to go back the other way, in the hope of finding shelter from the beasts that hunt at dusk in the deserted village.

(Deduct 1 point from your *Endurance* score and add 1 point to your *Terror* score.)

Turn to **10**.

240

Cowed by your dark majesty, the First Mate staggers away from you, making for the steps that lead up and out of the cargo hold. But as he departs, he utters an ancient Romanian curse and hurls something at you. It is a bottle.

The bottle hits you and smashes, covering you with holy water. The cry you utter is a scream of agony, as the blessed liquid eats into your undead flesh as if it were acid.

Roll one die and add 4 to the number rolled; deduct this many points from your *Endurance* score. (Alternatively, pick a card and deduct that many *Endurance* points, unless it is a picture card, in which case deduct 10 *Endurance* points.)

If you are still alive, deduct 10 *Blood* points and turn to **545**.

241

The lunatic suddenly jumps up from the bed, snarling like a beast, and before Dr Seward or any of the asylum's attendants can stop him, grabs you by the throat and pushes you against the wall of his cell.

Dr Seward acts swiftly, seizing the madman and pulling him from you, crying out for help.

As the attendants rush to restrain Mr Renfield, Dr Seward leads you from the cell. The experience leaves you feeling shaken and upset.

(Lose 2 *Endurance* points and add 1 to your *Terror* score.)

Once he has given you a restorative brandy, the doctor leaves for the station to meet Professor Van Helsing, while you wait in your room for Jonathan to arrive.

Turn to **592**.

242

MINA HARKER'S JOURNAL

23 September

Jonathan is better after a bad night. I am so glad that he has plenty of work to do, for that keeps his mind off terrible things...

Deeply saddened as you are by the passing of your dear friend Lucy, nonetheless you are able to take some small pleasure in seeing Jonathan shake off the insidious malaise that had seemed to follow him home from the continent.

You rejoice that your husband is not weighed down by the responsibility of his new position, now that he is the senior partner of the firm of Hawkins, Oldman & Lee, with all that that entails, and feel proud to see him rising to the height of his advancement and keeping pace with all the duties that have come upon him.

Knowing that he will be away all day till late, with your household duties done for the day, your mind turns to the journal he kept whilst he was away for all those months in Transylvania.

If you want to read Jonathan's journal while you are alone, turn to **272**. If you prefer not to know what torments he was forced to endure whilst staying in that benighted region, turn to **307**.

243

The bats swoop overhead but do not attack, and simply fly off again into the night.

Gain 2 *Blood* points and turn to **309**.

244

Having given blood twice in four days takes an additional toll on your body, leaving you feeling weak and lethargic.

Deduct 1 point from your *Combat* score and then turn to **212**.

245

This is your chance. The vampire is clearly feeling vulnerable. You confront your nemesis, driven by the desire to make him pay for all the crimes he has committed, all the lives that he has taken in order to sustain his own abominable existence.

But which weapon from your arsenal will you bring to bear against him?

Holy symbols and warding charms?	Turn to **420**.
Holy water (if you have some)?	Turn to **445**.
The Knight's Shield (if you have it)?	Turn to **575**.
Cold steel?	Turn to **350**.
Silver bullets (if you have some)?	Turn to **892**.
The Pen is Mightier special ability (if you still can)?	Turn to **300**.

246

You are traumatised by your ordeal and wish you had never taken a position with Mr Hawkins of Exeter, let alone made the journey to Transylvania, especially when you recall the rumours that abound regarding what happened to your senior colleague Mr Renfield, after he visited this benighted country.

Add 2 points to your *Terror* score and turn to **303**.

247

As you land the killing blow, the Texan drops to the ground, his life's-blood pouring from multiple wounds into the snow, and a gloating smile spreads across the gypsy woman's face. She is the witch-priestess of the snake-cult the Szgany belong to, and servant of the Voivode of Wallachia, the Son of the Devil, Count Dracula.

And now you are bound to the snake-cult too, your former friends and loved ones forgotten...

Your adventure is over.

THE END

248

The door has become warped by time, and the old wood is now swollen within its stone aperture.

If you want to try to force the draughty door open, turn to **337**. If not, turn to **308**.

249

"Excellent!" says Van Helsing once you are paired up. "I will take Madam Mina to Veresti by train, and then by carriage, following the route Jonathan journeyed, from Bistritz over the Borgo Pass, and thus we will find our way to Castle Dracula. There, Madam Mina's hypnotic power will surely help, for we shall find our way all dark and unknown otherwise after the first sunrise when we are near that fateful place. There is much to be done, and many places to be sanctified, so that his nest of vipers be obliterated."

* * * *

Less than two hours after your macabre visit to the graveyard of St Peter's you are on your way, travelling westwards on horseback towards the Carpathian Mountains, following the course of the Sereth River as closely as you can.

If you have the code word *Vânători* ticked off, turn to **12**. If not, turn to **981**.

250

LETTER FROM MISS LUCY WESTENRA TO MISS MINA MURRAY

24 May 1897

My dearest Mina, thanks, and thanks, and thanks again for your sweet letter. It is so nice to hear about your work as an assistant schoolmistress, and to hear about Jonathan's travels. I had never even heard of Transylvania until you wrote to me. It must be nice to see strange countries, but I am sure you must be missing him desperately, and long to hear all his news. But I have some news of my own I must share with you.

My dear, it never rains but it pours. Here am I, who shall be 20 in September, and yet I never had a proposal till today, not a real proposal, and today I had three. Just fancy! Three proposals in one day!

Well, my dear, number one came just before lunch. I told you of him, Dr John Seward. He is only 29, and he has an immense lunatic asylum under his own care. He would just do for you, if you were not already engaged to Jonathan, for he is handsome, well off, and of good birth.

He spoke to me, Mina, very straightforwardly. He told me how dear I was to him, though he had known me so little, and what his life would be with me to help and cheer him. He was going to tell me how unhappy he would be if I did not care for him, but when he saw me cry he said he was a brute and would not add to my present trouble. Then he broke off and asked if I could love him in time, and when I shook my head his hands trembled, and then with some hesitation he asked me if I cared for anyone else. I felt a sort of duty to tell him that there was someone. Then he stood up, took both my hands in his and said he hoped I would be happy, and that if I ever wanted a friend I must count him one of my best.

Number two came after lunch. He is such a nice fellow, an American from Texas, and he looks so young and so fresh that it seems almost impossible that he has been to so many places and has had such adventures. Mr Quincey P. Morris found me alone, sat down beside me, and looked as happy and jolly as he could, but I could see all the same that he was very nervous. He took my hand in his, and said ever so sweetly...

"Miss Lucy, I know I ain't good enough to regulate the fixin's of your little shoes, but I guess if you wait till you find a man that is you will go join them seven young women with the lamps when you quit. Won't you just hitch up alongside of me and let us go down the long road together, driving in double harness?"

Well, he did look so good humoured and so jolly that it didn't seem half so hard to refuse him as it did poor Dr Seward. So I said, as lightly as I could, that I did not know anything of hitching, and that I wasn't broken to harness at all yet. And then, my dear, before I could say another word he began pouring out a perfect torrent of love-making, laying his very heart and soul at my feet. I suppose he saw something in my face which checked him, for he suddenly stopped, and said with a sort of manly fervour...

"Lucy, you are an honest-hearted girl, I know. I should not be here speaking to you as I am now if I did not believe you clean of grit, right through to the very depths of your soul. Tell me, like one good fellow to another, is there anyone else that you care for? And if there is, I'll never trouble you a hair's breadth again, but will be, if you will let me, a very faithful friend."

I burst into tears, I am afraid, my dear, and I really felt very badly. I am glad to say that, though I was crying, I was able to look into Mr Morris' brave eyes, and I told him out straight...

"Yes, there is someone I love, though he has not told me yet that he even loves me." I was right to speak to him so frankly, for quite a light came then into his face, and he put out both his hands and took mine, I think I put them into his, and said in a hearty way...

"That's my brave girl. It's better worth being late for a chance of winning you than being in time for any other girl in the world. Don't cry, my dear. If it's for me, I'm a hard nut to crack, and I take it standing up. If that other fellow doesn't know his happiness, well, he'd better look for it soon, or he'll have to deal with me."

He stood up with my two hands in his, and as he looked down into my face, he said, "Little girl, your honesty and pluck have made me a friend, and that's rarer than a lover. Thank you for your sweet honesty to me, and goodbye."

He wrung my hand, and taking up his hat, went straight out of the room without looking back, without a tear or a quiver or a pause.

Oh, about number three, I needn't tell you of number three, need I? Besides, it was all so confused. It seemed only a moment from his coming into the room till both his arms were round me, and he was kissing me. I am very, very happy, and I don't know what I have done to deserve it, but I am to become Mrs Arthur Holmwood! I must only try in the future to show that I am not ungrateful to God for all His goodness to me in sending me such a lover, such a husband, and such a friend. Goodbye.

Ever your loving...

Lucy

Turn to 278.

251

You make a search of every inch of ground, and even go down into the vaults, but find nothing there but fragments of old coffins and piles of dust. Then you turn your attention to the boxes filled with earth.

Lying inside one of them, on a pile of newly dug earth, is the Count! You cannot tell whether he is dead or merely asleep, for his eyes are open and stony but lacking the glassiness of death. His lips are as red as ever, but there is no sign of movement.

You bend over him, searching for any sign of life, but there is no pulse, no breath, no beating of the heart.

But then, as your eyes become accustomed to the gloom permeating the crypt, you notice something that fills your very soul with horror. For the Count looks as if his youth has been half-restored to him, for the white of his hair has given way to iron-grey, his cheeks are fuller, and on his lips you see gouts of fresh blood. Even the deep, burning eyes seem set amongst swollen flesh, for the lids and pouches underneath are bloated.

It seems as if the vile creature is gorged with blood, and he lies inside the box, like a filthy leech, exhausted by his feast.

(Add 2 points to your *Terror* score.)

There is a mocking smile on the Count's bloated face. This is the being you are helping to transfer to London, where perhaps, for centuries to come, he might amongst its teeming millions satiate his lust for blood, thereby creating an ever-widening circle of lich-leeches to batten upon the helpless.

That realisation drives you to the edge of madness, but it is quickly followed by another; that you are in a unique position to put a halt to the Count's plans of conquest and empire-building.

If you want to kill the Count as he lies in his deathless state of suspended animation, turn to **281**. If you feel you dare not attempt such a thing, turn to **342**.

252

You do not get out of the way of the rat-swarm in time, and they come for you, squeaking furiously, their yellow chisel-teeth bared.

If you want to use *The Pen is Mightier* special ability, and you still can, cross off one use and turn to **314**. If not, turn to **506**.

253

If you have the code word *Inventa* ticked off, turn to **677**. If not, turn to **711**.

254

Making yourself as mist again, you escape through the open bedroom window and vanish into the night.

As Harker is clearly one of the Vampire-Hunters, none of your London lairs are secure from their predations. But you had the foresight to hide one of the boxes filled with Transylvanian soil yourself, in the basement of the Lyceum Theatre – which is currently staging a production of *The Strange Case of Dr Jekyll and Mr Hyde*, with Sir Henry Irving in the dual role of the tormented Henry Jekyll and the felonious Edward Hyde.

From Purfleet, you make your way back to London's Covent Garden and enter the theatre unseen, before heading to the dusty basement prop store. At the back of the undercroft, hidden behind a piece of scenery from some Shakespearean tragedy, you find the precious box of earth, that you slept in aboard the doomed *Demeter*, undisturbed.

With dawn breaking over the sleeping city and feeling drained after all that you have had to endure this night, you become as mist once more and seep through the narrow gaps between the planks, materialising once more inside the box, the touch of the mouldering earth of your homeland renewing you body and soul.

As you lie there, you go over all that has happened and what it means for your plans for the British Empire. With the boxes that were stored at Carfax House destroyed, you have to assume that those you had hidden at your other London properties are also at risk of discovery.

However, there is more kept at 138 Piccadilly than just boxes of earth; there are all manner of papers and, even more importantly, money. Money that will be most necessary if you are forced to change your plans and beat a hasty retreat to Transylvania.

Deciding to return to your townhouse to collect anything that may be necessary for your journey, you rouse yourself after midday and set off across London by hansom to Piccadilly. But London traffic being what it is, when you finally arrive it is to find the front door ajar and a locksmith standing outside, packing up his tools. The Vampire-Hunters must have made it here ahead of you!

Rather than stop outside the house, you instruct the driver to take you to the Green Park. You disembark and make your way round to the stone-flagged courtyard that is located behind the house. It is easy for you to scale the outside of the building and enter through an upper window.

From there, you make your way to the study you have been making use of on the first floor and collect what papers and money you think you might need, depending on how events play out, and having equipped yourself thus, make your way downstairs.

Take an ESP test. If you pass the test, turn to **370**. If you fail the test, turn to **302**.

255

"Mehmed has issued an edict that his soldiers may not exit their tents during the night," you tell your counsellors.

"Then that is when we should attack, my lord!" Petru declares. "Strike when they are least expecting it and catch them off-guard."

"But our forces are still outnumbered five times over," you remind him.

"Then we should stay where we are," Radu says, "and concentrate on strengthening the city's defences. But the decision is, of course, yours to make, my prince."

What do you think is the wisest decision?

Do you want to lead an attack on the Ottoman camp this very night, in the hope of catching Mehmed and his Janissaries off-guard (turn to **220**), or do you want to prepare for the siege that is surely inevitable now (turn to **785**)?

256

Leaving the nun on gate duty in a trance-like state, you set off into the hospital in search of the one the Weird Sisters claimed might have a part to play in thwarting your plans.

The Mattins Bell suddenly starts to ring, but not to summon the sisters to a service within the convent chapel; its loud clanging is sounding the alarm. Someone must have found the stupefied nun, and the gate open.

Aware that it is only a matter of time before you are discovered and knowing that your powers will be severely diminished as long as you remain on consecrated ground, you decide the most sensible course of action would be to leave the convent-hospital the same way you entered.

You have not gone far when you run into an older nun, who is also heading for the gatehouse, with another of her sisterhood close on her heels.

When the lantern she carries illuminates your features, she gives a gasp of horror, even as the nun accompanying her cries, "Sister Agatha, look out!"

Recovering herself quickly, she takes a crucifix from beneath her robes and holds it out towards you, hissing the words, "Begone, monster!"

If you have the code word *Elesett* ticked off, turn to **936**. If not, turn to **855**.

257

15 October, Varna

You travel night and day, arriving in Varna at about five o'clock in the evening. Arthur goes to the Consulate to see if any telegram has arrived for him – having arranged with Lloyd's to be sent a daily wire stating if the *Czarina Catherine* has been reported – while the rest of you make your way to the Hotel Odessus.

In a drawer in a bedside table in your room, you find a well-thumbed English copy of the Holy Bible. (If you want to take it, add the Holy Bible to your Adventure Sheet.)

Arthur eventually returns with four telegrams, but Dracula's ship

has not been reported to Lloyd's from anywhere. You are evidently in good time and will be ready and waiting for the Count when he arrives.

Turn to **640**.

258

From the top of the staircase, you enter room after room of the abandoned house, each one as empty and lifeless as the one before. The walls are fluffy and heavy with dust, and in the corners are masses of spider's webs, where the dust has also gathered so that they look like old, tattered rags, the weight having half torn them down.

The beams of light cast by your lamps criss-cross each other, the opacity of your bodies throwing great shadows on the walls. But you cannot shake the feeling that there is someone else amongst you. The feeling would appear to be common to you all, for you can't help noticing that the others keep looking over their shoulders at every sound and every new shadow.

(Add 1 to your *Terror* score and gain 2 *Blood* points.)

You also begin to feel that perhaps you should have chosen to follow the corridor leading away from the entrance hall. When you make the suggestion the others readily agree, and so you all go back downstairs.

Turn to **287**.

259

The thing that now wears Lucy's form suddenly gives an angry snarl, eyes blazing with unholy light. Overcome by her own monstrous bloodlust, the horror scatters the children with a blood-curdling scream.

But then, seemingly restoring some measure of self-control, she opens her arms to you. "Come to me, John," she says languidly, a wanton smile on her crimson lips. "My arms are hungry for you. Come and we can lie together."

Take an ESP test. If you pass the test, turn to **319**, but if you fail the test, turn to **346**.

260

The wolves suddenly take fright at something and freeze, crouching low. And then, just as suddenly, they take off into the blizzard.

Cross off one use of *The Pen is Mightier* special ability and turn to **53**.

261

There is the sharp crack of a pistol discharging nearby and the wolf-man is knocked off its feet as a bullet from the Texan's gun hits it right between its yellow predator's eyes.

Cross off one use of *The Pen is Mightier* special ability and turn to **291**.

262

You slink back to the cargo hold and secrete yourself away like some vile grub within the precious box of earth that has harboured you on your journey from deepest, darkest Transylvania to where you are now, in the North Atlantic, off the coast of France.

Turn to **432**.

263

The waking nightmare you have found yourself in is too much to bear and you faint from shock, as the spectral dead close in on you en masse...

* * * *

Gradually there comes the vague beginnings of consciousness, then a sense of dreadful weariness, and slowly your senses return. Your body is wracked with pain, and yet you find yourself unable to move. You are aware of an icy feeling at the back of your neck and all down your spine.

But there is in your breast a sensation of warmth, which you find, by comparison, delicious, and yet also a heavy weight that is making it difficult for you to breathe. A wild desire to be free grows within you as you become aware of the low panting of some animal close by.

Feeling a warm rasping at your throat, you come to a state of full consciousness at last, and realise some great animal is lying on top of you and licking at your neck!

You dare not move, but through half-closed lashes you see above you the great flaming eyes of a gigantic wolf. Its sharp white teeth gleam within a gaping red mouth, and you can feel its hot breath, fierce and acrid upon you.

(Add 2 points to your *Terror* score.)

The wolf gives a low growl, and you fear for your life. But then, coming from seemingly very far away, you hear a "Holloa! Holloa!" as of many voices calling out in unison.

Risking all, you raise your head and look in the direction whence the sound came, but the cemetery blocks your view. As the wolf starts to yelp, you see a red glare moving through the grove of cypresses, as though following the sound.

As the voices draw closer, the wolf's yelping intensifies. Nearer comes the red glow, dancing over the white pall which stretches into the darkness around you. Then all at once, from beyond the trees, there comes a troop of horsemen bearing torches.

The wolf rises from you then and makes to flee, as one of the horsemen – who are soldiers, judging by their caps and long military cloaks – raises a carbine and takes aim as the animal slinks away, and a shot follows. Moving at a gallop, the troop rides forward – some towards you, others in pursuit of the wolf as it disappears amongst the snow-clad trees.

Several of the soldiers jump down from their horses and kneel beside you. One of them raises your head and places his hand over your breast.

"Good news, comrades!" he cries in German. "His heart still beats!"

Turn to **294**.

264

You deftly sidestep out of the way, and the wagon bounces over the cobbles and out of the gate.

Turn to **236**.

265

Letter addressed to Mr R. M. Renfield, solicitor at Hawkins, Oldman & Lee, of Exeter, England

8 November 1896

My dear Mr Renfield –

I am very much looking forward to your visit. I am anxious to purchase a property in England, so that I might visit and learn what it means to be a gentleman in your fine country.

While you will doubtless find the Carpathians cold, the welcome that you will receive upon your arrival will be warm.

Yours

DRACULA

In due course, Mr Renfield arrives, when the Carpathians are already blanketed with snow, as they will remain for another five months at least.

Despite his long and arduous journey from England, you find him in good spirits and eager to get started on all matters legal, for while he is clearly excited at the prospect of being the guest of a nobleman in an ancient castle, he is keen to return home to his family before Christmas, which suits your plans very well.

Two days after he arrives at your castle home, the two of you are going through some of the paperwork associated with the purchase of a certain Carfax House in Purfleet – an ancient pile with a suitably gothic history of its own – when you decide it is the perfect time to enact your plan.

You fix your burning, blood-red eyes on his and invoke the power of hypnosis that is just one of the gifts your altered state has given you.

If your rank is that of *Nosferatu*, turn to **290**. If your rank is that of *Count Dracula*, turn to **318**.

266

The hold becomes filled with the squeaking of dozens of rats, the same rats that live in the ship's bilges and gnaw at the cargo carried aboard the *Demeter* – and even steal the sailors' food from their plates, when they can find nothing else to eat.

Compelled to do your bidding, the plague of rats runs at the terrified First Mate, nipping at his ankles, or dropping onto him from roof-joists, and in doing so drive the terrified man from the hold.

Turn to **545**.

267

Rising from the bed, Lucy suddenly lunges at Arthur, her mouth open wide and her fingers contorted into cruel talons.

You grab him with both hands and pull him out of harm's way, but in the process expose yourself to Lucy's uncontained savagery. She digs her fingernails deep into the flesh of your forearm and as she rakes them free, drawing blood from five deep gouges.

Lose 2 *Endurance* points, add 1 to your *Terror* score, and then turn to **297**.

268

As Harker's horrified gaze falls upon you, you meet it with your own transfixing, basilisk stare.

If your rank is that of *Prince of Darkness*, turn to **305**. If not, turn to **326**.

269

Apparently, some of the boxes of experimental earth that were delivered to Carfax House have since been moved to some other place, as yet unknown. It is Jonathan who is given the job of locating them, and you are sure that his eye for detail and logical lawyer's mind are more than up to the task.

But the memory of last night's nightmare worries at you, like a terrier worrying at the carcass of a rat it has caught.

If you want to seek out Dr Seward, in the hope that he might be able to prescribe something to help you sleep better tonight, turn to **338**. If you would prefer not to bother the young doctor, when he must have so much on his mind, turn to **298**.

270

The following night, when you go in search of prey again – unable to restrain the beast within, relishing how you feel having fed on the crew of the Russian schooner – you find a wiry-looking individual at the wheel. But while he might not be as heavily built as the Second Mate was, or as cunning as the mariner who tried to trap you under the sail, he poses possibly the greatest threat you have yet encountered aboard the *Demeter*.

He is bedecked with holy charms, rosary beads and crucifixes. Just to go near him makes your unnatural flesh crawl.

But he is aware of your presence now and to leave him alive would be to risk the crew hunting you down in the hold.

Divide your *Blood* score by 10, rounding fractions up. Then roll 1 die, and if the number rolled is equal to or less than the resulting total, turn to **983**, but if it is greater, turn to **470**.

271

You quit the palace and Târgoviște that very night, and set off alone on horseback, heading north deeper into the Carpathian Mountains. But it is a harder task than you might once have imagined and only after many weeks of searching – during which time you not only lose your steed but also your princely rings and raiment, when you are attacked by bandits – you come to a cleft in the rock at the foot of a towering mountain, that looks like a splintered canine fang, possessing nothing but the clothes on your back and your sword.

Creeping inside, you stumble through the darkness, guided only by the echoes of your own footsteps, and the blind hope that you have truly found the Scholomance at last. As the grey crack of twilight fades behind you, lights suddenly flare before you and you feel the razor-edge of a knife-blade cut into the flesh of your throat.

"Why have you come to this place?" a voice that sounds more snake-like than human hisses from the shadows between the blazing torches.

"I am Prince Vlad –" you begin but the serpentine voice cuts you off abruptly.

"We know who you are, Vlad Tepes, the Impaler. Vlad Dracula, the Son of the Dragon. Who you are is not the reason why you have come to Broken Tooth Mountain."

"I seek the power to crush my enemies," you reply, steeling yourself.

"And what price are you willing to pay for such power?" comes the sibilant hiss again.

"Whatever it takes," you say without a moment's hesitation.

"Even if it costs you your soul?"

This time you do pause before answering, but only for a moment. "Even that."

"Then step this way."

The knife-blade is removed from your throat and the bobbing torches lead you deeper into the darkness beneath the mountain until you find yourself in what appears to be a temple carved out of a cave.

On the far side of the temple-space stands a stone altar, but rather than bearing the icons of Christianity, it is covered with carvings of intertwining snakes and etched with curious symbols that speak to you of distant desert lands and ancient civilisations buried beneath the sands.

Standing on top of the altar is an alabaster statue of a huge white serpent – or maybe it is a wingless dragon – with a human figure trapped in its carved coils, and before that a golden goblet.

The voice returns, giving the strident command, "Kneel before Balaur! Kneel before great Apophis!"

"I kneel before no man–" you begin, before being struck violently from behind. You fall to your knees on the stony floor of the cave.

And then the owner of the voice enters the circle of light cast by the torches before the altar.

The woman is dressed in flowing silken robes, and when she passes in front of the torches, you can see the silhouette of her shapely body quite clearly through the near-transparent fabric. Her luxurious black hair falls in wavy tresses over her shoulders, framing a face that is a picture of beauty, and upon her head she wears a circlet of gold, shaped to resemble a rearing hooded cobra. Her olive skin is smooth, her lips are full and red, but, for all her other comely attributes, you are unable to tear your gaze away from her eyes. They are dark, and ringed with kohl, and while they sparkle in the flickering torchlight, they are also the oldest eyes you have ever seen.

"Are you sure you are ready to submit to Balaur?" the priestess challenges you, and you could have sworn that when she blinked, her eyes had the slitted pupils of a snake, if only for a moment.

Are you sure you are prepared to do this for your country and its people?

How do you want to reply?

"I am ready to submit to Balaur!"	Turn to **345**.
"Vlad Tepes submits to no one!"	Turn to **310**.

215

272

Locking yourself in your room, you begin to read the journal Jonathan kept while he was Dracula's guest. You do not finish until the sun is setting and you hear Jonathan's key in the door.

Poor dear! How he must have suffered, whether what you have read is the truth or merely the projections of an overactive imagination.

You wonder if there is any truth at all in his terrible stories of bloodthirsty wolves, phantom women, and the coffin-dwelling Count. They certainly terrify you and to think that they might have happened to your dear husband makes it doubly worse!

(Add 2 points to your *Terror* score.)

Did your husband come down with his brain fever and then write all those terrible things, or, impossible as it seems, could there be some kernel of truth behind his rambling diary entries?

He certainly believes it all himself. He seemed quite certain that he recognised the man you saw walking abroad on the streets of the capital, and in his journal Jonathan said that the fearful Count was coming to London. If the monstrous Count has come to London, with its teeming millions…

You sense that some fearful solemn duty will come knocking at your door before too long. And if it does, you and Jonathan cannot permit yourselves to shrink from it.

Tick off the code word *Scientia*, deduct 1 *Blood* point, and turn to **307**.

273

Choosing somewhere you haven't been already, where do you want to explore next?

The basement?	Turn to **656**.
The ground floor?	Turn to **253**.
The first floor?	Turn to **542**.
The second floor?	Turn to **434**.
The attic?	Turn to **323**.

274

It turns out that the boxes in the Walworth property are safe, but for how long will they remain undiscovered? Deeming it sensible to relocate them, the very next day you visit Harris & Sons, Moving and Shipment Company, of Orange Master's Yard, Soho, and instruct a pair of cart-men – the weak-minded Mr Smollet and Mr Snelling – to collect the boxes and take them to a scrap merchant's yard you have recently come into possession of, at 76 Totter's Lane, in the district of Shoreditch.

Choosing somewhere you haven't been yet, which property do you want to check next?

The printers' warehouse in Mile End?	Turn to **70**.
Carfax House in Purfleet?	Turn to **155**.

275

The wretch is dead, and his blood is a rare tonic, spiced with lingering traces of fear and hopelessness.

Gain 2 *Blood* points, and 1 *Suspicion* point, and restore up to 4 *Endurance* points.

If your *Suspicion* score is 9 points or higher, turn to **162**. If not, turn to **270**.

276

You leap up from the couch, trying to decide whether you should flee or somehow prepare to defend yourself against these horrors.

Do you want to:

Run from the chamber as fast as you can?	Turn to **373**.
Prepare to fight these monsters?	Turn to **403**.
Use your lamp against them somehow?	Turn to **464**.
Throw some Antique Coins at them (if you have some)?	Turn to **494**.
Throw some Good Luck Tokens at them (if you have some)?	Turn to **514**.
Brandish a Crucifix before them (if you have one)?	Turn to **544**.

277

The Westminster Gazette: Extra Special

25 September

THE HAMPSTEAD HORROR – ANOTHER CHILD INJURED –

THE BLOOFER LADY

We have just received intelligence that another child, missed last night, was only discovered late in the morning under a furze bush at the Shooter's Hill side of Hampstead Heath, which is, perhaps, less frequented than the other parts. It has the same tiny wound in the throat as has been noticed in other cases. It was terribly weak, and looked quite emaciated. It too, when partially restored, had the common story to tell of being lured away by the "Bloofer Lady".

You peruse the paper as you enjoy a breakfast of dead cat.

Since settling into the Piccadilly property, you have taken to purchasing a newspaper every day. A week has passed since you last visited Lucy and in that time she has passed away, her death being reported in both the local and national press, because of her betrothal to Arthur Holmwood who, since his father's death, is now the new Lord Godalming with all that such a title entails.

There can be no doubt in your mind that this 'Bloofer Lady' the press has become obsessed with is the same young woman you turned. She has barely been in her grave five minutes and yet she is already walking abroad at night, now that she is free of the shackles of life's mortal coil.

Lucy Westenra is the first of your get on foreign shores, but she will not be the last. Through her you hope to turn Lord Godalming, who should then provide you with access to the Royal family and the Widow of Windsor herself. However, for your plans of conquest to succeed, you will need to create an army of nosferatu, to fight alongside the Transylvanian strigoi you have had transported to England.

One of those you have had your eye on is a very beautiful girl, who favours a big cart-wheel hat, and who you first saw sitting in a carriage outside Guiliano's jewellery shop just a stone's throw from your townhouse lair. She is always accompanied by a gentleman companion.

But the next time you catch sight of her, as you are going among the crowds on Piccadilly – as any visiting foreign gentleman might – you see that she is travelling alone.

If you wish to follow her, with the intention of seducing her, as you did Lucy Westenra, turn to **966**. If not, turn to **189**.

278

MINA MURRAY'S JOURNAL

24 July, Whitby

Lucy met me at the station, looking sweeter and lovelier than ever, and we drove up to the house at the Crescent in which they have rooms...

Whitby is simply a lovely place. The river Esk runs through a deep valley, which broadens out as it comes near the harbour. A great viaduct runs across, with high piers, through which the view seems somehow further away than it really is. The valley is beautifully green, and it is so steep that when you are on the high land on either side you look right across it, unless you are near enough to see down.

The houses of the old town are all red-roofed and seem piled up one over the other anyhow. Right over the town is the ruin of Whitby Abbey, which was sacked by the Danes. It is a most noble ruin, of immense size. There is a legend that a white lady is seen in one of the windows. Between it and the town there is the parish church, which is surrounded by a large graveyard, full of tombstones.

As far as you are concerned, this is the nicest spot in Whitby, for it has a full view of the harbour and all up the bay to where the headland called Kettleness stretches out into the sea. It descends so steeply that part of the bank has fallen away, and some of the graves have been destroyed.

In one place, part of the stonework stretches out over the sandy pathway far below. There are walks, with seats beside them, through the churchyard, and people go there to look at the beautiful view and enjoy the fresh sea breeze, as do you.

Indeed, it is while you are sitting enjoying the view yourself one day, while taking your daily constitutional with Lucy, that you overhear the talk of three old men, who are sitting on the seat beside you. They seem to do nothing all day but sit here and talk. It seems they have a legend hereabouts that when a ship is lost, bells are heard out at sea.

The old man sitting nearest to you appears to be very old, for his face is gnarled and twisted like the bark of a tree. You get to talking and he tells you that he is nearly 100, and that he was a sailor in the Greenland fishing fleet when Waterloo was fought, and that his name is Mr Swales.

As he seems eager to make conversation, do you want to ask him about the local legend of the submerged bells (turn to **296**), the legend of the white lady (turn to **316**), or will you merely remark upon the view (turn to **456**)?

279

You have no choice but to defend yourselves against the giant bats. You and Arthur take on one of the creatures each. (In this battle, you have the initiative.)

GIANT BAT   COMBAT 6   ENDURANCE 5

Arthur dispatches his opponent with economic thrusts and slices of his rapier blade. If you succeed in killing the horror that is attacking you, turn to **309**.

280

At the Professor's urging, you return to the lounge and only once the rats have fled does he dare go back to the vermin-infested compartment. He returns some minutes later to inform you that not only has the coffin and its grotesque occupant vanished, leaving nothing but muddy smears behind, but so has the ratty gentleman.

Turn to **509**.

281

There is no weapon to hand, so you seize one of the shovels the Szgany have been using to fill the boxes and, lifting it high, prepare to strike the Count's head from his body.

But as you do so, the head turns, and the eyes fall upon you, blazing with basilisk horror.

Take a Terror test. If you pass the test, turn to **311**. If you fail the test, turn to **342**.

282

Moving with the practised ease of a trained hunter, Quincey strikes you on the side of your head with the butt of his knife and you fall to the ground unconscious...

Helping you up, as you come to again, and supporting you with one arm – having seemingly shed his snake-skin – Quincey helps you back to the horses, and into the saddle of your steed, whilst keeping his Winchester trained on the gypsies the whole time.

None of them makes a move to stop you as you set off into the Borgo Pass.

Deduct 2 points from your *ESP* score, tick off the code word *Ṭigani*, and then turn to **26**.

283

The pounding of footsteps on the deck, from the other end of the ship is evidence that what you feared happening has happened – the mariner's desperate shouts have brought the rest of the crew running. (Gain 3 *Suspicion* points.)

Do you want to stand and fight (turn to **315**), or do you want to attempt to flee, shrouding yourself in darkness, with the intention of returning to the cargo hold before any of the men actually spot you (turn to **262**)?

284

Of the nine crewmen who set out aboard the *Demeter* from Varna, only the Captain now remains. Not knowing what else to do, and with no one else to help steer the ship, the wretched man lashes himself to the wheel, fastening his hands, one over the other, to one of the spokes, and binding a crucifix and set of rosary beads about both wrists, hoping that it will prove some protection against your predations.

But you have no interest in killing the Captain – fear and exposure to the elements will do that soon enough. Instead, you ensure that a steady wind is always at your back, the schooner leaping from wave to wave as it rushes headlong over the North Sea.

Eventually, steered by nothing more than the wind and the hand of a dead man, the *Demeter* finds Whitby harbour and, without showing any sign of slowing, the ship pitches herself up on the accumulation of sand and gravel that has collected at the south-east corner of the pier jutting under the East Cliff, washed there by many tides and many storms.

As the ship grinds to an abrupt stop against the shingle, taking the form of a monstrous dog, you jump from the bow onto the sand, leaving your precious boxes of earth to be collected by those who have been tasked to resolve the matter, through the letters you sent ahead of you months ago.

You make straight for the cliff, seeking shelter elsewhere, considering it too dangerous to remain in situ in your box of earth, just in case anyone investigating the doom that befell the *Demeter* decides to examine the contents of the crates.

But the soil of your homeland offers you a measure of protection, and so you need to find an alternative refuge where you can lay low for a while. And you know just the kind of place that will suffice.

You set about sniffing out a suitable sanctuary, heading for the church you can see silhouetted against the moon at the top of the cliff. For where there is a church there will also be a churchyard.

However, it turns out that the route to your hiding place will not be an easy one, for it impinges upon another's territory. At the entrance to a coal merchant's yard at the bottom of the hill, close to the pier, you are confronted by a half-bred mastiff.

If you want to impose your will upon the dumb beast, so that it

lets you pass, deduct 3 *Blood* points and turn to **313**. If you do not want to fritter your abilities away against such a base foe, turn to **755**.

285

Making your way back through the hustle and bustle of the camp, unnoticed by the soldiers who are preparing to besiege your home, you ford the river once again and return to the hidden entrance to the secret tunnel by which you left Târgoviște in the first place. Captain Petru is waiting for you. Reunited, the two of you re-enter the palace.

Back in your throne room, you are joined by your wisest and most trusted advisors, the Captain of the Carpathian Guard, Radu the Monk, and your wife Erzebet.

If you have the code word *Stratégia* ticked off, turn to **255**. If not, turn to **785**.

286

You sense that you are drawing close to Castle Dracula, but at the same time you can feel your undead form weakening. (Deduct 4 *Blood* points.)

Gradually, over the yelping of the wolves, the rattling of the cart, the breathless snorting of the gypsies' horses, and the urgent shouts of the Szgany, your heightened senses become aware of other sounds; voices calling to one another in English, rather than in the half-forgotten tongue of the boyars, and gunshots. The Vampire-Hunters have caught up with you again at last.

The leiter-wagon suddenly slews to a halt and you realise that it is time to make your final stand against Harker and his allies.

Take another ESP test. If you pass the test, turn to **957**. If you fail the test, turn to **347**.

287

With the Professor leading, you set off along the passageway.

If the *Blood* score is equal to or greater than 6, turn to **288**. If it is lower than 6, turn to **734**.

288

As you make your way along the passageway, at the limit of your lamp beams you become aware of a mass of phosphorescence, which twinkles like stars.

You all instinctively come to a halt as you realise that a tidal wave of rats is surging towards you. These are no mere common black or brown rats, but monstrous horrors, each the size of a small dog. (Add 1 to your *Terror* score.)

They swarm along the corridor in ever-multiplying numbers, until the lamplight, shining on their dark bodies and glittering, baleful eyes, make the place look like a bank of earth set with fireflies.

Take an Agility test. If you pass the test, turn to **314**, but if you fail the test, turn to **252**.

289

Hissing and spitting like feral cats, the children launch themselves at you. You have no choice but to defend yourself, much as the thought of hurting any man, let alone a child, offends you. (In this battle, the children have the initiative.)

URCHINS   COMBAT 7   ENDURANCE 12

For the duration of this battle, you must reduce your *Combat Rating* by 1 point, as you do not really want to hurt the children. After 5 Combat Rounds, if you are still alive, or if you reduce the urchins' combined *Endurance* score to 6 points or fewer, whichever is sooner, turn to **259** at once.

290

It is an easy thing for you to dominate a lesser mind, such as Renfield's, and while you have him under hypnosis, you instruct him to act as your agent, acquiring the properties you require in and around London, and to prepare the way for an invasion force that will be under your command.

Take an ESP test, but add 2 to the total rolled with the two dice. If you pass the test, turn to **405**. If you fail the test, turn to **377**.

Alternatively, you can deduct 4 *Blood* points and turn to **405** straightaway, without having to take the test at all.

291

You suddenly find yourself surrounded by the rest of your party, as lupine shapes slink from between the overgrown gravestones.

Turn to **335**.

292

It is at that moment that help arrives, in the form of Barlow, Straker, and two more attendants from the asylum. As they surround Renfield, he turns on them like a cornered tiger.

You have never seen a lunatic in such a paroxysm of rage before, and you hope you never do again. It is a mercy you discovered his strength, and the danger he poses, before he could prove a threat to the general public. With strength and determination like his, he might have done wild work before he was caged.

Turn to **322**.

293

As you draw closer, you see that it is a moth – an *Acherontia atropos*, or Death's-Head Moth, to be precise, named thus because of the likeness of a skull and crossbones these lepidoptera have on their backs. The insect is beating its wings uselessly against the glass, with no comprehension of the fact that its efforts to break free are futile.

A second death's-head moth suddenly joins it at the window. And then another.

Hearing a great susurration behind you, as of a thousand fluttering insect wings, you turn to see a great mass of moths emerge from the shadows of the attic behind you. They batter you with their furry bodies, alighting on you and crawling all over your face, as if trying to smother you.

Take a Terror test. If you pass the test, turn to **224**. If you fail the test, turn to **374**.

294

Some brandy is poured down your throat, which goes some way to reviving you. (Regain 2 *Endurance* points.)

Opening your eyes fully, you look around. You see lights and shadows moving among the trees, and then the men who set off in pursuit of the wolf, come pouring out of the cemetery, pell-mell, like men possessed.

"Have you found him?" asks one of your rescuers.

The reply rings out hurriedly, "No! Come away quick – quick! This is no place to stay, and on this of all nights!"

"What was it?"

"It? 'It' indeed!" gibbers one of the new arrivals, clearly out of his wits.

"A wolf, and yet not a wolf!" cries another.

"No use trying for him without the sacred bullet," remarks a third.

"Serve us right for coming out on this night! Truly we have earned our thousand marks!" declares a fourth.

"There was blood on the broken marble," says the first. "The lightning never brought that there. And for him" – he turns his attention towards you now – "is he safe? Look at his throat!"

"The wolf was lying on him and keeping his blood warm," says the soldier holding your head, and who seems to be the least panic-stricken of the party. On his sleeve you make out the chevron of a petty officer. "His throat is all right; the skin is not pierced."

"What does it all mean?" asks another. "We should never have found him but for the yelping of the wolf."

"What became of it?" asks the officer.

"It went home," answers the first, whose long face is pallid and who is actually shaking with terror, as he glances around him fearfully. "There are graves enough there in which it may lie. Come, comrades – come quickly! Let us leave this cursed spot."

Several of the men help the officer put you on a horse, and he climbs into the saddle behind you. He gives the order to advance, and the hunting party rides away in swift military order.

* * * *

You ride through the night, until a red streak of sunlight appears over the horizon and is reflected like a path of blood over the waste of snow. Reaching the suburbs of Munich, the soldiers come across a stray carriage, into which you are lifted. The young officer drives you to the Quatre Saisons himself, a trooper following with his horse, while the others ride back to their barracks.

When you arrive at the hotel, Herr Delbruck rushes so quickly down the steps to meet you that it is apparent he has been watching from within, anxiously awaiting your return. Taking you by both hands, he solicitously leads you inside, while the officer salutes you and turns, as to withdraw.

If you want to insist that the officer comes with you to your room, so that you might thank him properly, turn to **324**. If you would prefer to retire, so that you might rest and recuperate after your night's adventures, turn to **354**.

295

You try to throw yourself out of the way but are not quite quick enough. One of the horses hits you, sending you spinning into the wooden planks of the open gate.

Lose 3 *Endurance* points and turn to **236**.

296

The old man's accent is very thick, but by concentrating and applying yourself, you work out the meaning behind his words, even if you do not understand every word directly.

It is now a well-known fact that during his reign, that old firebrand King Henry VIII sent out groups to destroy abbeys and churches of the Catholic faith as he built up his Church Of England, and one of those abbeys was Whitby Abbey, hence its present ruinous state.

On the King's instructions, the Abbey bells were removed, carried down the 199 steps that lead from St Mary's churchyard to the town, and loaded onto a ship that would then transport them to London, it being Henry's intention to sell them for scrap and keep the money for himself.

The people of Whitby were devastated; not only had their beautiful abbey been torn down but now they were going to lose the familiar chimes that had rung out through the day, every day of the year. The locals prayed that something might happen so that their bells would not be taken away.

And incredibly their wish came true. Inexplicably the ship sank, and it is said to still be there, just off the Black Nab under the North Sea. Sailors and fishermen have since said that if you sail to the shoals on a clear night you can still hear the currents ringing the bells.

Turn to **336**.

297

Lucy hisses like a serpent, baring her pronounced canines. Her face is contorted in a monstrous grimace, her eyes like hard, bloodshot pebbles.

A spasm of rage passes like a shadow across her face and the sharp teeth clamp together. Then her eyes close and she collapses onto the bed in a dead faint.

Only a matter of moments later, she opens her eyes again, and you see that they have regained their former softness. She puts out her pale, thin hand and Van Helsing takes it in his. Drawing his hand close to her, Lucy kisses it.

"My true friend," she says in a faint voice. "My true friend and his. Please look after Arthur and give me peace!"

"I swear!" the Professor says solemnly. Then he turns to Arthur. "Come, take her hand in yours, and kiss her on the forehead but once."

The lovers' eyes meet one last time and in a look they say their farewells. Lucy's breathing becomes laboured, and then all of a sudden she expels her last breath.

"It is over," Van Helsing says. "She is dead."

You take Arthur by the arm and lead him away to the drawing room, where he sits down, puts his face in his hands, and breaks down in tears.

You return to Lucy's room and find Van Helsing staring at her, his face sterner than ever. Standing beside him you say, "She is at peace at last. And that is an end to it."

He turns to you and says with grave solemnity, "Not so, alas! It is only the beginning."

Turn to **339**.

298

You spend the day fretfully walking the grounds, reading in your room, and conversing with the attendants of Carfax Asylum, but you are unable to settle to any one thing. You try to get some rest but find yourself unable to sleep while your husband is away.

Jonathan returns from London, at last, later that evening. After dinner, while the men meet again in Dr Seward's study to discuss developments, you retire to bed, for you feel oh so terribly tired.

Turn to **497**.

299

You want to run, but where before you were incapacitated by pleasure, now your body is paralysed by fear.

The unnatural monsters fall upon you, opening fresh wounds upon your arms and legs and gorging themselves on the life-blood that pours from them. (Lose 6 *Endurance* points.)

If you are still alive, you come to your senses at last and struggle to fight your way free of the horrors.

If you want to use *The Pen is Mightier* special ability, cross off one use and turn to **618**. If not, turn to **344**.

300

You steel yourself, ready to end the monster once and for all, when suddenly, and entirely unexpectedly, he turns tail and flees, his cloak flapping behind him like great bat wings.

Dracula moves so fast he is a black blur against the crisp white snow. One minute you believe he is a wolf, and then his blurring flight reminds you more of a flock of agitated bats, and then it is as if he is nothing more than smoke.

Cross off one use of *The Pen is Mightier* special ability and deduct 1 point from your *Combat* score, for not facing your foe when he was vulnerable; then turn to **970**.

301

The Professor is the first to step forward and enter the house. "*In manus tuas, Domine!*" he mutters, crossing himself as he passes over the threshold.

Once you are all inside, you close the door behind you and ignite your lamps.

The whole place is thick with dust. The floor is seemingly inches deep with it. On a table in the hall, you find a great bunch of keys, with a time-yellowed label on each. They have been used several times, for there are several rents in the blanket of dust covering the table.

If you have a map of Carfax House, multiply the number of rooms in the house by 15 and turn to the section which is the same as the final total. If not, turn to **328**.

302

Although you can sense them within, you have no inkling as to where the Vampire-Hunters might actually be or how many of them have invaded your home. That is until you open the door to the dining-room, located at the back of the house on the ground floor, and find them all waiting within.

A moment of recognition passes between you, and then Mina's protectors hurl themselves at you.

Turn to **620**.

303

Soon you are hemmed in by trees, which in places arch right over the roadway, so it is as if you are passing through a tunnel. Great frowning rocks guard the track on either side.

The rising wind moans and whistles through the rocks, and the branches of the trees crash together as you speed along. It grows colder still, and fine, powdery snow begins to fall. Soon, the caleche, the driver, the horses, and you are covered with a white blanket.

The baying of wolves cuts through the keening wind and sounds so close you wonder if the animals are closing in on you from every side.

Suddenly, away to your left, you see an inconstant light, like a flickering blue flame. The driver has clearly seen it too, for he brings the caleche to an abrupt halt and, without a word of explanation, jumps to the ground, disappearing into the darkness.

You are left alone, while the howling of the wolves draws closer.

Do you also want to disembark and set off after the driver (turn to **333**), or will you remain where you are and hope that the gypsy returns soon (turn to **363**)?

304

Hearing a deep-throated shout from your left, you turn abruptly to see one of the Szgany boyars bearing down on you, the warrior's steed foaming at the lips, whirling a flashing curved blade in the hand that is not holding tight to the horse's reins.

If you want to use *The Pen is Mightier* special ability, and you still can, cross off one use and turn to **76**. If not, turn to **334**.

305

Seeing you as you really are – nosferatu – paralyses your would-be murderer into inaction, but only for a moment. Harker brings the shovel down hard, but at the last moment he is unable to commit to the act of killing you and the instrument turns in his hand. Rather than beheading you, its sharp edge is merely deflected from your forehead. (Lose 2 *Endurance* points.)

Harker staggers away from your resting place, making no effort to hide his revulsion, the shovel falling from his shaking hands, and then he is gone.

You know that he will pose no further threat to you, for his mind is broken.

But no matter, you have no further need of him now. All the paperwork is in place, and you will leave for England yourself, soon. Then it will be up to the Sisters to decide his fate.

* * * *

The very next day, fifty boxes bearing the seal of the Dracul family, and filled with earth – not to mention the bodies from the catacombs – are loaded onto wagons by the Szgany and you commence your long journey to England.

Turn to **385**.

306

Two days after leaving London, you are relaxing in your compartment alone aboard the Orient Express, as the train passes through a snowstorm in the Austrian Tyrol, when there comes a knock at the door. From the other side comes a muffled, "Cabin service."

Cabin service? You didn't order any cabin service.

As you are rising, to see who it is, the door is forced from the outside and a young man bursts in. He is wearing an ill-fitting porter's uniform and wielding a large silver steak knife.

"Before you die, I want you to know who it is that kills you in the name of Lord Dracula!" he snarls.

"Who are you?" you gasp in bewilderment.

"I am Johnny Alucard!" he declares and throws himself at you.

If you want to use *The Pen is Mightier* special ability, cross off one use and turn to **362**. If not, turn to **332**.

307

LETTER, VAN HELSING TO MRS HARKER

24 September

Dear Madam,

I pray you to pardon my writing, for I sent to you sad news of Miss Lucy Westenra's death. By the kindness of Lord Godalming, I am empowered to read her letters and papers, for I am deeply concerned about certain matters vitally important. In them I found some letters from you, which show what great friends you were and how you loved her.

Oh, Madam Mina, by that love, I implore you, help me. It is for others' good that I ask to redress a great wrong, and to lift many terrible troubles that may be more great than you can know.

May I see you? You can trust me. I am a friend of Dr John Seward and of Lord Godalming (that was Miss Lucy's Arthur). I will come to Exeter to see you at once if you tell me I can.

I implore your pardon, madam. I have read your letters to poor Lucy, and know how good you are and how your husband has suffered; so I pray you, if it may be, enlighten him not, lest it may cause him harm.

Again I beg your pardon, and please forgive me.

Van Helsing.

Turn to **359**.

308

Unable to open the door, you turn from it and keep following the passageway instead.

Turn to **489**.

309

The first of November comes, and the boat passes from the Sereth into the narrower channel of the Bistritza river. But it is not until the fifth that you get your first glimpse of Castle Dracula atop its crag, still a league or more away, when the *Fantomă* finally stops at the isolated village of Strasba at the foot of the Borgo Pass. (Restore up to 4 *Endurance* points.)

You can go no further by boat, and so Arthur buys a pair of fine steeds from a farrier so that you can continue your journey on horseback.

Even though night is falling, and it has started to snow, you cannot wait until morning before continuing on your way, and so you set off into the encroaching darkness.

As you leave what feels like the last outpost of civilisation behind, you are accompanied by the howling of wolves that you know haunt the mountain forests.

You cannot see the wolves, even though you can feel their eyes on you, watching from the darkness of the forest. You try to put their presence from your mind and focus instead on following the track that is leading you ever deeper into the Carpathian Mountains.

If you have the code word *Vârcolac* ticked off, turn to **437**. If not, turn to **659**.

310

"I thought as much!" the priestess of the snake-cult declares. "You are not worthy to serve the Great Serpent!"

Before you can say anything in your defence, or do anything to save yourself, the knife-blade returns and is pulled swiftly across your throat. Blood spurts from the wound, which the foul witch catches in the golden goblet.

The last thing you see, as your life literally ebbs away before your eyes, is the woman excitedly put the chalice to her lips and begin to drink...

THE END

311

The sight seems to paralyse you, but you fight the feeling and bring the shovel down, although it turns in your hand and, rather than beheading the monster, its sharp edge merely makes a deep gash above the forehead.

Your stagger away from the Count's resting place in revulsion, the shovel falling from palsied fingers, and the last glimpse you have is of the bloated, blood-stained face, a grin of malice fixed upon it, which would have held its own in the nethermost hell.

Tick off the code word *Borzalom*, deduct 1 *Blood* point, and then turn to **342**.

312

The dog is a terrible thing to behold, with its burning red stare, slavering jaws, and thick black coat. It seems to you to almost be more wolf than dog, like a hellhound conjured up from a pious man's nightmares.

(Add 2 to your *Terror* score.)

Baring its sharp teeth, the beast starts to bark loudly, causing you to cry out involuntarily in fear.

If you have the code word *Barghest* ticked off, turn to **716**. If not, turn to **736**.

313

You are not the only one abroad this night, and pass a young woman on the clifftop, her long blonde hair blowing free about her face in the wind, her dress buttoned up to the collar.

Scouring the graveyard that surrounds the dark church with your supernatural senses, you find what you are looking for – the grave of a suicide.

Your dog body melting into mist, you slip between the cracks of a broken tombstone and settle down to share the grave with the skeleton of the suicide who was laid to rest here 24 years ago.

* * * *

The cold, English clay in which you now reside, does not sustain you like the mouldering earth of your homeland does, but you still consider it wise not to return to your box to sleep until it, and the other crates containing your undead invasion force are in place, in and around London. As a result, you know that you will need to feed again soon.

With the townsfolk of Whitby no doubt on edge, and more watchful than ever – following the arrival of the doomed *Demeter* and the discovery of her dead captain – rather than walk abroad in search of prey, you send your mind out into the night, broadcasting a siren call, to see if you can detect any who might respond to your summons.

Your mind alights upon two such souls. One is possessed of a firm resolve, the bulwarks of her mind strong, while the other is pliable

and suggestible, at once innocent and naïve but also flirtatious and seeking something more from life. It is to this mind that you call and, sure enough, several days later, she comes to the graveyard at night, in a fugue state, her conscious having no inkling as to what her subconscious is making her do.

* * * *

She comes to you, sleep-walking from the other side of the town, wearing only a nightdress, her shapely form visible beneath the gauzy shift. Her hair is as red as blood and her skin as white as marble. It is almost as if she were dead already, so pale is her flesh, the contours of her skull enhanced by the shadows cast by the moon.

Her feet and the hem of her nightdress are filthy with mud, from walking the streets of Whitby to the top of the East Cliff, but she is heedless of the dirt and the cuts the soles of her feet have sustained.

You are waiting for her, as she enters the graveyard, and beckon her to join you upon a bench overlooking the sea. But the view is of no interest to you, only the swan-like neck of the young woman, and the slow, steady beat of the pulse in her veins. She reclines upon the seat, offering herself to you. You do not need to be asked twice.

Piercing the alabaster-white skin of her throat with your elongated fangs, you start to drink. As you do so, a psychic bond forms between you, and you learn that her name is Lucy Westenra, just nineteen years of age, that she is betrothed to Sir Arthur Holmwood, heir to the Godalming lands and title, and that she seeks a swift marriage for she is yearning to discover all that the pleasures of the flesh have to offer. But there is no pleasure so great as that of draining the vital spark of a living human being and, if you were to make her your bride, you would share with her pleasures as yet undreamt of.

(Gain 2 *Blood* points.)

A cry of "Lucy! Lucy!" suddenly pierces the night, interrupting your feast, and you pull back from the young woman's gore-stained throat.

It is the young blonde-haired woman you passed on the cliff path the night you arrived at this seaside town. But more than that, she is the owner of the other mind, the one you sensed that was so firm in its resolve. She has clearly followed her friend through the sleeping town to the churchyard at the top of the cliff. A new name comes unbidden into your mind – Mina Murray – for whatever Lucy knows, you now know too.

By the time she rounds the corner of the church, you have vanished, returning to your temporary resting place, and leaving Mina to guide Lucy back to their lodging house on the other side of town.

Roll one die (or pick a card). If the number rolled is odd (or the card is red), turn to **927**. If the number rolled is even (or the card is black), turn to **83**.

314

Throwing yourself against the cold stone wall of the musty passageway, you watch in revulsion as the rats' rippling bodies surge past you, until they vanish into the house.

Turn to **606**.

315

Certain now that if the crew know you are on board the ship they will not rest until they find your secret sanctuary, you assume your beast-form to take them on in battle and rob them of their resolve by using one of the most powerful weapons at your disposal – fear!

Fight the crew of the *Demeter* together. (You have the initiative in this battle).

	COMBAT	ENDURANCE
SCARED SAILOR	7	7
SUPERSTITIOUS STEERSMAN	8	8
FIRST MATE	9	9
CAPTAIN	10	9

If you slay all of the sailors, turn to **358**.

316

Mr Swales' accent is very strong, but by concentrating and applying yourself, you understand that Whitby Abbey is supposedly haunted by Saint Hilda who founded the monastery there. Her ghost appears at a high window wrapped in a shroud.

However, she is not the only ghost to call the ruins home. The ghost of Constance de Beverley is also said to haunt the Abbey. She was a nun who broke her sacred vows, falling in love with a knight called Marmion. She was found out and bricked up alive in the dungeon of the Abbey as her punishment. Her poor ghost has been seen cowering and begging release in the winding stairway leading from the dungeon.

Turn to **336**.

317

Smollet the cart-man's physique suggests that although he is undoubtedly strong – he would not be able to do his job otherwise – over the years much of the muscle has turned to fat. He is slow and lumbering, but that does not mean he will be easy to stop. (In this battle, you have the initiative.)

SMOLLET   COMBAT 6   ENDURANCE 9

If you win the fight, turn to **389**.

318

It is an easy thing for you to dominate a lesser mind, such as Renfield's, and while you have him under hypnosis, you instruct him to act as your agent, acquiring the properties you require in and around London, to prepare the way for an invasion force that will be under your command.

Take an ESP test, but deduct 2 from total rolled with the two dice. If you pass the test, turn to **405**. If you fail the test, turn to **377**.

Alternatively, you can deduct 2 *Blood* points and turn to **405** straightaway, without having to take the test at all.

319

You somehow manage to resist her hypnotic spell, and in that moment, what remains of your love for Lucy burns away, leaving only hatred behind. You determine to put an end to the Bloofer Lady yourself, here and now, and will gladly do so.

Suddenly you are aware of a commotion all around you and turn to see your companions running between the gravestones as they come to your aid.

Giving a frustrated scream, Lucy flies past you, moving with unnatural speed, heading in the direction of the Westenra family tomb.

"After her!" cries Van Helsing, and the four of you set off in pursuit.

Turn to **669**.

320

Almost as quickly as she starts to feed, the Countess breaks off again and takes a step backward, staring at you, aghast, her mouth and chin smeared with your corrupted blood.

"You belong to another!" she gasps in horror. "You belong to… Him!"

Gain 3 *Blood* points and turn to **608**.

321

You run from Dr Callistratus's compartment before you are forced to bear witness to any more of the horrific transformation that is consuming his body. But you are still left shaken by your ordeal.

Add 1 point to your *Terror* score and turn to **509**.

322

DR SEWARD'S DIARY

(Kept in phonograph)

20 August

Renfield is safe now. Jack Sheppard himself couldn't get free from the strait waistcoat that keeps him restrained...

Renfield is also chained to the wall in the padded room, after escaping from his cell the night before. His cries are at times awful, but the silences that follow are worse, for he intends murder in every movement.

As you look in on him through the trap in the cell door, you hear him speak the first coherent words you have heard come out of his mouth since he was recaptured.

"I shall be patient, Master. It is coming, coming, coming!"

Who is this 'Master' he addresses in this way? And what does he believe is on its way?

You realise the only way you are going to get any answers to your questions is by speaking to him.

* * * *

He is still in the strait waistcoat and in the padded room when you interview him, but the suffused look has gone from his face, and his eyes hold something of their old pleading look.

As you enter the cell, flanked by two burly attendants – Barlow and Straker – Renfield gets to his feet and draws as close to you as his restraints will allow.

"They think I could hurt you!" he says in a whisper, all the while looking furtively at your attendants. "Fancy me hurting you! The fools!"

He certainly does not appear to be possessed of the same mania that seized him the previous night.

"Please, my dear Doctor, you can see that I am not a danger to anyone. Instruct them to release me from these restraints."

Will you instruct the attendants to free Renfield from the strait waistcoat (turn to **372**), or would you prefer that he remains restrained while you question him (turn to **352**)?

323

Climbing all the way to the top of the house, you enter the cramped attic space. There is more furniture here, kept under cobwebbed dustsheets, and you can make out where you are going quite easily as light enters the loft through a series of smeary windows.

You dare risk lifting a few of the sheets, to see precisely what it is they are enshrouding, but you find only chairs, occasional tables, and bookshelves.

As you are about to go back downstairs, something fluttering against a window in the far corner of the attic attracts your attention.

If you want to take a closer look, turn to **293**. If you would prefer to go back downstairs and search somewhere else, turn to **273**.

324

Over a glass of wine, you thank the officer and his brave comrades for saving you. The Riesling is as effective a restorative as a good night's sleep. (Add 3 points to your *Endurance* score.)

The officer replies, saying simply that he is more than glad to have been able to help and that Herr Delbruck had been the one to first take steps to make all the search party pleased; at which ambiguous utterance the maitre d'hotel smiles, while the officer pleads duty and withdraws.

Turn to **354**.

325

You arm yourself just in time, as the Janissaries thrust the spear-sharp points of their halberds at you. (Your opponents have the initiative in this battle, and you must fight them both at the same time.)

	COMBAT	ENDURANCE
First JANISSARY GUARD	9	8
Second JANISSARY GUARD	8	9

If you defeat the sentries, gain 2 *Blood* points. But how long did the fight last? If it lasted for 8 Combat Rounds or fewer, turn to **435**. If it lasted for more than 8 Combat Rounds, turn to **580**.

326

Divide your *Blood* score by 10, rounding fractions up. Then roll 1 die, and if the number rolled is equal to or less than the resulting total, turn to **305**, but if it is greater, turn to **238**.

Alternatively, you can deduct 3 *Blood* points and turn to **305** immediately, without having to make the dice roll.

327

"Come, sisters," cries the bat-winged harpy, with you hearing the archaic ungodly tongue she is speaking as English inside your head, "quickly, let us put this animal out of his misery, and then drain him of every last drop of blood!"

In this battle your opponents have the initiative, and you must fight the Weird Sisters all at the same time.

	COMBAT	ENDURANCE
SUCCUBUS	7	8
LAMIA	9	10
SIREN	8	9

If you are still alive after five Combat Rounds, or as soon as you reduce the *Endurance* score of one of the fiends to 4 points, whichever is sooner, turn to **618**.

328

In front of you, a broad stone staircase leads upwards, while to the right of the stairs a passageway leads off into the gloom of the house.

Your companions discuss which way to go but the four of them cannot reach a consensus of opinion; they are split precisely down the middle, two voting to head up the stairs and two thinking that you should follow the stone passageway. The one thing you all agree on is that you should stick together.

"It would appear that you, my friend, have the deciding vote," Van Helsing says gruffly. "So what is it to be?"

How will you reply?

"We should go upstairs."	Turn to **258**.
"Let's follow the passageway."	Turn to **287**.

329

JONATHAN HARKER'S JOURNAL

26 September

I thought never to write in this diary again, but the time has come...

Upon returning to Exeter, you find the demands of your new position as senior partner of the firm of Hawkins, Oldman & Lee, preoccupy your mind so much that you have little time to think of anything else, least of all the deprivations you suffered during your time in Transylvania. You rise to the challenge that now presents itself, following your advancement, and manage to keep pace with all the duties that are now yours and yours alone.

Coming home from work one evening in late September, you find Mina already has supper ready, and after you have eaten, she tells you that during the day she was interviewed by one Professor Van Helsing of Amsterdam, who had questions to ask her about Lucy Westenra's protracted illness.

She in turn shared with him how anxious she has been about you, and even showed him the journal you kept while you were Dracula's guest. Incredibly, he confirmed that everything you had written within it to be true. Knowing that someone else believes

247

you helps you put any lingering doubts regarding your own sanity from your mind, which makes a new man of you!

Now that you know you are not insane, you no longer feel as afraid as you did, not even of the Count.

(Deduct 1 point from your *Terror* score. Then restore your *Agility*, *Combat* and *Endurance* scores to their starting levels.)

Dracula has succeeded after all, then, in getting to London, and has somehow become younger in the process, but how? It would seem that this Van Helsing is the man to unmask him and hunt him down, if he is anything as Mina describes.

* * * *

The following morning you call at the hotel where the Professor is staying and meet him for yourself. When you come into the room where he is and introduce yourself, he seems surprised.

Taking you by the shoulder, and turning your face to the light, he says, "But Madam Mina told me you were ill, that you had had a shock."

"I was ill, and I have had a shock," you reply, smiling, "but you have cured me already."

"But how?" asks the kindly, strong-faced old man.

"I was in doubt, and I did not know what to trust, even the evidence of my own senses. Not knowing what to trust, I did not know what to do. Professor, you don't know what it is to doubt everything, even yourself."

"You will give me your hand, will you not? And let us be friends for all our lives."

You shake hands, and Van Helsing is so earnest and so kind that it makes you feel quite emotional.

"And now," he says, "may I ask you for your help? I have a great task to complete."

"Does what you have to do concern the Count?" you ask.

"It does," is his solemn response.

"Then I am with you heart and soul," you tell him.

* * * *

Van Helsing tells you that he must return to London and so you see him to the station.

As you are parting he says, "Perhaps you will come to town if I send for you and bring Madam Mina too."

"We shall both come when you will," you tell him.

Van Helsing is flicking through a copy of *The Westminster Gazette*, while you are waiting for the train to depart, when something catches his eye, and his cheeks lose all their colour.

As he reads the piece in question, quite intently, he groans to himself: *"Mein Gott! Mein Gott!* So soon! So soon!"

Just then the whistle blows, and the train moves off. This shakes him from his reverie and, remembering himself, he leans out of the window and waves, calling, "Love to Madam Mina. I shall write as soon as ever I can."

Turn to **839**.

330

The men back away, panting for breath, steeling themselves for another assault against your person.

Do you want to make the most of this lull in the fighting to flee the Piccadilly townhouse while you still can (turn to **485**), or would you prefer to press on with the battle against the Vampire-Hunters (turn to **390**)?

Sensing the unease felt by another member of your party, you turn to see Arthur staring out of the vaulted door of the chapel, into the dark passage beyond.

You follow his gaze, and for an instant your heart stands still, for you are convinced you can see highlights of an evil face – the ridge of the nose, the red eyes, the red lips, the awful pallor – staring back at you from the shadows.

It is only for a moment, and the illusion is dispelled as Lord Godalming says, "I thought I saw a face, but it was only the shadows," and then resumes his examination of the wooden crates.

But you, not satisfied that it was only a trick of the light, or lack of it, boldly step into the passage, just to be sure.

There is no sign of anyone there, and as there are no corners, no doors, indeed no aperture of any kind, but only the solid walls of the passage, there could be no hiding-place.

Deciding that the impression of the face was the product of both fear and your over-active imagination, you say nothing to the others and return to the chapel.

Add 1 point to your *ESP* score and 1 point to your *Terror* score, deduct 1 *Blood* point, and then turn to **564**.

332

You barely have time to seize a weapon of your own before the would-be murderer and disciple of Dracula is on top of you. (In this battle your opponent has the initiative.)

JOHNNY ALUCARD COMBAT 8 ENDURANCE 8

If you are still alive after 4 Combat Rounds, or if you reduce Alucard's *Endurance* score to 4 points or fewer, whichever is sooner, turn to **362**.

333

The howling of the wolves has stopped, and leaving the carriage and horses, you step off the road in your pursuit of the driver. And then you see him, back-lit by the ghostly flicker of the strange blue flames. You freeze, observing his actions from afar.

You watch as the man gathers up a few stones and forms them into something like a pyramid.

Just then, the moon, sailing through the black clouds, appears behind the jagged crest of a beetling, pine-clad rock, and by its light you see that you are surrounded by a ring of wolves, with glistening white teeth and lolling hot red tongues, as well as long, sinewy limbs and shaggy hair. They are a hundred times more terrible in the grim silence which holds them than even when they howled, and you feel the paralysis of fear grip you tightly. (Add 1 point to your *Terror* score.)

All at once the wolves begin to howl again, as if the moonlight has had some peculiar effect on them, and the horses behind you whinny in terror. Hearing a booming voice raised in a tone of imperious command, your attention is drawn back to the gypsy. With a sweep of his long arms, as if he is brushing aside some impalpable obstacle, the wolves fall back.

At that moment, a cloud passes across the face of the moon, and you are plunged into darkness. Free of the fearful paralysis, you hurry back to the carriage, your heart pounding in your chest – before the driver spots you and realises you followed him – and take your seat once more, wrapped in the cloak and rug.

Tick off the code word *Lángok* and then turn to **363**.

334

Bellowing the same war-cry favoured by the soldiers of the armies of Vlad Tepes, the Voivode of Wallachia, over 400 years ago, the boyar swings his keenly-sharp blade at your head. (In this battle, your opponent has the initiative.)

SZGANY BOYAR   COMBAT 9   ENDURANCE 8

If you kill the berserk boyar, turn to **76**.

335

"Werewolves," comes Van Helsing's voice from behind you and for the first time you realise that all six of you have been reunited in tracking down the wolves. Only now the hunters have become the hunted.

The pack circles your small band of brave souls – they have you entirely surrounded – and then they attack.

The six of you form a rough circle. Nine Werewolves attack in total. Roll one die for each Werewolf and check below to see not only who each one attacks but how many of the monsters that individual is able to deal with by themselves.

Die Roll	Vampire-Hunter	Werewolves dealt with
1	Professor Van Helsing	2
2	Dr Seward	1
3	Arthur	2
4	Quincey Morris	3
5	Jonathan Harker – YOU!	See below
6	Mina Harker	1

Any Werewolves that are dealt with by any of your companions are crossed off the list. You will have to deal with any that attack you directly. However, for every use of *The Pen is Mightier* special ability you cross off, you may remove one Werewolf from the total number you have to fight. The Werewolves will have the initiative in the battle and each one has the following stats:

WEREWOLF   COMBAT 8   ENDURANCE 8

If you manage to defeat all your opponents, make a note of how many Werewolves remain. For example, if two Werewolves attacked Mina, she will have only been able to dispatch one of them.

If there are no Werewolves left alive, turn to **406**. If there is at least one still to be dealt with, turn to **426**.

336

"But I wouldn't worry maself about such stories, miss. Them things be all wore out. Mind, I don't say that they never was, but I do say they wasn't in my time. Such legends all be very well for day-trippers, an' them feet-folks from York and Leeds that be always eatin' cured herrings and drinkin' tea, and lookin' to buy cheap jet – but not for a nice young lady like you."

Lucy joins you then, looking sweetly pretty in her white lawn frock. She has acquired a healthy complexion since she has been staying here. The old men do not waste any time in coming and sitting near her, when she sits down. Even your old friend appears enamoured of her, but you are keen to keep him on the subject of the local legends.

"It be all fool-talk," Mr Swales says brusquely, "lock, stock, and barrel, and that's what it be and nowt else. Stories of curses, wafts, barghests, an' bogles, an' all, are only fit to set bairns an' dizzy women a-blubbering."

Wafts, barghests and bogles, must be dialect names for different types of sprites and other supernatural creatures.

Which of them do you want to ask the old man about?

Wafts?	Turn to **356**.
Barghests?	Turn to **376**.
Bogles?	Turn to **416**.

If you would prefer to leave the old fellow be, and not to bother him further, turn to **456**.

337

Taking a few steps back, mustering all your strength, you charge at the door, with your shoulder square on to the iron-studded oak.

Take an Endurance test. If you pass the test, turn to **399**, but if you fail the test, turn to **367**.

338

You find Dr Seward in his study, where he and Professor Van Helsing are discussing the list of Mr Renfield's extraordinary psychoses and character defects. They stop the moment you enter the room.

"Can we be certain that it was merely a nightmare?" the Professor ponders once you have described the nature of your disturbing dream. "Perhaps it is not enough that we simply leave you behind when we embark upon our dark endeavours. Perhaps we should do more to help you protect yourself, should the need arise."

Dr Seward agrees and so the Professor suggests three different ways in which he and Lucy's suitors might help you.

"Our brave Lord Godalming is skilled with the sword, while Mr Morris, our bold American friend, is the master of the revolver. Both could no doubt teach you how to protect yourself with each. For my part, I have always tried to keep an open mind concerning all things and have schooled myself in methods of meditation and hypnosis. I have even made some study of more esoteric practices, such as psychography, telepathy, and extra sensory perception. It may be that I can pass on some of what I have learnt to you. Unfortunately, for any such training to be worthwhile, there is only time to focus on one form today."

Who do you want to help you?

Lord Godalming?	Turn to **394**.
Quincey Morris?	Turn to **422**.
Professor Van Helsing?	Turn to **364**.

339

The funeral is arranged for the 22 September, so that Lucy and her mother might be buried together. Because Arthur has to be back the day after that to attend his father's funeral, there is not time to notify everyone who might have liked to have been there to see Lucy off.

After the undertaker has been, you go to look at what has been done for poor Lucy this one last time. There is a mortuary air about the room in which Lucy and her mother are lying, festooned with tall wax candles. You are startled by her beauty; all her loveliness has come back to her in death so that you can hardly believe you are looking at a corpse.

The Professor adds wild garlic blooms to the other flowers that have been put in the room and places a little gold crucifix over Lucy's mouth. And that is how she remains until the day of her internment, with Van Helsing patrolling the house, never out of sight of the room where poor Lucy lies in her coffin.

* * * *

If you wish to continue the story as Dr John Seward, turn to **999**. However, you may choose to take on the role of Jonathan Harker (turn to **329**), or the recently married Mina Harker, if you prefer (turn to **242**).

340

You meet Professor Van Helsing at the station the next day and from there take a hansom to Hillingham, Lucy's home, in Hampstead. During the journey you tell your mentor that Lucy's fiancé Arthur has placed his absolute trust in you.

"You must tell him what you think," the older man says, steepling his fingers before his face, "for this is a matter of life and death – maybe more."

"What do you mean, Professor?" you challenge him, but he will not give you any further clue, merely tapping his nose with a finger.

Upon reaching Hillingham, you find Lucy in the conservatory and cannot hide your delight at finding her more cheerful than on the day you first assessed her. She certainly looks better, having lost something of the ghastly aspect that so upset you before. Her breathing is normal as well.

She is very sweet to the Professor and does her best to make him feel at ease, though you can see the effort etched in the poor girl's face. Van Helsing evidently sees it too, and so he begins to chat about everything other than diseases and yourselves.

"My dear young miss," he says at last, "those who love you told me you were down in spirit, and ghastly pale. To them I say 'Pouf!'" – and he snaps his fingers – "but you and I shall show them how wrong they are. How can he" – he points at you then – "know anything of young ladies? He has his madmen to play with!"

Van Helsing sends you out into the garden, so that he can talk with Lucy in private. Presently he comes to the window and calls you in again, but his expression is worryingly grave.

"I have made careful examination," he says, "but there is no functional cause. I agree that there has been much blood lost, but her condition is in no way anaemic. And yet there is cause; there is always cause for everything.

"I must go back home and think. You must send me a telegram every day, and if there be cause I shall come again. The disease – for not to be well is a disease – interests me, and the young miss interests me too."

He will not be drawn further on the matter, even when the two of you are alone again in the carriage on the way back to the London docks.

Once the two of you have parted company, you write to Arthur, as you promised you would, relating all that happened during the Professor's visit.

But the Professor's words, regarding your duty to your patients, makes you feel guilty for neglecting Renfield and the rest.

So how will you spend the day tomorrow? With Miss Lucy (turn to **841**), or back in Purfleet at your asylum (turn to **811**)?

341

In time, your feeding begins to take its toll on Lucy's physical and spiritual health, as her body starts to undergo the transformation necessary for her to become the mother of a new race of nosferatu under your command. For to become your bride, first she has to die.

Her mother, concerned by her daughter's worsening condition, calls physicians to attend her, but none of them can fathom what is wrong with her. In the end Mrs Westenra takes her daughter back to the family home in London, and you follow.

* * * *

Your precious boxes of 'common earth' are now installed within the chapel of Carfax House in Purfleet. From there you set your mind to the task of spreading them throughout the capital, hiring weak-willed men, who it is easy for you to dominate and place in your thrall, to distribute some of the boxes to the various properties you have recently purchased.

You are the proud owner of three properties within the capital – a former printers' warehouse in Mile End, a rundown end-of-terrace house in Walworth, and a grand townhouse on Piccadilly, that overlooks the Green Park – not to mention the Carfax House estate in the county of Essex, along the Thames to the east. You decide to make the Piccadilly townhouse your centre of operations, inviting a tramp to join you there simply to murder him and use his blood to consecrate the house, so that you can come and go freely as you please. (Gain 2 *Blood* points.)

From there it is only a few miles to Hampstead Heath, where the Westenra family live in Hillingham House. While you continue to visit Lucy, from time to time, to suckle from the open wound in her neck – that she has unconsciously taken to hiding from her mother by wearing a black velvet choker – you spend your time in continued studying, learning all you can about London and all it has to offer a newly-installed debonair foreigner gentleman.

Turn to **368**.

342

A feeling of dread and impending doom comes over you then, and you flee the chapel as quickly as you can, desperate to return to the daylight and the security of your own chambers.

Your courage spent, you ascend to the Count's room and leave again by the window, crawling back up the castle wall. Regaining your room, you throw yourself panting on the bed.

(Add 1 point to your *Terror* score.)

Slowly you become aware of a gypsy song, sung by merry voices, coming from far off but drawing closer, and accompanied by the rolling of heavy wheels and the cracking of whips. The Szgany have returned.

Turn to **607**.

343

Your heart thudding within your chest, you draw back the sheet. You cannot stop the gasp of fear that escapes your lips as you lay eyes upon the wizened thing that is lying on the bed.

In the brief glimpse you take in before you flee the chamber in horror, you believe it is the body of an old man, but it looks like it has been entirely drained of blood. In that split second's look, you see the contours of the skeleton beneath the emaciated husk of the man quite clearly.

Add 1 point to your *Terror* score and turn to **273**.

344

If you are wielding the Dragon Sword, turn to **433**. If not, turn to **327**.

345

"Then to begin," she says, indicating the goblet on the altar, "all you have to do is take up the goblet and drink."

No rough hands hinder you as you get to your feet once more and approach the altar. Taking hold of the goblet in one hand you find that it is fixed to the altar somehow. Gripping it with both hands you try again, but still the chalice will not move.

"This is some kind of trick," you say. "A test. The goblet cannot be taken."

"Can it not?" the woman says, picking up the golden cup in one delicate, alabaster hand, before placing it back down. "Now you try."

And you do, but still you cannot lift it, and so, gritting your teeth, you bring all your strength to bear.

Take an Endurance test. If you pass the test, turn to **375**, but if you fail the test, turn to **310**.

346

Your vision swims and Lucy is an innocent beauty once more, her purity restored.

"Come to me, John," she says again, and you cannot resist her. This is all you have ever wanted.

Your pulse racing, you welcome Lucy's cold embrace, and in that moment your broken heart is healed. And then Lucy sinks her fangs into your jugular and drinks deeply of your blood, as leaden drowsiness overcomes you.

"You are mine now, dear Dr Seward," you hear her say, as if through a dream, "and you will do my bidding, and that of my master."

You are unable to resist as she draws a fingernail across her exposed decolletage and presses your head to her breast, encouraging you to drink of her corrupted blood.

The oaths you have sworn to your friends, and the promises you made to Lucy's memory are all forgotten. You are a creature of darkness now, ready to rip the hearts from the weak. The reign of the vampiric doctor is about to begin.

Your adventure is over.

THE END

347

Your wolves and gypsies are putting up a spirited defence, but the Vampire-Hunters are relentless. You feel you need to throw yourself into the fray and turn the tide of battle in your favour.

Divide your *Blood* score by 10, rounding fractions up. Then roll 1 die, and if the number rolled is equal or less than the resulting total, turn to **786**. If it is greater, turn to **419**.

348

TELEGRAM, MRS HARKER, EXETER, TO VAN HELSING, THE BERKLEY HOTEL, LONDON

29 September

Am coming up by train. Jonathan at Whitby. Important news. Mina Harker.

It is only a matter of days before you hear from Professor Van Helsing again, asking you both to travel to London, to meet with Lucy's former suitors who are to join you and Jonathan in putting an end to the Count's nefarious schemes. But he also sets Jonathan the task of finding out what happened to the cargo that was brought to England on board the doomed *Demeter*.

While Jonathan sets off for Whitby, to try to trace that horrid cargo of the Count's, you take the train alone from Exeter to London. You arrive later that day at Paddington Station, where you are met by Lucy's brave Dr Seward. You recognise him immediately, telling him, "I knew you from Lucy's description of you."

You ride the Underground together across London, and upon reaching Fenchurch Street Station, from there take another train, this time travelling to Purfleet. In due course you arrive at Carfax Asylum, where you discover that Dr Seward has had his housekeeper prepare a sitting room and bedroom for you.

Having tidied yourself up, after a long day of travel, you go down to Dr Seward's study. At the door you pause, as you can hear him talking with someone. You knock and he immediately calls out, "Come in!"

You enter, but to your intense surprise, there is no one with him.

"I hope I did not keep you waiting," you say, "but I stayed at the door as I heard you talking and thought there was someone with you."

"Oh, I was only entering my diary," he replies with a smile. "I keep it in this."

As he speaks, he lays a hand on the device on the table opposite him, which you instantly recognise as a phonograph.

"Why, this beats even shorthand!" you blurt out excitedly. "May I hear it say something?"

"Certainly," he replies, and makes the necessary changes to set it up for play-back. But then he pauses, a troubled look on his face. "The fact is I only keep my diary in it, which is almost entirely about my patients, that is, I mean…"

"You helped to attend dear Lucy at the end," you tell him, trying to help him out of his embarrassment. "Let me hear how she died, for she was very, very dear to me."

He takes some persuading, but in the end he agrees. "Do you know, although I have kept the diary for months, I never once considered how I was going to find any particular part of it, in case I wanted to look it up."

Your mind is made up, for the diary of a doctor who attended Lucy might have something to add to the sum of your knowledge about the terrible being you must run to ground. And so, you say, quite boldly, "Then, Dr Seward, you had better let me copy it out for you on my typewriter."

You set to work immediately. You have already transcribed your own diary, starting from the day you arrived in Whitby, as well as that horrible journal Jonathan kept while he was in Transylvania. You do not complete your task until late the following afternoon.

In transcribing the good doctor's phonograph cylinders, you become morbidly fascinated by his zoophagous patient, Mr Renfield, to the point where you wonder what it would be like to meet him.

Do you want to take your courage in both hands and ask to see the deranged lunatic (turn to **186**), or would you prefer to have nothing to do with the madman, no matter how much his case might intrigue you (turn to **152**)?

263

349

Snelling is wiry, with an almost athletic physique. (In this battle, your opponent has the initiative.)

SNELLING   COMBAT 8   ENDURANCE 7

If you win the fight, turn to **389**.

350

Shrieking like a banshee, the King of Vampires attacks.

(In this battle, you have the initiative, and remember to deduct any damage you have already caused Dracula before you begin.)

DRACULA THE UN-DEAD   COMBAT 11   ENDURANCE 20

If you manage to win the battle in 12 Combat Rounds or fewer, turn to **379** at once. If after 12 Combat Rounds both you and Dracula are still alive, turn to **510**.

351

You stagger away from the dissolving Dr Callistratus and out of his private compartment, but you cannot take your eyes off the horrific transformation that is literally consuming his body.

Soon, where the cornered killer once stood there is nothing but a blood-soaked carpet and a pile of steaming bones.

Add 2 points to your *Terror* score and turn to **509**.

352

After what happened, you cannot bring yourself to trust Renfield. He is possessed of a great many manias, all acting in consort, and that makes him dangerously unpredictable.

However, as you try to question him, he remains stubbornly quiet again and uncooperative. Even the offer of a full-grown cat will not encourage him to speak.

His only response is, "I don't take any stock in cats. I have more to think of now, and I can wait. I can wait."

If you want to change your mind and instruct the attendants to release him from the strait waistcoat, turn to **372**. If not, then the interview is most definitely over; turn to **423**.

353

(Add the Tincture of Wolfsbane to the Equipment Box on your Adventure Sheet.)

The potion is contained within a grubby glass bottle, stoppered with a wax plug, and is of a vivid purple hue.

If you want to break the seal and drink the potion down straightaway, turn to **393**. If you would prefer to stow it away for safekeeping, in case you might want to use it later instead, turn to **413**.

354

"But Herr Delbruck," you enquire, when the officer has gone, "how did you know I was lost?"

"The driver, Johann, came hither with the remains of his carriage, which had been upset when the horses ran away."

"But surely you would not send a search party of soldiers merely on this account?"

"Oh no!" he replies. "But even before the coachman arrived, I received this telegram from the Boyar whose guest you are," and he takes from his pocket a piece of paper, which he hands to you, and you begin to read:

```
Bistritz.

Be careful of my guest - his safety is most precious to
me. Should aught happen to him, or if he be missed, spare
nothing to find him and ensure his safety. He is English
and therefore adventurous. There are often dangers from
snow and wolves and night.
```

> Lose not a moment if you suspect harm to him. I answer your zeal with my fortune.
>
> Dracula

As you hold the telegram in your hand, the room seems to whirl around you, and if the attentive Herr Delbruck had not been there to steady you, there is no doubt in your mind that you would have fallen.

The feeling grows upon you that you are in some way the sport of opposing forces, the mere idea of which threatens to paralyse you. You are certainly under some form of mysterious protection, for a message had come from a distant country, just in the nick of time, to save you from the dangers posed by snow, sleep, and the jaws of a wolf.

Add 1 point to your *Terror* score and turn to **384**.

355

"Werewolves," comes Van Helsing's voice from behind you and for the first time you realise that all six of you have been reunited in tracking down the wolves. Only now the hunters have become the hunted.

The others form a rough circle around you as the pack begins to circle your small band of brave souls, and then attacks.

There are nine Werewolves in total. Roll one die (or pick a card) for each of your five companions; if the number rolled is odd (or the card is red), that individual battles one Werewolf, but if the number rolled is even (or the card is black), that individual takes on two of the monsters. Total up how many Werewolves are engaged by your companions.

If there are no Werewolves left unaccounted for, turn to **406**. If there is at least one still to be dealt with, turn to **492**.

356

According to Mr Swales, a Waft is the phantasmal semblance of a living person. Such apparitions are far from benign but soul-stealing killers, for the appearance of such a spectre is supposed to foretell the death of the poor person in question.

They are also known by another name to the more academically orientated and that is the *Doppelgänger*. The name is German in origin and means 'double-goer'.

Turn to **436**.

357

DR SEWARD'S DIARY

(Kept in phonograph)

13 September

Called at the Berkley and found Van Helsing, as usual, on time...

The pair of you, student and mentor, arrive at Hillingham at eight o'clock. It is a lovely morning and the bright sunshine and all the fresh feeling of early autumn seems like the completion of nature's annual work.

As one of the family's maidservants admits you to the house, you meet Mrs Westenra coming out of the morning room. She greets you warmly, with the words, "You will be glad to know that Lucy is better. The dear child is still asleep. I looked in on her but did not go in, so as not to disturb her."

"Then my diagnosis was correct!" the Professor smiles, rubbing his hands together in delight, and looking quite jubilant. "My treatment is working."

"You cannot take all the credit yourself, Professor," Mrs Westenra replies. "Lucy's state this morning is due in part to me."

"How do you mean, madam," Van Helsing asks.

"Well, I was anxious about the child in the night, and went into her room. She was sleeping soundly, but the room was awfully stuffy. Those horrible, strong-smelling flowers were everywhere, even around her neck, and I feared their heavy odour would be too much for her in her weakened state, so I took them away and opened the window to let in a little fresh air."

The Professor's face turns grey, and as Lucy's mother moves off into her boudoir, he pulls you suddenly and forcibly up the stairs after him, saying, "This poor mother, in her ignorance and by her own actions, risks losing her daughter, body and soul!"

Bursting into Lucy's room, you rush to draw up the blind while Van Helsing goes to her bed. He wears a look of stern sadness and infinite pity as he looks upon poor Lucy's face, which now has the same waxy pallor as before.

"As I expected," he says, as he sets out his instruments to perform yet another blood transfusion.

You begin to take off your coat, knowing what must done, but he stops you.

"No!" he says. "Today you must operate. I shall provide."

If you are happy to allow Van Helsing to provide Lucy with the vital fluid she needs, turn to **387**. If you insist that you, being the younger and the stronger, should be the blood donor, turn to **417**.

358

Every last one of the crew of the *Demeter* is dead by your hand. But in killing the seamen, you have doomed yourself.

There is now no one left to sail the ship and ensure it makes land safely. You cannot flee the ship either, as your kind are unable to cross moving water and you are surrounded by the roiling sea.

You give voice to your fury with a howl of rage. In response, thunder rumbles across the stormy sky and flashes of lightning streak down from the heavens around the ship. One of them strikes the main mast, shearing off the top in an explosion of flame. The splintered oak plummets towards the deck, the ragged end spearing your body, which crumbles to dust, as the long centuries catch up with you at last, the wind carrying that dust away to be scattered over the ocean.

Your adventure, like your unnatural undead existence, is over.

THE END

359

You cannot help but feel excited as the time draws near for Professor Van Helsing's visit. Even though the reason for his coming is to find out more about Lucy's illness, you hope that he will also be able to throw some light upon your poor husband's experience. And as he attended your dear friend in her dying days, he can tell you all about her. She must have told him of her sleep-walking adventure on the cliff, and now he wants you to tell him what you know.

That awful night on the cliff must have made her ill. Caught up in your own affairs – what with your journey to Buda-Pesth, your marriage to Jonathan, and your subsequent return to England, and Mr Hawkins' sudden passing – you had almost forgotten how poorly she was afterwards.

Professor Van Helsing must be a good man as well as a clever one if he is a friend to both Arthur and Dr Seward, and if they brought him all the way from Holland to look after Lucy.

* * * *

It is half-past two o'clock when the knock comes. In a few minutes Mary your maidservant opens the door, and announces, "Professor Van Helsing."

You rise and bow, and he comes towards you. He is a man of medium weight, strongly built, with his shoulders set back over a broad, deep chest. The poise of his head strikes you at once as being indicative of thought and power.

"Mrs Harker, is it not? That was Miss Mina Murray?"

You nod.

"Madam Mina, it is on account of the dead that I come."

Taking your hand, he says, "I have read your letters to Miss Lucy and I know that you were with her at Whitby. She sometimes kept a diary, and in it she traced by inference certain things to an incidence of sleep-walking, in which she puts down that you saved her. Please tell me all that you can remember of that night."

And so, you relate how you woke to find Lucy gone from her bed and followed her to the churchyard atop the East Cliff, only to see her attacked by some manner of red-eyed beast. The Professor listens intently as you tell your story and only speaks when you are done.

"Madam Mina, is there anything else that I should know about your time in Whitby? Did you witness anything else out of the ordinary? Anything you observed yourself, or any strange occurrences you heard about at the time perhaps?"

How many of the following code words do you have ticked off? *Azrael, Barghest, Demeter.*

None?	Turn to **378**.
One?	Turn to **398**.
Two?	Turn to **418**.
Three?	Turn to **438**.

360

"I seek an audience with Sultan Mehmed bin Murad," you tell them.

Turn to **435**.

She looks so appealingly at you that you cannot refuse her, so take her down to the ward to meet Renfield. Going into his cell ahead of her, you tell your patient that a lady would like to see him, to which he simply answers, "Why?"

"She is going through the house, and wants to see everyone in it," you lie.

"Oh, very well," he concedes, "let her come in, by all means, but just wait a minute while I tidy up the place."

His method of tidying is most peculiar, for he simply swallows all the flies and spiders he keeps in his boxes, before you can stop him. When he has completed his disgusting task, he says quite cheerfully, "Let the lady come in," and sits down on the edge of his bed with his head down, but his eyelids raised so that he can see her as she enters.

For a moment you think he might harbour some secret homicidal intent, and so you take care to stand where you can seize him at once if he so much as looks like he might be about to spring at her.

Mrs Harker comes into the room with an easy gracefulness that would command the respect of any lunatic. Smiling pleasantly, and holding out her hand, she says, "Good evening, Mr Renfield."

He makes no immediate reply but studies her intently, a frown on his face. This look soon gives way to an expression of wonder, which then merges with apparent doubt.

"You're not the girl the doctor wanted to marry, are you?" Renfield says at last. "You can't be, you know, for she's dead."

"Oh no! I have a husband of my own," she replies. "I am Mrs Harker."

"Then what are you doing here?"

"My husband and I are staying with Dr Seward for a short while."

"Then don't stay."

The lunatic's words take you by surprise, as unexpected as they are considerate.

"But why not?" she asks him.

"I used to believe that by consuming a multitude of living things, no matter how low in the scale of creation, I might indefinitely prolong my life," he says, changing the subject, a distant look coming into his bulging eyes. "At times I held the belief so strongly that I actually tried to take human life. The doctor here will bear me out that on one occasion I tried to kill him for the purpose of strengthening my vital powers, by assimilating his life by consuming his blood. For the blood is the life, is that not true, Doctor?"

"It is time we left," you say, looking at your watch, aware that it is time you went to the station to meet Van Helsing.

She comes at once, only stopping at the door to address Renfield one last time: "Goodbye, and I hope I may see you again, under auspices pleasanter to yourself."

To your astonishment, Mr Renfield replies, "Goodbye, my dear. I pray to God I may never see your sweet face again. May He bless and keep you!"

Tick off the code word *Psychopathia* and turn to **391**.

362

There is a commotion in the gangway outside your cabin and a shout of, "Stop, villain!"

Looking about him in agitation, Alucard suddenly breaks off from the battle and flees towards the rear of the train.

A moment later, Arthur Holmwood and Quincey Morris appear at your door. "Are you all right?" Arthur asks.

Before you can reply there is a sudden squeal of metal on metal, as the train's wheels seize, and the Orient Express comes to an abrupt stop, which sends the three of you tumbling to the floor. Someone, no doubt your would-be murderer, must have pulled the emergency brake.

If you want to head after him, towards the rear of the train, turn to **411**. If not, turn to **383**.

363

As abruptly as he vanished, the man suddenly reappears and takes his seat again, without a word, and you resume your journey.

You can't help feeling possessed of an uncanny sense of looming dread, and the time seems interminable as you continue on your way, now in almost complete darkness, for the rolling clouds obscure the moon.

You sense that you are ascending, punctuated with periods of quick descent, until you become conscious of the fact that the driver is in the act of pulling the horses into the courtyard of a vast, ruined castle, from whose tall black windows comes no ray of light, and whose broken battlements show as a jagged line against the sky.

In the gloom, the courtyard appears to be of considerable size, and several dark ways lead from it under great round arches.

The caleche comes to a halt, and the gypsy driver jumps down, holding out his hand to assist you to alight. You cannot help but notice his prodigious strength; his hand is like a steel vice that could crush yours, if he so wished.

He takes your personal belongings from the carriage and places them on the ground beside you.

You are standing in front of a great door – clearly ancient and studded with large, blunt-headed iron nails – set within a projecting doorway of carved stone, although the carvings have been much worn by time and the weather.

As you stand there, awestruck, the driver jumps back into his seat and with a shake of the reins, sets the horses moving again. Trap, driver and all disappear into one of the deeply-shadowed openings.

You can see no sign of a bell, or knocker upon the door, so you simply stand there, in the courtyard, in silence, not knowing what else to do. You doubt your voice could penetrate these frowning walls even if you were to announce your arrival.

And as you stand there, you realise that this is the same place Mr Renfield visited before you, an expedition from which he returned a broken man.

273

You hear a heavy step approaching from behind the great door and see through the chinks the jaundiced gleam of a bobbing light. There is the sound of rattling chains, the clanking of massive bolts being drawn back, and a key is turned with the loud grating noise of long disuse, and finally the great door swings back.

Within, stands a tall, old man, clean shaven, save for an extravagant white moustache, and clad in black from head to foot. He holds in his hand an antique silver lamp, the flame burning within throwing long, quivering shadows as it flickers in the draught of the open door.

He motions to you, with an antiquated courtly gesture. "Welcome to my house!" he says in excellent English, but with a strange intonation. "Enter freely, go safely, and leave something of the happiness you bring."

You step over the threshold, and the old man moves forward impulsively. Holding out his hand, he grasps yours with a strength that makes you wince. It seems as cold as ice, more like the hand of a dead man than one of the living.

"Count Dracula?" you ask.

The old man bows, in his courtly fashion. "I am Dracula, and I bid you welcome, Mr Harker, to my house. Come in, the night air is chill, and you must need to eat and rest."

Taking your luggage before you can forestall him, he leads you inside the castle.

"It is late, and my people are not available. Let me see to your comfort myself."

Despite your protestations, he insists on carrying your bags along an echoing passage, and then up a great winding stair, and along another great landing, on whose stone floor your steps ring heavily. At the end of this passageway, the Count throws open a heavy door, and you are delighted to see a well-lit room beyond.

Inside, a grand dining-table has been set for supper, while a great fire of logs flames and flares within the hearth.

The Count puts down your bags, closes the door, and, crossing the room, opens another, which leads into a small octagonal room lit by a single lamp. Passing through this, he opens yet another door, motioning for you to follow. It is a great bedroom, warmed by another log fire, which sends a hollow roar up the wide chimney.

It is a most welcome sight, for you are exhausted after your traumatic journey to the Count's home.

The Count leaves your bags inside the room and withdraws, saying, "You will want to refresh yourself, after your journey. I trust you will find all you wish. When you are ready, come into the other room, where you will find your supper prepared."

It is past midnight. If you want to politely decline your host's offer of supper, and retire for what remains of the night, turn to **371**. If you would prefer to have something to eat before retiring, turn to **146**.

364

The Professor generously gives of both his time and his knowledge, sharing with you what he has learned over years of study and practical experimentation. But how receptive a student are you?

Roll one die and then divide the number rolled by 2, rounding fractions up. Add this many points to your *ESP* score. (Alternatively, pick a card: if it is an Ace, add 1 point to your *ESP* score; if it is a 2, add 2 points to your *ESP* score; if it is anything else, add 3 points to your *ESP* score.)

Turn to **449**.

365

"Werewolves," comes Van Helsing's voice from behind you and for the first time you realise that all six of you have been reunited in tracking down the wolves. Only now the hunters have become the hunted.

The pack circles your small band of brave souls – they have you entirely surrounded – and then they attack.

The six of you form a rough circle. Nine Werewolves attack in total. Roll one die for each Werewolf and check below to see not only who each one attacks but how many of the monsters that individual is able to deal with, without assistance.

Die Roll	Vampire-Hunter	Werewolves dealt with
1	Professor Van Helsing	2
2	Dr Seward – YOU!	See below
3	Arthur	2
4	Quincey Morris	3
5	Jonathan Harker	2
6	Mina Harker	1

Any Werewolves that are dealt with by any of your companions are crossed off the list. You will have to deal with any that attack you directly. However, for every use of *The Pen is Mightier* special ability you cross off, you may remove one Werewolf from the total number you have to fight. The Werewolves will have the initiative in the battle and each one has the following stats:

WEREWOLF   COMBAT 8   ENDURANCE 8

If you manage to defeat all of your opponents, make a note of how many Werewolves remain. For example, if three Werewolves attacked Van Helsing, the old man will have only been able to deal with two of them.

If there are no Werewolves left alive, turn to **406**. If there is at least one still to be dealt with, turn to **426**.

366

Jumping down from your horse, you run at the Szgany, hoping to take them by surprise and in the confusion barge past them before scrambling up onto the cart.

Take an Agility test. If you pass the test, turn to **421**, but if you fail the test, turn to **386**.

367

You slam into the door, but it does not budge an inch. Your shoulder, however, is left bruised and sore.

Lose 2 *Endurance* points and turn to **308**.

368

Able to move about freely during the hours of daylight, now that you are able to sleep in the soil of your homeland once more (even if it is with your powers diminished, the true source of your supernatural strength being bound to the night), on one occasion you visit London's famous Zoological Gardens. And it is there that you encounter the wolf Bersicker.

You have fed well, since arriving in London, and have regained your youthful good looks, seeming to be no older than the day you died. Appropriately attired, in the manner and fashion of an English gentleman, you do not stand out among the other people visiting the zoo.

But while your fellow visitors go about their business, oblivious to your true nature, the animals are unsettled by the presence of an apex predator. As you approach the wolf enclosure, the three grey wolves that reside there start yelping and howling, while the biggest of them starts tearing at the bars of the cage, as if desperate to get out.

Hearing the noise, one of the zoo's attendants comes running.

"Keeper," you call out, "these wolves seem upset at something."

"Maybe it's you," he replies, eyeing you suspiciously.

You smile. "Oh no, they wouldn't like me."

"Oh yes, they would. They always likes a bone or two to clean their teeth on about teatime, and you have a bagful."

His voice peters out into silence as he realises that the wolves are now lying down, calm again, and the big one that was savaging the bars even lets the attendant stroke its ears.

Copying him, you put your hand through the bars and stroke the old wolf's ears as well. The man is visibly taken aback.

"Take care, Bersicker is quick."

"Do not fear, I am used to wolves," you tell him.

"Are you in the business yourself?" the keeper asks incredulously, taking off his hat as if as a mark of respect.

"No, not exactly in the business, but I have made pets of several."

With that, you raise your own hat and take your leave of the wolves and their keeper.

* * * *

That night, you set out once more for Hillingham, but this time you do not go alone. Seeing the wolf Bersicker at the zoo reminded you of your shared kinship with the children of the night, and so you stop at the Zoological Gardens once more, breaking the bars of the wolf's cage with your bare hands and setting the beast free.

The old wolf joins you, and the two of you run together through the sleeping London streets as far as Hampstead Heath and the Westenra residence. Once there, you assume the form of a bat once more and fly up to Lucy's bedroom window. But finding it both closed and locked, you are forced to smash the glass to get in.

With her mother sleeping in the room next door, and oblivious to your presence, you do what you came here to do. Once you have fed, you fly out through the broken windowpane and set off on the return journey to Piccadilly, Bersicker still following.

(Gain 4 *Blood* points and 6 *Endurance* points.)

Flying over the rhododendron bushes that form an avenue either side of the drive that leads up to the house from the road, you are startled to see a young man running along it towards you. Judging by his elevated heartrate, he is just as surprised to see you, but his pulse quickens again when the wolf emerges from the shrubbery in front of him.

Thanks to the bond you share with your would-be bride, you realise that this unexpected night-time caller is Dr John Seward, an alienist as well as her personal physician.

Do you want to:

Fly away, as fast as you can into the night?	Turn to **397**.
Attack the doctor directly yourself?	Turn to **176**.
Send Bersicker to attack him?	Turn to **198**.

369

Realising that you and Arthur are not simply a couple of toffs who will crumble as soon as they are threatened with violence, the men quickly decide that discretion is the better part of valour and turn tail and run. Before you can stop them, they climb on board the cart again, and take up the reins, leaving the yard as quickly as they can.

Cross off one use of *The Pen is Mightier* special ability, gain 2 *Blood* points, and then turn to **409**.

370

You have no inkling as to where the Vampire-Hunters might be, or how many of them have invaded your home, until you put your hand to the dining-room door. You can sense the presence of anxious men within the room beyond, and if they are there, there can be no doubt that they will have found what you had stored there.

Do you want to enter the dining-room, with the intention of putting an end to them all, here and now (turn to **715**), or fearing that the game is up, do you want to make your escape while they are still unaware that the very creature they have come here to kill is there in the house with them (turn to **455**)?

371

Your sleep is disturbed by visions of skull-faced phantasms, wolves, and women with skin the colour of ivory, but you are unable to rouse yourself from your nightmares. When you do eventually awake, you realise it is late in the day.

Having dressed, you go into the room where supper was laid out the night before and find a cold breakfast waiting for you, with a hot pot of coffee keeping warm on the hearth.

There is also a card waiting for you on the table:

My Friend –

I have to be absent for a while. Do not wait for me.

D.

You set to and enjoy a hearty meal. (Gain 2 *Endurance* points if you dined last night, but gain 3 *Endurance* points if you did not sup with your host.)

When you are done, you look for a bell to let the servants know you have finished but are unable to find one. There are other odd deficiencies in the house as well, especially when you consider the evidences of wealth that are all around you.

The table service is of gold, and so beautifully wrought that it must be of immense value. The curtains and upholstery of the chairs and sofas, and the hangings of your bed, are of the costliest and most extravagant fabrics; they must have been of incredible value when they were made, for they are clearly centuries old, although they are in excellent order.

But you have not seen a servant anywhere or heard anything near the castle except for the howling of wolves.

The other strange thing is that in none of the rooms is there a mirror; you had to get the shaving glass from your bag before you could either shave or brush your hair.

When you are done with your meal – but whether to call it breakfast or dinner you do not know, for it was between five and six o'clock when you ate – you look for something to read, to help you pass the time, but there is absolutely nothing within the room.

Seeing the sun sinking towards the mountains through one window, you determine that the door by which you first came upon your suite of rooms is in the southern wall. Your bedroom lies through the door in the western wall and opposite, on the eastern side of the dining-room, there is another door, and between these two, in the north wall, there is a fourth.

Ignoring the way back to your bedroom, do you want to try the door to the:

East?	Turn to **401**.
North?	Turn to **431**.
South?	Turn to **451**.

372

Satisfied with your patient's present condition, you direct that he be relieved. The attendants hesitate before finally carrying out your wishes without protest.

"So tell me, Mr Renfield," you say. "What compelled you to visit the old house last night?"

He looks furtively at the attendants before coming close to you and saying, in a whisper, "The Master summoned me. I am his slave; I cannot deny him."

"Who is he, this Master of yours?" you press him.

"He is the one who comes! He is the Master of Life! He is the one who shall bestow his bounteous gifts upon me!"

"And does he await you in Carfax House?" you ask.

"Not yet. I must be patient. I shall be patient. For when he comes, his coming shall be glorious, and all false rulers shall succumb in the presence of his dark majesty!"

(Tick off the code word *Slave*.)

Renfield is suddenly seized by a terrible fit – that has him arching his back and foaming at the mouth, his arms and legs thrashing as he falls to the floor in near bone-breaking contortions – that the attendants have to restrain him again, to prevent him from hurting himself. The paroxysm is so violent that it exhausts him, and he loses consciousness.

* * * *

For three nights after that Renfield behaves in the same manner; he is violent during the day but then quiet from moonrise to sunrise. It almost seems as if there is some influence that comes and goes, and you begin to wonder whether under that same influence he might try to escape again.

If you want to put your theory to the test, by setting sane wits against mad ones, turn to **392**. If you would prefer not to risk it, turn to **423**.

373

With lightning-fast reactions, the shape-changers launch themselves at you. The three monsters knock you to the floor, latching lamprey-mouths onto your wrists and neck. Their teeth puncture your flesh, and you feel the very lifeblood being drawn from your veins.

Roll one die and add 3; deduct this many *Endurance* points. (Alternatively, pick a card and deduct its face value from your *Endurance* score, unless it is 10 or a picture card, in which case deduct 9 points from your *Endurance* score.)

If you are still alive after being the victim of the fiends' feeding frenzy, turn to **618**.

374

Several moths are trying to crawl up your nose and as you open your mouth to give an involuntary cry of horror, several more scuttle between your lips. And all the time you can hear nothing but the amplified buzzing flutter of their wings in your ears.

Add 1 point to your *Terror* score and then turn to **224**.

375

Sweat beading your brow, the goblet suddenly comes free of the altar, as if whatever esoteric spell holding it in place has been broken.

But as you raise the cup to your lips, the snake statue is suddenly stone no more and the serpent goes to bite you.

Take an Agility test. If you pass the test, turn to **430**, but if you fail the test, turn to **402**.

376

The Barghest is a well-known apparition in Whitby and indeed throughout Yorkshire. It is a huge black hellhound with glowing eyes that stalks the streets of the town by night.

"'Tis said that if ye hear the howl of the Barghest, then ye not long for this life!" Mr Swales pronounces, a gleam in his old eyes.

Tick off the code word *Barghest* and then turn to **436**.

377

While it is easy for you to dominate the weaker-willed Renfield, you have not learnt the finesse needed not to overwhelm a victim of your hypnotic powers, since you have never needed to before.

The psychic link forms a conduit between your two minds, and while you plant your instructions inside his head, he sees you for what you really are for the first time, witnessing, as if first-hand, the atrocities you have committed to keep yourself alive throughout the centuries.

In that moment his mind breaks, and while you are still focused on imposing your will upon the wretched soul, he takes up a letter opener from the table and drives it through your heart, demonstrating the kind of strength that is only possessed by the insane.

In that moment you appreciate that you have doomed yourself, and then relief washes over you as you realise that the sentence of eternity has been overturned. Your mortal remains crumble to dust and you are allowed to die properly at last, as Renfield retreats to a corner, sobbing like a baby, and takes a penknife to his own throat.

Your adventure, like your undying existence, is over.

THE END

378

Wrack your brains as you might, you cannot think of anything else that might be of use to the Professor in his investigations.

Turn to **457**.

379

Your blade shears through the vampire's throat. A look of horror twisting his face, Dracula staggers away from you, clutching at the wound, as blood pumps between his clawing fingers.

Then suddenly Quincey Morris is there, and with a shout of rage and effort, he plunges his great Bowie knife into the monster's heart.

Before your very eyes, and almost in the drawing of a breath, the vampire's entire body crumbles into grave dust – first the flesh and then the skeleton beneath – which disperses on the wind, and in a moment is gone.

Turn to **75**.

380

The wolves and the gypsies have flown, other than those whose corpses litter the ground all around you, while Castle Dracula is nothing more than a grim silhouette against the darkening sky.

But then there comes a terrible convulsion of the earth that sends your party falling to their knees. At the same moment, with a roar that seems to shake the very heavens, the whole castle and even the crag upon which it stands seem to rise into the air and scatter into fragments, while a mighty cloud of black and yellow smoke blasts upwards from the sundered ground. When the smoke clears, nothing of Dracula's ghost-haunted lair remains.

After the cataclysmic destruction of the castle, an eerie stillness falls like a funeral pall over the mountains, as the thunder-clap of the castle's destruction rolls away over the valleys and chasms of the Carpathians.

While the rest of you get to your feet, Quincey Morris remains on the ground, leaning on one elbow, a hand pressed to his side, and you can see the blood still gushing through his fingers. You go over to him – as does Dr Seward, Lord Godalming, Professor Van Helsing, and your dear Mina – and kneel behind him, laying the wounded man's head against your shoulder.

With a feeble sigh of effort, he takes Mina's hand in his, and seeing the anguish of her heart in her face, he smiles and says, "I am only too happy to have been of any service! Oh, God!" he cries suddenly, struggling into a sitting position and pointing at your wife. "It was worth dying for this. Look!"

Mina's face suddenly seems bathed in a rosy light and, as with one impulse, the other gentlemen sink to their knees. A deep and earnest "Amen" breaks from the lips of everyone as, following Quincey's pointing finger, your eyes rest upon the unblemished skin of your wife's forehead.

"Now God be thanked that all has not been in vain!" the Texan gasps. "See! The snow is not more stainless than her forehead! The curse has passed away!"

And to your bitter grief, but with a smile on his lips, Quincey dies, a gallant gentleman to the end.

Turn to **1000**.

381

Recovering himself, Professor Van Helsing gets to his feet and, his silvered blade suddenly in his hand, he thrusts it into the maddened doctor's chest.

Callistratus lets out a high-pitched scream and, before your very eyes, his skin starts to melt, blood pouring from the exposed musculature beneath as his flesh dissolves.

Take a Terror test. If you pass the test, turn to **321**. If you fail the test, turn to **351**.

382

The month marches on, each sunset bringing you closer to the day that has been designated as your dying day.

And then one day, as you wait within your chambers, a despairing feeling growing over you, you hear in the distance a gypsy song, sung by merry voices, coming from far off but drawing closer, and accompanied by the rolling of heavy wheels and the cracking of whips. The Szgany have returned.

Turn to **607**.

383

Peering out of your compartment window, you see a figure running along the edge of the track, only to be enveloped by the swirling snowstorm.

You don't see much point in following Alucard; you are a thousand feet up in the Tyrols after all. Where's he going to go? He'll freeze to death before he can reach the next station on foot.

Arthur goes to speak to the guard and the Orient Express is soon on its way again.

Add 2 to the *Blood* score and turn to **257**.

384

JONATHAN HARKER'S JOURNAL

3 May

Left Munich at 8.35 p.m. on 1st May, arriving at Vienna early next morning. The impression I had was that we were leaving the West and entering the East. We left in pretty good time, and came after nightfall to Klausenburgh...

It is on the dark side of twilight when you finally reach your destination, Bistritz. Being practically on the frontier – for the Borgo Pass leads from it into Bukovina – it has suffered a very stormy existence, and it certainly shows the marks of the fires that ravaged the town fifty years ago.

Following the directions Count Dracula relayed to your office before you left England – following Renfield's return and the poor man's descent into madness – you make your way to the Golden Krone Hotel, a thoroughly old-fashioned place where the Count has arranged lodgings for you.

You are greeted by a cheery-looking elderly woman, wearing the usual peasant dress. She bows, and says, "The Herr Englishman?"

"Yes," you confirm, "Jonathan Harker."

The old woman smiles and gives some message to an equally elderly gentleman in white shirtsleeves, who had followed her to the door. He disappears, but returns a moment later with a letter, which he passes to you:

My Friend –

Welcome to the Carpathians. I am anxiously expecting you. Sleep well tonight. At three tomorrow the diligence will start for Bukovina; a place on it is kept for you. At the Borgo Pass my carriage will await you and bring you to me.

I trust that you will enjoy your stay in my beautiful land.

Your friend,

DRACULA

Turn to **407**.

385

LOG OF THE 'DEMETER'

Varna to Whitby

6 July ~ *We finished taking in cargo, silver sand and boxes of earth. At noon set sail. East wind, fresh. Crew, five hands . . . two mates, cook, and myself (captain).*

11 July ~ *At dawn entered Bosphorus. Boarded by Turkish customs officers. Backsheesh. All correct. Under way at 4 p.m.*

12 July ~ *Through Dardanelles. More Customs officers and flagboat of guarding squadron. Backsheesh again. Work of officers thorough, but quick. Want us off soon. At dark passed into Archipelago.*

13 July ~ *Passed Cape Matapan. Crew dissatisfied about something. Seemed scared, but would not speak out.*

14 July ~ *Was somewhat anxious about crew. Men all steady fellows, who sailed with me before. Mate could not make out what was wrong; they only told him there was something, and crossed themselves. Mate lost temper with one of them that day and struck him. Expected fierce quarrel, but all was quiet.*

Turn to **453**.

386

As you try to elbow the gypsies out of the way, one of them delivers a punch to your stomach that throws you backwards into the snow.

Lose 2 *Endurance* points and, if you are still alive, turn to **733**.

387

The Professor takes off his own coat and rolls up his shirt sleeve.

Again the operation. Again the application of the narcotic. Again some return of colour to Lucy's chalky cheeks, and the regular breathing of healthy sleep.

After he has rested, Van Helsing seeks out Mrs Westenra to tell her that she must not remove anything from Lucy's room without consulting him first.

Turn to **487**.

388

Catching sight of you, the sentries cross their halberds, barring the way to you.

"Halt! Who goes there?" one of them demands.

How will you respond? Will you ask to see the Sultan (turn to **360**), or prepare to defend yourself (turn to **325**)?

389

Arthur finishes off his opponent too and in no time at all, both cart-men are lying dead in the yard behind the house. You cannot imagine what ties of loyalty they owe the Count that they would willingly sacrifice themselves to save him. The only reason you can think of is that they were somehow in his thrall.

Turn to **409**.

390

Continue your battle with all five of the desperate men but note that you now have the initiative.

At any time during the battle, if you wish, you may deduct 4 *Blood* points to eliminate one of the Vampire-Hunters; however, you may only do so once.

If you slay all the Vampire-Hunters, gain 8 *Blood* points and turn to **800**. However, if you lose the battle, turn to **605**.

391

"I must go to the station to meet Van Helsing," you tell Mrs Harker. "I think it would be best if you awaited your husband's return in the rooms I have provided for you both."

* * *

When the Professor alights from the train carriage onto the platform at Purfleet station, it is with the eager nimbleness of a schoolboy.

"Ah, John, my friend, how goes all? Well?" he asks, rushing up to you. "I have been busy and have settled all my affairs in Amsterdam, so I may stay here for as long as is necessary. Is Madam Mina with you? And her husband?"

As you drive to the house, you tell him of all that has passed, and of how Mrs Harker has, at her own suggestion, transcribed all of the diaries and created a chronicle of the whole sorry debacle.

"Ah, that wonderful Madam Mina!" he exclaims. "She has a brain that a man should have were he much gifted, and a woman's heart. The good Lord fashioned her for a purpose, believe me."

Turn to **592**.

392

Renfield escaped before without anybody else's help, but tonight it shall be an entirely different matter.

You give orders to the night attendant merely to shut him in the padded room. And sure enough, in the middle of the night, you are called to the ward again, for your patient has once more escaped. This time, Renfield waited until an attendant was entering the room to inspect it, then dashed out past him and flew down the passage.

You send word for the attendants to follow and set off once more for the grounds of the deserted house, convinced that is where you will you find him.

And sure enough, you find him pressed against the old chapel door of Carfax House. When he sees you, he becomes furious and were it not for the fact that the attendants seize him in time, you are sure he would have tried to kill you. (Add 1 point to your *Terror* score.)

But then he suddenly grows calm. Catching Renfield's eye you follow it, and see a large bat, flapping its silent and ghostly way to the west across the moonlit sky.

Bats usually wheel about, but this one goes straight on, as if it knows where it is bound, or has some intention of its own.

Your patient grows calmer with every passing second and presently says, "You needn't tie me. I shall go quietly."

And, true to his word, he returns with you to the asylum without giving you any trouble. But you can't help feeling that there is something ominous in his calm, and you certainly shall not forget this night.

Tick off the code word *Desmodontinae* and turn to **423**.

393

The concoction smells terrible, but you don't let that put you off. Holding your nose and taking a deep breath, you gulp it down in one go.

It does not take long for the potion to take effect and you vomit the contents of your stomach into the river from the side of the wharf.

But then that's hardly surprising, seeing as how the potion's active ingredient is of the *aconitum* genus of plants, also known as 'Monkshood', or 'The Queen of Poisons'.

You are left with a painful burning sensation in your abdomen, and your face and mouth tingle with numbness.

Lose 4 *Endurance* points and for the duration of the next battle you have to fight, reduce your *Combat Rating* by 1 point. However, if you have the code words *Lycanthropy* or *Lyssavirus* ticked off, you may now deselect them.

If you are still alive, strike the Tincture of Wolfsbane from your Equipment Box and then turn to **413**.

394

In an empty room in the asylum, Arthur teaches you how to hold a sword correctly, how to lunge, how to parry, and how to riposte. But how receptive a pupil are you?

Roll one die and then divide the number rolled by 2, rounding fractions up. Add this many points to your *Combat* score. (Alternatively, pick a card: if it is an Ace, add 1 point to your *Combat* score; if it is a 2, add 2 points to your *Combat* score; if it is anything else, add 3 points to your *Combat* score.)

Turn to **449**.

395

The gypsy dead, you turn your attention to the crate of earth. Pushing your blade under the lid, you set about prising it open.

"Let me help you with that," comes a familiar Texan drawl. Quincey is back on his feet, even though he is clutching bloody fingers to his left side. And so, the two of you set about opening the portentous box.

Seeing themselves covered by the guns of your fellow Vampire-Hunters, and entirely at their mercy, the gypsies prostrate themselves on the ground and offer no further resistance.

Under the efforts of both of you, the lid begins to yield at last; the nails come free with a sharp screeching sound, and you throw the box open.

And there is the Count, lying within the box upon the earth, some of the mud scattered over him. His face is deathly pale, like a waxen image.

But as you raise your weapon to finish him, his eye-lids flick open. Catching sight of the sinking sun, the look of hate within his blazing blood-red eyes turns to triumph, and his features take on a demonic leer that is painted crimson by the sunset.

Take a Terror test, adding 1 to the dice roll if you have the code word *Borzalom* ticked off. If you pass the test, turn to **19**. If you fail the test, turn to **39**.

396

You drive at once to Hillingham and, keeping your cab at the gate, head up the avenue alone. As you do so, you become aware of something moving through the rhododendron bushes that line the avenue to your right.

Suddenly, a great, grey wolf emerges from the shrubbery, while from over the hedge flies a huge bat.

If you have the code word *Eptesicus* ticked off, turn to **751**. If not, turn to **781**.

397

Giving a shrill cry, you fly off again into the night, the wolf following you. However, the doctor is not so ready to let bygones be bygones and, taking a pistol from his jacket pocket, takes a shot. It hits.

(Deduct 4 *Endurance* points and 3 *Blood* points.)

If you are still alive, turn to **221**.

398

As you share your secrets regarding those morbid summer months in Whitby, you can barely believe the tales you are telling yourself. But nonetheless, the Professor listens attentively to everything you have to say.

"Oh, but I am grateful to you, you so clever woman," he says when you are finished, clasping your hands in his. "There are darknesses in life, and there are lights. You are one of the lights."

Deduct 1 *Blood* point and turn to **457**.

399

You make contact with the door and it bangs open, to reveal a yawning gulf beyond. Wherever the door led to once upon a time, tumbled into the abyss long ago, as the castle fell into ruin over the course of the unforgiving centuries.

Take an Agility test. If you pass the test, turn to **459**, but if you fail the test, turn to **429**.

400

You have won, and it is a prize more valuable than all the gold in the coffers of Castle Dracula! You have destroyed those who were ranged against you, determined to thwart your plans of conquest. Now nothing and no one has the power to stop you.

Soon London will be yours, and then England will fall beneath the iron fist of the rule of the one once known as Prince Vlad Tepes – Vlad the Impaler. By the time anyone realises what is going on, it will be too late to do anything about it.

Today the British Empire. Tomorrow the world!

THE END

401

You try the door in the eastern wall of the chamber, opposite your bedroom, but it is firmly locked. There is no way you are going to be able to open it.

You are going to have to try another door, but will it be the door to the north (turn to **431**), or the door to the south (turn to **451**)?

402

Moving faster than your eye can follow, the snake sinks its fangs into your hand and injects its venom into your bloodstream.

Roll one die and add 1 to the number rolled; deduct this many points from your *Endurance* score. (Alternatively, pick a card and deduct that many *Endurance* points, unless it is greater than 7 or a picture card, in which case deduct 7 *Endurance* points.)

If you are still alive, turn to **430**.

403

Standing your ground, your heart thumping against the bony cage that contains it, you prepare to face the horrors of Castle Dracula.

If you want to use *The Pen is Mightier* special ability, cross off one use and turn to **618**. If not, turn to **344**.

404

Entering one room you are taken aback to see what looks like a body lying on the bed, covered by a dirty sheet.

Do you want to approach the bed and pull back the sheet (turn to **343**), or would you prefer to leave the room, and the second floor, and continue your search elsewhere (turn to **273**)?

405

"Yes, master," Renfield says, staring at you dumbly, his eyes pits of despair, for in the depths of his soul he knows what you have become over the centuries and that he is powerless to resist your will.

With the necessary paperwork now bearing your signature, and your instructions implanted within his mind, you send the solicitor on his way, your Szgany coachman, Medve, carrying him as far as the end of the Borgo Pass, where he joins the Bistritz stage and embarks upon his journey home.

* * * *

You do not hear anything else from England until February the following year, when Mr Hawkins writes to you again. Apologising for the lack of correspondence, he explains that upon his return to Exeter, Mr Renfield lost his mind – murdering his family on Christmas Day – and ended up being incarcerated within an asylum for the clinically insane. The madman had consigned the documents you had signed to the sea, whilst crossing the English Channel by steamship.

Hawkins apologises most profusely for this unfortunate state of affairs but finishes by saying that he has a new employee – a young man who has recently qualified as a solicitor – who is keen to make his mark and prove his worth to Messrs Hawkins, Oldman & Lee. If you are willing, Hawkins will send him to Transylvania to conduct affairs on his behalf.

You reply by letter, stating that you would like that very much indeed, and wishing Mr Renfield a speedy recovery, knowing full well what caused the poor man's mind to fracture.

Clearly your influence over him was too great. You will have to try a different approach with his replacement.

Turn to **440**.

406

The shape-changers lie dead at your feet. In death, the bodies of the Werewolves begin to lose their lupine shape until they look like ordinary men and women, their naked bodies clothed in blood, the horrific injuries they suffered at your hands plain to see in the wan moonlight.

Add one use of *The Pen is Mightier* special ability to your Adventure Sheet, deduct 1 *Blood* point, and then turn to **619**.

407

Your bed is comfortable, and the town is quiet after sundown, but you still do not sleep well, for your dreams are haunted by wolves and worse.

How many of the following code words do you have ticked off? *Superstition, Suicide, Succubus, Spectre.*

Four?	Turn to **468**.
Two or three?	Turn to **447**.
Fewer than two?	Turn to **498**.

408

Professor Van Helsing's words fade into the background as your subconscious seeks to tell you something, and you find your attention wandering to the window. The curtains have not yet been drawn, and you can see something there, a dark shape scratching at the glass, clinging to the windowsill.

"There's something at the window!" you cry, interrupting the Professor, but then it is gone.

Quincey Morris jumps to his feet and rushes out of the room, while Arthur flies to the window and throws up the sash.

From outside the house comes the sound of a pistol shot, and a moment later you hear Quincey call to the rest of you, still in the study: "It was a bat, and a big brute too!"

"Did you hit it?" asks Van Helsing.

"I don't know," comes Quincey's reply, "but I fancy not. It flew away into the wood."

Deduct 1 *Blood* point and turn to **427**.

409

There is no time to lose! If the Count is having the remaining boxes of earth moved – no doubt to stop you and your fellow Vampire-Hunters from destroying them – you had better join Van Helsing at the property in Piccadilly as fast as you can.

If the *Blood* score is equal to or greater than 8, turn to **439**. If it is lower than 8, turn to **876**.

410

Count Dracula may have begun to make you like him, when he forced you to drink his blood, but you are not his creature yet. Resisting the vampire's compelling summons, you swear to God you will finish him yourself!

However, between you and the box stands a warrior of the Szgany, a brute with the build and stature of a bear rather than that of a man. Nonetheless, you tighten your grip on your sabre and pistol and prepare to put him down, before he can do the same to you.

Turn to **505**.

411

You are the first one back on your feet and make your way after Alucard at a run. Coming to the end of your carriage, you find a door to the outside world open and the blizzard blowing in. Steeling yourself against the cold, you head outside, followed by your fellow Vampire-Hunters.

To your right rises the icy face of the mountain pass. To your left, on the other side of the track, a sheer cliff drops away to the snow-buried rocks below.

Ahead of you, you can just make out a black shape heading back along the train into the whirling snow, and you set off after it.

Suddenly shots are fired, the echo of them ricocheting from the wall of black rock and grey ice. And then you hear the dread rumble of an imminent avalanche.

Giving up on your pursuit of Alucard, you turn and race back towards the train, your boots crunching on the snow and ballast lying between the tracks.

Take an Endurance test. If you pass the test, turn to **482**, but if you fail the test, turn to **443**.

412

The effort of scaling the castle wall takes a great toll on your body, a body that has suffered so many torments since you became a prisoner of Castle Dracula, and you no longer have the strength you need to save yourself.

Clinging to the wall like a limpet, your arms start to shake as your weary muscles become possessed by a palsy, and you can hold on no longer. At the last you give in freely to the exhaustion and let go, knowing that you can climb no further, and yet at the same time not wanting the mistresses of the castle to find you still there when night falls. And so, you consign your body to the abyss.

Your adventure is over.

THE END

413

Within thirty minutes you are on your way, travelling by steam-launch along the Sereth River.

The boat – the *Fantomă* – is large and you were fortunate that Arthur's readily-given money was able to secure you passage on board, although you are not the only ones the captain is taking upstream.

If you have the code word *Orvos* ticked off, turn to **11**. If not, turn to **788**.

414

The riot is finally quelled by Barlow, Straker, and the other attendants. With the inmates back in their cells – Renfield included – it is gone midnight before you are able to retire to your bed yourself.

Turn to **941**.

415

Jonathan and Quincey heave the great box of earth from the back of the cart, letting it drop onto the ground, lest the gypsies try to ride off with it again, and then set about prising it open.

Seeing themselves covered by the guns of your fellow Vampire-Hunters, and entirely at their mercy, the gypsies prostrate themselves on the ground and offer no further resistance.

Thanks to the efforts of both men, the lid of the box yields at last; the nails come free with a sharp screeching sound, and the top of the box is thrown back.

You gasp, upon seeing the Count, lying within the box of earth, some of the mouldering soil scattered over him. His face is deathly pale, like a waxen image.

But as Jonathan and your Texan friend bring their weapons to bear to finish the vampire, suddenly the monster's eyes flick open, and he glares at them with a horrible, vindictive look.

Catching sight of the sinking sun, the look of hate within his blazing blood-red eyes turns to triumph and his features take on a demonic leer.

Fast as a striking snake, Dracula lashes out and Quincey falls, while Jonathan is thrown fifteen feet through the air to land hard in the snow. Dr Seward and the Professor then rush forward but before they can lay a finger on the vampire, they are cast back as Dracula bends the whirling wind to his will, hurling them to the ground as well.

You are the only one of the Vampire-Hunters left standing. And then you hear his voice speaking inside your head: *Come to me, Mina. Join me. Be one with me.*

Without even realising what you are doing, you move towards him as if drawn by some magnetic force.

The power of Dracula is irresistible – but resist you must!

Take a Terror test, subtracting 2 from the dice roll if you are in possession of the Seal of Solomon. If you pass the test, turn to **19**. If you fail the test, turn to **773**.

416

A Bogle is a troublesome, shape-shifting goblin, a notorious bugbear of local legend that traditionally haunts crossroads in out of the way places.

Turn to **436**.

417

Again the operation. Again the application of the narcotic. Again some return of colour to Lucy's chalky cheeks, and the regular breathing of healthy sleep.

(Deduct half your remaining *Endurance* points, rounding fractions down.)

But this time, as your blood flows from your veins into Lucy's, you feel as if something is transferred from her into you. And you see…

A great bat, its broad wings beating against the window, moonlight limning its elongated fangs…

You feel as if you are seeing something that Lucy saw first.

(Add 2 points to your *ESP* score.)

How many of the following code words do you have ticked off? *Transfusion, Haemorrhage.*

None?	Turn to **487**.
One?	Turn to **444**.
Two?	Turn to **463**.

418

And so, you share with the Professor every strange thing that occurred while you were staying in Whitby with Lucy and Mrs Westenra.

Hearing yourself tell another human being what happened, you would barely be able to believe such tall tales yourself, if it were not for the fact that you witnessed such terrible things first-hand.

When you are done, Van Helsing takes your hands in his and, his bushy eyebrows beetling, says, "Oh, Madam Mina, how can I express what I owe you? I am grateful to you, you so clever woman, and if ever Abraham Van Helsing can do anything for you or yours, I trust you will let me know."

Deduct 2 *Blood* points and turn to **457**.

419

Before you can burst free of your coffin and join the fray, the box is tipped off the back of the cart and crashes onto the ground, where it breaks open.

As you struggle free of the splintered crate, you are only dimly aware of the bodies of wolves and gypsies littering the ground all around you. Your more pressing concern is the mob of Vampire-Hunters bearing down on you with swords and crucifixes in hand.

You must fight the Vampire-Hunters all at the same time, and while you have the initiative in this battle, you must deduct 2 points when calculating your *Combat Rating*, due to the proliferation of crucifixes, holy wafers and other charms they have adorned themselves with.

	COMBAT	ENDURANCE
JONATHAN HARKER	10	11
ARTHUR HOLMWOOD	8	9
QUINCEY MORRIS	9	9
DOCTOR SEWARD	9	10
PROFESSOR VAN HELSING	8	8

If you wish, at any time during the battle, you may deduct 4 *Blood* points to eliminate one of the Vampire-Hunters; however, you may only do so once.

If you slaughter all of those who have raced the setting sun to slay you, gain 6 *Blood* points and turn to **666**. But if you lose the battle, turn to **605**.

420

How many protective talismans can you bring to bear against the vampire?

Consult the list below to see how many points your blessed artefacts add up to:

Golden Crucifix	+1 point
Good Luck Tokens	+1 point
Silver Crucifix	+2 points
Sacred Wafer	+2 points
Garlic Garland	+1 point
Holy Bible	+2 points
Seal of Solomon	+2 points
Knight's Shield	+1 point

Once you have calculated your points total, roll two dice; if the number rolled is equal to or less than your total, turn to **510**, but if the number rolled is greater than your points total, turn to **350**.

Alternatively, pick a card, noting that picture cards are worth 11 and an Ace is worth 12; if the value of the card is equal to or less than your total, turn to **510**; if the value of the card picked is greater than your score, turn to **350**.

421

Outmanoeuvring the Szgany, you pull yourself up onto the cart, as your companions engage the gypsies in battle. Before you is the last of the great wooden boxes containing the cursed earth of Dracula's homeland, and the vampiric Count cocooned within it.

Pulling free the ropes holding it in place and putting your shoulder behind it, you give the crate a shove, hoping to send it toppling to the ground.

Take an Endurance test. If you pass the test, turn to **461**, but if you fail the test, turn to **481**.

422

Quincey takes you out into the garden, where he soon has you shooting at flowerpots he has placed on a low wall. The revolver he gives you to use has a powerful kick, and the report of it firing makes you start, but you gradually become more used to it.

Roll one die and then divide the number rolled by 2, rounding fractions up. Add this many points to your *Combat* score. (Alternatively, pick a card: if it is an Ace, add 1 point to your *Combat* score; if it is a 2, add 2 points to your *Combat* score; if it is anything else, add 3 points to your *Combat* score.)

Record the Revolver in the Equipment Box on your Adventure Sheet and turn to **449**.

423

Some days later, you receive news of your beloved Lucy, from your friend, and her betrothed, the Hon. Arthur Holmwood, and your preoccupation with Renfield is forgotten in an instant.

Turn to **691**.

424

After dinner, you engage in posting up your books, a duty, which, through the press of other work and your many visits to Lucy, has fallen woefully into arrears.

It is as you are occupied in this task that someone suddenly bursts into your study. Turning, you are surprised to see Mr Renfield making straight for you, a dinner knife in his hand.

Take an Agility test. If you pass the test, turn to **573**, but if you fail the test, turn to **604**.

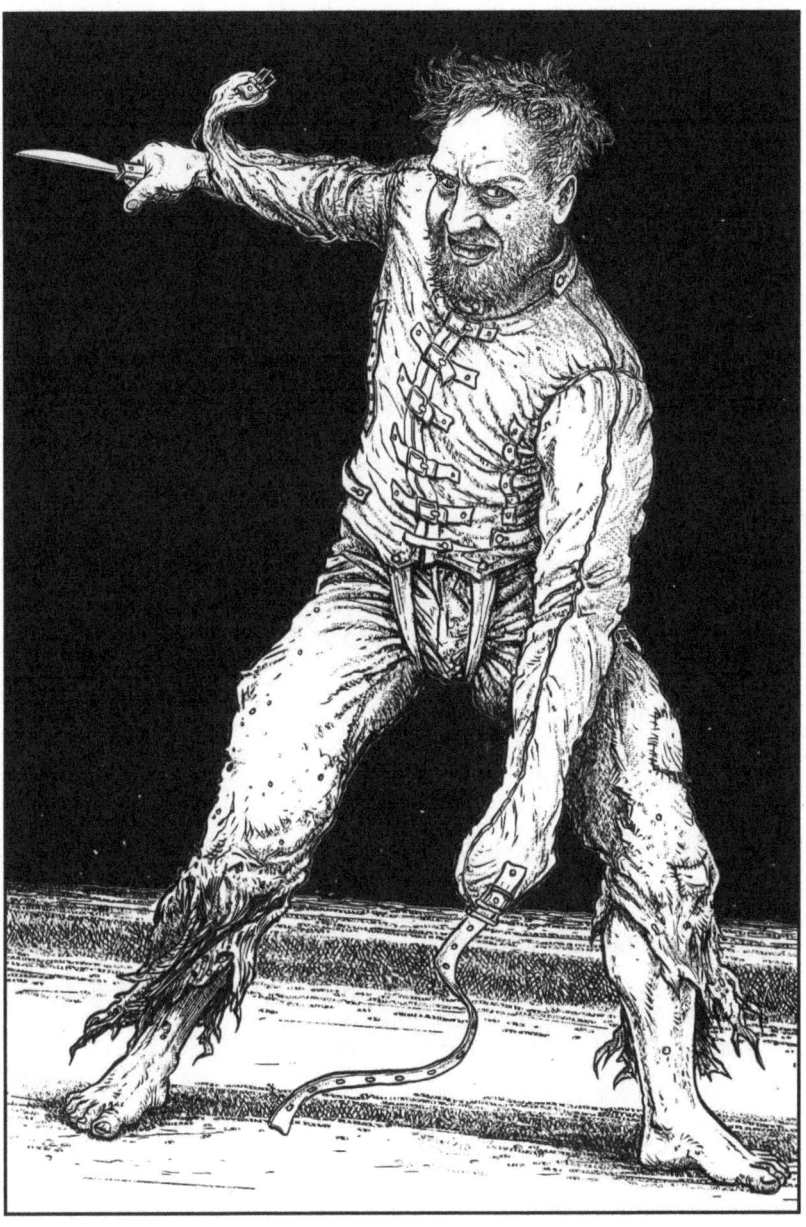

425

Leaving the chapel, you fly over the wall that separates the grounds of Carfax House from the adjoining property, which, it turns out, is an insane asylum.

You sense the presence of Lucy's friend Mina within and swear, there and then, to have your revenge on those who infiltrated the chapel – and in doing so put your plans of conquest in jeopardy – by making her your creature.

However, you will not be able to enter Carfax Asylum without being invited in, and you know that Mina's mind is too strong for her to ever offer you such an invitation.

But all is not lost, for there is another incarcerated within, who is known to you, and who you already know you will be able to influence to gain access.

You approach the window of a particular cell on the ground floor of the house, your physical body becoming incorporeal mist. A familiar face comes to the window, eyes and mouth open in wonder.

"Master?" Renfield gasps. His expression of disbelief becomes one of joy. "You came back to me, just as you promised you would."

"Yes, Renfield, I am here. Now invite me in."

"Have you brought me more lives to consume, like you sent me the flies? Great big fat ones with steel and sapphire on their wings; and big moths, in the night, with skull and crossbones on their backs?"

"Yes," you reply, your sharp white teeth glinting in the moonlight, "and not merely buzzing flies, and moths. Rats too! Hundreds, thousands, millions of them – and every one a life. And dogs to eat them, and cats too. All lives! All red blood, with years of life in it!"

Behind you, a dark mass spreads over the lawns of the asylum, as a great horde of rats answers your subconscious summons, their eyes blazing red like yours in the darkness.

"All these lives will I give you – aye, and many more besides, through countless ages – if you will but invite me in.

Opening the sash, Renfield says, "Enter, my Lord and Master! "

The sash is only open an inch, but you enter the lunatic's cell as easily as the light of the moon can enter through the tiniest crack.

"Come in, come in! I told Doctor Seward that you would come, but I do not think he believed me. And Madam Mina."

You pause on your way to the cell door. Suddenly everything makes sense. Renfield has given you away to Lucy's personal physician, and now you find her friend staying at his hospital. This is no coincidence. The lunatic is ultimately responsible for what you witnessed at Carfax House chapel this night.

In your rage, you launch yourself at the wretch. But Renfield has the strength of a madman and is not as weak as you might have thought. (In this battle, you have the initiative.)

RENFIELD   COMBAT 8   ENDURANCE 10

After 7 Combat Rounds, or as soon as you reduce Renfield's *Endurance* score to 4 points or fewer, whichever is sooner, turn to **885** at once. Alternatively, you may spend 3 *Blood* points and turn to **885** straightaway.

426

Are you carrying a Silver Crucifix? If so, turn to **448**. If not, turn to **472**.

427

"There is no time to lose!" urges the Professor. "We must find those boxes, and if we encounter our enemy, we must kill this monster in his lair. But if he eludes us, we must nonetheless sterilise the earth they contain, so that he can never again seek shelter within them. And if any have been removed, we must trace their whereabouts."

If you wish to continue the story as Jonathan Harker, turn to **4**. If you want to continue as Mina Harker, turn to **229**. And if you want to continue the adventure as Dr John Seward, turn to **446**.

428

The doctor goes into a berserk rage, and it is all you can do to fend off his flailing fists. (In this battle, Dr Callistratus has the initiative.)

DOCTOR CALLISTRATUS   COMBAT 9   ENDURANCE 8

If you are still alive after 4 Combat Rounds, or you reduce your opponent's *Endurance* score to 4 points or fewer, whichever is sooner, turn to **381**.

429

Momentum carries you over the threshold and you plunge into the abyss. You fall a thousand feet before you hit the bottom, your body smashed to pieces on the water-swept boulders of a spring river in spate.

Your imprisonment and your adventure, like your life, is over.

THE END

430

You pull your hand out of the way sharply. And then the snake is stone again, an alabaster serpent wrapped around a wretched human form, and you wonder if what you thought you saw was merely an illusion conjured by the flickering torchlight and your own exhausted mind.

"Drink!" the priestess exhorts you, her eyes glittering like rubies in the flame-lit darkness. They are the same colour as the claret-red liquid contained within the goblet.

Do you want to drink from the cup (turn to **467**), or will you hurl it to the ground (turn to **310**)?

431

The door opens and, finding yourself in a library, you set about scouring the shelves. You are delighted, if not slightly surprised, to discover the archive contains a vast number of English books – whole shelves full of them, in fact – as well as bound volumes of magazines and newspapers, although you notice that none of them are particularly recent.

The books are varied in nature – history, geography, politics, political economy, botany, geology, law – but all relate to England and English life.

Do you want to continue to examine the English books contained within the Count's library (turn to **471**), or would you prefer to look for something pertaining to the region of Transylvania and its customs (turn to **491**)?

432

LOG OF THE 'DEMETER'

30 July – Last night. Rejoiced we are nearing England. Weather fine, all sails set. Retired worn out; slept soundly; awaked by mate telling me that both man of watch and steersman missing. Only self and mate and two hands left to work ship.

1 August – Two days of fog, and not a sail sighted. Had hoped when in the English Channel to be able to signal for help or get in somewhere. Not having power to work sails, have to run before wind. Dare not lower, as could not raise them again. We seem to be drifting to some terrible doom. Mate now more demoralised than either of men. His stronger nature seems to have worked inwardly against himself. Men are beyond fear, working stolidly and patiently, with minds made up to worst. They are Russian, he Romanian.

If your *Suspicion* score is 9 points or higher, turn to **162**. If your *Suspicion* score is 8 points or lower, turn to **479**.

433

The monsters recoil in horror when they realise you intend to defend yourself using the ornate Dragon Sword.

"Come, sisters," declares the bat-winged harpy, with you hearing her archaic ungodly tongue as English inside your head, "quickly, let us put the animal down, and then we can drain his body of every last drop of blood!"

In this battle you have the initiative, but you must fight the Weird Sisters two at a time.

	COMBAT	ENDURANCE
SUCCUBUS	7	8
LAMIA	9	10
SIREN	8	9

If you are still alive after five Combat Rounds, or as soon as you reduce the *Endurance* score of one of the fiends to 4 points or fewer, whichever is sooner, turn to **618**.

434

On the second floor you find nothing but a number of dusty bedrooms, and notice that in some the mirrors have been turned to face the wall.

If you want to spend more time conducting a thorough search of the bedrooms, turn to **404**. If you would rather look elsewhere, turn to **273**.

435

You enter the tent. Inside it is even more opulent than it is outside, adorned with silk drapes and fine Persian rugs and cushions scattered over the floor.

In the centre of the pavilion is a table, upon which lies a map. Standing around the table are the commanders of Mehmed's forces, and the Conqueror himself. As you enter the tent, he looks up. Years may have passed since you last saw each other, but you cannot hide your identity from the flint-hard stare of the man who you grew up alongside at the court of Sultan Murad the Second.

"Vlad, my brother," he addresses you, a cruel smile curling his lips. "Have you come to pay me what you owe, or are you here to assassinate me in front of my men?"

Before you can answer him, you are seized. Knowing that certain death awaits you if you stay, bringing all your warrior's strength to bear, you break free from the men holding you and run from the tent.

Turn to **580**.

436

"But take no heed, miss," Mr Swales goes on. "Such things be nowt but air-blebs. They, an' all grim signs and warnin's, all be the inventions of parsons, an' book-learnin' busybodies, an' railway touters, to scare half-wits, an' to get folks to do somethin' that they don't otherwise incline to do."

But nonetheless, all this talk of spectres and the supernatural leaves you feeling uneasy to your very core.

Add 1 point to your *Terror* score and turn to **456**.

437

Your thoughts are distracted from the howling of the wolves when you realise that there is something wrong with Arthur. He is shaking, as if terribly cold or suffering from a fever, and seems barely able to stay upright in the saddle.

He cannot continue like this. Bringing your steed alongside his, you take the other horse's reins and bring both mounts to a halt. Helping Arthur down from his horse, you lay him down at the side of the road. As you do so, the moon appears from behind a cloud, full and round, and by its light you see that he is sweating profusely, his face knotted in an expression of pain.

But then his features begin to take on a pronounced wolfish appearance.

If you have a Tincture of Wolfsbane, turn to **466**. If not, turn to **566**.

438

You tell the Professor about the wreck of the *Demeter*, and your encounter with the black dog, and share with him the wretched fate suffered by Mr Swales, the poor old man.

"Oh, Madam Mina," he says when you are done, "how can I express what I owe you? I am grateful to you, you so clever woman." Here he takes your hands in his and, his bushy eyebrows beetling, says ever so earnestly. "If ever Abraham Van Helsing can do anything for you or yours, I trust you will let me know. It will be a pleasure and delight if I may serve you as a friend. There are darknesses in life, and there are lights. You are one of the lights."

Deduct 3 *Blood* points, gain one additional use of *The Pen is Mightier* special ability, and then turn to **457**.

439

As you set off again – intending to hail a cab to carry you to Piccadilly – you are startled by the sound of barking. Two large dogs – pit bulls, or so you believe – dash out from the shaded entrance to an alley. Seeing you and Arthur, they race towards you, growling and snarling, foam flying from their flapping lips.

If you want to use *The Pen is Mightier* special ability now, turn to **460**. If not, turn to **477**.

440

April comes, and with it the long-awaited thaw, although there are parts of the Carpathians that will keep their snow and ice all year long.

And then, one night, you are summoned by the Weird Sisters, to their chamber.

* * * *

Some hundred years after your first death, three seeresses found their way to your castle home, seeking to escape persecution by the authorities, as Europe became the victim of a hysterical plague of witch-hunts. In return for your protection, they offered you whatever you wanted, and you took it all. After all, eternity is a long time to be without female companionship.

But once you had shared your gift with them, their powers grew, until your relationship with them became less like that of a lord and his mistresses and more like an uneasy alliance, with you keeping to your part of the castle while they claimed the east wing as their own.

But when they deign to put out their siren-call to you, you know that it must be a matter of great importance to all of you...

* * * *

As you enter their opulently-adorned chamber, the three vampyre women surround you. Two are dark, with high aquiline noses and great dark, piercing eyes, that glow red like hot coals – Lamia and Melusina – while the other, Lilith, is fair, with great masses of golden hair and eyes like pale sapphires. Their brilliant white teeth shine like pearls against the ruby of their voluptuous lips as they smile lasciviously at you.

"We have a message," Lamia begins.

"A warning, from our master," Melusina continues.

"*I* am your master!" you snarl at them.

"Our true master," Lilith bites back. "And yours."

"Then tell me, what is this message?"

Roll one die (or pick a card). If the number rolled is odd (or the card is red), turn to **474**. If the number rolled is even (or the card is black), turn to **512**.

441

The two madmen are suddenly grabbed from behind, by a pair of burly attendants. It is Barlow and Straker. You have never been so pleased to see them in all the time you have been in charge of Carfax Asylum, and tell them so.

Turn to **414**.

442

As you negotiate the broken battlements of the ancient stronghold – the abyss of the gorge yawning beneath you, and the sun sinking lower and lower in the sky with startling alacrity – you round the corner of the castle only to find yourself at a dead-end.

The walled courtyard lies before you, but between you and it is a great cleft in the rock upon which the castle was raised. You have no choice but to jump for it.

Take an Agility test. If you pass the test, turn to **503**, but if you fail the test, turn to **473**.

443

Before you can reach the safety of the train, the avalanche hits. Totally exposed as you are, a wall of snow, a million tons in weight, hits you and drives you off the edge of the cliff. You are dead before you even hit the rocks a thousand feet below.

Your adventure is over.

THE END

444

The experience of giving blood again, leaves you feeling exhausted.

Deduct 1 point from your *Combat* score and turn to **487**.

445

Taking the phial of holy water from your pocket, you unstopper it and splash its contents over the vampire looming in front of you. You are so close, it is impossible to miss.

Roll one die and add 1 to the number rolled; this is the amount of damage in *Endurance* points you have caused the vampire already. (Alternatively, pick a card to determine the amount of damage, and if the card picked is 8 or above or a picture card, you have caused 7 points of damage.)

Dracula recoils from you, shrieking in agony, as the holy water eats away at his undead flesh like acid, giving you time to try something else.

How do you want to follow up your attack? Will you use:

Holy symbols and warding charms?	Turn to **420**.
The Knight's Shield (if you have it)?	Turn to **575**.
Cold steel?	Turn to **350**.
Silver bullets (if you have some)?	Turn to **892**.
The Pen is Mightier special ability (if you still can)?	Turn to **300**.

446

Arthur, Quincey Morris, Jonathan Harker, Van Helsing and yourself set about preparing for your raid on Carfax House, while Mrs Harker retires to bed, it being deemed that a nocturnal raid on a vampire's potential lair is no place for a woman.

But as you are getting ready to set out, an urgent message reaches you, via one of the attendants, that Renfield wishes to see you at once.

Knowing now that the madman seems to have some sort of psychic connection with the one you seek to destroy, it might be worth taking the time to pay him a visit. But then again, the longer you leave it before you venture into the grounds of Carfax House, the more likely your quarry is to evade your brave band.

If you agree to speak with Renfield, turn to **469**. If you feel that the task Professor Van Helsing has set you all upon is more pressing, and that now is not the time to see the lunatic, turn to **159**.

447

You are deeply disturbed by your horrid dreams and it is a feeling that remains with you after you wake.

Lose 1 *Combat* point and turn to **498**.

448

The Silver Crucifix will repel one Werewolf, causing it to take flight and flee the graveyard.

If all the Werewolves have been dealt with now, turn to **568**. If not, turn to **472**.

449

Dr Seward also prepares a laudanum-based concoction to help you sleep better. (Record the Sleeping Draught on your Adventure Sheet.)

Jonathan returns from London later that evening, and after dinner, while the men meet again in Dr Seward's study to discuss developments, you retire to bed, for you feel oh so terribly tired.

If you want to take the Sleeping Draught, turn to **478**. If you would prefer to fall asleep naturally, if you can, turn to **497**.

450

"How fortunate it is for us, Mr Harker, that you copied those plans of the house," says Van Helsing, as you unfold the map you made of the mansion. "Now which is the way to the chapel?"

You lead the way, and soon find yourself opposite a low, arched oaken door, ribbed with iron bands.

Turn to **606**.

451

Warily, feeling uneasy at the idea of going about the castle before you have asked the Count's permission, you put your hand to the door and push it open.

Suddenly, Count Dracula is there before you at the threshold.

(Add 1 point to your *Terror* score.)

"Mr Harker," he says, offering you a smile. As his lips run back over his gums, the long, sharp, canine teeth appear more pronounced. "Can I help you?"

His rank breath washes over you, causing you to recoil as a horrible feeling of nausea comes over you.

"I merely wished to explore your wonderful castle," you say weakly when you have recovered yourself, although the sense of nausea remains.

Deduct 1 point from your *Combat* score and turn to **533**.

452

You feel panic threaten to overwhelm you as the flies bombard your face, trying to get into your ears, your mouth, and up your nose, and you are aware of countless spiders now climbing up the inside of your trouser legs, no doubt intent on doing the same. And so, it is in desperation that you fight to keep the vermin off you and prevent them from biting and stinging you. (In this fight, the vermin have the initiative.)

VERMIN   COMBAT 7   ENDURANCE 8

If you manage to reduce the combined *Endurance* score of the Vermin to zero, add 1 more point to your *Terror* score and turn to **232**.

453

You have been at sea for ten days, remaining hidden in the cargo hold of the Russian schooner, the *Demeter*, having left Castle Dracula one day shy of a week before that.

But the need to feed is becoming too strong for you to suppress it any longer. And besides, you will need to replenish yourself for all that needs to be done when you reach England. And so, that night, you make yourself like smoke and escape the confines of your earth-filled box, in search of prey.

It is raining, and you find one of the crew enjoying a surreptitious smoke in the shelter of a lifeboat. The steady drumming of his heartbeat is loud in your ears.

Unable to contain yourself any longer, you make yourself corporeal again and spring at the man, armed with nothing more than fingers that have become talons, viciously sharp teeth, and an insatiable thirst for blood.

The deckhand springs to his feet and grabs the object closest to him, that he can use to defend himself – an old whaling harpoon. (In this battle, you have the initiative.)

DECKHAND   COMBAT 7   ENDURANCE 8

If you wish, you may spend 3 *Blood* points to automatically win this battle (turn to **475**).

If not, conduct the battle as normal and, if you defeat the deckhand, gain 2 *Blood* points and then turn to **475**.

454

You pick up the cloth bag and immediately feel how heavy it is, and hear a jangling sound. Intrigued, you open it to find several antique coins; you believe they are golden ducats.

On one side they are stamped with the image of a serpent, or a dragon. On the other there is a shield split vertically, with a crescent moon and a six-rayed star below it on the left-hand field, and inside the second field three horizontal bars. Around the edge of the coat-of-arms in Cyrillic letters is the legend *'Vlad Voivod'*.

(If you want to take the Golden Ducats with you, record them in the Equipment Box on your Adventure Sheet.)

What do you want to do now? Choosing something you haven't tried already, will you:

Examine the newspaper clippings?	Turn to **484**.
Take a closer look at the fish tank under the table?	Turn to **504**.
Leave the study and search elsewhere?	Turn to **273**.

455

Knowing that these men – these mere mortals – have come here to kill you threatens to unleash the enraged beast that lurks just beneath your mask of gentlemanly civility.

Divide your *Blood* score by 10, rounding fractions up. Then roll 1 die, and if the number rolled is equal or less than the resulting total, turn to **560**. If it is greater, turn to **715**.

456

"You see all these stones?" he says, pointing with his walking-stick at the headstones that rise from the turf of the churchyard in its picturesque spot. You confirm that you do. "It's a wonder they don't tumble down with the weight of lies wrote on them. 'Here lies the body' or 'Sacred to the memory' wrote on all of them, an' yet in nigh half of them there be no bodies buried there at all, an' the memories of them no-one cares a pinch of snuff about, much less sacred. Lies, all of them, nothin' but lies!"

"Oh, Mr Swales," you interject, "you can't be serious. Surely these tombstones are not all wrong?"

"There may be a poorish few not wrong," he admits, "but there be scores of these graves that be empty. Why, I could name ye a dozen whose bones lie in the Greenland seas, or where the currents may have drifted them."

He points to a stone at your feet, which has been laid down as a slab, upon which the seat you are sitting on rests, close to the edge of the cliff. "Read the lies written there," he says gruffly.

"Sacred to the memory of George Canon," Lucy says, leaning over and reading the words carved into it, "who died, in the hope of a glorious resurrection, on July 29, 1873, falling from the rocks at Kettleness. This tomb was erected by his sorrowing mother to her dearly beloved son. Really, Mr Swales, I don't see anything funny in that," she says, addressing the old man directly.

"You don't see aught funny?" laughs the old man. "That's because ye don't know the sorrowin' mother was a hell-cat that hated him because he was a hunchback. Deformed he was, an' he hated her so that he committed suicide in order that she mightn't get an insurance she put on his life. He blew the top of his head off with an old musket they kept for scarin' crows. That's the way he fell off the rocks. And, as to hopes of a glorious resurrection, I've often heard him say maself that he hoped he'd go to hell, for his mother was so pious that she'd be sure to go to heaven, an' he didn't want to go where she was."

He hammers the stone with his stick. "A pack of lies!"

"Oh, why did you tell us this?" demands Lucy. "It is my favourite seat, and I cannot leave it, and now I find I must go on sitting over the grave of a suicide."

"That won't hurt ye," says Mr Swales. "Why, I've sat here off an' on for nigh twenty years past, an' it hasn't done me no harm. Don't ye worry about them that lie under ye, or that don't lie there either!"

The church clock strikes six, at which the old man labours to get up, saying, "I must be goin' now. My granddaughter doesn't like to be kept waitin' when the tea is ready. My service to ye, ladies!" And with that he hobbles off.

Turn to **476**.

457

"Now Madam, tell me of your husband. Is he quite well?"

Seizing the opportunity, you share with the Professor your concerns about Jonathan: you tell him how your beloved came into the care of Sister Agatha and the nuns of the Hospital of St Joseph and Ste Mary in Buda-Pesth; how the Sister wrote to you on his behalf, summoning you to his bedside; of the terrible brain fever he suffered, and the hallucinations of the terrible things he believed he had witnessed in Castle Dracula brought on by the malady.

"Is all that fever gone," Van Helsing asks, "and is he strong and hearty?"

"He was almost recovered, but has been greatly upset by Mr Hawkins' death," you reply. "And when we were in London on Thursday last, he had a relapse."

"A shock, and so soon after a brain fever! That is not good. What kind of shock was it?"

"He thought he saw someone who recalled to his mind something terrible, something which led to his brain fever. Since yesterday I have been in a sort of fever of my own, a fever of doubt. Please be kind, and do not think me foolish that I have even half believed some very strange things."

"I have learned not to think little of anyone's beliefs," the Professor reassures you. "I try to keep an open mind when it comes to strange things, extraordinary things that would make one wonder if one was mad or sane."

Hearing Van Helsing's words, you feel like a great weight has been taken off your mind and decide it would be best if he were to read Jonathan's journal and draw his own conclusions regarding your husband's condition, which he duly does, reading at a rapid speed that is quite astonishing.

When he is done, he closes the notebook and smiling at you says, "You may sleep without doubt. Strange and terrible as your husband's diary is, it is true. I will pledge my life on it! And knowing now what he did, and the courage he displayed in doing so, I believe that he will be all right. But I would speak with him myself."

* * * *

And that is precisely what he does the very next morning, when Jonathan calls upon him at his hotel.

To have his terrible tale believed by another, and to have it confirmed that he has not lost his sanity, and by such a man of science and intellect as Professor Van Helsing, makes a new man of him. And seeing the transformation that has come over your husband lifts your own spirits and helps banish some of your fears for the future.

(Deduct 1 point from your *Terror* score.)

Jonathan returns from seeing the Professor off at the station and tells you that he has agreed, on behalf of both of you, that you will travel up to London again, if he should send for you. Your husband has spoken for you, and in this matter you are both of one mind.

Turn to **348**.

458

"The killer," you say, pausing to take a deep breath and steal yourself, "is Dr Callistratus!"

"This is preposterous!" protests the doctor, but there is a wolfish glint in his eye when he looks at you, akin to that of a hungry predator eyeing up its next meal.

"To the doctor's compartment!" Van Helsing announces, leading the way from the lounge towards the rear of the carriage.

Before the suspected killer can stop the pair of you, you are standing at the door to his private berth, and with a grand flourish the Professor pulls it open.

You gasp in shock at what awaits you within. Resting on the seats as well as the floor of the compartment are several large travelling cases. Some of them are open and you see that they all contain countless bottles of blood.

Shrieking like a banshee, Dr Callistratus tears his way through the appalled onlookers, smashing the Professor's head into the wall and causing him to slump to the floor stunned.

Backing into the compartment to escape him you nonetheless find yourself face to face with the enraged doctor.

If you want to use *The Pen is Mightier* special ability, cross off one use and turn to **381**. If not, turn to **428**.

459

You manage to grab the door handle and stop yourself from plunging into the abyss. Pulling the door firmly shut again, you keep following the passageway instead.

Turn to **489**.

460

Arthur takes out his pistol and opens fire on the dogs, while you follow his lead.

Before the rabid animals can get anywhere near you, they are both lying dead in the street.

Cross off one use of *The Pen is Mightier* special ability and turn to **876**.

461

The box slides off the back of the cart and crashes to the ground. But much to your annoyance, while one corner splinters, disgorging some of the mouldering black soil onto the snow, it otherwise remains firmly sealed.

Hearing a cry and seeking out the source of the sound among the melee of Szgany and Vampire-Hunters, you see Quincey Morris engaged in battle with a brute of a gypsy; the man appears to have the build and stature of a bear.

Seeing that the American is in trouble, you leap down from the leiter to assist him.

Turn to **505**.

462

You might have once sworn an oath to do no harm but faced by a pair of heavily-muscled madmen such as these, you seize a broken chair leg from the floor and prepare to defend yourself. (In this battle your opponents have the initiative, and you must fight them at the same time.)

	COMBAT	ENDURANCE
First LUNATIC	8	9
Second LUNATIC	8	8

If you are still alive after 6 Combat Rounds, or if you reduce the *Endurance* score of one of the Lunatics to 3 points or fewer, whichever is sooner, turn to **441** at once.

463

The experience of repeatedly giving blood leaves you feeling drained and listless.

Deduct 1 point from both your *Agility* and *Combat* scores, and then turn to **487**.

464

Not knowing what else to do, in your panicked terror, you hurl the lamp at the vile trio. They dart out of the way and the lantern lands in a corner of the room, where it sets light to the gossamer hangings adorning the room.

Shrieking like banshees, the mistresses of this dark place come for you then.

If you want to use *The Pen is Mightier* special ability, cross off one use and turn to **586**. If not, turn to **649**.

465

Considering many of Mehmed's Janissaries come from Wallachian bloodstock, with your strong Slavic features and thick facial hair, no one questions your right to be here within the camp.

As you approach the entrance to the pavilion, the two sentries cross their axe-headed halberds, barring the way to you. You salute and pass the time of day with them, the Turkish that you were forced to learn when you were a 'guest' at the palace of Mehmed's father, when you were still but a boy, proving of use again to you now. In this way, you manage to discover a little more of what the Sultan has planned. You learn that he has ordered his soldiers not to leave their tents during the night, so as to not cause panic in case of an attack.

(Tick off the code word *Stratégia*.)

Do you now want to leave the camp (turn to **285**), or do you want to tell the guards you have an important message to pass on and ask to enter the tent (turn to **435**)?

466

Arthur appears to be undergoing some terrible transformation that you cannot believe could be explained by modern medicine and so perhaps the old woman's folk remedy will be able to help, where science cannot.

If you want to break the seal on the bottle and make Arthur drink the potion, turn to **486**. If not, turn to **566**.

467

Putting the goblet to your lips, you gulp down its rich, red contents.

Your body is immediately wracked by the most excruciating pain, while your mind is assailed by the most terrifying sights. You see...

Giant snakes, blood dripping from their over-sized fangs... people impaled on stakes writhing in agony as they try to pull themselves off the greased, wooden posts... a table laid for a feast where the prize dish is a platter of dead babies... three rare beauties, now appearing to be human, now as monstrous snake-women, and now as decomposing corpses... a mirrored lake, deep beneath the earth, and something pallid circling its freezing depths...

Take a Combat test. If you pass the test, turn to **555**. If you fail the test, turn to **488**.

468

The Countess returns to you in your dream, screaming as the lightning bolt explodes through her, and as the echoes of the thunderclap die away, you hear the howling of wolves from all around you.

When you wake at last, you are left feeling badly shaken by your nightmare, no longer entirely sure how much of it actually happened to you and how much is merely a figment of your tormented mind.

Add 1 point to your *Terror* score, lose 1 *Combat* point, and then turn to **498**.

Leaving the others to complete the preparations for the raid, you follow the attendant down to the ward. You find Renfield in a state of considerable excitement, but far more rational in his speech and manner than ever before. There is even a certain dignity in the man's manner.

"Doctor," he addresses you as you enter his cell, "I beg you to release me at once from this asylum and send me home. As you can see, you have cured me, and I am now as sane as at least the majority of men who are in full possession of their liberties. I am sure that you, Dr Seward, who are a humanitarian as well as a scientist, will deem it a moral duty to deal with me as one to be considered as under exceptional circumstances."

You are staggered, for you find yourself convinced, despite your prior knowledge of the man's character and history, that his reason has indeed been restored.

"You certainly appear to be improving very rapidly," you tell him. "We will have a longer chat in the morning, and I will see what I can do regards meeting your wishes."

But your response does not satisfy him at all: "I fear, Dr Seward, you do not understand. I desire to go at once, here, now, this very hour, this very moment, if I may."

He looks at you keenly, and seeing no affirmation in your face says, "Then I suppose I must provide an alternative reason for my request. Let me ask for this concession, boon, privilege, what you will, for the sake of others."

You start to wonder if this sudden change of his intellectual method is yet another form or phase of his madness, and so decide to let him go on a little longer, knowing from experience that he will give himself away in the end.

"Can you not tell me the real reason for wishing to be free tonight?" you press him.

He shakes his head sadly, a look of poignant regret on his face.

"Come, Mr Renfield. You claim the privilege of reason in the highest degree, since you seek to impress me with your complete reasonableness. You do this, whose sanity I have reason to doubt, since you are not yet released from medical treatment for this very defect. If you will not help me in my effort to choose the wisest course, how can I perform the duty which you yourself put upon me?"

He shakes his head again. "I have nothing to say. I am not my own master in the matter. I can only ask you to trust me. If I am refused, the responsibility of what will happen next does not rest with me."

"Then we are done here," you tell him, going towards the door.

"Then you shall reap what you sow!" he suddenly screams.

Much to your horror, a cloud of flies emerges from the red hole of his mouth, filling the room with their disgusting black bodies and causing the attendants to retreat in horror, the buzzing of their wings like a hurricane roar in your ears.

After the flies come the spiders, hundreds of them, crawling from between the madman's lips. Descending to the stone-flagged floor on threads of silk, they scuttle towards you. (Add 2 points to your *Terror* score.)

If you want to use *The Pen is Mightier* special ability, and you still can, cross off one use and turn to **232**. If not, turn to **452**.

470

Hissing in fury and frustration, you throw yourself at the superstitious steersman. As you do so, he pulls a blade from his belt that shines silver. (In this battle, you have the initiative.)

SUPERSTITIOUS STEERSMAN   COMBAT 8   ENDURANCE 8

If you wish, you may spend 3 *Blood* points and turn to **118** at once.

If not, conduct the battle as normal, but every time the Steersman manages to strike you, deduct 3 *Endurance* points rather than the usual 2, as the silvered blade burns your unholy undead flesh. If you win the battle, you may then turn to **118**.

471

There are even such reference books as the *London Directory*, *Whitaker's Almanac*, and the *Army and Navy Lists*, among the Count's collection. And it gladdens your heart when you stumble upon the *Law List*.

While you are looking at the books, the door opens, and the Count enters the library.

Turn to **614**.

472

Do you have any Silver Bullets? If so, turn to **35**. If not, turn to **492**.

473

You throw yourself forwards but you are not enough of an athlete to make it across the gap.

You miss the courtyard wall and drop like a stone into the shadows of the chasm below. But your bold leap has carried you clear of the rocks that lie at the bottom of the abyss and after falling for several seconds that feel like an eternity, you enter the churning current that plunges through the gorge.

Roll one die and add 1; deduct this many *Endurance* points. (Alternatively, pick a card and deduct its face value from your *Endurance* score, unless it is 8 or above or a picture card, in which case deduct 7 points from your *Endurance* score.)

If you are still alive, turn to **627**.

474

The Weird Sisters begin to chant, their voices becoming as one:

> "Four women in your future lie;
> Countess, Sister, Lover, Wife.
> The first would make your slave her own,
> The last shall haunt your afterlife."

"A Countess?" you say, when they are done. "I am the only one of royal blood within Castle Dracula."

"Not here, in Gratz, two hundred and fifty leagues to the west, where the Countess Dolingen rules the night," Melusina says. "She lies in wait for the one you are expecting and shall arise this Walpurgis Night and put her own plans into play."

"Enough of your lies! You speak with forked tongues. I have spent decades refining my schemes. They are infallible!"

With that, you turn on your heel and quit the women's wing.

Lilith's tinkling laughter follows you, echoing along the passageway: "Women were ever your weakness, my Lord Impaler!"

Turn to **535**.

475

The deckhand dead, you drink your fill of his blood. (Restore up to 4 *Endurance* points.)

When you are done, what do you want to do with the man's body?

If you want to throw it overboard, turn to **526**. If you just want to leave it where it is, in the hope of keeping the crew cowed and in a state of fear, that will only make their blood more delicious, turn to **695**.

476

MINA MURRAY'S JOURNAL

26 July, Whitby

I am anxious, and it soothes me to express myself here. I am unhappy about Lucy and about Jonathan...

You have not heard from Jonathan, your fiancé, for some time, and were getting quite concerned, until yesterday, when his employer, dear Mr Hawkins, who is always so kind, sent you a letter from him. It is only a line, dated from Castle Dracula, and says that he is just starting for home.

But that is so unlike him. You cannot understand his brevity, and it does little to relieve your sense of unease. On top of that, Lucy has lately taken to her old habit of walking in her sleep. Her mother, Mrs Westenra, has spoken to you about it, and you have decided to lock the door of the room you share every night. Apparently, Lucy's late father had the same habit, and would get up in the night and dress himself, and go out, if he were not stopped.

Lucy is to be married in the autumn and is already planning out her dresses and how her house is to be arranged. You sympathise with her, for your mind is preoccupied with the same concerns, only you and Jonathan will start married life in a very simple way and will have to try to make both ends meet. Lucy's fiancé, is the Hon. Arthur Holmwood, only son of Lord Godalming, and is coming up to Whitby as soon as he can leave town, for his father is not very well, and you think your dear friend is counting the moments till he comes.

* * * *

Another week goes by without further word from Jonathan, and each night you are wakened by Lucy moving about the room; you feel that she is watching you. Every night it is the same; she tries the door, and finding it locked, goes about the room searching for the key.

The anxiety, and perpetually being awakened each night is beginning to tell on you, and you have become nervous and wakeful yourself.

(Lose 1 *Combat* point and add 1 to your *Terror* score.)

And so, the days tick by, following the same uncomfortably familiar pattern.

Turn to **496**.

477

Suspecting that the dogs are carriers of rabies, you and Arthur prepare to put them down before they can bite either of you, taking on one of them each. (In this battle the dog has the initiative.)

RABID DOG   COMBAT 6   ENDURANCE 6

If you defeat the dog, turn to **692**.

478

You finish the Sleeping Draught in one go and then get into bed and wait for it to take effect.

You can feel it doing you good from within even as you feel your eyelids grow heavy.

Gain 4 *Endurance* points, strike the Sleeping Draught from your Adventure Sheet, tick off the code word *Sedative*, and then turn to **497**.

479

You do not risk emerging from your hiding place the following night, suspecting that the remaining members of the crew will be on the lookout for anything untoward.

When you do emerge again to hunt, the *Demeter* is shrouded in thick fog, the weather itself working to protect your passage, now that you are so close to making land in England.

Although London is your ultimate destination, you considered that the Port of London itself would be too busy a place to put into harbour, too full of stevedores and officious people who might ask difficult questions regarding a cargo of experimental earth, and too ready to undertake a meticulous examination of such a cargo. That is why you chose the harbour-town of Whitby, on the north-east coast as your point of disembarkation.

The *Demeter* cannot continue sailing at night without someone keeping watch, to steer and make sure the ship does not run aground on any rocks, or collide with another vessel – especially here, in the notoriously busy English Channel. And so it is that you find a terrified sailor manning the helm, alone.

Starting at his own shadow, so nervous is the sailor, he lays eyes on you before you can surprise him and, abandoning his position without a second thought, he makes a dash for the Captain's cabin.

Take an Agility test. If you pass the test, turn to **499**, but if you fail the test, turn to **530**.

480

The four of you file out of the tomb again, Van Helsing coming last and locking the door behind him. After the terror of that vault, how sweet it is to breathe fresh air that has no taint of death and decay!

Under Quincey's direction, Arthur makes for the northern perimeter, Van Helsing goes east, Quincey himself takes the southern stretch of the cemetery, while you head for the line of yew trees on the western side of the churchyard.

As you approach the ancient evergreens, you hear the rustle of movement before you and half a dozen small figures emerge from the shadows that coalesce between the trees. As they move towards you, you gasp to see that they are young children, ranging in age from three to seven, or so you would imagine. Their clothes are dishevelled, and their faces appear unnaturally pale.

A ray of moonlight breaks through the clouds and you see a red-haired woman dressed in a white grave-gown, standing behind them. Your heart grows cold as ice; you would know those tumbling red locks anywhere.

"My dear John," she says. "How sweet of you to come visit me."

There is something diabolically honeyed in the tone of her voice, which rings through your brain. You recognise the features of Lucy Westenra, but their former sweetness has turned to adamantine, heartless cruelty.

(Add 1 point to your *Terror* score.)

"I have not come to visit you," you reply, your voice tremulous with fear. "I am here to stop you."

"Stop me?" You have never seen such baffled malice on a face before and trust you never shall again. "Do you hear that, my children? The doctor wishes to put an end to your Mama. We cannot allow that, can we?"

"No, Mama," say the wan-faced children, sounding half-asleep.

To your horror, the scruffy urchins advance, a feral hatred burning in their bloodshot eyes.

If you want to use *The Pen is Mightier* special ability, and you still can, turn to **259**. If not, turn to **289**.

481

It is no good – the box is simply too heavy. It would require a superhuman feat of strength to shift it by yourself.

A roar from behind causes you to turn around in shock and surprise, as a huge bear of a man grabs the side of the cart with both hands and heaves, tipping both you and the box onto the ground.

You land awkwardly on top of the box, bruising your ribs and crushing your sword-arm under you, as well as jarring your knee.

(Lose 3 *Endurance* points, 1 *Agility* point, and 1 *Combat* point.)

If you are still alive, turn to **505**.

482

You make it back to the train, and your companions pull you back on board, just as the avalanche hits. The Orient Express rocks under the impact but thankfully its wheels remain on the tracks.

It takes a day for the driver, fireman and other staff to dig the train out, but eventually you are on your way again, which is more than you can say for Johnny Alucard, who now lies buried under the snow on the rocks a thousand feet below.

Turn to **257**.

483

You ride your horses hard for days, pushing them still harder and harder, and barely resting, so desperate are you to reach Castle Dracula before your quarry does.

If you have the code word *Lángok* ticked off, turn to **991**. If not, turn to **8**.

484

Someone has taken the trouble to cut out a series of articles from various different local and national newspapers. Among them is one about a Russian schooner that ran aground on the North Yorkshire coast in Whitby, dated 8 August, and another from *The Pall Mall Gazette*, dated 18 September, regarding a wolf escaping from London Zoo, and a third bearing the lurid headline 'Bloofer Lady Strikes Again!'

What do you want to do now? Choosing something you haven't done already, will you:

Examine the black velvet bag?	Turn to **454**.
Take a closer look at the fish tank under the table?	Turn to **504**.
Leave the study and search elsewhere?	Turn to **273**.

485

There is only one way out for you now, so you hurl yourself through the un-shuttered dining-room window. Amidst the crash and glitter of falling glass, you land in the stone-flagged yard below.

The Vampire-Hunters rush to the window, only to see you spring from the ground unhurt. Crossing the yard, you push open the stable door, but there hesitate and turn to face your pursuers.

"You think you can confound my plans?" you bellow. "You shall be sorry, each one of you! You think you have left me without a place to rest, but I have more! My revenge is just begun! It is a plan I have devised over the centuries and time is on my side. Your girls that you all love are mine already, and through them you and others shall become my creatures yet, to do my bidding and to be my jackals when I want to feed!"

That said, you pass quickly through the door and are gone.

Turn to **635**.

486

As you put the phial to Arthur's lips, he starts to resist your efforts to help him, and the more you try to force him to consume the Tincture of Wolfsbane the harder he fights back.

Take a Combat test. If you pass the test, turn to **517**. If you fail the test, turn to **537**.

487

Van Helsing tells you that he will watch over Lucy both this night and the next and will send you word when he needs you to come. And so, you return to the asylum to see to the needs of the other patients in your care.

Take an ESP test. If you pass the test, turn to **527**. If you fail the test, turn to **424**.

488

Even for one such as you – a soul steeped in violence and bloodshed, and all manner of terrible atrocities, committed either at your command or by your own hand – can barely stomach the horrible visions that are assaulting your senses.

Take an ESP test. If you pass the test, turn to **555**. If you fail the test, turn to **520**.

489

Yellow moonlight floods in through the diamond panes of the curtainless windows, softening the wealth of dust, which covers everything, and disguises in some measure the ravages of time and moths. You are glad you thought to bring a lamp with you, for there is a dread loneliness about the place that chills your heart and makes your nerves tremble. (Add 1 to your *Terror* score.)

Descending a short flight of crumbling steps, you find yourself in an octagonal chamber, not unlike the one that separates your bedroom from the dining-room in your apartment. Two doors lead off to left and right, while ahead of you, another short flight of steps leads to what appears to be an opulent chamber bedecked with silken drapes.

The door to your left is adorned with a pair of ancient, curved swords, their blades pitted and tarnished by time. The door to your right bears the same dragon crest as is carved into the chimneybreast above the fireplace in your dining-room.

Do you want to:

Try the door to your left?	Turn to **672**.
Try the door to your right?	Turn to **529**.
Ignore both doors and descend the steps to the opulent chamber below?	Turn to **59**.

490

There is no time to lose, and there is nothing less at risk now than your own immortal soul! For if the menfolk – your brave, would-be saviours – do not find the remaining boxes of earth, and finish off the vampire quickly, you will end up like poor dear Lucy.

Fortunately, however, your dear husband Jonathan helped Count Dracula acquire not just Carfax House, but three other properties, all located in London: one in Piccadilly, one in Walworth, and one in Mile End.

"I think the house in Piccadilly is key," Professor Van Helsing says, when the six of you meet again, later that morning, in Dr Seward's study, which has become the Vampire-Hunters' committee room. "He must have many belongings hidden somewhere, and why not somewhere so central, so quiet, and from where he can come and go by the front or the back at all hours? I think we should search there."

"But what of the properties in Walworth and Mile End?" asks Arthur. "We cannot risk leaving any earths for that old fox to run to."

And so, it is agreed; Arthur Holmwood and Quincey Morris will visit the properties in Walworth and Mile End, while Jonathan and Dr Seward will go with the Professor to the large townhouse in Piccadilly. There is nothing for you to do but wait for them all to return safely, you hope, later this evening.

After the men have gone, you retire to your room, where you write up recent events in your journal. You are feeling very tired after the goings-on of the previous night, and soon fall asleep where you are sitting, in a chair by the window, the morning sunlight warming your skin…

Take an ESP test. If you pass the test, turn to **511**, but if you fail the test, turn to **543**.

491

You eventually find what you are looking for; a book dating from the 18th century about the peoples of the Carpathians, written in German. Poring over it you are able to translate certain passages and one about something called the '*Strigoi*', intrigues you in particular.

According to the tome, *Strigoi* are troubled spirits that are said to have risen from the grave, sometimes in order to take revenge for some crime perpetrated against them in life and sometimes at the behest of a demonic sorcerer.

While you are studying the book, the door opens – making you start. The Count enters and you instinctively slam the book shut in surprise.

Tick off the code word *Strigoi* and turn to **614**.

492

As your companions are busy dealing with their own opponents, it is up to you to do away with any that remain.

If you want to use *The Pen is Mightier* special ability, and you still can, turn to **528**. If not, turn to **548**.

493

There before you stands a pair of burly inmates, their heads shaven, to help keep them free of lice, the long sleeves of the strait-waistcoats they are wearing dragging along the stone-flagged floor of the ward behind them.

If you want to use *The Pen is Mightier* special ability, cross off one use and turn to **441**. If not, turn to **462**.

494

Pulling handfuls of the coins from your pockets, you hurl them at the weird women. Some of them actually touch the twisted flesh of their unnatural bodies, and where it does so it burns.

(If you end up having to fight the monstrous mistresses of this dark place, you may reduce all their *Endurance* scores by 2 points before battle begins.)

Screaming in pain and fury, with claws bared, they go for you then.

If you want to use *The Pen is Mightier* special ability, cross off one use and turn to **618**. If not, turn to **433**.

495

Pulling yourself up to your full height, carrying yourself like the prince among men that you are, you stride confidently towards the grand marquee.

If you have the code word *Rejtett* ticked off, turn to **465**. If not, turn to **388**.

496

MINA MURRAY'S JOURNAL

6 August, Whitby

Last night was very threatening, and the fishermen say that we are in for a storm...

Today is a grey day, the sun hidden in thick clouds, despite the time of year, high over Kettleness. Despite the uninspiring conditions, you make the walk from the Crescent, down into the town, and up the 199 steps on the other side of the River Esk, to your favourite spot on the cliff path at the edge of the churchyard. But you make it alone, Lucy feeling listless after a particularly unsettled night's somnambulism.

The sea tumbles in over the shallows and the sandy flats with a roar, while the horizon is lost in a grey mist. The clouds are piled up like giant rocks, and there is a low rumble over the sea that sounds like some presage of doom. You can see fishing boats racing for home, rising and dipping in the ground swell as they sweep into the harbour, bending to the scuppers.

You are not alone on the headland. Old Mr Swales is making straight for you along the cliff path, while the coastguard has joined you and is looking out to sea, spyglass in hand.

If you want to go and meet Mr Swales, curious as to what he could possibly want, turn to **516**. If you would rather not have anything more to do with the cantankerous fellow, turn to **556**.

497

Despite everything that is besetting your weary mind, you are so drowsy you fall asleep quickly...

As with the previous night, you dream you are in your bedroom in the asylum, which is filled with the same white mist as before, and you feel the same vague terror that came to you before, and the sensation that something else is there in the room with you.

Standing beside the bed, as if he has just stepped out of the mist – or rather, as if the mist has somehow become him – is a tall, thin man, dressed all in black.

You know him at once, from your husband's description of him; the waxen face, the high aquiline nose, the parted ruddy lips, with the sharp white teeth showing between, and the crimson eyes.

(Add 1 point to your *Terror* score.)

If you have the code word *Sedative* ticked off, turn to **613**. If not, turn **534**.

498

You rise early the next day and set about preparing for your onward journey. You learn that your landlord also received a letter from the Count, directing him to secure the best place on the Bukovina coach for you.

Do you want to ask him how this was arranged (turn to **522**), ask the landlord and his wife what they know of Count Dracula (turn to **552**), or do you simply want to finish packing (turn to **602**)?

499

Moving with all alacrity, you put yourself between the desperate fellow and the protection of the Captain's cabin. In response, he takes out a cleaver, no doubt pilfered from the ship's galley, and prepares to sell his life dear. (You have the initiative in this battle.)

SCARED SAILOR   COMBAT 7   ENDURANCE 7

If you do away with your opponent before he can do away with you, turn to **275**. Alternatively, you may spend 3 *Blood* points and turn to **275** straightaway.

500

DR SEWARD'S DIARY

(Kept in phonograph)

25 May 1897

Ebb tide in appetite today. Cannot eat, cannot rest, so diary instead. Since my rebuff of yesterday I have a sort of empty feeling...

It took all your courage to finally ask Miss Lucy Westenra if she would do you the honour of becoming Mrs John Seward, but she politely declined, an act which caused her to burst into tears. You can't help chastising yourself for being a brute to put her through such an ordeal, but the ordeal for you is far from over. Nothing in the world seems of sufficient importance to be worth doing now.

The only cure for a malady such as yours is to lose yourself in your work. And with that in mind, now that you are safely ensconced within the walls of Carfax Asylum once more, you go among the patients. Your attention is soon focused on one of the residents whose case interests you greatly: Mr R. M. Renfield, aged 59.

You have observed that Mr Renfield is of a sanguine temperament, morbidly excitable, but also prone to periods of gloom. Your staff have remarked to you, on more than one occasion, that he is also possessed of great physical strength, despite his gaunt appearance, for he is neither tall, nor heavily-muscled, and indeed has very little flesh on his bones.

The more time you invest in trying to understand the man, and his peculiar manic obsessions, the more his case fascinates you.

He had no recorded history of mental health issues until the breakdown occurred that resulted in him being sent to your asylum for containment and treatment. The reason for his mental collapse was reported as being the result of stress, following an extended sojourn somewhere in eastern Europe, on behalf of his employer, one Mr Peter Hawkins, of the firm of solicitors Hawkins, Oldman & Lee of Exeter.

No matter how he might have behaved before the breakdown, he is now self-absorbed and incredibly secretive, but also driven by some greater purpose. You only wish that you could pinpoint the subject of the latter.

He has one redeeming quality, his love of animals, although the pets he keeps in his cell are of odd sorts. He has recently taken to catching flies, and you decide to ask him about his newfound hobby when you are next on your rounds.

But when that time comes, you are shocked to see the vast quantity of flies he has collected, heaped on the sill of his single barred window to the outside world.

Do you want to:

Tell him he must remove the flies from his cell?	Turn to **538**.
Ask him why he is collecting the flies?	Turn to **518**.
Ask him about his trip to Eastern Europe?	Turn to **558**.

501

You wake suddenly in the middle of the night, from a horrible dream in which you are being pursued across the moors by a great black dog, to find Lucy getting dressed, as if she intends to go out.

Most disturbing of all, however, is that when you ask her where she thinks she is going she doesn't reply, and you realise she is sleep-walking!

You manage to undress her again without waking her and get her back to bed.

But before the coming of dawn, the same thing happens again. You stop her while her hand is still on the handle of the bedroom door.

It is a very strange thing, this sleep-walking, for as soon as her will is thwarted in any physical way, her intention, if there is any, disappears, and she yields herself almost exactly to the routine of her life.

Tick off the code word *Somnambulism* and then turn to **541**.

502

There are eight of these monstrously mutated rats in total.

Hearing your approach with their sharp ears and picking up your scent even over the all-pervasive stench of maggot-eaten flesh, the monstrous rats scamper across the floor towards you.

If you want to use *The Pen is Mightier* special ability, and you still can, turn to **562**. If not, turn to **588**.

503

You have made it! You land hard on the ragged battlements, grazing your knees, but you are safe.

(Lose 2 *Endurance* points, but also deduct 1 point from your *Terror* score.)

You descend to the courtyard floor and from there pass beneath the great arched entrance, and set out after the Szgany, down the steep path, heading for the valley far below.

Turn to **627**.

504

Getting down on your hands and knees you peer over the rim of the fish tank. The stink of the filthy water makes you recoil, just as something launches itself out of the tank straight at you.

The thing is composed of a gelatinous crimson body and eight arms connected by a webbing of skin. Having no warning of the creature's imminent attack, it manages to latch its rubbery limbs onto your sword-arm, and you cry out in pain as the rows of fleshy spines that line each one dig into your skin.

You manage to pull the horror from you with your free hand and it plops back into the tank, sloshing water over the floorboards. Whatever the creature has done to you leaves a lingering tingling numbness. (Deduct 2 *Endurance* points and 1 *Combat* point.)

It is then that you notice the smudged label on the side of the tank that read, '*Vampyroteuthis infernalis*'.

Not wanting to fall foul of the vampire squid from hell a second time, you decide to vacate the study as quickly as possible and look elsewhere.

Turn to **273**.

505

Giving voice to a terrible roar, the great bear of a man starts to change. His body appears to swell underneath his great fur coat and sharp claws rip through the fingertips of the thick leather gloves he is wearing. He fixes you with blazing red eyes and bares a mouth full of ursid fangs.

You stagger away from the monstrous skin-changer in appalled horror.

(Add 1 point to your *Terror* score.)

If you want to use *The Pen is Mightier* special ability, and you still can, turn to **615**. If not, make a note that in the battle to come, your enemy has the initiative and turn to **928**.

506

You have no choice but to defend yourself against the swarming rodents. (In this battle, the rats have the initiative.)

RAT SWARM   COMBAT 6   ENDURANCE 9

If you manage to reduce the swarm's *Endurance* score to zero, turn to **546**.

507

As the group splits up, preparing to jimmy the lids from the crates, you descend from the rafters, assuming your true undead form as you materialise among them.

"It is the devil himself!" Harker cries. "Look out, Quincey! Look out, Professor!" At his bellowed warning, the bushy-moustached American and the older man both manage to evade your sweeping talons.

The men are clearly scared half out of their wits, but they are also possessed of a grim purpose and, rather than flee the chapel screaming, they strike back with both their man-made weapons and their spiritual ones.

You must fight the Vampire-Hunters all at the same time, and while you have the initiative in this battle, you must deduct 2 points when calculating your *Combat Rating*, due to the proliferation of crucifixes, holy wafers and rosary beads the men carry about them.

	COMBAT	ENDURANCE
HARKER	10	11
HOLMWOOD	8	9
QUINCEY THE AMERICAN	9	9
DOCTOR SEWARD	9	10
THE PROFESSOR	8	8

At any time during the battle, if you wish, you may deduct 4 *Blood* points to eliminate one of the Vampire-Hunters; however, you may only do so once.

If you kill all of the Vampire-Hunters, gain 10 *Blood* points and turn to **400**. If you lose the battle, turn to **605**.

508

The reaction of the grave-leech is enough to convince you that the thing must die, and you bring the hammer down, striking with all your might.

The thing in the coffin writhes in agony and a hideous, blood-curdling screech comes from its lips. The body shakes, twisting in wild contortions, the sharp white teeth champing together till the lips are cut, and the mouth is smeared with a crimson foam.

But, as the Professor instructed you, now you have begun the grisly work you do not falter, even as foul, black blood wells up from the pierced muscle, some of it spurting into your face.

And then, at last, the writhing and quivering of the body passes, until finally it lies still, and the terrible task is done.

The hammer falls from your numb fingers, and you collapse against the side of Lucy's coffin, sweat pouring from your forehead, and your breath coming in broken gasps.

Turn to **124**.

509

You have done it! You have exposed the murderer of the young steward.

(Add 1 use of *The Pen is Mightier* special ability to your Adventure Sheet.)

Everyone returns to their own compartments and you and the Professor spend the rest of the train journey in your own company, grabbing a little rest while you still can.

Turn to **107**.

510

In the face of your righteous assault, hissing in fury, the undead wretch suddenly turns tail and flees – a black blur against the crisp white snow. One minute he is moving so fast you believe he is a wolf, and then his blurring flight reminds you more of a flock of agitated bats, and then it is as if he is nothing more than smoke.

Turn to **970**.

511

As you sleep, you dream...

You are travelling along Piccadilly, keeping to the shadows of the tall buildings, unseen by the London masses taking their daily constitutional in the Green Park. It is as if you are seeing through another's eyes.

A grim building rises before you, the number on its door '138'. You reach for the door with fingers that end in chisel-sharp nails...

* * * *

You suddenly start awake, your heart pounding and the wafer-burn on your forehead throbbing.

What did you just see? Was it a dream? Was it a vision of the future? Or was it happening right now? Whatever the truth, you are sure Jonathan and those other brave fellows are in danger.

Summoning Dr Seward's housekeeper, you dictate a telegram to be delivered to 138 Piccadilly at once, warning them that Dracula is on his way, if he is not there already.

Deduct 1 *Blood* point and then turn to **563**.

512

The Weird Sisters begin to chant then, as if speaking as one:

> *"Four women in your future lie;*
> *Countess, Sister, Lover, Wife.*
> *The first shall make your slave her own,*
> *The second curse your afterlife."*

"A Countess?" you say, when they are done. "I am the only one of royal blood within Castle Dracula."

"Not here, in Gratz, two hundred and fifty leagues to the west, where the Countess Dolingen rules the night," Melusina says. "She lies in wait for the one you are expecting and shall arise this Walpurgis Night and put her own plans into play."

"And who is this Sister, the second?"

"She does not know it yet, in fact she may never know it, but she will help to bring about your end," Lamia says.

"And where would I find her?"

"In her convent-sanctuary, overlooking the twin cities of Buda and Pesth," Lilith replies.

At hearing this, you cannot hold back your laughter. "She is a *nun*?"

"She is old and she is wise," Lilith warns you. "A deadly combination."

You have heard enough. The Weird Sisters will play their little games, but you want no further part in them.

Tick off the code word *Apáca* and turn to **535**.

513

You manage to dodge out of the way as the chair hurtles past, missing your head by a hair's breadth.

Turn to **493**.

514

The talismans your fellow passengers aboard the coach from Bistritz gave to you – the mountain ash, lucky rabbit's feet and tiny silver charms – are in the pockets of your waistcoat, which you happen to be wearing. Taking them out, you throw them at the monstrous fiends.

In response, in their rage, they hurl themselves at you, wounding you before you are able to cause them any harm. (Lose 4 *Endurance* points and remove the Good Luck Tokens from your Adventure Sheet.)

In the altercation you drop your lamp, which rolls across the floor to a corner of the room, where it promptly sets light to the gossamer hangings that adorn the chamber.

Shrieking like banshees, the mistresses of this dark place prepare to put an end to you.

If you want to use *The Pen is Mightier* special ability, cross off one use and turn to **586**. If not, turn to **649**.

515

You are momentarily taken aback; you recognise the tall gypsy, with the long brown beard and great black hat. It is the coachman who first brought you to Dracula's castle six months ago.

Giving voice to a terrible roar, the great bear of a man starts to change. His body appears to swell underneath his great fur coat and sharp claws rip through the fingertips of the thick leather gloves he is wearing. He fixes you with blazing red eyes and bares a mouth full of ursid fangs.

You witnessed many terrible things while you were a guest of the Count, and you are not going to let this shape-changing Szgany cow you into submission.

If you want to use *The Pen is Mightier* special ability, and you still can, turn to **615**. If not, make a note that in the battle to come you have the initiative and turn to **928**.

516

Taking your hands in his, Mr Swales says, in a surprisingly gentle way, "I'm afraid, my deary, that I must have shocked you by all the wicked things I've been sayin' about the dead, and such like, but I didn't mean any of them, and I want you to remember that when I'm gone.

"Someday soon the Angel of Death will sound his trumpet for me. And if he should come this very night I'd not refuse his call, for a hundred years is too much for any man to expect, and death be all that we can rightly depend on.

"There's something in the wind that smells like death. It's in the air and I feel it comin'."

Mr Swales removes his hat, his mouth moving as if he is praying. After a few minutes' reverential silence, he shakes hands with you, blesses you, and finally says goodbye, before hobbling off again.

Tick off the code word *Azrael* and then turn to **556**.

517

Desperation and determination lending you the strength you need, you manage to pour the foul-smelling concoction into his mouth and hold his nose, forcing him to swallow it.

You release your hold on him and stagger back as Arthur is seized by a terrible palsy. So violently is he shaking that you wonder if he is having a fit.

He is suddenly, violently sick, throwing up remnants of the last meal he ate in Strasba into the snow. But when he has finished vomiting, the terrible shaking subsides and he begins to look more human again, in every sense.

Turn to **659**.

518

"Why do you collect the flies, Mr Renfield?" you ask. "What can be your purpose in doing so?"

"My purpose, Doctor Seward?" your patient replies. "Why, I have been entrusted with the greatest purpose of all."

"And what is that?" you press him.

"To complete the work I was entrusted with, by my Master."

"Do you mean by your employer, Mr Hawkins?"

"No, not him! The Master! The one who is coming for me."

"But who is this Master of yours? Tell me."

"No, I have said too much already. I must say no more," Renfield hisses, suddenly retreating into a shadowy corner of his cell.

(Tick off the code word *Monomania*.)

Will you now tell him he must remove the flies from his cell (turn to **538**), or ask him to tell you more about his business trip to Eastern Europe (turn to **558**)?

519

Van Helsing springs forward, holding up a golden crucifix before Lucy. She recoils from it immediately, hissing and spitting, her face contorted by rage. In the same instant, her hypnotic spell is broken and Arthur falters. A look of bewilderment on his face, he breaks off his attack.

Cross off one use of *The Pen is Mightier* special ability and turn to **579**.

520

The horrors assailing your mind and the agonising paroxysms wracking your body are more than you can bear. Something suddenly snaps – something other than your mind, which has already been broken by the experience – and you bite through your own tongue as you somehow manage to break your neck, so violent are your convulsions.

Your adventure, like your life, is over.

THE END

521

You wake slowly the next morning to the first light of day streaming in through the window of the bedroom you share with Lucy, and her bed empty.

You are fully awake in a flash and, pulling on your dressing-gown, run downstairs in search of your friend. There is no one else up, it being just after dawn.

You find her in the garden, with her arms draped over an ornamental urn and fast asleep. She is still in her nightdress and her feet are filthy with mud.

How long can she have been like this?

You gently rouse her and lead her back into the house, still in a semi-comatose state, and help her wash her feet and get out of her night things.

But something about Lucy's disappearance, her dishevelled state, and her lack of any memory of where she went or what she was doing out at night, leaves you feeling deeply unsettled.

Add 1 point to your *Terror* score and turn to **541**.

522

As soon as you make inquiries as to the details, the landlord becomes somewhat reticent and pretends that he cannot understand your German, even though he has answered all your questions up until now without any problem at all.

You persist, and the elderly couple exchange frightened looks. Finally, the landlord mumbles something about having been sent money in a letter, insisting that that is all he knows.

Do you now want to ask him and his wife whether they know Count Dracula (turn to **552**), or will you simply return to your room and finishing preparing for your journey (turn to **602**)?

523

Entering the study, you realise that there are a variety of living things among the items on display. There is a glass jar containing a soupy green liquid, that looks like stagnant pond water, which is full of writhing black leeches; another container covered with a fine meshed netting, to which cling dozens, if not hundreds, of mosquitoes; and a vivarium containing a dead rat seething with blood-sucking ticks.

On the desk in front of the cabinet is the skeleton of a bat, poised on a stand with the finger-bones of its wings outstretched. You also see the leathery body of a lamprey pinned out on a fluid-stained board, apparently mid-dissection. In addition, there is a pile of newspaper clippings and a black velvet bag embroidered with gold thread.

But it is what you see resting on the floor under the table that fascinates you the most. It looks like a large fish tank, but you can see nothing through the inky water filling it.

Do you want to:

Flick through the newspaper clippings?	Turn to **484**.
Examine the black velvet bag?	Turn to **454**.
Take a closer look at the fish tank under the table?	Turn to **504**.
Leave the study and search elsewhere?	Turn to **273**.

524

The scar upon her forehead starts to pulse and you know then that she cannot resist you.

"And now, Mina, it is time for your baptism – your baptism of blood," you tell her, pointing to where her husband stands, struck dumb with horror and unable to move.

Shrieking like a banshee, Mina flies to her husband and he, all the fight having left him, does nothing as she sinks her fangs into his throat and starts to feed.

As the Szgany dispatch the exhausted Professor and the wailing Doctor Seward, whose mind is now as broken as those poor wretches it was once his responsibility to care for, you prepare to meet the last desperate charge of the English nobleman and his American friend. (In this battle, you have the initiative.)

	COMBAT	ENDURANCE
ARTHUR HOLMWOOD	8	9
QUINCEY MORRIS	9	9

At any time during the battle, if you wish you may spend 4 *Blood* points to eliminate one of your opponents, but you may only do so once.

If you kill Holmwood and Morris, gain 6 *Blood* points and turn to **585**. However, if you lose the battle, turn to **605**.

525

Making your way further into the Turkish camp, you come upon a great golden pavilion. It is at least three times the size of the largest of the other tents and far grander.

Standing guard either side of the awning that shades the entrance to the marquee are two tall Janissaries, that look like they could have been chiselled from granite, their faces hidden by full, thick beards, in the preferred style of the Ottomans. They are both armed with axe-headed halberds.

The tent stands apart from the others, meaning that you will not be able to approach unseen.

Do you want to approach the pavilion boldly (turn to **495**), or do you think it would be wiser to retreat from Mehmed's encampment and return to Târgoviște, armed with the knowledge you have already acquired about the make-up of the Conqueror's forces (turn to **285**)?

526

You cast the deckhand's limp, bloodless body over the gunwale into the sea, there to become food for the dwellers of the deep.

But the man's disappearance does not go unnoticed and fuels the fire that feeds the crew's suspicions that this voyage is cursed.

Gain 1 *Suspicion* point and turn to **730**.

527

Three nights after you last left Hillingham, you are forced to endure the most vivid dream...

* * * *

You are running through the streets of London, but in the form of a wolf rather than that of a man. People flee before you in terror until, eventually, you find yourself in the grounds of the Westenra family home once more. Only now you are no longer a wolf but a bat, and you enter the house through an open window.

Flying through the darkened rooms you see the bodies of the servants, lying limply on the ground, looking like nothing more than abandoned ragdolls. Ignoring them, you continue up the stairs to Lucy's room.

Putting your hand to the door, human again now, you open it to find your beloved fast asleep. But as you approach the bed, Lucy suddenly sits bolt upright, her red hair writhing about her head like tongues of flame. Her eyes snap open but the whites are drowned in blood, and hissing, she opens her mouth to reveal elongated snake-like fangs!

* * * *

You wake with a start, your bed drenched in sweat.

What can it all mean? You are beginning to wonder if your habit of living amongst the insane is beginning to tell upon your own brain.

Nonetheless, all the next day your memory of that terrible dream returns to haunt you. At sunset, your dream-sent visions return with greater intensity and you start to fear that it was not a nightmare at all but some grim prophecy.

If you want to drop everything and travel to Hillingham now, even though it will take you half the night to get there, turn to **396**. If not, turn to **424**.

528

As you are preparing to deal with what resistance remains, Arthur suddenly appears at your side and runs one of the beasts through with his rapier-blade.

If all the Werewolves have now been dealt with, turn to **568**. If not, turn to **548**.

529

The door opens and you enter another gloom-haunted room. Ancient, moth-eaten war-banners and pennants hang from the high walls of the chamber, while, picked out in the light cast by your lamp, you see a dust-shrouded suit of armour. It has something of the dragon about it, the mail reminding you of scales, while the faceplate of the helm projects as with a reptilian snout. You wonder which of the Count's ancestors last wore it into battle.

Perhaps it was the imperious figure who peers down from you from a canvas on the wall behind the suit of armour, among the motionless flags.

The armour has been posed as if it was still occupied, arms crossed in front of the breastplate, the gauntlets together, resting on the hilt of a magnificent sword, the tip of which is balanced in a groove in the wooden plinth on which it stands.

The blade does not appear to have suffered the unkind attentions of time, unlike the suit itself and the rest of the room's adornments, and you wonder how it would feel in your hand.

If you want to take up the sword, turn to **559**. If not, turn to **642**.

530

Fear and adrenaline lending him a strength and speed he never knew he had, the terrified sailor makes it to the door to the Captain's cabin before you catch up with him, and, in your beast-form, bring him crashing down onto the deck.

One bite of your terrible jaws puts an end to his life in an instant, and you drag his body back to the cargo hold to enjoy at your leisure. (Gain 2 *Blood* points and restore up to 4 *Endurance* points.)

However, the ruckus outside the Captain's cabin cannot have gone unnoticed. (Also gain 2 *Suspicion* points.)

Turn to **958**.

531

Reacting lightning-fast, you manage to evade the striking snake and then, in a stunning display of dexterity, grab hold of it and cast it into the fire.

But Quincey's quick-draw skills fail him now and the other albino serpent sinks its fangs into his hand before he can wrest it from him and crush its head beneath his cowboy-booted heel.

He staggers backwards, gritting his teeth against the pain.

"Quincey!" you call out to him. "Quincey, are you all right?"

Slowly your American friend opens his eyes and as they focus on you, you see madness there.

Quincey takes his great Bowie knife from its sheath, but rather than threatening the nearest gypsy with it, he staggers towards you, murder in his gaze.

If you want to use *The Pen is Mightier* special ability, and you still can, cross off one use and turn to **37**. If not, turn to **17**.

532

There are four of these overgrown rats altogether, dining on the flesh of the dead.

Their noses start to twitch, as they pick up your scent, even over the lingering stench of decay permeating the warehouse. Squeaking furiously, they abandon their scavengers' feast and scamper towards you.

If you want to use *The Pen is Mightier* special ability, and you still can, turn to **562**. If not, turn to **628**.

533

"You may go anywhere you wish within the castle, except where the doors are locked, where of course you will not wish to go," the Count says gravely. "There is a reason that all things are as they are. We are in Transylvania, and Transylvania is not England. Our ways are not your ways, and there shall be to you many strange things. From what you have told me of your experiences already, you know something of what strange things there may be."

If you have the code word *Lángok* ticked off, turn to **553**. It not, turn to **654**.

534

Your heart seems to stand still. You try to scream but find yourself somehow paralysed.

Take an ESP test. If you pass the test, turn to **554**, but if you fail the test, turn to **613**.

535

Walpurgis Night approaches and your mind returns to the Weird Sisters' warning. Despite having used your contacts to book him lodgings at every stop he will make on the way to you, concerned for Mr Harker's wellbeing, in the light of the Sisters' prophecy, you compose a telegram that you charge Medve with carrying to Bistritz, to be sent from the telegraph station there that you yourself paid to be built, so as to be able to keep in touch with the wider world.

```
Bistritz.
Be careful of my guest - his safety is most precious to
me. Should aught happen to him, or if he be missed, spare
nothing to find him and ensure his safety. He is English
and therefore adventurous. There are often dangers from
snow and wolves and night.
Lose not a moment if you suspect harm to him. I answer
your zeal with my fortune.
Dracula
```

But having sent it, you cannot shake the unwelcome knowledge of all that could happen to Mr Harker between Munich and here.

If you have the code word *Apáca* ticked off, turn to **565**.

If not, do you want to venture far afield on Walpurgis Night yourself, to ensure that nothing untoward befalls this second solicitor (turn to **645**), or, if you are confident no ill shall befall him, turn to **590**.

536

Varney the Vampire goes for you then and you are forced to defend yourself. (In this battle your opponent has the initiative.)

VARNEY THE VAMPIRE   COMBAT 11   ENDURANCE 12

If you slay the vampire, turn to **125**. If you wish, rather than having to fight him, you may deduct 6 *Blood* points and then turn to **125** anyway.

537

Suddenly possessed of incredible strength, Arthur hurls you from him and you fly through the air before landing painfully on your back in the snow, hitting a rock that was concealed by a drift.

Lose 2 *Endurance* points and, if you are still alive, turn to **566**.

538

"Mr Renfield, your new hobby is most unhygienic!" you exclaim. "I must insist that you remove the flies from your cell forthwith."

Such a look passes over his face then that you half expect him to break out into a furious rage, but to your astonishment, he does not.

After a moment's thought he says, "May I have three days, Doctor Seward? Give me three days and I shall clear them all away."

Impressed with his calm and measured response to your request, you agree to his, and continue your rounds.

Turn to **631**.

539

Professor Van Helsing is suddenly there by your side, his silvered blade in his hand. With one clean thrust he plunges it into the transformed Countess's heart. She gives a yowl of frustration and pain and slides from the blade onto the carpeted floor.

And then, before your very eyes, Carmilla's cat-body dissolves into a cloud of golden motes of dust which twinkle once before fading into nothingness.

Turn to **509**.

540

Making it out of the cave, the screams of the dying dragon-worm reverberating from the cavern behind you, you sprint through the catacombs as those ancient tunnels start to collapse.

Adrenaline gives you the strength to make it back to the crypt and from there into the ancient fortress, as paintings and displays of armour are shaken from their mountings around you, until you burst through the doors of Castle Dracula into the courtyard. From there you flee through the gates and re-join your friends, only then allowing yourself to fall to your knees in the snow, utterly exhausted.

Turn to **75**.

541

The night's strange distractions are forgotten when news reaches the Crescent that the poor sea captain, who was found lashed to the wheel of the *Demeter*, is to be buried today.

If you want to attend the funeral yourself, turn to **603**. If not, turn to **561**.

542

Most of the rooms on the first floor are empty, the few pieces of furniture you do find draped in heavy dustsheets. However, at the back of the house you come upon a study that looks like one of the cabinets of curiosities that were popular a century ago.

A large glass-fronted piece of furniture, that is a cross between a display case and a bookcase, dominates one wall, and in front of it is a desk piled with papers that is as cluttered as the cabinet. You see animal skulls, intriguing fossils, geodes, pieces of meteorite, polished fans of coral, West African carved figurines, and a plethora of other curios.

If you want to enter the cabinet of curiosities to take a closer look, turn to **523**. If you would rather leave the first floor and see what else you can find elsewhere, turn to **273**.

543

As you sleep, you dream...

* * * *

You find yourself back in Whitby, and night has fallen. You are walking the silent streets of the sleeping fishing port, wearing nothing but your nightdress.

You climb the 199 steps to St Mary's Church and there, at the top of the East Cliff, sit down on your favourite seat to rest.

But as you sit there, gazing out at the schooner wracked by the storm-tossed waves, the moon-cast shadows seem to coalesce around you, and you see two glowing coals set amidst the blackness, while moonlight shines from the tips of two elongated fangs...

* * * *

You suddenly start awake, your heart pounding and the wafer-burn on your forehead throbbing. And in that moment you fear you will never be free of the curse of the vampire!

Add 1 point to your *Terror* score, gain 3 *Blood* points, and then turn to **563**.

544

You brandish the crucifix the old woman gave you before the unnatural harridans. In response, they howl like banshees and recoil from you, so you decide to press home your advantage and fight your way free of their domain.

(If you end up actually fighting the foul fiends, you may reduce all their *Combat* scores by 1 point.)

If you want to use *The Pen is Mightier* special ability, cross off one use and turn to **618**. If not, turn to **344**.

545

LOG OF THE 'DEMETER'

4 August ~ Still fog, which the sunrise cannot pierce. I know there is sunrise because I am a sailor, why else I know not. I dared not go below, I dared not leave the helm; so here all night I stayed, and in the dimness of the night I saw It, Him! God forgive me, but the mate was right to jump overboard. It was better to die like a man; to die like a sailor in blue water no man can object. But I am captain, and I must not leave my ship. But I shall baffle this fiend or monster, for I shall tie my hands to the wheel when my strength begins to fail, and along with them I shall tie that which He, It, dare not touch; and then, come good wind or foul, I shall save my soul, and my honour as a captain. I am growing weaker, and the night is coming on. If He can look me in the face again, I may not have time to act. If we are wrecked, mayhap this account may be found, and those who find it may understand. If not... well, then all men shall know that I have been true to my trust. God and the Blessed Virgin and the saints help a poor ignorant soul trying to do his duty...

Turn to **284**.

546

You watch in revulsion as the remainder of the rats push past you and disappear into the abandoned building.

Were you injured at all by the rats? If so, turn to **576**. If not, turn to **622**.

547

Leaving your rooms, you roam the castle, descending its long staircases and exploring its great vaulted galleries, but just run up against one dead-end or one locked door after another, until soon you fear that you will never be able to escape this place. (Add 1 to your *Terror* score.)

In the end you are forced to admit defeat; there is no way for you to penetrate the Count's lair from inside the castle and seeing as you dare not venture forth from your window and scale the castle walls to reach it, you will simply have to return to your rooms and wait for fate to play its hand.

Turn to **382**.

548

Any Werewolves that remain have the following stats, although you have the initiative in the battle.

WEREWOLF   COMBAT 7   ENDURANCE 7

If you win the fight, turn to **568**.

549

It is as if Arthur no longer knows you, no matter how much you cry his name, desperately hoping to make him see sense somehow. You realise you have no choice but to defend yourself against the bewitched wretch. (In this battle you have the initiative.)

ARTHUR   COMBAT 8   ENDURANCE 9

You do not want to hurt your friend, and you certainly don't want to kill him, so you fight merely to incapacitate him and put him out of the fight.

For the duration of this battle, you must reduce your *Combat Rating* by 1 point, as you are trying to knock Arthur out, rather than kill him. If you win two consecutive Combat Rounds, or if you reduce Arthur's Endurance score to 4 points or fewer, whichever happens first, you succeed in knocking him out – turn to **579** at once.

550

The Janissary dead, it is a simple matter for you to remove his hauberk and pull it on over your own leather armour. Putting on his helmet and arming yourself with his scimitar completes your disguise.

Tick off the code word *Rejtett* and turn to **525**.

551

His ugly face is twisted by a manic grin, the inmate fixes you with wildly staring eyes and, giving voice to an animalistic snarl, launches himself at you.

If you want to use *The Pen is Mightier* special ability, cross off one use and turn to **688**. If not, turn to **748**.

552

"Do you know Count Dracula?" you ask. "And what can you tell me of his castle home?"

At that the landlord and his wife cross themselves, saying that they know nothing at all, and simply refuse to say any more. What can be unnerving them so?

Their unsettled disposition leaves you feeling on edge too.

Tick off the code word *Babona* and turn to **602**.

553

Talk of strange things causes you to call to mind the coachman's actions the preceding night, on the way to Castle Dracula, and your encounter with the wolf pack.

If you want to ask the Count about what you witnessed, turn to **584**. If not, turn to **654**.

554

In that instant you realise that this is not a dream at all but the horrible waking truth – this creature of the night is actually in the room with you, standing beside your bed!

"Silence!" the man hisses in a keen, cutting whisper.

You try to scream out, but no sound comes from your paralysed vocal cords.

He places one cold hand upon your shoulder and, holding you tight, bares your throat with the other, saying as he does so, "I require a little refreshment to reward my exertions."

Take a Terror test. If you pass the test, turn to **574**. If you fail the test, turn to **613**.

555

Part of you realises that the visions are not real – *cannot be real!* – no matter how convincing they seem to be. As soon as you realise that, you are able to start to fight back against them, until you dispel the last of them – a vision of a black dog onboard a ship, surrounded by the bodies of dead sailors – and wake to find yourself buried in a shallow grave. You burst free of the earth as a sense of impending doom threatens to overwhelm you, not knowing how much time has passed – is it minutes or months, seconds or centuries?

* * * *

From that moment on, your Scholomance training begins in earnest, as you are inducted into the secrets of necromancy.

You also find that after your sojourn in the soil of your homeland, your senses have become sharper, your hearing heightened, and your reactions quicker. You find that you are physically stronger too, and you are even able to catch glimpses of the surface thoughts of others.

(Add 1 point to your *Agility* and *Combat* scores, 2 points to your *ESP* score, and 4 points to your *Endurance* score. Also gain 6 *Blood* points.)

You feel as if you are no longer quite human, as if you are slowly transforming into something else, and a hunger for battle and bloodshed greater than you have ever known now burns within you.

Soon there is no one, among all the worshippers of Balaur-Apophis, who can best you in battle, none who are as fast as you or as agile as you, nor as ruthless.

"You are ready," the high priestess declares one day. "Go out into the world again and drive the enemy from our lands. But never forget the promise you made the Great Serpent, for one day that debt will come due."

The Priestess and the rest of the cult's devotees lead you from the tunnels that riddle the depths of the mountain, back to the cave by which you first entered Broken Tooth Mountain, but they do not follow as you step out into the light of a new dawn.

It takes a moment for your eyes to adjust to the light, having been underground for... In fact, you have no idea how long you have been in the catacomb-like caverns. And so, not wasting another second, you head south for Târgoviște.

* * * *

Days later, when you finally come in sight of the capital and your palace once more, you are horrified to find the city besieged, nearby farms and villages having been put to the torch. You might have gained the power to stop Mehmed but are you too late for it to make any difference?

Pushing on into the thick of the fray, driven by a hungry fire in your belly and a savage fury in your heart, you slake your thirst for revenge on the first of the enemy you come upon, amidst the chaos and confusion of the smoke-smothered battlefield.

The two Janissaries will not know what has hit them. (In this battle, you have the initiative, but you must fight the soldiers at the same time.)

	COMBAT	ENDURANCE
First JANISSARY	8	8
Second JANISSARY	8	7

If you slay your opponents, turn to **638**.

556

"Good lord!" the coastguard suddenly cries.

He has his spyglass to his eye and is looking through it at a strange ship, out at sea, that is knocking about in the queerest way.

"She's a Russian, by the look of her," he goes on, "but she doesn't seem to know her mind one bit. She seems to see the storm coming but can't decide whether to run up north in the open, or to put in here."

It certainly looks to you like she is being steered mighty strangely, as if there's no hand on the wheel at all, for the ship changes about with every puff of wind.

"We'll hear more of her before this time tomorrow," the coastguard says sagely.

* * * *

You return to the house on the Crescent where you are staying but that night are woken a little after midnight, as the tempest breaks. Lucy is tossing and turning in her bed, moaning faintly, but she does not get up. You, however, cannot sleep for thinking of the ship you saw struggling against the tide.

Do you want to sneak out of the house, and return to the East Cliff to watch for the ship (turn to **578**), or do you want to remain where you are and pray that sleep takes you again before too long (turn to **793**)?

557

In your vespertilian form, you fly towards an open window, but as soon as you come within a yard of the aging edifice, you are suddenly overwhelmed by agonising pain. It is as if you have struck an invisible barrier, a zone of righteousness that burns your undead form; it is as painful as if you had been cast onto a bonfire.

Either lose 8 *Endurance* points, 3 *Agility* points, 2 *Combat* points, and 2 *ESP* points, or deduct 6 *Blood* points. Make the necessary alterations to your Adventure Sheet and then decide what you are going to do next.

If you want to approach the main entrance via the bridge, if you haven't done so already, turn to **721**. If you think it would be wisest to give up trying to enter the Hospital of St Joseph and Ste Mary, and at least try to return to Castle Dracula before sunrise, turn to **810**.

558

"I understand you recently spent some time abroad," you say.

"That's right," Renfield replies, warily.

"Eastern Europe, wasn't it?"

"Yes. Transylvania."

"And what was the reason for your trip?"

"I had business with... a client. I was assisting him with the purchase of certain properties in and around London," he says, maintaining a calm, almost professional, demeanour.

"And who was this client?"

"That I cannot reveal. It is a secret," Renfield replies. And in the next instant a startling change comes over him.

One moment he is the respected West Country solicitor, the next he is transformed into a bestial savage.

"The Master!" he screams, foam flying from between gritted teeth. "The Master!"

Before the attendants can come to your aid, Renfield throws himself at you. Grabbing you by the throat with both hands, he starts to throttle you, as you fight to free yourself from his vice-like grip.

Take a Combat test. If you pass the test, turn to **581**. If you fail the test, turn to **611**.

559

Carefully unclasping the gauntlet fingers, you ease the sword from the place where it has rested for God alone knows how long.

Take an ESP test. If you pass the test, turn to **589**. If not, turn to **616**.

560

You flee from the house through the front door, not caring who sees you, sending the locksmith who is still outside reeling.

Turn to **635**.

561

Despite deciding not to attend the funeral, you do suggest to Lucy that the two of you go for a walk – secretly hoping that if she is physically tired after a day's exertions she will not sleep-walk again tonight – and thankfully she agrees.

You take her out for a long walk by the cliffs to Robin Hood's Bay and back. As you set off for the cliff path, it seems to you that every boat in the harbour is there for the sea captain's send off.

You have a lovely walk. Lucy is in good spirits, owing, you think, to some curious cows that come nosing towards you in a field close to the lighthouse, and frighten the wits out of you! You share a capital 'severe tea' at Robin Hood's Bay in a sweet little old-fashioned inn, sitting at a bow window that looks right over the seaweed-covered rocks of the strand. Then you walk home again with some – or rather many – stoppages to rest, and with your hearts full of a constant dread of wild bulls.

As you had hoped, by the time you return to the rented house on the Crescent, Lucy is suitably tired, and you intend to creep off to bed as soon as you can. But your plans are thwarted when the young curate of St Mary's calls in, and Mrs Westenra asks him to stay for supper.

Turn to **948**.

562

The Texan suddenly opens fire upon the giant rats, a large pistol gripped tightly in each hand, filling the close confines of the warehouse with a cacophony of gunshots and thick blue smoke.

Less than a minute later, the barking of the guns is replaced by a dull clicking, their chambers empty, and the rats are dead.

Leaving the property – intending to come back again once this nightmare is over and clear up after yourselves properly – you head back to the main thoroughfare, hoping to meet with the others at Dracula's house on Piccadilly.

Turn to **876**.

563

You are greatly relieved when your husband and the other Vampire-Hunters return to Purfleet that evening and you greet them at the door, daring to hope that they might bring with them good news.

But when you see their faces, and how your own dear Jonathan appears to have transformed from a vigorous young man in his prime to a haggard old soul in the space of one day – his white hair matching well with the hollow burning eyes and grief-written lines etched into his face – you feel the colour drain from your own cheeks and can scarce hold back the tears.

"I can never thank you all enough," you tell the Vampire-Hunters, and taking Jonathan's grey head in your hands you kiss it, saying, "Oh, my poor darling!"

(Add 1 point to your *Terror* score.)

Turn to **583**.

564

"And now, my friends," the Professor addresses you, "we have a duty to do. We must sterilise the earth that he has brought from a far distant land for such fell use. It is sacred to him because it is of his homeland, but we will sanctify it in God's name, purifying it and denying the Evil One his sanctuary."

As he speaks, he takes from his bag a screwdriver and a wrench and opens one of the crates. The earth it contains is redolent with the odours of damp and mildew. Taking up tools, the rest of you prepare to follow the Professor's example.

Using your knife, you prise open one of the crates and immediately recoil in horror; you can see dead fingers and the mottled pate of a head half-buried within the soil. Your horror is only compounded when the fingers suddenly start to twitch, and you stagger back in appalled disbelief.

Before your very eyes, a hand emerges from the mouldering loam, followed by another, and together they heave the body buried within the box from the stinking earth. Its features are half-rotted away, and its skin – that is like old, white leather – is stretched over the bones of its ribcage.

Take a Terror test. If you pass the test, turn to **780**. If you fail the test, turn to **814**.

565

And then there is the matter of the forewarning you have received about the part a certain Sister of Holy Orders may have to play in your unfolding plans and Machiavellian machinations.

If you want to seek out this mysterious nun in Buda-Pesth, turn to **680**.

If not, but you want to venture forth this Walpurgis Night yourself, to ensure that nothing untoward befalls this second solicitor, turn to **645**.

Failing that, if you are sure that you have done enough to ensure his safe arrival, turn to **590**.

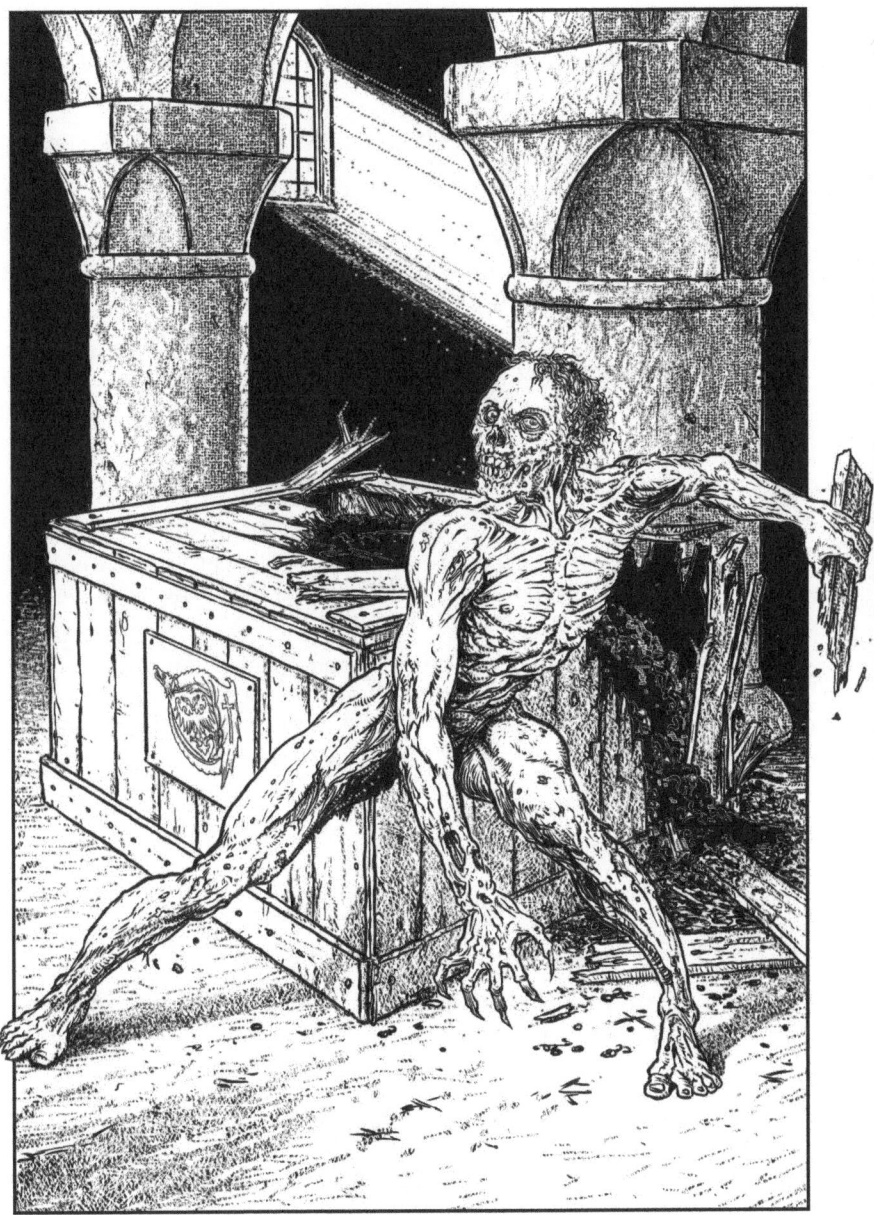

566

Before your eyes, Arthur undergoes a horrifying transformation. His face becomes covered with thick hair while his nose and mouth become a lupine snout.

And it is not only his face that is changing; as you watch, his nails lengthen, and the tips of his fingers start to bleed as the talons push through the skin.

A low growl rises from Arthur's chest and he fixes you with beady jaundice-yellow eyes. It is as if he doesn't know you anymore. And then, snarling, he attacks.

If you want to call upon *The Pen is Mightier* special ability, cross off one use and turn to **629**. If not, turn to **596**.

567

Suddenly desiring to return to the daylight and the security of your own chambers, you go back the way you came, leaving the Count's room by the window, and crawl again up the castle wall. Regaining your room, you throw yourself panting onto the bed.

Slowly you become aware of a gypsy song, sung by merry voices, coming from far off but drawing closer, and accompanied by the rolling of heavy wheels and the cracking of whips. The Szgany have returned.

Turn to **607**.

568

The pack is gone, the wolves either fled or dead.

If you were injured at all during the battle in the graveyard, turn to **599**. If not, turn to **619**.

569

You have no choice but to defend yourself against the hissing hellcat. (In this battle, your opponent has the initiative.)

WERECAT   COMBAT 8   ENDURNACE 8

If you are still alive after 4 Combat Rounds, or if you reduce the Werecat's *Endurance* score to 4 points or fewer, whichever is sooner, turn to **539**.

570

Before you can even make it out of the cave, a great chunk of rock comes free of the ceiling and crashes down beside you. While it doesn't strike you directly, the impact causes you to stumble and fall to the ground, grazing knees and elbows and banging your head on the rocky floor.

Lose 3 *Endurance* points and, if you are still conscious, turn to **540**.

571

You cannot resist. Accepting the cup, you drink deeply. It tastes like one of the full-bodied rustic reds you have been forced to tolerate whilst travelling through Eastern Europe.

Turn to **78**.

572

You are so shocked by your discovery that you run from the cellar, wailing in terror, and climb the servants' stairs two at a time to the ground floor.

Add 1 point to your *Terror* score and turn to **273**.

573

Renfield's face is distorted with terrible passion, and he is clearly dangerous whilst in this state. You try to keep the table between you and the lunatic, but he slashes at you with his stolen blade and manages to catch you on the wrist with its gleaming edge.

Lose 2 *Endurance* points and turn to **633**.

574

By sheer strength of will, you manage to break free of the Count's hypnotic spell. But his grip is like iron and so, as adrenaline rushes through your body, adding fuel to the fire of your fear, you struggle to free yourself from his clutches.

Take a Combat test. If you pass the test, turn to **594**. If you fail the test, turn to **613**.

575

You raise the shield before Dracula, and he recoils, hissing and spitting, as he is confronted by the cross of St George that adorns it. But the vampire is getting desperate now, and such a device won't hold him at bay for long.

If you want to use *The Pen is Mightier* special ability, turn to **300**. If not, turn to **350**.

576

You pause to examine the bite marks on your leg. A fear creeps over you – the fear that your injuries might be infected, that the rats might have been carriers of some terrible disease.

Roll one die (or pick a card); if the number rolled is even (or the card is black), turn to **622**, but if the number rolled is odd (or the card is red), turn to **597**.

577

Breaking free of the lunatic's strangle hold, you turn to face your attacker.

Roll one die (or pick a card). If the number rolled is odd (or the card is red), turn to **493**. If the number rolled is even (or the card is black), turn to **551**.

578

You dress quickly, and leaving the bedroom, you lock the door behind you, taking the key with you, in case Lucy's disturbed sleep should lead to another incidence of sleep-walking.

Exiting the house without anyone knowing, by the back door, you make your way hurriedly through the town, and up the 199 steps to the East Cliff churchyard, all the while the wind roaring like thunder and threatening to blow you off your feet. But you make it to the lookout point in the end and find the coastguard. Several officers are preparing to test the new searchlight that has been installed there for the first time.

It is as if the whole aspect of nature has become convulsed. The waves rise in growing fury, each over-topping its fellow, and the sea becomes a devouring monster. White-crested waves beat madly at the beach and rush up the cliffs. Others break over the piers at the entrance to the harbour, their spume drenching the lanthorns of the lighthouses there.

But it is difficult to see much else, since masses of sea-fog are drifting inland; white, wet wreaths, which sweep by in ghostly fashion, so dank and damp and cold that it needs but little imagination to think that they are the spirits of those lost at sea, reaching for their living brethren with the clammy hands of death.

The mist clears from time to time, and you can see the sea for some distance in the glare of the lightning, which comes thick and fast, followed by such peals of thunder that the whole sky seems to tremble.

The officers of the coastguard finally manage to fire up the searchlight and before long discover the schooner you saw earlier, all sails set, and an involuntary shudder goes through you when you realise the terrible danger it is in. Between the vessel and the port lies a great reef on which many good ships have floundered before, and with the wind blowing from its present quarter, it will be quite impossible for her to make the entrance to the harbour with the gale threatening to force her onto the shoals.

It is nearly the hour of high tide, but the waves are so great that in their troughs you can almost see the shallows of the shore. Then comes another rush of sea-fog, a mass of dank mist that seems to smother everything in a grey pall.

The wind suddenly shifts to the north-east, and the remnant of the sea-fog melts before the mighty billows. And swept before the blast, leaping from wave to wave as it rushes headlong, the strange schooner unbelievably gains the safety of the harbour.

The searchlight follows her passage, and another shudder runs through you, for now you can see lashed to the helm is a corpse, with drooping head, soaked by the sea, which swings horribly to and fro with the motion of the ship. (Add 1 point to your *Terror* score.)

Without slowing, the schooner rushes across the harbour, pitching herself up on the accumulation of sand and gravel washed by many tides and many storms into the southeast corner of the pier jutting under the East Cliff, known locally as Tate Hill Pier.

The vessel drives up onto the shore, the sand piling around her hull as it ploughs its way through the beach, the keel splintering as it does so, every spar, rope and stay straining, as the foremast comes crashing down.

But strangest of all, the very instant the ship touches the shore, an immense black dog springs up on deck from below and jumps from the bow of the schooner onto the sand. It makes straight for the cliff, from where you are watching these strange events unfold. In fact, it seems to be coming straight towards you.

(Tick off the code word *Bogey*.)

If you want to flee from the beast, turn to **598**. If you are determined to stand your ground, turn to **661**.

579

Lucy rushes past you, heading straight for the tomb.

Do you want to block her way (turn to **609**), or would you prefer not to obstruct her (turn to **669**)?

580

The commotion has alerted other Turks nearby to your presence within the camp. Before you can retrace your footsteps and make your escape, you find yourself surrounded and taken prisoner. As soon as the evidence of your murderous behaviour is discovered, without even facing trial, you are sentenced to death.

With the protestations of who you really are on your lips, one of the Janissaries unsheathes his sword and, with one clean strike, removes your head from your shoulders.

Your adventure is over before it has barely begun.

THE END

581

You manage to break the lunatic's hold on your neck, but the damage has already been done. As several attendants ensure he remains inside his cell, another helps you get out before you can come to any further harm.

Deduct 2 *Endurance* points, add 1 to your *Terror* score, and gain 3 *Blood* points.

Now turn to **631**.

582

Mina's steps falter while her features reveal some inner turmoil she is going through.

"Come to me, Mina," you call to her again. "Be one with me."

"Yes, Master," she mumbles, through gritted teeth, as she joins you.

And then suddenly there is a blade in her hand and, with one savage yet fluid motion, she slices its keen edge across your throat. (Lose 3 *Endurance* points and 3 *Blood* points.) If she had been but one step closer, she might have ended you!

Blinded by fury, you lift her off the ground with one hand and hurl her away from you into the snow.

A split second later, Harker and the American are before you, their own weapons drawn. (Your attackers have the initiative in this battle.)

	COMBAT	ENDURANCE
JONATHAN HARKER	10	11
QUINCEY MORRIS	9	9

At any time during the battle, if you wish, you may spend 4 *Blood* points to eliminate one of your opponents, but you may only use this trick once.

If you kill Harker and Morris, gain 6 *Blood* points and turn to **666**. However, if you lose the battle, turn to **605**.

583

That night, Quincey Morris keeps watch outside your room, should the vampire seek to attack you again. As a result, you sleep well; better than you have for many a night.

But as the grey of the coming dawn is making the windows into sharp oblongs, and the gas flame is like a speck rather than a disc of light, you find yourself fully awake, an idea having formed in your mind that you cannot shake.

Waking your husband, you tell him to call the Professor, for you want to see him at once.

When he asks why, you say, "I have an idea. I suppose it must have come in the night and matured without my knowing it. Go quick, dearest, the time is getting close."

Two or three minutes later, Professor Van Helsing is in the room, in his dressing-gown, while Arthur and Quincey are standing with Dr Seward at the door asking questions.

"Oh, my dear Madam Mina," says the Professor, rubbing his hands together in glee, "this is indeed a change. We have got our old Madam Mina back! And what can I do for you?"

"I want you to hypnotise me!" you tell him. "Do it before the dawn, for I feel that then I can speak, and speak freely. Be quick, for the time is short!"

Without a word, he motions for you to sit up in bed. Looking fixedly at you, he starts to make passes in front of your face, from over the top of your head downward, with each hand in turn. You gaze at him fixedly for a few minutes, but gradually your eyelids grow heavy, and you close your eyes...

Take an ESP test. If you pass the test, turn to **634**, but if you fail the test, turn to **612**.

584

It is evident that the Count is in the mood to talk, if only for talking's sake, and so you do. Growing bolder, you ask him why the coachman went to the spot where he had seen the blue flames.

"It is a commonly held belief," your host says, "that on a certain night of the year – last night, in fact, when all evil spirits are supposed to have unchecked sway – a blue flame is seen over the place where treasure has been concealed."

"There is buried treasure hidden in the Carpathian Mountains?" you say.

"Of that there can be little doubt," the Count goes on, "for this whole region has been fought over for centuries by the Wallachian, the Saxon, and the Turk. Why, there is hardly a foot of soil in all Transylvania that has not been enriched by the blood of men – patriots or invaders. When the Austrian and the Hungarian came up in hordes, men and women, the aged and the children, went out to meet them, triggering artificial avalanches above the treacherous passes. And when the invader was triumphant, he found but little, for whatever there was had been sheltered in the friendly soil."

Gain 2 *Blood* points and turn to **654**.

585

Your enemies are defeated; you are free of them at last!

The mountains bathed bronze by the last of its light, the sun sinks below the western horizon.

Answering your summons, Mina joins you at your side, her witless husband stumbling after her and looking like some forlorn puppy. With Harker's wife as your new queen, you shall sire a brave dynasty of nosferatu.

But you have had enough of England to last you an entire afterlife, and the British Empire is dead to you now.

If there is one thing eternal life has taught you, it is patience. And so, you will wait, as long as it takes, to rebuild your undead army. When you are ready, and only then, you will put your plans of conquest into action.

Perhaps you will set your sights on the New World instead, and live your own American dream...

THE END

586

The window of the chamber suddenly flies open, and a terrible tornado sweeps through the room, extinguishing the flames. In its wake comes the Count.

Turn to **679**.

587

Recovering themselves, your fellow Vampire-Hunters rally and advance on the Count, crucifixes and wafers held out before them, while Van Helsing intones the words of the exorcism prayer in Latin.

The Count's face twists into an expression of baffled hatred and hellish rage, as he cowers before the sacred symbols, and his waxy skin acquires a vile jaundiced hue.

The next instant, with a sinuous dive, he flies across the room and throws himself at the un-shuttered window. Amidst the crash and glitter of falling glass, he tumbles into the stone-flagged yard below.

You join the others in running to the window and see your quarry spring unhurt from the ground. Crossing the yard, he pushes open the stable door, but there hesitates and turns.

"You think you can confound my plans? You shall be sorry, each one of you! You think you have left me without a place to rest, but I have more! My revenge is just begun! It is a plan I have devised over the centuries and time is on my side. Your girls that you all love are mine already, and through them you and others shall become my creatures yet, to do my bidding and to be my jackals when I want to feed!"

And then he passes quickly through the door and is gone.

Turn to **910**.

588

The rodents' unnatural appetites can only be sated now by human flesh. (The rats have the initiative in this battle, and you must fight the four that are coming for you two at a time.)

	COMBAT	ENDURANCE
First GIANT RAT	5	6
Second GIANT RAT	6	5
Third GIANT RAT	5	5
Fourth GIANT RAT	6	6

If you manage to do away with all the rats, turn to **658**.

589

The room suddenly starts to spin as your vision blurs. But in your mind's eye, you see another kind of vision altogether…

You are caught up in the midst of battle. In the distance rise the ramparts of a mighty fortress-town but it is obscured by the smoke that rises from the battlefield. You see infantry soldiers and cavalrymen in dated armour, bearing the standards of the Ottoman Empire, intent on breaching the defences of the town, but they are brought up short when the smoke clears, revealing a forest of the impaled – hundreds of men, women, and even children, writhing in agony on stakes that have been rammed into the ground, row upon row of them, as far as the eye can see…

And then the hordes of charging Turks and the forest of stakes impaled with prisoners of war are just figures in a mosaic that you now see covers the ceiling of the chamber, while you are lying on the floor staring up at it.

Picking yourself up again, you study the mysterious blade, searching for an explanation for the strange visions that assailed you.

Add 1 point to your *ESP* score and turn to **616**.

590

Rather than travelling too far afield this night, you instead visit a village in the valley beneath Broken Tooth Mountain, reminding the peasant populace why they are right to fear the night, drinking the blood of a woodcutter in an attempt to quiet the insatiable beast that dwells within you.

Tick off the code word *Rabszolga* and turn to **810**.

591

Putting up your hand you politely refuse the drink, expecting the woman to move on to Quincey or offer it to someone else. But she is insistent. Perhaps you have offended her by not drinking but you make your excuses, explaining that you still have some way to go this night and need to keep a clear head. And yet she still will not take no for an answer and tries to put the goblet to your lips.

If you have the code word *Lycanthropy* ticked off, turn to **571**.

If not, *Take a Combat test*, adding 1 point to the dice roll if you have the code word *Lyssavirus* ticked off. If you pass the test, turn to **844**. If you fail the test, turn to **571**.

592

Two hours after supper, six of you gather in Dr Seward's study, and take your places around the table, like some impromptu committee. Professor Van Helsing takes the head of the table and makes the necessary introductions.

"My friends, in recent days we have all witnessed terrible things and have seen evidence of a corrupting evil working within the world, but I believe that we six have a chance to put an end to it, for we are uniquely blessed that our band has many skills that will help us to overcome our enemy and thwart his dastardly plans for conquest.

"We have Mr Harker, who not only survived the horrors he encountered within the monster's lair but had the courage to escape its confines, and whose solicitor's eye for detail has only increased our knowledge, and thereby the likely success of our scheme, since returning to England.

"And we have Mrs Harker, who has also witnessed first-hand the powers the blackguard can command, and whose scrupulous secretarial skills mean that we have as complete a record of the monster's actions to date as it is possible to have.

"Thanks to Lord Godalming's considerable resources, we need not want for anything in our fight against this foreign invader. Be it bullets, or train tickets, he has kindly said that he will cover all costs. And along with Arthur's generosity, we have Mr Quincey Morris's courage and redoubtable combat skills. With this brave Texan in our midst, we shall take the fight to the enemy and win!

"Then there is my friend, Dr John Seward, whose medical knowledge rivals my own, and whose insights into the workings of the mind are even greater. Fortuitously – or is it the hand of fate aiding us in our endeavour – his study of a patient in his care, a certain Mr Renfield, himself formerly an employee of Hawkins, Oldman & Lee in Exeter, has helped us learn where we must begin the hunt for the fiend.

"But before we do, I must tell you something of the kind of enemy we now face. For you must understand that there are such things as vampires; and there is much evidence that they exist. I admit that at first I myself was a sceptic, and – alas! – had I known from the outset what I now know to be true, the life of dear Miss Westenra might have been saved. But sadly, she is gone, and so we

must work to ensure that other poor souls perish not, whilst we can save them.

"The nosferatu do not die like the bee when he stings but once. He is stronger, and being stronger, has more power to do evil. This vampire which we now seek to destroy has the strength of twenty men. He has grown cunning through the ages and, through the power of necromancy, the dead are his to command. He is the devil himself, able to bend the elements to his will – the storm, the fog, the thunder – and he can command the meaner forms of life: the rat, the bat, the moth, and the wolf. He can even make himself invisible.

"How then are we to begin our crusade to put an end to him? How shall we find where he is hiding, and having found it, how shall we put an end to him? My friends, it is a terrible task that we are about to undertake, and there may be consequences that would make a brave man shudder. But if we fail in our task he will surely win.

"And to fail here, is not merely a matter of life or death. It is that we become as he is; foul things of the night without compassion or conscience, preying on the bodies and the souls of those we love best, the gates of heaven shut to us forever, abhorred by all, a blot on the face of God's creation.

"It is our duty to face him and destroy him, and who would shrink from such a duty? What say you? Are you with me?"

Everyone replies raucously in the affirmative. You all agree, wholeheartedly, not to rest until the monster has been vanquished. And so, you all join hands, and your solemn pact is made.

"And now," says Van Helsing, "let us share all we have learnt about the monster we face," and he proceeds to go round the table, asking each of you in turn to share with the rest what you have personally experienced, witnessed and discovered.

How many of the following code words do you have ticked off?

Anthropophagy, Arachnophilia, Barbastella, Bogey, Cadaver, Demeter, Desmodontinae, Eptesicus, Exsanguination, Lunatic, Monomania, Psychopathia, Quinquaginta, Sárkány, Scientia, Slave, Somnambulism, Strigoi, Térkép, Tükör, Zoophagous

1 – 3	Turn to **869**.
4 – 6	Turn to **889**.
7 – 9	Turn to **978**.
10 – 12	Turn to **909**.
13 or more	Turn to **939**.

593

In the form of a bat – *Desmodontinae gigantica*, to be precise – you follow the winding path of the Thames from central London to Purfleet.

But as you approach Carfax House, your preternatural senses alert you to the presence of a number of souls that are familiar to you nearby. It is as if they call out to you, and one in particular. Following the siren-lure of the souls, you are drawn to the more modern property that adjoins yours, and to one window in particular.

The curtains have not yet been drawn and, clinging onto the windowsill, you peer inside. Six people are seated around a large table in what appears to be a study. You recognise four of them.

There is Jonathan Harker, whom you thought was still in Transylvania, the wretched plaything of the Weird Sisters; he must have a stronger spirit than you gave him credit for. Next to him is the blonde-haired woman you met in Whitby, Lucy's friend Mina; from the way she and Harker are clutching each other's hands so desperately, and the golden wedding band on the ring-finger of her left hand, it would appear that the pair are now man and wife. Opposite them is Lucy's personal physician, Dr Seward, whom you met at Hillingham House.

The others you recognise solely from the memories you absorbed from Lucy. Sitting next to the alienist is Arthur Holmwood, the new Lord Godalming. The other two, a young man with a bushy moustache and dressed after the fashion of the American cowboys you have read about in some of the books in your carefully curated library, and an older man, who is grey of hair and beard, and who appears to be chairing the meeting, are Quincey Morris and Professor Abraham Van Helsing respectively.

And at the limits of your senses, you are sure there is another soul somewhere nearby who is also known to you already.

But before you can discover why the meeting has been called, Mina turns her head and looks straight out of the window, in your direction. She starts pointing urgently, and the American with the bushy moustache, jumps up from his seat and rushes out of the room.

He appears a moment later, from around the corner of the building and, catching sight of you, draws a pistol from a holster slung at his hip. He takes aim and fires, as Holmwood throws up the sash. But you are already on your way by then, flapping through the air on large leathery wings, heading for the sanctuary of the chapel that adjoins Carfax House.

You are pleased to find the twenty-nine strigoi-boxes still stored there wholly intact and decide to wait out the rest of the night hanging from the rafters of the desecrated chapel, intending to return to 138 Piccadilly after sunset the following evening.

However, at around midnight, when the full moon is high in the heavens, your rest is disturbed when the five men you saw meeting earlier this very night burst into the chapel, armed with swords and pistols, and brandishing holy charms, as if they know what has been hidden here and intend to cleanse the desecrated sanctuary.

Do you want to reveal yourself and attack the intruders (turn to **507**), or would you prefer to make your escape from this well-prepared party before they realise you are here (turn to **425**)?

594

The ferocity of your need to free yourself takes your captor by surprise and, incredibly, you actually manage to slip his grasp. But your newfound freedom only lasts a moment.

"Enough!" snaps the Count, lashing out at you with long, sharp fingernails.

He strikes you across the face and sends you flying across the room. (Lose 3 *Endurance* points.)

Crossing the room without seeming to take a single step, the Count lifts you from where you lie with one strong hand.

Turn to **613**.

595

How long did your battle with the bear-man last?

If it was fewer than 10 Combat Rounds in duration, turn to **395**. If the battle lasted for more than 10 Combat Rounds, turn to **933**.

If the battle lasted exactly 10 Combat Rounds, roll one die (or pick a card); if the number rolled is odd (or the card is red), turn to **993**, and if the number rolled is even (or the card is black), turn to **395**.

596

Seemingly more akin to a beast now than a member of the English aristocracy, the Wolf-Man, whom you once considered a friend, launches himself at you. (In this battle, the Wolf-Man has the initiative.)

WOLF-MAN   COMBAT 8   ENDURANCE 8

Because you do not want to hurt Arthur, you must reduce your *Combat Rating* by 1 point for the duration of this battle. If you win two consecutive Combat Rounds, or if you manage to reduce the Wolf-Man's *Endurance* score to 4 points or fewer, turn to **629** at once.

597

The skin around the bite marks is angry and inflamed, and you can't help thinking that this unwelcome encounter with the rats may return to haunt you in the future.

Lose 2 more *Endurance* points, tick off the code word *Pestis*, and then turn to **622**.

598

You take to your heels and run.

Take an Agility test and an Endurance test. If you pass both tests, turn to **641**, but if you fail either test, turn to **621** at once.

599

You survey the bite-marks and claw-marks marring your flesh and a cold knot forms in the pit of your stomach. You will need to clean your wounds when you get back to your hotel, but you can't help wondering if the harm caused by the Werewolves might run deeper than mere physical injuries.

Tick off the code word *Lycanthropy* and gain 3 *Blood* points. If you have the code word *Lyssavirus* ticked off, gain 1 more *Blood* point.

Now turn to **619**.

600

With your final, fatal thrust, you plunge the tip of your blade into the monster's heart. A look of shock seizes its warped, ophidian features, its mouth open in a gasp of disbelief. Pulling the blade free again, with a last scything blow, you take the monster's head from its shoulders.

The headless corpse starts to crumble to dust before it even hits the floor. At the same time, the monstrous worm starts to twist and jerk uncontrollably.

While Count Dracula has lived for centuries, that demonic worm has existed, in hiding beneath the surface of the world, for countless aeons, dominating the wills of lesser beings for millennia, travelling from Egypt, to Rome, and ultimately to the mountains of Transylvania.

But with the vessel of its unholy spirit destroyed, the bond between demon god and undead slave takes its toll on the dragon.

The ground shakes as the worm writhes in its tormented death-throes and great stalactites fall from the roof of the cathedral-like cavern, to splash into the black waters of the lake.

You have to get out of there as fast as you possibly can. Turning tail, you run for the archway that will lead you back to the catacombs.

Take an Agility test and an Endurance test. If you fail either test, turn to **570**. If you pass both tests, turn to **540**.

601

Stepping back out of the cellar, you give yourself a moment to recover your breath before retreating upstairs.

Turn to **273**.

602

You return to your room to finish packing. Just as you are about to leave, the old lady visits you there and says, in an almost hysterical manner, "Must you go? Oh! Young Herr, must you go?"

She is in such an excited state that she loses her grip on what little German she has, mixing it up with some other language you do not know at all.

"I must go at once," you tell her sternly, "for I am engaged on important business."

"Do you know what day it is?" she asks, managing to compose herself a little.

Do you want to answer the old woman's question (turn to **636**), or will you shoo her out of your room, having had enough of her histrionics (turn to **687**)?

603

Every boat in the harbour seems to be there for the poor sea captain.

Do you want to go up early to watch the procession (turn to **997**), or would you rather follow the coffin as it is carried up the 199 steps to St Mary's churchyard (turn to **973**)?

604

A patient getting into the Superintendent's study of his own accord is almost unheard of! But Renfield is clearly in the depths of a psychotic episode.

You try to keep the table between you, but the lunatic is too quick and too strong for you. Before you can get your balance, he slashes at you with the knife, cutting your left wrist rather severely.

Deduct 3 *Endurance* points 1 *Combat* point, and then turn to **633**.

605

The faith and the strength of the Vampire-Hunters combined is too great for you to overcome. They overwhelm you, one of them thrusting a silver crucifix into your face to keep you at bay, while another takes up a sharpened whitethorn stake and drives it through your heart.

As the black, withered organ crumbles to dust, time catches up with you and the rest of your body rapidly starts to decay.

Your adventure, just like your unholy, centuries-long vampiric existence, is over.

THE END

606

"This is the spot," announces the Professor in a half-whisper, as he opens the door.

You are expecting some unpleasantness, but you doubt that any among your party ever expected to be confronted by such an odour as the one that assails you now from the neglected chapel.

The sanctuary is small and close, and its long disuse has made the air stagnant and foul. There is an earthy smell, which cuts through the fouler air, but as to the odour itself, you believe it to be composed of all the ills of mortality, mixed with the pungent, acrid smell of blood, as if the very corruption has itself been corrupted.

It is as if every breath exhaled by the monster you seek has clung to the place, intensifying its loathsome foulness.

Take an Endurance test. If you pass the test, turn to **644**, but if you fail the test, turn to **681**.

607

There is the sound of many feet tramping and dying away in some passage, which sends up a clanging echo. There comes the crash of weights being set down heavily, doubtless the boxes, with their freight of earth, and then the sound of hammering as they are nailed shut.

You watch from your window as the boxes are loaded into the wagon awaiting them in the courtyard, and then – accompanied again by the roll of wheels and the crack of whips – the Szgany depart once more.

You know then that you are alone in the castle with those Weird Sisters – those devils of the Pit! – but you swear you will not remain here to become their plaything.

Without pausing for even a moment, you ease yourself out of your bedroom window – the only means of escape from the castle available to you – and brave the vertiginous castle walls, intent on finding a way out of your prison or die in the attempt. For even death is a more desirable fate than being left to the mercy of those shape-shifting hell-cats!

Take an Endurance test. If you pass, turn to **442**, but if you fail the test, turn to **412**.

608

"No!" Carmilla cries, her spell over you broken. And then, in the next instant, she starts to change.

Her flowing blonde hair seems to grow to cover her skin, only now it is no longer hair but fur, and she is no longer a beautiful woman but something more akin to a cat.

Hissing and spitting, the transformed Countess bares her sharp teeth and pounces.

If you want to use *The Pen is Mightier* special ability, cross off one use and turn to **539**. If not, turn to **569**.

609

Never before have you seen such baffled malice as you do when you stand between Lucy and her resting place, and you trust you never shall again.

Her complexion becomes livid, and her eyes seem to throw out sparks of hellfire. Her brows become wrinkled, as though the folds of flesh were the coils of Medusa's snakes, and her blood-stained mouth stretches, as in the passion masks of the Ancient Greeks. If ever looks could kill, you see it in that moment, as the handmaiden of death throws herself at you.

If you want to employ *The Pen is Mightier* special ability, and you still can, turn to **669**. If not, turn to **639**.

610

Your vision starts to dim, growing grey around the edges, as the throttling hands squeeze even harder. Clawing at the huge hands with your own desperate fingers, you struggle against the dying of the light, but it is no good – you cannot break their hold. (Lose another 2 *Endurance* points and add 1 point to your *Terror* score.)

On the verge of blacking out, you become aware of an altercation behind you, hear a gruff shout, a breathless grunt, and at last the pressure on your neck eases and the callused hands slip free.

As your vision starts to return, with the merciful release of the throttling hands, you see Barlow's face come into focus before your eyes and hear his gruff voice: "Are you all right, sir?"

"Nothing a glass of brandy won't fix," you croak, your voice a hoarse whisper.

Barlow gives a gruff laugh. "Purely medicinal I'm sure, sir."

Turn to **414**.

611

You cannot free yourself from the lunatic's grasp and find yourself at the edge of unconsciousness before your staff can wrestle Renfield from you, and by then the damage has been done.

While Renfield is forced into a strait waistcoat, a pair of attendants have to virtually carry you from his cell, back to your office.

Deduct 3 *Endurance* points, add 2 to your *Terror* score, and gain 3 *Blood* points.

Now turn to **631**.

612

You hear Van Helsing's voice coming to you, as if from far away: "Where are you?"

You open your eyes, but all is darkness.

"I do not know," you reply. You can feel a gentle rocking motion. "It is all strange to me!"

"What do you see?" comes Van Helsing's voice again.

"I can see nothing. It is all dark."

"What do you hear?"

You focus on the sounds coming to you from beyond the darkness.

"The lapping of water. It is gurgling by, and little waves leap. I can hear them on the outside."

"You are on a ship?"

"Yes!"

You can hear men stamping overhead as they run about, and the creaking of a chain. But there is something else; a low, bestial growling.

Your host has sensed your presence. Just as you are aware of where your enemy is hiding, so he knows that you are spying on him.

"He knows I am here!" you cry, as you feel something like gore-soiled claws sinking into the very being of your immortal soul.

"Come away! Come away!" you hear Van Helsing calling you. "Return to us Madam Mina. Awake!"

Gain 2 *Blood* points and add 2 to your *Terror* score, then turn to **663**.

613

You are unable to resist as the Count places his reeking mouth upon your throat, piercing the pulsing vein in your neck with his snake-like fangs, and starts to drink.

You feel your strength ebbing from your body. There is now no doubt in your mind that this is not some hideous nightmare – much as you might wish it were – but that the undead fiend is actually here, in your bedchamber, gorging himself upon your very life's essence!

When he finally takes his foul, sneering mouth away, it is gory with fresh blood – your blood!

Roll one die and add 1; deduct this many *Endurance* points. (Alternatively, pick a card and deduct its face value from your *Endurance* score, unless it is 8 or above, or a picture card, in which case deduct 7 points from your *Endurance* score.)

If you are still alive, turn to **632**.

614

"I am glad you found your way in here, for I am sure there is much that will interest you. These companions" – at this he lays his hand on some of the books – "have been good friends to me, and for some years past, ever since I had the idea of going to London, have given me many, many hours of pleasure. Through them I have come to know your great England, and to know her is to love her. I long to go through the crowded streets of your mighty London, to be in the midst of the whirl and rush of humanity.

"But alas! As yet, I only know your tongue through books. To you, my friend, I look that I know how to speak it. You shall, I trust, rest here with me a while, so that by our talking I may learn the English intonation."

You accede to the Count's entreaty and in return ask if you might use the library whenever you choose.

Turn to **533**.

615

"You look like you need a hand!" announces Quincey, joining you before the cart, and before the bear of a man has a chance to react, sinks all twelve inches of his Bowie knife between the Szgany's ribs.

The Transylvanian gives a terrible howl of pain and rage and, even as his legs give way beneath him, lashes out with his razor-sharp claws, the brave American going down on his knees in the snow.

Turn to **395**.

616

The greatsword is a magnificent example of the metallurgist's art. The quillons of its cross-guard have been fashioned in the shape of stylised dragon heads; the eye-sockets set with exquisitely-cut rubies.

Engraved into the blade itself, in an ornamented script, is what you take to be the name its maker gave it:

EFIL EHT SI DOOLB EHT

As long as you are wielding the blade in battle you may add 2 points when calculating your *Combat Rating*, and if you wound an opponent with it, you may subtract 1 additional point of damage.

Record the Dragon Sword on your Adventure Sheet, noting that you can only carry one bladed weapon at a time, and then turn to **642**.

617

And so, you find yourself facing Count Dracula, Voivode of Wallachia and Lord of the Undead, alone, with nothing but weapons forged of steel to save you.

The only thing that is to your advantage is that the vampire is not at his strongest during the hours of daylight. (In this battle, Dracula has the initiative.)

COUNT DRACULA   COMBAT 11   ENDURANCE 20

If you are still alive after 7 Combat Rounds, or if you reduce your enemy's *Endurance* score to 12 points or fewer, whichever is sooner, turn to **587** at once.

618

You are suddenly aware of the presence of the Count, as you are cast backwards to the corner of the room by the force of the furious storm that announces his arrival.

Turn to **679**.

619

Skinsky and the Werewolves cannot furnish you with the answers you need, regarding Dracula's whereabouts, so the six of you leave the wolf-haunted graveyard and make your way back through the town to the hotel where you are to spend the night.

Tick off the code word *Vânători* and then turn to **678**.

620

Weapons drawn, the Vampire-Hunters attack en masse.

You must fight them all at the same time, and you must deduct 1 point when calculating your *Combat Rating*, for they are protected by silver crucifixes and garlands of garlic, that would repel you completely were it not for the very desperate nature of this battle. (The Vampire-Hunters have the initiative.)

	COMBAT	ENDURANCE
JONATHAN HARKER	10	11
ARTHUR HOLMWOOD	8	9
QUINCEY MORRIS	9	9
DOCTOR SEWARD	9	10
PROFESSOR VAN HELSING	8	8

After 8 Combat Rounds, or as soon as you manage to reduce the *Endurance* score of one of the Vampire-Hunters to 3 points or fewer, whichever is sooner, turn to **330** at once.

621

As you hare off across the graveyard, your foot catches in a hole where one of the old tombs has crumbled inwards and you fall, twisting your ankle and bruising yourself on the cracked coffin-stone.

(Lose 3 *Endurance* points and 1 *Agility* point.)

If you want to make use of *The Pen is Mightier* special ability, cross off one use and turn to **641**. If not, make a note that the dog has the initiative and then turn to **312**.

622

Your party has not got away scot-free after your encounter with the monstrous rats and once all wounds have been treated, as best they can be, you set off again.

Following the trail left by the vile rodents, convinced that it will lead you to your desired destination, sure enough, you soon find yourselves before a low, arched oaken door, banded with iron.

Turn to **606**.

623

"Why, I couldn't hurt a fly."

The woman is so close you can feel her breath on your face and the sickly-sweet aroma of her perfume threatens to overwhelm you. But you cannot tear your eyes away from hers.

You are not the only one transfixed by her beauty, for no one else makes a move to help you when the Countess Carmilla suddenly goes for your neck, fast as a striking snake.

You feel her teeth pierce the flesh, but even then you do not resist as she begins to gorge herself on your blood.

(Lose 4 *Endurance* points.)

If you are still alive, turn to **320**.

624

There remains one thing left to do, and then your grisly work here is done. Taking up a heavy-bladed knife, the Professor removes the heads of each of the vampyres in turn, intoning the words "*Agnus Dei, qui tollis peccata mundi, dona eis requiem*" as he does so.

When he is finished, the two of you set about searching the catacombs again. In a secluded crypt you find one great tomb, more lordly than all the rest and nobly proportioned. Carved into the black granite you see but one word: *DRACULA*.

"This is the undead home of the King Vampire!" Van Helsing exclaims.

Heaving aside the great stone lid of the sarcophagus and finding it empty, you raise a prayer of thanks to the Lord.

Before you leave the crypt, the Professor lays some of the sacrament in the tomb and sprinkles it with holy water, declaring, "And so our enemy is banished from his own tomb, undead forever!"

Shaken by your ordeal but feeling the first stirrings of hope in your breast, when you consider what the two of you have accomplished here, you leave the haunted castle and return to your camp, to watch the road and see who shall reach the ruin first – your fellow Vampire-Hunters, or the Vampire King himself.

Deduct 2 *Blood* points and reduce your *Terror* score by up to 2 points; then turn to **194**.

625

As you stalk towards the Janissary, your foot catches against the guy-rope of a tent, which twangs as you pull yourself free.

The Janissary spins round, his scimitar suddenly in his hand. Abandoning any further subterfuge, you go for the man, determined to silence him before he can call for help. (In this battle, you have the initiative.)

JANISSARY   COMBAT 8   ENDURANCE 8

If you manage to defeat the Turk, how long did the fight last? If it lasted for 7 Combat Rounds or fewer, turn to **550**. If it lasted for more than 7 Combat Rounds, turn to **580**.

626

Half expecting to find the undercroft of the house flooded with raw sewage, you enter a mouldering wine-cellar and almost step in the mess of offal and intestines covering the floor in a slick of stinking viscera.

Lying on the packed earth floor is the eviscerated corpse of some unidentifiable wretch, his face frozen in a rictus of terror, his glazed eyes no doubt still staring at his killer, even though he is long gone from this place.

Take a Terror test. If you pass the test, turn to **601**. If you fail the test, turn to **572**.

417

627

How do you wish to proceed from here?

If you want to continue the story as Jonathan Harker, turn to **647**, but if you want to assume the role of Dr John Seward, turn to **691**.

628

The mutated rats' unnatural appetites can only be sated by fresh meat. (The vermin have the initiative in this battle, and you must fight them at the same time.)

	COMBAT	ENDURANCE
First GIANT RAT	5	6
Second GIANT RAT	6	5

If you kill both of them, turn to **658**.

629

You land a savage blow against the side of the Wolf-Man's head that is hard enough to knock him senseless. A cloud passes before the face of the moon again and, before its monochrome light fades altogether, you see Arthur's features start to revert to their original human state.

After a few moments he slowly comes to, but has no recollection of what just happened. You are going to have to watch your companion like a hawk from now on.

Tick off the code word *Vârcolac* and turn to **659**.

630

You raise your arms above your head to protect yourself, but it is not enough to stop the flying chair hitting you and knocking you to the floor. (Lose 2 *Endurance* points.)

As you are reeling from your altercation with the improvised missile, you feel rough hands close around your neck and start to squeeze.

Take a Combat test. If you pass the test, turn to **577**. If you fail the test, turn to **610**.

631

As the weeks pass, Renfield turns his mind from flies to spiders. On one of your occasional visits, he shows you a box in which he keeps several particularly large specimens.

He has clearly been feeding them his flies, since his store of the insects has been drastically diminished. That said, he has used half the food provided for him by the asylum kitchens to attract more *musca* – bluebottles, houseflies, horseflies and the like – from outside, into his room.

It is not long before the spiders become as great a nuisance as the flies were, and at your next visit you feel compelled to tell him that he must get rid of his collection of arachnids. He looks so sad at your pronouncement that you almost feel inclined to relent.

But then, all of a sudden, a horrid blowfly, bloated with some carrion food, buzzes into the room. Quick as a flash, he catches it, plucking it out of the air, and holds it exultantly for a few moments between finger and thumb, and then pops it into his mouth!

You have seen all manner of disgusting things whilst working at Carfax Asylum, but nothing has unsettled you quite so much as Renfield's consumption of the blowfly.

Having eaten the fly, he picks up a little notebook that he has in his possession and jots something down.

How will you react to what you have just witnessed? Will you:

Scold him for eating the fly?	Turn to **671**.
Tell him to dispose of his collection of spiders?	Turn to **651**.
Ask to see his notebook?	Turn to **701**.

632

Then he speaks to you mockingly: "And so you, like the others, would play your brains against mine. You would help these men to hunt me and frustrate me in my designs! You know now, and they will know before long, what it is to cross my path. They should have kept their energies for use closer to home. Whilst they played wits against me – against me who commanded nations, and fought for them, hundreds of years before they were born! – I was undermining their efforts.

"And you, their best beloved one, are now to me, flesh of my flesh; blood of my blood; kin of my kin; and shall be my companion and my helper. You are to be punished for what you have done, in aiding those who would thwart me. Now you shall come to my call. When I command it, you shall cross land or sea to do my bidding!"

With that he pulls open his shirt, and with his long sharp nails opens the skin of his chest. As viscous, black blood begins to ooze forth, he takes both your hands in one of his, holding them tight, and with the other forces your mouth to the wound, so that you must either suffocate or swallow some of the foul, dead fluid.

Oh, what have you done to deserve such a fate? May God take pity on you, a wretched soul in worse than mortal peril!

The door suddenly bursts open and the brave Vampire-Hunters rush into the room.

The scene that greets them would appal a priest. You are highlighted by the moonlight streaming in through the window, and they cannot help but see that your face and the front of your nightdress are filthy with blood. And then they lay eyes on the Count!

As your attacker throws you onto the bed, the brave Professor leaps forward, a Sacred Wafer in his hand held out towards the monster.

The Count stops abruptly and cowers back. As the rest of the menfolk raise their silver crucifixes, Dracula cowers further back still.

The moonlight suddenly fails, as a great black cloud sails across the sky.

When the gaslight springs up under Quincey's match a moment later, you see nothing but a faint vapour, that trails out through the window and then is gone.

Your husband rushes forward and gathers you up in his arms, his face a ghastly white.

"Are we too late?" the Professor cries, moving towards you, the Sacred Wafer still tight in his hand. "I have to know!" And with that, he presses it against your forehead.

You give voice to a fearful scream and recoil in pain. (Lose 3 *Endurance* points.)

The others stare at you in horror, for where the wafer touched your skin it has burned your flesh as surely as if it had been a piece of white-hot metal.

You sink to your knees, sobbing and pulling your hair over your face, wailing, "Unclean! I am unclean! Even the Almighty shuns my polluted flesh! I must bear this mark of shame upon my forehead until the Judgment Day!"

Jonathan falls to the floor beside you, consumed with impotent grief, and for a few minutes your sorrowful hearts beat together, whilst your friends turn away, their eyes running with silent tears.

Gain 6 *Blood* points and turn **693**.

633

Screaming, "The blood is the life! The blood is the life!" like a man possessed, Renfield goes for you.

If you wish to use *The Pen is Mightier* special ability, cross off one use and turn to **662**. If not, turn to **698**.

634

You hear Van Helsing's voice coming to you, as if from far away: "Where are you?"

You open your eyes, but all is darkness.

"I do not know," you reply. You can feel a gentle rocking motion.

"It is all strange to me!"

"What do you see?" comes Van Helsing's voice again.

"I can see nothing. It is all dark."

"What do you hear?"

You focus on the sounds coming to you from beyond the darkness.

"The lapping of water. It is gurgling by, and little waves leap. I can hear them on the outside."

"You are on a ship?"

"Yes!"

"What else do you hear?"

"The sound of men stamping overhead as they run about."

There is the creaking of a chain, and the loud tinkle as the check of the capstan falls into the ratchet as well, and you tell the Professor so.

"What are you doing?"

"I am still, oh so still. It is like death!"

Add 1 to your *ESP* score and turn to **663**.

635

With the Piccadilly property discovered and the strigoi-boxes kept there destroyed, there is only one course of action left open to you. You must give up on your scheme for seizing control of the British Empire – at least in the short term – and return to Transylvania, where you will be able to regroup and revise your plans. There is no time to lose, for the longer you delay, the more likely the Vampire-Hunters are to catch up with you.

But you have an ace in the hole that they are not even aware of; Harker's wife, Mina. She is already on the path to becoming your thrall and the only thing that can reverse her transformation is your second death. Until such a thing comes to pass, the psychic bond that exists between you – now that you have partaken of each other's blood – will remain, and in this way you will be able to spy on the Vampire-Hunters' progress, should they pursue you to the continent.

* * * *

Acquiring a cart, you return to the Lyceum Theatre. Retrieving the box you hid there, you single-handedly load it onto the wagon and set off for the Port of London.

Arriving at Doolittle's Wharf, not long after five o'clock, you enquire as to which ships are sailing for the Black Sea and, because you reward answers to your questions with money, you are soon introduced to Captain Donelson of the *Czarina Catherine*.

The gruff Scotsman agrees to transport your curious cargo to Varna, in Bulgaria, for an exorbitant fee – but one you can easily afford – and, abandoning all pretence, you astound everyone when you lift the great box down from the cart by yourself. Having stowed it on board, you assure the captain you will return to check on the crate when you have seen to the business of filling in the necessary shipping forms. Who would have thought the afterlife would involve so much paperwork?

But having been paid, Donelson is keen to set sail, and you fear he has no intention of waiting for you to return. At your behest, a thin mist begins to creep up from the river, growing in intensity until a dense fog envelops the ship and all those around her.

Funnily enough, the fog does not depart until you return and board the *Czarina Catherine* to check on your cargo, going down into the hold with the mate to see that it is stowed securely.

As the fog melts away again, the ship sails on the ebb tide, and, unknown to the crew, with you on board, buried inside your box of earth, away from prying eyes.

* * * *

You dare not feed on the crew of the *Czarina Catherine*, as you did the poor wretches aboard the *Demeter*, for fear of giving away your hiding place. But the voyage is long, and weeks of enforced abstinence drains you of your strength, until the youthful Count is gone, replaced by something that is little more than an emaciated corpse. (Deduct 6 *Blood* points.)

But during the voyage you are able to use your psychic link with Mina Harker to your advantage, for while she can gain an impression of where you are, the musty interior of a crate of earth aboard a sailing ship reveals little as to your whereabouts. Her interactions with the rest of the Vampire-Hunters, on the other hand, tell you a very great deal.

As you suspected they would be, the men are relentless in their pursuit of you, but they believe you are returning to the port of Varna. And so, while Captain Donelson sleeps, you reach out with your mind and impose your will upon him, implanting the suggestion that he would do better to dock at Galatz, in Romania, another two hundred miles further up the coast of the Black Sea.

* * * *

The *Czarina Catherine* reaches Galatz twenty-five days after leaving London, with dawn still but a rumour on the eastern horizon.

An hour before sun-up, a certain Immanuel Hildesheim comes aboard with an order, sent to him from England – within a letter, written by you under the alias of Mr de Ville, that also included an English bank note to cover any necessary costs – instructing him to receive a box marked for one Count Dracula. Captain Donelson is all too happy to see it go.

Your precious box is passed into the hands of one Petrof Skinsky, an agent who dealt with the Slovaks who trade down the river to the port on your outward journey.

Only now do you emerge from your peculiar carriage, to deal directly with Skinsky. There was only so much you could arrange before you had to leave London in haste, and you still need to arrange passage upriver to Transylvania and your home, Castle Dracula. You meet with the man in the inauspicious setting of the graveyard of the Church of St Peter, to make arrangements to have your box transported upriver to Strasba.

Do you want to meet with Skinsky again, the following night, to double-check that everything is in order (turn to **740**), or will you trust in the agent's ability to do his job and remain hidden inside the box and simply wait for it to be loaded onto a boat and taken upriver (turn to **140**)?

636

"Of course! It is the fourth of May," you reply.

"I know that," she says, shaking her head, "but do you know what day it is?"

"I'm sorry, I don't understand."

"It is the eve of St. George's Day. Do you not know that tonight, when the clock strikes midnight, all the evil things in the world will have full sway? Do you know where you are going, and what you are going to?"

She is so obviously distressed that you try to comfort the old woman, but without any success.

Finally, she drops to her knees, still imploring you not to go, or at least to wait a day or two before heading off.

Her reaction to you leaving seems ridiculously over the top and makes you feel deeply uncomfortable. After all, there is business to be done and you cannot allow anything to delay you.

"I am on important business," you tell her. "I must go."

Realising that you will not be deterred, the old woman rises and dries her eyes. She takes a small, golden crucifix from where it hangs about her neck and offers it to you.

"Madam, please," you say, "I am an English Churchman." As such, you have been taught that such trinkets are idolatrous. And yet it seems ungracious to refuse an old lady who means well and who is in such a state of mind.

"For your mother's sake," she insists, offering you the rosary.

If you want to accept the proffered gift, turn to **667**. If not, turn to **687**.

637

And so, you find yourself facing Count Dracula, Voivode of Wallachia and Lord of the Undead, alone, with nothing but weapons forged of steel to save you.

The only thing that is to your advantage is that the vampire is not at his strongest during the hours of daylight. (In this battle you have the initiative.)

COUNT DRACULA　　　　　　COMBAT 11　　ENDURANCE 20

If you are still alive after 7 Combat Rounds, or if you reduce your enemy's *Endurance* score to 12 points or fewer, whichever is sooner, turn to **587** at once.

638

Divide your *Blood* score by 10, rounding fractions up. Then roll 1 die, and if the number rolled is equal or less than the resulting total, turn to **875**. If it is greater, turn to **665**.

639

And in that moment, what remains of your love for Lucy is corrupted into hatred. You determine to put an end to the Bloofer Lady yourself, here and now, and will do so, with savage delight. (In this battle, you have the initiative.)

THE BLOOFER LADY   COMBAT 9   ENDURANCE 10

After 5 Combat Rounds, or if you manage to reduce the Lucy-creature's *Endurance* score to 5 points or fewer, whichever comes first, turn to **669**.

640

17 October, Varna

Arthur has been busy in the short time your party has been in Bulgaria and has used his money and influence to secure papers guaranteeing you the right to board the *Czarina Catherine* when it docks and open its dread cargo of Transylvanian earth.

There and then, in the bowels of the ship, between you, you will cut off Dracula's head and drive a stake through his heart. Professor Van Helsing believes the Count's body will simply crumble to dust.

You feel that the end is close, and that belief fills you with courage.

Deduct 1 point from your *Terror* score and turn to **703**.

641

The great black dog hurtles past you and disappears into the night, but your close call with the beast leaves you shaken.

(Add 1 point to your *Terror* score.)

Not wanting to stay out a moment longer, as the officers of the coastguard and local fishermen go to board the beached vessel, you hurry back to the Westenras' house on the Crescent and the security of your own bed.

Turn to **774**.

642

Leaving the room again, do you want to try the door opposite you – the one bearing the twin Janissary sabres – if you haven't already done so (turn to **672**), or do you want to descend the steps to the next chamber (turn to **59**)?

643

As the dark-haired vampyre flies at you, you raise your blade to protect yourself, and in her rage she unwittingly throws herself onto its tip, which pierces her heart.

Cross off one use of *The Pen is Mightier* special ability and turn to **624**.

644

In any other circumstance, such a stench would bring your enterprise to an end at once. But this is no ordinary situation, and the vital purpose that has brought you here gives you the strength to rise above merely physical considerations.

After the involuntary drawing back at the first nauseous whiff, every member of your party presses on into the chapel.

Turn to **707**.

645

Taking wing, you fly from Castle Dracula, swooping over the peaks and valleys of Wallachia, and soaring above the forests and farms that pass beneath you in the blink of an eye, covering hundreds of miles in only a matter of hours.

On the other side of the Bavarian mountains, you are drawn towards a bleak, open road that traverses a high, windswept plateau. Another road, that appears little used, branches from it and charts another route through a winding valley.

Something is pulling you onwards through the night, towards that valley; a force you can only describe as destiny.

But if you are to face the Countess Dolingen this night, and on her home soil, you decide it would be best to travel in the company of wolves.

Landing, you take on the aspect of a wolf. Giving voice to a mournful howl, you are answered by a dozen more. They come from the hills, the forests, their lairs underground, forgotten caves, all answering your call. When you set off again, it is at the head of an entire pack of the animals.

In this way, you come to a wide stretch of open country, shut in by hills all around. Their sides are covered with trees, which spread down to the plain, dotting in clumps the gentler slopes and hollows that are visible here and there. The winding road curves close to one of the densest of these thickets before vanishing behind it.

And then the snow begins to fall. Darker and darker grows the sky, while the snow falls faster and heavier.

Your heightened senses detect the presence of another, like you, not far away. The Sisters were right; the Englishman is in danger.

You race on through the falling snow, leading the pack towards the ruins of an abandoned village that your sharp eyes can now make out through the dense trees and falling snow. You sense the presence of a mortal being too – and not another wolf or a bat, but a man – your wolfish ears picking up the thudding of the pulse in his veins. It must be the young solicitor, Harker.

A shrill, screeching cry cuts through the encroaching night, and you cast your eyes heavenward to see a cloud of monstrous bats descending on you and your lupine slaves from out of the darkness.

If your rank is that of *Count Dracula* or higher, turn to **795**. If not, turn to **675**.

646

The gypsies make room for you by the campfire and their welcome warms you even more than the burning logs. You start to relax, feeling the tension ease from your tired body. Soon you find a bowl of goulash in your hands and tuck in gladly to the hot, meaty stew. (Regain 4 *Endurance* points.)

Someone picks up a mandora and starts playing, while a young woman starts to dance, stamping out the rhythm of the tune as she swirls her bright red shawl around her.

You and Quincey are just finishing your meal when a hush falls over the gypsies and you look up to see another woman emerge from the back of one of the wagons, descend the wooden steps and enter the circle. Her black hair falls in wavy tresses over her shoulders, framing a face that is a picture of beauty. Her olive skin is smooth, her lips are full and red, but it is her eyes that cause you to stare at her for an impolitely long time. They are dark, and ringed with kohl, and while they sparkle in the firelight, you also feel like they are the oldest eyes you have ever seen.

In her hands, she carries a golden goblet and, approaching you, offers it to you. With a nod of her head, she indicates that she expects you to drink from the claret-red liquid contained within.

If you want to drink from the proffered cup, turn to **571**. If you want to politely decline, turn to **591**.

647

It is night. A full moon rides high in the cloud-chased sky above you, while all around you is darkness, except where the moonlight reflects from the eyes of circling wolves.

You run, guttural growls rising from the bellies of the beasts as they set off in eager pursuit. The twig-clawed fingers of branches catch you as you flee, tugging at your clothes, tangling in your hair, and tearing at your skin. You are trapped within the very heart of darkness, and it can only be a matter of time before the predators run down their prey…

* * * *

You wake to the sound of a church bell tolling and sunlight streaming through a high mullioned window to strike the crisp white sheets of the bed in which you are lying. In that moment of waking confusion, you struggle to recall where you are and how you got there.

The last thing you remember clearly is escaping from Castle Dracula. You remember fleeing through the forest, and have vague recollections of a train journey, but there is nothing else.

You try to sit up, propping yourself up on your elbows, but even that slight exertion is too much for you, and you fall back onto the bed, sweating and trembling from the effort.

It is at that moment that a door opens and a woman, wearing the habit and wimple of a nun, enters the room.

"Ah, Mr Harker," she says, addressing you by name, "you are awake."

"Where am I?" you ask in a faltering voice. Your throat is dry, and your lips are gummed with old saliva.

"You are convalescing at the Hospital of St Joseph and Ste Mary, in Buda-Pesth."

Buda-Pesth? But that is hundreds of miles from where you started your journey.

"And who are you?"

"I am Sister Agatha," the nun says, "and I, and my sisters, have been nursing you ever since you arrived here, almost six weeks ago."

Sister Agatha's Hungarian accent is strong, but her English is excellent. She proceeds to tell you that when you arrived you were suffering from a violent brain fever, and had also suffered numerous other injuries, which have all been treated and are healing well, but that it will still be some weeks before you will be able to leave the sanatorium.

Your thoughts immediately turn to your beloved Mina, and you ask Sister Agatha if she will write to her on your behalf, since you are not even strong enough to write yourself, conveying your love and begging her to join you in Buda-Pesth, which she duly does.

Turn to **13**.

648

There is something so inhuman about the figure's movement that it sobers you all up from the shock of his unexpected arrival.

But before any of you can so much as raise a hand to stop him he lashes out, sending Arthur and Quincey flying to opposite corners of the room before they can even draw their weapons, and sweeps the other Vampire-Hunters aside with a lightning fast attack, that leave them all reeling, until you are the last man standing.

The Count is suddenly there before you, and a snarl passes over his face, revealing pointed, elongated eye-teeth. For all his veneer of noble breeding, you see him for what he really is then, a bestial monster that lives only to hunt and steal the lives of others.

Take a Terror test. If you pass the test, turn to **686**. If you fail the test, turn to **746**.

649

"Come, sisters," cries the snake-tailed horror, and you hear her archaic ungodly tongue as English inside your head, "quickly, let us put this wretch out of his misery, and then we will drain him of every last drop of blood!"

In this battle the Weird Sisters have the initiative, and you must fight them two at a time. However, you also have the added problem that the drapes are on fire, and the flames make it harder for you to see what you are fighting, while the smoke gets into your lungs, making you cough and generally hampering your efforts.

For every Combat Round the battle lasts, you must decrease your *Combat Rating* by the same number of points as the number of Combat Rounds the battle has lasted so far. So for the first Combat Round you must reduce your Combat Rating by 1 point, but for the second Combat Round you must reduce it by 2 points, and so on.

	COMBAT	ENDURANCE
SUCCUBUS	7	8
LAMIA	9	10
SIREN	8	9

If you are still alive after five Combat Rounds, or as soon as you reduce the *Endurance* score of one of the fiends to 4 points, whichever is sooner, turn to **586**.

650

Breaking eye-contact with the horror, you screw your courage to the sticking place, determined to put an end to the undying Count once and for all, although you fear it may be the last thing you ever do. (In this battle, your nemesis has the initiative.)

DRACULA, SON OF THE DRAGON   COMBAT 10   ENDURANCE 12

If you somehow win your battle against the skin-shedding vampire, turn to **600**.

651

Renfield suddenly looks so very sad, having received your instruction, that you relent a little, telling him that he must get rid of some of them at least. He cheerfully acquiesces to this and says that he will fulfil your wishes within three days.

If you now want to ask to see his notebook, turn to **701**. If you do not want to tempt fate and risk upsetting Renfield, and would rather be about your rounds, turn to **729**.

652

"I believe the murderer to be you, Countess Carmilla," you say, pointing at the beautiful aristocrat.

"You can't mean that surely," she says, rising from her seat and approaching you, trapping your gaze with her sparkling sapphire eyes. "You can't seriously believe I am the killer."

Take an ESP test. If you pass the test, turn to **608**. If you fail the test, turn to **623**.

653

LETTER FROM DR SEWARD TO THE HONOURABLE ARTHUR HOLMWOOD

2 September

My dear old fellow, with regard to Miss Westenra's health I hasten to let you know at once that, in my opinion, there is not any functional disturbance or any malady that I know of. At the same time, I am not by any means satisfied with her appearance; she is woefully different from what she was when I saw her last.

I found Miss Westenra in seemingly gay spirits. Her mother was present, and in a few seconds I made up my mind that she was trying to mislead her mother and prevent her from being anxious.

After lunch, Mrs. Westenra went to lie down, and Lucy was left with me. We went into her boudoir, and as soon as the door was closed, the mask fell from her face and she sank down into a chair with a great sigh, and hid her eyes with her hand. When I saw that her high spirits had failed, I at once took advantage of her reaction to make a diagnosis.

I could easily see that she is somewhat bloodless, but I could not see the usual anaemic signs, and by chance I was actually able to test the quality of her blood, for in opening a window, which was stiff, she cut her hand slightly with broken glass. It was a slight matter in itself, but I secured a few drops of the blood and have analysed them.

The analysis shows that Lucy is in a vigorous state of health. In other physical matters I was quite satisfied that there is no need for anxiety; but as there must be a cause somewhere, I have come to the conclusion that it must be something mental.

She complains of difficulty in breathing satisfactorily at times, and of heavy, lethargic sleep, with dreams that frighten her, but regarding which she can remember nothing. She says that as a child she used to walk in her sleep, and that when in Whitby the habit came back, and that once she walked out in the night and went to East

Cliff, where Miss Murray found her; but she assures me that of late the habit has not returned.

I am in doubt, and so have done the best thing I know of; I have written to my old friend and master, Professor Van Helsing, of Amsterdam, who knows as much about obscure diseases as anyone in the world. He is a philosopher and a metaphysician, and one of the most advanced scientists of his day; and he has, I believe, an absolutely open mind.

I have asked him to come at once. We shall visit Miss Westenra together.

Yours always,

John Seward

Turn to **340**.

654

"Come," the Count says, "tell me of London and of the houses you have procured for me there."

And so, you pore over the plans, deeds and other paperwork you brought with you, all the way from Exeter, concerning the Count's new properties in Piccadilly, Walworth, and Mile End, and the jewel in the crown – his own English estate.

"The estate is called Carfax," you explain. "It contains some twenty acres in all and is surrounded by a high stone wall. There are a great many trees, which make it gloomy in places, and there is a small lake, fed by subterranean springs, the water flowing away in a fair-sized stream.

"The house itself is very large and of all periods, and dates back to medieval times. One part is of immensely thick stone, with only a few windows high up and heavily barred with iron. It looks like part of a keep and is close to an old chapel."

You set up the portable lithograph projector you have carried with you all the way from England, and much to the Count's delight, project views of the house onto a bare stone wall, which you took with your Kodak from the cardinal points of the compass.

"There are very few other properties close at hand," you go on, "one being a very large house only recently converted into a private lunatic asylum. I should point out, however, that the asylum is not visible from the grounds."

"I am glad this Carfax is old and big," the Count says, when you are finished. "I myself am of an old family, and to live in a new house would kill me. I rejoice also that there is a chapel of old times. We Transylvanian nobles love not to think that our bones may lie amongst the common dead. Moreover, I love the shade and the shadow, and would be alone with my thoughts when I may."

Perhaps is it the light cast by the flickering lamps in the room, but his smile seems to you malignant and somehow saturnine.

After Count Dracula has put his signature to the necessary legal documents, he makes his excuses and leaves. You pull together your papers and write a letter to accompany them, finally preparing everything to post to Mr Hawkins back in Exeter.

As you are putting your papers together, you notice an atlas lying on a table.

If you would like to take a look at the atlas, turn to **684**. If not, turn to **713**.

655

Taking a dagger from its sheath at your belt, unheard, you slip the razor-sharp blade between the man's ribs and into his heart, clasping your other hand over his mouth, stifling his gasp of surprise and gently lowering him to the ground as his life force leaves him.

Gain 2 *Blood* points and turn to **550**.

656

As you make your way down the servants' stairs into the basement of the house, the terrible smell permeating the places worsens, until you feel your gorge rise and worry that you might retch at any moment.

If you want to persist with your investigation of the basement, turn to **626**. If you would prefer to look somewhere else, turn to **273**.

657

Suddenly Professor Van Helsing is at your side, crucifix in hand as he chants, *"Agnus Dei, qui tollis peccata mundi, dona eis requiem!"*

It is as if even just the sight of the crucifix and the sound of the holy Latinate words cause the vampire pain, and he recoils physically, hissing and spitting like a wildcat.

Cross off one use of *The Pen is Mightier* special ability and turn to **587**.

658

The sharp crack of a pistol shot echoes through the warehouse and then nothing but silence remains. The rats are dead.

Leaving the property – intending to come back again, once this nightmare is over, and clear up after yourselves properly – you head back to the main thoroughfare, hoping to meet with the others at Dracula's house on Piccadilly.

If you were injured two or more times during your battle with the giant rats, turn to **824**. If you were only injured once, or even not at all, turn to **876**.

659

The snow is falling more heavily now, so you decide that it would be best if you take this opportunity to stop and make camp, intending to continue on your way at sunrise. Finding some shelter for the horses under an overhanging rock, you make a fire to keep the cold and the wolves at bay.

You barely sleep a wink, the howling of the wolves and your own fear of failing to catch your nemesis before he reaches his castle home both keeping you awake. With dawn still only a rumour purpling the eastern sky above the snow-clad mountain peaks, the two of you mount up and continue on your way.

If the *Blood* score is 10 points or higher, turn to **888**. If it is less than 10 points, turn to **483**.

660

16 October, Varna

Despite the fact that you can feel yourself getting stronger day by day, and the colour is returning to your cheeks, you also find yourself needing to sleep a great deal. Indeed, you slept for almost the whole journey to Varna aboard the Orient Express.

Professor Van Helsing comes to you again that evening, to hypnotise you, as he has continued to do at both dawn and dusk, every day since that first time in Carfax Asylum.

As soon as you are under, you find yourself in darkness once more and sense the lapping of waves and rushing water, and sails snapping in favourable winds.

Gain 2 *Blood* points and turn to **703**.

661

You were right – the dog is heading straight for you!

Making the churchyard, scrambling over the tombstones that project from the crumbling cliff, it bounds towards you, a monstrous, black-furred thing, its eyes seeming to glow like hot coals in the darkness.

Take an ESP test. If you pass the test, turn to **641**, but if you fail the test, turn to **683**.

662

Before he can cause you greater injury, even though it is not in your nature to strike your patients, fuelled by fear and adrenaline you manage to land a punch that sends him sprawling on his back on the floor.

Your wrist is bleeding freely, and a small pool collects on the carpet. Moments later, Barlow and Straker rush in, in pursuit of the scoundrel, only to find him lying on his belly licking up your blood like a dog! The sight of him, slavering over that vital fluid, positively sickens you. (Add 1 to your *Terror* score.)

He is soon secured, and the attendants drag him back to his cell, his cries of "The blood is the life!" echoing back to you from the ward.

You bind your arm, all too well aware that you cannot afford to lose any more blood. The prolonged strain of Lucy's illness is telling on you, and you need to rest.

After your latest traumatic run-in with Mr Renfield, you realise that you are not going to achieve anything worthwhile tonight and so retire to bed, happy that Van Helsing has not summoned you, so you need not forego your sleep.

Turn to **722**.

663

Blinking yourself awake, you find yourself back in your room at the asylum. The first thing you see is the expression of intense concentration on the Professor's face and the beads of sweat covering his forehead.

It is growing lighter, and as Jonathan pulls up the blind, a rosy light diffuses through the room.

"Have I been talking in my sleep?" you ask in a dreamy manner, stifling a yawn.

Turn to **718**.

664

As lithe as a panther, you leap into the room, moving almost too fast for the men to see.

The first of them to recover himself is your pawn-turned-nemesis, Harker, and he comes for you with a great silver-bladed knife.

If your rank is that of *Emperor of the Dead*, or you are willing to spend 3 *Blood* points, turn to **170**. If not, make a note that you have the initiative in the battle to come and turn to **990**.

665

Overcome by an insatiable bloodlust, that will not be denied, you sink your teeth into the throat of first one, and then the other Janissary, gorging yourself on their blood as if you were no better than a savage beast.

Only when your thirst for blood has been sated do you cast their lifeless bodies aside and turn back to the battle unfolding all around you.

Gain 8 *Blood* points and then turn to **875**.

666

Your enemies are defeated; you are free of them at last!

The mountains bathed bronze by the last of its light, the sun sinks below the western horizon.

Answering your summons, Mina joins you at your side. She will not remain a widow for long, and with her as your queen you shall sire a whole new dynasty of nosferatu.

But you have had enough of England to last you an entire afterlife, and the British Empire is dead to you now.

If there is one thing eternal life has taught you, it is patience. And so, you will wait, as long as it takes, to rebuild your undead army. When you are ready, and only then, you will put your plans of conquest into action again.

Perhaps you will set your sights on the New World instead this time, and live out your own American dream...

THE END

667

You submit and allow her to hang the crucifix round your neck.

(Record the Golden Crucifix on your Adventure Sheet.)

Whether it is the old lady's fear, or the many ghostly traditions of this strange, un-English place, or the crucifix itself, you do not feel nearly as easy in your mind as usual.

Tick off the code word *Kereszt* and then turn to **687**.

668

Ignoring Barlow's advice, you make your way to Dandrige Ward where the attendants are engaged in what appears to be an all-out war with the unleashed inmates, as they attempt to bring the riot under control.

You suddenly become aware of something hurtling through the air towards you.

Take an Agility test. If you pass the test, turn to **513**, but if you fail the test, turn to **630**.

669

You look on with horrified amazement as the creature, whose body is as corporeal as yours, suddenly melts into mist, and in this state passes through the interstice in the door of the tomb, where scarce a knife blade could pass.

Flinging open the door to the tomb, the Professor leads the charge, and you follow his stuttering lamp down the marble steps, into the near dark of the crypt.

You arrive at the bottom a split second after your old tutor, and just in time to see the Bloofer Lady climb back into the coffin that birthed it.

Turn to **74**.

670

24 October, Varna

Ten days after your party arrived in Bulgaria, Arthur finally receives word of the *Czarina Catherine*.

TELEGRAM, RUFUS SMITH, LONDON, TO LORD GODALMING, CARE H. B. M. VICE CONSUL, VARNA

24 October

Czarina Catherine reported this morning from Dardanelles.

Everyone reacts with wild excitement to the news, all except for Mrs Harker. She alone among your party shows no sign of emotion.

She has changed greatly during the past three weeks. She is lethargic, sleeping for much of the day as well as the night, and though she seems strong and well, and is getting back some of her colour, you and Van Helsing talk of her often in private.

The Professor tells you that he examines her teeth very carefully, whenever she is hypnotised, and says that so long as they do not begin to sharpen there is no active danger of a change in her. But if this change does come, it will be necessary to take steps, and you both know what those steps would have to be.

It is only about 24 hours' sail from the Dardanelles to Varna, at the rate the *Czarina Catherine* has come from London. She should therefore arrive sometime in the morning.

You and Van Helsing are both men of science, but the Professor also entertains all sorts of curious ideas, none of which have proven to be false so far. Perhaps you should be more like your old tutor.

The Professor has shared all manner of outlandish superstitions with you during your time on the Orient Express, one of which concerned how silver is anathema to the creatures of darkness.

Quincey Morris has furnished you all with rifles and pistols, guns being a curiously American obsession, but how do you know that ordinary bullets will stop a being that is already, to all intents and purposes, as medical science would have it, dead? Your musings lead you to the only logical conclusion: what if the bullets fired by your guns were not of lead but of silver?

If you want to try to acquire some silver bullets, turn to **768**. If not, turn to **703**.

671

Renfield weathers your scolding as an errant schoolboy might weather the reprimands of his housemaster.

"The fly was very good and very wholesome," he says quietly. "It is life, strong life, and gives life to me."

Much as his proud reaction repulses you, it does give you an idea, or at least the rudiment of one.

(Tick off the code word *Arachnophilia*.)

What do you want to do now? Will you:

Tell him to dispose of his collection of spiders?	Turn to **651**.
Ask to see his notebook?	Turn to **701**.
Be on your way?	Turn to **729**.

672

The door is unlocked and, opening it, you step into a room shrouded in darkness. You raise your lamp above your head and its welcome light is reflected back from a thousand captured treasures.

The room is full of trophies, recovered from battlefields hundreds of years ago. They are mostly the arms and armour of Janissaries – like the crossed swords secured to the door – the elite infantry of the Ottoman Turks that Count Dracula told you invaded his ancestral lands centuries ago. They must have been taken as spoils of war by one of Dracula's ancestors.

Well, as they say, to the victor the spoils.

A number of items in particular pique your interest: a fanned arrangement of swords; an open box of the kind apothecaries used to carry with them, containing a number of glass bottles; a large chest, that has its lid closed; an ornate flask supported upon a brass stand.

What do you want to do? Will you:

Take a closer look at the swords?	Turn to **3**.
Take a closer look at the apothecary's box?	Turn to **769**.
Take a closer look at the large chest?	Turn to **829**.
Take a closer look at the flask in the brass stand?	Turn to **702**.
Leave the room?	Turn to **36**.

673

As the Professor defends himself against the predations of a dark-haired horror, you are left facing an exquisitely voluptuous specimen, her radiant beauty twisted into a hideous gargoyle leer. (In this battle, the Vampyre has the initiative.)

VAMPYRE   COMBAT 9   ENDURANCE 10

If you manage to slay the vampyre, turn to **624**.

674

MINA MURRAY'S JOURNAL

19 August, Whitby

At last, news of Jonathan. The dear fellow has been ill, and that is why he did not write. I am not afraid to think it or to say it, now that I know...

Mr Hawkins sent the letter on to you, and wrote himself, the good Christian soul that he is. You are to leave in the morning and travel to be with your fiancé in Buda-Pesth, and help nurse him if necessary, and ultimately bring him home.

Mr Hawkins says it would not be a bad thing if the two of you were to be married while you are there. You have cried over the good Sister's letter until you can feel it wet against your bosom, where it lies. For it is of Jonathan and must be near your heart.

Your journey is mapped out, and your luggage ready; you are only taking one change of dress. Lucy will take your trunk to London and keep it until you send for it.

* * * *

If you wish to continue the story as Mina Murray, turn to **13**. If you want to continue as Dr John Seward, turn to **691**.

675

Clearly directed by the mind of another – the other of your kind whose territory you have violated by coming here – the bats swoop down and attack the wolves.

Divide your *Blood* score by 10, rounding fractions up. Then roll 1 die, and if the number rolled is equal or less than the resulting total, turn to **705**. If it is greater, turn to **739**.

676

Renfield is lying in his cell in a glittering pool of blood. It is immediately apparent that he has received some terrible injuries. His face is horribly bruised, as though it has been beaten against the floor.

"I think his back is broken," Simmons says. "See, both his right arm and leg and the whole side of his face are paralysed, but how such a thing could have happened is a mystery to me. He could have damaged his face like that by beating his own head on the floor – I saw a young woman do it once at the Eversfield Asylum before anyone could lay hands on her – and I suppose he could have broken his neck by falling out of bed, if he got in an awkward kink. But for the life of me I can't imagine how the two things occurred together.

Renfield is breathing stertorously, another indication that he has suffered some terrible injury, but then suddenly his eyes open, and become fixed in a wild, helpless stare.

"I have had a terrible dream, and it has left me so weak that I cannot move," he whispers weakly. "What's wrong with my face? It feels all swollen, and it smarts dreadfully."

He tries to turn his head, but even that slight effort causes his eyes to grow glassy.

"Tell us your dream, Mr Renfield." Van Helsing says in a quiet grave tone.

"Give me some water, my lips are dry; and I shall try to tell you."

Quincey hurries off but soon returns with a glass and a decanter of brandy. His parched lips moistened, the patient revives a little.

Fixing you with a piercing look of agonised confusion he says, "I must not deceive myself; it was no dream, but all a grim reality."

His eyes suddenly start roving the room.

"Quick, Doctor, quick. I am dying! I feel that I have but a few minutes! Wet my lips with brandy again. I have something that I must say before I die."

More brandy is offered, and the wretch begins his tale of woe.

"It was that night after you left me, Dr Seward, when I implored you to let me go away. I couldn't speak then, for I felt my tongue was tied; but I was as sane then as I am now. I was in an agony of despair for a long time after you left me; it seemed hours. Then there came a sudden peace. My brain seemed to become cool again, and I realised where I was. He came to me then."

You stifle a gasp. There can only be one individual to whom he is referring.

"He came up to the window in the mist, as I had seen Him often before; but He was solid then not a ghost, and His eyes were fierce like a man's when angry. He was laughing with his red mouth; the sharp white teeth glinted in the moonlight when He turned to look back over the belt of trees. I wouldn't ask Him to come in at first, though I knew He wanted to just as He had wanted all along. Then He began promising me things not in words but by doing them."

"How?" asks the Professor.

"By making them happen; just as He used to send in the flies when the sun was shining. Great big fat ones with steel and sapphire on their wings; and big moths, in the night, with skull and crossbones on their backs.

"Then He began to whisper: 'Rats, rats, rats! Hundreds, thousands, millions of them, and every one a life; and dogs to eat them, and cats too. All lives! All red blood, with years of life in it; and not merely buzzing flies!' I laughed at Him, for I wanted to see what He could do.

"He beckoned me to the window. I got up and looked out, and He raised His hands, and seemed to call out without using any words. A dark mass spread over the grass, coming on like the shape of a flame of fire; and then He moved the mist to the right and left, and I could see that there were thousands of rats with their eyes blazing red like His, only smaller. He held up His hand, and they all stopped; and I thought He seemed to be saying: 'All these lives will I give you, aye, and many more and greater, through countless ages, if you will fall down and worship me!'

"A red cloud, like the colour of blood, seemed to close over my eyes; and before I knew what I was doing, I found myself opening the sash and saying to Him: 'Come in, Lord and Master!' The rats were all gone, but He slid into the room through the sash, though it was only open an inch wide."

Renfield's voice is becoming weaker, so Quincey moistens his lips with the brandy again, and he continues. But it seems as though his memory has gone on working in the interval for his story has advanced further.

"All day I waited to hear from Him, but He did not send me anything, not even a blowfly, and when the moon got up I was pretty angry with Him. When He slid in through the window, though it was shut, and did not even knock, I got mad with Him.

"He sneered at me, and His white face looked out of the mist with His red eyes gleaming, and He went on as though He owned the whole place, and I was no one. He didn't even smell the same as he went by me. I couldn't hold Him. I thought that, somehow, Mrs Harker had come into the room."

You manage to remain silent, upon hearing this revelation, although your body starts to shake uncontrollably.

"When Mrs Harker came in to see me this afternoon, she wasn't the same; it was like tea after the teapot had been watered. I didn't know that she was here till she spoke; and she didn't look the same. I don't care for pale people; I like them with lots of blood in them, and hers had all seemed to have run out.

"I didn't think of it at the time, but when she went away, I began to think, and it made me mad to know that He had been taking the life out of her. So when He came tonight, I was ready for Him.

"I saw the mist stealing in, and I grabbed it tight. I had heard that madmen have unnatural strength; and as I knew I was a madman at times anyhow I resolved to use my power. Aye, and He felt it too, for He had to come out of the mist to struggle with me. I held tight; and I thought I was going to win, for I didn't mean Him to take any more of her life, till I saw His eyes. They burned into me, and my strength became like water. He slipped through it, and when I tried to cling to Him, He raised me up and flung me down. There was a red cloud before me, and a noise like thunder, and the mist seemed to steal away under the door."

His voice is becoming fainter and his breathing more stertorous, until his last breath escapes him as a gargling death-rattle.

"We know the worst now," says Van Helsing, turning to address you all. "He is here, and we know his purpose. It may not be too late. Let us be armed, the same as we were the other night."

Glad that you have grown into the habit of carrying your knife and revolver with you at all times now, you run from Renfield's cell, after Van Helsing, and take the stairs to the first floor two at a time, arriving at the door to the room where Mina is sleeping in mere moments.

"Beware!" the Professor warns, as you seize hold of the door handle. "Alas, it is no common enemy we face."

Turning the handle, the five of you burst into the room together.

The scene that greets you appals you; you feel the hackles on the back of your neck rise and your heart seems to stand still.

In the moonlight streaming in through the window, you see the white-clad figure of Mina kneeling on the edge of the bed, her face and the front of her nightdress filthy with blood. By her side stands a tall, thin man, clad in black. It is the Count!

As your party bursts into the room, the monster turns, his expression that of some hell-born demon. His eyes burn with devilish passion, the great nostrils of his white aquiline nose flare open, and the white sharp teeth, behind the full lips of the blood-dripping mouth, champ together like those of some wild beast.

With a wrench, he throws his victim onto the bed and springs at you.

Take an Agility test. If you pass the test, turn to **724**, but if you fail the test, turn to **744**.

677

The Professor joins you in the dining room. Even though you know what to expect when you open the boxes this time, it does not mean that your heart does not beat a tattoo against its cage of ribs.

Eight boxes could mean that you will have to deal with eight of the Transylvanian undead, and so you decide not to advance your plan any further until the others have joined you.

While you are waiting, keeping a wary eye on the damp-smelling crates for any sign of movement, you open a window that looks out across a narrow stone-flagged yard at the blank face of a stable, pointed to look like the front of a miniature house.

As the sun's orbit carries its light across the back of the house, a beam of sunlight strikes one of the wooden boxes.

Almost at once you hear a scraping sound coming from inside the box, followed by a succession of rasping cries from half a dozen others.

You take up your tools of death just in time, as first one box is broken open by whatever lies hidden within, and then another, and another. In an explosion of earth and enormous splinters, six pallid corpses burst from their wooden prisons.

(Add 1 point to your *Terror* score.)

If you want to use *The Pen is Mightier* special ability, and you still can, turn to **976**. If not, turn to **996**.

678

If you want to continue the story as Mina Harker, turn to **45**. If not, turn to **25**.

679

Dracula grasps the slender neck of the succubus in his steely grip. His eyes are transformed with fury, as if the flames of hellfire burn behind them. His teeth champ with rage, and his pallid cheeks flush red with passion. Never before have you imagined such wrath, even of the demons of the pit!

With a fierce sweep of his arm, he hurls the woman from him, before driving the other two back as well. In a voice which, although almost a whisper, seems to cut through the air and ring from the cold stone walls of the chamber, he declares, "How dare you touch him, any of you? How dare you cast eyes on him when I had forbidden it? This man belongs to me! Beware how you meddle with him, or you will have to deal with me!"

Climbing, like a spider, into the shadows that hang about the dome of the chamber like cobwebs, the succubus turns and answers him with the words: "You yourself never loved. You never love!"

A mirthless, soulless laughter rings through the room, from the foul fiends, and it makes you feel faint to hear it.

"Yes, I too can love," the Count replies. "You yourselves can tell it from the past. Is it not so?"

And then his voice takes on a guttural growl.

"I promise that when I am done with him you shall kiss him at your will. Now go!"

"Are we to have nothing tonight?" one of the unnatural women says, pointing at a bag on the floor that was not there before Dracula's arrival.

The bag suddenly moves, as if there is some living being within it.

The Count says nothing but merely nods. One of the women pounces on the bag then, tearing it open. You quite clearly hear a gasp, followed by a low wail, as of a half-smothered child.

The other women gather around the bag, muttering almost motherly, soothing sounds, but which sound to you like the purrs of hunting felines. (Add 2 points to your *Terror* score.)

And then, aghast with the horror of it all, you mercifully pass out.

Turn to **709**.

680

There is only one convent-sanctuary that fits the Sisters' prophecy. The Hospital of St Joseph and Ste Mary, stands atop a crag, on the east bank of the River Danube, overlooking the Hungarian capital of Buda-Pesth.

The moon has passed the zenith and is making for the horizon again as you fly down, out of the sky towards the holy house. There are not many hours of the night left, and the longer you spend during the hours of daylight away from the sanctuary of the soil of your homeland, the weaker you will become.

Do you want to try to gain entry unseen, via a high window (turn to **557**), or will you risk brazenly approaching the main entrance via the bridge that leads to the hospital (turn to **721**)?

681

In any other circumstance, such a stench would bring your enterprise to an end at once. But this is no ordinary situation, and you cannot give up on the vital mission that has brought you here. But that doesn't stop you from feeling nauseous and lightheaded.

Lose 2 *Endurance* points and for as long as you remain within the chapel, if you find yourself engaged in battle, you must reduce your *Combat Rating* by 1 point.

Turn to **707**.

682

The room suddenly goes dark, but only for a moment. As the dim glow of the gas-lamps returns, you scan the lounge only to see that everyone is still there, except for the Bulgarian mystic. Count Yorga has vanished.

"Quickly," Professor Van Helsing declares, "to the Count's compartment!"

There is no sign of the mysterious Bulgarian in his berth either, but you do find all manner of occult paraphernalia laid out as if he was going to conduct some dark satanic rite. As well as a horned ram's skull, a kris knife and a pair of black candles, there is a gold signet ring, and etched into it the image of a six-pointed star inside a circle.

"The Seal of Solomon," Van Helsing says, handing it to you. "Keep it safe, Madam Mina, for this ring is a powerful talisman."

(If you want to keep the signet ring, record the Seal of Solomon in the Equipment Box on your Adventure Sheet.)

Turn to **509**.

683

The dog's crazed flight slows to a trot until it stops on the path before you, and a threatening, deep-throated growl rises from its chest. You can't help doubting that this encounter will end well, and you steel your nerves, fearing the worst.

If you want to make use of *The Pen is Mightier* special ability, cross off one use and turn to **641**. If not, make a note that you have the initiative and then turn to **312**.

684

The book falls open naturally at a map of England, as if that page has been much studied. Looking at it, you find in certain places little rings have been marked, and on closer inspection you notice that one lies near to Purfleet, to the east of London where the Count's new estate lies. The other two locations marked in this way are your hometown of Exeter, and Whitby on the north Yorkshire coast.

Tick off the code word *Térkép* and then turn to **713**.

685

Creeping up behind the man as he finishes his business, you prepare to pounce.

Take an Agility test. If you pass the test, turn to **655**, but if you fail the test, turn to **625**.

686

Snarling like a caged beast, his face twisting into a demonic visage, Dracula attacks.

If you want to use *The Pen is Mightier* special ability, and you still can, turn to **657**. If not, turn to **637**.

687

You cannot tarry any longer; your coach awaits, as does your client, Count Dracula.

While the landlord and the driver take care of your luggage, you board the coach and take the only remaining seat, the carriage being quite full. The coachman has not yet taken his seat and you can see him talking to the landlady.

A crowd begins to gather at the entrance to the inn and you become convinced the gossips are talking about you, for every now and then they cast pitying glances in your direction. You can hear a lot of repeated strange words.

Do you want to look up their meaning in the dictionary you have brought with you on your expedition to Eastern Europe (turn to **717**), or will you just settle yourself for the doubtless long journey ahead (turn to **747**)?

688

Barlow suddenly appears and deliveries a powerful blow to the back of the madman's head with his cosh. The wretch drops to the ground, unconscious.

"Are you all right, sir?" Barlow asks.

"Nothing a glass of brandy won't fix," you reply. "Purely medicinal, you understand?"

Barlow gives a gruff laugh. "Of course, sir."

Turn to **414**.

689

"Oh, my dear Madam Mina," says the Professor, rubbing his hands together in delight, "this is indeed a change. We have got our old Madam Mina back! And what can I do for you?"

"I want you to hypnotise me!" she tells him. "Do it before the dawn, for I feel that then I can speak, and speak freely. Be quick, for the time is short!"

Without a word, he motions for Mina to sit up in bed. Looking fixedly at her, he starts to make passes in front of her, from over the top of her head downward, with each hand in turn. She in turn gazes at him for a few minutes, until gradually her eyes close and she sits stock still. It is only by the gentle heaving of her bosom that you can tell she is alive.

The Professor makes a few more passes and then stops, and you can see that his forehead is covered with great beads of perspiration.

His subject opens her eyes, but she does not seem the same woman. There is a far-away look in her eyes, and her voice is possessed of a sad dreamy quality.

The stillness is broken by Van Helsing's voice speaking in a low level tone: "Where are you?"

"I do not know." Her answer comes in a neutral way, as though she is interpreting something only she can see and hear. "It is all strange to me!"

"What do you see?" Van Helsing asks.

"I can see nothing. It is all dark."

"What do you hear?" You detect the strain in the Professor's patient voice.

"The lapping of water. It is gurgling by, and little waves leap. I can hear them on the outside."

"Then you are on a ship?"

"Yes!"

"What else do you hear?"

"The sound of men stamping overhead as they run about. There is the creaking of a chain, and the loud tinkle as the check of the capstan falls into the ratchet."

"What are you doing?"

"I am still, oh so still. It is like death!" Her voice fades away into a deep breath, as of one sleeping, and her eyes close again.

Van Helsing places his hands on Mina's shoulders and lays her head down softly on her pillow. She lies like a sleeping child for a few moments, and then, with a long sigh, awakens again and stares in wonder to see you all watching her.

"Have I been talking in my sleep?" she asks as she stifles a yawn.

Turn to **718**.

690

Breaking eye-contact with the horror, you prepare to put an end to the undying Count once and for all, if it is the last thing you ever do. (In this battle, you have the initiative.)

DRACULA, SON OF THE DRAGON   COMBAT 10   ENDURANCE 12

If you win your battle against the skin-shedding vampire, turn to **600**.

691

LETTER FROM THE HONOURABLE ARTHUR HOLMWOOD TO DR SEWARD

31 August

My dear Jack,

I want you to do me a favour. Lucy is ill – that is she has no special disease, but she looks awful, and is getting worse every day. I have asked her if there is any cause; I do not dare to ask her mother, for to disturb the poor lady's mind about her daughter in her present state of health would be fatal.

I am sure that there is something preying on my dear girl's mind. I am almost distracted when I think of her. To look at her gives me a pang. I told her I would ask you to see her. It will be a painful task for you, I know, old friend, but it is for her sake, and I must not hesitate to ask, or you to act.

You are to come to lunch at Hillingham tomorrow, two o'clock, so as not to arouse any suspicion in Mrs. Westenra.

I am filled with anxiety, and want to consult with you alone, as soon as I can, but I have been summoned to see my father, who is worse.

Do not fail!

Arthur

Turn to **653**.

692

Arthur runs the other dog through with his sword, a last defiant growl escaping the animal's throat as it dies.

Were you injured at all by the rabid dog that attacked you? If so, turn to **712**. If not, turn to **876**.

693

"It may be that you may have to bear that mark till God himself sees fit to redress all the wrongs of the earth and of His children," Van Helsing says gravely. "And oh, Madam Mina, my dear, may we who love you be there when that red scar passes away, and leaves your forehead as pure as the heart we know.

"Till then we must bear our Cross, as His Son did in obedience to His Will. It may be that we are chosen instruments of His good pleasure, and that we ascend to His bidding; through tears and blood; through doubts and fears, and all that makes the difference between God and man."

* * * *

If you wish to continue the story as Jonathan Harker, turn to **24**. If you want to continue it as Mina Harker, turn to **490**. And if you want to continue the adventure as Dr John Seward, turn to **54**.

694

LETTER, SISTER AGATHA, HOSPITAL OF ST JOSEPH AND STE MARY, BUDA-PESTH, TO MISS WILHELMINA MURRAY

12 August

Dear Madam.

I write by desire of Mr Jonathan Harker, who is himself not strong enough to write, though progressing well, thanks to God and St Joseph and Ste Mary. He has been under our care for nearly six weeks, suffering from a violent brain fever. He wishes me to convey his love, and to say that by this post I write for him to Mr Peter Hawkins, Exeter, to say, with his dutiful respects, that he is sorry for his delay, and that all of his work is completed.

He will require some few weeks' rest in our sanatorium in the hills, but will then return. He wishes me to say that he has not sufficient money with him, and that he would like to pay for his staying here, so that others who need shall not be wanting for help.

Yours, with sympathy and all blessings,

Sister Agatha.

P.S. – My patient being asleep, I open this to let you know something more. He has told me all about you, and that you are shortly to be his wife. All blessings to you both! He has had some fearful shock, so says our doctor, and in his delirium his ravings have been dreadful; of wolves and poison and blood; of ghosts and demons; and I fear to say of what. Be careful with him always that there may be nothing to excite him of this kind for a long time to come; the traces of such an illness as his do not lightly die away. We should have written long ago, but we knew nothing of his friends.

Be assured that he is well cared for. He has won all our hearts by his sweetness and gentleness. He is truly getting on well, and I have no doubt will in a few weeks be all himself. But be careful of him for safety's sake. There are, I pray God and St Joseph and Ste Mary, many, many, happy years for you both.

Turn to **674**.

695

Leaving the deckhand's drained carcass for the next man on watch to find will certainly induce a sense of fear in the rest of the crew, but it will also alert them to the fact that there is a killer on board the *Demeter* with them.

Gain 2 *Suspicion* points and turn to **730**.

696

It is some time before Mehmed the Conqueror sends his armies into Wallachia again, but when he does, so great are the numbers of his forces that he clearly intends to lay waste to all before him, as punishment for you sending him running with his tail between his legs last time.

As the Sultan's forces – three hundred thousand strong – march on Târgoviște, you ride at the head of your Carpathian Guard, Captain Petru beside you, equally with only one intention – to sever the head of the snake; to assassinate Mehmed the Second, and send his army fleeing Wallachia in fear.

If your rank is that of *Voivode of Wallachia* or higher, turn to **735**. If not, turn to **765**.

697

Without any further delay, Professor Van Helsing places the tip of his whitethorn stake over the fair maiden's breast and, raising the hammer high above his head, sets about his butcher's work.

A horrid screeching rises from Dracula's undead concubine as Van Helsing drives the stake home, blood as thick and black as tar spurting from the wound. But as one vampyre dies, so her Weird Sisters awaken.

They explode out of their coffins and come for you both, their banshee cries filling the echoing sepulchre with their screams.

If you want to employ *The Pen is Mightier* special ability, and you still can, turn to **643**. If not, turn to **673**.

698

Renfield's bloodshot eyes bulge from his head and spittle flies from his lips as he lashes out at you again with the dinner knife. (In this battle Renfield has the initiative.)

RENFIELD   COMBAT 8   ENDURANCE 10

If you win two consecutive Combat Rounds against the lunatic, turn to **662** at once. If not, but you are still alive after 4 Combat Rounds, or if you reduce Renfield's *Endurance* score to 5 points or fewer, whichever comes first, then turn to **662**.

699

You are sure that the house has more secrets that have yet to be discovered, and so you return to the hall.

Tick off the code word *Inventa* and turn to **273**, noting that you can now revisit the ground floor when you are ready.

700

"I am a lonely traveller who seeks shelter for the night," you say. "Won't you let me in, my dear?"

"You will find plenty of inns and hostels open to travellers down in the town, even at this late hour," she replies curtly, and promptly slams the hatch shut.

Despite being only a novice, the young woman's faith is strong, and your supernatural powers hold no sway over her.

Clearly you are not going to gain entry here.

If you want to try to gain entry via a high window, turn to **557**. Alternatively, if you think you would do better to not waste any more time trying to enter this house of God, and would rather attempt to return to Castle Dracula before sunrise, turn to **810**.

701

"May I take a look at your notebook, Mr Renfield?" you ask.

"I would prefer that you didn't, Doctor," he replies, tensing.

"But for me to be able to treat you effectively, I need to understand what is preoccupying your thoughts."

"But I am not ill, Doctor. In fact, I see things more clearly now than I ever did before."

Clearly the thought of letting another into his private world causes him great anxiety.

You turn to one of the attendants who is present with you inside Renfield's cell. "Barlow, get it for me."

Barlow snatches the notebook from Renfield's shaking hands and passes it to you. Flicking through it you see whole pages filled with masses of figures, generally single numbers added up in batches, and then the totals added in batches again, as though Renfield is keeping some account.

And then suddenly, spitting like a wildcat, he leaps on you and claws the notebook from your hands, tearing the flesh of your hands and forearms with his ragged fingernails as he does so.

Roll one die and add 2, then divide the total by 2, rounding fractions up. Deduct this many *Endurance* points. (Alternatively, pick a card and deduct its face value from your *Endurance* score, unless it is 5 or above, or a picture card, in which case deduct 4 points from your *Endurance* score.)

You know that when Renfield is in the grip of his mania, he is no better than a wild animal and cannot be reasoned with. Accompanied by your attendants, you leave his cell and continue your rounds.

Turn to **729**.

702

Holding your lamp close to the crystal phial, you marvel at the intricate filigree that holds it within a lattice of silver. It appears to be filled with black smoke, shot-through with glittering particles, which shifts and swirls as you look at it.

If you want to pull the stopper from the phial, turn to **731**.

If you would rather leave the stopper firmly in place, choosing something you haven't tried already, will you:

Take a closer look at the swords?	Turn to **3**.
Take a closer look at the apothecary's box?	Turn to **769**.
Take a closer look at the large chest?	Turn to **829**.
Leave the room?	Turn to **36**.

703

26 October, Varna

Over a week of waiting, and still no tidings of the *Czarina Catherine*. But she ought to be here by now. That she is still at sea is apparent, but where?

The next day there is still no news and Van Helsing makes it plain that he is anxious the Count is somehow escaping the trap you have laid for him.

And then, on 28 October, news at last!

```
TELEGRAM, RUFUS SMITH, LONDON, TO LORD GODALMING,
       CARE H. B. M. VICE CONSUL, VARNA

                    28 October

Czarina Catherine reported entering Galatz at one o'clock
today.
```

The revelation that Count Dracula has evaded you is a shock to everyone. Van Helsing raises his fist to the sky, as if in remonstrance with the Almighty Himself, Arthur grows very pale, and Quincey Morris tightens his belt, which you know means 'to action'.

"It must have been while Mrs Harker was under hypnosis," the Professor says at last. "Just as our own dear Mina can move her mind to where he is, the Count must have sent his spirit to read her thoughts, and in doing so learned that we were already here, waiting for him. Now he is making every effort to escape us."

* * * *

Galatz is more than two hundred miles away in Romania. The next train for Galatz leaves at 6:30 tomorrow morning, so your party spends the rest of the day preparing for the journey: Arthur arranges the train tickets; papers are obtained so that you might board the *Czarina Catherine* at Galatz; and Quincey Morris visits the Vice Consul to ensure that all will run smoothly with his counterpart in Romania.

And so, on the morning of the 29 October, you board the train for Galatz.

Turn to **725**.

704

Turning right out of your berth, at the end of the carriage you find a huddle of concerned passengers peering at something on the floor of the companionway that connects the traveller compartments. As you join the muttering, shuffling quartet, they make room for you and you see that one of the stewards is lying on the floor. You are appalled to see the look of horror frozen in his glazed eyes and the waxy pallor of his skin. The poor wretch is quite clearly dead.

"Let me through!" comes the voice of the Dutchman, and the huddle moves again as he crouches down to inspect the body. "Who found the victim?" he asks at last.

"I did," says a short, nervous-looking man, putting up his hand. There is something unpleasantly of the rat about him.

"Ladies and gentlemen, might I ask you to gather in the lounge?" directs the Professor and your fellow passengers seem compelled to obey.

Before you and Van Helsing join them, the old man shares what he discovered with you. "There are two puncture wounds on the poor victim's neck," he explains, "and I believe he died from extreme exsanguination."

Could there be *another* vampire on board the train with you? You are certain it is not the Count, for you are convinced your psychic bond would have alerted you to his presence. But then that must mean there is another blood-sucker abroad.

* * * *

In the lounge car, Professor Van Helsing opens proceedings. There are six of you gathered together: the ratty man who found the body; a handsome, middle-aged man with a widow's peak, his hair greying at the temples, and who is wearing a curious talisman set with a bloodstone; a beautiful blonde-haired young woman, with skin as smooth and white as ivory and bright red rosebud lips; and a wolfish-looking older man wearing a velvet smoking jacket, who has strangely pointed ears.

"Ladies and gentlemen," the Professor begins. "I have gathered you here because this very night, aboard this train, a murder has been committed. We are travelling in the last carriage on the train. I was here in the lounge with the barman when the murder was committed, no one passed this way and there is no sign of anyone

having exited the carriage by any other means, so I can only conclude that the killer was someone travelling in this carriage."

The assembled passengers exchange glances and gasps of horror, all arguing their innocence.

"How do you propose to deduce which of them is the murderer?" you ask the Professor.

"We must interview them, one at a time, and by cross-referencing their answers to our questions, the guilty party's lies will find them out. But Madam Mina, who we should interview first I will leave up to you."

Who do you want to interview first?

The ratty little man?	Turn to **727**.
The handsome, middle-aged man?	Turn to **742**.
The beautiful young woman?	Turn to **767**.
The wolfish-looking older man?	Turn to **787**.

705

Conduct the battle between the bats and the wolves yourself. The wolf pack has the initiative in this battle, and you may add a 2 point bonus when calculating the wolves' *Combat Rating*.

	COMBAT	ENDURANCE
CLOUD OF BATS	8	18
PACK OF WOLVES	7	24

If the wolves reduce the bats' combined *Endurance* score to 6 points or fewer, turn to **815** at once. However, if the bats reduce the wolves' combined *Endurance* score to 12 points or fewer, turn to **761** immediately.

You realise that you have subconsciously taken hold of your silver crucifix. It is as if a mighty power is creeping along your arm, a power against which the vampire has no resistance, and that knowledge gives you the strength to break the Count's hypnotic hold over you.

Snarling like a caged beast, his face twisting into a demonic visage, Dracula attacks.

If you want to use *The Pen is Mightier* special ability, and you still can, turn to **657**. If not, turn to **617**.

707

Inside the chapel, resting upon the packed earth floor, are dozens of bulky, wooden crates, their lids nailed shut.

"The first thing we must do is count the boxes," says the Professor.

It does not take long to ascertain the number, and to the horror of you all, there are only twenty-nine left out of the fifty that the Count had transported to England on board the Russian schooner.

Take an ESP test. If you pass the test, turn to **331**, but if you fail the test, turn to **564**.

708

"The murderer is Count Yorga!" you declare.

Turn to **682**.

709

JONATHAN HARKER'S JOURNAL

19 May

```
I awoke in my own bed. The Count must have carried me
here. As I look round this room, although it has been to
me so full of fear, it is now a sort of sanctuary, for
nothing can be more dreadful than those awful women,
who are waiting to suck my blood...
```

As you try to piece together your memories of what happened last night, you realise that your host is also now your saviour. However, he knows that you went against his wishes, by exploring the women's wing of the castle.

(Any weapons you may have collected are gone. Remove them from your Adventure Sheet.)

At nightfall, the Count visits you in your rooms again, and asks you to write three more letters: one saying that your work is almost done, and that you will start for home again within a few days; another saying that you are setting out the morning after the date the letter is sent; and the third saying that you have left the castle and are back in Bistritz.

"The first should be dated June 12," he instructs you, "the second June 19, and the third June 29. Posts are few and uncertain, Mr Harker," he goes on, as if by way of explanation, even though you know it is only an excuse. "You writing these letters now will put the minds of your friends at ease."

You know better than to try to resist him, and now you know how long you have left to live. You can only hope that something may occur within the next month that will provide you with a chance to escape.

* * * *

It is almost ten days before such an opportunity presents itself, or at any rate of being able to send word home.

A band of Szgany arrives at the castle and sets up camp within the courtyard. They are gypsies, peculiar to this part of the world. You have read in the Count's library that they attach themselves to some great noble, or boyar, and call themselves by his name. They are fearless and without religion, save superstition, and they speak their own variety of the Romany tongue, but their loyalty is without question.

Perhaps you could write some letters home and try to get the Szgany to have them posted (turn to **738**). Alternatively, you could wait and see if a proper chance to escape presents itself (turn to **766**). But then, fearing that you do not have long left to live, you could try to take on the Count directly, by ambushing him the next time he comes to visit you in your chambers (turn to **857**).

710

This serpentine shape-changer fixes you with its hypnotic ophidian gaze and you feel your resolve start to weaken.

Take a Terror test. If you pass the test, turn to **690**. If you fail the test, turn to **650**.

711

It is in the dining room – which lies off the hall at the back of the house – that you find eight boxes, like those you found in the unhallowed chapel of Carfax House, the dust-covered dining table and chairs having been moved to the edges of the room to accommodate them.

If you want to proceed to deal with the boxes, as required, turn to **677**. If you would prefer to continue searching the property, with the intention of returning here later, turn to **699**.

712

You can already feel yourself starting to get sick, as you start to sweat and shake.

(Lose another 2 *Endurance* points and deduct 1 point from both your *Agility* score and your *Combat* score.)

You dread to think what might lie ahead of you in your future.

(Add 1 to your *Terror* score.)

If you are still alive, tick off the code word *Lyssavirus* and then turn to **876**.

713

The door opens and Count Dracula returns unexpectedly.

"Still at your books?" Before you can reply he says, "Come! I am informed that your supper is ready."

An excellent meal awaits you in the next room, laid out on the table. The Count excuses himself, explaining that he has already dined out. (Regain 2 *Endurance* points.)

The two of you talk late into the night, until all at once you hear a cock crow and the Count jumps to his feet, saying, "Why there is the morning again! How remiss I am to let you stay up so long," and with a courtly bow he quickly leaves you.

Turn to **743**.

714

MINA MURRAY'S JOURNAL

17 August, Whitby

No diary for two whole days. I have not had the heart to write. Some sort of shadowy pall seems to be coming over our happiness...

There is still no news from Jonathan, and Lucy seems to be growing weaker, whilst you fear her mother's days are numbering to a close.

You do not understand how Lucy can be wasting away as she is. She eats well and sleeps well, and enjoys the fresh air, but all the time the roses in her cheeks are fading, and she is getting weaker and more languid day by day. Worst of all, at night you hear her gasping for air.

You keep the key to your door fastened to your wrist at night, but she still gets up and walks about the room or sits at the open window. Last night you found her leaning out when you woke up, and when you tried to wake her you could not rouse her.

She was in a faint. When you did finally manage to restore her, she was weak as water, and cried silently between long, painful struggles for breath. When you asked her how she came to be at the window, she simply shook her head and turned away.

You have studied her throat while she lay sleeping and were horrified to find that the tiny wounds have not healed. If anything, they are larger than before, and the edges of them are faintly white. Unless they heal within a day or two, you determine to insist on the doctor taking a look at them.

Turn to **694**.

715

Unable to help yourself, you throw open the door and burst into the dining-room.

Take an Agility test. If you pass the test, turn to **664**, but if you fail the test, turn to **825**.

716

It is the Barghest beast old Mr Swales told you of! He told you that if you hear its howl then your time is at hand, but he didn't tell you that the phantom dog came to drag you to Hell itself!

Picking up a splinter of stone from a broken gravestone, you prepare to sell your soul dear.

(The Barghest has the initiative in this battle, and for the duration of the fight you must reduce your *Combat Rating* by 1 point.)

BARGHEST   COMBAT 7   ENDURANCE 8

If you are still alive after 6 Combat Rounds, or if you reduce the Barghest's *Endurance* score to 4 points or fewer, whichever is sooner, turn to **754** at once.

717

When you discover what the words mean you can't help being reminded of the old adage, "Ignorance is bliss". For among them are *Ordog*, meaning 'Satan', *Pokol* – "hell", *Stregoica* – "witch", *Vrolok* and *Vlkoslak* – both of which mean something like "werewolf" or "vampire". You are left wishing you had not bothered to seek to know the meaning of the words.

You make a mental note to ask the Count about these dark superstitions when you meet at last.

Tick off the code word *Gonosz* and turn to **747**.

718

"There is not a moment to lose," says the Professor urgently, "for it may not yet be too late to thwart the Enemy's plans! That ship, wherever it was, was weighing anchor whilst Madam Mina spoke. There are many ships weighing anchor at the moment in your so great Port of London. Which of them is it that we seek?

"We can know now what was in the Count's mind, when he fled the house in Piccadilly. He meant to escape. He saw that, with but one earth-box left and a pack of men following like dogs after a fox, this London was no place for him. And so, he has taken his last box of earth on board a ship. He thinks to escape, but we will follow him. The old fox is wily, but so too am I."

"But why do we need to seek him further," Arthur asks, "when he is already gone away from us?"

At this the Professor looks gravely at Arthur: "Because he can live for centuries, whereas Madam Mina is but a mortal woman. Time is now to be dreaded since he put that mark upon her throat. Now, more than ever, must we hunt him down, even if we have to follow him to the jaws of Hell!"

* * * *

If you wish to continue the story as Jonathan Harker, turn to **46**. If you want to continue as Mina Harker, turn to **66**. If you want to continue the adventure as Dr John Seward, turn to **16**.

719

You might have once sworn an oath to do no harm but faced by a lunatic in the middle of a psychotic episode, you have no choice but to defend yourself. (You have the initiative in this battle.)

LUNATIC   COMBAT 9   ENDURANCE 9

If you are still alive after 4 Combat Rounds, or if you reduce the madman's *Endurance* score to 4 points or fewer, whichever is sooner, turn to **688**.

720

Removing your royal raiment, accompanied by Captain Petru, you leave the palace by one of a dozen secret tunnels that worm their way beneath the capital, and emerge close to the banks of the river. Wading across at a shallow point, you enter the encampment unseen and begin to creep between the pavilions, learning what you can about the organisation of Mehmed's forces as you do so.

Rounding the corner of one tent, you see a lone Turkish soldier relieving himself – while twenty yards away his fellow Janissaries are busy sharpening weapons and polishing armour – and it gives you an idea. If you stole his armour, you could disguise yourself and go about the camp unhindered.

If you want to sneak up on the soldier, with the intention of stealing his armour, turn to **685**. If you would rather not risk drawing the attention of the man's fellow Janissaries and prefer to continue going about the camp as you are currently, turn to **525**.

721

Flying down to the causeway that links the hospital to an adjoining peak, you assume your human guise once more.

As you stride confidently across the bridge, a hatch opens in the sealed gate and a face appears behind its iron grille, her anxious innocence illuminated by the lantern the young nun is holding in one hand.

"Hello? Who goes there?" she demands, peering out into the darkness. You would know she is in a highly agitated state from the quiver in her voice, if you hadn't already detected the quickening of the pulse in her veins.

Appearing suddenly at the gate, you make the nun start, and she gives a startled gasp.

"Good evening, Sister," you begin, fixing her gaze with yours.

Take an ESP test. If you pass the test, turn to **988**. If you fail the test, turn to **700**.

Alternatively, you may deduct 3 *Blood* points, if you want, and turn to **988** without having to take the test in the first place.

722

TELEGRAM, VAN HELSING, ANTWERP, TO SEWARD, CARFAX

17 September

```
Do not fail to be at Hillingham tonight. If not watching
all the time, frequently visit and see that flowers are as
placed, very important, do not fail. Shall be with you as
soon as possible after arrival.
```

You cannot believe it! Van Helsing's telegram arrives early on the morning of 18 September, but a whole day late! The Professor's dire warning fills you with dismay, for you know by bitter experience what may occur in the course of an entire night – a night that has been lost because of the late arrival of his telegram!

Of course, it is possible that all may still be well, but you find yourself fixating on what you fear might have happened. You feel that there is some dreadful doom hanging over your endeavours, that every possible accident seems to thwart your efforts to keep Lucy alive at every turn.

You set off immediately, boarding the first train to London and – even you, a man of science – praying that nothing has befallen Lucy during the night.

* * * *

You drive at once to Hillingham and, keeping your cab at the gate, head up the avenue alone. Ascending the steps to the front door, you knock gently and ring as quietly as possible, hoping to only bring a housemaid to the door. When there is no response, you knock and ring again, but still there is no answer.

Cursing the laziness of the servants, you ring and knock a third time, more impatiently, but without receiving a response.

A creeping dread steals into your heart; is this desolation another link in the chain of doom that seems to be drawing tight around you? Is it a house of death to which you have come, too late?

Knowing that minutes, even seconds of delay might lead to hours of danger for Lucy, you circle the house, searching for another way in.

But you can find no other means of ingress. Every window and door on the ground floor is fastened and locked. Baffled, you return to the front porch.

Turn to **42**.

723

You can't quite put your finger on it, but something doesn't feel quite right. You sense danger nearby, but is it the gypsies who are a threat to you or is it the wolves lurking within the forest?

If you want to draw your weapon, in case you need to defend yourself in a hurry, turn to **843**. If not, turn to **646**.

724

You throw yourself out of the Count's path as he lands with a snarl in the midst of your party.

Turn to **790**.

725

The train from Varna to Galatz is nothing like the Orient Express. You are forced to make do with compartments interspersed throughout the train and are unable to purloin any that are adjacent to one another.

You are returning to your compartment from the dining car after supper when you see a curious, hunchbacked fellow – dressed in rough clothes and bald but for a few straggly wisps of hair – exit a berth at the far end of the carriage and head in the direction of the luggage van.

There is something about his surreptitious manner that arouses your suspicions.

If you want to find out where he is going, turn to **798**. If you would prefer to leave well alone and retire for the night, turn to **881**?

726

It's no good, the vampire is simply too powerful. How did you ever imagine you could get the better of a creature that has survived down through the centuries thanks to a combination of animal cunning, a warlord's ruthlessness, and sheer physical power?

Dracula seizes you with one hand and, lifting your feet from the floor, sinks his teeth into your neck and starts to drink...

Your adventure is over.

THE END

727

The man is German and goes by the name of Herr Knock. He claims he is manservant to Graf Orlok of Wisborg and is accompanying his employer to his ancestral home in Transylvania.

"Where is your master?" Van Helsing demands.

"My master is sleeping and cannot be disturbed," he replies.

Taking you to one side, the Professor says, "What do you think we should do? Should we disturb the Graf?"

How will you reply?

"Wake Graf Orlok."	Turn to **732**.
"Interview the handsome, middle-aged man."	Turn to **742**.
"Question the beautiful young woman."	Turn to **767**.
"Interrogate the wolfish-looking older man."	Turn to **787**.
"Let us draw this matter to an end."	Turn to **987**.

728

You bring the pommel of your sword down hard on the Professor's head and he crumples to his knees. But it seems to have had the desired effect.

As he woozily gets to his feet again, he looks at you with unfocused eyes and says, "What was I in the middle of doing?"

"Killing vampires," you say, pointing at the blonde-haired vampyre lying prone in her coffin.

Turn to **697**.

729

There is a method to Renfield's madness, and the rudimentary idea you have in your mind is growing. You judge it best to keep away from your friend for a few days, so that you might notice if there is any change. And yet things remain as they were, except that he parts with some of his pets and acquires a new one.

You learn from your staff that he has managed to get hold of a sparrow and has already partially tamed it. His means of taming is obvious, for already his collection of spiders has diminished. Those that remain, however, are well fed, for he still brings in the flies by tempting them with his food.

* * * *

The next time you visit Renfield's cell, you are surprised to discover that he has a whole colony of sparrows, and his flies and spiders are almost obliterated. You are barely through the cell door when he runs up to you, an obsequious expression on his face, saying that he has a great favour to ask you: "A very great favour, my dear Doctor Seward."

"What is it?" you ask.

"A kitten," he replies, with a sort of rapture in his voice and bearing. "A nice, little, sleek, playful kitten, that I can play with, and teach, and feed, and feed, and feed!"

His request does not totally take you by surprise, since you have noticed how his pets have continued to increase in size and liveliness.

How do you wish to respond to his request?

"Would you not rather have a cat?"	Turn to **749**.
"We'll see, but I can't make any promises."	Turn to **783**.
"No, absolutely not! Such a thing is out of the question!"	Turn to **803**.

730

LOG OF THE 'DEMETER'

17 July ~ Yesterday, one of the men, Olgaren, came to my cabin, and in an awestruck way confided to me that he thought there was a strange man aboard the ship. He said that in his watch he had been sheltering behind the deck-house, as there was a rain-storm, when he saw a tall, thin man, who was not like any of the crew, come up the companion-way, and go along the deck forward, and disappear. He followed cautiously, but when he got to the bows found no one, and the hatchways were all closed. He was in a panic of superstitious fear, and I am afraid the panic may spread. To allay it, I shall to-day search the entire ship carefully from stem to stern.

Later in the day I got together the whole crew, and told them, as they evidently thought there was someone in the ship, we would search from stem to stern. First mate angry; said it was folly, and to yield to such foolish ideas would demoralise the men; said he would engage to keep them out of trouble with a handspike. I let him take the helm, while the rest began thorough search, all keeping abreast, with lanterns: we left no corner unsearched. As there were only the big wooden boxes, there were no odd corners where a man could hide. Men much relieved when search over, and went back to work cheerfully. First mate scowled, but said nothing.

22 July ~ Rough weather last three days, and all hands busy with sails so no time to be frightened. Men seem to have forgotten their dread. Mate cheerful again, and all on good terms. Praised men for work in bad weather. Passed Gibraltar and out through Straits. All well.

Turn to **771**.

731

You pull the stopper from the flask. There is a great rushing of air, as if the wind outside has somehow found a way to penetrate the castle, and the room is plunged into darkness.

At first you think the wind has extinguished your lamp, but then the gloom clears again. And yet, in that brief moment of total darkness, you can't shake the feeling that you saw something like a pair of glittering golden eyes peering at you from within a cloud of black smoke, as if the darkness was in fact a tangible thing. (Add 1 point to your *Terror* score.)

Choosing something you haven't tried already, will you:

Take a closer look at the swords?	Turn to **3**.
Take a closer look at the apothecary's box?	Turn to **769**.
Take a closer look at the large chest?	Turn to **829**.
Leave the room?	Turn to **890**.

732

Deaf to the ratty man's protests, you and the Professor lead the way as your fellow passengers accompany you to the Graf's compartment. Upon reaching it, Van Helsing does not hesitate but pulls the door open without knocking, only to be greeted by a horrible scene.

Leaning against a seat is an open coffin. You can see that it is half-filled with mouldering grave-dirt, and lying atop the foul soil is a hideous, rake-thin figure. It is a man, entirely bald and with exaggeratedly pointed ears, like those of a rat or a bat. Two elongated fangs protrude over his bottom lip and the man has his arms folded across his chest, his fingers ending in long, claw-like nails. Milling about the floor of the compartment are dozens of rats!

You are assailed by a horrendous stench, that you have no doubt is emanating from the coffin. As you stare in appalled horror at the rats, the man's eyes flick open, and a venomous hiss escapes from his mouth.

The rats suddenly pour out of the compartment towards you and there are cries of panic as everyone tries to get out of the way. But as you and the Professor were the first at the door, you cannot escape the vile vermin and their sharp, chisel-like teeth.

Roll one die and deduct this many *Endurance* points. Alternatively, pick a card and deduct that many *Endurance* points, unless it is greater than 7 or a picture card, in which case deduct 6 *Endurance* points.

If you are still alive, add 2 points to your *Terror* score and turn to **280**.

733

Your sword and revolver in hand, you prepare to face Dracula's loyal Szgany in battle.

If you want to use *The Pen is Mightier* special ability, cross off one use and turn to **904**. If not, turn to **792**.

734

You soon find yourselves opposite a low, arched oaken door, ribbed with iron bands.

Turn to **606**.

735

You lead the charge of the Carpathian Guard against the Ottoman cavalry, which turns and breaks before you. Those among the Turkish infantry who do not flee in the horsemen's wake are trampled beneath the hooves of your own Wallachian cavaliers.

Turn to **840**.

736

Picking up a splinter of stone from a broken gravestone, you prepare to defend yourself as best you can against the black dog's snapping jaws and gouging claws. (Which one of you has the initiative will depend on how you got to this point.)

BLACK DOG   COMBAT 7   ENDURANCE 8

If you are still alive after 6 Combat Rounds, or if you reduce the Barghest's *Endurance* score to 4 points or fewer, whichever is sooner, turn to **754** at once.

737

"His red eyes again!" Lucy murmurs in her sleep as you tuck her up under the covers, and in mere moments she is sleeping peacefully again.

Turn to **714**.

738

You write one letter to Mina in shorthand, explaining your situation but without mention of the horrors you have been forced to endure – it would frighten her to death if you were to expose your heart to her – and one to Mr Hawkins, simply asking him to communicate with your fiancée.

The letters sealed, you let them drop through the bars of your window, along with a gold sovereign, to the courtyard below, using such sign language as you can to communicate with the gypsy folk that you want to have them posted.

The man who picks them up presses them to his heart and bows, putting them inside his cap for safekeeping.

You can do no more, and so steal back to the library to read.

* * * *

That evening, after nightfall, the Count comes to your rooms. He has a pair of letters with him. Sitting down beside you, he says in his smoothest voice, "The Szgany have given me these, of which, though I know not whence they come, I shall, of course, take care."

As he begins to open the letters, your pulse quickens.

"See! One is from you, and to my friend Mr Hawkins. The other…" – he catches sight of the strange shorthand symbols as he opens the envelope, and a dark look comes upon him, his eyes blazing wickedly – "… is a vile thing, an outrage upon friendship and hospitality! It is not signed, so it cannot matter to us."

He calmly holds both letter and envelope in the flame of the lamp till they are consumed.

"The letter to Hawkins, that I shall of course send on, since it is yours, and your letters are sacred to me."

With that, he leaves, and you hear the key turn softly in the lock.

If seems you have no choice now, but to wait, for you know that to try to charge the heavy oak door would be to break yourself rather than the ancient lock, and hope that you are not merely waiting for death.

Add 1 point to your *Terror* score and gain 2 *Blood* points, then turn to **766**.

739

Conduct the battle between the Cloud of Bats and the Pack of Wolves but note that the Bats have the initiative in this battle.

	COMBAT	ENDURANCE
CLOUD OF BATS	8	18
PACK OF WOLVES	7	24

If the bats reduce the wolves' combined *Endurance* score to 12 points or fewer, turn to **761** immediately. However, if the wolves reduce the bats' combined *Endurance* score to 6 points or fewer, turn to **815** at once.

740

"Is everything ready?" you ask, when you meet by moonlight in the graveyard again.

"The box will be loaded onto the boat this very night and should reach Strasba five days from now."

"Excellent," you say, "then all that remains is for me to ensure that there are no loose ends."

"Wh-What do you mean?" Skinsky stammers, his face turning white and his heartrate starting to quicken.

If your rank is that of *Emperor of the Dead*, or you are willing to spend 3 *Blood* points, turn to **40**. If not, turn to **860**.

741

"I will go with you," you tell the Professor and a broad smile spreads across his face in response.

And so, it is agreed. While you and Van Helsing make your way to the Piccadilly property, between them, the others will visit the other properties in Walworth and Mile End, in search of the missing boxes of Transylvanian soil.

* * * *

Upon reaching the corner of Arlington Street, you exit the cab you hired upon arriving at Fenchurch Street Station, and the two of you stroll into the Green Park, trying to blend in with the members of the general public partaking of their daily constitutional in the afternoon sunshine.

Your pulse quickens as you catch sight of the house on which your hopes are centred. It looms grim and silent in its deserted condition amongst its more lively and spruce-looking neighbours. Choosing your moment, you and the Professor approach the front door.

Taking out a bunch of skeleton keys, and selecting one, Van Helsing slides it into the lock. After fumbling about for a bit, he tries a second and then a third. At the fourth attempt, all at once the door opens at a slight push, and the two of you enter the hallway beyond. The place smells vile, like the old chapel at Carfax.

A staircase ascends and descends through the Piccadilly property. You decide to split up so that you might search the house more quickly.

Where will you begin your search?

The basement?	Turn to **656**.
The ground floor?	Turn to **711**.
The first floor?	Turn to **542**.
The second floor?	Turn to **434**.
The attic?	Turn to **323**.

742

The handsome, middle-aged man calls himself Count Yorga, and claims to be a Bulgarian mystic, who is travelling to Veresti at the behest of a wealthy client. When Van Helsing asks him why his wealthy client has summoned him, he replies that he is to conduct a séance, so that she might speak again with her dead husband.

"I could perform a séance now, if you like," Yorga offers. "If I could summon the dead man's spirit he could tell us who the murderer is himself."

"What do you think, Madam Mina?" says Van Helsing. "We have witnessed many strange things ourselves in recent months. Who is to say that this Count Yorga is not capable of contacting the dead? Should we ask him to use his powers to aid us in our investigation? I leave the decision in your hands."

Do you want to:

Ask Count Yorga to conduct a séance?	Turn to **817**.
Interview the ratty little man?	Turn to **727**.
Question the beautiful young woman?	Turn to **767**.
Interrogate the wolfish-looking older man?	Turn to **787**.
Draw this matter to an end?	Turn to **987**.

743

You only sleep a few hours and, feeling that you cannot sleep any longer, you get up. You hang up your shaving glass by the window, and are just beginning to shave, when an inexplicable shiver passes through you, as if someone just stepped over your grave.

Take an ESP test. If you pass the test, turn to **804**. If you fail the test, turn to **834**.

744

The Count is fast as a striking cobra. He lands in front of you, and with one swipe of his taloned hand, sends you flying across the room and into the door frame.

Lose 3 *Endurance* points and turn to **790**.

745

At sunset, Professor Van Helsing comes to your berth to hypnotise you again. Making yourself comfortable, as best you can, you focus on the Professor's voice and the languid movements of his hands.

Take an ESP test. If you pass the test, turn to **821**, but if you fail the test, turn to **851**.

746

The Count's expression transforms into a cold stare of lion-like disdain and from the look in his blood-red gaze alone you know that to the vampire you are no more than prey, the mouse to his cat. It is pointless to resist him.

But deep down, your distant inner voice is calling out to you, telling you that you must fight the vampire's hypnotic influence.

Take a Combat test. If you pass the test, turn to **706**. If you fail the test, turn to **726**.

747

By the time the coach sets off, the crowd round the inn door has swelled quite considerably, and the locals all make the sign of the cross and point two fingers towards you. You wonder what this gesture can mean.

Do you want to ask one of your fellow passengers what it means (turn to **772**), or would you rather not know (turn to **802**)?

748

You might have once sworn an oath to do no harm but faced by a lunatic in the middle of a psychotic episode, you have no choice but to defend yourself. (In this battle, your opponent has the initiative.)

LUNATIC   COMBAT 9   ENDURANCE 9

If you are still alive after 4 Combat Rounds, or if you reduce the madman's *Endurance* score to 4 points or fewer, whichever is sooner, turn to **688**.

749

His eagerness betrays him as he answers: "Oh, yes, I would like a cat! I only asked for a kitten lest you should refuse me a cat. No one would refuse me a kitten, would they?"

But you shake your head then, saying that at present you fear such a thing would not be possible, but you will bear his request in mind and think on it further.

Turn to **783**.

750

The True History of Vlad the Impaler

17 June 1462

The Sultan Mehmed the Conqueror besieged Prince Vlad the Third and discovered him in a certain mountain where the Wallachian was supported by the natural strength of the place. There Vlad had hidden himself along with 24,000 of his men who had willingly followed him. When Vlad realised that he would either perish from hunger or fall into the hands of his cruel enemy, and considering both eventualities unworthy of brave men, he dared commit an act worthy of being remembered.

As the sun rises over the Principality of Wallachia, from the walls of your palace in Târgoviște you see its rays illuminate the Turkish encampment that lies outside the city. The proliferation of tents covers the land south of the river, as far as the eye can see – an area that rivals the ground covered by the capital itself.

You estimate that the Ottoman army must still number somewhere in the region of 150,000 fighting men, despite many having succumbed to the radical scorched earth policy carried out by your own forces as they retreated before the Turkish advance – poisoning wells, creating marshes by diverting the waters of small rivers, setting pit-traps, and even sending sick people suffering from leprosy, tuberculosis and bubonic plague into their midst.

"My lord, the Sultan prepares for war," Captain Petru of your Carpathian Guard declares from his place beside you on the battlements.

"Mehmed has a long memory," you reply, "and is not a man given to forgiveness."

"It is not so long since you had his envoys killed by nailing their turbans to their heads, my prince," Radu, your wisest counsellor, reminds you.

"But when the heathen would not take no for an answer, what other message could my lord have sent?" your wife, Erzebet, snaps back.

"Mehmed's taxes are unfair and unjust," you reply calmly, never once taking your eyes from the painted pavilions, shining brightly in the morning sunlight.

"Is ten thousand ducats really too high a price to pay to keep the heathen horde from our door?" Radu challenges.

You turn on him then, with fire in your eyes. "And what of the thousand boys he also demanded, to be trained as Janissaries to fight in his armies? That was too high a price to pay! My sworn duty to my people is not to be auctioned off to the highest bidder."

"Then we must prepare to be besieged, for the Ottomans have us trapped."

Perhaps Radu is right. You have some 30,000 men holed up in Târgoviște; an impressive number, no doubt, but not when the Ottomans outnumber your brave Wallachians five to one. The only thing that might turn the odds in your favour would be if you were able to gain some insight into the organisation of Mehmed's troops and the Sultan's battle plans.

If you want to command Captain Petru to prepare for Târgoviște to be besieged, turn to **785**. Alternatively, if you want to risk sneaking into the Ottoman camp to acquire the information you so desperately need, turn to **720**.

751

There is something horribly familiar about the bat; the size of its wing-span, its hooked claws, its ugly snub face, and its elongated fangs. You are convinced it is the same bat you saw when you sat up, watching over Lucy, the night after you and Van Helsing observed the puncture marks on her neck for the first time.

And in that moment, you make the horrible connection between the bats' fangs and the ragged wounds on Lucy's throat. Can it be that this thing has been responsible for her unexplained blood loss all this time?

Add 1 point to your *Terror* score, tick off the code word *Exsanguination*, and turn to **781**.

752

"Ah, English! What-what?" says the older man in heavily accented English, a broad smile splitting his face and a gold tooth glinting in the firelight. "Tally-ho! Stiff upper lip, what-what?"

He bows respectfully then, his moment of frivolity having passed, and says, "Welcome! Come in peace, go safely, and leave something of the happiness you bring."

Take an ESP test. If you pass the test, turn to **723**. If you fail the test, turn to **646**.

753

DR SEWARD'S DIARY

(Kept in phonograph)

29 September

Last night, at a little before ten o'clock, Arthur, Quincey and myself, called on Van Helsing at the Berkley Hotel...

With you all gathered together in his rooms, the Professor proceeds to update Arthur and Quincey, telling them how the two of you visited the Westenra family tomb and, upon forcing it open, found Lucy's coffin to be empty.

"This is too much!" Arthur says, rising in anger. "I am willing to be patient in all things that are reasonable, but in this, this desecration of her grave..." He breaks off, unable to continue.

"If I could spare you this pain, God knows I would," counters Van Helsing, "but this night our feet must tread thorny paths. Hear what I have to say, and then you will at least know what I intend."

"That sounds fair enough," agrees Quincey.

After a pause, Van Helsing goes on. "Miss Lucy is dead, is she not? If so, then no harm can be done to her. But if she is not dead..."

"Good God!" Arthur cries, jumping to his feet. "What do you mean? Has there been a mistake? Has she been buried alive?"

"I did not say she was alive, but she may be un-dead."

"Undead? Not alive? Say what you mean, man! Is this all some horrible nightmare?"

"There are mysteries which men can only guess at, which age by age they may solve only in part. And believe me, we are on the verge of one now. But I know what we must do, if we are to ensure Lucy's eternal rest."

"Tell me! What must we do?" Arthur demands.

"We must cut off her head and fill her mouth with garlic, and then drive a stake through her heart."

"Heavens, no!" Arthur cries in a storm of passion. "I will not consent to the mutilation of her dead body! Professor Van Helsing, you test me too far. What did that poor, sweet girl do to you that you should want to dishonour her grave?"

"Lord Godalming," Van Helsing says sternly, rising to his feet, "I have a duty to both the living and the dead. Come with us now, that you may see what John and I have already seen. And if later I intend the same course of action, we will see how you answer then."

* * * *

It is fifteen minutes to midnight when the four of you enter the churchyard at Kingstead over the wall. The night is dark, with occasional gleams of moonlight between the dents of the heavy clouds scudding across the sky. As a precaution, all of you are armed.

Reaching the Westenra tomb, the Professor unlocks the door again, and the rest of you follow as he makes his way inside, a shuttered lantern held high in one hand.

Arthur looks on, very pale and silent, as Van Helsing sets about opening Lucy's coffin once more, and when the lid has been removed, he steps forward warily. He recoils instantly, with a gasp: "The coffin is empty!"

For several moments no one says a word. The silence is broken at last by Quincey Morris: "Professor, your word is all I need. I wouldn't ask such a thing ordinarily, for I would not wish to dishonour your name, but is this your doing?"

"I swear to you by all I hold sacred that I have not removed nor touched her body. Two nights ago, John and I came here with good purpose, and I opened her coffin, which was then sealed up, and we found it, as it is now, empty.

"Yesterday I came before sundown. I waited here all the night till the sun rose, but I saw nothing. It was most probable that it was because I had laid garlic over the clamps of the doors to the tomb, which the undead cannot bear, and other things which they shun. Last night there was no exodus, so today, before sunset, I took away the garlic. And so, it is we find this coffin empty.

"But Lucy will return before too long, I am sure of it. We must close the tomb, and bar her from entering it again."

"But we are here already," says Arthur. "Would it not make more sense to lie in wait for her here?"

"I say we treat this like a good old-fashioned Texas round-up, and split up to search the cemetery for her," says Quincey, phlegmatically.

"And what do you think would be for the best, John?" Van Helsing says, turning to you. "It would appear you have the casting vote."

Whose idea do you think is best?

If you agree with Van Helsing that the tomb must be sealed, to stop Lucy from re-entering, turn to **776**. If you think that Arthur is right, and that you should set an ambush for her inside the tomb, turn to **15**. But if you think that Quincey's idea is the best, and that you should split up and search the graveyard for her, turn to **480**.

754

The beast abruptly breaks off its attack, and hares off into the night, leaving you alone in the churchyard.

The coastguard are already occupied with the stricken schooner, as are a shoal of local fishermen. Not wishing to remain here a moment longer, half fearing the dog may return at any moment, you hurry back through the town to the Westenras' house on the Crescent and the security of your own bed.

Gain 2 *Blood* points and turn to **774**.

755

There is no sign of its owner, but the brute recognises you as a threat and goes for you. (In this battle, the Mastiff has the initiative.)

MASTIFF   COMBAT 8   ENDURANCE 6

If you win, you tear out the guard dog's throat with your teeth and slit open its belly; gain 1 *Blood* point and turn to **313**.

756

Somehow, against all the odds, you manage to break the monster's hypnotic spell. But now you are almost face to face with the vampire.

Turn to **245**.

757

You get up quietly and peer out into the night. The soft effect of the moonlight over the sea and sky, merge together in one great silent mystery that is beautiful beyond words.

A shadow suddenly falls across your face and you start as something hits the glass. There at the window is a huge bat, clawing at the panes, as if desperate to get inside. It must be at least six feet from wingtip to wingtip!

(Add 1 point to your *Terror* score.)

"His red eyes again!" Lucy cries and you pull the blind shut, as the bat flits away across the harbour, as if making for the abbey.

When you come back from the window, Lucy has already lain down once more and appears to be sleeping peacefully! She does not stir again all night.

Tick off the code word *Barbastella* and then turn to **714**.

758

"Must kill the vampire," the old man says again.

Reluctantly, you unsheathe your fencing blade. You do not want to hurt Van Helsing, but unfortunately, in his hypnotised state, he has no compunction about killing you. (In this battle the Professor has the initiative.)

PROFESSOR VAN HELSING   COMBAT 8   ENDURANCE 8

Because you are trying not to hurt the Professor, you must reduce your *Combat Rating* by 1 point for the duration of this battle. If you win two consecutive Combat Rounds, or if you manage to reduce Van Helsing's *Endurance* score to 4 points or fewer, turn to **728** at once.

759

In a moment, you are at Harker's side, your hungry eyes fixed on the blood tricking over his chin. The beast fully in control now, you make to grab for his throat!

Your hand touches the string of beads around his neck, from which hangs a small golden crucifix, the sanctified icon burning your fingers. (Lose 2 *Endurance* points.)

You recoil at once, the beast within hissing in frustration, allowing you to regain control once more as it slinks back into the dark depths of your soul.

"Take care how you cut yourself," you growl. "In this country it is more dangerous than you think."

You seize hold of the shaving glass, in which the room and Harker are reflected, but you are not. "And this is the wretched thing that has done the mischief. It is a foul bauble of man's vanity. Away with it!"

With that, you fling it out of the window, to smash into a thousand pieces on the stones of the courtyard far below.

Gain 2 *Blood* points, tick off the code word *Árulás*, and then turn to **201**.

760

Quincey Morris's wolf-hunters set off again, towards the edge of the graveyard.

Suddenly you hear the sharp crack of a twig breaking underfoot.

The Texan freezes, raising an arm, signalling for the rest of you to do the same. "They're here," he says in a dry whisper.

You peer into the gloom ahead of you but can see nothing. As you stand there, your ears straining for any sound, you become aware of a panting breath coming from the left.

Slowly turning your head, you see them – several hunched shapes, perched on top of gravestones or crouched, half-hidden behind large stone crypts. From their moon-silhouetted postures they look like they walk on two legs like men, but their bodies are covered with thick grey fur, they have sharply-pointed ears, like those of a German Shepherd, and their eyes shine redly in the reflected light of the moon.

Add 1 point to your *Terror* score and then *Take a Terror test*. If you pass the test, turn to **335**. If you fail the test, turn to **108**.

761

Chastened by the bats' savage and relentless attack, the pack breaks, the wolves heading for the wooded slopes of the confining hills.

Your own animal form suffers a number of savage injuries. (Roll one die and add 1 to the number rolled; deduct this many points from your *Endurance* score. Alternatively, pick a card and deduct that many *Endurance* points, unless it is greater than 7 or a picture card, in which case deduct 7 *Endurance* points.)

Deduct 2 *Blood* points and then turn to **815**.

762

In a lull in the fighting, you see the way to the cart clear.

If you want to seize the opportunity and make a dash for the wagon, turn to **421**. If not, turn to **933**.

763

This snake-like thing that was once Count Dracula tries to transfix you with its hypnotic ophidian gaze but you cannot succumb to the curse of the vampire now. You will not be denied your revenge!

Cross off one use of *The Pen is Mightier* special ability and turn to **690**.

764

The door to the dining room suddenly bursts open and something as black and as lithe as a panther leaps into the room.

You happen to be standing closest to the door and are sent flying. You land heavily on the floor, slamming your shoulder into the remains of a broken crate.

Lose 2 *Endurance* points and turn to **648**.

765

But before you can face the man you once called brother, in single combat, your charge is met by the Sultan's own elite cavalry – the Yaya. Shouting a bloodthirsty battle-cry, you prepare to engage the nearest of the Ottoman riders. (In this battle, you have the initiative.)

YAYA CAVALRYMAN   COMBAT 9   ENDURANCE 8

If you defeat your opponent, gain 2 *Blood* points and turn to **840**.

766

Almost another three weeks pass before an appropriate opportunity presents itself. On the morning of 17 June, as you are sitting on the edge of your bed cudgelling your brains, you hear the cracking of whips, and the pounding and scraping of horses' hooves coming up the rocky path beyond the courtyard.

Hurrying to the window, you see two leiter-wagons drive into the yard, each drawn by eight sturdy horses, and at the head of each pair a Slovak, with his wide hat, great nail-studded belt, dirty sheepskin, and high boots.

You cry out to them, and they look up at you stupidly, pointing as they talk among themselves. But just then, the hetman of the Szgany appears, and seeing them pointing to your window, says something at which they laugh, and resolutely turn away.

The wagons contain great square boxes, with handles of thick rope. They are evidently empty, considering the ease with which the Slovaks manoeuvre them, and by their resonance as they are roughly deposited within the courtyard.

Once they have all been unloaded and stacked in a great heap in one corner of the yard, the Szgany pay the Slovaks, who leave.

* * * *

That night you hear the sound of mattock and spade echoing through the castle walls. The Szgany are quartered somewhere in the castle and are doing work of some kind for the Count.

But then another sound makes you start. It is the low, piteous howling of dogs, somewhere far below in the valley.

A couple of sleepless hours pass, and you hear a sharp wail elsewhere in the castle, which is quickly suppressed. Then there is silence, an awful silence that chills you to the bone. You are reminded of the horror to which you were forced to bear witness the night you were attacked by the fiend-like women.

And then you hear another sound, this time out in the courtyard. It is the agonised cry of a woman.

Do you want to go to the window to see what is going on (turn to **796**), or would you prefer to stay where you are and not involve yourself in affairs that it is not within your power to influence (turn to **827**)?

767

Her name, she tells you, is Carmilla, Countess of Karnstein. She claims to be undertaking the journey to visit a childhood friend in the forest region of Styria, where she lives with her father, a wealthy English widower who has chosen to retire to Austria.

Fixing you with eyes as blue and sparkling as sapphires, she says, "You can't believe me capable of such a thing, can you, my dear?" running a perfectly-manicured fingertip over the collar of your dress.

She is so close to you that you can smell her breath, which is as sickly-sweet as week-old pot pourri, and you find yourself answering breathlessly, "No, of course not."

(Lose 1 *ESP* point.)

"Madam Mina," the Professor says, taking you firmly by the arm, and shaking you from your reverie, "I believe we are not ready to make a declaration of guilt or otherwise, just yet. Or are we?"

Do you want to:

Interview the ratty little man?	Turn to **727**.
Question the handsome, middle-aged man?	Turn to **742**.
Interrogate the wolfish-looking older man?	Turn to **787**.
Draw this matter to an end?	Turn to **987**.

768

In a secluded backstreet, you find a gunsmith who will make some bullets for you – for a price – but he does not have any silver from which to make them.

If you want to give him the Silver Crucifix Van Helsing gave you, so that he can melt it down and use the precious metal to fashion some Silver Bullets for you, turn to **21**. If you do not want to sacrifice your Silver Crucifix in this way, turn to **703**.

769

The bottles stored in the box contain the dry residue of a dozen philtres, potions, elixirs and sleeping draughts. But there is one that is still liquid. It is clear, colourless and – as you discover when you remove its ground glass bung and give it a sniff – odourless.

If you want to drink the potion, turn to **799**.

If you would prefer to replace the stopper and return the bottle to its place within the velvet-lined box, what do you want to do instead? Making sure you choose an option you haven't selected already, will you:

Take a closer look at the swords?	Turn to **3**.
Take a closer look at the large chest?	Turn to **829**.
Take a closer look at the flask in the brass stand?	Turn to **702**.
Leave the room?	Turn to **890**.

770

At a mere thought from yourself, the vermin that were preoccupied with scavenging what they could from the piles of rotting waste littering the street rush the vampire in a flood of black furry bodies.

While he is distracted in this way, you land your first strike before he can even muster any kind of defence. (You have the initiative in this battle.)

VARNEY THE VAMPIRE   COMBAT 11   ENDURANCE 10

If you slay the vampire, turn to **125**. Alternatively, rather than having to fight Varney, you may deduct 6 *Blood* points and turn to **125** straightway.

771

Another eight days pass before you are compelled to leave your sanctuary once more and go in search of fresh blood to provide you with sustenance.

You find it in the form of a sallow crewman who is stumbling across the deck, as the ship is buffeted by violent winds, making for the crew quarters. Your sudden appearance gives him the fright of his life.

If your rank is that of *Prince of Darkness* or higher, turn to **806**. If not, turn to **169**.

772

Not without some difficulty, you manage to get one of your fellow passengers – a man dressed in thick furs – to tell you what the gesture means.

"It is a charm, to guard against the Evil Eye," he says, in thickly-accented English.

Tick off the code word *Varázslat* and turn to **802**.

773

The scar caused by the touch of the sacred wafer begins to tingle with a pleasing warmth and, in that moment, you know the vampire has won. It is the last thought you will ever have, as Mrs Mina Harker.

"And now, Mina, it is time for your baptism – your baptism of blood," Dracula says. He points to your husband who is lying in a broken heap on the ground and barely conscious.

You kneel down beside Jonathan and he groans as you take him in your arms. Whispering words of comfort in his ear you say, "It is all right my beloved. All will be well. I will take away your pain."

You kiss his forehead, and then you kiss his lips, and finally his neck. Baring new white fangs, you sink your teeth into his throat and start to feed.

Jonathan was your first love, and he is also your first kill. For you are now a vampire, totally subservient to your dark lord and master, Count Dracula.

Your adventure is over.

THE END

774

The orange glow of dawn is teasing at the East Cliff and the ruins of the Abbey before you manage to fall asleep again and you rise late, to find your friend already up and about.

You join Lucy and her mother in the conservatory for a late breakfast and find them poring over a report in the local paper, *The Dailygraph*, about the shipwreck you witnessed during the night.

"It says here that the captain of the schooner was found dead, bound to the ship's wheel," Lucy says with ghoulish delight. "How absolutely ghastly!"

How will you respond?

"May I see the article myself, Lucy?"	Turn to **853**.
"Why don't we go down to the harbour and see the ship for ourselves?"	Turn to **883**.
"I think it's best we don't go out today; no doubt there will be police and day-trippers all over the town."	Turn to **823**.

775

Crouching beside the comatose crewman, you sink your teeth into his neck and drink. But it is some moments before you become aware of the sharp but sweet aftertaste, and then an unpleasant feeling comes over you. Your head starts to swim, and your vision begins to blur.

The man is unconscious because he is drunk on vodka. (Temporarily deduct 1 point when calculating your *Combat Rating* for the next battle you are involved in.)

Turn to **960**.

776

The four of you file out of the tomb again, Van Helsing coming last and locking the door behind him.

After the terror of that vault, how sweet it is to breathe fresh air that has no taint of death and decay. Nonetheless, each in his own way is solemn and overcome. Arthur is silent, as he strives to make sense of the mystery, Quincey is phlegmatic in the manner of a man who accepts all things in a spirit of cool bravery, while you are half-inclined to throw aside doubt and to accept Van Helsing's conclusions.

As to the Professor, he is busily employed in his own curious way. First he takes from his bag a mass of what looks like thin, wafer-like biscuit, which has been carefully rolled up in a white napkin. Next, he takes out a double-handful of some whitish stuff, that you think must be dough or putty. Crumbling up the wafer, he works it into the mass between his hands, before rolling it into thin strips, which he then pushes into the crevices between the door and its setting in the wall of the tomb.

Seeing your puzzled look, he says, by way of explanation, "I am closing the tomb, using the Host I brought from Amsterdam, so that the undead may not enter."

Before the Professor can finish his work, Quincey gives a whistle, and points down the avenue of yew trees. There you see a dim, white figure approaching the tomb, with something held to its breast.

At that moment, a ray of moonlight breaks through the clouds and you see that it is a red-haired woman in a white grave-gown, a fair-haired child in her arms. Your heart grows cold as ice, and you hear Arthur give a wail that is a marriage of horror and disbelief.

Now that she is close enough, you recognise the features of Lucy Westenra, but they are somehow changed; the sweetness has turned to adamantine, heartless cruelty, and her purity to voluptuous wantonness.

At Van Helsing's direction, the four of you line up before the door of the tomb. The light of his lantern falls on her face, and you see that her lips are crimson with fresh blood, and that the stream has trickled over her chin and stained the white of her death-robe.

(Add 1 to your *Terror* score.)

When the thing that bears Lucy's shape becomes aware of you all, it draws back with an angry snarl, eyes blazing with unholy light. Without any care for its well-being, she callously flings the child to the ground, growling over it as a dog growls over a bone. The infant gives a sharp cry, and lies there wailing, the cold-blooded act wringing a groan from Arthur.

Turning her attention to Lord Godalming then, she advances towards him with outstretched arms, and a wanton smile on her lips. "Come to me, Arthur," she says languorously. "My arms are hungry for you. Come and we can lie together. Come, my husband, come!"

There is something diabolically sweet in the tone of her voice, which rings through your brain even though the words are addressed to another.

As for Arthur, he appears to be under a spell, his arms open wide as if to accept her embrace and draw her to him.

"Arthur, these others mean me harm," she says. "Protect me, my husband."

Too late, you realise what the Lucy-creature has done.

"Yes, my dearly departed," Arthur says, turning towards you, the club he is carrying gripped tight in his hand.

Suddenly Lucy flies at Quincey, while Arthur focuses his murderous rage upon you.

If you want to use *The Pen is Mightier* special ability, and you still can, turn to **519**. If not, turn to **549**.

777

Again you awake in the night, and this time find Lucy sitting up in bed, pointing at the window, as brilliant moonlight streams into the room.

If you want to approach the window to see what Lucy is looking at, turn to **757**. If you simply want to tuck her back into bed, turn to **737**.

778

You launch yourself at the Mariner before he can alert the rest of the crew to your presence. (Who has the initiative will depend upon how you reached this point.)

MARINER   COMBAT 9   ENDURANCE 9

If you slay the seaman, turn to **974**. Alternatively, you may spend 3 *Blood* points and turn to **974** without having to fight the battle.

779

Rising from the desk you turn the key and open the door. You are suddenly aware of a large man standing before you, dressed in the garb of an inmate, his hands clasped together above his head, and then he deliveries a powerful, double-fisted strike, that sends you reeling back into the room. (Deduct 2 *Endurance* points.)

If you want to use *The Pen is Mightier* special ability, cross off one use and turn to **688**. If not, turn to **748**.

780

In Dracula's native Transylvania, they are called '*Strigoi*', restless souls that rise from the grave, often at the behest of a powerful necromancer.

A maggot-eaten black tongue darts from between ragged lips and the unliving horror hisses as it clambers out of the crate that has kept it confined these past three months.

(Add 1 to your *Terror* score.)

You are only dimly aware that its venomous hiss is underscored by the horrified cries of your companions as other corpses start to break free of their wooden prisons.

If you want to use *The Pen is Mightier* special ability, and you still can, turn to **867**. If not, turn to **837**.

781

The wolf growls, baring large, vicious-looking, yellow teeth, and you see that its muzzle is covered in gore.

If you want to use *The Pen is Mightier* special ability, cross off one use and turn to **908**. If not, turn to **818**.

782

Realising that the two of you are horribly outnumbered, you shout to Quincey to retreat. Throwing yourself back into the saddle, you turn your horse about and ride back out of the wood, even though the clawing fingers of trees tear at your face and hands.

Lose 1 *Endurance* point and turn to **26**.

783

His face falls and you read the tell-tale signs within his expression that warn you of danger. There is a sudden fierce sidelong look that you have observed in others to mean the patient is about to suffer a psychotic episode.

The man is no more than an undeveloped homicidal maniac, and you deem your session with him to be over.

Turn to **893**.

784

Suppressing your bloodlust, you approach the young man and seize the shaving mirror – in which the room and Harker are reflected, but not you – saying, "This is a wretched thing, a foul bauble of man's vanity. Away with it!" and fling it out of the window.

Turn to **201**.

785

Overseen by Captain Petru, your army mans the battlements of Târgoviște, secures the gates, and prepares to repel the invaders.

Back in the throne room of your castle, you take counsel from your two most trusted advisors.

"My lord," Radu begins, approaching your throne with his head bowed. "The city walls are strong, and your soldiers are among the greatest in the world, but if Sultan Mehmed besieges Târgoviște, people will die. Wallachian people. I beg you, Prince Vlad, to reconsider and pay the Sultan what he is due."

"You mean give him what he wants – money and boys?" you rail.

"The royal coffers contain more than enough gold, while the gift of one thousand fine sons of Wallachia could save the lives of more than five times as many of her proud people."

"Spoken like a true coward!" Erzebet hisses like a hell-cat, unable to contain herself any longer. "Husband, now is not the time to capitulate to the heathen Turk. Now is the time to make a bold statement, one that would make Mehmed sick to his stomach and not even dare approach the gates of our ancient capital."

"Do you have something in mind, my queen?" you challenge her.

"I do. Force those who have derided your laws to make amends for their crimes to their prince and their fellow countrymen. Make those who have shunned our society work again, for the greater good."

Whose advice will you take?

Will you wait for Mehmed to arrive, with the intention of giving him what he wants (turn to **85**), or will you issue a command that will make the Conqueror fearful of even approaching Târgoviște (turn to **115**)?

786

As the molten iron orb of the sun disappears behind the snow-capped peaks of the Carpathian Mountains, you burst from the crate in an explosion of soil and splinters.

In that moment, everyone freezes – Vampire-Hunters, Szgany, even the wolf pack – all eyes fixing upon you. But in the next moment, Harker and the American recover themselves, leaping onto the back of the wagon to finish you.

As Seward and Van Helsing futilely attempt to fight back against the knot of Szgany steadily tightening around them, you prepare to put paid to the two Vampire-Hunters and bring an end to their pathetic schemes. (You have the initiative in this battle.)

	COMBAT	ENDURANCE
JONATHAN HARKER	10	11
QUINCEY MORRIS	9	9

At any time during the battle, if you wish, you may spend 4 *Blood* points to eliminate one of your opponents, but you may only do so once.

If you kill Harker and Morris, gain 6 *Blood* points and turn to **666**. However, if you lose the battle, turn to **605**.

787

"My name is Dr Callistratus," the man tells you, "and I am an expert in diseases of the blood. I am returning to the facility for the criminally insane where I work. I travelled to Varna to meet with Dr Ravna to discuss my research regarding blood-typing, so that transfusions can been conducted safely."

"Blood transfusions, you say?" Van Helsing replies, his interest piqued. "I have had some experience of such myself."

"Then perhaps we could compare notes. In fact, there seems no time like the present, for surely when we reach Veresti we must go our separate ways."

The Professor seems ready to accompany Dr Callistratus to his berth right at this moment. If you want to accompany the two men, turn to **458**. If not, you stop Van Helsing with a mere touch of his arm and suggest an alternative course of action. But what?

Do you want to interrogate the ratty little man (turn to **727**), question the handsome, middle-aged man (turn to **742**), interview the beautiful young woman (turn to **767**), or draw this matter to a conclusion (turn to **987**)?

788

Your cabin is cramped and uncomfortable and so you and Arthur decide to go up on deck for a while, at least until you are ready to retire to bed.

You are lulled by the chugging of the steam engine, while the captain's burly stokers keep the furnace fuelled with coke.

Hearing a piercing cry, you look up to see a pair of enormous bats flapping towards you on their great leathery wings. The wingspan of each of them must be at least six feet and they have elongated fangs.

If you want to employ *The Pen is Mightier* special ability, and you still can, turn to **243**. If not, turn to **279**.

789

Professor Van Helsing suddenly stops and stares into your eyes, slack-jawed.

"You do not wish to hurt me," you tell him. "You have sworn upon your life to protect me from harm. This one has no power over you."

The Professor blinks heavily several times, as upon waking. Focusing on you again he says, "What was I in the middle of doing?"

"Killing vampires," you say, pointing at the blonde-haired vampyre lying prone in her coffin.

Turn to **697**.

790

The Professor is suddenly there in front of the Count, the Sacred Wafer in his hand, which he holds out towards the monster.

The Count stops abruptly and cowers back. As the rest of you raise your silver crucifixes, he cowers back further still as you advance upon him.

The moonlight suddenly fails, as a great black cloud sails across the sky.

When the gaslight springs up under Quincey's match a moment later, you see nothing but a faint vapour, that trails out through the window and then is gone.

You rush forward to help Mina, who suddenly gives a scream so wild, so ear-piercing, and so despairing that it breaks your heart to hear it. You gather her up in your arms, and for a few seconds she lies there, in helpless disarray.

Her face is of a ghastly pallor, which is only accentuated by the blood that smears her lips and cheeks and chin. From her throat trickles a thin stream of blood, and when you look into her eyes you see that they are mad with terror.

"Are we too late?" the Professor cries, rushing forward, the Sacred Wafer still tight in his hand. "I have to know!" And with that, before you can stop him, he presses it against Mina's forehead.

She gives another fearful scream and recoils in pain. Where the wafer touched her skin, it has burned her flesh as though it were a piece of white-hot metal.

Mina sinks to her knees, sobbing and pulling her beautiful hair over her face, and wails, "Unclean! I am unclean! Even the Almighty shuns my polluted flesh! I must bear this mark of shame upon my forehead until the Judgment Day!"

Falling to the floor beside her, consumed with impotent grief, you put your arms around her and hold her tight. For a few minutes your sorrowful hearts beat together, whilst your friends turn away, their eyes running with silent tears.

Add 2 points to your *Terror* score, gain 6 *Blood* points, and then turn **693**.

791

The Second Mate's blood revitalises you and the very next night you walk abroad again. It is not only the desire for blood that drives you – you take pleasure in tormenting the crew of the *Demeter*. Eternity is such a long time; you have to make the most of any opportunity to relieve the endless ennui.

But the thrill of the hunt is negated when you emerge from the cargo hold only to almost trip over a body lying at the top of the creaking wooden staircase. The man is not dead – you can sense his relaxed heartbeat – but he is clearly comatose.

If you want to stop to drink the unconscious man's blood, turn to **775**. If you would rather ignore him and go in search of more challenging prey, turn to **986**.

792

If the *Blood* score is 12 points or higher, turn to **874**. If it is lower than 12 points, turn to **836**.

793

You wake late the following morning, to find your dear friend already dressed and gone down to breakfast.

You join Lucy and her mother in the conservatory where they are poring over a report in the local paper, *The Dailygraph*. Apparently the ship you saw struggling out at sea the previous afternoon ran aground during the night.

You are intrigued and keen to learn more about what unfolded during the storm.

If you want to read the article in the paper yourself, turn to **853**. If you want to suggest to Lucy that the two of you take a stroll down to the harbour to see the shipwreck, turn to **883**.

794

Inexplicably, you sense that the five of you have company in the house; someone – or some*thing* – else is here.

You take a step back from the door to the hall a moment before it flies open and something as black and as lithe as a panther bounds into the room.

Turn to **648**.

795

You give a guttural snarl, and at your command the swirling snowstorm increases in intensity, the biting wind, howling in sympathy with the wolf pack, battering the bats and whisking them away on the wind.

Turn to **815**.

796

Peering between the bars of your window, you see a woman with dishevelled hair, at the entrance to the courtyard.

But when she sees your face at the window, she throws herself forward and shouts, in a voice laden with menace, "Monster, give me my child!"

Throwing herself onto her knees, raising up her hands in supplication, she makes the same desperate plea, over and over, tearing her hair and beating her breast. She disappears from view, but you can hear the beating of her hands against the castle door.

From somewhere high overhead, you fancy you hear the harsh whispering voice of the Count, calling to the children of the night, and it is answered from far and wide by the howling of wolves.

Before many more minutes have passed, a pack of the wild animals pours through the archway into the courtyard.

You see the woman try to run, but the wolves drag her down before she can reach the gate. You cannot tear your eyes away as the creatures tear her to shreds.

Before long the wolves stream away again, back to their forests, licking the ruddy gore from their muzzles. Nothing is left of the wretched peasant save for a bloody smear on the cobbles of the courtyard.

You are left shaken by what you have witnessed but you do not pity the woman, for you know all too well her child's fate, and she is better off dead than having to live with that terrible knowledge.

(Add 2 points to your *Terror* score and deduct 1 point from your *Combat* score.)

How will you ever escape from this dreadful, benighted place, that gloom and fear have made their dwelling place?

If you want to continue to wait for fate to play its hand, turn to **947**. If you would rather seize control of your fate and act now, turn to **132**.

797

You wake with the dawn, and hear birds chirping outside your bedroom window. Lucy rouses too, and you are glad to see that she is even better than on the previous morning. Her old cheerful manner seems to have returned, and she comes and snuggles in beside you, and tells you all about Arthur.

You, in turn, tell her how anxious you are about Jonathan, and she does her best to comfort you. She succeeds somewhat, for, though sympathy cannot alter the facts, it can make them more bearable.

Gain 2 *Blood* points and then turn to **714**.

798

Taking care not to draw attention to yourself, you set off after the strange figure, the train rocking along the track as it crosses the Bulgarian-Romanian border.

By the time you reach the luggage van, the hunchback seems to have disappeared, but your attention is drawn to a number of large cases and packing crates. To one has been tied a label, upon which has been written, in German, 'Scientific equipment', while another bears a name: 'Frankenstein'.

"Can I help you, *mein Herr*?" comes a voice from behind you, making you start and setting your heart racing. It is the hunchback.

"No, no," you bluster, "I was merely looking for…"

"The dining car perhaps?" suggests the other.

"Yes, yes, the dining car," you reply.

"It is zat way," he says, pointing back along the luggage van.

"Thank you," you say and start to move towards the exit. "Good evening."

"*Guten nacht, mein Herr*," the hunchback replies.

You hurry back to your compartment in a state of high agitation, and do not leave it again until morning.

Tick off the code word *Orvos* and turn to **881**.

799

You take a cautious sip, and when the liquid fails to burn your lips or tongue, you down the contents of the bottle. Almost immediately you feel a welcome calm spread throughout your body. You feel the tension ease from your muscles, and there is peace and comfort in every breath you take. At the same time, you feel as if a befuddling cloud has lifted from your mind, your senses becoming sharper.

(Deduct 1 point from your *Terror* score and add 1 point to your *Combat* score.)

Choosing something you haven't done yet, will you:

Take a closer look at the swords?	Turn to **3**.
Take a closer look at the large chest?	Turn to **829**.
Take a closer look at the flask in the brass stand?	Turn to **702**.
Leave the room?	Turn to **890**.

800

Your enemies either dead or dying – and Harker's silver-bladed knife lying safely out of reach of any of them – you settle down to feed and replenish your strength.

You have won! You have destroyed those who were ranged against you, determined to thwart your plans of conquest. Now nothing and no one has the power to stop you.

Soon London will be yours, and then England will fall beneath the iron fist of the rule of the one once known as Prince Vlad Tepes – Vlad the Impaler. By the time anyone realises what is going on, it will be too late to stop you.

Today the British Empire. Tomorrow the world!

THE END

801

What can you do but agree?

"I pray you will not discourse of things other than business in your letters," the Count says, handing you three sheets of note paper and three envelopes. "It will please your friends to know that you are well, and that you look forward to getting home to them. Is it not so?"

He smiles then, his sharp, canine teeth lying over the red underlip, and you vow to yourself that you will be careful what you write, for your host will be able to read the letters before sending them.

You write two letters, one to your employer Mr Hawkins and one to your beloved fiancée Mina. The Count himself composes several notes: one directed to Samuel F. Billington of Whitby; another to Herr Lautner of the Bulgarian port of Varna; a third to Coutts & Co., the London bankers; and the fourth to Herren Klopstock & Billreuth, bankers of Buda-Pesth.

Adding the missives you have penned to his pile, the Count rises and says, "I trust you will forgive me, but I have much work to do in private this evening. You will, I hope, find all things as you wish."

At the door he stops and turns.

"Let me warn you, my young friend, that should you leave these rooms you will not fall asleep in any other part of the castle. It is old, and has many memories, and there are bad dreams for those who sleep unwisely."

And then he is gone, leaving you wondering whether any dream could be more terrible than the unnatural net of gloom and mystery which you feel is closing around you.

Turn to **172**.

802

The driver cracks the whip over the four small horses tethered to the traces, and you set off on your journey. But you will never forget your final glimpse of the inn yard and the crowd gathered round the wide archway, all crossing themselves.

But you soon lose sight of the inn and your recollection of ghostly fears in the beauty of the scenery as the carriage bounces along the road travelling eastwards.

Before you lies a green sloping land, full of forests and woods, and here and there steep hills crowned with clumps of trees or farmhouses. Everywhere you see a bewildering mass of fruit blossom – apple, plum, pear, cherry – and as you drive by, you can see the green grass under the trees spangled with fallen petals.

The road is rugged, but the coach seems to fly over it with feverish haste; the driver clearly does not want to lose any time in reaching the Borgo Pass, where you will meet the carriage that will carry you to your final destination, Castle Dracula.

The verdant swelling hills eventually give way to forested slopes that rise up to the lofty steeps of the Carpathian Mountains themselves. They tower over the road – which is little more than a rutted track – to left and right, as the afternoon sun falls full upon them, drawing out the glorious colours of the season – deep blue and purple in the shadows of the peaks, green and brown where grass and rock mingle – and an endless perspective of jagged rock and pointed crags, until these too become lost in the distance, where the snowy peaks rise grandly. Here and there you glimpse rifts in the mountains, through which the sinking sun highlights the white gleam of cascading waterfalls.

As the coach winds on its endless way, the sun sinking lower and lower behind you in the west, the shadows of evening creep closer. Here and there you pass Cszeks and Slovaks, and by the roadside you see many crosses and the occasional wayside shrine. As you sweep past them, your fellow travellers cross themselves. You have never known such a superstitious land.

The temperature drops and the growing twilight merges the gloom of the trees into one dark mistiness. In the deep valleys between the spurs of the hills, dark firs stand out here and there against the background of late-lying snow.

Sometimes the way is so steep that, despite the driver's obvious haste, the horses can only go slowly, but he only halts the team for a moment's pause to light the carriage lamps.

As it grows dark, your fellow passengers become agitated, urging him to hurry. He urges the horses on with wild cries of encouragement and his long whip, with which he lashes them mercilessly.

Through the encroaching darkness you make out a patch of grey light. The excitement of the other passengers grows, as the coach rocks on its great leather springs, swaying like a boat tossed on a stormy sea. Then the mountains seem to crowd closer again on either side, and you realise you must be entering the Borgo Pass.

One by one, several of the passengers offer you gifts, odd tokens and trinkets, which they press upon you with an earnestness it would be hard to deny.

If you want to accept these gifts, turn to **832**. If you want to refuse them, turn to **117**.

803

Renfield gives you a sudden fierce sidelong look, which in other patients you have observed is a precursor to a psychotic episode.

You turn and make for the door, but before you can reach it the lunatic pounces on your back and knocks you to the floor. (Lose 2 *Endurance* points.)

If you wish to make use of *The Pen is Mightier* special ability, cross off one use and turn to **863**. If not, turn to **833**.

804

You turn to see the Count enter your chamber. "Good morning," he says, bowing courteously.

Turning back to your shaving mirror, you see the whole room displayed behind you but there is no sign of anyone in it other than yourself! The Count is close to you, just over your shoulder, but there is no reflection of him in the mirror!

(Add 1 point to your *Terror* score and tick off the code word *Tükör*.)

Seeing your horrified reaction, the Count hisses and seizes the shaving glass. "This is the wretched thing that has done the mischief. It is a foul bauble of man's vanity. Away with it!"

Turn to **954**.

805

Ignoring the weakened vampire, you charge into the shallows of the lake, weapon in hand, but before you can even lay a blow against its leathery hide, the albino monster bends down and snaps you up in its mouth, biting your body in half.

Your adventure, like your life, is over.

THE END

806

The man's face suddenly goes white, a rictus of horror seizing hold of his features. In the very next moment, he gives a strangled gasp, clutches at his chest with one hand, and then pole-axes onto the deck. You have scared the man to death!

Rather than leave a perfectly good meal to waste, you puncture an artery and drink deeply. When you are done, you consign his body to a watery grave.

Restore up to 4 *Endurance* points and gain 2 *Blood* points. Then turn to **873**.

807

It is hopeless – the vampire's will is simply too strong to resist.

If you are still able to use *The Pen is Mightier* special ability, and you want to use it now, cross off one use and turn to **756**. If not, turn to **773**.

808

Unlocking the door, you pull it open to find not Barlow standing there, but one of the inmates of the asylum. His ugly face is twisted by a manic grin. He fixes you with mad staring eyes and says, in an impeccable impersonation of Barlow's voice, "Time for your medicine, Dr Seward!"

If you want to use *The Pen is Mightier* special ability, cross off one use and turn to **688**. If not, turn to **748**.

809

DR SEWARD'S DIARY

(Kept in phonograph)

29 September

When we arrived at the Berkley Hotel, Van Helsing found a telegram waiting for him...

"It is good news at last!" the Professor exclaims in delight, upon reading the telegram. "The wonderful Madam Mina, pearl among women, arrives today, but I cannot stay. She must go to your house, John. You must meet her at the station."

Over a cup of tea, he tells you about the diary kept by a young solicitor, one Jonathan Harker, during a trip he undertook to Transylvania, and also of what his wife, Mrs Harker, witnessed when she was staying in Whitby with Lucy.

* * * *

Later, with Van Helsing having already set off for Amsterdam, by way of Liverpool Street, you make your way to Paddington, arriving before Mrs Harker's train gets in.

The crowd melts away, following the hustle and bustle that is common to all arrival platforms, and just as you are beginning to feel that you might have missed your guest, a sweet-faced, dainty-looking girl approaches you, and after a quick glance says, "Dr Seward, is it not?"

"And you must be Mrs Harker!" you reply, whereupon she holds out her hand.

"I knew you from the description of poor dear Lucy, but…" She stops suddenly, and a quick blush spreads over her face. The blush that rises to your own cheeks is a tacit answer to her own, that thankfully puts you both at ease.

Getting her luggage for her, which you see includes a typewriter, together you take the Underground to Fenchurch Street, and from there board the train to Purfleet. In due course you arrive at Carfax Asylum, where your housekeeper has a sitting room and a bedroom prepared for Mrs Harker.

* * * *

While Mrs Harker retires to her room to rest after a long day spent travelling, you shut yourself away in your study to make a record of the day's events on a fresh cylinder on your phonograph.

Presently you hear a gentle knock at the door and, breaking off from your recording, at your cry of "Come in!" Mrs Harker enters the room.

"I hope I did not keep you waiting," she says, "but I stayed at the door as I heard you talking and thought there was someone with you."

"Oh," you reply with a smile, "I was only entering my diary."

You lay a hand on the phonograph. "I keep it in this."

"Why, this beats even shorthand!" she blurts out excitedly. "May I hear it say something?"

"Certainly," you reply, setting the machine to speak rather than record. But then you pause, suddenly aware of what you might be about to reveal to this woman, who is, after all, a complete stranger. "The fact is I only keep my diary in it, which is almost entirely about my patients, that is, I mean…"

"You helped to attend dear Lucy at the end," she tells you. "Let me hear how she died, for she was very, very dear to me. I would be very grateful."

It takes some cajoling, but in the end you agree.

"Do you know, although I have kept the diary for months, I never once thought about how I was going to find any particular part of it, in case I wanted to look it up," you confess.

"Then, Dr Seward, you had better let me copy it out for you on my typewriter," she says.

* * * *

Van Helsing was right; Mrs Harker really is a pearl among women. She spends the rest of the evening typing, and recommences her work the following morning, transcribing not just your diary, but also her husband's foreign journal and her own account, begun when she went to stay with Lucy in Whitby, back in May.

She does not complete the task until late that afternoon. When she presents the bundle of typewritten pages to you at five o'clock, the act is accompanied by a question.

"Dr Seward, may I ask you a favour?" she asks sweetly. You can see why Lucy loved her so. "I want to see your patient, Mr Renfield. Do let me see him. What you have said of him in your diary interests me greatly."

If you want to grant Mrs Harker an audience with your zoophagous patient, turn to **361**. If not, turn to **391**.

810

JONATHAN HARKER'S JOURNAL

5 May 1897. The Castle —

The grey of the morning has passed, and the sun is high over the distant horizon, which seems jagged, whether with trees or hill I know not...

Mr Harker of Hawkins, Oldman & Lee arrives at Castle Dracula at last and you immediately do all you can to make him welcome. The young Englishman is clearly overwhelmed to find himself visiting such a grand and ancient place so steeped in history. You show him to the guest quarters – the same rooms where Mr Renfield stayed, while he was your guest – and relish the opportunity to not only show off your library but also to practise your English.

Mindful that you must be careful not to let what happened with Renfield happen again, you instruct Harker not to leave his quarters and wander into other parts of the castle. After all, you fear what might happen should he encounter the Weird Sisters, while you are out hunting. You also make sure to secure the front door and keep the key to its great iron lock about your person at all times; for while locked doors mean nothing to a creature such as you, they are very good at keeping mere mortals where you want them to remain.

* * * *

You soon settle into a comfortable routine, whereby you sleep in your sarcophagus in the crypt deep beneath the castle during the day, and spend the nights talking with your guest, keen to learn all that you can about London and the ways of the English. Harker, in turn, takes the opportunity to go through the papers he has brought with him, regarding your property purchases. You do not let on that Mr Renfield has gone through these with you already, for fear of alerting your guest to the danger he is in.

But only three days after Harker's arrival, you enter his chamber to find him in the process of shaving, having hung a mirror by the window. Your sudden appearance startles the young man and he spins round. It is then that you see he has nicked himself, and the sight of the crimson cut threatens to unleash the beast that lies dormant within you.

Divide your *Blood* score by 10, rounding fractions up. Then roll 1 die, and if the number rolled is equal to or less than the resulting total, turn to **784**. If it is greater, turn to **759**.

811

DR SEWARD'S DIARY

(Kept in phonograph)

4 September

Zoophagous patient still keeps up our interest in him. He had only one outburst and that was yesterday at an unusual time...

Back at Purfleet, your time is soon taken up by Mr Renfield. According to his attendants, just before the stroke of noon, the previous day, he began to grow restless and soon became so violent that it took all their strength to subdue him, until he sank into a kind of melancholy, in which state he has remained ever since.

"His screams whilst he was in his paroxysm were truly appalling," Straker tells you.

You spend the morning attending to some of the other patients who were frightened by Renfield's outburst. After the dinner hour you find your patient brooding in a corner of the padded room, with a sullen, woebegone look on his face.

When you look on him again, at five o'clock that evening, you find him seemingly as happy and contented as he used to be. He has returned to the practice of catching flies and eating them, and is keeping a tally of his captures by making nail-marks on the edge of the door, between the ridges of padding.

He comes over to you and says, in a very humble, almost cringing, way, "My dear Doctor, I must apologise for my poor conduct of late, but I would be so much happier if I could return to my own cell. And my happiness would only be compounded if you would return my notebook to me as well."

What do you want to do? Will you accede to Renfield's request (turn to **871**), or will you tell him that he must stay where he is for the time being (turn to **901**)?

812

Your preternatural senses tell you that there is someone else here. You can hear the quickening pulse in his veins as clearly as you can hear the wind moaning about the masts of the schooner.

You leap out of the way, just as one of the ship's heavy, calico sails comes crashing down, almost on top of you. Standing by the mizzenmast is a mariner, his hands on the ropes, having triggered the improvised trap himself.

He cries out for help in his native Russian, declaiming that he has found the monster. You are going to have to finish him quickly before he gives the game away altogether.

Make a note that in the battle to come you have the initiative, add 2 points to your *Suspicion* score, and then turn to **778**.

813

As Quincey takes on two of the burly gypsies, you find yourself facing a bear of a man, who is actually wearing a bearskin. (You have the initiative in this battle.)

GYPSY   COMBAT 9   ENDURANCE 9

If you win your duel with the gypsy, as the Texan dispatches both of his opponents, half a dozen more prepare to take their place.

Turn to **782**.

814

Frozen to the spot in fear, your limbs feel too heavy to move, as the unliving horror clambers out of the crate that has kept it confined, a maggot-eaten lump of black flesh hissing from between rotted lips.

Add 2 points to your *Terror* score and turn to **837**.

815

You sense that Harker and the other malign entity are near now. Bounding through the snow, you pass the boundary wall of the abandoned village's derelict graveyard.

Running on all fours, you race along an avenue of cypress trees that leads to a square stone building. The snow is falling thickly now but a ray of moonlight manages to pierce the black mass of drifting cloud, illuminating the marble mausoleum, its great bronze portal, and the figure standing before the open door. You can hear the thumping of the man's panicked heart quite clearly.

At that instant, another figure appears within the doorway – a beautiful woman, her skin as smooth and white as marble, and just as cold. You do not detect a second heartbeat.

If your rank is that of *Count Dracula* or higher, turn to **62**. If not, turn to **850**.

816

Your curiosity getting the better of you, you take the crowbar in hand and lever off the lid of the box. More of the chilling fog immediately fills the air, but then just as quickly begins to clear and the contents of the crate are revealed to you.

The box has been lined with straw and then packed with ice, and laid within the ice are all manner of body parts, which are all clearly human. You see a huge arm, an enormous foot, and a ham-like fist of a hand, the skin livid with a tracery of purple veins. And in the middle of the crate is a human head that is missing the top of its skull and the blancmange-like grey matter of a brain.

You take a step back in horror.

Add 1 point to your *Terror* score and then *Take an ESP test*. If you pass the test, turn to **97**, but if you fail the test, turn to **71**.

817

With the Professor's help, Count Yorga arranges six chairs around one of the lounge tables and invites those present to sit, forming a circle. Van Helsing is on your right, and the beautiful blonde-haired young woman manoeuvres herself so that she is on your left.

Count Yorga invites you all to join hands, and you give a sharp intake of breath when you feel how cold the Countess's hand is.

The lights in the lounge are dimmed and the Bulgarian mystic begins to chant under his breath in a language you do not understand. It could just be the reflection of the lamps in the facets of the bloodstone, but his medallion seems possessed of a ruddy glow.

Roll one die and then turn to the appropriate section number.

Die Roll

1	Turn to **852**.
2	Turn to **877**.
3	Turn to **891**.
4	Turn to **911**.
5	Turn to **931**.
6	Turn to **838**.

818

Snarling, the wolf springs at you.

Take a Terror test. If you pass the test, turn to **848**. If you fail the test, turn to **878**.

819

You unsheathe your sabre and, dodging a clumsy swipe with the hammer from the Professor, make your move.

Cross off one use of *The Pen is Mightier* special ability and turn to **728**.

820

The Professor is suddenly there in front of the Count, the Sacred Wafer in his hand, which he holds out towards the monster.

The Count stops abruptly and cowers back. The rest of you raise your silver crucifixes, and he cowers further back still as you advance upon him.

The moonlight suddenly fails, as a great black cloud sails across the sky.

When the gaslight springs up under Quincey's match a moment later, you see nothing but a faint vapour, that trails out through the window and then is gone.

Harker rushes forward to help his wife, who suddenly gives a scream so wild, so ear-piercing, and so despairing that it will ring in your ears till your dying day. Her husband gathers her up in his arms, while she just lies there in helpless disarray.

Her face is of a ghastly pallor, which is only accentuated by the blood that smears her lips and cheeks and chin. From her throat trickles a thin stream of blood, and when your eyes meets hers, you see that they are mad with terror.

"Are we too late?" the Professor cries, rushing forward, the Sacred Wafer still tight in his hand. "I have to know!" And with that, before you can stop him, he presses it against Mrs Harker's forehead.

She gives another fearful scream and recoils in pain. Where the wafer touched her skin, it has burned her flesh as though it had been a piece of white-hot metal.

The wretched woman sinks to her knees, sobbing and pulling her beautiful hair over her face, whilst wailing: "Unclean! I am unclean! Even the Almighty shuns my polluted flesh! I must bear this mark of shame upon my forehead until the Judgment Day!"

Falling to his knees beside her, consumed with impotent grief, her husband put his arms around her and holds her tight. You are forced to turn away, for you do not want him to see that your eyes are also running with silent tears.

Add 1 point to your *Terror* score, gain 6 *Blood* points, and then turn **693**.

821

Despite the calm and isolation of your carriage, and the lulling motion of the train rocking on its tracks, you do not yield to the Professor's hypnotic influence as readily as before.

But when you do, you find your senses are far from the train and describe to Van Helsing everything you feel.

"Something is going out; I can feel it pass me like a cold wind. I can hear, far off, confused sounds as of men talking in strange tongues, fierce-falling water, and the howling of wolves."

You stop suddenly, as a shudder runs through you, and you wake from the trance, feeling cold and exhausted. But thanks to what you have told him, Van Helsing believes he has some idea of where the Count is now.

Deduct 1 *Blood* point and turn to **881**.

822

MINA MURRAY'S JOURNAL

13 August, Whitby

Another quiet day, and to bed with the key on my wrist, as I have done every night since Lucy's nocturnal flight to the churchyard...

Having secured both the door and the key, you retire to bed. You do not expect any trouble tonight.

Take an ESP test. If you pass the test, turn to **777**, but if you fail the test, turn to **797**.

823

That night, with the last remnants of the previous night's storm sending scuds of cloud racing across the bay beyond the harbour wall, you and Lucy retire to bed, the rattling of the chimney pots and the moaning of the wind about the eaves of the house your only lullaby.

Take an ESP test. If you pass the test, turn to **501**, but if you fail the test, turn to **521**.

824

Unknown to you, the rats' mouths were infested with a strain of deadly flesh-eating bacteria, after consuming the flesh of the Count's Strigoi shock-troops.

Lose 2 more *Endurance* points and 1 *Agility* point, unless you have the *Pestis* code word ticked off, in which case lose 4 more *Endurance* points and 2 *Agility* points!

Now turn to **876**.

825

As soon as they set eyes on you, the Vampire-Hunters throw themselves at you.

Take a Combat test and an Endurance test. If you pass both tests, turn to **940**. If you fail either test, turn to **620**.

826

You hesitate, a small voice somewhere within your hindbrain warning you that something isn't right.

There comes an almighty crash and the door splinters down the middle. There comes a second crash and the split widens. And now large fingers appear through the crack, and strong hands start to prise the planks apart.

An ugly face bearing a manic grin pushes through the gap, wild eyes rolling in their sockets, and the lunatic at your door growls, "Here's Johnny!"

Reaching a meaty hand through the hole, the monstrous madman manages to unlock the door and lets himself into your study. But you are ready for him.

If you want to use *The Pen is Mightier* special ability, cross off one use and turn to **688**. If not, turn to **719**.

827

The woman's cries give way to the hammering of her hands against the castle door. And then you hear another noise, the howling of wolves drawing closer, until you are convinced there must be a pack of the beasts gathering in the courtyard below.

The woman's desperate screams rend the night air again until they are abruptly silenced. You hear the wolves depart not long after. (Add 1 to your *Terror* score.)

How will you ever escape from this dreadful, benighted place, that gloom and fear have made their dwelling place?

If you want to continue to wait for fate to play its hand, turn to **947**. If you would rather seize control of your fate and act now, turn to **132**.

828

And then the child pounces. You have no choice but to defend yourself as the urchin slashes at you with ragged fingernails. (In this battle, you have the initiative.)

URCHIN   COMBAT 6   ENDURANCE 5

For the duration of this battle you must reduce your *Combat Rating* by 1 point, as you do not really want to hurt the child. After 5 Combat Rounds, if you are still alive, or if you reduce the urchin's *Endurance* score to 2 points or fewer, whichever is sooner, turn to **993** at once.

829

Finding the strongbox unlocked, as you lift the heavy lid the light from your lamp is reflected back at you from what looks like a king's ransom in silver coins.

You cannot help but gasp and wonder how much ancient wealth is hidden away within the Count's castle.

Picking up one of the coins, you scrutinise it more closely. One side is covered with Arabic calligraphic script, but on the other is the face of a bearded, hawk-nosed sultan, with a turban on his head. Around the edge of the image is what appears to be a name: *Sultani Mehmed II*.

If you want to fill your pockets with the antique coins, turn to **859**. If you would rather leave the treasure hoard untouched, turn to **890**.

830

Enraged, you tear through the sail, ready to bring hellish retribution down upon the head of the one who sprung the trap.

Make a note that in the battle to come your opponent has the initiative and then turn to **778**.

831

"It is the insignia of the Order of the Dragon," your host explains, "a noble chivalric brotherhood of knights whose initiates vowed to defend the Cross and fight the enemies of Christianity, the Turks of the Ottoman Empire in particular!"

Tick off the code word *Sárkány* and then turn to **861**.

832

The items are a curious collection of lucky rabbit's feet, tiny silver charms, and mountain ash. But knowing that your fellow passengers are genuinely concerned for your well-being does help to allay some of your fears.

(Deduct 1 point from your *Terror* score, record the Good Luck Tokens on your Adventure Sheet, and tick off the code word *Szerencse*.)

Turn to **117**.

833

Renfield tears at your back with splintered fingernails and even tries to bite you as you struggle to fight him off.

(In this battle Renfield has the initiative, and you must deduct 1 point when calculating your *Combat Rating* each Combat Round, as you are lying face down on the floor, with the madman on top of you.)

RENFIELD   COMBAT 8   ENDURANCE 10

If you are still alive after 4 Combat Rounds, or if you reduce Renfield's *Endurance* score to 5 points or fewer, whichever is sooner, turn to **863** at once.

834

You suddenly feel a hand on your shoulder.

"Good morning," comes the Count's voice in your ear.

You start in surprise, amazed that you had not seen him approach, since the reflection of the glass covers the whole room behind you.

You turn again to the shaving mirror, to see how you could have been mistaken. This time there can be no error, for the Count is close to you – you can see him over your shoulder – but there is no reflection of him in the mirror!

(Add 1 point to your *Terror* score and tick off the code word *Tükör*.)

It is then that you see that you have cut yourself shaving, and blood is tricking over your chin. (Lose 1 *Endurance* point.)

In that instant, the Count's eyes blaze with demoniac fury and he suddenly makes to grab your throat!

If you are wearing a Golden Crucifix about your neck, turn to **864**. If not, turn to **894**.

835

Not wishing to delay a moment longer, realising that this might be your only chance to stop Dracula once and for all, you set off after the vampire again.

You follow his malign spoor through the labyrinthine passageways of the catacombs, aware that with every turn you take you are travelling deeper into the crag upon which the castle stands.

Time loses all meaning as you pursue the vampire who knows where, until you turn a corner and pass through an archway bearing the carving of a dragon upon its keystone and you enter a vast cavern.

Your lantern cannot penetrate the darkness at the back of the cave, but you can see that you are not far from the edge of a subterranean lake. Standing at the water's edge is your quarry.

A low chanting echoes from the walls and stalactite-hung roof of the natural domed chamber and it takes you a moment to realise it is coming from the Count's lips.

As you step forward, with your weapon raised to deal the undead monster a killing blow, there is a disturbance in the previously still black waters of the lake, and you watch in disbelieving horror as something truly monstrous rises from the water.

It looks like a huge white worm, as wide across as a man is tall, but with obsidian pearls for eyes. It opens a horribly-fanged mouth big enough to swallow you whole and gives voice to a roar that freezes the blood in your veins and shakes the very rock upon which you are standing.

You are going to have to act fast.

Will you attack the monstrous white worm (turn to **805**), or the vampire (turn to **984**)?

836

A gypsy comes flying out of the throng, a keen-edged axe raised above his head, and engages you in battle. (You have the initiative in this fight.)

GYPSY   COMBAT 8   ENDURANCE 7

If you defeat the gypsy, gain 2 *Blood* points and turn to **904**.

837

You can do nothing but tighten your grip on the revolver and the knife in your hands and ready yourself to meet the living corpse's attack. (In this battle, the Strigoi has the initiative.)

STRIGOI   COMBAT 7   ENDURANCE 7

If you finish off the horror, turn to **897**.

838

Take an ESP test. If you pass the test, turn to **961**. If you fail the test, turn to **852**.

839

JONATHAN HARKER'S JOURNAL

29 September

When I received Mr Billington's courteous message, that he would give me any information in his power, I thought it best to go down to Whitby and make, on the spot, such enquiries as I wanted...

It is only a matter of days before you hear from Professor Van Helsing again, asking you and Mina to travel to London, to meet with Lucy's former suitors who are also intent on putting an end to the Count's malicious schemes.

But he also sets you the task of tracing that horrid cargo of Dracula's – the boxes of soil from his homeland that he had brought to England aboard the doomed *Demeter* – to where it was delivered in London.

Billington Junior meets you at the station, and brings you to his father's house, where they have already decided that you must stay the night. They are hospitable, believing that one should give a guest everything and leave him free to do as he likes.

Understanding that time is of the essence and that your stay will, by necessity, be short, Mr Billington already has all the papers concerning the consignment of boxes ready for you in his office.

Among them is one of the letters which you saw on the Count's table before you knew of his diabolical plans. It soon becomes evident that Dracula prepared for every obstacle which might be placed in the way of his intentions being carried out.

Then you come upon an invoice, that sets you on the path to uncovering the information you came here seeking.

Fifty cases of common earth, to be used for experimental purposes.

There is also a copy of a letter sent to a company by the name of Carter Paterson, and their reply.

This is all the information Mr Billington can furnish you with, so you go down to the port and speak with the coastguards, the Customs officers, and the harbour-master.

They all have something to say about the arrival of the *Demeter*, on that dark and stormy night, but none of them can expand upon the simple description, "Fifty cases of common earth."

You see the station-master next, and he is able to put you in communication with the men who had actually received the boxes, but all they can tell you is that the boxes were "mortal heavy" and that shifting them was "dry work."

* * * *

Returning to London the next day, you arrive at King's Cross and from there travel to Carter Paterson's central office, where you are met with the utmost courtesy. They look up the transaction in their ledger, and by the end of the working day you have all the papers connected with the delivery of the boxes to Carfax House in Purfleet, including a roughly-drawn map of the property that shows 30 rooms in the main house, and a set of skeleton keys attached to a tag bearing the number '145'. (Record the Map and the Skeleton Keys, along with the numbers associated with them, on your Adventure Sheet.)

That evening, as you take a cab from Purfleet station to Carfax Asylum – where you are to be reunited with your wife, Mina, and Professor Van Helsing – you are certain of one thing: that all the boxes that arrived at Whitby from Varna in the hold of the *Demeter* were safely deposited in the old chapel at Carfax. There should be fifty of them there, unless any have since been removed.

Tick off the code word *Quinquaginta* and turn to **592**.

840

The Ottoman cavalry broken, you press on, breaching the defences the Turks have raised around their camp in your desire to hunt down your enemy and put an end of this unholy invasion of your homeland.

But before you can do that, you will have to fight your way through the devoted Janissary soldiers who guard his hiding place, and who have sworn to protect him unto death – their own!

The two soldiers you vent your ire upon do not know what has hit them. (In this battle, you have the initiative, but you must fight the soldiers at the same time.)

	COMBAT	ENDURANCE
First JANISSARY	8	8
Second JANISSARY	8	7

If you slaughter your opponents, gain 4 *Blood* points and turn to **875**.

841

DR SEWARD'S DIARY

(Kept in phonograph)

4 September

I have been to see Miss Westenra, whom I found much better...

It does your heart good to see Lucy looking so well, although she is clearly not totally recovered. She has a good appetite, her nights have not been troubled by any more incidents of sleep-walking, and her colour is gradually coming back.

(Deduct 1 *Terror* point.)

You return to Purfleet that evening. As you are standing at the gate, watching the sunset, you hear Renfield yelling. It is a shock to turn from the smoky beauty of a sunset over London, with its lurid lights and inky shadows, and all the marvellous tints that come on foul clouds even as on foul water, to face the grim sternness of Carfax Asylum, with its wealth of breathing misery, and your own desolate heart to endure it all.

You reach Renfield's cell in time to see the red disc of the sun sink below the horizon. As it does so, he becomes less frenzied until he slides onto the floor, now no more than an inert mass. But within only a few minutes he gets to his feet again and looks around him, quite calm now.

As you watch, he goes straight over to the window and brushes away the crumbs of sugar he has sprinkled there. Then he takes his fly box and empties it outside, finally throwing the box itself away. Shutting the window, he sits down on his bed.

"Are you not going to keep flies anymore?" you ask him.

"No," he says. "I am sick of all that rubbish!"

He is certainly a fascinating subject for study. If only you could get some glimpse into his mind to understand the reason for his outbursts. Can it be that there is some malign influence of the sun at periods which affects certain natures, as the moon does others?

Tick off the code word *Lunatic* and then turn to **921**.

842

As you round the corner of the church, the cloud has passed and you see Lucy once again, transfixed within a beam of brilliant moonlight, lying with her head hanging over the back of the seat. She is quite alone, and there is no sign of another living thing anywhere nearby.

She is asleep, her lips parted and her breathing coming in long, heavy gasps, as if she is striving to fill her lungs with every breath.

As you draw closer, she puts up her hand and pulls up the collar of her nightdress, as though she is feeling the cold. You fling the warm shawl over her and pull the edges tight around her neck – dreading that she might come down with some deadly chill from the cold night air, unclad as she is – fastening it at her throat with your brooch.

Once she is safely wrapped up, you put your shoes on her feet, and then begin, very gently, to wake her. When she does not respond, wishing to get her home at once, you shake her forcibly, until finally she opens her eyes.

When you tell her to come home with you, Lucy rises without a word, with the obedience of a child. As you leave the churchyard, the gravel hurts your feet, making you wince, but you press on. You make it all the way back to the Crescent without meeting a soul. When you get in, you both wash your feet, and having said a prayer of thankfulness together, you tuck Lucy up in bed.

However, you are sorry to notice that your clumsiness with the brooch has hurt her, for the skin at her throat is pierced. You must have pinched a piece of loose skin and transfixed it, for there are two little red points, like pin-pricks, and on the band of her nightdress there is a drop of blood.

Before falling asleep, she implores you not to say a word to anyone, least of all her mother, about her sleep-walking adventures. Despite hesitating at first, in the end you accede to her demands.

However, before returning to bed yourself, you make sure you lock the door, tying the key to your wrist, so hopefully you will not be disturbed again.

Turn to **822**.

843

In response to your aggressive challenge, the gypsies arm themselves with knives and axes and rush towards you, roaring their incomprehensible battle-cries.

If you want to call upon *The Pen is Mightier* special ability, cross off one use and turn to **782**. If not, turn to **813**.

844

The gypsy woman hisses in anger at your continued refusal to drink. Perhaps you have offended her by declining the hospitality she has offered you.

You are taken aback when you suddenly realise that her naked arms are entwined with a pair of snakes that are an eerie milky white in colour. You know you're not imagining their presence when Quincey gives a cry of alarm and drops his empty goulash bowl on the ground.

And then suddenly the snakes strike simultaneously, one for each of you!

Take an Agility test. If you pass the test, turn to **531**, but if you fail the test, turn to **57**.

845

You will not stand for such appalling intolerance, no matter who Varney the Vampire claims to be.

Transforming yourself into something that is part-bat and part-wolf, you tower over the terrified vampire for a moment, drinking in his fear, before grabbing hold of him and tearing his decaying body limb from limb.

Turn to **125**.

846

"Who is it?" you call.

"Barlow, Dr Seward," comes a familiar gruff voice from the other side, and you rise from your seat to open the door.

Take an ESP test. If you pass the test, turn to **826**. If you fail the test, turn to **808**.

847

Opening your eyes wide, you ensnare Van Helsing's gaze within yours.

In as calm a voice as you can manage you say, "Professor, look into my eyes…"

Take an ESP test. If you pass the test, turn to **789**. If you fail the test, turn to **758**.

848

You have no idea what a wolf is doing in North Hampstead, but you do not let that fact trouble you as you pull a scalpel from your doctor's bag and prepare to defend yourself. (In this battle, you have the initiative.)

WOLF   COMBAT 7   ENDURANCE 7

After four Combat Rounds, or if you manage to reduce the Wolf's *Endurance* score to 3 points or fewer, turn to **908** at once.

849

The crewman arms himself with a hunting knife, that he had secreted about his person, and you prepare to fight back using your own weapons – your dreadful fangs, claws, and a killer's instinct. (In this battle, you have the initiative.)

CREWMAN   COMBAT 8   ENDURANCE 7

The sailor grunts with effort and cries out in horror as you fight, and you fear that someone will have heard your altercation. (Gain 1 *Suspicion* point.)

If you wish, you may spend 3 *Blood* points and turn to **806** without having to fight the man.

If not, conduct the battle as normal and if you reduce the Crewman's *Endurance* score to 2 points or below, turn to **806** at once.

850

Transforming into a bipedal beast that is still more wolf than man as you run, you grab hold of the Englishman from behind and hurl him out of harm's way into the snow.

But the occupant of the tomb is ready for you, becoming a bat-like monster herself, quite capable of matching you in battle, in both tooth and claw. (In this battle, the Vampyre has the initiative.)

VAMPYRE   COMBAT 9   ENDURANCE 11

If you kill the undead Countess, turn to **884**. Alternatively, you may choose to deduct 3 *Blood* points and turn to **907** straightaway, without having to engage in battle.

851

It is no good; no matter how long the Professor perseveres, even though you eventually enter a trance-like state, your senses remain trapped on board the train. It is as if your mental connection to the Count has been broken.

Lose 1 *ESP* point and turn to **881**.

852

The lights dim still further and then it is as if the flickering gas-flames detach from the lamps and drift towards the table where you and your fellow passengers are sitting. As they do so they start to swell, the will-o'-the-wisps taking on vague humanoid forms.

You see wailing faces and silently screaming skull-visages closing in on you. Panic threatens to overwhelm you and you tear your hands free of the grip of your fellow seekers after knowledge.

The moment the circle is broken, the phantoms are dispelled, and the lounge is filled with a warm orange glow once again.

The others are looking at you with bewildered expressions, all apart from the Countess who has a lascivious smile on her perfect rosebud lips.

"What is it, my dear?" Van Helsing asks, concerned.

"The ghosts!" you reply, in a state of agitation. "Did you not see them?"

"I saw nothing," he replies. "And I do not believe anyone else did either."

Add 1 point to your *Terror* score and turn to **987**.

853

The Whitby correspondent responsible for the piece makes much of the fact that last night's storm was one of the greatest and most sudden on record, and after describing the changes in the weather over the course of the evening, focuses on the fate of the Russian schooner and the gruesome details surrounding the discovery of the ship's captain bound to the helm.

Having made the harbour, the ship's headlong flight only came to an end when it ran ashore, at which moment numerous onlookers witnessed an immense dog leap from the deck of the ship and bound up the East Cliff, to disappear into the darkness beyond the graveyard.

The reporter was one of a small group who saw the dead seaman whilst he was actually lashed to the wheel. The man was fastened by his hands, tied one over the other to one of the spokes. And what is more, between the inner hand and the wood was a crucifix, the set of beads on which it was fastened being around both wrists and wheel, and all kept fast by the binding cords. The flapping and buffeting of the sails had worked through the rudder of the wheel and had dragged him to and fro, so that the cords with which he was tied had cut the flesh to the bone.

The helmsman was examined by a surgeon, who declared that he must have been dead for two days. The coastguard said that the man must have tied himself to the wheel, fastening the knots with his teeth.

It is needless to say that the dead steersman was removed from the place where he held his honourable watch and ward till death and placed in the mortuary to await inquest.

(Tick off the code word *Demeter*.)

Having read all you want to about the derelict ship that found her way so miraculously into Whitby harbour in the storm, do you want to suggest to Lucy that the two of you take a stroll down to the seafront to see the wreck for yourselves (turn to **883**), or will you advise that you think it better the two of you remain at the Crescent today, especially considering Lucy's delicate state at present (turn to **823**)?

854

LOG OF THE 'DEMETER'

29 July – Another tragedy. Had single watch to-night, as crew too tired to double. When morning watch came on deck could find no one except steersman. Raised outcry, and all came on deck. Thorough search, but no one found. Are now without second mate, and crew in a panic. Mate and I agreed to go armed henceforth and wait for any sign of cause.

Turn to **791**.

855

Even as you bear down on her, Sister Agatha starts to chant an invocation in Latin.

It suddenly feels as if your body is ablaze, your corrupted blood boiling within your veins. Such is the pain that you have no choice but to flee from the convent-hospital, defeated by the very one you came here to destroy.

Either lose 8 *Endurance* points, 3 *Agility* points, 2 *Combat* points, and 2 *ESP* points, or deduct 6 *Blood* points.

Make the necessary alterations to your Adventure Sheet and, if you are still alive, turn to **810**.

856

You have granted the corpses true death at last, and Van Helsing, you are relieved to see, has done the same. All that there remains for you to do is to purify the soil of Dracula's homeland while you wait for your friends to arrive.

* * * *

Within half an hour, the rest of your party has joined you inside the house at 138 Piccadilly. Lord Godalming reports there were six boxes of earth at the Walworth address, and that the undead creatures nailed up inside them were destroyed when exposed to direct sunlight.

Quincey Morris then explains that the bodies in the boxes that had been stored in the old printers' warehouse in Mile End had already been eaten by a pack of rats, the diet of corrupted flesh having had an equally corrupting effect on the rodents.

"So six boxes at the Walworth property," says the Professor, "another six in Mile End, and eight boxes of earth here."

With a sinking feeling in the pit of your stomach, you already know what he is going to say next before he says it.

"Which means there is still one outstanding from the original fifty Dracula had transported to England. One box that has somehow escaped detection. But where can it be?"

Take an ESP test. If you pass the test, turn to **794**, but if you fail the test, turn to **764.**

857

You plan out your ambush meticulously and wait for the opportunity to present itself when you might put your plan into action.

That very night, when you hear the key turn in the lock, you position yourself by the door, a knife from the dining table in your hand.

The door opens a crack, and the Count steals into the room. In that instant, you bring the hand holding the knife down in a stabbing motion. But before you know it, the Count seizes your wrist in his iron grip. You drop the knife in shock. In a second his other hand is around your throat, and his eyes burn with infernal fire as he turns them upon you.

Take a Terror test. If you pass the test, turn to **887**. If you fail the test, turn to **917**.

858

And then the unnatural child springs at you, with all the agility of a cat. You have no choice but to defend yourself, much as the thought of hurting the child appals you. (In this battle, the child has the initiative.)

URCHIN COMBAT 6 ENDURANCE 5

For the duration of this battle you must reduce your *Combat Rating* by 1 point, as you do not really want to hurt the child. After 5 Combat Rounds, if you are still alive, or if you reduce the urchin's *Endurance* score to 2 points or fewer, whichever is sooner, turn to **993** at once.

859

You fill your pockets with coins, until you can carry no more.

Add the Antique Coins to your Adventure Sheet and turn to **890**.

860

"What loose ends?" Skinsky demands, clearly highly agitated now.

"You," you say, your voice a guttural growl. In a form that is neither wolf nor man, you attack as Skinsky pulls a heavy kukri knife from his belt to defend himself. (In this battle, you have the initiative.)

PETROF SKINSKY COMBAT 9 ENDURANCE 9

If you kill the agent, gain 2 *Blood* points and turn to **40**. Alternatively, rather than having to fight Skinsky at all, you may deduct 3 *Blood* points and turn to **40** straightaway.

861

"But enough of the past," says the Count. "Let us focus our thoughts on future prosperity and the preparations for my forthcoming journey to English shores.

"I wish you to write to our mutual friend, Mr Hawkins," he says, laying a heavy hand on your shoulder, "and to any other you wish, saying that you shall stay with me until a month from now."

"Do you wish me to stay so long?" you ask, and your heart grows cold at the thought.

"I desire it very much. You will rest here with me a while, so that I may learn more of your English ways."

Will you acquiesce to the Count's wishes (turn to **801**), or will you tell him that you have business in England that will not wait another month (turn to **989**)?

862

The inhuman quality of the face stops you dead in your tracks as fear seizes your heart, and it is all you can do not to swoon or turn on your heels and flee. But your friend needs you, and so you press on regardless.

As you enter the churchyard, the church building comes between you and the seat, and for a moment or two you lose sight of Lucy.

Add 1 point to your *Terror* score, gain 2 *Blood* points, and then turn to **842**.

863

The attendants rush into the cell and drag the lunatic from you, beating him into submission with their discipline sticks.

He deserves nothing less – the man is an undeveloped homicidal maniac! – but you are left shaken by his sudden, unprovoked attack.

Add 1 point to your *Terror* score and turn to **893**.

864

You instinctively draw away, and the Count's hand touches the string of beads that hold the Crucifix. It brings about an instant change in him, and his fury passes so quickly you wonder if it was ever there at all.

Turn to **924**.

865

As you pause to light the lantern you had the presence of mind to grab from among your belongings before setting off after the Count, the wick flares into life, illuminating an ornamental stone shield above a cracked archway. The coat-of-arms is superimposed with the carved relief of a mighty dragon, its wings and tail curled about it.

The vampire's trail does not lead that way, but further into the darkness of the catacombs.

Do you want to keep following the Count (turn to **835**), or do you want to see what lies beyond the archway (turn to **895**)?

866

Hurrying to your study, you shut the door firmly behind you and turn the key in the lock. The shouts of both the psychotic patients and the agitated attendants struggling to contain the riot rise through the floor from the ward below and echo like wailing ghosts in the stairwells.

To take your mind of it, you sit down at your desk and look through the reports your colleague Dr Hennessey has written up each day while you were away, for you to peruse upon your return. One in particular grabs your attention as you flick through them:

With regard to patient, Renfield, he has had another outbreak. This afternoon a carrier's cart with two men made a call at the empty house whose grounds abut onto ours – the house to which, you will remember, the patient twice ran away. The men stopped at our gate to ask the porter their way. I was myself looking out of the study window, and saw one of them come up to the house.

As he passed the window of Renfield's room, the patient called him all the foul names he could lay his tongue to. The man, who seemed a decent fellow enough, contented himself by telling him to "shut up for a foul-mouthed beggar," whereon our man accused him of robbing him and wanting to murder him and said that he would hinder him if he were to swing for it.

I opened the window and signed to the man not to notice. "Lor' bless yer, sir," he said. "I wouldn't mind what was said to me in a bloomin' madhouse. I pity ye and the guv'nor for havin' to live in the house with a wild beast like that." Then he asked his way civilly enough, and I told him where the gate of the empty house was.

He went away, followed by threats and curses and revilings from our man. I went down to see if I could make out any cause for his anger. I found him, to my astonishment, quite composed and most genial in his manner. I tried to get him to talk of the incident, but he blandly asked me questions as to what I meant, and led me to believe that he was completely oblivious of the affair.

It was, I am sorry to say, however, only another instance of his cunning, for within half an hour I heard of him again. This time he had broken out through the window of his room, and was running down the avenue. I called to the attendants to follow me, and ran after him, for I feared he was intent on some mischief.

My fear was justified when I saw the same cart which had passed before coming down the road, having on it some great wooden boxes. The men were wiping their foreheads, and were flushed in the face, as if with violent exercise. Before I could get up to him the patient rushed at them, and pulling one of them off the cart, began to knock his head against the ground. If I had not seized him just at that moment I believe he would have killed the man there and then.

The other fellow jumped down and struck him over the head with the butt-end of his heavy whip. It was a terrible blow; but he did not seem to mind it, but seized him also, and struggled with the three of us. You know I am no light weight, and the others were both burly men.

At first he was silent in his fighting; but as we began to master him, and the attendants were putting a strait-waistcoat on him, he began to shout: "They shan't murder me by inches! I'll fight for my Lord and Master!" and all sorts of similar incoherent ravings. It was with very considerable difficulty that they got him back to the house and put him in the padded room. One of the attendants, Hardy, had a finger broken. However, I set it all right; and he is going on well.

The two carriers were at first loud in their threats of actions for damages, and promised to rain all the penalties of the law on us. But after a stiff glass of grog, and with each a sovereign in hand, they made light of the attack.

I took their names and addresses, in case they might be needed. They are Jack Smollet, of Budding's Rents, King George's Road, Great Walworth, and Thomas Snelling, Peter Farley's Row, Guide Court, Bethnal Green. They are both in the employment of Harris & Sons, Moving and Shipment Company, Orange Master's Yard, Soho.

(Tick off the code word *Scientia*.)

You start as there comes a loud knock at your door. Will you:

Open the door?	Turn to **779**.
Ask who it is?	Turn to **846**.
Ignore it and keep reading Dr Hennessey's report?	Turn to **826**.

867

(Cross off one use of *The Pen is Mightier* special ability.)

Suddenly the Texan is by your side, and you start as he discharges his Smith & Wesson right next to your ear.

The air is filled with a pink mist and flying bone fragments, as the corpse falls to the ground, missing its head.

Turn to **914**.

868

Long snake-like fangs protruding from his mouth, the Snake-Man moves in for the kill. (In this battle you have the initiative.)

SNAKE-MAN   COMBAT 9   ENDURANCE 9

If the Snake-Man wins two consecutive Combat Rounds, turn to **282** at once. If you manage to win the fight without your opponent winning two consecutive Combat Rounds, turn to **247**.

869

Disappointingly, as a group you have not actually learned that much and seem to have more questions than answers regarding the fiend and his plans.

Gain 4 *Blood* points and turn to **978**.

870

Dismounting, you and Quincey lead your horses by the reins between the trees towards the flickering firelight. You emerge into a clearing at the centre of which a large fire is blazing. Positioned around it are a number of brightly-painted and ornately-decorated covered wagons. Sitting around the fire is a group of burly men and slight women, dressed in the native dress of Transylvanian gypsies; the men are wearing thick sheepskin jackets and large, fur-lined hats, while the women's heads are covered by shawls or bright red bandanas, and all manner of jangling trinkets hang from their wrists and headscarves.

As you approach the camp, several of the men get to their feet and approach you, and you are all too aware of the rifles they are carrying in their hands, not to mention the axes and long knives they have tucked into their thick leather belts.

One of the broad-shouldered men, whose thick black beard is streaked with grey, says something to you in what you assume is his native tongue.

How will you respond? If you want to draw your own weapon, turn to **843**. If you would prefer to say something in your own language, turn to **752**.

871

Thinking it best to humour your patient, you agree to his request.

When you call on him later that day, you find that he has sprinkled the sugar intended for his tea on the windowsill and has started to catch the flies that land to feed on the sweet, white granules. However, rather than consume them himself, he is storing them in a matchbox, just as he did previously, and is currently searching the corners of his cell for a spider.

Becoming aware of your presence he turns to you resolutely, and says as politely as he can, "Doctor, won't you be very good to me and let me have a little more sugar? I think it would be very good for me."

"And the flies?" you ask.

"Yes! The flies like it too, and I like the flies, therefore I like it."

You procure him a double supply and leave him as happy as any man in the world.

Turn to **921**.

872

"Let me come with you, Professor," you press him. "Dracula's concubines pose no threat to me, but they could yet cause you harm. Do not go into that benighted place alone. Let me accompany you and we shall do what needs to be done together."

There is something about the purring persuasive tone of your voice that the old man cannot resist, and so he relents. Van Helsing clears a path for you through the holy circle and, having armed yourself, you follow as the Professor makes his way up the hill, through the snow, towards the castle.

Already knowing the route, by dint of having read the dreadful diary Jonathan kept during his stay here, you find your way to the old chapel within the bowels of the castle and descend to the catacombs beneath it. The air here is oppressive, as if thick with sulphurous fumes.

"We know we have at least three graves to find," the Professor says in a low voice, "three graves that are inhabited." He swallows hard, his mouth suddenly dry. "The maw of the wolf would be better to rest in than the grave of the vampire," he mutters.

Regardless, you begin your search.

Within one shadowy alcove you find three ancient coffins. Their stone lids are missing and inside each one lies one of the vampyre women, sleeping the sleep of undeath. They appear so full of life and voluptuous beauty that you cannot help but think of poor Lucy, and how Van Helsing said she appeared after she had been turned by the Count.

The Professor joins you within the alcove and steps up to the first coffin, a blacksmith's hammer and a wooden stake clutched in his hands.

"Such beauty," he mutters, his voice barely audible.

But rather than plunge the stake into the vampyre's heart, he stares at the coffin's occupant, as if transfixed by the flowing blonde locks cascading over the swell of her bosom. She appears no older than you, but in truth she could have been born centuries ago.

"I wonder how many men, who set forth to do such a task as mine in times past, found their heart fail them at the last, and then their nerve."

Still he does not move.

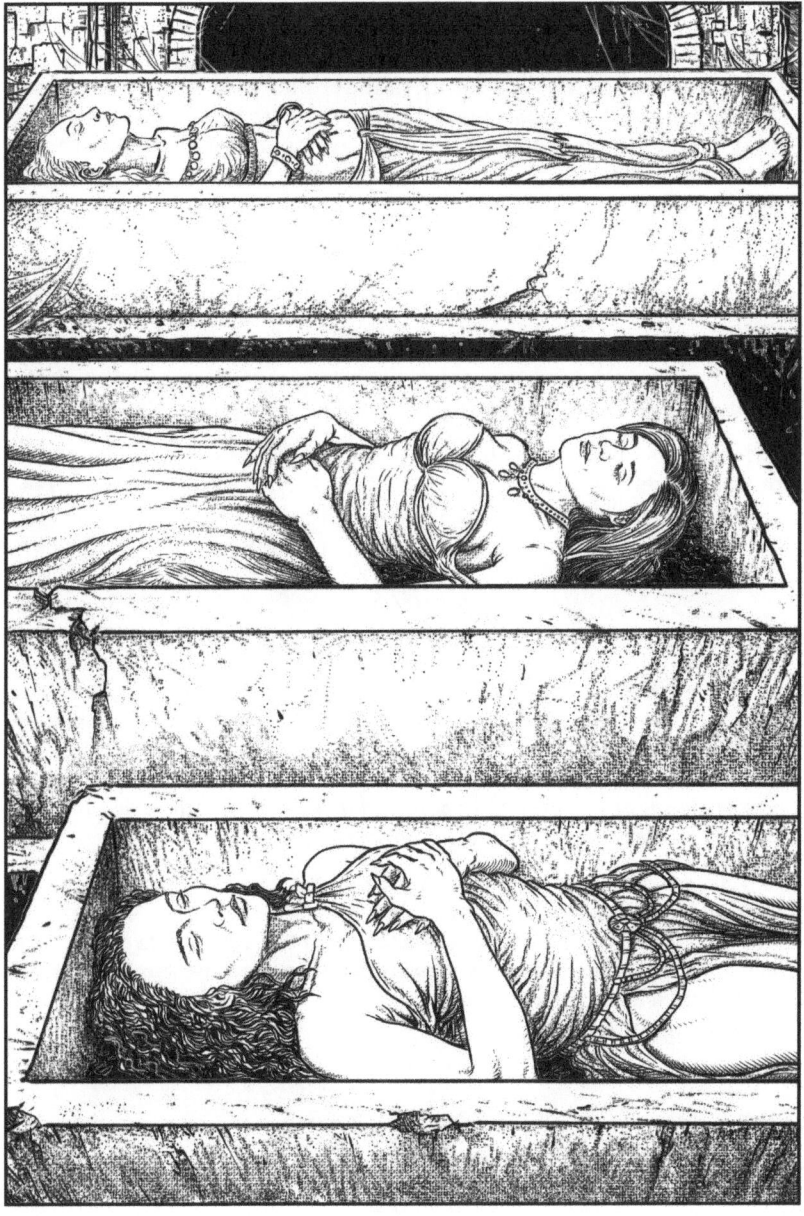

Then the eyes of the fair woman open and she fixes the Professor with an ophidian stare.

You feel relief wash over you as you hear him say, "I must kill the vampire." But in the next moment that relief turns to horror as Van Helsing turns towards you. He raises the hammer and the stake as if he intends to bludgeon you with one and stab you with the other, and says again, his voice barely more than a murmur, "Kill the vampire."

What are you going to do? Will you:

Prepare to defend yourself against the Professor?	Turn to **758**.
Use *The Pen is Mightier* special ability (if you still can)?	Turn to **819**.
Try to hypnotise Van Helsing yourself?	Turn to **847**.
Attack the vampyre woman who has the Professor in her power?	Turn to **994**.

873

LOG OF THE 'DEMETER'

24 July ~ There seems some doom over this ship. Already a hand short, and entering on the Bay of Biscay with wild weather ahead, and yet last night another man lost, disappeared. Like the first, he came off his watch and was not seen again. Men all in a panic of fear; sent a round robin, asking to have double watch, as they fear to be alone. Mate angry. Fear there will be some trouble, as either he or the men will do some violence.

28 July ~ Four days in hell, knocking about in a sort of maelstrom, and the wind a tempest. No sleep for anyone. Men all worn out. Hardly know how to set a watch, since no one fit to go on. Second mate volunteered to steer and watch, and let men snatch a few hours' sleep. Wind abating; seas still terrific, but feel them less, as ship is steadier.

Turn to **898**.

874

Just as you are about to join with your companions in battling the gypsies, the sound of savage snarling behind you alerts you to the fact that a pair of large wolves is bearing down on your position. You have no choice but to turn and fight tooth and nail against the vicious predators. (In this battle, the wolves have the initiative, and you must fight them at the same time.)

	COMBAT	ENDURANCE
First WOLF	6	6
Second WOLF	7	6

If you manage to slay the wolves, gain 4 *Blood* points and then turn to **904**.

875

Soaked in Ottoman blood, you find yourself standing before a familiar golden pavilion. It is the Sultan's tent. Your nemesis is within your reach at last.

You rush inside, and a grim smile of satisfaction spreads across your blood-splattered face when you see Mehmed standing there, scimitar in hand and clad in golden scale armour.

"My Lord Impaler," he says, bowing, but never once taking his eyes off you, not even for a moment, "we meet again."

"And for the last time," you declare, raising your blade once more, intending to bring it down on his head and end this interminable war.

But before you can land a blow against the Sultan, a figure swathed in black, emerges from the shadows at the back of the tent, taking you by surprise.

You have heard rumours of the black-clad Magi who serve the Sultan; curious mystics – sorcerers, some say – from distant desert lands, who have sworn allegiance to the Conqueror. You dread to think what Mehmed must have promised them in return for their blasphemous, sorcerous assistance.

The figure is holding what appears to be a crystal flask in one hand. It is wrapped within a cocoon of intricate silverwork and the Magus is raising it up, almost reverently, in one hand.

And then the Magus plucks the ground glass stopper from the throat of the flask and a thick black smoke starts to pour from within the bottle. It forms a cloud before you, shot-through with glittering golden particles.

You watch, almost hypnotised, as the motes of light shift and swirl, and for the briefest moment they appear to come together as a pair of golden eyes that fix on you, as if staring into your soul.

You have heard of such smoky spirits before too. It must be one of the supernatural entities that are called Djinn.

How do you want to react to the Djinn's sudden manifestation? Will you:

Command it to begone?	Turn to **905**.
Attack the Djinn?	Turn to **925**.

876

Back on the main thoroughfare, you catch a cab and set off for 138 Piccadilly.

As it turns out, your destination is a silently sinister, abandoned building, that looks even more grim compared to its more lively and spruce-looking neighbours.

Taking the doorknocker in hand, you bang it against the brass plate three times. You are admitted a few moments later by a harassed-looking Van Helsing.

The rest of your courageous band is already gathered in the shadowy hallway. Now that you have joined them, you all report back on the location and destruction of the remaining boxes of Transylvanian earth.

"Six boxes at the Walworth property you say?" – Lord Godalming confirms that that is correct – "And another six at Mile End?" the Professor goes on, looking at Quincey Morris, who nods in agreement. "And eight boxes of earth here."

With a sinking feeling in the pit of your stomach, you already know what he is going to say next before he says it.

"Which means there is still one outstanding from the original fifty Dracula had transported to England. One box that has somehow escaped detection. But where can it be?"

Take an ESP test. If you pass the test, turn to **794**, but if you fail the test, turn to **764**.

877

The lights dim still further and then suddenly go out. The six of you sit there in silence, as Count Yorga stops chanting.

And then another sound reaches your ears, as if from a long way off. It is the squeaking of rats. The squeaking grows steadily louder until it sounds like a swarm of the vermin are there with you in the lounge, and although you can see nothing you are sure you can feel their supple bodies brushing against your legs.

At the same time, the ratty man starts to gibber in fear, whimpering under his breath, "Forgive me, Master. Forgive me, Master."

You have had enough and tear your hands free of the grip of your fellow séance-goers, breaking the circle.

At once the spectral rats are dispelled and the lights in the lounge glow back into life.

Add 1 point to your *Terror* score and turn to **987**.

878

What on earth is a wolf doing running loose about North Hampstead? And is Lucy all right?

But such questions fly from your head as the wolf bears down on you, snarling, its jaws slavering. Having the presence of mind to pull a scalpel from your medical bag, you prepare to defend yourself against the beast as best you can. (In this battle, the wolf has the initiative.)

WOLF   COMBAT 7   ENDURANCE 7

After four Combat Rounds, or if you manage to reduce the Wolf's *Endurance* score to 3 points or fewer, turn to **908** immediately.

879

Thrusting her crucifix into the face of your thrall, Sister Agatha sends the young woman reeling, and then turns her attention back to you.

Deduct 2 *Blood* points and turn to **855**.

880

Dismounting, you and Quincey lead your horses by the reins between the trees towards the flickering light. You emerge into a clearing at the centre of which a large fire is blazing. Positioned around it are a number of brightly-painted and ornately-decorated covered wagons. Sitting around the fire is a group of burly men and slight women, dressed in the native attire of Transylvanian gypsies; the men are wearing thick sheepskin jackets and large, fur-lined hats, while the women's heads are covered by shawls or bright red bandanas, and all manner of jangling trinkets hang from their wrists and headscarves.

You freeze, a gasp catching in your throat. These gypsies are clad in the same garb as the Szgany who laboured within Castle Dracula, filling the boxes the Count had transported all the way to England.

Catching sight of the two of you, several of the men get to their feet and approach, and you are all too aware of the rifles they are carrying in their hands, not to mention the axes and long knives they have tucked into their thick leather belts.

One of the broad-shouldered men, whose thick black beard is streaked with grey, says something to you in what you assume is his native tongue.

How will you respond? If you want to draw your own weapon, turn to **843**. If you would prefer to say something in your own language, turn to **752**.

881

30 October, Galatz

You arrive at Galatz as the sun is rising on the morning of 30 October, on fire with anxiety and eagerness. By nine o'clock your party is boarding the *Czarina Catherine*, which lies at anchor in the river harbour, in order to interview its captain, a Scotsman named Donelson.

Captain Donelson willingly shares the details of his voyage. "I never had so favourable a run in all my life," he begins. "Man, but it made us afeard, for we thought that we should have to pay for it with some rare piece o' ill luck. It's no' right to run from London to the Black Sea with a wind behind ye, as though the Devil himself were blowing on yer sail. And all the time we could no' see a thing; a fog fell on us and travelled with us, till we came to the Dardanelles.

"When we got past the Bosphorus the men began to grumble. Some o' them, Romanians, came and asked me to heave overboard a big box that had been put on board by a queer lookin' old man just before we left London. I had seen them looking at the fellow and put out their two fingers when they saw him to guard against the evil eye. Man, but the superstitions of foreigners are perfectly ridiculous! I sent them about their business pretty quick.

"We had a fair way and deep water all the time after that, even though the unnatural fog descended again, and two days ago, when the morning sun came through the mist, we found ourselves just in the river opposite Galatz.

"An hour before sun-up, a man came aboard with an order, written to him from England, to receive a box marked for one

Count Dracula. He had his papers, and I was glad to be rid o' the damn thing, for I was beginning to feel uneasy about it maeself."

"What was the name of the man who took it?" asks Van Helsing.

At that, Captain Donelson steps down into his cabin and produces a receipt signed 'Immanuel Hildesheim', and bearing the address 'Burgenstrasse 16'.

* * * *

You find Hildesheim in his office at Number 16 Burgenstrasse. He is reluctant to share any information with you to begin with, but as soon as Arthur opens his wallet, and after a little bargaining, he finally tells you what he knows.

He had received a letter from Mr de Ville of London, telling him to receive, if possible before sunrise so as to avoid customs, a box which would arrive at Galatz on board the *Czarina Catherine*. This he was to pass into the hands of one Petrof Skinsky, an individual who dealt with the Slovaks who traded down the river to the port. He was paid for his work by an English bank note, which had been duly cashed for gold at the Danube International Bank. When Skinsky had come to him, he took him to the ship and passed the box into the charge of the other man.

You have no choice other than to set about searching for this Skinsky, but it is dusk before you find yourselves at the door to his lodgings. One of his neighbours reveals that he left two days ago, but no one knows where he was travelling to. It seems you are at a standstill again.

But whilst you are discussing what you should do next, a boy comes running and, gasping for breath, tells you that Skinsky has been found inside the graveyard of St Peter's church.

And so it is, as dusk falls and a full moon rises, providing you with enough light to see by, your party enters the churchyard in search of answers.

"There!" shouts Arthur, pointing to a nearby tomb. You can see the amorphous black shadow of something lying atop the cold stone.

Just as you make to move towards the tomb and examine it further, a mournful howl cuts through the deepening darkness that makes everyone start.

"Sounds like a wolf," Quincey says, his hand automatically going to the pistol holstered at his waist.

"Then we must be quick about our business and tarry no longer than is necessary," says Van Helsing.

"I don't like the idea of being caught unawares by a wolf," drawls the Texan. "I'd rather be the hunter than the hunted. Anyone else want to come with me?"

As your party begins to split into two distinct groups, who do you want to follow further into the graveyard? Will you:

Go with Van Helsing to examine the body
on the tomb?   Turn to **912**.

Join Quincey Morris in hunting for wolves?   Turn to **982**.

882

You press on, unperturbed by the unnatural nature of whatever it is that is attacking your friend.

"Lucy!" you call out to her, as another cloud passes before the face of the moon.

She does not answer, and you run on to the entrance of the churchyard. As you enter, the squat church building is between you and the seat, and for a minute you lose sight of her.

Add 1 point to your *ESP* score and then turn to **842**.

883

Lucy readily agrees, and so that afternoon the two of you join the other sticky-beaks and nosey-parkers who have come to the East Pier to see the derelict for themselves and discover the latest gossip concerning its almost supernatural arrival.

But it turns out the *Demeter's* secrets are stranger than the circumstances of its arrival. The ship is almost entirely in ballast of silver sand, with only a small amount of cargo, a number of great wooden boxes filled with mould! This cargo was signed over to a Whitby solicitor, Mr S. F. Billington, who went aboard this morning to take formal possession of the boxes of scientific earth.

The Russian consul too, acting for the charter-party, took formal possession of the ship, and paid all harbour duties owing.

There is also a good deal of interest concerning the hound, which appears to have disappeared entirely from the town. General consensus of opinion is that it has made its way to the moors, where it is hiding even now.

This thought terrifies you, for it is evidently a fierce brute; early this morning a half-bred mastiff belonging to a coal merchant close to Tate Hill Pier, was found dead in the roadway opposite its master's yard. It had been fighting, and manifestly against a savage opponent, for its throat was torn out, and its belly was slit open as if with a savage claw.

Lucy announces that the gruesome details of these mysterious events make her feel quite faint, and you have heard enough yourself, so you agree to return to the Crescent and not go out again today.

Add 1 to your *Terror* score and turn to **823**.

884

The vanquished vampyre hangs limp in your clawed hands. As the last of her un-life leaves her body, you lock your wolfish jaws about her neck and drink deeply of her vampiric power.

Gain 4 *Blood* points and turn to **907**.

885

Raising the wretch above your head, you hurl his body against the stone floor of the cell with such force that his back is broken.

Knowingly or otherwise, Renfield betrayed you; he does not deserve the gift of eternal life you could have bestowed upon him.

Becoming like mist again, you slip under the cell door and move through the corridors of the sprawling house unseen. In this fashion, you find your way to one room in particular and there find Lucy's friend – and Harker's beloved – Mina, asleep in bed.

Your first instinct is to kill her while she sleeps, and have those who have set themselves against you driven to distraction by her murder. But then you think again; you did not rise to become

Voivode of Wallachia without being able to turn an enemy's weakness to your advantage.

Mina is doubtless precious, not just to Harker but his allies as well. Killing her could make them even more dangerous, Harker in particular, for a man who has nothing to lose is willing to risk everything to achieve his ultimate goal. And who knows who else might be in on their plans? No, what you need is a spy in the enemy camp.

"Mina," you call to her in a keen, cutting whisper. She wakes with a start. Her eyes fix on you and the colour drains from her cheeks as a look of terror seizes her pretty face.

Gripping her firmly by the shoulder with one hand, you force her head back with the other, exposing her throat.

"First, a little refreshment to reward my exertions."

Bound by your curse now, she looks at you sidelong in bewilderment, whimpering as you place your mouth upon her throat. She swoons as you sink your fangs into her neck. As you drink, her strength becomes your strength, her knowledge your knowledge.

All your questions are answered then, how Harker escaped the Weird Sisters, how he and this woman were married, how Harker saw you abroad in London, and how Professor Van Helsing – Doctor Seward's mentor and teacher – interviewed her and realised that Lucy Westenra had been the victim of a vampire attack, all of which led to them resolving to hunt you down and put an end to you, aided by Lucy's betrothed, Arthur Holmwood, and another of her suitors, the American Quincey Morris.

"So you, like the others, would play your brains against mine. You would help these men to hunt me and frustrate me in my designs! You know now, and they will know before long, what it is to cross my path. They should have kept their energies for use closer to home. Whilst they played wits against me – against *me* who commanded nations, and fought for them, hundreds of years before any of you were born!

"I have made their beloved one, flesh of my flesh; blood of my blood; kin of my kin; and you shall be my companion and my helper. You are to be punished for what you have done, in aiding those who would thwart me. Now you shall come when I call. When I command it, you shall cross land or sea to do my bidding!"

With that, you open a vein in your breast. As the viscous, black fluid begins to ooze forth, you clasp her hands tight in one of yours, and with the other press her mouth to the wound, so that she must either suffocate or swallow some of your corrupted blood.

The door to the room is suddenly flung open, and the five men burst into the room. They cry out in horror at the scene that greets them, for by the moonlight streaming in through the window, they can see the white-clad figure of Mina kneeling on the edge of the bed, her face and the front of her nightdress filthy with your blood, while you tower over her.

Do you want to spring at the stupefied men and attack, while they are still in a state of horrified paralysis (turn to **110**), or do you want to make your escape before they can gather their wits and attack you themselves (turn to **254**)?

886

DR SEWARD'S DIARY

(Kept in phonograph)

26 September

Truly there is no such thing as finality. Not a week since I said 'finis', and yet here I am starting fresh again, or rather going on with the record...

Four days after the funeral of Lucy Westenra, on the evening of 26 September, Professor Van Helsing bounds into your study at Carfax Asylum, having spent the previous day and night in Exeter, and thrusts last night's *Westminster Gazette* in front of your nose.

"What do you think of that?" he asks, pointing out a piece about children being lured away at Hampstead.

You do not think much of it, as you read over the story, until you reach the passage where it describes the wounds found on the children's throats.

"The wounds they describe are like those on Lucy's neck."

"And what do you make of that?"

"I do not know what to make of it," you protest wearily, "only that, I suppose, whatever injured her must have injured these children too."

"Do you mean to tell me, John, that you have no suspicions as to what poor Lucy died of, not after all the evidence you have seen with your own eyes?"

"Of nervous prostration following a great loss of blood."

"And how was that blood lost?"

You can only shake your head in reply.

"You are a clever man, John," Van Helsing says, sitting down beside you, "but you are too prejudiced. You do not let your eyes see nor your ears hear, and you pay no heed to that which is outside your personal experience. Do you not think that there are things which you cannot understand, and yet which are; that some people can see things that others cannot? Science cannot explain everything!

"Do you not know that there are bats in the Pampas of South America that come out at night and open the veins of cattle and horses and suck them dry of their blood? Or that in some islands of the Western seas there are bats as big as foxes that hang from the branches of trees all day, only to descend on sailors sleeping on deck, because it is so hot, who are then found to be dead men by the morning?"

"Good God, Professor!" you cry. "Do you mean to tell me that Lucy was bitten by such a bat, and that such a thing is here, in London, in the nineteenth century? Professor, let me be your student again, so that I may apply your knowledge as you go on. I feel like a novice lumbering through a bog in the mist!"

"Then you must believe."

"Believe what?"

"Believe in things that you cannot. Do not let some previous conviction blind you to the truth."

"You mean you want me to keep an open mind."

"Ah, you remain my favourite pupil. Do you think those holes in the children's throats were made by the same creature that made the holes in Miss Lucy?"

"I suppose so," you reply.

"Then you are wrong. Oh, that it were so! But alas, no. It is something far, far worse. They were made by Miss Lucy!"

"Professor Van Helsing," you say, sheer anger rising inside you, "are you mad? You really think that Lucy is this Bloofer Lady the children talk of?"

"Would that I were!" he rails. "But tonight, I will prove to you that I am right, although I dearly wish that I was wrong. Dare you come with me?"

"Where are we going?" you ask him in bewilderment.

"That I will let you decide. I have learned from my friend Dr Vincent at the North Hospital that the latest young victim of the Bloofer Lady is being treated there. So we could visit the child at the hospital, or" – and at this he takes a key from his pocket – "we could visit the churchyard where Lucy lies interred. This is the key to the Westenra family tomb."

Your heart sinks, fearing that some dreadful ordeal awaits you. So, how will you answer?

"The hospital."   Turn to **903**.

"The churchyard."   Turn to **923**.

887

You hold the Count's furious gaze and manage not to pass out from fright.

"Is this how you repay my hospitality?" the Count roars. "Is this the betrayal I must suffer for taking you into the heart of my home?"

You cannot answer; his hold on your throat prevents you from speaking.

Rather than release the pressure, he merely tightens his grip. You pull at his fingers, trying to free yourself, but it is to no avail. As you are starting to pass out, with one sharp twist, in his rage he breaks your neck as easily as you would snap a twig.

Your adventure is over.

THE END

888

The road climbs steadily away from the river and you enter a range of wooded crags. It does not feel like you have gone many miles when you become aware of a slavering panting sound chasing you along the road.

"Wolves," Arthur growls, glancing back over his shoulder.

Turning in the saddle you look for yourself and see a number of lithe, dark shapes bounding along the road after you, their eyes shining silver in the moonlight.

You spur your desperate steed onwards but, hearing a savage snarl to your right, turn your attention back to your pursuers. The leader of the pack – a hulking, grey-furred beast, that seems almost as big as a bear – has caught up with you.

If you want to use *The Pen is Mightier* special ability, and you still can, turn to **22**. If not, turn to **43**.

889

It does not take you long to share what you know, as between you, you have not actually learned very much. You hope that the Professor has learnt more than you during his sojourns to Amsterdam.

Gain 2 *Blood* points and turn to **978**.

890

You slowly become aware of a whispering sound within the room. At first you think it must be a breeze blowing under a door, or through a crack in the wall, but as you listen more intently, you become convinced you can hear words within the susurration.

Curiosity getting the better of you, you close in on the source of the sound until you are standing before a table upon which rests a silver stand. Something is clearly resting on the stand, but a dusty silken cloth has been draped over it.

If you want to remove the cloth, turn to **949**. If not, turn to **919**.

891

The lights dim still further and then it is as if the flickering gas-flames detach from the lamps and drift towards the table where you and your fellow passengers are sitting. These conjured will-o'-the-wisps come to rest above the beautiful woman to your left and in their lambent glow she seems to sparkle, as if caught in a cascade of golden mote-shot light.

You stare at her in wonder, your hand slipping from hers.

As soon as the circle is broken, the golden glow vanishes from above the woman and is restored to the lounge lamps once more.

Turn to **987**.

892

Your pistol loaded with the remaining silver bullets, you take aim at the vampire and fire.

You have time to fire your gun three times. If all three shots hit Dracula, turn to **510**.

If not, for every shot that hits the vampire, make a note that you have already caused him 4 *Endurance* points damage; you will deduct these when you come to fight him.

Turn to **350**.

893

Unable to rid your mind of the homicidal look Renfield gave you, you feel compelled to visit him again that same evening, but this time ensuring there is a securely locked door between you.

When you come to his stinking cell, you find him sitting in a corner brooding. But when he becomes aware of your presence, he throws himself on his knees and implores you to let him have a kitten.

"My salvation depends upon it!" he cries forlornly.

But you remain firm and tell him that he cannot have such an animal, whereupon, without a word, he returns to his corner and sits down, gnawing at his fingers.

* * * *

After an unsettled night's sleep, you visit Renfield again very early the next morning, before the attendants make their rounds.

You find him up and humming a tune as he spreads out sugar, which he has saved, on his windowsill. He is clearly beginning his fly catching again, but cheerfully and with good grace.

Looking around for his birds, and not seeing them, you ask him where they have gone.

"All the little birds have flown," he replies, without turning round.

You can see a few feathers scattered about the room, and on his pillow you notice there is a drop of blood, but you think nothing more of it.

* * * *

One of the attendants, Straker, comes to see you in your office later that same day, and reports that Renfield has been very sick, disgorging a whole lot of feathers.

"My belief is, Doctor," he says, "that he has eaten his birds, and that he just took and ate them raw!"

* * * *

That night you give Renfield a strong opiate, enough to make even him sleep, and take away his pocketbook for closer scrutiny.

What you learn is that your Mr Renfield is a very peculiar kind of homicidal maniac. You will have to invent a new classification for him.

It is clear to you now that he desires to absorb as many lives as he can, and he has set out to achieve this in a cumulative way. He gave many flies to one spider and many spiders to one bird. He wanted a cat to eat all his birds and you can't help wondering what might have come next. (Tick off the code word *Zoophagous* and add 1 point to your *Terror* score.)

He has closed the account most accurately, and today has started a new record.

* * * *

If you want to continue the story as Dr Seward, turn to **906**. If you would prefer to continue the adventure as Mina Murray, turn to **476**.

894

The Count's hands close around your neck and he pulls you towards him, crushing your throat in his steely grip, as his reeking mouth opens wide.

(Add 1 *Terror* point and deduct 2 *Endurance* points.)

"Sir!" you gasp, in panicked desperation. "You are strangling me!"

Suddenly the burning red light in Count Dracula's eyes fades and he regains his previous composed demeanour, loosening his hands from about your throat.

Turn to **924**.

895

Beyond the archway is a dank passageway that ultimately leads to what appears to be a curious chapel, in which stands a stone altar. But rather than bearing the icons of Christianity, it reminds you of a shrine such as might be found in the ruins of ancient Rome or perhaps even Egypt.

The altar is covered with carvings of intertwining snakes while on top of it is an alabaster statue of a huge white serpent – or it could be a wingless dragon – a human figure trapped in its sculpted coils.

But what stops you in your tracks is the greatsword that is also lying on the altar, its polished blade gleaming in the light of your lantern. The quillons of its cross-guard have been fashioned to look like stylised dragon heads, their eye-sockets set with exquisitely-cut rubies.

Engraved into the blade itself, in an ornamented script, is what you take to be the name its maker gave it:

EFIL EHT SI DOOLB EHT

As long as you are wielding the blade in battle you may add 2 points when calculating your *Combat Rating*, and if you wound an opponent with it, you cause 1 additional point of damage.

Record the Dragon Sword on your Adventure Sheet but make a note that you may only use one weapon at a time – then turn to **835**.

896

Confronted by a plethora of holy symbols, sacred artefacts and superstitious charms, all three Strigoi retreat from you and so you press home your attack. As you advance upon them, their leathery skin blackens like charred parchment and their flesh withers, while the bones beneath crumble to dust.

Restore one use of *The Pen is Mightier* special ability and turn to **856**.

897

With a final powerful swing of your heavy knife, you decapitate your attacker.

Turn to **914**.

898

The more you let the beast feed, the more it wants to feed, or so it seems. Not even a week has passed when you emerge again, at night, to hunt. While the rest of the crew hides below decks, the Second Mate has been left to steer the ship alone.

Perhaps it is the Russian's own sixth sense working overtime, or perhaps it is just chance that he happens to turn your way as you are attempting to creep up on him, but it gives him time to arm himself with a broken marlinspike.

He is a large man, muscular, and you suspect has spent time serving in the military, judging from the fighting stance he assumes.

He lunges at you with his makeshift weapon, and you catch the metal point between your hands before it can pierce your chest. And then you are wrestling with the Second Mate for control of the marlinspike.

Take a Combat test. If you pass the test, turn to **929**. If you fail the test, turn to **950**.

899

"Will you play with me?" the child asks again, a trickle of dark red blood escaping the corner of its mouth, as it reaches for you with fingers that are knotted into arthritic talons.

Take a Terror test. If you pass the test, turn to **828**. If you fail the test, turn to **858**.

900

You wake with a start, panting for breath and your heart pounding. Your horrible nightmare has shaken you to the very core of your being. (Add 1 point to your *Terror* score.)

There is no sign of the Professor and the holy circle remains unbroken. Dusk is laying its mantle over the mountains and so you put more wood on the fire, rousing it back into life.

As your eyes are searching the gathering gloom again for your guardian, you suddenly catch sight of him, approaching from the direction of the castle. From his gait, he appears almost overcome with exhaustion and is carrying something.

As he draws closer you see that he is holding the severed heads of the three vampyre women by the long tresses of their hair, and in his other hand he still holds the knife that carried out the bloody deed.

"It is done," he says, throwing his grim trophies onto the fire. "Hardly had my knife severed the head of each before the whole body crumbled to dust."

Seeing the Vampire-Hunter standing there, so noble and so proud, afraid to do naught in protection of your immortal soul, you feel a stirring within your breast, and you are filled with the wanton desire to plant kisses upon his face and neck.

"Come to me, Professor," you say in a lascivious tone. "Let me wrap you within my arms and comfort you."

"Madam Mina?" he gasps, as if seeing you for the first time. "What has come over you?"

"Come to me," you say again, your outstretched arms reaching for him, to enfold him within your embrace. "Lie here with me. Be as one with me."

"No, Madam Mina, I shall not!" he rails. "You do not know what you are saying. You do not want this!"

"Oh, but I do," you reply, licking your lips with the tip of your tongue and giving a cry of pain and delight as it catches on the sharpened points of your elongated canines. "I want you, Professor Van Helsing."

You will not take no for an answer, and as you advance upon the old man, he tightens his grip on the bloody knife, ready to defend himself.

If you want to call upon *The Pen is Mightier* special ability, cross off one use and turn to **964**. If not, turn to **918**.

901

No one sleeps well that night, for Renfield's screams echo through the cold corridors of the asylum, and the terrible words he utters between the blood-curdling howls, disturb the balance of the minds of the other inmates.

When you do grab a few minutes' shut-eye, you imagine yourself a fly, trapped between the lunatic's filthy fingertips, as he moves you inexorably towards his champing mouth, his teeth black and rotten from decay and with hairy black flies' legs and iridescent wings stuck between them.

Add 1 point to your *Terror* score and deduct 2 *Endurance* points as a result of your nightmare-plagued slumber.

Turn to **921**.

902

The something raises its head and from where you are you get the impression of a colourless bestial face. From sunken hollows within the hideous visage, two red gleaming eyes fix you with a bloody stare.

Take a Terror test. If you pass the test, turn to **882**. If you fail the test, turn to **862**.

903

The afternoon is passing quickly and so you hasten to the hospital. You find the child awake, it having slept for much of the day, and taken some food. Indeed, it appears to be doing well.

But when Dr Vincent takes the bandage from its throat and shows you the puncture marks and worried at flesh, there can be no mistaking the similarity to those you saw on Lucy's neck.

You ask Dr Vincent what he attributes them to, and he tells you that he believes it was probably caused by a bite of some animal, perhaps a rat, or possibly a bat. "Some sailor may have brought one home, and it managed to escape," he says, "or perhaps one escaped from the Zoological Gardens. These things do occur, you know. Only ten days ago a wolf got out."

* * * *

By the time you leave the hospital, the sun has already dipped below the horizon.

"And now I think we should visit the churchyard at Kingstead, where Miss Lucy lies," Van Helsing says, and you see no reason to argue with him.

Turn to **923**.

904

You fight with a righteous, vengeful fury, against which no mere servant of the vampire can stand, and another foe falls to your blade.

If the *Blood* score is 15 points or higher, turn to **933**. If the *Blood* score is lower than 15, turn to **762**.

905

"Begone, demon!" you command the Djinn, and are somewhat taken aback when you see a shudder pass through its nebulous form. The thick black smoke then pours itself back into the flask, still held in the stunned Magus's hands.

Deduct 3 *Blood* points and turn to **33**.

906

DR SEWARD'S DIARY

(Kept in phonograph)

19 August

Strange and sudden change in Renfield last night. About eight o'clock he began to get excited and sniff about as a dog does when settling...

It is Straker who summons you, after Renfield, who is usually respectful to the attendant, and at times even servile, would not condescend to talk with him at all.

You visit him yourself at just after nine o'clock, but he treats you with the same indifference he demonstrated towards Straker. It is as if he is possessed by some form of religious mania, and he will soon think of himself as God! You must continue to observe him carefully, for a strong man with both homicidal and religious mania might be dangerous.

For half an hour or more Renfield keeps getting excited to a greater and greater degree. And then, all at once, that shifty look comes into his eyes, which you have noticed is always there when this madman has seized upon an idea, and with it the shifty movement of the head. He becomes quiet again and sits on the edge of his bed, resignedly staring into space with lacklustre eyes.

In an attempt to ascertain whether he is feigning this sudden apathy, or whether it is the real thing, you try to get him to talk to you about his pets, a theme that has never failed to excite his attention in the past.

"Bother them all!" he snaps testily. "I don't care a pin about them!"

"What?" you say, taken aback. "You don't mean to tell me you don't care about spiders?" Spiders being his hobby again at present.

To this challenge he replies enigmatically, "The bridesmaids rejoice the eyes that await the coming of the bride, but when the bride draws nigh, then her maids shine not so brightly."

He will not explain himself further but remains obstinately seated on his bed.

You are weary this night and in low spirits, and so end your assessment of Renfield and return to your study. You cannot stop thinking about Lucy, and how different things might have been if she had but accepted your proposal of marriage.

Regardless of how tired and overwrought you feel, you fear tonight shall be a sleepless one. Of course, to save yourself from such sleepless misery, you could take a measure of chloral – that modern Morpheus! – although you must be careful not to let it grow to become a habit.

If you want to take a dose of the sleeping draught, turn to **926**. If you would prefer not to, in case you become reliant on the sedative, turn to **945**.

907

The mortal remains of the Countess Dolingen of Gratz crumble to dust, as time and age catches up with her at last.

The Englishman lies unmoving in the snow, and while you can still sense his heartbeat, it is weak and fluttering. You are sure that the maitre d'hotel of the Quatre Saisons will even now be acting on your missive, sending people to find the missing man, but if they do not get here soon, Harker will likely die of exposure before they can reach him. It is up to you to keep him alive.

And so, in the form of a wolf, you lie down on top of him, covering his body with yours. The heat of this animal form gives warmth to his chilled body.

* * * *

Time passes, during which the man beneath you moans and whimpers, as if wracked by horrible dreams, until at last you sense the thundering pulses of both men and horses, and a cry of "Holloa! Holloa!" rings through the trees.

You cry out in response, in your wolf-voice, your yelps drawing the hunters to the spot where Harker lies. You can see a red glare moving through the grove of cypresses, dancing over the white pall which stretches into the darkness around you, and steadily drawing closer. All at once, from beyond the trees, there comes a troop of horsemen bearing torches.

You rise, knowing that the Englishman will be safe now, and head towards the snow-clad trees that lie beyond the cemetery wall. As you do so, one of the horsemen – who are soldiers, judging by their caps and long military cloaks – raises a carbine, takes aim, and fires, the shot zipping over your head.

Moving at a gallop, the troop splits into two distinct groups – one that rides towards where Harker is lying in the snow, slowly gaining consciousness, and another that is clearly coming in pursuit of you.

Do you want to turn and meet the hunters' charge (turn to **932**), or will you increase your pace in the hope of fleeing this place (turn to **975**)?

908

Suddenly the bat gives a piercing cry and takes off into the night. The wolf howls, as if in response, and takes off after it, disappearing down the road into the darkness.

Your heart racing, you follow the wolf's path back through the rhododendrons, wondering where it can possibly have come from and desperately hoping that Lucy has not suffered some terrible, night-time visitation.

If the *Blood* score is equal to or greater than 3, turn to **938**. If it is lower, turn to **992**.

909

You feel heartened to hear every member of your band share what they have learned about the fiend and his ways, as you begin to believe that, between you, you might actually be able to stop him.

Deduct 1 *Blood* point and 1 *Terror* point, and then turn to **978**.

910

Although you all set off in pursuit, you find the stable door is bolted, and by the time you manage to force it open the Count has fled, leaving no sign of his passing. It is late afternoon and sunset is not far off. With heavy hearts you have to accept that the game is up.

"Let us go back to Madam Mina," Van Helsing says. "All we can do just now is done, and we can there, at least, protect her. But we need not despair. There is but one more box of earth, and we must not rest until we find it. When that is done, all may yet be well."

You can see that the purpose of his words is to comfort Harker as best he can. The poor fellow is quite broken, now and again giving a low groan that he cannot suppress as he thinks of his wife, and her present condition.

Harker has been quite overwhelmed by what has befallen his precious Mina. Yesterday he was a frank, happy-looking man, with a strong, youthful face, full of energy, and with dark brown hair. But today he has the appearance of a drawn, haggard old man, whose white hair matches well with the hollow burning eyes and grief-written lines of his face.

* * * *

It is with sad hearts you return to Purfleet, where you find Mrs Harker waiting for you, with an appearance of cheerfulness that does her bravery and unselfishness honour. But when she sees your faces, her own becomes as pale as death.

Turn to **971**.

911

The gas-lamps dim still further as Count Yorga continues his chanting. But then you become aware of another sound, as if the liquid from a spilled drink is dribbling off the edge of the table.

Following the sound to its source, you are horrified to see that the wolfish-looking man now appears to be sitting under a dripping cascade of blood that is pouring from the roof of the carriage.

You are so appalled by this gory vision that you break hands with your companions. The lights in the lounge abruptly come back to full brightness.

Add 1 point to your *Terror* score and turn to **987**.

912

As you approach the tomb, it quickly becomes apparent that it is the corpse of the man you have been searching for. But what can have happened to him?

The Professor examines the body as best he can by the light of the moon.

"His throat has been torn out," he says gravely. "It looks like the work of some wild beast."

At that moment the howling starts up again, only this time it sounds like a whole pack of wolves.

"There is nothing more we can learn from Herr Skinsky," Van Helsing says, his eyes searching the encroaching gloom for Quincey Morris.

If you want to go looking for Quincey yourself, turn to **982**. If you would prefer to champion the idea of leaving the graveyard as quickly as possible, turn to **942**.

913

Finding the small pyramid of stones half-buried by the snow, you start to hack at the frozen ground with the point of your knife. Your companion joins you, without passing comment, and soon you have dug deep enough to reveal the treasure that was hidden here who knows how many years ago.

It is a wooden chest. Pulling it free of the earth, you smash the lock with the butt of your revolver and throw open the lid. The chest contains a curious collection of items – ancient gold coins, a tarnished knife, a helmet, a rusted chainmail shirt – that look like they could have belonged to some crusader knight who must have died centuries ago.

The coins doubtless have some value, but the ancient armour and the knife are useless now. At the bottom of the casket, you find the knight's shield; it is in a poor state of repair, but it is still emblazoned with the red cross of St George.

If you want to take the Knight's Shield with you, record it on your Adventure Sheet. You may use the shield to protect yourself in battle, but if you do this, you may not use your revolver at the same time. You must also reduce your *Combat* score by 1 point for as long as you are using the shield, but you may reduce any damage you suffer by 1 point too.

You cannot delay here any longer, and so, mounting your steed, you set off again after your quarry – turn to **968**.

914

The chapel is suddenly awash with noise, the desperate cries of your compatriots, the crack of pistol-shots, and the tearing of wood echoing from its vaulted roof as more Strigoi break free of their confinement and attack your fellow Vampire-Hunters.

You throw yourself into the fray, in an effort to aid them in their hour of need.

You need to work out how many of the unleashed Strigoi you and your companions manage to destroy.

Take an Agility test, a Combat test, an Endurance test, an ESP test, and a Terror test. Then roll one die (or pick a card). You may also choose to spend one use of *The Pen is Mightier* special ability. Having done all these things, consult the list below to see how many points you have scored.

Passed the *Agility test*	+1 point
Passed the *Combat test*	+1 point
Passed the *Endurance test*	+2 points
Passed the *ESP test*	+1 point
Passed the *Terror test*	+1 point
The number rolled is even (or the card is black)	+1 point
Used *The Pen is Mightier* special ability	+2 points

You have the *Strigoi* code word ticked off +1 point

You have the *Pestis* code word ticked off −1 point

Once you have calculated your points total, turn to **937**.

915

The novice nun's initial invitation revoked by the Sister's declamation, you race for the gatehouse and away from the Hospital of St Joseph and Ste Mary, feeling your skin start to blister and burn, as the holy aura of the place starts to overwhelm you.

Roll one die and add 1 to the number rolled; deduct this many points from your *Endurance* score. (Alternatively, pick a card and deduct that many *Endurance* points, unless it is greater than 7 or a picture card, in which case deduct 7 *Endurance* points.)

If you lose 4 *Endurance* points or more, also deduct 1 *Agility* point and 1 *Combat* point.

Turn to **810**.

916

Two of the Strigoi wither when exposed to votive symbols, leaving just one for you to deal with via the tried and tested method of close quarters combat. (In this battle, you have the initiative.)

STRIGOI   COMBAT 6   ENDURANCE 6

If you manage to destroy the remaining resurrected corpse, turn to **856**.

917

In the face of the Count's fury, you pass out from shock.

(Lose 2 *Endurance* points, add 2 points to your *Terror* score, and gain 2 *Blood* points.)

* * * *

When you come to again, you are lying on a couch, and the Count has gone.

Driven almost mad by fear, you dare not leave the room again, and so have no choice but to wait for whatever dark fate the future has in store for you to come to pass.

Turn to **947**.

918

"Come to me, Professor," you say again, unable to help yourself. "Do not resist. Come to me. Come. Come!"

Reluctantly, Van Helsing raises his knife, prepared to finish you if it means that, in the end, he can finish Count Dracula. (In this battle you have the initiative.)

PROFESSOR VAN HELSING   COMBAT 8   ENDURANCE 8

If the Professor wins two consecutive Combat Rounds, turn to **964** at once. If you manage to win the fight without Van Helsing ever winning two consecutive Combat Rounds, turn to **944**.

919

Unnerved more by the thought of what could be making the sound than the whispering itself, you decide not to tarry here any longer.

Add 1 point to your *Terror* score and then turn to **59**.

920

Although you all set off in pursuit, you find the stable door is bolted, and by the time you manage to force it open the Count has fled, leaving no sign of his passing. It is late afternoon and sunset is not far off. With heavy hearts you have to accept that the game is up.

"Let us go back to Madam Mina," Van Helsing says. "All we can do just now is done, and we can there, at least, protect her. But we need not despair. There is but one more box of earth, and we must not rest until we find it. When that is done, all may yet be well."

You know that the Professor is trying to offer you comfort, as best he can, but having battled the Count inside the house only for him to escape you once again, you feel the weight of your grief overcome you, and cannot help but give voice to a groan of despair as you think of your wife, and what the monster has done to her.

Catching your reflection in the blade of your knife you are shocked into inaction. Yesterday you could have considered yourself a generally happy-looking man, with a strong, youthful face, full of energy, and with a mane of dark brown hair. Today you barely recognise yourself. It is as if you are looking into the face of your father; you have acquired the appearance of a drawn, haggard old man, your white head of hair matching well with the hollow burning eyes and grief-written lines etched into your face.

(Add 1 point to your *Terror* score, and deduct 1 point from your *Agility* score, and 1 point from your *Combat* score.)

* * * *

With sad hearts your party returns to Carfax Asylum, where you find Mina waiting for you, with an appearance of cheerfulness that does her bravery and unselfishness honour. But when she sees you, the colour drains from her face.

For a second or two she closes her eyes, as if in secret prayer, before opening them again.

"I can never thank you all enough," she says. Taking your grey head in her hands she kisses you, whispering through her tears, "Oh, my poor darling!"

Turn to **951**.

921

You continue to make regular visits to check on your other patient, Miss Lucy Westenra, and when you make a house call next, on Monday 6 September, you find that her condition has worsened again.

Mrs Westenra is naturally anxious about her daughter and consults with you professionally about her. You tell her that you will summon your old master, Professor Van Helsing, the great specialist, to come at once, and that you will treat her together.

And so you send a telegram to Van Helsing, asking him to return to England with haste, and you write a letter to poor Arthur, updating him on Lucy's condition.

* * * *

Van Helsing arrives from Amsterdam the very next day.

The first thing he says to you when you meet at Liverpool Street Station is, "Have you said anything to our young friend, Lucy's lover, Arthur?"

"I only wrote to him telling him that you were coming, as Miss Westenra was not so well," is your answer.

"Quite right! Better he not know as yet. Let me caution you, my good friend John. You deal with madmen, but all men are mad in some way or other. You and I shall keep what we know here, and here."

At this he touches you on the heart and on the forehead, and then touches himself in the same way.

"You were always a careful student, and your case book was ever more full than the rest," he goes on gravely. "I trust you still practise that good habit, for knowledge is stronger than memory and we should not trust the weaker. Record everything – no detail is too small – even your doubts and surmises. We learn from failure, not from success!"

* * * *

When you arrive at Hillingham, you are met by Mrs Westenra. She is understandably concerned for her daughter, but fully aware of her own failing health, you set down a rule that she should not be present with Lucy, or think of her illness more than is absolutely required. She assents readily, and Van Helsing and yourself are shown up to Lucy's room by a maidservant.

If you were shocked when you saw her yesterday, you are horrified by the change you see in her today.

She is as white as a ghost. The red blush has gone even from her lips and gums, the bones of her face stand out prominently, and her breathing is painful to hear. Lucy lies there motionless and does not even have the strength to speak.

Van Helsing's face sets like marble, and his eyebrows converge till they almost touch over his nose. He guides you out of the room again and the instant the door is closed, he says in a harsh whisper, "My God! This is dreadful! There is no time to lose, or she will die for sheer want of blood. We must carry out a blood transfusion at once. But who shall be the donor? You or me?"

Roll one die (or pick a card). If the number rolled is odd (or the card is red), turn to **7**. If the number rolled is even (or the card is black), turn to **27**.

922

"Lucy! Lucy!" you call out in fright, as another cloud passes before the face of the moon.

Your friend does not answer, and you run on to the entrance of the churchyard. As you enter, the squat church building is between you and the seat, and for a minute you lose sight of her.

Gain 2 *Blood* points and then turn to **842**.

923

It is after ten o'clock when you reach the wall of the churchyard, and are forced to help each other climb over, the gates to the cemetery being locked. After some searching, for it is very dark, you find the Westenra tomb.

Using the key, the Professor opens the creaking door, and the two of you enter. Once inside, Van Helsing takes a matchbox and a piece of candle from his bag and makes a light.

The flowers that were placed in the tomb, at the same time as Lucy's coffin, hang lank and dead, their white petals turning to the colour of rust, their green leaves and stems to browns, lending the place a gruesome air. The reflection of the feeble glimmer of the candle's illumination from the time-discoloured stone, the dust-encrusted mortar, the dank iron and tarnished brass, and the clouded silver-plating of ancient coffin handles only add to the miserable atmosphere within the place.

Locating Lucy's coffin among those of her ancestors, Van Helsing takes a set of tools from his bag and sets about opening it.

When he is done, your heart thudding in your chest, you help him lift off the lid, dreading what you might find.

"Are you satisfied now, my friend?" he asks, as you stare in shock at the empty coffin.

"Lucy's body is not here!" you exclaim in horror.

(Add 2 points to your *Terror* score.)

"And how do you account for that?"

"Perhaps a body-snatcher?" you suggest. "Some of the undertaker's people may have stolen it." But even as you say the words, you feel that such a suggestion is mere folly.

"If you must have more proof, come with me."

Arming yourself with a crowbar from the Professor's bag of tools, you leave the tomb again, much to your great relief.

Locking the door once more Van Helsing says, "We must keep watch. You on one side of the churchyard and I on the other. Where would you prefer to perform your sentry duty?"

How will you answer?

"The western side of the churchyard, in the shelter of the yew trees." Turn to **943**.

"The eastern side of the churchyard, by the boundary wall." Turn to **963**.

924

"Take care how you cut yourself," he growls. "In this country it is more dangerous than you think."

He seizes the shaving glass. "And this is the wretched thing that has done the mischief. It is a foul bauble of man's vanity. Away with it!"

Gain 2 *Blood* points and turn to **954**.

925

Sweeping your blade through the smoke, you are surprised and thrilled when you hear what sounds like a shrill shriek of pain, and a few drops of inky black liquid drip onto the ornate rug at your feet.

If the Djinn can bleed, then it can be killed. But equally, that which bleeds can also manifest claws with which to defend itself against an attacker. (In this battle, you have the initiative.)

DJINN   COMBAT 10   ENDURANCE 7

If you win your battle with the supernatural spirit, how long did the battle last? If it lasted for 8 Combat Rounds or fewer, turn to **33**. If it lasted for more than 8 Combat Rounds, turn to **113**.

926

You pour a measure of the sedative solution into a glass and swallow it down. It does not take long for its soporific properties to take effect and you lie down on your unmade bed without even getting undressed, and let sweet, dreamless oblivion take you.

Turn to **322**.

927

Having formed a bond with the young redhead, you continue to feed from her, when you can, even flying to the house where she is staying, in the form of a bat, in order to drink her blood.

But her friend Mina seems to have an uncanny awareness of what you are doing and thwarts you at almost every turn, so that you gain little sustenance from the wretched creature you have chosen to help you create a new dynasty of the undead on English shores, at the very heart of the British Empire.

Gain 2 *Blood* points, restore up to 4 *Endurance* points, and turn to **341**.

928

"You look like you could do with a hand!" Quincey Morris says, joining you beside the cart. But before he can make good on his offer of help, the giant gypsy gives a terrible roar and lashes out. Quincey gasps as the brute's razor-sharp claws rake his ribs, and collapses onto the snow.

You engage the Szgany shape-changer before he becomes a bear entirely. (Who has the initiative in this battle will depend on how you arrived at this point.)

WEREBEAR   COMBAT 10   ENDURANCE 10

If you win the fight, turn to **595**.

929

You wrench the spike from the ruffian's hands and cast it away from you. It spears through the air and lands amidst the waves a good distance from the ship.

But the Second Mate is not done yet, picking up an axe, he goes for you with that instead. (You have the initiative in this battle.)

SECOND MATE   COMBAT 10   ENDURANCE 10

If you wish, you may spend 3 *Blood* points to automatically kill the Russian – make the appropriate adjustments on your Adventure Sheet and turn to **980**.

If not, conduct the battle as normal. If you win the fight, how long did it last? If it lasted for 10 Combat Rounds or fewer, turn to **980**. If it lasted for more than 10 Combat Rounds, turn to **995**.

930

As you pause to light the lantern you had the presence of mind to grab from among your belongings before setting off after the Count, the wick flares into life, illuminating an ornamental stone shield above a cracked archway. The coat-of-arms is superimposed with the carved relief of a mighty dragon, its wings and tail curled about it.

You recognise it at once. It is the insignia of the Order of the Dragon, the noble brotherhood of knights to which Count Dracula once belonged.

The vampire's trail does not lead that way, but further into the darkness of the catacombs.

Do you want to keep following the Count (turn to **835**), or do you want to see what lies beyond the archway (turn to **895**)?

931

The gas-lamps dim and Count Yorga intones in a heavily-accented voice, "Is there anybody there?"

For a moment his question is met with nothing but silence. But then, as if coming from very far off, you hear a disembodied phantasmal voice cry out, "Mina? Mina, is that you?"

"Lucy?" you reply in barely more than a whisper, as the temperature in the lounge suddenly drops dramatically.

"It is you!" the disembodied voice declares in delight, sounding both louder and closer now. "Oh, Mina, how I've missed you!"

"Lucy!" you call out, tears running down your cheeks. "Where are you? Are you all right?"

"There's no time for that," Lucy replies. "You must listen to me. He knows you are coming for him. He knows you are coming..."

And then, just as suddenly as it manifested, the voice fades and is gone.

(Add 1 point to your *ESP* score and deduct 1 *Blood* point.)

Breaking hands with your companions, you wipe the tears from your eyes as the light in the carriage rises once more. The séance is over.

What do you want to do now?

Interview the ratty little man?	Turn to **727**.
Question the beautiful young woman?	Turn to **767**.
Interrogate the wolfish-looking older man?	Turn to **787**.
Draw this matter to its conclusion?	Turn to **987**.

932

You turn, snarling like a cornered animal, and rise onto your hind-legs, become something more than wolf but less than human – the ultimate predator! (In this battle, the Hunters have the initiative, but you can fight them one at a time.)

	COMBAT	ENDURANCE
First HUNTER	7	7
Second HUNTER	8	8
Third HUNTER	8	7

As soon as you manage to defeat one of the soldiers, you may choose to flee the battle; deduct 4 *Endurance* points and turn to **975**. But if you fight to the bitter end and win, turn to **955**.

Alternatively, you can choose to deduct 3 *Blood* points and turn to **975** straightaway.

933

As the molten iron orb of the sun disappears behind the snow-capped peaks of the Carpathian Mountains, accompanied by a terrible splintering sound, something monstrous bursts through the lid of the box.

In that moment, everyone freezes – Vampire-Hunters, Szgany, and even the pack of wolves – and all eyes fix upon the vampire.

Dracula rises from the crate of earth in all his dark majesty, terrible and glorious, indomitable and unconquerable, an expression of twisted fury on his ancient face. And you see him at last for the hideous undying horror he really is, for before he was a vampire he was already a monster.

He fixes you with blazing, blood-red eyes and says, "Come to me, my child."

If you have the code word *Lycanthropy* ticked off, turn to **30**. If not, turn to **100**.

934

Roll one die (or pick a card). If the number rolled is odd (or the card is red), turn to **23**. If the number rolled is even (or the card is black), turn to **304**.

935

You are also struck by the heavy beam that is attached to the bottom of the sail. (Lose 4 *Endurance* points.)

Enraged now, your animalistic nature coming to the fore, you tear through the calico with claws bared.

Make a note that in the battle to come your opponent has the initiative and then turn to **778**.

936

Screeching like a banshee, an apparition suddenly flies towards you from the direction of the gate, its white robes flapping behind it. It is the novice you met at the entrance to the hospital, and whose blood you partook of.

Her fingers locked like hooked talons, she launches herself at the Sister, the older woman crying out in alarm as the novice tries to scratch her face with her fingernails. "Leave my master alone!" she screams.

If you want to make your escape while Sister Agatha is preoccupied with the ravening harridan, turn to **915**. If you want to use this opportunity to strike Sister Agatha down, turn to **879**.

937

The number of points you have scored is the total number of Strigoi that have already been dealt with, one way or another, by your brave band. Deduct this total from 20, then divide the remaining number by four, rounding fractions up; this is the total number of Strigoi you personally still have to fight. Each of them has the following stats, and you must fight any remaining Strigoi at the same time. (In this battle, you have the initiative.)

| STRIGOI | COMBAT 6 | ENDURANCE 6 |

If you manage to put down all of the undead host, turn to **967**.

938

You make your way round to the back of the large house. You can see no lamps lit in any of the windows and there are no audible signs of disturbance – the place is as quiet as the grave – so you hear the skittering of disturbed earth coming from a walled section of the garden quite clearly.

Warily, you make your way across the moonlit lawn as clouds smother the face of the lambent orb, to what you soon realise is the cemetery where the Westenra family's pets have been buried over the years.

Something is worrying at one of the tiny graves, the name of the headstone unreadable in the darkness. You wonder if it's a fox, and approach with caution, picking up a stone ornament, in the form of a chubby cherub, on the way.

The clouds abruptly pass from before the moon and cold realisation forms a ball of ice in the pit of your stomach. The creature is not digging up the grave, it is trying to pull itself out of the hole it has excavated with its claws. The horrid thing is nothing more than ragged scraps of mangy fur, matted with clods of earth, clinging to the ossified carcass of a dog.

(Add 2 points to your *Terror* score.)

The resurrected dog does not growl, but finally manage to free itself from the ground and starts to move towards you, with jerky, almost insect-like, movements.

If you want to use *The Pen is Mightier* special ability, cross off one use and turn to **952**. If not, turn to **972**.

939

As each member of your party shares what they have discovered about the fiend and his evil ways – all too often as a result of first-hand experience – you are filled with the hope that, as a group, you are capable of stopping the monster.

Deduct 2 *Blood* points and 1 *Terror* point, and add 1 point to another attribute of your choice; then turn to **978**.

940

In a display of incredible, supernatural strength, you hurl the men from you, sending them crashing into the furniture.

But your pawn-turned-nemesis, Harker, was not involved in the initial assault, and he comes for you now, with a great silver-bladed knife in one hand.

If your rank is that of *Emperor of the Dead*, or you are willing to spend 3 *Blood* points, turn to **170** now. If not, make a note that Harker has the initiative in the battle to come and turn to **990**.

941

The Westminster Gazette

25 September

A HAMPSTEAD MYSTERY

During the past two or three days, several cases have occurred of young children straying from home or neglecting to return from their playing on the Heath. In all these cases the children were too young to give any properly intelligible account of themselves, but the consensus of their excuses is that they had been with a "Bloofer Lady".

It has always been late in the evening when they have been missed, and on two occasions the children have not been found until early the following morning. It is generally supposed in the neighbourhood that, as the first child missed gave as his reason for being away that a "Bloofer

Lady" had asked him to come for a walk, the others had picked up the phrase and used it as occasion served.

However, all those children who have been missed at night, have been slightly torn or wounded in the throat. The wounds seem such as might be made by a rat or a small dog, and although of not much importance individually, would tend to show that whatever animal inflicts them has a system or method of its own.

The police of the division have been instructed to keep a sharp look-out for straying children, especially the very young, in and around Hampstead Heath, and for any stray dog which may be about.

Turn to **886**.

942

"We should be away from this place," you say. "This is not England and who knows what horrors might await the unwary in a Romanian graveyard at night."

Everyone else reluctantly agrees, and so your party hastily makes its way – Quincey and the Professor included – back through the town to the hotel where you are to spend the night.

Turn to **678**.

943

You take your place behind a yew tree and commence your lonely vigil.

You hear a distant clock strike twelve, and then one, and two. You are chilled and unnerved, angry with the Professor for taking you on such a nocturnal errand, and with yourself for agreeing to go with him.

Suddenly you see something like a white streak pass between two dark yew trees, at the side of the churchyard. At the same time, you see a dark figure move off from the Professor's side of the burial ground, moving after it, and so you set off too.

A little way off, beyond the line of scattered juniper trees that border the pathway to the church, you see the apparition flit in the direction of the tomb.

Hearing a rustle of movement where you first spotted the white figure, you approach the place and find the Professor holding, in his arms, a tiny child.

"Are you satisfied now?" he asks, holding the sleeping infant out to you.

Striking a match, you check the child's throat, and see that it is without scratch or scar of any kind.

"We were just in time," the Professor says thankfully.

But now your only concerns are for the child's well-being and set off for home. At the edge of Hampstead Heath, hearing a policeman's heavy tramp, you lay the child on the pathway, where he might find it, realising that if you were to engage in conversation with the Peeler you would have to give an account of your movements during the night.

As you leave, without making a sound, you hear the policeman's exclamation of astonishment and know then that the child will be reunited with its mother before too long.

Dawn is colouring the clouds laid above the eastern horizon salmon pink when Van Helsing turns to you and says, "My mind is made up. Let us go. You return home for tonight to your asylum and see that all is well. As for me, I have things to do. Meet me again at the Berkley Hotel two nights from now at ten o'clock. I shall send for Arthur to come too, and also that so fine young American, Quincey Morris. We shall all have work to do then."

Turn to **753**.

944

As Professor Van Helsing lies dying in your arms, his precious blood spoiling the pristine snow, he whispers his final words to you: "I forgive you, Mina."

You hesitate for a moment, wondering what he can possibly mean, and then sink your fangs into his throat, gorging yourself on the hot blood even as his failing heart stops beating.

You have made your first kill. Professor Van Helsing is dead by your hand. You are now the Count's creature, loyal only to His Dark Majesty, the oaths you swore to your friends and your husband forgotten. Indeed, you decide that Jonathan will be the next to feel your kiss.

While Van Helsing might be your first kill, Jonathan will be the first vampire you sire, and then you can live together forever, in service to Count Dracula, Voivode of Wallachia, King of Vampires and Emperor of the Dead.

Your adventure is over.

THE END

945

You retire to bed, but as you feared, you lie there, tossing and turning, and hear the clock strike twice. But it is then that the night watchman comes to see you, sent up from the ward, to share most dire news with you – Renfield has escaped from his cell!

You throw on your clothes and run down to the ward at once. Your zoophagous madman is too dangerous a person to be roaming about freely. You join the attendant Barlow at the door to Renfield's cell.

"I saw him not ten minutes before," Barlow says. "When I looked through the observation trap in the door, I thought he was asleep. But then I heard a harsh grating sound, and I ran back in time to see Mr Renfield's feet disappear through the space he had made by wrenching out the bars of the window!"

The madman is truly possessed of a terrifying strength!

The two of you hurry to the window and peer out into the darkness. Renfield only had his night gear on and so cannot have gone far.

Do you want to follow Renfield out through the window, and set off in pursuit of the madman (turn to **965**), or would you prefer to keep watching from the window, to see where he might have gone (turn to **69**)?

946

One of the unholy creatures crumbles to dust when exposed to your protective artefacts, leaving two for you to deal with using your sword and pistol. (In this battle, you have the initiative, but you must fight the Strigoi at the same time.)

	COMBAT	ENDURANCE
First STRIGOI	6	6
Second STRIGOI	7	6

If you manage to do away with the Transylvanian terrors, turn to **856**.

947

The twenty-ninth day of June arrives, the date of the last letter the Count instructed you to write, and you know that you are almost out of time.

The Count has taken steps to prove that the letters are genuine, and not written under coercion, for he has left the castle again, in the same lizard-like fashion as you have seen him adopt before, but this time wearing a suit of your own clothes – the same suit in which you made the journey to this accursed place.

This then has been his evil scheme all along; allowing others to see you – as they think, believing him to be you – so that he may both leave evidence that you have been seen in the towns or villages posting your own letters, and that any wickedness which he may do shall be attributed to you by the local people.

As you watch him climb down the wall, headfirst, you wish you had a gun, or some other lethal weapon, that you might destroy him. But you fear that no weapon wrought by man's hand alone would have any effect on him.

You dare not wait to see him return, and so return to the library, and read there until you fall sleep.

* * * *

You are awakened by the Count himself, who looks at you as grimly as any man could look.

"Tomorrow, my friend, we must part," he says. "You return to your beautiful England, I to some work which may have such an end that we may never meet. Your letter home has been despatched. Tomorrow I shall not be here, but all shall be ready for your journey. In the morning come the Szgany, for they have some labours of their own here, but when they are gone, my carriage shall come for you, and shall bear you to the Borgo Pass, to meet the stagecoach that travels the road from Bukovina to Bistritz."

"Why may I not go tonight?" you ask, determined to test his sincerity.

"Because, dear sir, my coachman and horses are away on a mission."

"But it would be my pleasure to walk."

He smiles such a soft, smooth, diabolical smile, that you know there is some dark intention hidden beneath his veneer of civility. "And what of your baggage?"

"I do not care about it," you say, and truly you do not – not anymore. "I can send for it some other time."

"Come then, my young friend," says the Count. "Not an hour shall you wait in my house against your will, though sad am I at your going, and that you so suddenly desire it. Come!"

With a stately gravity, he takes up the lamp and leads you through the castle, down the stairs and along the hall. Upon reaching the door, he draws back the ponderous bolts, unhooks the heavy chains, and begins to draw it open. You cannot believe your luck!

But as the door begins to open, you hear the howling of wolves without, growing steadily louder and angrier.

With slavering jaws, bloody teeth, and their blunt-clawed feet, they come right up to the threshold until only the Count stands between you and the pack.

"Shut the door!" you hear yourself cry at the last possible moment. "I shall wait till morning."

With one sweep of his powerful arm, the Count throws the door shut, and the great bolts clang and echo through the hall as they shoot back into place.

In silence, you return to the library, and after a minute or two retire to your bedchamber.

Take an ESP test. If you pass the test, turn to **977**. If you fail the test, turn to **382**.

948

That night, you complete that day's entry in your journal with Lucy breathing softly in her sleep in the bed next to yours. She seems much improved, and you would be quite content if you only had news of Jonathan, God bless and keep him.

You in turn fall asleep as soon as you close your diary…

* * * *

Suddenly finding yourself wide awake, you sit up, with a horrible sense of fear clawing at your heart, and a distinct feeling of emptiness around you.

The room is dark, so you steal across to Lucy's bed and feel for her, but the sheets are empty. Lighting a match, you have your worst fears confirmed; Lucy is not in the room.

The door is shut but not locked, just as you left it the night before. Not wanting to wake Lucy's mother, who has been more than usually ill of late, you throw on some clothes and set out to look for Lucy yourself.

When you cannot find her anywhere inside the house, taking a heavy shawl with you, you head out into the sleeping town.

The clock strikes one as you leave the Crescent and there is not another soul in sight. You run along the North Terrace, but see no sign of the white figure, clad in nothing but her nightdress, that you are expecting.

At the edge of the West Cliff, above the pier, you look across to the East Cliff, in hope or fear – you're not sure which – of seeing Lucy in your favourite seat.

The moon is bright and full, with heavy, black, driving clouds, which throw the whole scene into a fleeting diorama of light and shade as they sail across it. For a moment you can see nothing, but then the shadow of a cloud moves on, revealing first the abbey ruins, followed by the church and then the churchyard.

And there, on the seat in question, the silver light of the moon strikes a half-reclining snowy white figure. Before the scene is obscured by shadow again, it seems to you as though something dark is standing behind the seat and bent over it. But what it was – whether man or beast – you do not know.

You do not wait to catch another glance but throw yourself down the steep steps to the pier and along by the fish-market to the bridge, which is the only way to reach the East Cliff. The town seems dead, for not another soul do you see abroad.

Your knees tremble and your breath becomes laboured as you toil up the endless steps to the abbey. It seems to you as though your feet are weighted with lead and every joint in your body restricted with rust.

Reaching the top of the winding steps, you can see the seat and there is undoubtedly something long and black bending over the white figure reclining upon it.

Take an ESP test. If you pass the test, turn to **902**, but if you fail the test, turn to **922**.

949

Pulling the cloth free, you immediately take a step back, giving your revulsion a voice, as you find yourself face to face with what appears to be a mummified head; the wrinkled grey-green flesh is as dry as a desert tomb and the eyes have dried up and turned to dust long ago. The straggly hairs of a beard still cover the sunken hollows of its cheeks and the bony point of its chin, while the top of the head is covered by an ancient turban.

And then you hear the whispering again, and realise it is issuing from between the dead man's dried-up lips.

Take a Terror test. If you pass the test, turn to **99**. If you fail the test, turn to **128**.

950

With an almighty tug, the brute wrenches the spike from of your grasp and tries to skewer you with it again. (The Second Mate has the initiative in this battle.)

SECOND MATE   COMBAT 10   ENDURANCE 10

If you wish, you may spend 3 *Blood* points to automatically kill the Russian – make the appropriate adjustments on your Adventure Sheet and turn to **980**.

If not, conduct the battle as normal. If you win the fight, how long did it last? If it lasted for 10 Combat Rounds or fewer, turn to **980**. If it lasted for more than 10 Combat Rounds, turn to **995**.

951

Mina awakens you early the next morning, as the grey of the coming dawn is turning the windows into sharp oblongs, and the gas flame is like a speck rather than a disc of light. "Go, call the Professor," she says hurriedly. "I want to see him at once."

"Why?" you ask.

"I have an idea. I suppose it must have come in the night and matured without me knowing it. He must hypnotise me before the dawn, and then I shall be able to speak. Go quick, dearest, the time is getting close."

Two or three minutes later, Professor Van Helsing is in the room, in his dressing-gown, while Arthur and Quincey are standing with Dr Seward at the door asking questions.

Turn to **689**.

952

The un-living horror takes two more jerky steps and then falls to pieces where it stands, whatever malign influence that gave it the semblance of life having passed from this place.

Barely able to countenance what you have witnessed here this night, and how you might reconcile what you have seen with your profound scientific beliefs, you dread to think what might await you inside the house.

Turn to **992**.

953

Quincey leads the way into the pass, and you stop some hours later, when the moon hangs high and full and cold in the cloud-chased sky.

As the pre-dawn colours the sky to the east pink, you mount up once more and press on.

Turn to **26**.

954

Opening the window with one wrench of his terrible hand, your host flings the mirror out of it. You hear the glass smash into a thousand pieces on the stones of the courtyard far below.

With that, the Count leaves again, without uttering another word.

When you go into the dining room, the Count is not there. He is not out on the stairs either but having ventured beyond the suite of rooms, you decide to explore further.

You soon stumble upon a room that faces towards the south. The view is magnificent, for the castle is on the very edge of a terrific precipice. A stone falling from the window would fall a thousand feet without touching anything! As far as the eye can see is a sea of green treetops, with occasionally a deep rift where there is a chasm. Here and there are silver threads where the rivers wind in deep gorges through the forests.

Exploring further, you find doors – doors, doors everywhere – but all locked and bolted. Only the windows in the castle walls seem to offer any available exit. The place is a veritable prison, and you are its prisoner!

* * * *

You find yourself thinking things that you dare not confess to your own soul, among them that you are the only living soul within Castle Dracula.

One thing is certain; the Count is the one who has made you a prisoner, and he alone is master of the secrets of this place, so you must keep your knowledge and your fears to yourself, for you will need your wits about you if you are to come through the other side of this ordeal.

You have hardly come to this conclusion when you hear the great door below shut, and suspect that the Count has returned. Hurriedly returning to your rooms, you are joined not long after by Count Dracula.

In an effort to hide your suspicions from him, and with a mind to finding out all you can that might help you effect an escape from your prison, you engage him on the subject of Transylvanian history, which he warms to wonderfully.

He speaks of battles in particular, striding about the room and acting out moments of pivotal action as if he had been present at them all, explaining that to a boyar like himself the pride of his house and name is his own pride, their glory his glory, and their fate his fate.

"And we Szekelys have a right to be proud," he exclaims, "for in our veins flows the blood of many brave races who fought for lordship of these lands. Is it a wonder that we were a conquering race, when in our veins runs the blood of Attila the Great? That when the Magyar, the Lombard, the Aver, the Bulgar, or the Turk poured in their thousands upon our borders we drove them back?

"And when shame fell upon my nation, when the flags of Wallach and the Magyar were trampled beneath the Crescent, who was it but one of my own race, who as Voivode, crossed the Danube and beat the Turk on his own ground?

"Mr Harker, the Szekelys – and the Draculas as their heart's blood, their brains, and their swords – can boast a record that upstart mushroom growths, such as the Hapsburgs and the Romanoffs, can never reach. But those warlike days are over, and blood is too precious a thing in these days of dishonourable peace, and the glories of the great races are now just a tale that is told."

The Count turns his gaze to a great crest in the shape of an ornamental shield bearing the bas-relief of a mighty dragon, its wings and tail curled about it – carved into the stonework above the mantelpiece.

If you want to ask him about the significance of the crest, turn to **831**. If you prefer to say nothing, turn to **861**.

955

The soldiers dead, their horses flee in terror, while you lap at the blood of the men pooling around their mauled bodies, its warmth melting the snow it touches.

(Gain 3 *Blood* points and restore up to 6 *Endurance* points.)

As you feed, a voice carries to your sharp ears: "Good news, comrades! His heart still beats!"

Certain now that the Englishman is safe, and your thirst slaked for the time being, you race away into the night.

If you have the code word *Apáca* ticked off, and want to act on it now, turn to **680**. If not, turn to **810**.

956

As the molten iron orb of the sun disappears behind the snow-capped peaks of the Carpathian Mountains, accompanied by a terrible splintering sound, something monstrous bursts through the lid of the box.

In that moment, everyone freezes – Vampire-Hunters, Szgany, even the pack of wolves – and all eyes fix upon the vampire.

Dracula rises from the crate of earth in all his dark majesty, terrible and glorious, indomitable and unconquerable, an expression of twisted fury on his face. And then his eyes fix upon yours.

"Come to me, Mina," he says. "Join me."

Without even realising what you are doing, you move towards him as if drawn by some magnetic force.

Seeing what is happening, your friends and your husband throw themselves at the vampire, but each one is cast aside as if he were no more than a flea. Here, in his home country, within sight of his ancient home, the power of Dracula is irresistible.

And yet their self-sacrifice distracts the monster, and you feel his grip on your body, mind and soul loosen slightly. But it is enough, and you try to fight back against the compulsion that is drawing you towards him.

Take a Combat test, adding 1 to the dice roll if the *Blood* score is 12 points or higher.

If you pass the test, turn to **756**. If you fail the test, turn to **807**.

957

But it would appear you have an ally of your own, in addition to the wolves and the Szgany. Mina Harker is here too. You call to her with your mind, and she is powerless to refuse you.

As the molten iron orb of the sun disappears behind the snow-capped peaks of the Carpathian Mountains, you burst from your crate of earth in an explosion of soil and splinters.

In that moment, everyone freezes – Vampire-Hunters, Szgany, and even the wolf pack – and all eyes fix upon you. But you have eyes only for one person.

Seeing a scar on Mina's forehead, bearing the imprint of a cross, you cannot help but smile, for you know that she is your creature now. All that there remains for her to complete her transformation, is for her to make her first kill.

"Come to me, Mina," you say, compelling her with your mind. "Join me."

Her will no longer her own, your new bride-to-be walks towards you through the snow that covers the ground, as if drawn by some magnetic force.

Divide your *Blood* score by 10, rounding fractions up. Then roll 1 die, and if the number rolled is equal or less than the resulting total, turn to **524**. If it is greater, turn to **582**.

958

LOG OF THE 'DEMETER'

2 August, midnight ~ Woke up from few minutes' sleep by hearing a cry, seemingly outside my port. Could see nothing in fog. Rushed on deck, and ran against mate. Tells me heard cry and ran, but no sign of man on watch. One more gone. Lord, help us! Mate says we must be past Straits of Dover, as in a moment of fog lifting he saw North Foreland, just as he heard the man cry out. If so we are now off in the North Sea, and only God can guide us in the fog, which seems to move with us; and God seems to have deserted us.

If your *Suspicion* score is 9 points or higher, turn to **162**; otherwise, turn to **270**.

959

It is suddenly as if you are within your own small bubble of calm, while the blizzard of battle whirls around you.

And then you hear the silky voice of the vampire inside your head:

You would help these men to hunt me and frustrate me in my designs! But you, their best beloved one, are now to me flesh of my flesh; blood of my blood; kin of my kin. You have aided in thwarting me, and yet you shall come when I call. And I call to you now. Come!

Take an ESP test, adding 1 to the dice roll if you have the code word *Lycanthropy* ticked off.

If you pass the test, turn to **410**. If you fail the test, turn to **979**.

960

The sudden rattling of a rope racing through a pulley takes you by surprise, but by the time you hear the trap being sprung, there is nothing you can do to avoid it. One of the ship's calico sails comes crashing down on top of you, trapping you beneath its heavy folds. But you will not remain trapped for long.

Add 1 *Suspicion* point and then *Take an Endurance test*. If you pass the test, turn to **830**, but if you fail the test, turn to **935**.

961

Your sixth sense is screaming at you that Count Yorga is hiding a dark secret and that he is the one you want.

Breaking hands with your companions, you jump to your feet, knocking your chair to the floor in the process, and declare, "Count Yorga, you are the killer! You murdered that poor young man!"

Turn to **682**.

962

The blood of the young woman is sweet and uncorrupted by alcohol or narcotics. Drinking it is like enjoying a fine Beaujolais.

(Gain 2 *Blood* points and restore up to 4 *Endurance* points.)

You do not take so much blood that she passes out, or her heart gives out; you just take enough to leave her swaying where she stands, her eyelids fluttering, as if she is on the verge of falling asleep.

Tick off the code word *Elesett* and turn to **256**.

963

You take your place on the far side of the churchyard, sheltered by the boundary wall, and you see the dark figure of Van Helsing head westwards, until the intervening headstones and yew trees hide him from your sight.

It is a lonely vigil. You hear a distant clock strike twelve, and then one, and two. You are chilled and unnerved, angry with the Professor for taking you on such a nocturnal errand, and with yourself for agreeing to go with him.

Hearing the disturbance of the loose earth atop a recently filled-in grave, you turn to see a child almost at your shoulder.

"Oh!" you gasp. "You made me start. What are you doing out here by yourself in the middle of the night?"

"We've been playing."

"Who has?" you ask, confused. The child – a boy – cannot be more than six years old.

"Me and the Bloofer Lady."

Your blood runs cold at mention of that name. As the child takes another step towards you, by the light of the moon you see that its face and hands are deathly pale, while the whites of its eyes are a deep crimson.

(Add 1 to your *Terror* score.)

"Will you play with me?" the child says smiling, exposing the sharp points of its elongated milk teeth, and your hand tightens on the crowbar.

If you want to employ *The Pen is Mightier* special ability, and you are still able to do so, cross off one use and turn to **993**. If not, turn to **899**.

964

Quick as a flash, Van Helsing strikes you over the head and grabs you with his free hand, squeezing a pressure point in your neck, and you lose consciousness immediately…

You come to again, not many minutes later, to find the Professor rubbing your face with cold snow. Thankfully the lascivious madness that had possessed you has passed, and you feel yourself once more.

You apologise profusely to the Professor for what you have subjected him to, but he dismisses it out of hand, such is this kind-hearted Dutchman's generosity of spirit.

Deduct 1 point from your *ESP* score and turn to **194**.

965

Barlow is a bulky man – giving him the strength to deal with unnaturally strong inmates like Renfield – and cannot squeeze through the window, but you can. And so, with Barlow's aid, you go out, feet foremost, and drop the six feet that remain to the ground.

Take an Agility test. If you pass the test, turn to **199**, but if you fail the test, turn to **985**.

966

As dusk falls and the shops start to shut up for the night, the girl boards the familiar carriage, which subsequently sets off along Piccadilly, heading for the centre of town. You hail a hansom of your own and instruct the driver, exerting the full force of your will, to follow it.

The carriage takes a circuitous route through the city streets until it finally enters a rundown area of Limehouse that is due for redevelopment, its mysterious passenger disembarking outside a boarded-up tannery. This hardly seems like the kind of place befitting of a young lady as refined as the girl in the cart-wheel hat.

Intrigued more than ever now, you dismiss the hansom and follow her through a narrow archway into a dark alleyway. The alleyway leads to another street, where vermin feed on piles of rotting rubbish that have been dumped on the cobbles.

You are rather surprised to find the young woman waiting for you, a serene smile on her perfect lips, but you are even more surprised when a figure emerges from a shadowed doorway and steps into the road between you. He is dressed in the manner of an eighteenth-century nobleman and looks like he has just stepped out of the pages of a James Malcolm Rymer novel.

"She's already taken," the man says, his intonation marking him out as a member of the British upper class, "my dear Penny Dreadful, isn't it, that she can't walk the streets of our fine city without receiving unwanted attention from a foreign upstart like you? And talking of this fine city, she's already taken too, sir!"

"And who are you," you demand, your voice a bestial growl, "to claim the capital of the British Empire as your own?"

"I have been known by many names over the years, as, no doubt, have you. I have gone by both Marmaduke Bannerworth and Sir Runnagate Bannerworth in the past, but now those who know of my existence at all know me as Sir Francis Varney. I know why you are here, and I know what you intend to do, but I am here to tell you, sir, that there isn't room in London for two vampires!"

With that, Varney sheds his human disguise, and you see him as he really is – a decomposing corpse!

What is your current rank?

Count Dracula, or below?	Turn to **536**.
Prince of Darkness?	Turn to **770**.
King of Vampires?	Turn to **845**.

967

With the destruction of the last of the living corpses, it seems as if some evil presence has quit the place and you feel your spirits rise, as the shadow of dread slips from you like a robe.

(Deduct 1 point from your *Terror* score.)

"Now we understand the Count's plan all the better," Van Helsing muses as he surveys the dismembered corpses that lie among the broken boxes. "He seeks to conquer this fair isle, and he brought an army to England to help him accomplish his goal. He wishes to tear down the established order and build an empire of the undead in its place! His old warlord habits have not left him."

You exchange horrified looks with your companions as the terrible truth that has been revealed to you starts to sink in.

"But come," the Professor goes on, "we must finish our work here to ensure that Dracula can never resurrect his strigoi to fight for him again."

Taking a tinderbox and matches from his bag, utilising the splintered planks of the broken boxes in which Dracula had hidden his vanguard of the undead, he prepares for each of you a blazing torch and between you, you set about creating a number of bonfires within the chapel.

The boxes and bodies already starting to burn, you leave the chapel, closing the door behind you, and quit the accursed Carfax House.

The morning is quickening in the east when you emerge from the shadowed entrance hall.

"Our night has been eminently successful," Van Helsing declares, smiling broadly. "Our first, and perhaps our most difficult and dangerous step has been accomplished, without troubling Madam Mina's waking or sleeping thoughts with sights and sounds and smells of horror, which she might never forget. And we know that twenty-one boxes have been moved from Carfax House.

"Our priority now must be to find those remaining boxes and cleanse them of all that might lie hidden within."

Turn to **20**.

968

The snow is falling more heavily now, and swirls about fiercely, for a high wind has started to blow. However, through pauses in the snow flurries, you see your quarry; the band of Szgany gypsies accompanying the leiter-wagon carrying the last remaining box of earth – and, no doubt, the fiend himself – towards Castle Dracula.

Beyond the white waste of snow, you make out the looming shadowy presence of the Count's decaying home, silhouetted against the sinking red orb of the sun.

"They are racing for the sunset!" your companion shouts over the panting of the horses, the pounding of their iron-shod hooves on the road, the clatter of the wagon, the moaning wind, and the howling of wolves. "We may be too late!"

If the *Blood* score is 12 points or higher, turn to **934**. If the *Blood* score is lower than 12, turn to **76**.

969

DR SEWARD'S DIARY

(Kept in phonograph)

22 September

It is over. Arthur has gone back to Ring, and has taken Quincey Morris with him. What a fine fellow is Quincey! If America can go on breeding men like that, she will be a power in the world indeed...

After the funeral, Arthur and Quincey go away together to the station, while Professor Van Helsing sets off for Amsterdam, promising to return tomorrow night. You return to Carfax Asylum in Purfleet alone, your only companion for the journey your own darkly melancholic thoughts.

As soon as the carriage pulls up outside the gates, you can hear the uproar that has consumed the place. Entering the building, you are greeted with a vision of bedlam.

You are met by Barlow. Blood runs from a crescent of tooth-marks in his cheek.

"What's going on?" you demand, feeling your ire rising.

"It's Renfield, Doctor," the burly attendant replies, a weary look in his eyes. "He got out of his cell again and proceeded to release the rest of the inmates on Dandrige Ward. We're in the process of containing the breakout. You should retire to your office, Doctor, and lock the door, for your own safety. I will come for you when the patients are back in their cells."

If you want to do as Barlow suggests and lock yourself in your office, turn to **866**. If you think you would be of more use on the ward, turn to **668**.

970

With their master flown, the wolves slink back into the trees, their hackles raised and growling in fear. Without the vampire's presence impelling them to fight back, the Szgany give up as well, too many of their number having already fallen to your bullets and blades.

Abandoning your companions, you set off in pursuit of your nemesis.

The supernatural monster leaves no footprints, but you have no trouble tracking him, thanks to the malodorous stench of the grave he leaves hanging in his wake, along with a lingering sense of evil.

You follow the fleeing Count through the dusty halls and cobwebbed corridors of his fortress stronghold, down a spiralling stone staircase and into the catacombs that lie buried beneath it.

If you have the code word *Sárkány* ticked off, turn to **930**. If not, turn to **865**.

971

You are woken early the next morning, as the grey of the coming dawn is turning the windows into sharp oblongs, by Professor Van Helsing, who has been summoned to attend Mrs Harker.

Two or three minutes later, Professor Van Helsing is in the room, in his dressing-gown, while you watch with Arthur and Quincey from the doorway.

Turn to **689**.

972

Its ribcage rattling, the bag of bones that was once a no doubt much-loved family pet launches itself at you. (In this battle, the skeletal dog has the initiative.)

SKELETAL DOG   COMBAT 6   ENDURANCE 6

If you reduce the dog's *Endurance* score to zero, turn to **952**.

973

The coffin is carried by the captains of the boats, all the way from Tate Hill Pier up to the churchyard, with a great many townsfolk and parishioners following after it, you and Lucy included. The poor fellow is finally laid to rest close to your favourite seat and you see everything.

Poor Lucy seems very upset. She is restless and uneasy throughout the funeral service and you cannot help but think that her walking at night is also taking its toll on her. But she will not admit that there is any cause for her restlessness, or if there is then she does not understand it herself.

There is an additional cause. You learn that poor Mr Swales was found dead this morning, on your very seat, his neck broken. The doctor who examined him at the scene said that he must have fallen back in the seat in some sort of fright, for there was a look of fear and horror on his face that you hear the men talking about, and that made even these hardy sea-faring folk shudder. Poor dear old man!

Add 1 point to your *Terror* score, tick off the code word *Cadaver*, and then turn to **948**.

974

As the swarthy man breathes his last, you drink, savouring the fear and resignation he is feeling directly through his blood. (Gain 2 *Blood* points and restore up to 4 *Endurance* points).

You then turn your attention to the sleeping sailor, who is snoring loudly, the worse for wear for drink. You slit his throat, purely out of spite.

Roll two dice. If the total rolled is equal to or greater than your *Suspicion* score, turn to **262**. If the total is less than your *Suspicion* score, turn to **283**.

975

You easily outpace the hunters' horses as they set off into the darkness of the snow-bound valley beyond the graveyard after you.

A voice carries to you on the wind: "Good news, comrades! His heart still beats!"

Certain now that the Englishman is safe, you race away into the night.

If you have the code word *Apáca* ticked off, and want to act on it now, turn to **680**. If not, turn to **810**.

976

(Cross off one use of *The Pen is Mightier* special ability.)

As the risen dead stalk towards you, with jerky, slack-jointed steps, you look for something else about your person that might repel the unholy horrors.

How many of the following items do you have in your possession? Golden Crucifix, Good Luck Tokens, Holy Water, Silver Crucifix, Garlic Garland, Sacred Wafer.

1-3	Turn to **946**.
4-5	Turn to **916**.
6	Turn to **896**.

977

You are about to lie down when you think you hear a whispering at your door. Going to it softly, you listen and hear the voice of the Count from the other side.

"Back! Back to your own place! Your time is not yet come. Wait! Have patience! Tonight is mine. Tomorrow night is yours!"

The Count's words are followed by a low ripple of laughter.

In a torment born of your desperation, you throw open the door, which remains unlocked, and see the three terrible women standing there in their terrible beauty, licking their swollen, blood-red lips.

They greet you with their mocking laughter before vanishing into the suffocating darkness.

Slamming the door, you fall to your knees, your head in your hands. Is the end so near?

Add 1 to your *Terror* score and turn to **382**.

978

When everyone else has had a chance to speak, Arthur rises from his seat at the table: "Professor, you mentioned that the monster has grown cunning through the ages. Not years, ages."

"The vampire cannot die by the mere passing of time, and he flourishes on the blood of the living," Van Helsing explains. "And having feasted, he can even grow younger. But he cannot flourish without this diet. Even Jonathan, who lived with him for weeks, never saw him eat! He casts no shadow and makes no reflection in a mirror. He can change his shape. He can come in the form of mist and he can see in the dark. He can do all these things, and yet, he is not free to come and go as he pleases.

"He may not enter anywhere unless he has been invited in. His power ceases with the coming of the day, at which time he must return to his hiding place within unhallowed ground, such as the grave of a suicide. It is also said that he cannot pass over running water.

"Then there are things which can harm him, including garlic, and holy artefacts; the crucifix, the Host. There are others, too: a branch of wild rose on his coffin will keep him from leaving it; a sacred bullet fired into the coffin will kill him truly dead, as will a stake driven through his heart, and having his head cut-off.

"If we can find where the monster is hiding, we can confine him to his coffin and destroy him, if we obey what we know. But we must ever be watchful and wary, for he is clever."

For a moment the only sound in the room is the ticking of the clock on the mantelpiece.

"So who was this Count Dracula when he was but a mortal man?" asks Arthur.

"I asked my friend Arminius, of Buda-Pesth University, to find out the answer to this very question, scouring all the ancient chronicles and documents that are available to him, and he is certain that he was once the Voivode Dracula, who won the title of warlord fighting against the Turks, at the very frontier of the Ottoman Empire, on the borders of Wallachia.

"Even then he was no common man; for at the time of his reign, and for centuries after, he was spoken of as the cleverest and the most cunning, as well as the bravest of the sons of the Land Beyond the Forest. That mighty intellect and iron resolution went with him to his grave, and are even now arrayed against us.

"The Draculas were a great and noble race, although there were rumours that certain scions had dealings with the Devil. They learned their secrets in the Scholomance, a school of black magic, hidden among the mountains. In one manuscript this very Dracula is spoken of as *'wampyr'*, a name we recognise all too well.

"And now we must decide upon a course of action." Picking up the chronological account, that comprises the contents of three diaries, as well as telegrams, letters and newspaper clippings, he says, "We have here much data, and we must proceed to plan our campaign. We know from the inquiry of Jonathan that from the castle to Whitby came fifty boxes of earth, all of which were delivered at Carfax. It seems to me, that our first step should be to ascertain whether they remain in the grounds of Carfax House, or whether any have been removed."

Take an ESP test. If you pass the test, turn to **408**, but if you fail the test, turn to **427**.

979

The wafer-scar upon your forehead burning with intense pain, try as you might, you cannot resist the vampire's siren summons. As soon as you succumb to Dracula's implacable will, the pain in the scar subsides.

Jonathan has climbed onto the cart and is hurriedly loosening the ropes that have kept the box in place during its journey here.

You calmly make your way through the melee of gypsies and Vampire-Hunters, none of them attempting to stop you, and startle your husband when you climb up onto the wagon beside him.

At first, he looks at you in delight, believing you are there to help him in his dreadful task. But his expression transforms into one of shock when you grab hold of his arm and hurl him from the back of the cart, possessed of a strength that surprises both of you.

Gain 2 *Blood* points and turn to **956**.

980

The Second Mate's blood is rich in iron and by drinking it you absorb some of the strength he enjoyed in life.

(Restore up to 6 *Endurance* points, gain 2 *Blood* points, and add 1 point to your *Suspicion* score as well.)

Having fed, and disposed of the Russian's body overboard, you return to your box of Transylvanian earth in the cargo hold.

Turn to **854**.

981

After three days on the road, you are feeling weary, having only had as much rest as was needful for the horses.

At Fundu you hear that the *Fantomă*, carrying one third of your party, has gone up the Bistritza. It is bitterly cold and there are signs of coming snow.

And then, on the fifth day since you left Galatz, with it having started snowing the night before, you reach the foot of the Borgo Pass.

Pressing on into the night, through the trees and the darkness and the snow, you see the flickering lights of a campfire.

Do you want to turn off the road and head towards the fire, in the hope of maybe warming your bones before continuing on your way (turn to **870**), or would you prefer to keep going along the Borgo Pass (turn to **953**)?

982

Quincey sets off towards the back wall of the graveyard, beyond which lies a dark stand of trees, certain that this is the direction from which the sound of wolves came. Arthur also joins your small hunting party as you hurry to keep up with the Texan.

"Do you remember, Art, when we had the pack after us at Tobolsk?" Quincey says his Winchester already in his hand. "What wouldn't we have given for a repeater apiece then!"

Before Arthur can answer, another mournful howl cuts through the night, bringing everyone to an abrupt halt.

Take an ESP test. If you pass the test, turn to **998**, but if you fail the test, turn to **760**.

983

Overcoming your own fear, you strike the wretch down without him even being able to retaliate, as you reveal your true form to the superstitious steersman.

Turn to **118**.

984

Ignoring the roaring serpent, you charge at Count Dracula, your weapon in your hand and a scream of defiance on your lips, as he turns to face you.

But you are stopped in your tracks when his face tears open, from the widow's peak at his forehead down to his chin, and his human visage sloughs away, revealing hideous nose-less features that are more reptile than man beneath.

The undead monster sheds both his cloak and his skin, his luxuriant black hair coming away with it. His jaws distend as they open impossibly wide, a sinuous forked tongue hissing from between long venomous fangs. (Add 1 point to your *Terror* score.)

If you are still able to use *The Pen is Mightier* special ability, and you want to use it now, turn to **763**. If not, turn to **710**.

985

Unable to see where you are landing in the darkness, you go over on your ankle. Wincing in pain, you set off at a hobble.

(Lose 1 *Agility* point and 2 *Endurance* points.)

"Last I saw, Mr Renfield went left and then headed straight towards the old house," Barlow calls down to you.

Setting off at a limping run, not wanting to give your quarry the chance to escape, as you pass through the belt of trees that rings the asylum grounds, you see a white figure disappear over the top of the high wall that separates your property from Carfax House.

Do you want to run back to the asylum to rally the troops (turn to **149**), or do you want to go it alone and follow Renfield over the wall before he can get any further away (turn to **129**)?

986

Leaving the comatose crewman where he is – you can always return to him later if it proves unwise to take another life this night – you set off across the deck.

Take an ESP test. If you pass the test, turn to **812**. If you fail the test, turn to **960**.

987

You do not believe you will learn anything more by continuing to question your companions; it is time to reveal the identity of the killer.

"I am sure that if we inspect the compartment of the killer we will find conclusive proof that will point the finger of accusation in their direction," says the Professor.

So who do you think killed the steward?

Herr Knock, the ratty little man?	Turn to **732**.
Count Yorga, the handsome, middle-aged man?	Turn to **708**.
Carmilla, Countess of Karnstein, the beautiful young woman?	Turn to **652**.
Dr Callistratus, the wolfish-looking older man?	Turn to **458**.

988

"I am a lonely traveller seeking shelter for the night," you say. "Won't you let me in, my dear?"

The impressionable young woman's eyes glaze over, and she says in a dreamy manner, "Of course, sir."

Drawing back the bolt, she opens the gate, admitting you with the words, "Enter and be welcome here."

You hesitate for a moment before crossing the threshold, but feeling nothing untoward, you enter the holy house.

The novice nun looks at you with a doe-eyed expression, as if waiting for your next instruction. Although her modesty is covered by her habit and wimple, it is almost as if she is offering her neck to you.

If you want to drink from her to replenish your vampiric strength, turn to **962**. If you want to resist temptation in this house of God, turn to **256**.

989

"I will take no refusal," says the Count, brooking no argument. "When Mr Hawkins informed me by letter that someone would come on his behalf, it was understood that my needs only were to be consulted."

By the light of the fire burning in the hearth, his eyes appear to glow crimson, as if with flames of their own, and you feel your resolve weaken under his furious gaze.

Add 1 to your *Terror* score and gain 2 *Blood* points.

Now turn to **801**.

990

The prematurely-aged solicitor-turned-Vampire-Hunter is driven by an almost insane fury – how else could he dare raise even a hand against you – but you are ready for him. (Who has the initiative in this battle will depend on how you have arrived at this point.)

HARKER   COMBAT 10   ENDURANCE 11

After 7 Combat Rounds, or as soon as you reduce Harker's *Endurance* score to 3 points or fewer, whichever is sooner, turn to **170** Immediately.

991

The road becomes hemmed in by trees, which in places arch right over the roadway, so it is as if you are passing through a tunnel. Great frowning crags guard the track on either side.

The rising wind moans and whistles through the rocks, and the branches of the trees crash together as you speed along. It grows colder still, as the snow continues to fall, while the baying of wolves cuts through the keening wind.

This place is eerily familiar to you. This is where the coachman stopped, before he delivered you to Castle Dracula, and hurried into the woods in the direction of the flickering blue flames.

If you want to break off your pursuit to see if you can find the exact spot again yourself, turn to **913**. If you think it better you keep riding for Castle Dracula, turn to **968**.

992

At the back of the house, you find fragments of broken glass on the gravel path, beneath Lucy's room, and looking up see the blind flapping between the shattered panes.

Now almost in a panic, you race back round to the front of the building and, not caring who you might disturb, bang on the door and ring the bell repeatedly. When no one comes to the door, you knock and ring again, cursing the laziness of the servants, as a terrible fear steals over you.

Is this desolation another link in the chain of doom that seems to be drawing tight around you? Is it a house of death to which you have come, too late?

Turn to **42**.

993

Suddenly Van Helsing appears, moving at a run between the tombstones.

"Begone, offspring of evil!" he cries, thrusting a silver crucifix into the child's face.

The boy gives a blood-curdling scream and, spitting and hissing like a cat, flees to the sanctuary of the shadows between the ancient yew trees on the other side of the churchyard.

"What was that?" you exclaim, shaking from the shock of your encounter with the urchin.

"She might not have been a mother in life – indeed, she was barely more than a child herself when she died – but in death she seeks to start a family of her own nonetheless," the Professor says cryptically.

"And what is that supposed to mean?" you challenge him.

The sky is overcast and somewhere far off an early cock crows.

"Come," he says, ignoring your inquiry, "my mind is made up. Let us go. You return home for tonight to your asylum and see that all is well. As for me, I have things to do. Meet me again at the Berkley Hotel two nights from now at ten o'clock. I shall send for Arthur to come too, and also that so fine young American, Quincey Morris. We shall all have work to do then."

Turn to **753**.

994

The Professor intervenes, stepping between you and the vampyre lying in her coffin.

He lashes out, striking you with the blacksmith's hammer. (Lose 2 *Endurance* points.)

You have no choice but to defend yourself – turn to **758**.

995

The Second Mate's blood is rich in iron and by drinking it you absorb some of the vitality he demonstrated in life.

(Restore up to 6 *Endurance* points, gain 2 *Blood* points, and add 2 points to your *Suspicion* score. You may also add a temporary 1 point bonus when calculating your *Combat Rating* for the duration of the next battle you are involved in.)

Having fed, and disposed of the Russian's body overboard, you return to your box of earth hidden in the cargo hold.

Turn to **854**.

996

You do not have the benefit of waiting for the other Vampire-Hunters to come to your aid, and so you and the Professor prepare to battle three of the rotten horrors each. It's a case of kill or be killed. (In this battle, you have the initiative, but you must fight the three Strigoi at the same time.)

	COMBAT	ENDURANCE
First STRIGOI	6	6
Second STRIGOI	7	6
Third STRIGOI	6	7

If you manage to dispatch the trio of Transylvanian terrors, turn to **856**.

997

Lucy goes with you, and the two of you head up early to your favourite seat, whilst the cortege of boats goes up the river to the Viaduct and then comes down again.

You are surprised but pleased to find old Mr Swales already there on your favourite bench, but as you pass along the path between the gravestones, you soon realise that something is wrong.

He is lying back against the seat, his head lolling at an unnatural angle, and when you draw close enough, you see that his eyes are open. They are glazed like two glass spheres, and there is a look of fear and horror on his face that makes you cry out in horror yourself.

(Add 2 points to your *Terror* score and tick off the code word *Cadaver*.)

Someone hears your cry of distress and raises the alarm. A doctor is summoned, and poor Mr Swales' body is carried away before the funeral service begins. But by then you are more concerned with the present condition of your friend than the final rest of the sea captain.

Lucy is understandably very upset, and she is restless and uneasy the whole time the funeral is taking place. However, you cannot help but think that her walking at night is also taking its toll.

Turn to **948**.

998

You suddenly receive a flash of insight and glimpse something in your mind's eye, tall, and thickly-furred, its claw-like hands and distended jaws red with gore. In the next instant, the horrible vision has gone.

(Add 1 point to your *Terror* score.)

"Wait!" you hiss, holding up your hand. "Something isn't right."

"We're hunting wolves in a Romanian graveyard while trying to track down a goddamn vampire," counters Quincey Morris. "Nothin' about this entire endeavour is 'right'."

If you want to insist that your hunting party returns to the Professor and that you all leave this place as quickly as you can, turn to **942**. If you would prefer to say no more, turn to **760**.

999

If the *Blood* score is 5 or higher, turn to **969**. If the *Blood* score is lower than 5, turn to **941**.

1000

JONATHAN HARKER'S JOURNAL

6 November 1904

Seven years ago, we all went through the flames; and the happiness of some of us since then is, we think, well worth the pain we endured. It is an added joy to Mina and to me that our boy's birthday is the same day as that on which Quincey Morris died.

His mother holds, I know, the secret belief that some of our brave friend's spirit has passed into him. His bundle of names links all our little band of men together; but we call him Quincey.

In the summer of this year, we made a journey to Transylvania, and went over the old ground which was, and is, to us so full of vivid and terrible memories. It was almost impossible to believe that the things which we

641

had seen with our own eyes and heard with our own ears were living truths. Every trace of all that had been was blotted out.

When we got home we were talking of the old time which we could all look back on without despair, for Godalming and Seward are both happily married. I took the papers from the safe where they had been ever since our return so long ago. We were struck with the fact that, in all the mass of material of which the record is composed, there is hardly one authentic document; nothing but a mass of typewriting, except the later notebooks of Mina and Seward and myself, and Van Helsing's memorandum. We could hardly ask anyone, even if we wished to, to accept these as proofs of so wild a story. Van Helsing summed it all up as he said, with our boy on his knee:

"We want no proofs; we ask none to believe us! This boy will someday know what a brave and gallant woman his mother is. Already he knows her sweetness and loving care; later on he will understand how some men so loved her, that they did dare much for her sake."

THE END

Acknowledgements

There are a number of people without whose help I could not have resurrected Bram Stoker's *Dracula* as an **ACE Gamebook** and so I would like to take the opportunity to thank them here.

First of all, my grateful thanks go to the illustrator, Hauke Kock, who took over art duties after the untimely passing of former collaborator Martin McKenna, and Nic Bonczyk of Mantikore-Verlag (my German publisher) who put us in touch. Hauke has done an astounding job, bringing the world of ***Dracula – Curse of the Vampire*** to life in all its macabre glory, and his portraiture is absolutely incredible.

Secondly, thank you to Emma Barnes at Snowbooks for her patience and support, and thirdly, to Anna Torborg, for doing such a fantastic job on the layout, and helping to turn out such a grotesquely glorious-looking book. I must also thank Kevin Abbotts, who created the bookmarks and the hyperlinked eBook version of the adventure.

Thanks are also due to Dacre Stoker, the great-grandnephew of Bram Stoker, who gave his blessing to this project, and Kim Newman, for all the inspiration his own ***Anno Dracula*** series has provided me with over the years.

But it would be most remiss of me if I failed to offer a huge and heartfelt thank you to everyone who pledged their support to this grim, gothic adventure from the outset, and joined me on my journey beyond the forest. Without them, this book would have remained dead and buried, rather than being allowed to crawl from the grave to horrify all with its bloodthirsty tale once more.

Kickstarter Backers

Rat

Bryan Howarth ✛ Jessica Rickardsson ✛ Alistair McLean ✛ Radouane Betayeb

Bat

Jason Archer

Wolf

Robert Biskin ✛ Shaun Kronenfeld ✛ Mark Crew ✛ Anthony Reddy ✛ Jason Lamb ✛ Guy Reisman ✛ Jadher Machado ✛ Cyril Keime ✛ Flavio Mortarino ✛ Tyler Byers ✛ Eric Monkman ✛ Xander Schrijen ✛ José Lomo ✛ Chris Blackford ✛ Violet Flohr ✛ James Smith ✛ Daniel J Taylor

Strigoi

Luke Sheridan ✛ Sue Lee ✛ Kjeld Froberg ✛ Javier Fernandez-Sanguino (Alarion) ✛ Jennifer Fuß ✛ Axel Riviere ✛ Jules Fattorini ✛ Hans Peter Bak ✛ Colin Deady ✛ Andrew Hartley ✛ Scott Moore ✛ Panagiotis Loukas ✛ Niki Lybæk ✛ Tim Shannon ✛ Jason Conlon ✛ Holger Finbarr Richter ✛ Christopher Semler ✛ PJ Montgomery ✛ Micah Atkinson ✛ Chris Jefferson ✛ Thea Shortman ✛ Mark Stoneham ✛ Victor Cheng ✛ Mark Lee Voss ✛ Adam Sparshott ✛ Derek Bizier ✛ Chuck McGrew ✛ Stephane Bechard ✛ Patrick Davey ✛ Paragrafka ✛ Nacho Blasco ✛ Robyn Taylor-Abbotts ✛ Brian Edwards ✛夏谷実✛ Jim Gray ✛ Paul Taylor ✛ Ols Jonas Petter Olsson ✛ Mark Lain ✛ Evie and Alex McKenzie ✛ Sapper Joe ✛ Gregor Allensworth ✛ Kamarul Azmi Kamaruzaman ✛ Michael J. Boucher ✛ Dan Ashley Hall ✛ Štěpán Hofmeister ✛ Richard Catherall ✛

Marc Kennedy ✤ Maikel Nepomuceno ✤ Michael Reilly ✤
Joe Tilbrook ✤ Tom Cottrell ✤ Peter "Wraithkal" Christiansen ✤
Scott Kuhn ✤ Andrew Alvis ✤ Panagiotis Vlamis ✤ Tom Lee ✤
Dane Barrett ✤ Olly McNeil ✤ James A. Hirons ✤
Crystal McCarty ✤ Richie Stevens ✤ Blitzbuff ✤ Philip W Rogers Jr
✤ Miss O. ✤ Prof. Dr. Oliver M. Traxel ✤ Tom Geraghty ✤
Scott Lewis ✤ Nicodemus ✤ Euan Ball ✤ Ian Ross ✤ Brett Schofield
✤ Professor Narok ✤ Joonseok Oh ✤ Michael Hartland ✤
Dave Bowen ✤ Henrik Spalk ✤ Kevin Harvey ✤ Colin Snoad ✤
Svein Børge Hjorthaug ✤ Pete Wood ✤ Andreas Rocha ✤
Mike Andrews ✤ Steven Jenkinson ✤ Tim Morris ✤
Balder Asmussen ✤ Fernand Vos ✤ NB Holden ✤
Della-Ann Sewell ✤ Olivier Leclair ✤ Tim Wild ✤
Zacharias Chun-Pong Leung 梁振邦 ✤ Jocelynn K ✤
Pang Peow Yeong & Family ✤ Colin Jackson ✤ DrLight ✤
Thomas Petit ✤ Lisa Sustaita ✤ Paul Gaston ✤ G R Jordan ✤
Beau Chambers ✤ Jesse Raymond Ames ✤
Xavier Miriam Leia Aixendri Moneny ✤ Zack Ronan McGinnis ✤
Duncan Lenox, Blaine Lenox, and Jason Lenox ✤
Robert Browning ✤ Paul Jones ✤ SamSam Forde ✤ Matt Molloy ✤
Jakob S. Pfafferodt ✤ Michael Hardy ✤ Rafi Rodriguez ✤
Martin Terrier ✤ Michael Knarr ✤ Martin Keown ✤
Vladimir Dzundza ✤ Mark Chaplin ✤ Richard Tidmarsh ✤
Ang Zuan Kee ✤ Chris Halliday ✤ Bay vonKhukuri ✤ Skorpio ✤
Rod Gillies ✤ Jan Snasel ✤ Debbie D'Amico ✤ Mattias Bengtsson ✤
James Cleverley ✤ Keith Matejka ✤ Richard Bunting ✤
Simon Day ✤ Jean-Baptiste PATYN ✤ Felicity Keane ✤
Adrián Soltész ✤ Mike Bingham ✤ Hayley Kitchen ✤
Ashley Harper ✤ Lee A. Chrimes ✤ Kieran Coghlan ✤ V Wood ✤
Sven "DOC" Berglowe ✤ Stephan Forkel ✤ Stuart Lloyd ✤ Bhajho
✤ Gál Zsigmond Gergely ✤ Zachary Bratcher ✤
Alex Allston ✤ Peter Cutting ✤ Dr tedster ✤ Argentium Thri'ile ✤
KM ✤ Joe McEvoy ✤ Sean F. Smith ✤
Chester Wrinklesdorf VIII ✤ Christopher Lush ✤ Michael Dodd
✤ Frankie B ✤ Sattawat Beernaert ✤ Steven Lord ✤ Rob Lord ✤
Kashif Sheikh ✤ Stefan Heidenreich ✤ Kevin Clifford ✤ Abi Dear
✤ Ed Fortune ✤ Alex Mair ✤ Holger Schrenk ✤ Fiachra Delea ✤
Nickolaus ✤ Dave Bartram ✤ Ken Nagasako ✤ Jason Baldwin ✤
M Rinaldi ✤ Swen Harder ✤ Anna Dobosz ✤ Justin Whitman ✤
John Dennis ✤ Jennifer Bryan ✤ Shyue Wen Ong ✤ Bob Olsson ✤
Greg Smith ✤ Mayer Brenner ✤ Bas van Zon ✤ Oliver Morris ✤
Elisa Lamont ✤ Charles Lister ✤ me@edmondkoo.com ✤
Tracy 'Rayhne' Fretwell ✤ Paul C Grimaldi ✤ Sibtain J. Adams ✤
Sebastian ✤ L. Luciel Miller ✤ Melanie Calion Mendoza ✤

Matt Leitzen ✚ Duncan Jarrett ✚ Caroline Sinclair ✚
Brice WITTMANN ✚ Mathias Mattiuzzo ✚ Kenny L. Koh ✚
Daniel Maxson ✚ Cristovao Neto ✚ Craig Andrews ✚
Talmor ✚ Pablo Pérez Gómez ✚
Brendan Clarke ✚ Ondrej Zastera ✚ Harris Larson ✚ Peter Halls ✚
Timothy Coulson ✚ Joey Kidd ✚ Sunex Amures ✚
Jenny Stevens-Ketland ✚ Travis Casey ✚ Timothy Burnett ✚
José Brinca ✚ James Boland ✚ Neil Parkin ✚ Phil Brumby ✚
Nathan Dunn ✚ Carl Shewry ✚ Claire Osborne ✚ Hervé Appriou
✚ Helen Donovan ✚ Steven Smith ✚ John Fitzgerald ✚
Jonathan Grey ✚ Jack Jacobs ✚ James Sampson ✚ Jeff Wilms ✚
David Gotteri ✚ Miguel Diaz Rodriguez ✚ Brian Twomey ✚
Rob Burke ✚ Frazer Barnard ✚ Sean Franks ✚ Hamad Alnajjar ✚
Paul Smith ✚ Darren Tietz ✚ John Conlan ✚ Lee Ambolt ✚
Alexis Anderson

Dracula Playing Cards & Dice

Richard Harrison ✚ Ken "Professor" Thronberry ✚
Joseph William Rochester Jr. ✚ Mel Hall ✚ Cleric Hellspeak ✚
Luis L ✚ Aron Tarbuck

Szgany

Alisher ✚ Ian Greenfield ✚ David (Lowrie) Gillson ✚
Y. K. Lee ✚ Rob Crewe ✚ Mario Villanueva ✚ David J. Williams ✚
Dave Tobin ✚ Matt Sheriff ✚ James Lawrence ✚ Andrew Wright ✚
Stephen Chadwick ✚ Graham Hart ✚ Marc Thorpe ✚
Ang NamLeng ✚ Andrew Shannon ✚ Michael Hartley ✚
Phil Gooch ✚ Daniel Northfield ✚ Gabor Geza Kiss ✚
Martin Gooch ✚ Michael Atkinson ✚ Andy Bow ✚
Darren Fillingham ✚ Anders Svensson ✚ Matt Taylor ✚
Doug Thomson ✚ Edd Duggan ✚ Magnus Johansson ✚
Jonny Hansen ✚ Steven Parry ✚ Laurent BOSC ✚ Stuart Claydon ✚
Steve Pitson ✚ Dominic Marcotte ✚ Justine Evans ✚
Christian Lindke ✚ Fenric Cayne ✚ Dr. Vitárius Gábor ✚ lek ✚
Drakkar Darkholme ✚ Mister Fluck ✚ Gonçalo Rodrigues ✚
Paul, Noah, Jona, Elya Brückner ✚ GregUrb VampyrSlayr ✚
Alucard ✚ Mighty Werewolf Vargarde ✚ Alexander Ballingall ✚
Chiel Jacobs ✚ Danielle Williamson ✚ Robin Horton ✚
Anthony Christopher Hackett ✚ Tom Bohac ✚ Maggie J. Kulzer
✚ Bradley J Anderson ✚ David Poppel ✚ Chris Aldis ✚ Jiminy ✚

Ashley Laycock ✢ James Danko ✢ Michael Loughlin ✢
Dennis Chang ✢ Darren Uren ✢ Paul Berry ✢ Mark Buckley ✢
Cristina Conforti ✢ Seth Martin ✢ Michael Lee ✢ Terry Adams ✢
Chris Trapp ✢ Dacre Stoker ✢ Borce Dimitrijovski ✢
Stefan Atanasov ✢ Ivan Kemenes ✢ Patrick Harrison ✢
Robert H Wilde ✢ Nicholas Chin ✢ Adrian Jankowiak ✢
Simone "OldMariner" Carlini ✢ Lawrence Lovoy

Werewolf

James Aukett ✢ Simon J. Painter ✢ Eddie Boshell ✢
Jeremy R Haupt ✢ Rms ✢ Ant O'Reilly ✢ Allan Matthews ✢
Phillip Bailey ✢ Jonathan Caines ✢ Benjamin Wicka ✢ Vin de Silva
✢ Lee Robinson ✢ Daniel Ley ✢ Jason Epstein ✢
Antonio Jorge Garcia Lentisco ✢ Seth Alexander

Vampire Hunter

Laurent JALICOUS aka Warlock-man ✢
Simon Scott ✢ René Batsford ✢
JASON VINCE. A.K.A. 'DREAM WALKER SPIRIT' ✢
Andrés Rodríguez Rodríguez ✢ Shane "Asharon" Sylvia ✢
Ron White ✢ Stuart Warren ✢ Fabrice Gatille ✢
Nasser Khalid Al Alawi ✢ Reba Phillips ✢ Kim Newman ✢
Suguru Oikawa ✢ Nicholas Chin ✢ Emma Owen

Vampire Count

KJ Shadmand ✢ Tim Shannon

Nosferatu

林立人 Lin Liren

He is Legend
Breathing New Life into an Undead Classic

I don't recall when I was first bitten by the vampire. I have a feeling that the bloodsucker in question, however, would have been Count Dracula, in the guise of the Hungarian-American actor Béla Lugosi, with his signature cape and widow's peak, but it would have been as a still photograph reproduced in a book rather than in the Tod Browning directed film, which I have still not seen to this day.

There were two books, however, which are the ones that immersed me in vampire lore – Carey Miller's *A Dictionary of Monsters and Mysterious Beasts*, and the *Usborne Supernatural Guide to Vampires, Werewolves & Demons*. The first was given to me by my mother, while the second I bought for myself from the school bookshop when I was about nine or ten years old, and both terrified and fascinated me in equal measure. Between them, they furnished me with what felt like an encyclopaedic amount of information about the undead rulers of the night; everything from how you could become one and ways they could be thwarted, to the historical origin of such beliefs and tales of infamous inhuman fiends who rose from the grave to feed on the vital essences of the living.

I didn't read Bram Stoker's *Dracula* until I was at university and only came to appreciate it more fully when I re-read it in order to write my own gamebook adaptation of the story. Strangely, this is something I resisted for a long time, and I believe it was my German publisher who eventually persuaded me to have a go, suggesting I write an ACE Gamebook for a more adult audience.

The reason for my hesitation? Simply because *Dracula* has been adapted so many times before, and I always want to bring something new to the public domain properties that I add to the ACE Gamebooks series. *Dracula – Curse of the Vampire* isn't even the first gamebook adaptation of the seminal gothic horror story. But having read up on the origins of Stoker's novel I began to see a way in and, from that moment on, it was as good as inevitable that I would tackle the tale of an enigmatic Transylvanian nobleman who travels to English shores with the intention of spreading his undead plague.

Monster Maker

Abraham "Bram" Stoker was born on 8 November 1847 at 15 Marino Crescent, Clontarf, on the northside of Dublin, Ireland. The third of seven children, Stoker was bedridden with an unknown illness until he started school at the age of seven, when, miraculously, he made a complete recovery. Of this time, Stoker wrote, "I was naturally thoughtful, and the leisure of long illness gave opportunity for many thoughts which were fruitful according to their kind in later years."

He grew up without further serious illnesses, excelling as an athlete at Trinity College, Dublin, which he attended from 1864 to 1870. He graduated with a BA in Mathematics, and pursued his MA in 1875. He was also auditor of the College Historical Society and president of the University Philosophical Society, the only student in the history of Trinity College to hold both positions. His first paper for the latter was on 'Sensationalism in Fiction and Society.'

As a student, Stoker became interested in the theatre, and later, while working for the Irish Civil Service, he became the theatre critic for the *Dublin Evening Mail*. The newspaper just happened to be co-owned by Sheridan Le Fanu, who was himself an author of gothic tales. In December 1876, having given a favourable review of Henry Irving's *Hamlet* at the Theatre Royal in Dublin, Irving invited Stoker for dinner at the hotel where he was staying, and the two men became friends.

In 1878, Stoker married Florence Balcombe – a celebrated beauty who had previously been wooed by none other than Oscar Wilde –, and on 31 December 1879, their only child was born, a son whom they christened Irving Noel Thornley Stoker.

The family moved to London, so that Stoker could take up the position of business manager at the Lyceum Theatre, where Henry Irving was based. Commanding, demanding and mesmerising, it was said that Irving himself inspired the character of Dracula. Stoker certainly idolised him, not unlike the wretched Renfield worships Count Dracula in the book.

Through his collaboration with Irving, Stoker started to move in high society circles, meeting both the celebrated American artist James Abbott McNeill Whistler, and the equally celebrated Scottish author Sir Arthur Conan Doyle, who happened to be a distant relative. In London, Stoker also met the writer Hall Caine, who became one of his closest friends, and to whom *Dracula* is dedicated.

Accompanying Irving when he went on tour, Stoker travelled the world, although he never visited Eastern Europe. He was invited to the White House with Irving twice, and knew both William McKinley and Theodore Roosevelt. He also met Walt Whitman, one of his literary idols, on one of his visits.

Stoker began writing novels while working for Irving. The first to be published in the UK was *The Snake's Pass* (1890), the plot of which is focused upon the legend of Saint Patrick defeating the King of the Snakes in Ireland. Before writing *Dracula*, Stoker met Ármin Vámbéry, a Hungarian-Jewish writer and traveller, and it is likely that the story of the blood-sucking Count grew out of Vámbéry's sinister stories of the Carpathian Mountains.

Written in Blood

Over the years, *Dracula* has become a true literary archetype, and the tale of the book's creation has become a legend in its own right. The story goes that, having dined on dressed crab one evening, Bram Stoker had a terrible nightmare. In this ghastly phantasmagoria, three vampiric women descended upon their victim, while their demonic master intoned, "This man belongs to me!"

When he awoke, Stoker wrote that fateful phrase down on a piece of paper. This was in March 1890, and when the novel was published in 1897, that very pronouncement appeared within the text, and has done in every edition of the seminal gothic horror novel since.

In 1890, Stoker joined the London Library (established in 1841), which is still located where it has always been, at No. 14 St James's Square, London. There he took notes from books such as the Reverend Sabine Baring-Gould's *The Book of Werewolves* (1865)[1], drawing together all manner of folkloric sources, and, in doing so, created an immortal myth that endures to this day.

He also referred to more modern reference books, for the time, so that he might describe the strange eastern European lands Harker travels through on his way to Dracula's home all the more convincingly. One of these was ***Round About the Carpathians***, by Andrew Crosse (1878), and another was ***An Account of the Principalities of Wallachia and Moldavia***, by William Wilkinson (1820), which he just so happened to pick up in the small harbour town of Whitby on the northeast coast of England. It was in this book that he first stumbled across the name 'Dracula'.

Stoker visited Whitby in the summer of 1890, staying at No. 6 on the Royal Crescent. He spent a week there alone, before his wife Florence joined him, mulling over his ideas for his new novel in a writer's retreat all of his own. With the gaunt, gothic ruins of its Abbey, Georgian terraces, and even the 199 steps that lead up from the harbour to the churchyard of St Mary's, the town became the backdrop to many of the book's most memorable scenes.

---

1   And which I am pleased to say is among my own collection of reference books.

Location, Location, Location

No. 6 the Royal Crescent is now a holiday let, so you can stay in the house where Stoker wrote at least parts of his undead masterpiece. Situated on the first floor of an impressive 18th century Georgian house, it is close to all the usual tourist amenities, and only 100 yards from the cliff lift down to a three-mile stretch of Blue Flag sandy beach.

Other locations that may have inspired Stoker while he was writing the novel include Slains Castle in Aberdeenshire, and the crypts of St. Michan's Church in Dublin.

No. 138 Piccadilly is believed to be Dracula's London townhouse, having been identified as such by several people – reportedly including Bernard Davies, co-founder of The Dracula Society – based on information and architectural details given in the book.

However, there is no such place as a Carfax House in Purfleet, Essex.

The Nature of the Beast

The notes Stoker made whilst researching and writing the novel (dating from 1890-96) are still kept at the Rosenbach Museum and Library in Philadelphia. They reveal that Stoker originally intended to break the novel into four parts.

On a piece of paper dated 14 March 1890 is Stoker's outline for Book I, called 'Styria'[2] – although the word 'Styria' was later crossed out and replaced with 'Transylvania to London'. There then follows a numbered list of things he intended to incorporate into the first part of the novel. They include, 'lawyer's letters', 'Munich', 'wolves', the arrival at the castle, 'loneliness', and 'the Kiss', as well as a reference to an 'old chapel' and 'carting earth'.

---

[2] Interestingly, Styria was the setting for Sheridan Le Fanu's gothic novella and vampire story *Carmilla*.

Among the jotted notes for Chapter 4 of Book I are the words Stoker heard in his dressed crab-induced dream: 'This man belongs to me.'

Other pieces of paper list the rules of the beast, which Stoker had collected from various vampiric sources. These include:

- *No looking-glass in Count's house — never can see him reflected in one. No shadow?*
- *Lights arranged to give no shadow.*
- *Never eats nor drinks.*
- *Carried or led over threshold.*
- *Enormous strength.*
- *See in the dark.*
- *Power of getting small or large.*
- *Influence over rats.*
- *Painters cannot paint him — their likenesses always like someone else.*
- *Insensible to music.*
- *Absolute despisal of death & the dead.*
- *Power of creating evil thoughts or banishing good ones in others present.*
- *Could not kodak him — come out black or like skeleton corpse.*

To begin with, the villain is referred to as 'Count Wampyr', but 'Wampyr' has been crossed out and replaced with 'Dracula', while at the top left corner of one page 'Count Dracula' appears, underlined!

Dracula was eventually published on 26 May 1897, by Archibald Constable and Company. The book had a *fin de siècle* yellow cover, which immediately identified it to the Victorian book-buying public as being something that was diabolical and *outré*. Yellow was the colour used for the jackets of disreputable French novels at the time, and by giving ***Dracula*** a cover of the same hue, the publisher intentionally aligned it with what was considered by many to be a more experimental.

The Un-dead

The original 541-page typescript of Dracula was believed to have been lost, until it was found in a barn in north-western Pennsylvania in the early 1980s. Consisting of typed sheets with many emendations, handwritten on the title page was 'The Un-dead'[3]. The author's name was shown at the bottom as Bram Stoker. The manuscript, including 150 pages that the editor had cut before publication, was purchased by billionaire Microsoft co-founder Paul Allen for an undisclosed amount.

Dying on Stage

Eight days before *Dracula* was published, the play *Dracula, or the Undead* was performed at the Lyceum Theatre, in London. I say performed, but it was really just a readthrough, conducted by members of Sir Henry Irving's company, which did not involve Sir Henry himself.

The script had been cobbled together, by Stoker, from galley proofs for the novel, purely so that he could secure the dramatic rights to his own work. It took an interminable four hours to 'perform', and when asked what he thought of it, Irving gave a dire one word review: "Dreadful!"

In 1924, however, the Irish actor, playwright and director Hamilton Deane produced a new, and far more well-received, stage adaptation of the book, and it is this that we have to thank for the popular perception of Dracula today.

Unable to find a scriptwriter to take on the project, Deane wrote ***Dracula: The Vampire Play in Three Acts*** himself, in a four-week period of inactivity while suffering with a severe cold. He then contacted Stoker's widow Florence and negotiated a deal for the dramatic rights.

---

[3] Which I used as the title of the short story I gave away to backers of the original *Dracula – Curse of the Vampire* Kickstarter.

Deane re-imagined Count Dracula as a more urbane and theatrically acceptable character who could more plausibly enter London society. It was his idea to have the Count wear a tuxedo and stand-up collar, and a flowing cape which concealed Dracula as he slipped through a trapdoor in the stage floor, giving the impression that he had disappeared into thin air. Deane also arranged to have a uniformed nurse available, ready to administer smelling salts in case anyone happened to faint during a performance.

The Vampyre

The trapdoor in the floor of a stage is known as a 'vampire-trap' precisely because it was a technical innovation first created for an 1820 performance of *The Vampire*, a play based on John Polidori's prose piece, *The Vampyre* (1819).

The Vampyre was itself inspired by a tale Lord Byron told as part of a story-telling contest held in 1816 – the 'Year Without a Summer' – at the Villa Diodati beside Lake Geneva in Switzerland. The weather being too cold and dreary to enjoy the usual outdoor holiday activities[4], the group retired indoors until dawn. Sitting around a log fire, the company proceeded to amuse themselves by reading German ghost stories translated into French from the book *Fantasmagoriana*. Byron then proposed that they, "each write a ghost story."

The same contest inspired the then 18-year-old Mary Shelley to write the novel *Frankenstein; or, The Modern Prometheus* (1818). While *Frankenstein* is now considered to be the first true work of science fiction, *The Vampyre* is often cited as being the progenitor of the romantic vampire genre of fantasy fiction.

---

[4] Since the world was locked in a long volcanic winter caused by the eruption of Mount Tambora in 1815.

The Children of the Night. What Music They Make!

The play was rewritten for its US debut, in 1927, by the American playwright John L. Balderston, and it went on to help grant the then-unknown Hungarian actor who took on the role of Dracula a special kind of immortality. The show ran for a year on Broadway, before enjoying another two years on tour, breaking all previous records for any touring show in the United States.

It is the Deane/Balderston adaptation upon which the classic Tod Browning film *Dracula* (1931) was based. The actor who had played Dracula on stage in the US managed to persuade the film's producers to cast him as the vampire in the celluloid version as well, partly because he asked for so little money[5].

The actor's name? Béla Lugosi.

Dawn of the Dead

1897 was a vintage year for the undead. Not only was *Dracula* was published that year, but it also witnessed the first exhibition of Philip Burne-Jones's controversial painting *The Vampire*. The piece depicted a predatory female looming over a supine man, and it was an image that inspired Rudyard Kipling to write a poem on a similar theme, also called *The Vampire*.

On top of that, 1897 was also the year in which the author and spiritualist Florence Marryat published her novel, *The Blood of the Vampire*. The central character of the story is Harriet Brandt, the daughter of a mad scientist and a mixed-race voodoo priestess, who drains the life force from anyone with whom she comes into contact.

---

[5]   Cheap by the standards of Hollywood, anyway.

An American Horror Story

Stoker originally tried to sell **Dracula** as being a true story, and among his papers – many of which were left to Trinity College – there is an 1896 clipping from the *New York World* newspaper bearing the headline "New England Vampire Scare."

Two hundred years after the Salem witch trials, farmers in the region became convinced that their relatives were returning from the grave to feed on the living. In 1854, in Jewett City, Connecticut, townspeople had exhumed several corpses that were suspected of being vampires.

This quintessential American vampire story, involves the 19-year-old Mercy Lena Brown, who lived in Exeter, Rhode Island. By 1892, the year Lena died, Exeter's population had dropped to 961, from a high in 1820 of more than 2,500. Farms were abandoned, many of them later to be seized and burned by the government. It was largely a subsistence farming community with barely fertile soil, and some parts of Exeter had become a veritable ghost town.

Tuberculosis – or 'consumption' – spread like a plague in New England in the 1730s, and by the 1800s the disease was the leading cause of death throughout the north-east. It was a horrible way to die, with a victim often suffering for years, their body visibly wasting away, before the end finally came. As one 18th century commentator put it, "The emaciated figure strikes one with terror, the forehead covered with drops of sweat; the cheeks painted with a livid crimson, the eyes sunk... the breath offensive, quick and laborious." Apparently symptoms, "progressed in such a way that it seemed like something was draining the life and blood out of somebody."

The Brown family, living on the eastern edge of Exeter, began to succumb to the disease in December 1882. Lena's mother, Mary Eliza, was the first, while Lena's sister, Mary Olive, a 20-year-old dressmaker, died the following year. Within a few years, Lena's brother Edwin sickened too and left for Colorado Springs, hoping that the climate would improve his health.

Lena herself didn't fall ill until nearly a decade after her mother and sister were buried. Her tuberculosis was the 'galloping' kind, which meant that she might have been infected but remained asymptomatic for years, only to fade fast after showing the first signs of the disease. Her January 1892 obituary was much terser than her sister's: "Miss Lena Brown, who has been suffering from consumption, died Sunday morning."

As Lena lay on her deathbed, her brother was, after a brief remission, taking a turn for the worse. Edwin had returned to Exeter from the Colorado resorts "in a dying condition," according to one account. But some of the Brown's neighbours, fearful for their own health, approached Lena's father, George Brown, and offered an alternative take on the recent tragedies. They suggested that perhaps an unseen diabolical force was preying on his family, and that one of the three Brown women wasn't dead at all, but instead secretly feasting on the living tissue and blood of Edwin. If the offending corpse was discovered and destroyed, then Edwin would surely recover.

On the morning of March 17, 1892, a party of men unearthed the bodies, as the family doctor and a *Providence Journal* correspondent looked on, so that they could check to see if there was any fresh blood in their hearts. After nearly a decade, Lena's sister and mother were barely more than bones, but Lena, "was in a fairly well-preserved state," the correspondent later wrote. "The heart and liver were removed, and in cutting open the heart, clotted and decomposed blood was found." Bear in mind, she had only been dead a few months, and it was wintertime.

Despite the doctor pointing out that Lena's lungs "showed diffuse tuberculous germs", the villagers nonetheless burned her heart and liver on a nearby rock, feeding her brother Edwin the ashes. He died less than two months later.

News of Lena Brown's exhumation spread. After the piece written by the reporter who witnessed the whole sorry business of Lena's grave being opened appeared in the *Providence Journal*, a well-known anthropologist by the name of George Stetson travelled to Rhode Island to investigate "the barbaric superstition" that seemed to be prevalent throughout the area.

Stetson's account of New England's vampires was published in the venerable **American Anthropologist** journal, and before long, even the foreign press was offering explanations for the phenomenon; perhaps the "neurotic" modern novel was the motivating cause for this New England madness, or maybe shrewd local farmers had simply been having a laugh at Stetson's expense. A writer for the London Post declared that whatever forces drove the "Yankee vampire," it was an American problem and most certainly not the product of a British folk tradition. In the **Boston Daily Globe**, another commentator went so far as to suggest that, "perhaps the frequent intermarriage of families in these back country districts may partially account for some of their characteristics."

But it was an 1896 *New York World* clipping that found its way into the papers of Bram Stoker, whose theatre company was touring the United States that same year. While some scholars believe that there wasn't enough time for the news accounts to have influenced *Dracula*, others see Lena in the character of Lucy – her very name a tantalising amalgam of 'Lena' and 'Mercy' – a consumptive-seeming teenage girl turned vampire, who is exhumed in one of the novel's most memorable scenes, her disinterment presided over by a medical practitioner, just as a doctor oversaw Lena's unearthing.

A Warning From Beyond the Grave

I should point out, before I go any further, that if you have not read through the adventure contained within this book yet, there are many spoilers ahead and they *will* spoil your enjoyment of the story!

Still here? Okay, you were warned...

Blood Relative

Dracula – Curse of the Vampire is quite different from the ACE Gamebooks that came before it for several reasons. For one thing, it is probably the adventure that follows the plot of its source material most closely. For another, while you are able to play as different characters in the book, you can also change which character you are playing as, actually during the course of a playthrough. And lastly, it is the longest gamebook I have ever written – almost 170,000 words in length, spread over 1,000 sections.

So, what was it I thought I could bring to the story that hadn't already been done by other people? In some ways, it was more a case of taking *Dracula* back to its roots and undoing the changes that had been made by other people. When people think of the eponymous Count today, they more often than not think of him as a handsome, misunderstood, romantic hero, doomed to a twilight existence due to some tragic heartbreak in his past, and motivated by his desire – not to say love – for Mina Murray.

However, if you go back to Stoker's novel, Dracula is a monster who has survived for centuries by preying on those weaker than himself; he is a black-hearted sorcerer who can command lesser creatures and even the elements to do his bidding. He is an apex predator, and not some desirable would-be paramour. The only reason he attacks Mina in the book, other than to acquire sustenance, is out of spite, to punish the men who would see him destroyed. In turn, Mina does not fall in love with Dracula; rather she is repelled by the undying Count, appalled by the violation he visits upon her, and does all she can to help her husband and his friends complete their mission and kill the monster.

Something else I wanted to do was make Jonathan Harker the heroic figure that I believe he is in Stoker's story. Too often, the West Country lawyer is side-lined in film adaptations, and comes across as weak in both mind and body. The truth, on the other hand, is that Harker goes through hell whilst kept prisoner in Castle Dracula, with his host slowly breaking his spirit, not to mention the literal horrors he encounters in the women's wing. Despite all this, he still manages to scale the exterior wall of the castle in order to penetrate Dracula's apartments, and comes close to putting an end to the vampire while he is sleeping in his coffin. And although he is unable to finish the job then, he still manages to escape the Weird Sisters, who keep him as their midnight-feast-cum-plaything, a feat that tests both his physical being and his imperilled soul. If you had been through such privations, I think you would forgive yourself if you suffered a nervous breakdown as a result. Nonetheless, Harker recovers, and he is the one who finds the strength of will to attack Dracula with a knife in the vampire's townhouse lair on London's Piccadilly, when all the other Vampire-Hunters are held at bay by shock and fear.

Of course, the problem with adapting ***Dracula*** as a solo-player gamebook, is that the story is told from various points of view, through diary entries, letters, telegrams, newspaper articles and the like. None of the protagonists in the story experience everything that happens in the book. In fact, the three main characters – Jonathan Harker, Mina Murray, and Dr John Seward – all have unique storylines that do not fully converge until almost two-thirds of the way through the novel. But rather than being a hindrance, this rather suited the ACE Gamebook series.

While some of the adventures – such as ***Beowulf Beastslayer, 'TWAS – The Krampus Night Before Christmas***, and the forthcoming ***Ronin 47*** – only allow you to play as one character throughout, others – ***The Wicked Wizard of Oz*** and **NEVERLAND – *Here Be Monsters!*** – allow you to play as one of several different individuals. The same is true of ***Dracula – Curse of the Vampire***, but how this adventure differs is in the way the reader can switch between characters during the course of one playthrough. With the addition of the Count himself as a playable character, the reader can experience every significant encounter that appears in Stoker's story first-hand.

I had already written a gamebook in which you could play as a vampire[6], but tackling the story of the granddaddy of all vampires would prove to be a unique challenge. For one thing, he starts his adventure as a mere mortal and ends up as a mighty undead lord, and for another, his story unfolds over the course of 435 years.

I am not the first one to do this, but I also wanted to reinstate the novel's original opening and ending. ***Dracula's Guest*** is a short story that was published posthumously in 1914, after Bram Stoker's death in 1912. It is told in the first person by a young Englishman, who is never mentioned by name, and relates what happens to him during a visit to Munich, in Germany, while on his way to Transylvania. Originally written as the first chapter of ***Dracula***, it was removed prior to publication as the publisher felt that it was superfluous to the story. I, however, do not, partly because it introduces the reader to the wonderfully mysterious Countess Dolingen of Gratz, who I made more of in Dracula's personal storyline in my adaptation.

Equally, the original ending of the book is much more dramatic, more akin to the sort of thing you would expect to find at the climax of a monster movie today, with Castle Dracula being destroyed by a huge explosion-cum-earthquake. How could I not include that in my own reimagining?

So far, so unoriginal. ***Dracula*** is a masterful piece of work, a truly seminal novel, but it is not without its problems. Many of these appear in the form of inconsistencies – Professor Van Helsing's grasp of the English language, for example – while others are to do with the pacing of the plot, particularly regarding Seward

---

6   One of three, in fact, in the now very hard to get hold of ***Shadows Over Sylvania*** – a Path to Victory adventure published by the Black Library for Games Workshop.

and Van Helsing's attempts to discover the reason for Lucy Westenra's worsening condition. Another problem with the book is that Dracula's motivations throughout are unclear. While it is hinted at by Van Helsing that the Count seeks to build himself a new empire, as he did in his flesh-and-blood life, this idea is never followed up. For my gamebook, I made much more of this, influenced in part by Kim Newman's ***Anno Dracula*** (1992). In my version, Dracula is quite clearly a megalomaniac, who plans to take over the British Empire, if not the world, and the fifty boxes of earth he has transported from his homeland to England contain an invasion force of animated corpses[7].

The one part of the story that is glossed over more than any other in adaptations is the Vampire-Hunters' pursuit of Dracula back to his bat-haunted home in Transylvania. In the novel, it reads rather like a gazetteer guide to how to travel across Europe, including how to deal with local dignitaries and acquire all the necessary permits. This does not make for a particularly thrilling adventure, even though the Crew of Light – as the Vampire-Hunters are sometimes referred to in works of literary criticism – do discover evidence of the dead left in Dracula's wake along the way, particularly regarding the fate of a certain Petrof Skinsky, who helps the Count smuggle his one remaining box of earth out of England. Taking these cues from Stoker's story, I built up what I hope is now a much more exciting chase sequence that carries the reader along at a breathless pace, to the inevitable denouement outside the gates of Castle Dracula.

---

7   An idea I came up with long before I saw Mark Gatiss and Steven Moffat's 2020 reimagining of ***Dracula***.

Bloodlines

Dracula has influenced countless creators since it was published in 1897 and Bram Stoker himself was influenced in turn by other, earlier vampire stories. In writing *Dracula – Curse of the Vampire*, I was able to pay homage to these tales myself. Although some might be more obvious than others, they include the penny dreadful *Varney the Vampire* (1847), written by James Malcolm Rymer, Sheridan Le Fanu's gothic novella *Carmilla* (1872), Stephen King's modern American horror classic *Salem's Lot* (1975), and the aforementioned, post-modernist, alternate history novel, *Anno Dracula* (1992), by Kim Newman.

Then there are the movies; F W Murnau's silent German Expressionist horror film *Nosferatu: A Symphony of Terror* (1922), Henry Cass's *Blood of the Vampire* (1958), Bob Kelljan's *Count Yorga, Vampire* (1970), the Alan Gibson-directed *Dracula A.D. 1972* (1972), Tom Holland's knowing cable TV culture-influenced *Fright Night* (1985), Francis Ford Coppola's Academy Award-winning old school style moving picture *Bram Stoker's Dracula* (1992), and Gary Shore's dark fantasy origin story *Dracula Untold* (2014). And those are just the vampire ones[8]!

Born of Blood

As with the film *Bram Stoker's Dracula* (1992), I took Dracula's personal story right back to the beginning and Prince Vlad Tepes III's 15th century battles against Mehmed II, or Mehmed the Conqueror. I have always been fascinated by the historical figure who gave the world the name Dracula; he is both reviled as a bloodthirsty psychopath – who thought nothing of impaling hundreds of his own subjects (including children!) or having the turbans of Turkish envoys from the Ottoman Empire nailed to their heads because they refused to remove them in his presence, even though they were prevented from doing so by their religious

---

[8] Other sources of filmic inspiration include *Murder on the Orient Express*, *The Wolfman*, and *Frankenstein*.

beliefs – and revered as a national hero by the people of Romania, due to the fact that he undoubtedly kept the region independent and Christian[9].

One of the fun things for me as an author was squaring the historical Voivode of Wallachia with the undying Count Dracula, working out what needed to have happened for one to become the other. Not only that, but it was great to explore the events of the novel from the point of view of its eponymous, monstrous antagonist.

While I wanted to stay true to Stoker's original, there were elements of the mythos that were added later, mainly through the numerous film adaptations, that I decided to keep. In the book, Dracula is described as having curiously elongated and pointed incisors, but I chose to make his vampiric teeth exaggerated canines, as they are in almost every vampire movie made after Murnau's ***Nosferatu***.

Another aspect I borrowed from the movies was Renfield's backstory. In the original novel, the insane Renfield has not obvious connection to Dracula other than his madness; it is as if his psychological state is what makes him susceptible to the vampire's influence. But then why aren't the other inmates of the Carfax madhouse affected in the same way? Neither are we told why Renfield has been incarcerated in a lunatic asylum in the first place.

However, some adaptations, most notably ***Bram Stroker's Dracula*** (1992), make passing reference to the fact that Renfield was a solicitor in the employ of the same firm as Jonathan Harker. This made sense to me, as it provided a valid reason for the wretch's psychic bond with his master, and also explained why the other inmates of Carfax asylum don't fall under the vampire's influence in the same way. But then the problem I had to overcome was, if Renfield has gone mad because of what he witnessed during his sojourn to Transylvania, how was it that he returned to England and was then sent to Dr Seward's primitive psychiatric hospital?

Finding a solution to this conundrum allowed me to develop Dracula and Renfield's relationship, and it was ultimately resolved during Dracula's unique journey through the adventure.

---

[9] It is even said that the Knights of Malta sang *Te Deum* in Vlad's name and proclaimed him 'Champion of Christ'!

I personally feel that the 59-year-old Mr R. M. Renfield is one of Stoker's greatest creations, and it would seem that modern medicine agrees. The character of the zoophagous maniac has influenced the study of real-life behaviour in psychiatric patients suffering from an obsession with drinking blood. The term Renfield Syndrome was coined by psychologist Richard Noll, in 1992, to describe clinical vampirism[10].

The symptoms that can be observed in someone suffering from Renfield Syndrome follow the pathology of the character in the novel and consist of several stages. Initially the patient exhibits zoophagia, in the form of a compulsion to eat insects, or to eat live animals or drink their blood. As the condition worsens, the behaviour grows more and more deviant, culminating in a compulsion to drink another person's blood in an act described as True-Vampirism. This state includes the intentional harming of another in order to consume their vital fluids, the same behaviour Renfield exhibits in the novel.

Bearing all this in mind, I find the wretched Renfield a far more disturbing and even more frightening individual than the undead Dracula. Perhaps it is precisely his humanity that makes him such an unsettling character.

Another thing I love about Stoker's story is the doomed voyage of the *Demeter*; the idea of the vampire preying on the crew of the ship that is transporting him to England, so as not to starve to death during the journey, until he eventually makes shore in the form of a monstrous dog, only to take refuge in the grave of a suicide. If this doesn't perfectly demonstrate how monstrous and inhuman Count Dracula really is, then I don't know what does.

Other familiar aspects of cinema's influence on the mythic story, however, were abandoned in favour of what Bram Stoker had originally intended. Therefore, the vampyre women who share Dracula's castle home are not his 'brides', even though in the original text it is implied that they might all have been his lovers in the past, the Count is able to move about during the hours of daylight, rather than being burned to a crisp by the sun's rays, and there is no Carfax Abbey in the story, merely the decaying Carfax House with derelict chapel attached.

Another change I decided to make myself was simply in the way that Van Helsing is addressed. In the book, he is a doctor as well as a professor, and is referred to by both titles. However, because

---

10   Although originally it was only supposed to be a joke term.

I already had Dr John Seward as one of the player characters, I wanted to make a clear distinction between him as his eccentric tutor, which is why Van Helsing is only ever addressed as Professor in my version.

One other notable change I made was concerning the identity of the mysterious coachman who collects Harker from the Bistritz-Bukovina stage, when it stops at the end of the Borgo Pass, and transports him to Castle Dracula. In Stoker's original, it is heavily implied that the coach driver is Dracula himself, but I made the conscious decision to make them different people, the driver becoming the master of Dracula's gypsy followers instead. This meant that I could set up a rather satisfying encounter at the end of the book.

I also made the Weird Sisters shape-changers. After all, if Dracula could turn himself into a dog, or a bat, or even mist, why wouldn't the women he had turned have similar shapeshifting abilities?

While we're on the subject of the castle's inhabitants, Stoker has only four creatures dwelling there when Harker visits – Dracula and the three Weird Sisters. There are no servants and yet Harker is welcomed with a hearty feast, and he is well-fed every day after that. But what no one talks about is what a good cook Dracula must be – either that or her has the Sisters slaving away in the kitchens night after night!

The Blood is the Life

Having covered all the necessary story beats and included all the relevant characters in my tale, when it came to the game aspect of the gamebook, I used the existing ACE ruleset, but with three important additions; the *ESP*, *Terror*, and *Blood* scores (although I was over 100 sections into writing the book before I finally settled on the additional rules and attributes I would use in the adventure).

ESP, as the term 'Extra-Sensory Perception' would imply, is a measure of how susceptible to the supernatural a character is. Dr Seward, a man of science, has a low *ESP* score, while Mina Murray, who is much more in tune with her emotions, has a higher *ESP* score.

When it was first published, **Dracula** was widely considered to be frightening, and many reviewers praised Stoker's prose for effectively sustaining the novel's persistent level of horror. To reflect this in my gamebook, I included the *Terror* score; quite simply, the more unsettling experiences a character has, and the more horrifying situations they are forced to endure, the more their *Terror* score increases, potentially up to the point where they will have a nervous breakdown and no longer be able to continue with the adventure.

And lastly, there's the *Blood* score. This acts as an indicator of how Dracula's plans of conquest are progressing. If you are playing as one of the Vampire-Hunters, the higher the *Blood* score, the better your enemy is doing but also the more aware he is of your efforts to stop him. If you are playing as Dracula, the higher the *Blood* score, the more formidable vampiric powers you are able to bring to bear against those who would stand in your way.

I originally intended the *Blood* score to be a *Blood Tracker*, possibly with its own unique page in the book. The idea was that you would tick off boxes when you were required to update the *Blood Tracker*, and some of those boxes would include a number to turn to when you reached them. The idea was that the more you drew attention to yourself, the more lethal servants the vampire would send to stop you. First it would be a bat, then a wolf, until later you would be fighting Szgany gypsies or even undead Strigoi.

In the end, I scrapped this idea, because it could have resulted in some totally out of context encounters. For example, the reader might run into a Strigoi before they had found the animated corpses hidden in the chapel of Carfax House, or they might have had to fight a wolf whilst they were onboard a train, which just seemed a step too far for me. Good game design is as much about what you leave out, as it is about what you put in[11].

There is another reason why **Dracula – Curse of the Vampire** is unusual, compared to my other ACE Gamebooks. The other adventures are full of battles, but despite this being a much longer book and adventure, there are far fewer situations where you end up resorting to fisticuffs, as it were. There are also just as many human combatants as there are monsters, due to the story's setting, in terms of both where and when it takes place.

---

11   However, I may reuse the *Blood Tracker* idea if I ever get round to designing the **Dracula – Curse of the Vampire** card game I have in mind.

You may have already noticed – at least you will if you have attempted the adventure –, but if you are playing as the Vampire-Hunters, the combative encounters with the major 'villains' you come up against – the seductive, vampiric Lucy Westenra, the zoophagous maniac Renfield, the ageless Gypsy Witch, and Dracula himself – are structured like Boss Battles in a video game. You will always have to deal with a lesser minion before facing off against the Big Bad themselves.

Blood Brothers

There was one final addition I made to the storyline for *Dracula – Curse of the Vampire*. As long time readers of my ACE Gamebooks series will know, when I base an adventure on a particular book, I have a habit of including elements from other works in the original author's canon. For example, in *Alice's Nightmare in Wonderland*, as well as featuring narrative elements from both *Alice's Adventures in Wonderland* and *Through the Looking-Glass, and What Alice Found There*, there is the potential to meet characters from *The Hunting of the Snark*, and even a reference to Lewis Carroll's poem *Phantasmagoria*.

While *Dracula* is Bram Stoker's best known work, and most highly-acclaimed, it is not his only work. Indeed, he had four novels published before *Dracula*, and another seven after it. His final novel was *The Lair of the White Worm*, a horror story inspired by the legend of the Lambton Worm, which is a source I have plumbed myself several times over the years[12]. While it was not well-received when it was published – H P Lovecraft himself stating that Stoker had ruined "a magnificent idea by a development almost infantile" –, it still contains some notable scenes and a particularly memorable monster.

I really wanted to include some element of *The Lair of the White Worm* in my adventure and eventually found my way in when I read up on the Scholomance, the school of black magic where Professor Van Helsing claims the members of the Dracula line were taught the dark arts by the Evil One himself.

---

12   See the Devilworm in my first published Fighting Fantasy gamebook *Spellbreaker* (1993), the *Pax Britannia* short story *Conqueror Worm* (2009), and, most recently, *The Serpent's Egg: A Dark Tale of the Cthulhu Mythos* (2013).

According to legend, this fabled school of black magic was located within Transylvania. It was hidden underground, and its students remained unexposed to sunlight for the seven years they spent studying there. Submerged in a mountaintop lake nearby was the dragon Zemu, or Balaur[13], a many-headed dragon or monstrous serpent from Romanian folklore. One of the ten graduating students would be chosen by the Devil to be the Weathermaker and ride the dragon in that duty, for whenever Balaur glanced at the clouds it would rain.

During the Iron Age in Europe, a Thracian people known as the Dacians were the ancient inhabitants of a region located near the Carpathian Mountains and west of the Black Sea; an area that includes mainly the present-day countries of Romania and Moldova. The Romans encountered the Dacians, and Trajan's Column in Rome includes a depiction of the Dacian Draco, a standard they carried before them into battle, which has the form of a dragon with open wolf-like jaws containing several metal tongues[14].

Among the Dacians, the Draco was seen as a special protective symbol, and played an important part in the religious life of the people. The body of the standard, depicting the serpentine Balaur, was seen by the people as a manifestation of the sky demon or 'heavenly dragon'. The dragon symbol is also present in the silver, snake-shaped Dacian bracelets, which were used as currency and votive offerings, as well as ornaments and high rank insignia in Classical antiquity.

This devotion to serpents was prevalent during this time and evidence of snake cults exists in several ancient cultures, including that of Ancient Egypt. Indeed, several characteristics of Egyptian culture and civilization can be identified in the prehistoric Dacian territories.

Within the Transylvania of Dracula there exist various tribes of Romani people, whom Stoker refers to as gypsies. The word 'gypsy' is a mid-16th century word, originally '*gipcyan*', which is

---

13   The term '*Balaur*' has been linked with the Albanian '*buljar*', meaning 'water snake', and possibly stems from the Thracian root, *bell-* or *ber-*, meaning 'beast' or 'monster', as in the name of the Greek mythological hero Bellerophon (literally 'beast-slayer').

14   The wolf had been the symbolic animal of the Carpathian people since the 10th century BC.

short for 'Egyptian'[15]. The Ancient Egyptians worshipped a vast pantheon of animal-headed deities that included many serpents. Most feared of them all was the demonic Apep, or Apophis[16].

And so, the connection was made. What if people travelled from Egypt to eastern Europe, bringing with them their snake worship and strange, occult practices, and what if their 'god' came with them, hiding from the light in a vast subterranean lake underneath a mountain?

The last thing that clinched it for me was the way in which a cobra's fangs can be seen in the elongated fangs of the vampire. And by merging *The Lair of the Worm* into the narrative tapestry, it also presented me with a unique origin story for the immortal Count.

Blood, Sweat and Tears

Having complete creative control over the ACE Gamebooks series, I am very particular about who illustrates the different titles and will happily delay a project until the right artist is available. When I sat down to plan *Dracula – Curse of the Vampire*, I knew from the get-go that I wanted Martin McKenna to illustrate the adventure, and it was his artwork I envisaged when I pictured certain scenes from the story in my head.

I was delighted when he agreed to illustrate the book. We had worked together before on the Fighting Fantasy gamebooks *Curse of the Mummy*, *Howl of the Werewolf*, and *Night of the Necromancer*, and he even ended up producing cover images for *Spellbreaker* and *Bloodbones*, when the series was taken over by Wizard Books. He also produced the stunning wraparound cover that appeared on *YOU ARE THE HERO – A History of Fighting Fantasy Gamebooks*, and even gave me permission to use other examples of his work in an artbook to be offered to backers as an additional reward, as part of the *Dracula – Curse of the Vampire* Kickstarter.

---

15 Because gypsies were popularly believed to have originally come from Egypt.

16 *The Book of the Dead* contains a spell to repel an evil snake in the underworld: "Get back! Crawl away! Get away from me, you snake! Go, be drowned in the Lake of the Abyss, at the place where your father commanded that the slaying of you should be carried out."

As Martin put in an email to me once, we were clearly inspired by similar things, and probably being close in age was a factor as well. When I sent him a brief for the artwork for a book, I always knew that the illustrations would either match what I had in my head precisely or would be even better than what I had imagined.

And so it was that, while I was writing *Dracula – Curse of the Vampire*, I started preparing the illustration brief for the book. I emailed Martin in January 2020, double-checking when he would be able to start work, but heard nothing back – and continued to hear nothing back until the end of June. It turned out that Martin's life – like the lives of many others in the Year of COVID – had taken an unfortunate turn during the pandemic and he warned me that it was unlikely he would be able to illustrate *Dracula – Curse of the Vampire* after all. But he did offer me a ray of hope; if he could find his feet again quickly, he said he could potentially start on the illustrations later in the year. That was the last time I heard from him.

Come the autumn I emailed Martin again, to see how he was, but received no reply. On Halloween 2020, a flippant comment on somebody else's Facebook page sent a chill down my spine, and following some investigative work on my part, I was dismayed to discover that Martin had died at the beginning of September. It turns out that the demons he was so good at drawing in Fighting Fantasy gamebooks were nothing compared to those he was fighting himself and he had taken his own life.

What I felt on hearing this news was nothing compared to what his family and friends were still going through, but it threw the future of the project into doubt. Although we had never met – we hadn't even spoken on the phone – it was still a horrible shock when I discovered that Martin had died. I had always intended for *Dracula – Curse of the Vampire* to be a collaboration with Martin. Did I want to continue writing the book if he could no longer go on that journey with me?

I did not resume writing the adventure until January 2021, and I am very grateful to the Kickstarter backers for their patience and understanding during this difficult time. I had already worked on the book for over a year, and only had Dracula's adventure left to write. For a while it almost felt like a step too far, but I had promised readers that the Count would be one of the playable characters in the gamebook and it felt like I would be leaving out a lot of what made my version of *Dracula* different from everyone else's if I didn't keep that promise. Now that the adventure is finished – all 1,000 sections and 167,000 words of it – I am very pleased that I did. Just don't ask me to write another gamebook as long as this one again!

Of course, no one could replace Martin, his style was his own, and for a while I considered publishing *Dracula – Curse of the Vampire* without any illustrations. But ultimately that felt fundamentally wrong to me; after all, the other ACE Gamebooks had illustrations. While no one could replicate what Martin would have brought to the book, another artist might be able to bring their own look to the project. The difficult question was, who?

This is where my German publisher, Nicolai Bonczyk of Mantikore-Verlag, came to the rescue, when he suggested Hauke Kock. I was not aware of Hauke's work, but he had illustrated numerous gamebooks for the German market, including some in Joe Dever's Lone Wolf series. I checked out his website and had to agree that he might just have what was needed to be able to illustrate *Dracula – Curse of the Vampire*. One of the things that made the task so challenging was that the artist who took over the project would have to draw various real people into their illustrations, and there were numerous other 'real' people to be illustrated, rather than just an endless parade of grotesque monsters[17].

So Hauke produced a couple of test pieces for me – one of Dracula crawling headfirst down the façade of Castle Dracula, and another of Abraham Van Helsing, whose likeness is based on the very real David Peterson, to whom this book is dedicated. What Hauke produced convinced me that he was the man for the job. The downside was that he wouldn't be able to start work until May 2021, which meant he would be under pressure to get everything finished in time for *Dracula – Curse of the Vampire* to make its revised publication date of October 2021.

While Hauke's illustrations are not what Martin would have produced, I think you will agree that he did an incredible job of bringing the scenes in the story to life, and to an incredibly tight deadline as well.

---

17   Although there are a few of those as well.

Hauke Kock's Sketchbook

As with the other ACE Gamebooks, I wanted to have portraits of the playable characters appear in the rules section of the book. However, it was Hauke's idea to present them in oval frames, helping to give them a certain late-19th century, Victorian vibe.

Vampire Count level backer KJ Shadmand as Jonathan Harker (top left), and Vampire Count level backer Tim Shannon as Dr John Seward (bottom left).

Since Dracula is the star of the show – I mean, he has his name on the cover of the book, for goodness' sake – getting his look right was vitally important. I also didn't want him to look like any other well-known actors who have played him on the big or small screen. In fact, the only person I wanted him to look like in any way whatsoever was Prince Vlad Tepes III.

Dracula actually appears in a total of fourteen[18] illustrations in the book, including all those that depict him in one of his many supernatural forms – such as the beast-man threatening the Captain of the doomed *Demeter*, the Black Dog that makes it to shore in Whitby, and the bat-beast Dr Seward encounters when he visits Hillingham House in the middle of the night – and the filler illustrations as well. Not bad for a demonic undead abomination who casts no reflection and whose image cannot be captured on film.

Hauke Kock's wood-cut style drawing of Vlad Tepes III (a.k.a. Dracula).

---

18   It could be fifteen, if you believe that the swarm of rats the Vampire-Hunters encounter in Carfax House are also possessed by Dracula's spirit; or sixteen, if you take the wolf filler illustration to be that of Dracula in lupine form, when he hunts down Countess Dolingen of Gratz.

Dracula descends.

Hauke's original sketch for the 'Harker sees Dracula descend the wall of the castle' scene, next to the revised version. The first, I felt, made Dracula look too young, and not monstrous enough. I also asked Hauke to lose the shoes for the revised design. The final drawing that appears in the book is slightly different again, making the monstrous Count appear older.

This is also one of the iconic scenes in the ***Dracula*** story for me, which helps make it stand out from any other vampire story before or since, which is why it also ended up being used as the cover image for ***Dracula – Curse of the Vampire***.

Old man Dracula, with a portrait of his younger self – Vald Tepes III – on the wall behind him.

The Wolf Enclosure at London Zoo.

Did you recognise any of the characters in this drawing of Dracula's visit to London Zoo? Dracula's style is based on Gary Oldman's look in the movie **Bram Stoker's Dracula** (1992), while US horror writer extraordinaire Stephen King has been cast in the role of Thomas Bilder, the keeper who, in the book, has responsibility for the wolf enclosure. UK horror writer and film critic Kim Newman and Nosferatu level backer Lin Liren look on from behind.

Taking a leaf out of Ian Livingstone's book, I had Hauke draw me into a couple of the illustrations in the book. Not that I'm saying writing **Dracula – Curse of the Vampire** *nearly drove me mad or anything...*

Varney the Vampire, the foppish 18th century undead bloodsucker from the serialised gothic horror story Varney the Vampire; or, The Feast of Blood, by James Malcolm Rymer and Thomas Peckett Prest. The penny dreadful predated Bram Stoker's book by fifty years.

Self-exhumation.

A rejected sketch for the Strigoi encountered by the Vampire-Hunters in the chapel of Carfax House. I felt that the box containing it looked too much like a coffin and wanted to make a clear distinction between the cargo of 'experimental earth' Dracula sent over to England from Transylvania and a conventional vessel for the dead, which would surely have aroused the attention of anyone who came into contact with them during their journey.

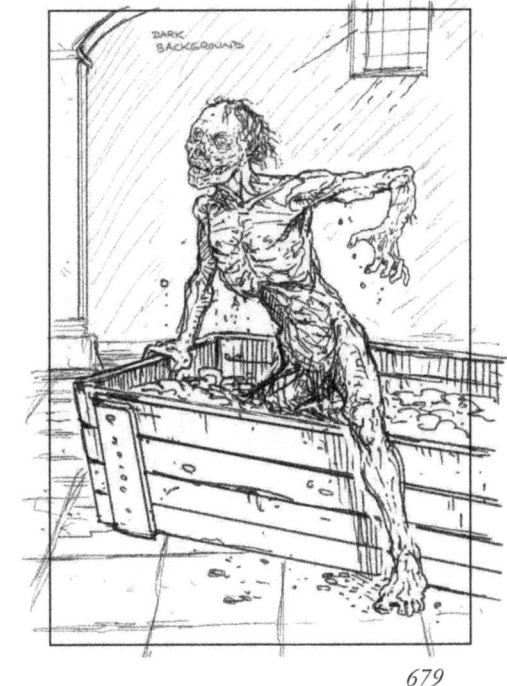

Two drawings of the Crew of Light, featuring more likenesses of certain Kickstarter backers.

Dracula forces Mina to drink his blood. Hauke himself suggested changing this image to a tighter close-up on the pair, which is what we went with for the final illustration.

The Usual Suspects.

More familiar faces. German actor Max Schreck (1879-1936) as Graf Orlok, from the film ***Nosferatu: A Symphony of Horror*** (1922), British actor and star of the silver screen Peter Cushing (1913-1994) as Dr Callistratus, from ***Blood of the Vampire*** (1958), and Christopher Lee (1922-2015), who happened to play Dracula in seven Hammer Horror films, this time cast as Count Yorga, from ***Count Yorga, Vampire*** (1970). And is that Rita Ora in the role of Carmilla, Countess Karnstein, from Sheridan le Fanu's gothic novella of the same name?

*In **Dracula**, it is implied that the Count's agent, Petrof Skinsky, is killed by the vampire in the form of a wild beast. However, for **Dracula – Curse of the Vampire**, I decided to add a whole pack of werewolves to the story.*

*One more familiar face, this time English actor Boris Karloff (1887-1969) as the Monster from the seminal horror film **Frankenstein** (1931).*

*This was the rough for one of Hauke's test pieces that he produced before he got the job of illustrating **Dracula – Curse of the Vampire**.*

This image comes from near the climax to the adventure, when Dracula's Szgany coachman transforms into a Werebear.

Two different versions of Dracula bursting out of his box of earth in sight of Castle Dracula.

While the image on the left is undeniably dramatic, it wasn't quite what I was looking for, partly because of how the reader can come upon this particular image. I was also keen to have Dracula looking less like a proto-Victorian gentleman by this point in the story, and slightly less human, which is why Hauke ended up inking the image on the right for the final illustration.

The Lair of the White Worm.

The final scene of the adventure, where Dracula is revealed to be a servant of the monstrous White Worm. The problem with this initial sketch was that the Worm looked too grub-like, more like some sort of massive, mutated larva. However, I dumped my original serpent image idea and kept the grub's head, because I loved how grotesque and different Hauke's design was, and just asked for the body to be slimmed down a little. At the same time, Hauke focused more attention on the transforming Dracula's head, as he sloughs his skin to become a true Son of the Dragon.

Bran Castle.

Commonly known outside Romania as 'Dracula's Castle', the 13th century Bran Castle is located on the Transylvanian side of the historical border with Wallachia. The medieval fortress stands on the very edge of a terrific precipice, and a stone falling from a window – such as the one Jonathan Harker looks out of, only to see Dracula crawling down the wall – would fall a thousand feet without hitting anything.

In 2014, Bran Castle, which happens to be a registered national monument as well as a popular tourist landmark, was put on the market for a blood-chilling £47 million, while in 2016, Airbnb ran a competition for guests to stay in the castle, complete with coffins instead of beds.

The Order of the Dragon.

Vlad II Dracul, the father of Vald the Impaler, took his name from the Order of the Dragon; a monarchical chilvaric order of knights, founded in 1408 by Sigsimund of Luxembourg, who was then King of Hungary, and later Holy Roman Emperor. Hauke redesigned the insignia of the order to become Dracula's personal coat-of-arms.

Miss Lucy Westenra, looking pale and interesting.

Mist Monsters.

When Dracula visits the wretched Renfield at Carfax Asylum, he passes through the bars of the lunatic's cell in the form of insubstantial mist. Hauke's first take on this filler image looked a little too much like a phantom octopus to me, so he then produced the far more impressive, revised sketch on the right.

Professor Van Helsing's 'medical' bag – if you're about the business of hunting vampires, you should never leave home without it.

An Undying Legacy

Almost fifteen years to the month after *Dracula* was published, after suffering a number of strokes, Stoker died at No. 26 St George's Square, London, on 20 April 1912. He was 64 years old. Some biographers attribute the cause of death to overwork, others to tertiary syphilis, but Bram Stoker's death certificate named the cause as "Locomotor ataxia 6 months." He was cremated, and his ashes placed in a display urn at Golders Green Crematorium in north London. But thanks to his own undying creation, Stoker achieved a form of immortality to rival that of the undead Count.

Dracula is regarded as one of the most significant pieces of English literature. Many of the book's characters have entered popular culture as archetypal versions of themselves; for example, Count Dracula has become the quintessential vampire, while Abraham Van Helsing is the iconic vampire-hunter. The novel has been adapted for film over 30 times, and its characters continue to appear in all manner of media – everything from comic books to television commercials.

The book has had such an impact on the world that the date of its initial publication, 26 May, is now celebrated as World Dracula Day, while the Bram Stoker Festival is an annual event held in the autumn, in Dublin. *Dracula's* influence also runs through the veins of the Whitby Goth Weekend, which is held in October, as close to Halloween as possible.

The novel has inspired academics, as much as it has Hollywood producers, and Bram's great-grandnephew, the Canadian-American author, sportsman and filmmaker Dacre Stoker, has co-written both a sequel and a prequel. The former, *Dracula the Un-dead* (2009), written by Dacre Stoker and Ian Holt, was based on Bram Stoker's own handwritten notes for characters and plot threads excised from the original edition of *Dracula*, while the latter, *Dracul* (2108), was written with J. D. Barker, and features a heavily-fictionalised version of Bram Stoker himself as the narrator of the story.

Whether it is thanks to the fact that it was the first genuinely unnerving gothic horror chiller that had mass appeal, whether it is thanks to the themes of the novel that are still just as relevant today – those of race, life, death, gender and sexuality, dominance and dependence, science versus religion, and the consequences of modernity –, or whether it is just because it is a rollicking adventure story, with a truly evil antagonist, *Dracula* has transcended the printed page to become a modern myth, which makes it open to endless reinterpretation. Even if the monstrously charming Count is killed, he always seems to manage to come back to life somehow, and long may he continue to do so.

Jonathan Green
London, June 2021

About the Author

Jonathan Green is a writer of speculative fiction, with more than seventy books to his name. Well known for his contributions to the Fighting Fantasy range of adventure gamebooks, he has also written fiction for such diverse properties as *Doctor Who*, *Star Wars: The Clone Wars*, *Warhammer*, *Warhammer 40,000*, *Sonic the Hedgehog*, *Teenage Mutant Ninja Turtles*, *Moshi Monsters*, *LEGO*, *Judge Dredd*, *Robin of Sherwood*, and *Frostgrave*.

He is the creator of the ***Pax Britannia*** series for Abaddon Books and has written eight novels, and numerous short stories, set within this steampunk universe, featuring the debonair dandy adventurer Ulysses Quicksilver. He is also the author of an increasing number of non-fiction titles, including the award-winning ***YOU ARE THE HERO – A History of Fighting Fantasy Gamebooks*** series.

He occasionally edits and compiles short story anthologies, such as the critically-acclaimed ***GAME OVER***, ***SHARKPUNK***, and ***Shakespeare Vs Cthulhu***, all of which are published by Snowbooks.

To find out more about ACE Gamebooks and his other projects, visit www.JonathanGreenAuthor.com and follow him on Twitter @jonathangreen.